Cover art by Yocla Book Cover Designs

Edited by Brieanna Robertson, Beth Fawcett, and Jessica Ripley

Published by Eighth Ripple Press

Print ISBN: 978-1-9990270-4-9

Ebook ISBN: 978-1-9990270-5-6

CONTENTS

ZERO FOX GIVEN

Chapter 1	3
Chapter 2	10
Chapter 3	18
Chapter 4	24
Chapter 5	32
Chapter 6	37
Chapter 7	44
Chapter 8	49
Chapter 9	56
Chapter 10	63
Chapter 11	71
Chapter 12	77
Chapter 13	84
Chapter 14	90
Chapter 15	101
Chapter 16	109
Chapter 17	116
Chapter 18	122
Chapter 19	127
Chapter 20	132
Chapter 21	145
Chapter 22	149
Chapter 23	157
Chapter 24	163
Chapter 25	169
Chapter 26	175
Chapter 27	181
Chapter 28	188
Chapter 29	197
Chapter 30	205

Chapter 31   212
Chapter 32   219

HOWL ALWAYS LOVE YOU

Chapter 1   225
Chapter 2   232
Chapter 3   240
Chapter 4   247
Chapter 5   254
Chapter 6   262
Chapter 7   272
Chapter 8   282
Chapter 9   290
Chapter 10   297
Chapter 11   304
Chapter 12   310
Chapter 13   320
Chapter 14   325
Chapter 15   330
Chapter 16   338
Chapter 17   348
Chapter 18   355
Chapter 19   361
Chapter 20   367
Chapter 21   373
Chapter 22   380
Chapter 23   385
Chapter 24   394
Chapter 25   401
Chapter 26   408
Chapter 27   417
Chapter 28   422

CAN'T BEAR TO BE WITHOUT YOU

Chapter 1   429

Chapter 2   436

Chapter 3   446

Chapter 4   454

Chapter 5   462

Chapter 6   471

Chapter 7   477

Chapter 8   485

Chapter 9   493

Chapter 10   497

Chapter 11   503

Chapter 12   509

Chapter 13   514

Chapter 14   522

Chapter 15   528

Chapter 16   535

Chapter 17   541

Chapter 18   549

Chapter 19   555

Chapter 20   561

Chapter 21   568

Chapter 22   571

Chapter 23   579

Chapter 24   582

Chapter 25   589

Chapter 26   597

Chapter 27   603

Chapter 28   611

Chapter 29   619

About the Author   625

Also by Mandy Rosko   627

DEDICATION

*This book is dedicated to all of my patrons from 2019 over on Patreon!
Thank you for your support! - Mandy*

*Nancy Mcdonald, Tami Gryder, Jessica Ripley, Nicole Henry, Barbara
Burdette, Johanna Snodgrass, Andi Downs, Alisha Derr, Nicole Cook,
Michelle Fortune, Teresa Ward, Sherry Smith, Angie Kyle, Melinda Miller,
Leslie Gordon, Saleena Chamberlin, Ramona Cabrera, Dusty Weller, Terri
Eaches.*

*Daria Donnelly, Kayla Reindl, Clare Parrott, Patricia Cassar, Sheryl Tegt-
meyer, Lori Martin, Anne Rindfliesch, Stacy Ittersagen, Megan Mills,
Christina Morgan, Monica Lynn Emery, Leanne Ede, Cassandra Hyden.*

*Anne Samson, Pauline Dixon, Rachelle Binkley, Rebekah Snyder, Michelle
Chantler, Thomas Werner, Kaer Baer, Sharron Anthony, Roxanne Johnson,
Rachel Morse, Karen, Marlene Eaton, Julie Spencer, Wendy Custer, Annette
Alex, Shelia Deal, Carolyn Lown, Mellissa, Jill Micklich, Confused Child,
Samalee Johnson, Sandy Folz, Janet Rodman, Jeanne Clark, David Friend.*

Lizzy, Soshanahlila, Alexandra Smith, Virginia Robinson, Donna Hogel,

Nanci Quinn, Janice Richmond, Stacey F, Barb Sands, Marcy Schwendiman, Charlotte Brincat, Sharon Manning-Lew, Teresa Albarran, Gerryann L., Denise Holder, Gail Powell, Rose Allen.

Opal Carew Lori Trask, Retiredhsmom, Maria T, Rachel Barckhaus, Laura Furuta, Angela Cowen, Diana Mason, Beth Wolfe, Toni Mcconnell, Valerie Cobb, Valerie Jondahl.

Tiffany Villeda, Iona Stewart, Samantha Quinones, Seen Cassell, Melissa Carlton, Ugo, Amanda Barker, Tricha Fely, Corrina Mayall, Ellen Swindall-Bailey, Alexis Abbott, Selena Kitt, Essie Munro, Anna Garcia-Centner, Biggi Ziegler, Jill Morrison, Alexia Falco, Kerrin Brittain, Ruth Roberts, Carol Ingham, Cynthia Powers, Tanya, Yolanda Pedroza, Belinda Jarrell, Miriam Loellgen, Pam Van Veen, Tammy Francis, Valerie Marshman.

MANDY ROSKO

CHAPTER 1

The lights flashed in a blinding rhythm that would give any normal person a seizure, the music blared so loudly Zelda's sensitive ears could barely pick up the beat, and yet she moved anyway. She probably looked like a complete idiot flailing around as she did, but she didn't care and no one seemed to notice in the sea of bodies.

Zelda Wolff had no idea how to dance, and yet here she was, having the time of her life. A few short weeks ago, the idea of being in a place like this would have made her heart seize up.

The heat of the bodies surrounding her, sweaty and lithe as they moved, pressing against her back, her sides, and her breasts, created a heady scent that pulled her in. Because she was a sweaty, moving body with them. On her own, if she did this, she would look so ridiculous. Together, she vanished into the crowd.

Now she understood why people loved this so much. It wasn't the dancing. Not really. This could barely be called dancing anyway. No. It was the feeling that came with it. The anonymity, the feeling of being desired, of feeling sexy in her own skin as the already tight black skirt clung to her curves like a painted on skin. Her long hair was loose. Zelda shook it out as everyone raised their hands up high.

Free. Light. Careless.

Reckless.

The eyes of the male standing next to her lit up. She didn't get around that often, but she knew what the smile on his face meant. What he wanted from her.

He was good-looking, too. In an old fashioned, James Dean kind of way. Gelled hair, blue jeans, and white T-shirt. The heat and sweat of the room let her see what was beneath that white T-shirt, too.

And she was impressed with what she saw.

The old Zelda would have shied away by now. Would have avoided eye contact because she didn't want to give off the wrong impression.

Now...well, why the hell not? That was the entire point of doing this. Of wearing these clothes, of letting her dark curls loose and showing off her body for the first time since...

Well, ever.

He reached for her hand. A thrill rushed through Zelda's arm as she allowed him to guide her away from the crowd of dancers.

Her heart beat. Her fox tail flicked behind her, and her ears twitched. This was it. For the first time since *it* had happened, she was going to have sex.

Good. This was going to be good. The dancing was one thing, but it wasn't nearly enough to make her forget.

The man said something to her. At first Zelda thought he might be trying to tell her his name. So difficult to tell with all the noise. She should have worn ear plugs.

She asked him to repeat himself.

He leaned in a little closer. She could smell the last thing he'd had to drink, obviously a bit of alcohol, but she also felt the warmth of his breath against her nape.

"Want a drink?"

Her tail swished.

Of all the things she was willing to do this night, that was one step too far.

"No thanks." Zelda smiled at him and hoped it looked good, that her makeup hadn't been smudged too badly from the sweaty dancing.

"I think I'd rather…" Zelda trailed off, something catching the corner of her eye.

It wasn't anything overly out of the ordinary. Just a man. A man in a leather jacket whose dark blue eyes scanned the crowd.

As though he was searching for someone.

Her spine stiffened.

James Dean put his hand on Zelda's waist. "You good?"

Zelda nodded quickly, turning her back to the man, forcing James Dean around so he was in front of her.

He laughed. "Okay."

"I'd like to go with you." Zelda put her smile back on, trying to look as pleasing as possible for this guy.

She needed this. She needed him to take her out of here. Right now. Her reckless fun suddenly didn't seem so fun anymore, and she needed to be gone from here.

"What's the matter?"

There were other people in this crowd who were shifters, so it shouldn't matter if that guy saw the back of her head, her ears, and tail. They shouldn't give her away.

She hoped.

"I…think I see my ex-boyfriend over there. I'd just like to get out of here with you before any drama starts."

The lie rolled right off her tongue. She was surprised with how easily it came.

James Dean's mouth quirked, as though he wanted to look over her shoulder and see for himself, but managed to stop himself.

"No problem." He took her by the hand. "My car's out back."

Sweet relief.

Zelda quickly followed him. He took her through the employee only area. Zelda heard the sounds of the kitchen as they prepared food for the few people who actually came here to eat.

"Do you know the people who work here?"

"Nope. Hurry," he said.

Zelda did, though the thought of rushing through the back halls of a club, being where she wasn't supposed to, thrilled her on some level.

Just like in a movie. The hero and heroine outrunning some terrible foe.

In her case, the foe wasn't just terrible, he was deadly.

A bouncer shouted at them as they ran, but then there was the door with the bright red EXIT sign above it.

They burst through. Home free.

"This way."

When James Dean said his car was *out back*, he wasn't kidding. The man pulled her down the back alley of the club, behind another restaurant, and down another dark alley.

Zelda's adrenaline began to simmer down, and the farther and farther away Mr. Dean pulled her from the lights of, well, anything, the more uneasy she became.

"Are you sure your car is around here?"

She began searching for any signs of a vehicle, something that would let her relax out of this state of mind that had her so utterly worked up.

"Yeah, it's this way."

He pulled her along a little farther. Zelda's heart lurched into her throat when James Dean shoved his hand into his pocket, but the only thing he pulled out was a set of keys. He clicked a button, and a distinct beeping noise sounded as the car lights flashed.

She hadn't even seen it there.

"Sorry." James Dean smiled at her, an innocent dimple appearing at his cheek. "It's just easier than paying for parking."

She supposed that made sense.

He opened the passenger door for her.

The sound of glass clinking, as though someone had knocked over a bottle, caught her attention real fast. Zelda spun around, searching through the darkness to see what had made that noise. There was some yellow light from bulbs at the few back doors, but nothing that really reached into the cracks of the alley.

"Everything okay?"

Zelda looked back at her suitor. For some reason, her gaze flitted down to the door he held open for her. It was an old fashioned sort of car. She didn't know much about vehicles, but Zelda was willing to bet this one was a classic of some sort. And the little hole where the lock popped in and out of, there was nothing there for her to press down on to lock the door.

Or pull on to unlock it.

Zelda's gaze slowly turned back up to the man she'd allowed to bring her out here. She smiled. She tried to. Her mouth didn't seem to hold it very well. "Let's go back to the club."

He blinked at her. His smile so easy-going, so handsome, that she wanted to melt right into it. "Go back? Why?"

"I just figured it might be a better idea to get to know each other a little more first. We can get those drinks you offered."

She wanted to go back more than anything. She'd allowed one guy looking out over the gyrating and pulsing crowd of people to scare her away from a public space where she would have been safe. That guy might not have anything to do with this at all. What if it was the handsome stranger with the cute and innocent smile she had to beware of all this time?

Zelda found herself backing away from the man, and his car, without meaning to.

James Dean's smile slowly melted from his face as he shut the door. "If you want to go back, I'll take you back."

Zelda blinked. "You...really?"

James Dean shrugged. "Yeah, sure. If you're not into it, then that's fine." He said it grudgingly, though.

She supposed that made sense. He'd thought he would be getting laid tonight, and then Zelda had to go ahead and ruin the mood.

"Well, I'm not saying I'm *not* into it." She definitely still wanted the sex.

James Dean cocked his head, his brows coming together as though confused by her signals. "Uh..."

"I just thought we could have a few drinks first. I think I need to loosen up, you know?"

James Dean smiled at her again. "Sure thing. Just let me grab my jacket."

She nodded, holding her arms and glancing behind her one last time as he went around to the driver's side of the door.

There was still no one there that she could see, but she couldn't help the feeling in her stomach—

A hand clamped hard around her mouth. A hand holding something that smelled sharp and…

Don't inhale.

Zelda fought. She squirmed and struggled, but James Dean's free arm curled around her waist and it was tight. Painful. The chemical smell of chloroform panicked her because she knew what would happen if she passed out. She knew where she would go to.

Who would see her. Who would end her life.

James Dean must have been either a shifter or a subhuman because his strength was immense. Zelda couldn't get him off.

Someone get him off me!

He released her. Just like that. Zelda couldn't get her legs to work beneath her in time to catch herself as she fell to her knees.

And glanced back just in time to see the man with those dark blue eyes, the man from the club, lift James Dean up into the air before slamming him down hard onto the filthy concrete.

"Don't fucking think so, pal."

James Dean flailed and struggled for all he was worth, but Blue Eyes held him down with relative ease.

He was bigger, after all. Still, it should have caused him some struggle to hold down his captive like that. Either he hid it well or it wasn't that difficult for him. Blue Eyes looked her way as he pressed down his victim and cuffed the man. Their eyes locked, and Zelda froze.

Something about the way he looked at her caught her off guard. Not even that, there was something in his eyes she could only see now that they both held their gazes. As though Zelda was downloading some information right from his brain and into hers.

It made Zelda's guts seize up and her heart clench, and a terrifying reality pressed upon her that she didn't want.

Not now. Not after she'd just gotten away from her ex.

Mate. That's what that look said, and now that the smell of chloroform was fading and she could think again, even his scent said what she didn't want it to say.

This wasn't some guy her alpha had chosen for her to breed with. This was her natural born mate.

Holy shit.

The man held James Dean down with the weight of his knee, ignoring the man's screams of innocence and his thrashing. He seemed to snap out of the haze so fast that Zelda wondered if she'd caught the frequency between them right. Or if her nose was working properly.

He yanked something out from the inside of his leather jacket. A cell phone. He actually dialed 911.

"My name is Victor Kincaid; I'm with Delany and Kincaid Security. I'm in the alley behind the Golden Palace Chinese Restaurant on 37th and Main. I've got a suspect here who was attacking one of my clients. Could you send over an ambulance and some officers to assist, please?"

Zelda blinked at that. Did he say *security*? And did he say *client*?

That couldn't be right, but she was too glad to be alive to care.

The way he looked at her now didn't seem to show any of the previous mind-blowing, rock your world revelations he'd seemed to be hit with earlier.

Maybe he wasn't her mate. Maybe Zelda was just misinterpreting the adrenaline rush that came with being rescued by a tall, dark, and handsome stranger.

The operator on the phone asked him, Victor, a few more questions, which he answered. Then, still on the phone, he looked right at her again with those piercing blue eyes.

"You okay? Are you hurt anywhere?" He sounded almost frantic about that.

Zelda shook her head. She felt dirty all over, and cold. The sweat she'd built up from dancing in the heat of the club didn't mesh well with the night air of late August.

"You're bleeding."

Zelda shook her head, ready to tell him that she wasn't bleeding and that she was fine. Except her hands stung. She looked down at her palms. There was blood there. Blood from the scratches she'd sustained when she'd fallen to her knees. Dirt and little rocks were embedded in her palms as well, some under the skin, and one of her nails had been broken right off.

Her knees weren't faring much better, and her tail was wet and filthy. Now that she was taking note of herself, Zelda could really start to feel the sting all over her body. The chloroform lingering on her face made her feel dirtier.

"I'm...I'm fine." She looked down at the man she'd been ready to walk off with, and all she felt for him now was disgust and contempt. He wasn't facing her. He had his gaze turned away. She couldn't tell if that was because he was a coward and couldn't look her in the face, or because Victor had turned his head away for him.

She looked back at Victor. "Thanks for saving me."

Zelda wasn't sure how to feel about the fact that Victor also seemed to have trouble holding her haze, even as he gave his gruff reply. "Don't mention it. It's my job."

That's right, he'd said something about her being a client.

Zelda pushed herself to her feet. She brushed herself off, ignoring the pain in her palms and knees when she did. "I don't know who you think I am, but I'm grateful for the mistake."

"It's no mistake. Your brother hired me to keep an eye on you after what you started saying about your husband."

"*Ex* husband," she corrected quickly. That was the first thing that needed to be made right in all of this. "And what do you mean? My brother called you? Why would he do that?" She'd told him not to.

Of course, something like that might be an odd question to a human, or even a subhuman. They didn't always understand the way pack life worked, and Victor sure did give her an odd stare.

"You want to know why your brother would call us to protect you when you accused your ex of murder?"

Zelda pressed her lips together. She suddenly felt a little more like her old self. Small and insignificant. She pushed it away. That wasn't her anymore. "Pack life is different than most humans know. We don't pull in any outside help."

He nodded. "Even at the expense of your own life. Got it."

That really made her cheeks heat.

A siren sounded in the distance. Zelda's ears twitched. She looked up, so did Victor.

He turned his attention back to her quickly. "For now, you're stuck with me. I'm your bodyguard."

That should have annoyed her; it should have set her on edge and brought up her defensive hackles. Instead, the sound of his voice as he told her she was stuck with him melted her insides like warm butter.

She had no idea what was happening right now, but already it felt kind of good.

THE FIRST THING Zelda did after the police came and questioned them was call her brother.

She had to do that at the police station for obvious reasons, and while her new *bodyguard* was giving her some small amount of space that she assumed was meant for privacy, the fact that he was still within sight of her made it fairly awkward to give her brother hell for doing this.

"I didn't know what else to do." Even through the phone, Link's voice came out sounding like a groan. "No one else was listening."

"You're supposed to leave it alone." Zelda glanced over at Victor.

He stood there, just twenty feet away, almost looking casual had it not been for the hand on his hip, and the way he seemed to be looking down both hallways, his blue hawk eyes seeking out any potential danger.

If he he handled all threats the same way he'd dealt with the man who'd tried to abduct her, then Zelda got the feeling she was going to be in fairly good hands.

"I can't leave it alone. You're my sister."

Zelda pressed her forehead against the wall. "Do you want the pack to throw you out?"

"Who fucking cares about the pack? I don't want you dead!"

His shout shocked her. Zelda yanked the phone from her ear. There was a long minute of silence between them.

"This isn't a game," Link said. "Not like when we were kids. Besides, Harry fucked off anyway. No one knows where he is."

That got her attention. "Really?"

Her ex was gone?

"Really."

"As in, he's on the run? What happened? Who's running the pack?"

"I guess the pack elders are. They came over and started asking questions. About you, about Harry and his friends. Gerard and Ben are gone too."

"They were the ones there," Zelda muttered.

"Yeah, and apparently Ben called the cops. He was the one who got the humans involved in this in the first place."

Her brother could have reached his hand through the phone and gut punched her and it wouldn't have felt as bad as this.

"Ben called the police? On Harry?"

They were best friends. At least, that had been the impression Zelda had been left with when she'd married Harry.

Gerard had been Harry's best man at the wedding, but Ben had been up there at the altar with him.

Wolves on one side of the aisle and foxes on the other.

Zelda could still feel the knotting in her stomach she'd gotten that day, even as she was being given away, not by her bother, her uncle, or her alpha, but by Maxwell, the alpha of the new wolf pack she was joining.

All that had gone through her head at the time was how much she didn't want to do it. How much she didn't want to get married to Harry or have his babies.

But he had looked handsome in that suit, and when he'd taken her hands, he'd told her she looked pretty in a soft, almost shy voice, and it hit her hard that he probably didn't want to do this either.

So she'd smiled and told herself she was going to make the best of it.

It hadn't occurred to her then, and it was still hitting her now, that the shy smiling man who had touched her and kissed her, danced with her, and then made love to her, could be a killer.

One year. She'd spent one year in that house with him, alone during the nights and waiting for him to come back from his wolf hunts during the days. She'd never once suspected he could be the sort of person who could poison a man.

Hell, she'd eaten his cooking.

Zelda shivered.

"Zel? Hey, you there?"

Zelda snapped out of it. "Yeah, I'm here. I'm fine."

"Are you sure?"

He sounded as though he wanted to make sure there was no one standing next to her holding a gun to her head.

She didn't like that. She felt guilty for making him think something like that. "I'm sorry. Trust me. Everything's okay, but how to did you get the money to pay for this? A bodyguard? Really?"

"Harry is missing," Link said, as though he needed to drive that point home. "There's no telling where that asshole is or what's going on. You were just attacked in a fucking dirty alley. You need to come home."

She couldn't come home. If she went home to her fox pack, to her brother and her uncle, they would take her in without a doubt.

There was no telling how the alpha would react. He was always just and fair, but being just and fair meant putting the majority of the pack above the minority. Risking everyone to suffer the wrath of a wolf pack because Link and Uncle Mike couldn't turn her away was something she couldn't live with.

She could still see the way Maxwell choked. The foam that had come from his mouth as he clutched at his throat over the table. Then Harry, pretending to show concern, had frantically given him the Heimlich.

Of course, he hadn't been choking, and Maxwell had died vomiting blood.

If she had to watch Link do that, or Uncle Mike, she would die. Zelda wouldn't be able to survive.

"I can't come home, but you don't have to have this guy here. He took care of me and everything's good now."

"Yeah, until the next time."

"There won't be a next time. I've got pepper spray with me."

"Were you able to use it when you were being attacked in a dark alley behind a club?"

Why did her brother have to be the sort of asshole who had to pick apart every single one of her arguments?

He didn't even give her the chance to answer.

"It doesn't matter anyway; Mike and I pooled together the money. He's sticking around you even if you come home."

"What?"

"Yeah. Are you fucking crazy? What are you even doing in places like that? You never used to go clubbing before."

Zelda glanced back at Victor. Her new bodyguard. He was looking away from her, though Zelda got the impression he had been listening.

He didn't have the ears or tail, but if he was a subhuman then he'd be able to hear the conversation no matter what.

She got the feeling that, despite the look he was giving off, he could definitely hear what she was saying.

"I don't need a bodyguard."

Even one as handsome as that guy.

Very few men had been able to make Zelda stop and really look, to make her jaw drop while she thought to herself, *Damn. That's one gorgeous hunk of man meat right there.*

Well, okay, even in her head, she never said it quite like *that*, but the point was the same. Victor was probably the third guy Zelda had ever seen in her entire life that made her stomach clench with actual butterflies. A guy that made her bite her lower lip, made her want to bite *his* lower lip.

Add that to the fact that he was her bodyguard and the sex meter in her chest just blew up right to her head, sending smoke signals out her ears.

It couldn't be more of a sexy trope if she were writing this into a romance novel. A sexy bodyguard and a woman in danger. If this actually was a romance novel, they'd be hitting the sack by the second act.

But it was just a flutter in her stomach. She probably had to throw up soon after nearly getting kidnapped and killed. That was all. She was only projecting this sense of lust onto him because he was unbelievably gorgeous, had saved her life, and was an actual bodyguard.

Hell, the next thing she knew, Zelda would find out he was a former Navy Seal and that he had a billion dollars in his account. Then he'd really be sex on wheels.

Link was still talking to her. Shit. She had to pay attention. Zelda only came back into the conversation when she heard him talking about bringing Uncle Mike onto the phone.

No. She couldn't handle that. Not right now. This wasn't something she could deal with when there was literally a hot guy she didn't know listening to every word she said.

"Hey, Link, I have to go, thanks for the call."

"Zel—"

She hung up on him, not entirely sure why her heart pounded so hard and fast.

Victor took note of it. He tilted his head to the side just a little. Then he stepped forward.

Zelda wanted to run. She wasn't sure why. The smell of him made her want to get even closer to him. She wanted to fall into his chest and feel for herself what it was like. Hard with muscle? Had to be with the way he looked. Did he feel as good as he looked? Would he hold her? Comfort her?

Zelda had to remember to take a breath when he was finally in front of her. As cool and collected as though he was not feeling these things she was.

"We need to talk."

CHAPTER 3

*Y*our brother and uncle paid me good money to watch after you. From the description they gave, you're not the type of woman to go into clubs like that. I was shocked when I finally tracked you down."

Zelda kept her fingers curled around her paper coffee cup. It warmed her. She wanted to look away from him. Her old self was still pushing forward the shame she felt, but she pushed it back with equal force, determined to meet his gaze.

"I'll pay them back for the money. I don't need a bodyguard."

He lifted a dark brow at her. Why did he have to have such perfect eyebrows? "You sure about that?"

Zelda took a sip of her coffee. It warmed her belly, and she smiled, batting her lashes a little. "Yup."

He didn't seem to react. It was a pity and caused her a bit of grief.

She'd spent good money to look this way. She'd thought she looked good enough, but there wasn't as much as a reaction out of this guy.

Maybe he was used to more beautiful women.

Victor sighed. "I can't tell you what to do. I can only make suggestions for your safety. Until your husband is found—"

"*Ex* husband," she corrected quickly.

Victor nodded. "Of course. My apologies. Until your ex is found, or at the very least, until we find out why that guy came after you, you might not want to put yourself in danger like that."

"I was in a public place having fun. I was only in danger when I stupidly left with someone I didn't know. It won't happen again."

Why did he have to smell so good? Seeing him up close like this, the both of them sitting around a small table at an all night coffee shop down the street from the station, he was the most perfect looking specimen she'd ever seen in her life.

Harry had been relatively good-looking. Good-looking enough for Zelda to breathe a sigh of relief the first time she'd seen him, but Victor was on a whole other level.

Even with the haven't-shaved-in-three-days look, she wanted to melt all over him.

Take me away. I'm yours.

She cleared her throat. "How much are you charging my family anyway?"

He grinned at her. He actually grinned.

"Sorry, can't disclose that."

Of course.

"So then, what does this mean? I'm still going to go out."

"It would be for the best if you didn't."

She grinned at him.

"But…" he continued. "If you're determined to self destruct, then there's not much I can do about it."

"Self destruct? What's that supposed to mean?"

"I don't know, you're a grown woman capable of making your own choices." Victor stood, and all of a sudden, Zelda didn't think he looked, or smelled, so sexy anymore. "I'll take you home. Unless you think one in the morning is too early."

This guy was going to be a problem. She could tell that already, but Zelda was discovering a few things about herself lately. One of them happened to be how much she enjoyed a challenge.

Challenging herself to throw caution to the wind. Challenging herself to buy this dress and these heels, to go out and do things she never would have done. They made her feel more alive than anything else in the entire world.

Maybe this would be a good challenge as well.

But just because he was a challenge didn't mean he was a problem that needed to be solved.

Zelda would butter him up a little first.

She stood, pulling her purse over her shoulder. "I'm ready to turn in. I think it was enough excitement for one night, don't you?"

He looked relieved. That was good. She didn't want to entirely push him away just yet.

"I'll drive you to your apartment."

"I've got a car."

"We can pick it up in the morning." Victor hadn't taken his coat off when he'd sat down for coffee with her, so he was already ready to go.

Zelda got the feeling a lot of that had to do with the fact that, despite the permit he most likely had for his gun, taking his jacket off and flashing his holster might not have been the best idea in the world for the mental well-being of the night staff.

Even being hyper aware of the fact that this man had a weapon, she couldn't help but note the strength in his voice.

The surety with which he thought he would be driving her home.

She tried to keep her smile pleasant. "I would really like to drive home on my own."

Victor looked at her. He studied her, as though thinking of his next move.

So calculating.

"How about this. If I let you do the driving, will that make you feel more comfortable?"

The question stunned her. "You would let me drive your car?"

"Why not?" He said it as though it was no big deal.

Zelda's tail twitched. Something was off about this. She could feel it in her bones. He was manipulating her somehow, and while that alone should have been enough to make her go running for the hills, there was something else about it that made her want to stick around. Which was crazy. Knowing she was being manipulated was not supposed to make her feel warm and good inside.

She got the feeling that, despite his lax attitude, there was really no choice in this.

"All right, but only if you're serious and I can drive."

He tossed her the keys. "Let's go."

Zelda caught them, shocked to feel the weight of them in her hands.

Victor went to the door and opened it. He looked at her, waiting for her. "After you."

Zelda steeled herself, straightened her back, and walked ahead. She felt the undeniable urge to walk with perfect posture, to keep her breasts high.

Not for him, though. She was sure she wasn't doing that for him.

No. She had to stop thinking like that. Zelda was a strong and capable woman. Just because walking with a little confidence so happened to thrust her breasts out and accented her curves had nothing to do with anything. Not with how the smell of him affected her, nothing.

His car was parked right out front. If Victor hadn't opened the door for her, she would have seen it through the glass.

And yet seeing it now reminded her of what she'd nearly done in that alley behind the buffet.

She was about to attempt to get into another car with a stranger.

Zelda's heart pounded. Victor went to the passenger side door.

"All right. Ready when you are."

Zelda nodded. She walked around to the driver's side, keeping her eyes on him, trying to be as inconspicuous as possible..

This time, she wasn't going to mess up. Her pepper spray was in her purse. She had the zipper open so she could get it easily this time if he grabbed her, and she wasn't about to be caught off guard.

Instead of pressing the button that would have unlocked the doors for her, she inserted the key into the door and unlocked it manually.

She got in.

She shut the door.

Victor still waited to be let inside. She reached over, her hand touching the passenger door, ready to open it and let him in.

Zelda pulled back instead, and Victor frowned, seeming to realize that something wasn't quite right in Oz.

He rapped the window with his knuckles. "Hey, you gonna let me in or what?"

Zelda inserted the key into ignition. She started the car.

Victor grabbed the door handle and pulled, as though that would magically unlock the door for him.

"Zelda, let me in. Come on. No one is here to hurt you."

She wanted to believe that, part of her did.

A big part.

But the fact that she'd nearly been taken for a spin by another guy she'd wanted to trust only hours before wasn't jiving with her. She didn't care if this guy was hired by her brother and her uncle. He could be literally anyone. If Harry was really missing, then who was to say this guy wasn't a plant?

"Zelda. Open the door."

Victor pulled something out of his pocket. Zelda's heart launched right into her throat at the thought of a weapon, but no. She heard the jingling of keys.

She put the vehicle into drive and pulled away from him before he could unlock the door. He chased after her. She let him, at first. She wanted him to hear her when she called out to him through the glass.

"If you're the real deal then you'll meet me at my place."

"Zelda!"

"I'll leave your car back at the club!"

Zelda sped off down the street, white-knuckling the heated steering wheel as she went.

She briefly watched Victor chase after her. He kept up a pretty good speed for a while, but of course he couldn't hold a candle to a moving vehicle.

Zelda laughed when he was far enough away that he wouldn't be able to catch her even if she ran against a stop light.

She'd just committed grand theft auto. The intent to leave the vehicle nice and safe in a spot where Victor could pick it up later wasn't the point. She'd still done it.

The old her never in a million years would have thought to do something as reckless as this.

Might as well keep going. There was no turning back now.

23

CHAPTER 4

*T*here was a heavy bang on Zelda's door not long after she returned home.

She went to the peep hole, and was kind of relieved, and nervous, to see Victor on the other side, his hands planted on his hips. The posture pushed his jacket back and exposed the gun holster.

He didn't look remotely happy.

"If I open the door, are you going to arrest me?"

He rolled his eyes up to the ceiling, as though asking for patience. "I'm not a cop."

That didn't stop him from putting that last guy in handcuffs, but, hey, what did she know about being a bodyguard?

Zelda kept the chain on the door as she unlocked it, which turned out to be a good thing as Victor tried to push his way inside when she opened it just the lightest amount.

The fire in his eyes was almost enough to make her step back.

Yeah, he definitely wasn't happy with her.

"You realize I could have you arrested for that shit, right?"

Zelda leaned against the door frame. "Yeah, it occurred to me while I was driving down the road. Though I'm hoping that leaving your car nice and safe in the club parking lot made up for it."

He actually smiled at her. Sort of. The half quirk of his lips looked as though he was more or less finding her reluctantly funny.

"Barely," he said.

"Come on. I had to pay to park that car and everything." She smiled innocently at him, as though this was the kind of banter they had all the time.

"Uh huh, and what were you going to do if you got home and someone was waiting for you here when you were alone? I was going to do a proper sweep of your apartment."

"I thought of that. I put a little piece of tape on the door so I would know if someone came in when I was away."

And when she got home and saw the tape still at the top corner of the door, untouched, she knew she was in the clear.

Victor didn't seem all that impressed. He shook his head at her. "That's literally the oldest trick in the book and if someone really wanted to get into your apartment, they could have done it. Even if they spotted the tape, because everyone knows that trick."Zelda bit her lips together. She didn't want to admit she only knew that trick because she'd searched Google.

"Any assailant could have tried getting in through one of your windows. You're only on the third floor. Any subhuman or shifter could have made it up there. Even some humans can get up here. And don't tell me you put tape on those windows, too. It wouldn't have mattered, and by the time you got inside to check it, would have been too late."

That had briefly occurred to her as well when she'd crossed her living room to check the sliding glass door to her balcony, and then again when she'd gone into her bedroom to check the window there.

Her apartment wasn't that great. It wasn't as if she'd had a lot of money saved up for something amazing after leaving Harry anyway, but it was still hers, her territory, and she wanted to protect it.

She wanted to stay where she could be independent for the first time.

"You gonna let me in or what?"

Zelda looked at him. She thought of her options, and knew she didn't exactly have any.

"If I wanted to hurt you, really hurt you, I could have kicked in this door by now. That little chain won't keep anyone out who really wants to get in."

Zelda had installed a strong chain, but she knew he was right. Short of it being as thick as her wrists, that bit of metal wouldn't keep out any alpha or beta shifter. Most subhumans could probably break it. Hell, many humans could probably break it, too.

She closed the door, slid the chain across the lock, then opened it.

Victor stood on the other side of the threshold, his face a mask she couldn't read, but his eyes still spoke loud and clear on how unhappy he was. He could be biting down on the inside of his cheek to keep from yelling at her right now.

"So, are you letting me get away with this because I'm a client?"

He lifted a brow at her. "Not quite."

What was that supposed to mean?

Did it mean…maybe he was picking up on the same smells and pheromones she was as well? Was he being affected the same way she was?

Even now as he stepped into her apartment, Zelda struggled against the urge to lift her hand to her nose. Anything to keep that sweet smelling scent from making her blood warm, and her sex from responding.

Zelda crossed her arms. She was out of that tight dress she'd been wearing back at the club and in her bathrobe. She didn't want him to see her nipples budding beneath the material.

"I was just about to have a bath, so, do what you need to do."

Victor nodded, letting out a grunting noise of some kind.

"I won't be a minute. For the most part, I'll be out in my car, and if you need anything, or you see anything, you can give me a call and I'll be right up." He reached into his jacket pocket and pulled out a card holder. He flipped it open and set one of the cards down on the little round table that held her odds and ends beneath her calendar. "Put that number in your contacts list."

Zelda took the card. She looked at it, then at the back of Victor's dark head of hair. Not that she was tall enough, but from what she could make out, he wasn't showing signs of hair loss. He was either late to that party or it wasn't happening for him.

Nice. Very nice. Not only did he have to smell like heaven in a hand basket, but he also had to have the scruffy beard thing going that she liked, he was fit, had a full head of hair.

If he kept this up, she wasn't going to be able to resist.

Zelda found herself following him around her apartment. He didn't say anything about that. Maybe he thought it was normal, or his other clients tended to supervise as he did this sort of thing as well.

Really, Zelda just couldn't get enough of that smell.

She needed it in her face at all times. That's what it felt like at the very least. She wanted it up her nostrils for as long as possible. The longer she held onto that scent, the more she could study it.

Zelda could almost taste it on her tongue. The fact that it was making her want to be alone in that bath wasn't helping her too much, but at the same time…didn't he notice this? Was this only happening in Zelda's head?

She'd been so sure the first time she saw him, the first time she'd smelled him, that it meant they were mates. Natural mates, the kind chosen by fate or nature, or whatever anyone out there wanted to call it.

She had been so sure…

But he didn't seem to be reacting to her at all. He checked her bedroom, opened her closet, and moved her clothes hangers aside to see if there was anyone hiding behind them. He was thorough.

"So, you're an armed bodyguard."

"That's what I am."

Ignore the smell. The sweet, musky smell that made her want to put her face to his neck and inhale long and deep.

Mostly, she wanted to press her breasts to his chest and see if that would have any impact on him. She wanted to see if she could seduce him.

Of all the people she'd danced with since leaving Harry, she'd never slept with any of them. She'd wanted to; she would have if her last choice hadn't been a kidnapping psycho.

Zelda shook off the scent of lust. "So, what are you going to do then? I mean, aside from sitting out in your car and waiting for someone to attack me?"

He looked back at her. "It's not exactly going to happen like that."

A thrill rushed through Zelda's chest. "So, you're going to stay here?"

She could make up the couch for him, then maybe pretend to forget he was there, walk out of her room in her slinky little nighty. The brand new one she'd bought after running to freedom.

She'd never worn it for Harry. She could grab a snack in it. He would wake up from the noise and see her there. He might even find her attractive. That little nighty did show off her long legs…

"I won't be sleeping here. You won't be seeing me when I sleep. When I need to, I'll go home."

Home?

"What do you mean? You're not going to be watching over me?"

She hadn't been all that excited over the idea of having someone tailing her when she was supposed to be having fun for the first time in her life. However, now that she was faced with the idea of not having someone around who would protect her when…*if* she was attacked again…

He smiled at her. "My partner will be watching over you when I'm not available to. Steve. He's a good guy. Don't steal his car and you'll get along just fine."

Zelda smiled. Now that it was done and over with, she couldn't believe she'd actually done it. "I really did steal your car, didn't I?"

"Yes, you did."

"And it doesn't hold any water with you that, at least when you were out of sight, I kept to the speed limit and made sure the car was dropped off nice and safe?"

Victor looked as though he wanted to be angry with her, but then he couldn't help but smile, and then laugh. He had such a nice smile, and a good laugh. God, why did she have to be reacting this way to him? Why couldn't he at least look at her as though she was having the same effect on him? At least then she could know whether this was real or not.

"Unfortunately, no. There's nothing in the law books that lets you off the hook for that. You're lucky you're cute."

Cute. He said she was cute. Not sexy. Or gorgeous. But *cute*.

For now, she'd take it.

"Okay. So, aside from you and your friend switching off to watch over me, what else is going to happen?"

Victor was clearly amused by the questions. Maybe it was because of how cute he thought she was.

"I'll be doing a search of your car after this. If you've got any plans or responsibilities, run them by me and I'll plan your routes, assess threats, that kind of thing."

"Uh huh, and are you going to look sexy doing all that as you do right now?"

Victor's brows raised. He turned away from her quickly.

Was that a blush on his face? She'd definitely embarrassed him. She couldn't believe she'd said it.

"I'll try not to distract you," Victor said. It was the only thing he said, then he got back to business. "I was able to look into you a little before I found you. You don't seem to be working right now, but I want to make sure. You got a job? Or anything under the table?"

This was something that Zelda bit her lips together about.

"I've got some money."

"No work?"

"I'm a fox shifter from a small pack and was married off to a wolf to join territories. If I was to get a job, it would be waiting tables."

"There's nothing wrong with that."

She couldn't help but think there was. She was in front of a guy who had a career in saving and protecting people.

She didn't have more than a high school education. Everyone knew college wouldn't be in her future. Not when she was going to be married off to whoever happened to make the best deal with her alpha.

And her, stupid girl she was, had been fairly content with the idea. She'd been happy to get her high school diploma, and then stick around the pack learning how to cook and sew and garden, learning how to be a good mother, basically.

She didn't want to knock those skills either, but it had been a comfortable life, waiting for her alpha to come to her and say someone had been chosen. The only thing that bothered her about the whole set up was that she didn't get a say in who she was married off to.

She should have asked questions. She should have pushed for college. She should have learned how to run her own business.

She liked gardening and flowers. Maybe if she'd gone to school, she could have her own store right now.

Maybe.

But she didn't. Now she was here.

"I just don't have a job right now."

"Okay, so then you're spending your savings." He looked at her patiently, as though waiting for her to admit to something.

He *knew*. She could tell right then and there that he knew.

"I took some money with me when I left." Her hackles might have been a bit raised up when she said that.

"I'm not accusing you of anything."

"Link told me there were people in Maxwell's pack who were accusing me of theft."

"If it was your husband's money, then as his wife, you're entitled to half of it anyway. If you found some cash beneath the mattress or in his wallet then it doesn't matter to me if you took it."

"I'm his ex wife. I don't care what the papers say right now. He's a fucking killer and there's no way in hell I'd ever go back to him."

"I agree with you. Your uncle and brother told me what happened."

"Great, and what did the rest of the pack say? Did you talk to them?"

"Steve and I both did, yes."

"And?"

He smiled at her. "Cooperate with me a little on this and you might find out."

Zelda thought about this a little while longer. "Do bodyguards normally go around asking questions like this? I mean, you're not investigating anything."

"I did have to investigate where you would be. Steve and I do a range of things. Mostly, he's the investigator, and I'm the muscle."

She thought about that. "Are you really a bodyguard?"

"When I'm hired to be, I am."

Something still wasn't settling right in her gut with this. She shouldn't have hung up on her brother. She should have demanded to know everything that was going on here.

"Well, tomorrow night, I'll be going out again."

"I would advise against that."

Zelda smiled, shrugged, and went to the fridge. It was always best to have a bottle of cool water with a hot bath. "I'm still going out."

He followed her, keeping at a short distance. "It would be better if you didn't. If I can keep a better eye on you without too many variables, it makes my job a lot easier."

"Well, I will do my best to take that into consideration."

She stopped herself before she could get any farther, an idea suddenly hitting her. A way for her to test if this was just hormones, or if she really was picking up on a mating scent.

Victor didn't look too pleased about her answer either, so she was happy to continue with this.

"Actually, I was thinking about staying home tomorrow night, on one condition."

"Great, let's hear it."

He was still trying to be professional with her. She liked that. It made a strange new thrill rise up inside her. As though this was a challenge for her to overcome.

"Kiss me. Right now, like you really mean it. And I'll stay in tomorrow night."

CHAPTER 5

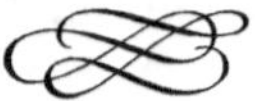

"No."

Zelda blinked. The seductive air she tried to put on whooshed out of her like a leaking balloon.

"Well, you could have pretended to think about it for a little before saying no."

He really could have, instead of mercilessly slamming her with the instant rejection.

Kind of made her want to put her glasses back on her face and cuddle up in one of her thick turtlenecks so she could start hiding again.

"It would be grossly unprofessional of me to do that." Victor's lips pulled up at the corner of his perfect mouth. His mannerism was gentle enough, but that didn't help her wounded pride.

Try and try again, though. Right?

"Well, you did call me cute." She stepped up to him, invading his personal space. He didn't step back from her. He watched her, holding his ground, as though he was in perfect control of this situation.

Zelda wanted to change that. She pressed herself against him. Through the robe, she felt the leather jacket he wore against her

32

breasts, and beneath that she felt the heat of his body, and the firm muscle beneath that.

She was so in tune with his body it was crazy. She felt him through his clothes as though they both stood there with nothing on.

"Just one little kiss?" She batted her lashes at him. "It won't take more than a few seconds."

And she intended to make sure it lasted as long as possible.

His face remained a neutral mask. He reached his hands up, his strong fingers clasping around her small wrists as he gently eased her back.

But it was too late. Zelda already felt the increase in heat from his body, and she saw the way his pupils went wide.

She was having a reaction on him. He just wasn't showing it.

"Sorry, can't do that either. If it makes you more comfortable, I won't call you cute ever again."

That wouldn't make her feel more comfortable. That would bother her something fierce. She wanted him to call her cute. She wanted him to tell her how much he wanted her, especially now that she knew for a fact he was denying the urge to touch her.

"Don't pout."

"Not pouting."

He let go of her wrists. Already she missed the tingle in her arms. The warmth of his touch shot up her arms and did something to her that she couldn't exactly explain.

She wanted it back. She wanted Victor to touch her again. Longer this time. Not just on her wrists either.

Zelda swallowed. "I…"

She choked before she could say it. She wanted him to touch her. She wanted his hands all over her body and her thighs around his waist while he thrust inside her.

She wanted him in bed with her. Or in her shower. On the couch, the kitchen floor, it didn't matter where because this was her mate and she needed him.

Victor shook his head. "Don't finish that thought. It's not gonna happen."

She looked at him, taking note of his face, his eyes.

And how absolutely serious he was. It *radiated* off him. Victor clenched his hands into fists, biting down on his lips briefly before speaking.

"You're my client. For now. I won't jeopardize your life by getting involved with you."

"You wouldn't be jeopardizing anything. You already saved me." She had to make him see that. She wanted his hands on her again.

She reached for him. Needing him to touch her. Needing to feel that again.

He pulled back when she touched his hands.

"No."

The rejection got her hard. Got her right in the chest. Zelda couldn't believe it.

She swallowed hard. "I think you're my mate."

Victor hissed.

Zelda winced.

Was it really that horrible of an idea?

"I'll give Steve a call. We'll figure something out."

"What are you going to do?"

"First, keep an eye on you until we can find out where your ex went off to. Chances are he was the one who sent that guy after you. We just have to get him talking then we'll know for sure." Victor rubbed his chin, briefly looking away from her. "I'll get Steve to watch over you full time. There are some other guys I know. We can bring them in on this for when Steve needs to sleep. Don't shake your head at me. This is the way it's going to be."

"It doesn't have to be. I like having you around."

"Next thing I'll do is find out if this mating thing is true or not."

He said it as though Zelda hadn't spoken a word. And she didn't like that, or the implication of what he said. "You think I'm lying?"

She'd left the wolf pack because they had accused her of lying. She didn't go home because she didn't want to put her brother and uncle through that either, or watch as the fox elders had to decide whether or not to believe her and pretend otherwise to keep the pack safe, or turn her away.

She couldn't even get someone to believe her on something as simple as a mating.

Un-fucking-believable.

She backed off from him. "So you're just going to dump me off on your friends? I thought you said my brother and uncle were paying you?"

"I'm not dumping you off. Steve and I are in business together and we know other people we trust in our line of work. You'll be perfectly safe and be treated with the respect you need. Having someone paid to protect you jumping into bed with you wouldn't exactly be a smart move."

"So you're saying I'm stupid for wanting this? Is that it?"

Where was this anger even coming from? She didn't entirely understand. Part of her got where he was coming from, she really did, but the idea that he wasn't going to be the one watching over her, when he was the only one she needed, cut her in a way that she'd never been cut before.

It was different from when she'd overheard Harry talking about what he'd done with Ben and Gerard, a different kind of shock, a different kind of pain, and it stung.

Victor's lips thinned. "I did a sweep of your apartment. Everything is clear. I'll do a check of your vehicle tomorrow, but for tonight, I'll call Steve over here. He'll be parked on the side of the road right over there."

He pointed. From where they stood, Zelda could see the spot he indicated out the far window.

"So you're leaving?"

"Until Steve gets here, no. I won't. We'll make sure there's always security with you."

"Uh huh, and while you're gone, you're going to do a little digging to make sure I'm not lying about you being my mate?"

"Just because I think you're a beautiful woman doesn't mean I'm mated to you."

"Humans can feel the pull of a mating with shifters. That does happen."

"I'm not entirely human."

She was shocked he'd revealed that about himself. The way he straightened his spine told her he didn't mean to let that horse loose either.

"So you're a subhuman. What kind of animal?"

"Since I can't shift, it hardly matters."

They looked at each other for what felt like a long minute before Victor made for the door.

Zelda opened her mouth, but nothing came out. She wanted to call out to him, to tell him the perfect words he needed to hear to keep him here with her, but her throat, and her brain, became stuck.

"Lock the door behind me," Victor said, as though she needed the reminder.

At the same time, the sound of the door shutting behind him, his lack of presence, and warmth, in the room did glue her feet to the floor.

She unstuck herself and marched to the door. She slid the chain back into place and turned the bolt, locking herself inside.

Zelda kept her hand on the door. The door her mate had touched.

The mate who would not touch her.

She pressed her back to the wood, biting down on her knuckle.

If he didn't want her…if he decided to remove himself entirely from the equation…

She wouldn't let him.

Zelda went to have her bath, grabbing her phone and Victor's card along the way so she could Google something.

She had the perfect idea.

Zelda sent Victor a quick text, then put her phone on mute and cleaned up for the night.

If this worked, it was going to be so much fun.

*E*ver since Zelda had left her husband, and her pack, and her family, behind, she'd decided to go a little rogue on certain things.

Which was why there was a sink full of dirty dishes in her small kitchen, why she had more shoes than she knew what to do with, all purchased with Harry's money—because screw him and he'd cheapened out on their first Christmas together, and her birthday—Zelda also didn't tidy up her room so much anymore either.

Which, now that she thought about it, made it kind of a good thing that she didn't manage to get Victor into her bedroom last night.

Either way, she'd turned into a bit of a slob, and one of the things that came with that was sleeping until almost one in the afternoon.

Regularly.

Staying up all night dancing and drinking seemed to have that effect. Mornings were something she slept through now instead of enjoyed as her husband went off to hunt for the pack.

She used to make the breakfast, do the dishes, the laundry, and then settle down with a good book all before lunch time.

Not so much anymore.

Her hair wasn't even brushed yet.

She checked her phone, her heart thudding a little harder than usual as she checked for a message from Victor.

There was one. She was glad to see it as she walked to her window.

She frowned at the sight of a black SUV she didn't recognize.

That did not look like Victor's Toyota. The color was the same, and it had gotten her hopes up a little, but that was about it.

She checked the message on her phone, then heaved a relieved sigh when she read Victor's message.

Steve gets off at 2PM. I'll be there early to watch over everything. If you leave, let him know. Text him when you get up so he knows you're aware of him, though he will message you. You have his number on the card.

She did, too. In fact, there was also a message from Steve telling her when he'd arrived. Last night at four-thirty in the morning. Well after she'd gone to sleep.

It was the next part of Victor's message that made Zelda smile all the more.

Couldn't find anyone to replace me just yet. We'll just have to hang tight for a little while longer.

Right. As if it was some kind of chore for Zelda to have her mate around.

With the amount of time she had left, there was more than enough for her to get dressed, do her makeup and hair, and even go down to introduce herself to Steve. She could bring him a coffee and one of the leftover cherry pastries she had in her fridge.

Just because she wasn't Suzy Q Homemaker anymore didn't mean she didn't still have the urges to be a good host.

She set to work.

VICTOR ARRIVED fifteen minutes earlier than his text said he would. Which was impressive considering Zelda wasn't home.

She'd told Steve where she was going for her class, and he dropped her off. She asked him to not tell Victor exactly what was here, which he refused to do. All that sucking up with the coffee and donuts hadn't done anything for her. Steve even smiled at her in a similar way to how Victor had as he'd disappointed her.

"Can't keep anything like this from my partner, can I?"

"It's not like it would hurt anything."

Steve looked up at the sign over the front door, his brown eyes sparkling. "No, but I still can't keep secrets from him. For your safety and everything."

He looked back at Zelda. He really was a handsome guy. Tall, broad in the shoulders without looking like he'd stuck needles into himself in order to keep that look either. Fit and healthy with a nice head of red-brown hair, though he kept himself better shaved than Victor did.

As handsome as he was, Zelda didn't feel that same pull towards Steve Delany as she did for Victor Kincaid. Steve smelled nice, too, but not nice enough that Zelda was dying for the man to touch her.

Steve reached out, gently patting her shoulder. "Don't worry about it. I'm sure that when he gets here, he'll like the surprise you've got set up for him."

When Victor arrived, even though Zelda was aware that Steve had told him where they were going, he did still manage to look surprised when he looked at the sign.

Victor blinked at it, looked at Zelda, and then at his partner. "I was hoping you were kidding."

Steve snorted. He looked way too amused by this. Zelda thought she was going to like having him around for when Victor couldn't be here.

"I'll go check out the perimeter. If you want, you can go inside with Miss Wolff to make sure everything is secure."

That was another reason why Zelda liked Steve. He called her *Miss Wolff.* He didn't need to be reminded again and again that she was no longer a *Mrs. Singer.*

If there was a way Zelda could go back in time and make it so that never happened at all, that would be fabulous.

Victor nodded, and Steve took off.

Zelda thought he would just get into his SUV and go when Victor's

Toyota pulled up, but she supposed that being in this line of work meant doing more than the obvious.

"After I confirm everything is in order inside, I won't be staying."

"What? Why?"

Victor rolled his eyes, though Zelda noted with a slight triumph that his mouth did that quirking thing at the corner.

"Don't play all innocent with me. I am not going in there and watching a bunch of woman in tight yoga pants doing a pole dancing class."

"It wasn't them I was hoping you would be looking at."

His dark blue gaze flitted to her before he looked away quickly.

Zelda grinned. She had him right where she wanted him. This was going to be perfect.

Or, maybe, not so much.

It turned out that a beginner's pole dancing class didn't have a lot to do with looking sexy and had more to do with listening to the instructor as she explained how to hold the pole, how many steps to take, to keep on her toes, to hold her shoulders back, and how to do a proper spin.

It was the most basic of beginner spins, apparently, the fireman, and Zelda couldn't seem to do. She couldn't get the spin going and kept sliding into the pole before going down onto her butt.

Luckily, everyone else in the class was smiling and having fun with their lesson, so no one seemed to notice the way Zelda struggled.

She really shouldn't have insisted that Victor stand by and watch. She'd managed to convince him to come inside, which he hadn't been happy about, and after Zelda explained to the instructor what he was and Victor showed his ID, he was allowed to stay.

It took a while for the other students to forget about him standing by the door, but Zelda didn't forget.

The man wore a pair of stereotypical sunglasses. He was just missing the earpiece to look entirely official. It didn't matter because she could feel his eyes on her as she danced.

Attempted to dance.

Fuck.

Zelda's ears twitched and her tail wouldn't hold still. She struggled to not glance back at him, but every time she did, she caught sight of that look on his face.

So serious, but he was holding back a smile. She could tell that much.

The asshole.

"Are you having some trouble here?"

Zelda jumped. "Oh, sorry."

She tried not to laugh at herself for being so nervous, but it was difficult.

The instructor shook her head. "Do not be sorry. You're doing very well."

Zelda looked to the other dancers in the class as they did their spins. Some had already mastered the spin, and there were a few others who kept themselves off their feet entirely.

They had either been practicing from home or were just showing off.

"You look nervous." The instructor glanced to Victor, who stood with his hands clasped in front of him, looking for all the world as though he wasn't seeing anything in front of him. Aware of everything around him, but capable of not showing it. Zelda never realized that could be such a skill before.

"I'm a little nervous."

Might as well not lie about it.

"Don't be," said the instructor. She had a soft French accent and a friendly air about her that gave off the impression of someone who was definitely in charge of this class, but at the same time, was every-one's friend who walked in. "Come now, show me your stance."

Zelda did.

"Okay, now your weight needs to be at the exterior while you hang on. If you lean too close, you'll spin into the pole. We don't want that. Hold the pole in your hand up high like a baseball bat. Yes. Just like that. Now, one step, two steps, three, and on the fourth you push yourself into the spin. There you go! Just like that. Good. Good."

Zelda felt pretty good about it, too. Now that she was doing it, a sense of pride came over her, and she couldn't believe she'd struggled with this earlier.

She did it again.

"Wow, this is easy!"

And kind of fun. It reminded her of being a kid again and climbing the jungle gym, or being on a swing set. She could do this all day long.

"Hey, Victor, you see that?"

She looked back at him, immediately seeking out the approval of her mate.

Victor coughed and adjusted his stance. "Yes. Very good."

Zelda's question seemed to remind the rest of the students that he was there, which put a brief damper on things before they went back to what they were doing and the instructor called for them to perform another kind of spin.

Right. Maybe Zelda shouldn't be reminding the other ladies in here that there was a man watching. Luckily, Victor just looked so professional as he stood there. He was easy for the others to ignore.

Not Zelda. She couldn't ignore him. She could never get him out of her head after this and she wanted him to see what her body could do.

She was a fox shifter. She could be graceful when the time called for it, and she was going to do it.

She spun around one more time before standing straight again, listening as the instructor showed them how to get the next move going.

It was getting a little hot in the studio as Zelda worked. She was getting sweaty. Not a good look, but at the very least, she was getting some good exercise. This was almost as fun as dancing, and there were fewer people around, so there wasn't the worry that someone would walk up to her, ask her to go home with them, and turn out to be a psycho.

The only man in here was Victor. She might be getting herself all sweaty and gross, totally not attractive at all, but this was definitely something Zelda could see herself doing again and again even when he wasn't here to watch.

How would she get a pole into her bedroom? Or in the living room of her apartment? It might be better to get Victor alone there so he could watch her for a private show. Even with these basic moves,

Zelda figured she could still make herself look good if she did her hair and makeup the right way.

Maybe got herself another slinky little dress…

Zelda's sensitive ears picked up on the vibrating noise that came from his cell phone. She glanced back quickly, just as Victor lifted the phone to his ear, answering as quietly as possible.

Those sunglasses might have been hiding his eyes, but Zelda was acutely aware of the grim set to his mouth, especially when he looked up at her.

She could see it right through those shades.

Her heart froze.

CHAPTER 7

"*H*arry was picked up?"

Zelda couldn't believe it. Her first instinct was to be shocked, then happy, but it was the look on Victor's face that had her not entirely convinced she was in the clear.

"This isn't a good thing?"

"He said he had nothing to do with sending that guy after you, who's still not talking."

She thought about it. They stood outside the dance studio. The call Victor had received was by and large more important than learning how to pole dance for him.

"He's got to be lying, though, right?"

"We can't rule anything out. I should contact your brother and your uncle to make sure they're up to date."

"They need their money's worth, I guess."

She didn't mean for it to come out sounding like that. Zelda was beyond embarrassed when Victor lifted a brow at her. He wasn't wearing the sunglasses anymore, so she could make out the clear confusion in his eyes.

"Never mind. I really should call Link back anyway. Should I go back to the police station? Will they want me to talk with him?"

"Eventually, I imagine," Victor said. He still had his phone in his hand. "They're going to want to question him themselves for a little while."

"Okay. How long will that take?"

Victor shrugged. "Hard to say. It depends on when he talks and if the detectives are satisfied with what he said. You accused him of murder and now the law is involved. If they see no reason to release him, then they won't."

"His pack will back him. They won't say anything against him."

Victor looked at her for a long minute. "Will they really not say anything? You're not just accusing him of murder, you're accusing him of murdering the previous alpha."

Zelda shook her head. "It doesn't matter. Even the people who weren't happy with what he did…"

"You're saying there are others who knew about this?"

"Well, not exactly, no. It's complicated."

"You need to un-complicate it." Victor stuck his phone into his pocket. He looked and sounded more serious than Zelda had seen him in the short time she'd known him. "You're going to be questioned about this. You need to have your story straight."

"I do have my story straight. It's just not as simple as the way you're making it out to be."

"Okay."

That was all he said. Zelda realized he was waiting for her to keep talking.

"For a subhuman, you sure don't know a lot about any of this. Some people probably would have had their suspicions, others didn't. The ones who suspected probably didn't like it, but Harry would have been the new alpha then, so it wouldn't have mattered. Who were they going to complain to? Harry? That makes no sense."

"They could always complain to the police."

Zelda glared at him.

Victor nodded. "Right."

"You think I knew about it, don't you?"

"I don't think that, and even if I did, it wouldn't matter what I think because it's my job to keep an eye on you."

"Until Harry is found. Which he was."

That part hit her again. If Harry had been picked up by the police, then that meant Victor wouldn't have to be her bodyguard any longer.

She could pursue him without his job getting in the way.

Of course, after this conversation, she wasn't sure how close she wanted to be to him just now.

"When will you not have to watch over me anymore?"

"It's not a matter of having to," he corrected. "Your brother and uncle are paying me to be here for you, and even then, I'm still looking for a replacement."

"You're only protecting me because you're being paid to?"

Victor sucked back a deep breath through his nose. "Don't do this."

"Don't do what? You're only watching me and keeping me safe because you're getting money out of it from my family."

"I'm a bodyguard, it's sort of how I make my living."

The sarcasm in his voice definitely wasn't helping anything.

"So you wouldn't have saved my life if you weren't being paid to do it?"

"That's literally not what I said."

"But you are saying it. You're only protecting me because you're being paid to."

Victor pinched the bridge between his eyes, a low groaning noise escaping his throat. "If I were to happen across a man or a woman alone in a dark alley then of course I would step in and do something. I'm actually trained for that so it's not a difficult decision to make. I am being paid to protect you, but even if I wasn't, I would have still done something to help you. Does that clear things up a little?"

Zelda clenched her hands into fists. "No, it doesn't."

She walked away from him, but she still caught the bewildered expression on his face, the way he raised his hands to his head, as though his mind was being blown. "How does that not clear anything up?"

"It just doesn't."

Zelda was so angry she couldn't even be appreciative of the fact that she'd finally managed to get Victor to show a little damned emotion.

Zelda went for her car, parked in the small lot along the side of the building. She was angry and she didn't want to have to justify it. She didn't care what reasons he had for why it made any sense. She just wanted to be away from him for a minute. Everything he said and did was annoying her now.

She couldn't go back into the studio. It occurred to Zelda that she could, but she didn't want to disrupt the classroom anymore.

"Where are you going?"

"None of your business."

"It is my business. It's my job to make sure you stay safe."

Zelda unlocked her car and sat down. She tried to pull the door shut, but Victor grabbed it before she could.

Zelda wet her lips. "Let go."

He didn't. "I need to know where you're going to be. If you want to go anywhere, that's fine. Just let me know so I can plan around it."

Zelda looked up at him, thinking of all the things she would like to do with that mouth of his, all the things she wanted him to do to her with that mouth, more specifically.

"All right. I'm going home."

He blinked down at her, as though he didn't quite believe her. "You're going home?"

"That so hard to believe?"

He took his hand away from the door and straightened, trusting her to not shut it and lock it. "Nothing else?"

She thought about it. It was a little early, but in a few hours she could go out.

"I'll be going dancing again."

Victor hissed. "After what happened last night?"

"It won't be to the same club."

"That hardly matters."

She shrugged. "Well, too bad. You're my bodyguard, I'm sure being in another club won't be a problem for you, what with all your skills in protecting people for money."

"You're angry at me for nothing. You have to see you're getting worked up for no reason."

It was the worked up comment that did it.

She glared at him, hard. Zelda felt a little of her fox come out and Victor actually took a step away from her.

"You fucking…asshole! *Worked up?* Are you serious?"

"All right. I'm sorry." He raised his hands, as though in surrender.

Zelda didn't care. She slammed the door shut, started her car, and then pulled out of the lot.

He was lucky she didn't steal his car again, but even with her fury at him, at his accusatory tone and telling her she was getting worked up, she was still able to enjoy watching as he scrambled for his vehicle and followed after her.

He was only a few cars behind, still too close as far as Zelda was concerned as she got onto the highway and headed back for her apartment.

Her pole dancing class was ruined because every man she ever liked turned out to either be a murderer, or a soulless bastard.

If Harry had been picked up then there was no harm in her going back to another club so she could go dancing, and if Victor didn't want her, then fine. Someone else would. Someone who didn't need to be paid to hang around her.

CHAPTER 8

$\mathcal{A}$fter a few hours at home to calm her head, Zelda had to admit she felt a little foolish for blowing up on Victor outside of the studio.

She couldn't even pin down exactly why she was angry with him. Not really.

Everything rubbed her the wrong way lately. It was as though she needed to be in control of all of her surroundings at all times, and whenever she wasn't, she flew off the handle for no reason.

She liked Victor and was attracted to him, she thought she smelled the scent of a mate on him, but it wasn't as though she'd ever had a mate before, a *true* mate, anyway. So how was she supposed to know what this felt like? How she was supposed to act?

But it wasn't him. It wasn't the mating scent she got from him. It was something else.

Something that hit her after Maxwell had died, and after she'd overheard Harry talking to Ben and Gerard downstairs.

Zelda had her shower and, her hair done up in a towel, walked to the freezer for her peanut butter and chocolate ice cream. She pulled the lid off and dug her spoon directly into the frozen goodness.

She'd put on almost eight pounds since she'd left Harry, deciding to eat pretty much whatever she wanted. Zelda was lucky in the fact that, so far, it had all gone straight to her boobs and her ass in a good way.

Had it not been for the beautiful, wonderful, miraculous metabolism that came with being a shifter, and her new habit to go out dancing every night, she would have put on a lot more than that eight pounds.

If she kept eating ice cream like this out of the tub, then, fox metabolism or no, she was going to have a lot more to worry about than just eight pounds. There was such a thing as being an overweight shifter.

But whatever. This one time wasn't going to kill anything, and she was going to work it all off on the dance floor tonight.

If Victor was there, fine; if he wasn't, then she was okay with that, too.

She went to the window to make sure his car was still out there.

Yup. Still there. The windows were tinted, but she knew he was sitting in the driver's seat.

She was a little relieved by that, but only a little.

Zelda got ready. She put her makeup on, using the best techniques she'd learned since leaving Harry. She'd always been told that her eyes were her best features, so she played that up as much as possible.

Lipstick had a nasty habit of getting onto her teeth, so the best solution for that was her lip stains. She loved her lip stains. She put on a dark red color, then lined her lips with a pencil liner to make them look fuller.

The pushup bra she'd splurged on at Victoria's Secret came next. She loved that bra and it was her absolute favorite with the way it lifted her boobs and accented the rest of her curves.

She kept her dark hair down. She liked it down; other people seemed to like it when it was down, the waves tossing and turning wildly in the flashing light of the dance floor.

That was where she wanted to be. In that space where she could forget herself. Forget everything. She'd already sent a text to her brother, but she wasn't ready to call him just yet and have a long, drawn-out conversation about her safety.

She wasn't interested in talking about how important her safety was when the one man she wanted to care the most was downstairs and…

Zelda sighed. There was no point in letting herself get all worked up over it, so she might as well go out.

She sent a text to Victor to let him know she was almost done and would be coming downstairs soon.

His short answer grated on Zelda's nerves all the more.

Got it

She nearly threw her phone across the room.

Instead, she went down to the parking garage of her building.

Victor was already down there. He'd moved his car and waited for her to get out of the elevator.

"I can drive you there."

"No need."

She was an independent woman now, and she was capable of driving herself to the places where she could have her fun.

Still, Victor followed her to her car.

"Wait a minute," he said sharply, taking her keys before she could so much as get the door open.

Zelda planted her hands on her hips. "What are you doing?"

She probably shouldn't have bothered with asking, since she could see what he was doing now that he was doing it. He was checking the back seat of her car to make sure no one was hiding in it. She wasn't sure what the rest was for.

"Why are you checking the engine?"

"I'm not." Victor let the car hood fall back into place with a heavy slam before he tossed the keys to her. "I'm checking to make sure the engine wasn't tampered with. Don't run me over. I want to check your brakes."

"My…" Zelda trailed off. She couldn't believe it. "That's going a little far, isn't it?"

"Maybe." He didn't seem to care that he was getting his suit dirty by lying on the concrete like that to check that her brake fluids weren't leaking everywhere.

"Do you always give short answers like that?"

Victor stood with an easy smile. "Sometimes."

Asshole. But he was an asshole she could smile at.

"Honestly, it would be better if I drove you."

"What sort of strong and powerful woman would I be if I relied on a chaperone like that?"

"I'm not your chaperone."

"You kind of are." Zelda got into her car, started the engine, and rolled down the window. "It could be worse, I could snag your car and you could take mine. We could race to the club."

Victor almost looked as though he was pretending to consider that. "Right. I'll follow you there."

IT WAS a little on the early side for her to be there at the club, but there were still people who were there. It was also easier to get in.

Just because Zelda had her special makeover and ditched her glasses for contacts didn't mean she was confident enough in her looks to be able to skip to the front of a long lineup of eager patrons.

She was shocked when Victor paid his way into the club as well.

"Don't you get special bodyguard privileges or something?"

"Not really," he responded. "Honestly, I'm glad you're here early. I had a bitch of a time getting passed the bouncer on that first night."

He did? She hadn't known that.

There were a few people on the dance floor, but not enough that Zelda really felt she could lose herself in a sea of bodies. There was enough open space there that other people would be able to see her awkward movements. She wouldn't be able to dance like a fool and then get off the stage to be another anonymous drinker in the crowd.

The only people here now were the ones taking advantage of the cheaper prices that came with being here three hours before the main crowd arrived. It was still light outside.

Feeling a little guilty for her behavior earlier, for blowing up on Victor when he was just trying to do his job, to do right by her, and uncomfortable with dancing right now, Zelda decided to offer a little olive branch.

"Want me to buy you a drink?"

He looked at her, brows raised a little. He'd taken off his sunglasses after coming into the dark club.

Zelda looked away from that stare. "Just, you know, for being so nice and everything. For helping me out. For saving my life."

From the corner of her eye, it looked as though he was smiling at her.

"Thanks for the offer, but I'll have to decline."

Zelda rolled her eyes. "Let me take a wild guess."

"No drinking on the job," he said, finishing the thought she was about to make.

Zelda's head fell back. "Come on! You've got to work with me a little here! I'm trying to be nice!"

"Uh huh, how about you buy me one of their overpriced water bottles? That's something I can keep with me."

That sounded okay. She and Victor walked to the bar and grabbed their seats.

Zelda ordered, flashing a smile. The bartender didn't have many patrons, so it was easy enough to bring her the Sangria she'd ordered, and Victor's water bottle.

She tapped her glass to his bottle. "Cheers."

His smile actually had a little mirth in it. "Cheers," he said.

Zelda took a drink.

Victor watched her, but he did it in such a way that it looked as though he was trying not to be too obvious.

There was no way he was bad at watching people. It was literally his job. Zelda did feel hyper aware of him, however. She wanted to be as close to him as possible. She wanted to know what it felt like to have him sitting next to her like this often.

Zelda swished her drink around a little before swallowing, desperately demanding her brain think up something to say.

"It's kind of nice having you actually sit next to me."

Victor smirked. "Sometimes I sit with clients."

He did? "Oh yeah?"

The idea that this wasn't something unusual or special got her in a way she didn't think was possible.

"On occasion. It works well to make the client feel comfortable, after all."

"Right." Zelda took another drink from her glass. "Any luck on finding a replacement for yourself? Seeing as how it's unprofessional to want to touch me while you're watching over me?"

Victor got the cap twisted off his water bottle, but Zelda's words seemed to catch him off guard.

"Look, this isn't to hurt you. It's not to punish you either."

"Is it because you don't like what you see?"

He grinned at her. Not one of his little held back smiles either. He looked at her as though he could eat her right up.

"Trust me, there's nothing wrong with how you look."

A little shiver passed through her tail and ears.

"Really?"

"Of course. Haven't you taken a look at yourself lately?"

He sounded so sincere. As if the idea that she could ever not realize how she looked had never occurred to her.

"You really don't know how beautiful you are, do you?"

Zelda's heart flipped. Her breath stuck in her throat for a long second before she let it out. Then she couldn't stop smiling.

"That wasn't very professional, was it?"

Victor brought his water to his lips. "Nope."

Zelda grinned.

"I think I can forget about everything else just for that."

Victor nodded. "Still not entirely sure why you were mad at me, but I'll take what I can get at this point."

Zelda wet her lips. She tried to hide the heat in her face behind her Sangria glass, but she wasn't sure it was working.

"So, when you're not my bodyguard anymore—"

"Even if it's Steve who takes over, you're still a client."

"Well, either way, when your agency isn't in charge of my safety anymore, are you free?"

He looked at her. Zelda was such a coward that she couldn't look back at him.

"I am."

This was good. This was going well.

"I'm not so used to doing this, but do you think that, since Harry was picked up, when your services aren't needed anymore, you might want to give me a call?"

That smile continued to melt everything in her gut. Zelda had never seen a smile so perfect.

Victor rubbed the scruff on his jaw. "I guess you're more accustomed to the guys pursuing you, aren't you?"

Zelda opened her mouth to deny that. To tell him that she wasn't used to either. To men asking for her number, or for her to do the asking.

She said nothing instead.

"Sorry," Victor said, apparently taking her silence to mean something else. "Didn't mean to get too personal."

"No, no, it's fine."

Zelda was smiling again. He hadn't said no, but she reminded herself that, since he was on the job, he couldn't come out and say yes either.

So, not saying no was sort of like a yes, wasn't it?

"Wanna dance?"

Zelda was suddenly overcome with energy and the drive to move her body. There still weren't a whole lot of people on the dance floor, but she wanted to be there. She wanted Victor to be there with her more than anything.

But since he wasn't going to join her for a dance, maybe she could show him what she could do instead.

That seemed like the better idea.

"No," he said predictably. "Sorry, I can't."

"Yeah, I figured, but if you want, you can stay here and watch my drink."

"I have to watch you, too."

She got up from her stool. "That's something of the point."

Even though there weren't as many bodies on the dance floor as she was used to, and even though she couldn't lose herself in the crowd, Zelda realized that was exactly what she liked about this.

Victor was up by the bar, looking down on her as the music thumped and the lights flashed.

Zelda felt only a brief moment of self-consciousness about being there, knowing Victor was watching her.

Then she started to move her hips, and it didn't matter. All her fears and doubts melted away from her as she lost herself in the swing of the pulsing music.

Even when she wasn't watching him, dipping down low before twisting back up again, she could feel his eyes on her as her fingers threaded through her dark curls.

Up high and then down low, bouncing around her shoulders.

She glanced his way, then smiled at the sight of his dark gaze.

Never had anyone's eyes smoldered as they looked at her before.

Well, that wasn't true; she'd experienced a few looks like that from the men she'd danced with ever since freeing herself from her marriage, her own constraints, and her limits, but this was different.

The way Victor looked at her was nothing at all like the way those other men had looked at her.

For one thing, Victor wasn't some random stranger she needed to kill some time with. He was important.

So she danced. She danced and lost herself in it as though there was the usual sea of people surrounding her.

Someone came to dance with her. Zelda felt the heat of his body. A man's body. She pretended it was Victor and let him. His hands came to rest on her hips.

They were strong hands, not entirely like Victor's. She felt some rings there. Victor wore no rings. Let alone on every finger.

Still, it worked out well.

She glanced Victor's way. That smoldering gaze was hard on her, but not angry.

No, it was more of a burning kind of hard.

Zelda smiled.

He wanted to be down here with here. She could tell that much as she danced with her mystery partner.

Part of her felt a little bad for teasing Victor like this, but she couldn't help herself. This was too much fun.

The music, the dancing, seeing a man's eyes while she was the only one he focused on.

Victor frowned, yanking Zelda out of the hazy dream she'd fallen into.

Frowning usually wasn't good.

Victor reached into his pocket and stood. He put his phone to his ear.

"Hey, what's the matter, baby?"

She'd stopped dancing and had barely noticed.

"Sorry. I think I need to go and see—"

The man grabbed her wrist. "Come on, that was fun."

Zelda's heart flew into her throat. She yanked her wrist away, but the man she'd been dancing with hadn't been holding on so tight.

He backed away, grinning with his hands raised. "Okay, okay."

His eyes wandered over to someone else. Zelda didn't care if he let her go because he really did just want a dance partner, or because he didn't want trouble from the bouncers if he got a little too handsy.

She cared about that look on Victor's face, and what he was saying on the phone.

Zelda left the dance floor. Her heart still jumped.

Apparently, she was affected a little more by the possibility of someone being after her than she'd thought. All that guy did was grab her and she'd almost felt herself jolted back into that dark alley. That wet cloth soaked with chloroform pressing hard against her mouth.

Zelda ducked and weaved around the patrons in the bar, the waitresses, and people who weren't paying attention. It was a little busier now. She hadn't noticed when all these people had come into the club, but she still had Victor in her sights at all times, and that meant he had her in sight as well. He waved for her to come on over.

Harry. This was something to do with Harry. She felt it.

Zelda made it to Victor's side, much more out of breath than she should have felt considering she hadn't been on the dance floor all that long.

"What's going on? What's happening?"

Victor glanced at her, though he kept his free hand to his ear to block out the music while his other hand held the phone tightly to his other ear.

He jerked his head to the door. Zelda followed him when he moved outside.

The shadows were long as the orange light of the sun sank deeper into the distance. It could barely be seen with all the buildings around, and there weren't even that many tall buildings on this side of town.

It was probably so much easier to hear what was being said to him now that he was outside.

"I hear you. She's with me now." Victor hesitated. Zelda put her hand to his arm.

"What is it? What's happening?"

Victor pressed his lips together.

"Right. I'll tell her. Do you want her to come over? Answer some questions?"

Zelda's stomach twisted and the fox ears on top of her head straightened right out.

She'd known this was going to happen. Zelda had already answered some questions by the police, and it had been too much. She didn't want to answer anymore, but she knew better than to think this wasn't going to happen. If they wanted more details, and if she wanted to help keep Harry away from her, then she was going to have to come in.

Victor hung up the phone, pocketing it.

"Harry's talking."

"Small relief that is," Zelda said, crossing her arms, though it was still true. "What's he saying? He's denying it, isn't he? Asshole."

"Actually, he confessed to everything."

Zelda blinked. "He what?"

"Yeah."

Her brain still wasn't processing that. "You could have punched me in the gut and it wouldn't have shocked me as much. Are you sure?"

"It's what the detective in charge of the case said." Victor didn't look like he was joking. Zelda hadn't known Victor long enough to be sure what his joking face was, but she was pretty sure this wasn't it.

"So, he confessed to killing Maxwell? That's great. This means you're not my bodyguard anymore."

Victor's smile was apologetic. "Maybe not. Harry's admitting to poisoning your alpha so he could take his place, but he's denying having anything to do with sending people after you."

"What?" A chill suddenly hit. Zelda rubbed her arms. "That can't be right. It's him. I know it is."

"Well, he's saying it's not. Gerard and Ben are still out there. Ben was the one who called in the tip to the police, but he hasn't turned himself in either."

"Why would he call the police just to send someone after me?"

Victor pushed back his suit jacket and planted his hands on his hips. A few people gave him an odd stare when his holster was exposed, but he didn't seem to care.

"Could be a number of reasons. Could be to throw suspicion off his trail. Or it could be nothing and he might not have anything to do with it. We don't know because he hasn't turned himself in."

"Okay, but Ben was always nice. I don't think it's him."

"Right. Well, the detective heading the case will be going back out to question some more people at your pack."

"Which one?"

"Both. The wolf and the fox pack. These guys are thorough."

"Like on TV?"

"Like better than TV," Victor said. He lifted his hand and reached out, as though to touch her shoulder.

He pulled back at the last second.

The disappointment building inside her didn't get the chance to spring before Victor took her by the hand. "You'll be okay. I won't let anyone come near you."

Victor's thumb stroked once across her hand before he let go. The touch was so brief that to have it and then lose it so suddenly brought a beautiful ache in her chest.

She wasn't going to be ungrateful for that touch, however. It was by and large the greatest feeling she'd ever had, to feel him touch her like that, no matter how fleeting.

"So, should I go into the station? Do they want to talk to me? Or do they want me to talk to him?"

"They might want to talk to you a little. It's a good idea if we go to them. The sooner we get this done, the better. Honestly, I know you're enjoying the single life and everything, being free from pack and responsibilities, but with your brother and uncle really is the safest place for you to be right now."

Zelda sucked back a heavy breath, letting it out slowly.

"I know you don't want to see your family hurt, but they can handle themselves."

"I doubt they can pay for your services forever."

Victor smiled. "Well, to be honest, they're not paying for my services."

Zelda frowned. "What?"

Victor crossed his arms. "I can't exactly ask Steve to work for free, he's got his own bills to pay, but whenever I'm on the clock, you don't have to worry about the cost. I already called Link and let him know."

Zelda blinked. She shook her head. "No, I mean, you can't do that."

"I already did."

She laughed, stunned to hear such a thing. "You can't just work for free!"

"I can and I am."

Zelda pressed her lips together. "If this is because of me, you don't have to do it."

"It's not because of you. It's for you." Victor wet his lips. He took one step closer, getting into her personal space. She felt the heat of his body. "I know you already know the reason why, but when it's not so unprofessional to talk about it, I can go into the details why I'm doing this when we get this resolved."

The fire in his dark blue eyes told her everything she needed to know. It made her stomach swirl with monster butterflies and her heart pound uncomfortably against her ribs. As though it was trying to break free from a prison.

"I think…I like the idea of that. Of talking."

Victor nodded. His face was such a mask, but she detected the signs of relief in those eyes. "Good. Would you mind if we took my car to the station?"

Zelda grinned. Her heart wouldn't stop beating and the adrenaline was getting to her. "You want me to steal your car again?"

"Actually, no. I want to drive you."

Zelda laughed. Victor grinned and shook his head.

"Sure. I wouldn't mind being in the passenger seat of your car this time around."

"Good. Let's go."

It wasn't exactly a date, and Victor was still keeping his distance from her, but at the same time, walking next to him to the parking lot, Zelda felt so much lighter on her feet. She would have reached out to hold his hand if she'd thought he would let her.

No. Just having her bodyguard walking beside her was enough.

Their cars were parked next to each other not too far from the sidewalk. Not quite halfway in. Victor had grumbled a little about wanting to park closer to the doors when they pulled up, but they were the closest spots that were together and nearest to the door.

"Hey!"

Victor's angry shout, then when he started running, startled Zelda at first.

Until she spotted the man running away from her car. Running as though his life depended on it.

Victor gave chase, not wasting one minute as he went after the guy.

Zelda tried to run with him, unsure if she should even bother, or stay right where she was.

She didn't have the choice. Her shoes made the decision for her.

It was impossible to run in heels. She didn't care what the movies said. There was no way in hell she was doing any running with the high heels she wore.

Zelda watched Victor vanish from sight as he chased that kid down. He had to be a kid. There had been a hood pulled up, but the shape of his body and height couldn't have made him much older than a teenager.

Zelda waited for Victor to turn around and come back, to reappear around the corner so she wouldn't be alone anymore, but he didn't.

He was gone. He'd gone after that kid who was...what? What was he doing?

She glanced towards her car. The heavy smell of oil suddenly caught her right in her nose. She went to have a look.

Victor had taken a look beneath her car before they'd left for the club. He'd put himself right down onto the floor and said something about her brake fluids. Zelda did that same thing, already with an idea in mind of what she was going to see before she saw it.

Dark dripping. With the shade of her car, it could have been black blood.

That guy, whoever he was, had just cut the wire for her breaks.

He'd tried to kill her.

CHAPTER 10

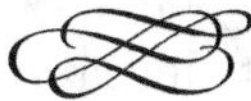

That had been two days ago. Two days, and nothing had happened since.

Not that it mattered. Zelda had been strung higher than a Goddamned kite after finding out someone tried to cut her brakes.

Someone Victor hadn't been able to catch when he'd returned to her.

He'd been gone for no more than three minutes. Four at the absolute most. Yet, it felt as though he'd been gone for ten thousand years as Zelda stayed there, by her car that was tampered with because someone wanted her to drive into a building, or another car, or a person.

And get killed.

She'd been so cold, and frozen. Zelda could hardly move. She'd thought about going back into the club, but her feet had been frozen. She wanted to run for someplace safe, but she couldn't.

So she waited with bated breath for Victor to come back to her.

When he did come back, his eyes wide and his face flushed, he ran to her, grabbed her shoulders and looked at her as though she was on the verge of vanishing right before his eyes.

She was a fox shifter, not a witch.

"You're okay? Are you all right?"

Zelda could hardly remember the details of it. Only that his grip had been painful, and that she couldn't seem to get all the words out of her mouth that she wanted.

She managed a nod, and that seemed to be enough. Victor let go of her shoulders, but Zelda wasn't sure what he did after that. He was on his phone then, yelling something into it, and then he was on the phone with someone else, and then they were in a cab.

She supposed Victor wasn't all that into driving either of their cars after someone had been caught messing with hers.

There was no choice after that. Victor took her back to her pack. Back to her brother and uncle.

Zelda didn't remember the ride home either. An hour long cab ride out of Washington and into Lakeview and she could hardly remember it.

Link and Mike were thrilled to see her, at first. Then Victor had to explain what went on, why they were back, and what to expect.

Her uncle Mike was furious, and in front of the entire pack, he screamed at her that she wasn't going anywhere anymore. She was staying put, and right then, Zelda was too stunned to fight him on it.

Now, after everything had been said and done, she was back in her old clothes, in her old house, sleeping alone in her old room, staring out her window, wondering if it was a mistake to come here.

The urge to flee and go back to Washington was getting the best of her. She kept looking to Uncle Mike's truck and thinking about how easy it would be to snatch his keys and get back to the city, find another apartment, or even a motel room for a couple of days until she got another place set up, and then go back to dancing the night away searching for someone to rock her Casba.

To make her forget.

To prove to herself that she was really no longer Harry's wife.

Hands touched her shoulders. Zelda jumped.

Mike pulled back, his eyes wide and his hands back, palms up. "Sorry. Sorry."

Zelda exhaled hard. Her heart pounded, but the embarrassing

shriek she'd just let out made her smile now that she knew there was really nothing for her to be worried about.

"No, no, it's okay. You just scared me a little."

"No kidding."

Mike grumbled a little about that part as he turned his back to her. She hadn't heard him walk in, but then again, he'd always been a quick fox.

On her dresser was a tray with two mugs on it.

Zelda smiled at the sight.

Her favorite mug was on there. The one with the reading owl.

My Weekend is Owl Booked.

She loved that mug. Reminded her of snow days from school when she'd burrito herself in her sheets and catch up with what Edward and Bella were up to, or reading *Wuthering Heights,* or the *Flowers in the Attic* series for the first time.

Mike hadn't liked it when he'd caught her reading that series at the tender age of thirteen.

"How did you know?"

"I always know what you like." He handed her the mug.

Zelda put it to her nose. She could smell the peach tea now that it was up close. Also her favorite.

"I used to know you inside and out."

Zelda caught the *used to* remark. She didn't know what to say about it, so she put the lip of the mug to her lips.

A long drink of hot tea felt good. She felt it slide all the way down her throat and into her belly. It still didn't seem to warm her the way she wanted it to.

There was still something that remained cold deep within her.

"The rest of the pack calm down yet?"

Mike shrugged, taking a look out her lace curtains. "Enough. They're not bitching anymore, but you know how people are. The ones who are scared won't say anything out loud, but they'll be festering with this for the next little while."

Zelda shook her head. "I don't want to be here if they don't want me here."

"I want you here." Mike looked at her hard. "Your brother wants you here."

Zelda pressed her lips together.

She couldn't escape her uncle's stare, however.

"Come on, out with it," he said, bringing his mug to his lips.

"Okay, well you and Link can want me here until the cows came home. I was the one who accused Harry of murder and now his pack is pissed. If they come here looking for a fight, that's going to be one fight we're not gonna win."

Mike nodded. "Which is why the police are now involved."

Zelda didn't know whether to laugh at a comment like that or cry. "I can't believe you guys got the humans involved."

Mike shrugged. "Not gonna lie, I'm all for keeping pack business in with pack business. The second it's my favorite niece on the line, I turn into a giant hypocrite."

He took another mouthful of tea. Zelda smiled at him.

Mike didn't show too much emotion. He tended to swing from one side to the other like that. At times, she could read him like a baby book. Easy. Obvious. Big colorful pictures and everything to go with it.

Other times, like now, his face could be a mask.

He'd mostly worn that mask for the first year when Link and Zelda lived with him, after her parents, his sister and brother-in-law, took off without a trace. His eyes remained distant, his mouth firm. His fox ears were stiff and pointed like triangles, and his tail hardly flicked or moved when he had that air about him.

Zelda's parents had promised to come back after a week, and then never did.

His mask slipped back into place when he didn't know what to do. That was the only thing Zelda could take away from a look like that.

"You're not a hypocrite."

"I don't mind being a hypocrite for you." He looked at her, forced a smile. "Besides, you're my girl. Of course I'm going to keep you around. Better here than God only knows where doing God only knows what."

"I wasn't doing anything dangerous."

"You were alone when we didn't know where Harry was. That was more than enough without knowing you were partying it up."

Heat rushed into Zelda's face.

Mike lifted a brow at her. "What? Did you think I wouldn't know?" He reached out, his hand ruffling her hair.

"Hey!" She pushed his hand away, but of course Mike only chuckled about it.

"I'm old, not stupid."

"You're not old."

He'd just turned forty not too long before Zelda took off. He could be an older brother. Sort of.

Still, the fifteen-year age difference had been enough for her mother to decide Mike was a good enough replacement before taking off.

Now that Zelda thought of it, she was the same age now as Mike had been when he'd agreed to babysit her and her brother that fateful day fifteen years ago.

She couldn't imagine what it would be like to be dumped with two ten-year-olds at her age now. Let alone two ten-year-olds who had cried night after night for their parents when the days stretched into months.

Link had been the one to outwardly display his anger more than Zelda had. She'd withdrawn into herself. Now Link was the calm one and she was the one running out and making a mess of things.

Zelda set her mug down, turned to her uncle, and put her arms around him. Mike froze.

"What's this?"

"You know what it is." Zelda squeezed him a little tighter. "Thank you."

He stroked her hair, his hands coming up and holding her back. She felt the press of his mouth on the top of her head.

They were silent for only a moment before Mike's soft voice spoke up. "Look, whatever you do, just be safe. If you want to go out and have fun, date guys—"

"Uncle Mike..."

"I'm serious. I don't get it, but you're an adult now. I can't tell you what to do. Just make sure you're safe when you do it."

Zelda thought about that for a moment. It was as though he knew he wouldn't be able to stop her. That he wouldn't have anything to say that would change her mind and make her want to stick around the pack, where it was safe and secure.

"I'll be safe." She squeezed her uncle a little tighter before pulling back. "At least you got me a sexy bodyguard to watch my back."

Mike shrugged. "Well, he's doing a decent job of it so far. He told me he's cutting his bill in half. I tried to talk him out of it, but he told me him and his partner will still be around. To be honest, I wanted to fight him on that a little more, but maybe he knew Link and I were... well, never mind."

"Right."

She decided to let that go. For now.

There was no easy way to explain to him just *why* Victor had cut the expenses the way he had. Much as Mike was pleased with the results Victor was putting out so far, she doubted he would like hearing the reason why Victor wasn't taking as much money.

Even now, she knew where Victor was. She could see him. His suit jacket was gone, and the sleeves of his white button-down were rolled up. The sunglasses were back on as he slowly paced around Mike's house.

He would appear, stick around for a minute, check the locks on the doors, the windows, that sort of thing, and then head to the back to do the same.

He was never out of sight for long. Even when he was, Zelda could still smell him all over the house she grew up in.

It was kind of nice.

With her view of him from the window, Zelda noted the way Victor reached to the ear piece he had on.

He'd purchased one of those hands-free Bluetooth accessories for his phone. He was so good at conversing with someone without making it look as though he was talking with anyone at all, but she saw it. She saw the way his jaw tightened.

She had to get out there. That was about her.

"I think I should go out there. Maybe bring him another water bottle. It's kind of hot out."

Mike looked at her, as though gauging whether or not to ask her to sit back.

He either figured the threat level wasn't worth it, or knew she didn't want to be cooped up in her room anymore, because he let her go.

"All right. Just stick close to the house, okay?"

"All right. And thanks for the tea." She kissed his cheek.

"Anytime." They headed out of her room. Zelda went to the kitchen, grabbing two bottles. "But just for next time, you know you and Link don't have to take turns watching over me, right?" Zelda glanced back at her uncle after closing the fridge. "When you're home, you're supposed to be resting."

Both her uncle and Link worked hard. Even for shifters, construction tended to take a lot out of them. Somehow, without her knowing it, they'd set up their shifts so that at least one of them would always be home when the other wasn't.

"I am resting," Mike said, sliding onto one of the stools in front of the counter.

Zelda could only shake her head at him.

It was kind of sweet. But it was also going to take a toll on both men.

"You and Link need to stay focused on your jobs. The last thing I need to hear about is that one or both of you accidentally caught yourselves or someone else with one of those nail guns."

"That is incredibly unlikely to happen."

"Either way." Zelda headed for the door. "Go and have a nap or something. I'll make dinner tonight."

"Have you decided how long you're staying then?"

Zelda paused, halfway outside. Her gaze darted to her hands. She finally looked at her uncle. "I don't know."

It was the truth. It wasn't what he wanted to hear, but at least she was telling the truth.

Nothing else had happened since Victor chased away the guy who cut her brakes, but she couldn't shake the feeling this wasn't over yet.

Even if the attacks stopped, at the bare minimum, there would be more questions she would have to answer with the police. A trial would be had. She might need to be a witness.

The wolf pack was definitely not taking her back. They hadn't even decided on a new alpha to replace Harry yet because, word had it, they were still half convinced he was coming back.

As expected, Mike definitely didn't look happy about her answer. His tail whipped around before he got control of it. His orange fox ears remained locked and pointed up high at the ceiling.

"Well, you keep on thinking about it. Go on now. Go keep that human hydrated. He's a lot better to have around than I would have thought."

"He's a subhuman, actually."

"Is he?" Mike seemed to think on that. "Makes sense, I guess."

Zelda grinned and left. When the door was shut behind her, she sobered up, ready to find out just what that call had been about, and why Victor hadn't looked the least bit pleased by it.

CHAPTER 11

*H*ow did I know you were going to come out here and see me?"

Zelda grinned up at him, holding out the water bottle for him. "Just thought you might like some company."

He took the offered bottle. She leaned against the tree he stood by. Victor kept his back straight.

"You didn't look so happy on the phone."

Victor grunted, taking a swig of the water. "Not really."

Zelda rubbed her hands up and down her thighs. Her old jeans were getting a touch tight on her. Time to stop with all the peanut butter ice cream.

Victor rubbed at his chin. He'd purchased a razor since coming here, so the chin scratch he grew had a bit more of a method to it.

"I just got off the phone with the detective involved in the case,"

"Is it normal for bodyguards and police to have this kind of working relationship?"

His mouth quirked. "He and I are old friends. It pays to know who people are in this line of work."

She believed him, considering all the information he was prone to getting.

"So, what happened?"

"Harry is still denying he sent anyone after you. He confessed to murdering your alpha. Well, the alpha of the wolf pack. Detectives will be sent on over there to let them know, and find out if they've got any plans for replacing him, and with who."

"They probably won't talk."

Victor nodded. "I know. Shifters like to keep to themselves."

A small heat crept into Zelda's chest. "Well, to be honest, having you around felt pretty good."

Victor wouldn't look at her. "There's something else."

Zelda frowned, waiting.

"That guy who tried to grab you in the alley the night we first met. He finally started talking. Came up with all kinds of excuses for why he was doing what he was doing. He even accused you of trying to steal from him."

Zelda pushed herself away from the tree, dropping her water, her hands clenching into fists. "That's bullshit!"

"I know. Don't worry. Another hour of questioning, comparing my statements, yours and his, and they figured out he was full of shit."

"Oh, well, good. Right?"

Victor nodded. "Right. The problem here is that they can't pin him down to whoever sent that guy after you to cut your brakes. He doesn't seem to know anything about Harry, Maxwell's murder, Ben, or Gerard. None of it."

"Well, he's got to be lying, right? I mean, of course he is. What are the odds that I would get attacked like that?"

"What are the odds that a beautiful woman with a couple of drinks in her would be lured into a dark alley and be attacked by some stranger she doesn't know?"

Zelda punched his arm. "Yeah, yeah, I get it." She hesitated. "Do the police believe him?"

Victor briefly pressed his lips together. "They'll keep probing him as much as his lawyer allows, but I trust the people involved here. If they think there's nothing else to be found, then that's likely all there is to it."

"You're telling me that was just some random guy?"

"From the looks of it, yes."

Zelda absorbed that information, thought a little more deeply about everything else Victor just said. "And...Harry had nothing to do with my attack?"

"We're not going to rule it out, but he's not confessing to it yet. They'll keep cross-checking the information they have. Cell phone records, texts he sent, where he's been. So far, unless something else comes up, it looks as though he's not the one who sent that guy to cut your brakes."

Victor's jaw tightened just then.

It still bothered him something fierce that he hadn't been able to catch that man. Zelda could feel it in the air around him whenever the subject came up. Or even when he was thinking about it. He got that tight, half-twisted look on his face. As though he could see the guy just ahead of him, just within reach, only for him to slip away.

Zelda reached out, grabbed Victor's shoulder. She squeezed it before letting go quickly, knowing he had a no touching policy.

"For what it's worth, thanks for coming back for me."

Victor looked at her, a dark brow lifted. "Of course I came back for you."

Now Zelda was the one pressing her lips together, struggling to keep the heat in her chest and neck from flooding into her cheeks.

She liked to think there was something more to his words there, but it was hard to say. He was so difficult to read at times.

"Well, either way, I'm glad you did. Sorry you didn't catch that guy, but I was getting worried there. Seeing you come back was kind of a relief."

"Honestly, I shouldn't have left you alone." Victor looked over Zelda's head and nodded.

Zelda had a look.

Steve, Victor's business partner, loosely waved to him before continuing on his rounds.

Victor had come here with Zelda alone, but his partner had eventually arrived to pick up the slack after what happened.

Zelda smiled. "My uncle seems to think you're only taking half pay because you're doing him a favor."

Victor stuffed his hands into his pockets. He glanced out around the property, the other houses in the distance between the trees. It was hard to see them with all the foliage in the way, but there were neighbors here.

"You didn't tell him otherwise, did you?"

Zelda shook her head. "No. I don't think he wants to hear that I'm getting a mating scent off you. Link might suspect something."

"Wouldn't be shocked if he knows."

"Really?"

Victor nodded. "He was looking at me funny the day I told them I was cutting costs."

"Honestly, are you sure you should be doing that?"

"I've got some cash saved. Like I said, I can't make a decision like that for Steve, but for me, I'm here for you."

This time, he did look at her, and even through those shades, Zelda felt her feet freeze to the ground, and her stomach twisted with mutated butterflies.

"Does this mean that you'll—"

"No."

The sharp answer caught her as though she'd been sucker punched in the stomach.

"Oh."

"Like I said, it's unprofessional. Just because I'm not taking pay for this doesn't mean I'm going to use that as an excuse. Far as I'm concerned, I'm still on the job. I would expect no less from Steve if he was to do the same with another client."

"Right."

Why did it feel like every time she got remotely close to getting somewhere with him, he had to go ahead and ruin it?

A soft touch on her fox ears pulled her back into the real world. They'd been pressed flat against her dark hair after the rejection, but that small, gentle touch was more than enough to perk them back up high again.

She looked at Victor. He was a step closer than she remembered him being, his sunglasses off, and he looked at her with those deep blue eyes in a way that melted the pit of her stomach.

"Don't pout. You make it hard for me to stand back when you pout."

Zelda shook her head. "I'm not pout—"

Victor's mouth cut her off with a kiss.

A sudden kiss. The kind of kiss that pulled all the air out of her lungs as she was overcome with sensation.

Heat. That came first. His scent was overpowering. A possessive musk that wrapped around her like a comforting blanket, one she wanted to lean into.

His mouth, soft at the lips but scratchy from his prickly beard all the way around. And then there was *taste.*

He dipped his tongue against the crease of her lips. Wet and warm. A thrill rushed through her as she instinctively opened her mouth, moaning softly as he licked inside…

And then he was gone.

Just as Zelda tried to press herself against him, as her nipples hardened and her body ached for more of that high-pitched pleasure that was there so sharply before, it was suddenly gone—he was gone.

Victor stepped back from her. Just one step, but it was more than enough for her to lose the feeling of his body heat.

His powerful body that had been holding her so closely just one minute ago before leaving her with nothing.

He smiled.

She shook her head. "No way, you can't just do that to me."

"It's not meant to torture you. It's something to leave you with. Until we find out what's going on. That way you won't need to think about bringing home any other guys. At least until I'm free for you."

Oh God. She was going to melt into a puddle at his feet.

Calm. She had to remain calm and collected. "All right. When do you think that will be?"

"Hard to say. Could be a few days, could be a few weeks. Even months."

"You've got to be shitting me."

He shrugged. "The case doesn't necessarily have to be closed. I just have to be satisfied that you're not going to be attacked again."

Zelda felt a soft twitch in the tiny muscles beneath her eye.

She pressed her lips together, straightened her back, and then inhaled a deep breath before letting it out again.

Slow and steady. She breathed again.

Victor still looked at her patiently, waiting for her response.

Knowing she had to agree.

"All right, fine. Makes sense."

Victor nodded. "Good."

She touched her mouth, then groaned, throwing her hands up into the air. "*Arrrgh*! You can't just do that to me!"

"You seemed to like it."

She pointed at him, a silent warning. A warning she knew didn't hold much weight with the way he smiled at her.

Zelda sighed. "Well, since you got me all hot and bothered with so much energy I don't know what to do with, I'm going to have to think of something to do."

The smile faltered. "Like what?"

Zelda shrugged. "Not sure. I was thinking of taking up drunken, naked painting."

Victor snorted. He actually snorted. "What?"

"Yeah," Zelda grinned. Now it was her turn to do a little of the torturing. "Yeah, I think it would be a little fun. I could wait until uncle Mike takes off and Link is asleep. Put on a little Bob Ross in my room, get a bottle of Vodka…"

"And this will calm you down…how?"

"You're my bodyguard." Zelda stepped into his space this time. She walked her fingers up his chest, to his neck. "You watching me do that, being unable to touch because of your kill-joy rules, seems like enough fun for me."

CHAPTER 12

There were no sexy Bob Ross painting sessions like Zelda had been hoping for.

She'd wanted to get back at Victor for his little kiss, but with so many people around, it seemed like an impossible task to accomplish.

Uncle Mike didn't go anywhere unless it was work related, and Link didn't seem interested in sleep. Or leaving her alone. He wanted to watch movies and play video games, like when they were still kids.

She wasn't sure what that was about, this need to spend every waking minute around her when he didn't have to go to work either, but Uncle Mike seemed to be in a similar position.

He brought her home a bracelet after work one day, and they had Chinese takeout, Shawarma, pizza, and even breakfast foods for dinner, her absolute favorites, every night since she came home.

Not that she wasn't grateful, but Zelda was starting to see through their spoiling. And starting to crave a salad.

Victor held back from her as well. Since she couldn't get the time alone she needed to pull off her sexy playtime, he seemed to distance himself.

He barely looked at her when she was with Link or Mike, or both of them.

That bothered her.

What, now that she couldn't play this game with him, he was going to back off? Just like that? For real? That seemed like such utter bullshit. It made her angry, and when Zelda was angry, her brother and uncle picked up on it, and they tried to spoil her even more.

It had been ten days since she'd come back to her pack. Nothing had happened. The wolf pack didn't come demanding answers. The police didn't make contact again, and Zelda was starting to think that maybe the whole ordeal had just...ended.

Kind of anti-climactic, but then again, she supposed that was the best way for it to happen. Probably how it usually went. Not everything was a romantic suspense movie.

Still, she wasn't going to put up with Mike and Link tip-toeing around her anymore.

Today they both had to go to work. They worked construction, and when they were contracted for a job, they took it seriously, so Zelda decided to get a little sneaky that morning.

She secretly told Uncle Mike that Link would be picking up dinner when he came home, and she told Link that Uncle Mike would be grabbing the food. They worked at the same location, but Link had begged off work a few hours earlier than usual to make sure he could be home with Zelda.

Some days it was Uncle Mike who did that. Meaning if they left for work together, Link would catch a ride home with someone else, or walk.

He caught a ride in, stepped inside the house, and then tilted his head at the sight of Zelda peeling potatoes.

He shook his head. "Are you serious?"

She nodded. "Very serious. I haven't made Shepard's pie in a long time."

And she had a salad ready to go as well. The veggies were already chopped and they sat in a nice salad bowl.

"Let me help."

Zelda pointed the knife at him before he could take another step closer.

"Stay the hell away from my kitchen when your hands look like that. Get out of here and wash up."

"Fine, but then I'm helping you."

"You're not going to help out anything. I've got it tonight."

"Zel..."

She shook her head. "Nope. Forget it. I appreciate you and Mike babying me a little, but you don't have to do that anymore. You guys worked all day, and I've been sitting around in yoga pants. The least I could do is cook."

"We would have just ordered takeout again."

Which cost money they barely had.

Victor wasn't taking money from her uncle and brother anymore, but they were still paying Steve. Uncle Mike and Link were still paranoid, and Zelda hated to be a burden on them. Emotional as well as financial.

She smiled, burying those thoughts. "Home cooked is just as good. Supposed to be better, actually. Why? You hate my cooking or something?"

"No, don't be an idiot." Link shook his head, heading for his room. He peeled off his dirty, sweaty T-shirt, and Zelda knew she'd won this one.

He'd take a shower, Uncle Mike would be home in an hour or two, and everything would be perfect.

"You know they're just worried about you."

Zelda jumped, exhaling hard at the sight of Victor standing in the doorway. "Jesus, you scared the hell out of me."

He leaned against the doorframe.

His clothes had become a touch more casual ever since he'd come to stay at the fox pack, though she could still see the strength and muscle beneath his long-sleeved black shirt and navy jeans. She could also make out parts of his gun holster on the inside of his leather jacket.

"So you're talking to me again?"

"I was never *not* talking to you." He looked taken aback by the accusation.

Zelda grabbed a carrot and started chopping it as though it had insulted her. "Uh huh."

Even from the corner of her eye, she noted the stupid smile on his face.

Why did he have to smile at her like that? Why did he always have to look as though he knew something she didn't?

She wasn't sure if she liked that. If his smile wasn't so damned sexy, there would be no question in her mind about how much she didn't like it.

He was lucky he was so good-looking.

And that he was her mate.

"I was giving you space to be with your family."

Yeah right. "Is that what you've been doing?"

"Yes, that's exactly what I've been doing. Anyone can tell how worried they are about you. They've spent almost every spare minute they have acting as though it's your birthday."

"That's because they feel bad," Zelda said. "Since they have nothing to feel badly about, I don't want them spending any more money on me when they don't have to."

"Which is why you're worth all of it."

Zelda stopped what she was doing. Her gaze shot to Victor. He had his hands fisted in the pockets of his leather jacket, and he smiled at her as though there was nothing unusual about what he'd just said.

Zelda's heart pulsed. She swallowed hard. She went back to her carrot, finishing it off, grabbing another. "And why would you say something like that?"

No answer.

Zelda cracked her knife down a little harder on the carrot.

"You know I can't answer a question like that. Not yet."

"Not until the case is closed."

"It doesn't even have to be closed. I just have to—"

"Be satisfied there is no inherit or prominent danger to my safety. Yes. I remember. You've said it about a thousand times."

She expected him to say something else, to comment on the tone of her voice, to ask her why she was angry with him if she understood why he was doing the things he was doing.

He didn't. He waited for her anger to simmer down.

She growled at that.

"I know it's frustrating."

She snorted.

"But this is the way it has to be. At least for now."

"Yeah, I know."

"I don't want to get between you and your family time anyway. They want to spend time with you."

"You're my mate. You're my family, too. If you want to be." She glanced up.

This time, she did expect an answer.

To see him pressing his lips together, holding something back, got to her in a way she didn't think possible. Her anger rushed to the surface again like a pot of over boiling water. She couldn't get it off the stove fast enough and her anger bubbled over the rim and hissed on every surface it touched.

That's what it felt like, and that's all she thought it was.

"Careful!"

Victor rushed to her. Zelda stood still, shocked that he was suddenly, finally, after days of staying at least ten feet away from her, getting into her personal space.

He yanked the dishtowel from its spot hanging on the handle of the stove. He took her hand and wrapped her fingers.

Zelda saw the blood before he could wrap up her fingers in time, which was when she finally registered the heat and stinging wasn't her anger. It was the pain from when she'd sliced herself with the knife.

"Shit. Dammit, oh no, it got all over my carrots."

"They're fine. You can cut up some more later. Come over here."

He squeezed her fingers so tightly that it hurt. The burn of his hand over hers was so much more than the sting of her cut.

But, and it was so stupid that she was even thinking like this, she didn't care. It didn't bother her in the least that his touch hurt. She only cared that he was actually touching her.

Zelda's fox ears twitched beneath her headband. Her tail swished.

An energy rushed through her body the likes of which she'd never felt before Victor had come into her life.

His smell, up close and personal, was heady. He didn't wear anything scented. Not even his deodorant had a smell, but *he* himself did have a smell. A good smell.

Victor held her hand between them, likely squashing them to stop any blood flow, but Zelda didn't care what he did. She leaned forward, pressing her forehead against his chest.

With his leather jacket open, she could feel the strength and muscle beneath his black shirt. His heart and his heat were right there. So close. She wanted to touch his skin and see if it would feel the same as when he'd kissed her for the first time.

"Zelda, you should step back a little."

"I don't want to."

"I need to see your fingers. You might need stitches."

"I doubt it."

She was a shifter. Tight bandages and her shifter healing should take care of the rest.

"Even a shifter needs stitches sometimes." His voice didn't quite sound right. Was that because of the way she leaned against him? Did he feel this as much as she did?

He had to. He wasn't a shifter, but he was a subhuman. He still had the same instincts she did. His lack of ears or a tail didn't mean he was blind and deaf to those wants and needs.

She couldn't believe that he was, and yet, despite those desires he definitely felt, he was a master at ignoring them.

He pulled away from her. Victor still held tightly to her hand, clenching it, the pain shooting through her, but it was worse when that space was between their bodies.

"I need to see your hand." Slowly, Victor began unwrapping the towel.

Zelda looked away, hissing a little.

She hadn't felt the knife going into her flesh the way she probably should have at the time, but when Victor stopped gripping her hand, the rush of blood back into her fingers made her feel a pain she wasn't entirely sure was real.

"The cut's deep, but you didn't slice anything off. You're lucky your nails got in the way."

"Yeah?"

She looked, noting the lines that filled with blood on her index and middle finger. Her thumb had only been sliced a little, but it still bled.

"So, do I need stitches?"

He examined her fingers with a frown, as though he really wanted to make sure everything was all right.

"Don't think so. Some bandages might do it." He looked at her, and seemed to freeze.

Zelda stared up at him.

"Just be careful."

She nodded. "Yeah, I will."

After another five seconds of neither of them moving, Zelda knew what to do.

She pushed herself to her toes just as he leaned down. His mouth covered hers. Zelda inhaled deep through her nose, breathing him in as his powerful hands gripped into her hair and slid around her waist.

When he pulled her body closer instead of pushing her away, Zelda could have sang.

Her body buzzed as his tongue brushed against her mouth. She opened for him, but she didn't welcome him inside. She pushed her tongue to meet his when he thrust it between her lips.

Her mouth buzzed, her entire body hummed as Victor held her close.

And when his hand brushed against the base of her tail, Zelda moaned.

Victor kissed her deep, taking what he wanted, as though he'd been starved for it.

As Zelda gripped the back of his neck and jacket, the cuts on her thumb and fingers screamed at her, but she ignored that until her brother's voice called to her from across the kitchen.

"What the hell?"

CHAPTER 13

*Z*elda jumped away from Victor harder and faster than she meant to. She had to grab onto the counter island where she'd been chopping and peeling her veggies just to keep her balance.

"Hey, Link. What are you doing there?"

He was freshly showered and wearing clean clothes, and looking at the two of them as though he'd just stepped in on something criminal.

He didn't keep that look trained on Zelda, however, before he looked at Victor, eyes flashing, his fox ears sharp and pointing to the ceiling while his tail slashed the air behind him.

"Dude, what the fucking hell are you doing?"

"It won't happen again."

"*What?*" Zelda looked sharply at Victor.

That damned mask he kept up was back on his face, as though the kiss had never happened. As though he was back to being the professional, stick up his ass bodyguard.

"No fucking shit it won't happen again."

"Link, calm down."

Link marched forward. "You were fucking my sister? That's why you wanted to stay here? That it?"

Zelda stepped between her brother and Victor before something

84

nasty happened that she didn't want to happen. Link barely seemed to notice her as he swung his fist over her shoulder Victor.

"Stop it! Link!"

Zelda was pushed aside. She barely realized what happened next, but when Link tried to punch Victor, it seemed Victor grabbed onto not just his wrist, but his whole arm.

Victor was the one who shoved Zelda away, and he angled his body in a way that he locked Link's arm, spun around, and flipped Link down onto his back, pinning him.

Zelda grabbed Victor by his jacket, pulling, tearing a bit more skin on her thumb. "Victor, get off of him!"

Link thrashed, cursing and promising all kinds of pain to Victor when he got to his feet.

Pain Zelda doubted he would be able to dish out.

"Calm down. Calm down and I'll let you up."

"Fuck you!"

"Victor, get off of him."

"If he attacks me again—"

"He won't. Link, relax."

Link twisted his head enough that he was able to look up at her, his cheeks flushed with exertion and fury. "What the fuck do you want me to relax about? He was the one—"

"Link, Victor is my mate."

Zelda had never watched a body so tight and tense melt so quickly. It was as though someone had splashed Link with cold water, shocking him with stupidity.

His ears flicked. He looked at Zelda with such wide eyes that she felt...badly for him.

She wasn't sure why. It wasn't as though she'd told him anything particularly horrific. There wasn't anything she'd said that was bad or wrong.

So why the reaction?

"Victor, let him up. Please. He won't do anything, right, Link?"

Link looked between her and Victor, as though thinking about his next move. He nodded. That was the important thing.

Victor backed off, taking his knee off of the middle of Link's back.

Link rushed to feet. He looked down at Victor, then at Zelda, as though debating his next move.

Victor easily, and calmly, pushed himself to his feet. He never took his eyes away from Link.

And in that moment, Zelda really felt the power and authority Victor held. He'd let her get away with a few things before, stealing his car, forcing him to come with her to a pole dancing class, but right now he felt positively...

Alpha.

Link finally looked at her. "Is this true?"

Zelda nodded. "Yeah, it's true."

And her fingers hurt again, a lot, so she reached back and took the dishtowel that Victor had held to her hand, covering her cuts with it.

Link looked at Victor, then back at her. "Are you sure?"

To his credit, Victor said nothing. The look he gave Link was all kinds of dangerous.

"Why is that so hard to believe?"

"Because." Link glanced at Victor one more time. "You just got out of a bad marriage. You could be trying to rebound on this guy and not even know it."

"You think Victor is taking advantage of me."

"His job is to protect you and keep you alive while Gerard and Ben are still out there, not make out with you and trick Mike and me into letting him stay here so he can mess around with you behind our backs."

"There has been no *messing around*," Victor said.

Zelda was impressed he'd said anything in the first place.

"Whatever, okay? I just saw you feeling up my sister. Asshole."

Zelda was getting embarrassed by this whole exchange. This wasn't the sort of conversation she wanted to have with her brother. "He means we haven't had sex yet, and I am not rebounding. I know better than that."

"It wouldn't be the first time something like this has happened, and even if you were rebounding, I don't give a shit, just don't let some guy take advantage of you when he's supposed to be watching your back."

Victor's chest heaved with a long breath. He seemed to hold it before letting it out, as though holding onto the last shreds of his patience.

When he didn't defend himself, that was when Zelda got angry.

"He is not taking advantage of me and he is watching my back! He's working for free to watch my back."

"I don't give a shit if he's working for free and I don't care if you think he's your mate. If he's not thinking about doing his job then Mike and I need to call someone else."

That caught Zelda off guard for a couple of reasons. She focused on the one that made her the angriest. "What do you mean *think* he's my mate? There's no *thinking* about this. He is."

Victor's voice was low, as though trying to comfort her. "Zelda."

She yanked her arm away when his hand touched it. She didn't want him to comfort her when he would barely allow himself to touch her.

Great. Now she was torn between her fury for her idiot brother and her anger for the guy who had saved her tail more than once.

"Why do you think I wouldn't know something like that for sure?" She didn't give Link the chance to explain himself. "Is it because you think I don't know how to handle myself?"

"You *don't* know how to handle yourself."

Zelda was taken aback. She honestly hadn't expected him to say that.

"Zel, you've been taken care of your entire life. We all knew you weren't into marrying Harry, but you did it anyway because it was what the pack wanted. Every step of the way someone's had to take care of you, and the one time you've lived on your own was after seeing Maxwell choking on his own vomit over the dinner table."

"Okay, stop."

He didn't stop. "And even then, you didn't get a job or sign up for school. You went off the deep end and started dressing in weird clothes and going to night clubs and other places you had no business being in. You don't know how to take care of yourself and now you expect me to believe that you've found your mate in the guy that Mike and I hired for you? Seriously?"

He asked it as though he expected an answer. He looked as though he genuinely wanted one.

Zelda couldn't give him one. Her throat closed, and her heart was heavy. She looked away from Link, but only so he couldn't see the burn in her eyes.

She might as well have not bothered at all.

"Shit, Zelda, come on. Don't do that."

She marched out of the kitchen. "Screw you."

Screw them both as far as she was concerned. She was out. She was going to her room and she was leaving Link to fix his own Goddamned dinner.

She slammed her bedroom door behind her, flopping onto her bed with the pink sheets.

She may have grabbed onto her pillow and smothered herself with it to try and cut off any crying that she may or may not have been doing, which she was never going to admit to anyone one way or the other.

She hated it so much. She hated it because her asshole brother was right. He knocked at her door, called her name softly and asked her to come back outside, but no way in hell was she going to do that. She didn't want to be seen by anyone. Not him. And definitely not Victor.

Because Link was right. Zelda didn't want to admit it even to herself in the quiet of her mind, but he was right.

She didn't know how to take care of herself, and when she watched Maxwell die at the dinner table, only a few seats down from her, something snapped.

She couldn't entirely explain what it was; maybe Victor could. He was another guy that seemed to know absolutely everything.

Christ, he'd even hinted to her at one point that he knew what was up.

She tried to remember his exact words. Had he said them when they were at the police station? Or was it when he'd searched her apartment after she'd stolen his car?

He'd said something to the effect of how her behavior was being manipulated by her experiences.

Basically, she'd seen something traumatizing and had decided to go off the deep end.

She'd put on makeup she'd never worn before, bought clothes she never would have worn, and shed her good girl persona for drinking, dancing, nightclubs, and even sex.

Even when she'd tried to take back her independence, to prove to herself that she could be something amazing, something powerful and strong, she hadn't proved anything but what a complete flake she could be.

It was probably why Victor wasn't touching her. He could give her that speech all he wanted about how unprofessional it was, but the two times he'd kissed her so far proved he could overlook that sort of thing, at least for a little while.

Her brother didn't respect her enough to believe in the choices she made. Uncle Mike was probably the same way, what with how he was babying her since she got back.

Victor was definitely the same.

And she couldn't blame them for it.

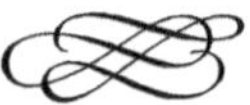

CHAPTER 14

Zelda stayed in her room feeling sorry for herself until someone barged inside.

She lifted her head from her pillow. She'd been dozing and hadn't realized it, which was probably why she was so sluggish to react when Victor grabbed her by her arm and yanked her out of bed.

"What, hey! What are you doing?"

"You're getting out of bed. You're not doing this."

"Let go of me!"

"No."

She hated it when he said no to her. He always did it with such conviction in his voice, as though he knew he was going to get what he wanted. As though every time he said the word no, people obeyed.

Zelda wasn't his Goddamned employee and he wasn't her alpha. Victor got her outside by the time she managed to yank her arm free.

"What the hell are you doing?"

Victor looked at her. Even when she'd taken his car for a joy ride, she'd never seen such intensity before. Impatient was too soft a word to describe what she saw in those eyes.

"You're not going to sit around in your room and sulk over nothing."

"What the hell gives you the right to decide that for me? If I want to go to bed and stay there I'll damn well do it!"

"Yeah? Well too damned bad. I had a talk with your uncle and brother and they agreed with me. You're coming out here."

"What?"

Uncle Mike came home?

She supposed that made sense. A quick look up at the sky told her how much time had passed. The sun was setting, the shadows long, and in the distance, the tips of the trees turned black against the contrasting sky.

She must have been in her room for hours. She definitely wasn't making dinner now.

Victor grabbed her arm and yanked her forward. He took a hold of her so quickly, and with such strength, that this time there was no chance for her to fight him off.

"Will you get *off* of me?"

"No. You're coming with me. I've got permission to do this, too. So don't bother fighting too much."

"I don't need anyone's permission to do anything!"

"No?"

Victor yanked her around, forcing her to face him.

It was odd to feel such power and strength in his body. If she went up against him in a fight, there would be nothing she could do about it.

With how nice he was to her lately, how sweetly he touched her, when he bothered to touch her, she sometimes forgot that he was a powerful male.

Not even fully human. Subhuman. How much was he holding himself back around her?

And Goddamn, why did she have to like that show of strength so much?

"What are you doing?"

A low growl rumbled in Victor's throat. Was he even aware he'd made that sound?

"Those people love you. They love you and care for you. They want to take care of you. Now is not the time for you to be laying your guilt trips on them."

Zelda glared at him. "Right, how dare I feel bad when my own brother tells me no one takes me seriously? That they still think I'm a child?"

"And whose fault is that?" Victor's teeth snapped.

Zelda fell back a step.

"You're a grown woman. You're an adult. You want to prove that? Then prove it. Don't run away when someone says something pseudo mean to you. You face it head on with your head held high and deal with it."

"That is so easy for you to say. Everything goes your way. You never had to grow up in a pack. You never had to deal with an arranged marriage."

"*No.*" Victor pointed his finger at her as though stabbing her through her heart with it. "You do not get to say that shit to me. You have no idea who the hell I am or where I've been."

"Oh, yeah right. *You've* had an arranged marriage to deal with that you had no say in?"

"Yes, I fucking did."

That information caught her off guard. So hard that it felt as though she'd been punched in the stomach with the information.

An uncertain laugh bubbled its way out of her gut instead. "What?"

He glared at her, not taking back his words.

She still couldn't believe it. "No, that's not possible."

"Why? Because I'm subhuman? Do you even know what that word means? What people think of when they say it? The answer is no, you don't. So don't give me this shit about how I don't understand anything."

"You're..." Zelda's first thought was to ask about his wife, but a quick glance down at his hand confirmed that he didn't have a ring there, and he never did. There was no trace even of an indent from having worn it. "What happened?"

Victor wet his lips. He propped his hands on his hips, the muscles in his arms and shoulders tight. Everything in his body language told her how he didn't want to say anything else to her. He'd likely only revealed so much to her because he'd wanted to shut her up with her pity party.

"Are you still married?"

"No. I never was."

That was one thing she didn't understand. "But you just said—"

"I know what I said."

Victor lifted his hand, as though he wanted to make some point, then dropped it with a sigh.

"She was the alpha's daughter in a neighboring pack. We were friends; she wasn't afraid to come near me because I couldn't shift. She was my best fucking friend, and somehow, my parents convinced her parents that an arranged union between the two of us wouldn't be such a bad thing. With her bloodline, I might even be able to give her children that wouldn't be defective."

Zelda pressed her lips together. She brought her hands up and rubbed her arms, suddenly feeling cold.

Hearing him say the word defective like that, as though he'd been called that more than once, probably by people who were supposed to love him...

Christ, now she wasn't angry with him anymore. Now she was torn between wanting to go and hug him and stay right where she was, embarrassed and ashamed.

"So you backed out of the marriage?"

"No. She did. Left me at the altar." Victor shook his head. "I loved her. I loved her so much and I was ready to marry her. She'd told me more than once how much she loved me, too, but I guess with pressure from her parents and mine...she only ever saw me as her friend. She didn't want to make a mistake she and I would both regret, so when it came time to say our vows, she just never showed up."

"That...I'm really sorry."

"Don't be." Victor shook his head. "I'm not."

Zelda blinked. "But you just said you were in love with her. She left you at the altar. That's...that's horrible."

"No, it wasn't. Think about it."

"I am. I don't get it."

Victor's shoulders sagged. He approached her, slowly, as though to make sure she didn't run. "I loved Angie, I thought she was going to have my children, and I was crushed when she didn't show up. I thought every negative thing you could think. About her, about myself. I thought she couldn't go through with marrying a defective subhuman, but that wasn't it, and when I got it, I got it."

He was toe to toe with her now, looking down at her, waiting for her to understand.

"What did you get?"

Victor's hands were on her shoulders. Gently, he rubbed her arms.

"That she didn't want the decision to be made for her. That she couldn't force herself to love someone she didn't love. Not even her best friend. She's still my best friend. We still talk."

A spike of jealousy caught Zelda in her belly. She didn't like the idea of Victor talking to other women. She crossed her arms.

"Do you still love her?"

He smiled, as though the idea of her closing herself off to him amused him. "Not like that. Not anymore, but there's still something you're missing."

"Yeah, what's that?" She was still swimming in her jealousy.

"That Angie had the choice, even when everyone around her told her she didn't. Even when her alpha, who was also her father, made the decision for her. A decision that would have been good for her pack. She backed out because, ultimately, it was her choice. It was her choice whether or not she was going to marry me, and it was your choice whether or not you were going to marry Harry, as much as it was your choice to leave. It was a good choice, by the way," he said.

"No kidding," Zelda replied. "I knew it was a good choice, the right choice, but I still can't believe I did it."

"And Angie couldn't believe it when she pulled together the guts to leave me. It wasn't just her family and pack she was disappointing. She knew how I felt, and she thought she knew how she felt. It took a lot of courage for her to do it, but she still did it."

"But I'm not courageous like you're ex girlfriend, okay? I couldn't have just walked away."

"That's the thing, *yes*, you could have. There's nothing Angie has that you don't already have; in fact, you've got it better than Angie did because her family didn't talk to her for two years after she did what she did. They're barely talking now. You've got a family that loves you and wants to make you happy, and I don't know, maybe that gets in your way sometimes, but you can't punish them or yourself because they're doing the best they know how to do."

Zelda tried to absorb all of that. It was difficult. She still wanted to fight. Her hackles were still raised high and everything inside her told her to back away from him. To deny everything he said.

Because if she admitted to herself that she did have courage, that she could make responsible decisions, then she would have to admit that she'd done a few things wrong.

"It's okay," Victor said. "It's okay to not get everything just the way you want it all to be all the time. It's okay to make mistakes. Just don't tell yourself that you don't have the courage to do something, because then you'll start to believe it. And if you believe it, every time someone says something remotely troubling to you, you'll regress."

"You mean run to my room and slam the door."

Victor grinned at her. "Yes, something like that."

Zelda's eyes burned. She looked away from Victor, but only because she was too ashamed and embarrassed. Of everything.

She could have been a collage graduate by now. She could have her life, her own home, her own responsibilities by now if she hadn't let herself lie down and let everyone make her decisions for her.

Victor sighed, his hands pulling away from her shoulders, taking their warmth with him.

Zelda was left standing there, cold and embarrassed.

"Come on. We can talk while we walk."

She rubbed at her face, desperately trying to get rid of the wet burn in her eyes. "Walk where?"

"Somewhere no one can listen in on us. I said a lot of private shit to you, and you look like you don't want anyone to overhear any of this either."

"What happened to facing your problems head on?"

Victor shook his head, that damned quirk of his lips coming back. "It's one thing to face an enemy when you're prepared for him, but everyone knows you don't go to a fight unprepared. Come on, let's go."

They weren't talking about fighting, but Zelda supposed she could see what he meant by that. She followed him.

Her pack was well lit, even in spaces where there were no houses. Victor didn't take her into the darkness of the trees, but to one of the open areas of the pack.

The trees had been cleared out a long time ago. Cars and trucks sometimes parked here whenever the pack was having a party. Picnic tables and barbecues were also brought out here if it was something more informal, like the Fourth of July, or a wedding.

Zelda shivered. "I got married in this spot," she said.

Victor looked at her, a brow lifting. "You did?"

Zelda nodded, suddenly kind of bashful about it. "It was one of my bridal requests. I wanted the marriage to take place in my own pack. As you can see, all the benches, and the gazebo is gone."

Victor glanced around. "Do you want to go somewhere else?"

Zelda *almost* said yes. She stopped herself, then shook her head. "No. Face it all head on, right?"

Victor grinned at that.

And only then did Zelda start to feel a little more normal. A little more relaxed.

"So, what are we going to do out here? You want to teach me about personal responsibility?"

"Maybe."

Zelda had to smile at him. "Okay, so I can work on not getting angry at my brother for not believing me when I said you're my mate, but what if I happen to like going out to parties? What if pole dancing lessons are something I want to do for the rest of my life?" An amazing thought suddenly hit her. "I could *teach* pole dancing lessons!"

"You would actually have to be good at it before you could get started."

Zelda punched him in the arm. The bastard snorted a laugh, but he barely flinched.

"I will get you back for that one."

"That's something of the point."

Zelda blinked at him.

Victor just smiled back at her, that same wicked grin. He took off his jacket. She noticed he didn't have his holster on.

"Where's your gun?"

"Left it with Steve. It's not the best idea in the world to have a loaded weapon on me if I'm going to teach you anything physical."

"Physical?" Her pulse raced at the thought.

"Not sex. I'm going to teach you some self-defense. We'll talk about how much going to nightclubs actually means to you later. This is more important."

"Wait, what? You're going to teach me self-defense? Really?"

"Of course. You're young and healthy, and the situation you're in requires some basic knowledge of self-defense."

The objections came immediately. "I can barely swat a fly. I don't even like laying out mouse traps because I think they're cruel, and I have to get Link or Uncle Mike to squash the spiders in the house."

"Flies, mice, and spiders aren't trying to do you any physical harm."

"I beg to differ!"

Victor may have smiled at her, but he still shrugged his shoulders, entirely uncaring for her plight against spiders and mice. "Beg to differ until the cows come home, when it's your life on the line, instinct to survive will take over and if you don't know how to harness that, you'll get a little more of what happened outside of that nightclub where you and I met."

Zelda shivered. She could still feel the hand around her mouth. The hand that had been holding a cloth wet with chloroform.

"Do you ever want to be in that position again?"

Zelda shook her head. "No."

Victor laced his fingers together and cracked his knuckles. "Okay, then this should be simple."

"But what can you teach me that would even work?"

Even when she wasn't playing at being a damsel, she was still as helpless as they came. Her bone structure didn't exactly bode well for a fight.

"You're a shifter, aren't you?"

Her fox ears flicked. "Yeah?"

"So, if someone grabs you, bring your teeth out and bite them. You could even shift into your animal shape. It's incredibly hard to hold onto a wriggling animal with claws and teeth."

Made sense. "I suppose."

Victor stepped up to her again, taking her hand, looking at her manicured nails. "These are an especially important weapon."

"My manicure?"

"Yes, exactly. Even if you can't focus enough to change, putting these into the eyes of your enemy will guarantee they will drop you. If someone has you like this,"—he grabbed her by the throat, but didn't hold on hard enough to cut off her airway—"most people will grab the wrists of their attacker, trying to pry them off."

"Because they can't breathe."

Zelda even tried to remove his hands, but he held on tight enough that she couldn't budge him.

"Yes, that makes sense, but if you go for their eyes, you'll be released so fast, and if you do a little damage, you'll have the chance to run while your assailant tries to recover. Try it on me."

She blinked at him. "What?"

He grinned, shaking his head. "I won't let you stick your nails in my eyes. I'll know it's coming."

"They why bother?"

"Because the point is the same. My instinct to protect my eyes will force me to release you, even if I see the attack coming. I will have to let you go. Try it."

She didn't want to. What if she accidentally got him in the eyes? It seemed gross, but, at the same time, he was clearly not going to release her until she gave him what he wanted.

And in a way, she wanted to make him proud.

So Zelda moved quickly, pushing her fingernails towards his eyes.

He released her and stepped back fast. Fast enough that she hadn't been able to get anywhere near his eyes, but he did let her go.

"Good. Very good."

"What if they're behind me?"

Victor nodded. "All right. Try this."

He came up behind her, looping his arm around her throat, but again, he didn't use enough pressure to cut off her airways, he just held on, preventing her from moving even when she struggled.

She didn't like it. It reminded her too much of the way that guy had grabbed her.

"Don't just fight like that. I'm up close and personal with you. You're within reach to just put your hands back and find my eyes."

She did, again. Victor released her quickly and stepped back, protecting his eyes.

Now Zelda was starting to feel a little more confident. "This really works?"

Victor nodded, pride in his gaze that hadn't been there a few minutes ago. "It does. And believe it or not, but turning yourself into dead weight also helps. It's incredibly difficult to carry someone like that, and if you're in the middle of a struggle, it can throw off your attacker. He might drop you. You get up and run for it."

Zelda put that information away for later. "Right. Okay, anything else I need to know?"

"Yes." Victor crossed his arms. "It's the most basic but most important thing. If I'm ever not around, and you have no way of running, remember this one key thing and it could save your life."

Zelda pressed her lips together. The idea of him not being around was…troubling, but she was willing to listen. "Okay, shoot."

Victor ticked off his fingers. "Stop your enemy from being able to move, to see, or to breathe, and you'll up your chances for survival."

"Okay." Zelda nodded. "How do I do all of that?"

Victor grinned. "It means to go for their eyes, their throat, or their knees and feet. I'll be showing you a little of all of that tonight."

Zelda shivered, but she had to admit, she was eager to learn. "Couldn't I just kick my attacker in the balls and run for it?"

"You'd be amazed at how well men actually protect that part of themselves." Victor shrugged. "If you can get the shot in, great, but someone trying to grab at you who happens to be a male will usually see a retaliation like that coming. They don't expect you to go for the eyes."

Zelda nodded. "Right. Okay, eyes, throat, and joints."

"Preferably the knee. You get a hard kick with the right angle in that spot and your attacker will go down."

Zelda made a mental note of that, already pumping herself up to practice with Victor.

It was such a powerful feeling. The sense of control Victor gave to her as he went over the steps was unlike anything she'd ever felt before in her life.

No longer did she feel like a helpless snowflake flitting through life, waiting to melt as the slightest possible infraction. She felt confident. Just as she had when she'd been on the dance floor with so many eyes on her.

Only now instead of sexy confident, she felt bad ass confident.

She could get used to that feeling.

CHAPTER 15

Zelda wasn't sure how long they practiced for, but it was a while. She was glad she'd been wearing comfortable clothes when she'd tried to make dinner earlier. The idea of Victor dragging her out of bed wearing a tight little skirt and high heels so he could teach her how to…not fight. That wasn't what it was, and when she'd asked him about it, he'd made sure to clarify himself about it, too.

He was not teaching her how to fight. He was teaching her how to survive in the event someone grabbed her.

When he finished with her, Zelda sweated from top to bottom, her t-shirt clung to her, and being grabbed and held onto so many times by her mate, just for him to suddenly release her whenever she went for his eyes, or tried to punch his throat, or even dig her nails into his beck, got to her on a level she never thought possible.

Her body responded to Victor sexually whenever he grabbed her.

It got to the point where she stopped trying too hard to get away.

How could she possibly want to escape him when he held her so tightly to his back? She felt his heart slamming against his chest and through her shoulder blade.

Her blood thrummed hot.

It was likely only a product of their physical activity. The heat they produced as they worked together. Still, Zelda couldn't help herself. She wanted him. She wanted Victor so badly that it hurt.

His breath rasped in her ear, making it flick from the warmth. "You're getting too tired for this."

It was sort of true, but she shook her head. "Not too tired for something else."

She never would have been so bold with Harry. Whenever he'd wanted sex, for the most part, she gave in. Not that he'd ever been demanding. For a psycho murderer, he'd been fairly accommodating with that aspect of their marriage.

But she'd always waited for him to make the first move. Even when it had occurred to her that she could ask for sex, she'd just waited for Harry to give her the look, or to notice when his hands had rested on her in a certain way. She'd never said no to him. She'd tell him when she wasn't feeling well, or when it was that time of the month for her, but now that she thought about it, she'd never told him no, and she'd never been the one to ask him for it in the first place.

How would he have reacted to her if she had asked for it, or if she had just flat out told him no?

With Victor, even though they had yet to have sex even once, the fact that he was so easy with the word no made her feel as though she could say it, too.

If and when the time came, which she doubted it ever would. Not with the way he touched her now.

Christ, he wasn't even touching her in any way that could be deemed as almost sexual, and her body still responded to him.

"You say you're not too tired for something else, but the fact that you keep dozing off makes me think otherwise."

"I'm not dozing off."

"You're barely paying attention. It's why I keep grabbing you. Why you're not out of my hands yet."

"I don't want to be out of your hands." She didn't want to struggle to get away from him. She didn't want to practice anymore. She wanted to stay out there with him and mate with him. Really mate with him.

She was tired of dancing around this.

The heat she felt all along his body, and the heat she felt rushing lower still, told her he wanted the same thing.

Victor backed off. He released her suddenly and without her having to do anything to push him away.

Disappointment filled her from top to bottom. Even knowing he didn't like the sight of her pouting, she couldn't help it.

"You know why I can't."

"Is it really because you're my bodyguard? Or is it because of what happened with you and your ex?"

Victor barely moved. He stared at her, long and hard, as though calculating his words carefully.

"This has nothing to do with Angie. I'm not afraid you will hurt me, Zelda. I'm afraid I will hurt you if I don't do my job properly. People get hurt if I don't pay attention on the job; that's sort of the point of me being here."

"You don't need to worry about that right now. We're safe right where we are. We're at my pack." She reached out, gently taking him by his hand. "No one will see us."

His nostrils flared. Zelda never in her life would have thought that to be something dangerous, but there was a warning in his eyes, in the tightness of his lips, in his expression in general.

"Steve is still out there. You're not even being paid for this anymore. Let him do it."

"I can't."

"Yes, you can."

Zelda pushed herself to her toes, her mouth finding his. She inhaled deeply through her nose as their mouths met, the briefest touch of his tongue against her lips making her heady and drunk on sensation.

Victor had only ever kissed her twice before, and those times weren't enough for her to get used to the feeling. Even when she was the one taking charge like this, she could barely bring herself to hold on.

A low growl rumbled inside Victor's chest. His strong, heated hands settled on Zelda's waist.

For a brief, terrible second, Zelda feared he would push her away, break off the kiss, and walk her back home.

He didn't. Victor's hands tightened on her waist, pulling her closer to his body heat, as though making sure she wouldn't go anywhere.

If Zelda had been a cat shifter, she would have purred. Instead, she did the next best thing and let out a sound of triumph as she threw her arms around Victor's neck, holding him tightly, pushing his mouth open and sliding her tongue inside to say a proper hello to his mouth.

Again with that rumbling sound. Zelda liked it. She liked the way Victor pushed his tongue back against hers before he pushed inside her mouth, as though it was now his turn to taste her.

Zelda moaned. The fact that Victor swallowed her kiss made the sensation that much better. Her body was on fire from the very tip of her tail to the top of her ears.

As Zelda pushed her body against Victor's, demanding more of him, something animal seemed to awaken in the man. His grip around her waist tightened. He pulled her so close that she was flush against him, her breasts pushing up against his powerful chest through her shirt and lace bra.

Zelda felt the steady drum of his heart. Her feet left the ground. Victor didn't even pull her up into his arms. He just lifted her a few inches off her feet and started walking with her.

As though she weighed nothing at all.

A hard surface pushed against the back of Zelda's legs. A shocked cry escaped her lips as she was pushed against the rough surface.

One of the picnic tables used for barbecuing. Zelda helped to lift her hips off the edge so Victor could push her onto the table itself. Their mouths briefly separated, and then came back together again only when Zelda grabbed Victor by his ears and yanked him forward.

He had such nice human ears. She loved the feel of them, the shell shape and their softness. They might have been the only soft thing on him because he kissed her like an alpha in heat.

Had he been a shifter instead of a subhuman, he very likely would have been an alpha.

Her alpha.

She opened her thighs for him, welcoming Victor between her legs just as she welcomed his tongue back between her lips. Her breasts felt tight. Zelda blindly reached out for one of Victor's hands, which were back on her waist, bringing one up to cup her breast beneath her shirt.

"You drive me crazy."

Victor's words were hot and heavy against her mouth. She felt the thrum of his body as he began to pull at the waist of her black yoga pants.

She lifted her hips just enough so Victor had an easier time of getting the elastic waist around the curve of her ass. Her tail thumped against the table now. The wood was rough and cold.

But Victor was so very warm, and as he pulled her black pants down her legs—being gentlemanly enough to not toss them on the grass, he put them next to her on the table instead—Zelda's body shivered.

She trembled as though filled with too much energy, as though her body was at capacity for how much anticipation and excitement she could handle.

Her sex felt swollen and wet. Zelda's thighs clenched eagerly as Victor worked the belt of his jeans, his fingers pulling down his zipper, the metal teeth spreading open for him.

"God, finally."

He looked at her, his eyes flashing with something she didn't entirely understand. More guilt for what he was doing?

No. Zelda couldn't have that. She kissed him again, licking teasingly at the crease of his lips, desperate to distract him.

She didn't want him to have any second thoughts about this.

Which was also why she angled her hips, curled her legs around his thighs, and pulled him closer.

The sudden move had an unexpected impact on her as well. Zelda moaned softly as she felt the heat of Victor's cock against her bare sex. Nothing separated them now.

All he had to do was push inside.

He moaned against her lips. Already he thrust his hips, his shaft sliding against her sex.

Zelda shuddered against the rush of pleasure. Her mouth left his, but it was as though her body reacted against her will now. She had no control.

A sigh escaped her throat as she dug her nails into the back of Victor's neck and in his hair. "Oh my God."

Victor said nothing. He continued to move his hips, as though he was also under the same spell. If he was still fighting with how wrong he felt it was for him to do this, he wasn't giving any indication of it. Or he was possibly too far gone for any of his previous excuses to matter.

Zelda was more than happy with that. She'd take whatever she could get at this point.

Victor didn't spend long teasing her. He thrust against the lips of her sex as though he only wanted to feel how wet she already was. Or slick his cock. Either way, when he reached down, taking his shaft in hand by the base, Zelda knew what to expect.

He lined up with her opening, pushing forward and sheathing himself inside her at the slightest give.

A single, hard, well-placed thrust, and Zelda felt her body come alive in ways she'd never thought possible.

She shouted, her thighs squeezing tightly around Victor's waist as he thrust into her again and again. She couldn't seem to hold on properly because already she was coming. Zelda was coming, and the consistent motion of Victor's hips pushed her climax even higher.

Until she collapsed against his body, hardly able to breathe, hardly able to think about anything other than the pleasant aftershocks, and how nice if felt to feel his thick cock still filling her.

Victor groaned low in his throat. He fucked into her wildly, as though he'd lost all control and could think about nothing else but reaching the end.

Zelda blinked, feeling sated and even kind of sleepy, but she remembered her manners.

She let her hands slide around his shoulders and chest. She touched him everywhere she could reach, pushing her fingers up beneath his shirt and finding his nipples.

"Come inside me. I want to feel it."

Another hard growl, another sound that made something within Zelda perk up.

She felt herself responding to him, to the motion of his body on top of her, the smell of him, the heat that radiated from him, and the way he moved inside her.

She almost couldn't believe it, and it was enough to make her burst out in a short laugh.

Zelda's pleasure was rising again. Already. After only having one of the best orgasms of her life about a minute ago. She felt her pleasure rising as naturally and easily as though she and Victor did this every day.

As though they were already well versed with each other's bodies.

And it was good enough for her.

Zelda reached down, her hand sliding against the folds of her sex.

Victor's eyes briefly widened when he realized what she was doing.

Touching herself while he was inside her. She couldn't imagine that was the kinkiest thing he'd ever seen, but she had never been daring enough to do that with Harry.

Zelda grinned, clenching her thighs around his waist, trying to make her inner walls tighter for him.

Victor groaned, turning his face away from her, though the movement of his lower half never stopped. "Why. The hell. Do you. Have. To. Be. So. Damn. *Perfect.*"

He moaned again, grabbing her by the bottom of her shirt and yanking it up, shoving aside her lace bra and exposing one of her breasts before Zelda could say anything to him, could respond to his comment.

Her nipple was in his mouth before she knew it. He teased it with his lips and tongue, but also his teeth.

So hard, hot, and wild. Zelda panted and gasped for breath and before she knew it, that rising sensation was on her again.

"Oh fuck, you've got to be kidding," she gasped.

Victor didn't seem to notice she'd said a word. The sounds of his grunting became harder, the motion of his hips more violent and sudden. He was almost there. She could feel it, and the thought made her want his pleasure, made Zelda need Victor to come inside her so much that it felt as though she was waiting for Christmas.

"Please. Hurry. I need...I *need* it."

Victor's spine briefly tensed. He groaned, and his neck tightened as warmth filled her from inside out.

Which was about when she realized they not only didn't use a condom, but she also hadn't taken her birth control since getting home.

Shit.

Whatever. She'd deal with it later. Zelda had what she wanted; now all she needed was to reach that sweet release herself.

So close. She was so close, her sex still sensitive and he was still inside her. Even without moving, the pleasure was great and then...

Then she was *there*, throwing her head back and sighing, spasming. Zelda's orgasm popped off as though by gunshot.

She blinked. Victor pulled himself off her, looking towards the source of that noise, which was not her.

"What—"

"Get dressed." He pulled away from her, righting his pants, his eyes alert and watching the trees around him. "Right now."

The sound of a popping gunshot hadn't been in her head as a sign of her sudden orgasm. No. Of course not. She couldn't just be that lucky.

Someone had actually fired a gun.

CHAPTER 16

"*C*ome on."

Zelda barely had her yoga pants over the round of her ass before Victor grabbed her wrist and started yanking her along. Through the trees and towards the sound of the gunfire.

Zelda could barely keep up with him. More than once his hard tugging nearly made her lose her balance, but also kept her on her feet.

She could hardly believe it. The fact that he was able to run that fast with her, faster than she could ever go, brought her inner fox to shame.

She wasn't the fastest for a shifter, but she'd still thought she could be graceful when the time came for it.

Yeah, apparently not.

Just as fast as Victor started running with her, he came to a sudden halt. Zelda banged into his back and this time did fall onto her ass because he released her hand.

And she just happened to land on the sharpest pinecone in the damn woods. She swore the point of it got her right beneath her tail and just above her ass crack.

"*Ow! Victor!*"

He didn't have to shush her. He motioned to her with his hand, as though asking her to wait, and though he wasn't facing her, it was the look in his eyes that told her now was most definitely not the time to test him.

Zelda dug the pinecone out from beneath her tail, wincing as it scratched that sensitive spot, but it was the look on Victor's face, the tightening of his jaw that did her in.

She almost forgot about the sounds of shouting, the sounds of tires squealing. The fact that her brother or uncle could be in trouble.

She pushed herself to her feet. Victor grabbed her just as she nearly stormed passed him.

"What are you doing? No, get back here."

"What if Mike and Link are hurt?"

"They'll be more hurt if they find out anything happened to you."

She wasn't talking about emotionally hurt and he damn well knew it.

His hand came up and covered her mouth before she could say a word.

"That was a gunshot. I don't know if it was friendly fire or where it came from and I do not have my weapon on me. Do not go out into the open until we know what's going on."

It made sense. It really did.

The little nagging bitch inside her head that had popped up ever since she'd taken off from her previous life didn't seem to care.

It was quite the struggle.

Zelda groaned, her body humming to get out there.

Victor wasn't having any of it.

"No."

All semblances of the man who had been between her legs, who had kissed her in the kitchen, and fucked like a wild animal, were entirely gone.

The moment was over, he wasn't wrapped around her little finger anymore, and it was just the serious alpha warrior in front of her who wanted to keep her alive.

"Fuck." Victor released her long enough to reach into his pocket.

He grabbed his phone, his thumb moving with all the precision and skill of a teenager as he shot off a long text.

Zelda could barely make out what it was he'd written, but she'd taken in enough before he'd hit send to know he was messaging Steve.

He looked up and away from his phone multiple times, as though searching the surrounding area for threats.

The tension in his shoulders was starting to get to Zelda. She didn't like it. Her tail whipped around behind her, and Zelda too started searching around for any signs of someone about to jump out of the bushes.

It wasn't a good feeling. A little too close to how she'd felt in that alley behind the club, or when Victor had chased off the man who cut her breaks.

The fact that Victor continued to glance at and growl at his phone meant he wasn't getting the reply he wanted. If any at all.

"Fuck. Come on. Come on."

"Hey."

Zelda screamed, jumping three feet in the air when a hand grabbed her shoulder.

Victor, still standing close by, dropped his phone, his fist swinging, and immediately he caught Link in the apple of his cheek before he was able to stop himself.

Zelda saw the entire thing in slow motion. The way Link's feet went up before he came back down hard.

He might have landed on the same pine cone she did from the sound he let out when he landed.

"Fuck!"

"Link!"

Zelda went to kneeling down. She put her hands behind his back, but he was already pushing himself up, his hand cupping his cheek.

"What the fuck?"

"Sorry. Thought you were…someone else."

Victor offered his hand. Zelda expected some macho fight, or for Link to growl at the offering and get up himself before going chest to chest with Victor.

He took the hand instead, still wincing from the pain in his face, and still glaring at Victor, but it didn't go any farther than that.

"Stupid prick. Watch what you're doing next time."

Victor paid no mind to Link's words before he went back to business. "What happened? We heard a gunshot."

"I don't know. Your boy went and ran off chasing someone down in his car."

Zelda didn't understand. "Wait, what?"

"Someone came onto pack territory who wasn't supposed to be here?" Victor asked.

Link shrugged. "I don't know. I just came out here to get my sister before something happened."

Zelda looked to Victor, trying, and failing, to keep from wringing her hands together. "What are you going to do?"

She already knew the answer as Victor shoved her towards Link. "Take her home. Keep the doors locked. Don't let anyone inside until I get back."

"Hey, wait a minute!" Zelda didn't seem to get a say in any of this as she was passed around like a hot potato.

And Link, her asshole brother, kept a firm grip on Zelda's arms as he nodded. "Right."

Men on missions were either the best or the worst. With her brother and her idiot mate, Zelda was leaning towards it being the worst.

"No, wait a minute." She struggled against her brother's grip, trying to get answers from Victor, who rushed off towards his car. "Where are you going?"

"Leave him alone. He's working."

And not getting paid. The only reason why Zelda kept that little jab to herself was because she knew it wasn't Link's fault, and he would only feel guilty to hear such a thing.

Victor didn't answer her and Link didn't stop yanking her towards their house. At some point, she stopped fighting it and went along with him because, well, there was someone with a gun out there and she clearly wasn't getting what she wanted.

Mike waited for them at the door. He looked relieved, but frowned at the sight of Link still rubbing at his face.

"What happened?"

"Fucker got me good," Link groaned.

Mike shut the door after them, locking it. He pulled Zelda into his arms. She went, comforted by his heat and the kiss he pressed to the top of her head, but he wouldn't stop looking at Link.

Link waved it off. "I'm fine. I just snuck up on him."

Mike grunted, though his next question to Zelda had her blood turn icy.

"What took you so long out there anyway?"

Her brain scrambled. "Uh, he was showing me some self-defense moves. I thought you knew that?"

"I did know that, but you smell…"

Zelda couldn't move. Everything inside her screamed to run away as Mike sniffed her, but her knees and feet were locked.

She knew he had his answer when he yanked his head back. "Oh."

Link growled low in his throat, shaking his head.

"He's my mate." She was getting sick of defending this, regardless of what Victor had already told her about it.

Still, it was because of Victor's words that she tried to hold onto her patience, to understand the men in her life a little more and be aware that they were coming from a good place.

Mike's mouth pressed to a thin line, and that was enough. Zelda pulled herself away from his arms. "He's my mate."

"I believe you."

Zelda blinked. "You do?" She growled in her brother's direction. "He doesn't."

Link crossed his arms, made a tsking sound, and walked off.

"Ignore him. He's just worried about you. What he doesn't like, and what I don't like either, is that this man is supposed to be protecting you. He's not supposed to be distracted by anything when he does that."

"That's what Steve's for."

Mike's jaw tightened. "Yes, well, I'm starting to feel a little less grateful about the fact that Victor stopped taking my money now that I know why."

"What? Why? Would you fire him if you could?"

"Damned straight I would. Mate or no mate."

And now that he couldn't and Victor was still technically doing a job, it left him in a tight spot.

Mike went to all the curtains, closing them. Zelda followed after him, reminded of the bigger problems they had on their hands.

She went to help him. He closed the curtains and Zelda dimmed the lights.

"Don't worry about that, sweetheart. I got it."

But he and Link had always had it. There was never a time in Zelda's life when she could remember not being taken care of by someone. Even her crazy parents, who took off on her and Link, dumping them onto Mike and promising to be right back had still shielded her from the realities of the world.

Before blasting her with a very real, very harsh one involving child abandonment.

"I'll get the kitchen." She marched off before Mike could stop her.

He sighed, following her.

She shut the kitchen curtains, which were little more than lace, so she figured the best idea would be to keep away from the glass for as long as possible until Victor or Steve sent her a message that everything was all right.

Mike turned out the lights. "All right, come out of there."

"Where are we going?" She could hear her brother stomping around the house. Likely he was doing the same thing. Locking windows, shutting curtains and turning out the lights.

"We're going into the basement, cuddling up with some blankets, and watching a few movies until this ends."

In that case, they were going to need some snacks. Zelda quickly went to the pantry, grabbed the leftover potato chips.

Mike stared at her with that look he used to give her whenever he thought she was doing something stupid. "You risked your life for that?"

"I stayed away from the window. Any soda downstairs?"

"Yes. Christ. Let's go. You and I need to have a little chat about your new bodyguard."

"Uncle Mike—"

"He's not banging you in my house."

Zelda snapped her lips shut. She stared hard at her uncle. He stared right back at her, as though waiting for her to say something, make an argument, or get testy with him.

Zelda swallowed over the large, incredibly awkward lump in her throat. "Uh, yeah. That sounds fine."

"Good. Let's go."

She was going to melt into a puddle and die before any stalker or crazy ex managed to get their hands on her. Zelda had no doubts in her mind about that.

Of course, her uncle's sort of demand, sort of request wasn't the last Zelda heard of her new relationship with Victor. Despite being an adult, and at one point being married, Mike had some questions for her as he sat on the other side of the couch.

The basement was small, but it had been made up well enough that, with the help of a dehumidifier, it made for a nice family room.

If Zelda could ignore the occasional spider.

As it was, she sat in her corer of the couch, wrapping the knit throw around her shoulders that usually hung off the back of the seat, her knees up, as though she was trying to shield herself from her uncle's questions about her sex life.

Questions which Link was apparently in no mood to hear when he came downstairs, pulled out his game console, and stuck his headphones in his hears.

"Now, I just want to make sure you're being safe."

It was right about then that Zelda wished she had a Nintendo console and noise cancelling headphones of her own. Since she didn't, she put up with the questions as best as she could, which was to say, not very well at all.

She wasn't exactly getting a birds and bees talk out of all of this, but it was one step away from that and still managed to be just as embarrassing as anything else.

"You know I love you, right?"

Zelda nodded, reaching for another potato chip from the bag and popping it into her mouth.

"You know I only want the best for you, right?"

"Mmhm." She reached for another. She was going to stuff her face and finish off the bag and still Mike would be asking her these questions.

Mike looked away from her. They weren't even watching the movie he'd put on.

Kind of hard to, considering the topic, and what was happening outside.

"Look, I'm sorry about what happened with Harry. If I'd known for one second he was like that...well, I never would have let you near him."

Zelda almost choked on the potato chips she was eating. "W-what? God, no! Uncle Mike, no, that isn't something I hold against you at all."

"I allowed it to happen." He leaned back in his seat, looking away from her and down at the soda can he thumbed in his hand. "I'm your guardian. I could have put a stop to that if I wanted to."

"I never asked you to stop it. It's okay. I was nervous about it, but I kind of wanted to marry him."

"Kind of."

Zelda pressed her lips together.

This was what Victor had been talking about. She let everyone take the blame for her, let everyone fight for her and protect her, and it had gotten to the point where, now as an adult, she couldn't even put her uncle's mind at ease about her shoddy marriage with Harry.

Zelda leaned over; she reached for his hand. Mike tensed when she took it, but then seemed to relax as she gave it a squeeze.

Zelda looked him right in the eye. She shook her head. "That's not on you. It's not on me either. It's not on anyone. Harry was, well...we know how he is now and that's not the point."

Mike growled. "You were *alone* with him."

"Yes, and I am fine now, and I know you don't like me being with Victor, but he's doing his best to keep me safe."

"That's not what I don't like about it." Mike pulled his hand away.

Zelda blinked. "Really? Then what don't you like?"

A dusting of color came over Mike's cheeks. He grumbled as he looked away from her again. "You're both adults, and if you're right about this mating thing, well, even if you're wrong, lust can get the better of two people and—"

"*Mike.*"

Zelda quickly glanced to Link, who sat in the corner, making sure he still couldn't hear a word of what was being said.

Luckily it looked as though he was going to remain blissfully ignorant of the horrifying things coming out of Mike's mouth as he hunted monsters in his game.

Mike raised his hands. "Look, I don't like thinking about it anymore than you like talking about it, but if his head can't be in the game then maybe he shouldn't be..."

He seemed to struggle for the words he wanted.

"Shouldn't be around me?"

"Well, not if you're actually his mate. That's not an option."

Zelda was stunned. "So then what's the problem?"

"The problem is as simple as I laid it out. I want him focused on his goal. Eyes on the prize and all that. If he can't then, all right, let him hang around you and show you a few things. He's already saved your ass a couple of times from what I've heard."

Zelda cleared her throat and shoved her hand back into the chip bag. She didn't like thinking of the updates Victor and his partner Steve had been giving to her uncle while they were in the middle of keeping her safe.

"But if he's going to be distracted, then I am more than happy to pay to bring someone else in."

"No, Mike, you really don't need to do that."

"Yes, actually I do. I appreciate Victor not taking our money after he realized what was going on. His partner even took a pay cut, which helped, but honestly, no more. Someone is trying to hurt you because Harry doesn't know how to get his shit together, and Steve and Victor are out there right now chasing someone down with a gun. I'll damn well pay for some extra people to stick around you if I have to and I'll be glad to do it."

Zelda's chest tightened painfully. She opened her mouth to say something, but of course nothing would come out of her closed throat.

So much was happening that she barely had a clue about. First to learn that Steve had also taken a pay cut, and now to hear her uncle say he was ready to keep paying to bring more people here to protect her…

She knew her uncle loved her. He'd put up with a lot of shit after getting two kids dumped on him, kids who were constantly demanding their parents who were never coming back, and were never grateful for his help until they were much older…

What had she ever done for him to deserve that kind of regard? She didn't like this feeling of shame that hit her so hard. Zelda hugged her legs tighter around herself.

She didn't know what to say. It was as if she was that shy introvert who married Harry all over again.

The person she'd never wanted to be again.

"Aw, sweetie, come here. Don't cry."

Mike pulled her to him. Zelda went, eagerly allowing herself to fall into his arms and letting him hold her like he used to.

She didn't always allow him to hug and comfort her like this, but when it became clear that mommy and daddy weren't coming home, she was the first to start accepting Mike's love. She felt just as small and powerless now as she did back then.

"Zel? You all right?"

Great. Link had taken off his headphones and was now standing over her, watching as she lost her composure and proved she couldn't handle serious issues by crying in the arms of the only father figure she'd had ever since she was little.

Mike waved Link away, which was good. Zelda wasn't in the mood to answer questions or to look at while she held tightly to Mike.

Mike and Link already thought she was a weak little girl in need of saving, and maybe this proved they were right.

The doorbell rang.

Zelda pulled her face away from Mike's chest, looking up at the ceiling. As though she would suddenly develop the power to see through it and the door upstairs.

"Uh, should I get that?"

Mike's phone vibrated. He reached for it, checked it.

"Yeah, that's Victor and Steve upstairs."

Mike started to rise. "Come on, up you get."

Now she really did feel like a kid, but at least with Victor back home and safe, there was one less thing for her to worry about.

She'd composed herself by the time she made it up the stairs. Mike rubbed her back as Link went to the door, opening it.

Zelda didn't get the chance to ask either of them to not tell Victor she'd been crying, because the instant Link opened the door, Victor damn near fell through it.

"Fuck!" he cursed.

"Victor!"

Zelda forgot about her embarrassment as she ran to him, smelling the blood, *seeing* it on his skin.

But it wasn't coming from him. Apparently, he'd only stumbled because of the weight he struggled to hold onto.

Steve's eyes were shut, and the blood, dark and heavy, seemed to be coming from the deep bite marks up and down his arms, as well as the slashes that had been made of his clothes.

"Call 911, right now. Lock the door. Hurry."

Link cursed, though he quickly did as he was told.

"What happened?" Mike immediately went into command mode. Sometimes Zelda thought he would have made a great alpha if he'd been born to it.

"Link, go get the First Aid kit."

Link nodded, his eyes a little on the wide side as he rushed off to do as he was told.

"What happened?" Even Zelda knew that you weren't supposed to move someone who was injured. If she knew that, then a guy like Victor who had all kinds of training and experience behind him should know it, too.

Which meant Victor had only brought Steve here with him as an absolute last resort.

"Who was it?" Mike asked when Victor didn't answer. "Who did this? Was it the wolves?"

Zelda didn't understand the hesitation, but Victor nodded. "Yeah. It was the wolves. We were ambushed on the side of the damn road."

CHAPTER 18

An ambulance came.

Because their pack wasn't exactly located in the middle of a bustling city or town, it took a little longer.

About twenty-four minutes.

Zelda knew because she was watching the clock.

When Maxwell had been poisoned, grasping as his throat and foam appearing at his mouth, it had also taken a while for paramedics to make it to him, and by the time they got there, it was long too late.

Zelda hadn't been keeping track of the minutes then, but she kept track now.

With her new understanding of how far away her pack and family lived from civilization, she had to wonder why packs chose to isolate themselves like this.

It seemed like a bad idea in the long run.

Luckily, unlike Maxwell, Steve stayed alive until the ambulance came. The police arrived with them.

Victor had dressed Steve's wounds quickly on the kitchen table. Zelda brought in clean water bowls for him to wipe away the blood, taking away the bloodied bowls when there was no point in using the water anymore.

It was the only thing she could do.

And seeing the long stretches of slashed flesh on Steve's chest made her feel sickeningly warm. Her ears were filled with an ongoing ringing sound and she couldn't stay for too long.

The smell of blood was making her sick.

Zelda didn't need to be sick when there was someone else who was in more need than her. The last thing Zelda wanted was for anyone to give her any kind of attention when a man was literally bleeding and injured in her house.

Had the situation not been so serious, she might have been proud of herself for holding it together.

Then Link had to remind her that everything was not yet right with the world.

"Thank fuck it's not a full moon tonight."

Zelda gasped. "I didn't even think of that."

She and Link stood just outside the kitchen. The paramedics were currently working on getting Steve onto a gurney. They flashed lights in his eyes and tried speaking with him, but Zelda didn't think they would have an answer.

She glanced into the kitchen just as the gurney lifted. Victor stayed beside Steve as they walked him out. Zelda and Link made sure to give them enough space to pass by.

And Zelda couldn't help but look at the back of Steve's head before he and the paramedics were out the door.

With the wounds he'd received, if Victor was right and they had been inflicted by the wolves from Maxwell's pack...

It wasn't exactly a guarantee that he would change into a wolf on the next full moon, but it was close enough that it might as well have been.

Victor had once told her that Steve was not a subhuman, but even if there was the tiniest drop of shifter blood in him, no matter how many generations back, it increased his chances even further of changing.

Hell, if the poor bastard didn't shift into a wolf on the next full moon, he would be beating the odds.

Mike sighed as he came to stand outside the kitchen. "Don't go in there for a while yet, kids. I don't know if the police are going to want to take pictures, or what their policy is."

"We're just going to leave the kitchen like that?" Link glanced back inside before quickly looking away, his eyes wide at the sight of all the blood on the floor.

Zelda didn't blame him.

"For now, yeah. I don't know how investigating works or what they'll need. Just don't touch anything for a while."

Link's expression became somber. "Yes, sir."

Zelda hadn't heard Link call their Uncle Mike sir in a long time.

Another reminder of just how serious all this had become.

The police came and asked their questions. They mostly spoke to Victor, who had seen all of the chaos happening.

Zelda may or may not have spied a little on them; she wasn't going to confirm or deny that it was what she was doing when she continually offered the officers refreshments. She recognized a couple of them from when she had been questioned after her first attack.

When she and Victor had met.

They declined her offer, which was good since all the sodas from the downstairs mini fridge were officially gone, and she was forbidden from going into the blood bath that was the kitchen.

So, instead, she stood just outside of the sitting room, arms crossed, listening in on whatever could be useful. She kept out of sight, but was well within hearing range with her fox ears as pointed as they were.

"There were four of them. Steve was already out of his car when I got there. At least two were on top of him."

"Which was when you fired your shot?"

Zelda could hear the tension in Victor's voice. "Right. I had my weapon on me at that time. I fired my gun into the air and the wolves backed off."

"Why did you come back here?"

"I was worried that waiting for police and an ambulance to come up here would take too long and we'd get attacked again. Steve was only partially conscious at that point."

"Why not call for help while in your car with the doors locked?"

"I should have done that; instead, I drove back here. I don't know where Steve's phone is, it might still be inside his car. Mine was beneath his bloody body on the passenger seat and I just moved."

It sounded very much as though Victor was annoyed with himself, as though he didn't like admitting to something like that.

Something like a weakness.

It never occurred to her that he could get frazzled, that he could lose himself to panic and move without thinking. It really might have been better if he'd dialed 911 while on the road, even if he still came back here. It might have saved another three or four minutes, allowing the paramedics to get here faster.

It didn't matter. Steve was alive and that was the only thing Zelda would focus on.

The police asked a few more questions. They took Victor's card, asked about his permit to carry a weapon, then took his phone number and other general information.

Zelda barely got away from the sitting room as the police came to a stand.

She ran on her toes to her room, hoping no one saw her as she went, which she doubted.

When the police knocked at her door, it was only to confirm that everything Victor said had been true.

They asked similar questions to Mike and Link, took so many pictures of the kitchen, and then gave the bad news.

"For now, until we can get everything we need out of this place, it might be for the best if you stayed somewhere else."

Zelda pressed her lips together. She glanced to the side at Mike. He didn't appear to have a reaction right away.

"You want us to stay in one of the other houses?"

The officer nodded. "This is a pack, right? Someone will take you in."

This guy was definitely a human. While most packs did have that sense of camaraderie, no one was obligated to bring anyone else into the home they'd paid for. Everyone still had their own private property and an expectation of personal space.

Mike didn't correct the officer, and the man continued. "Detectives and forensics are on their way. I don't know how much they'll want from here since it appears he wasn't attacked in this house, but they're going to scope out the road where the incident took place. Just make arrangements for the night in case you need to, which is, honestly, most likely. Most people wouldn't want to be around a mess like that anyway."

Mike nodded. Right.

A few other members of the pack stood in their front doors, drawn to the lights of the police cars and ambulance. The ambulance was long gone with its patient. The lights of one of the police cars flicked on, its siren *woop wooping* to life and then dying just as quickly as it drove away, leaving only one other car there.

There were still questions to be asked. Men in blue were still asking around, trying to find out who heard what, who could help solve what happened.

No one seemed to know if it was even Steve who had shot first. That was a scary thing even Zelda hadn't thought of. There were lots she didn't know about when it came to the law and police work.

Mike growled low in his throat as everyone suddenly turned their eyes to him, to his house when the ambulance was out of sight.

The officer speaking to them seemed to pick up on the tense air around him.

"Will you be having trouble finding other arrangements?"

CHAPTER 19

Zelda wasn't sure if anyone in the pack would be giving her or her family a place to stay for the night. Not because they were angry with her for leaving Harry behind, but there were many people here who had families of their own to watch out for.

The fact that Steve had chased off some people, and that they weren't even sure who shot first yet...

It wouldn't endear her or her uncle and brother to the people around here as possible house guests.

The officer didn't seem to pick up on that. No one told him either.

"We'll get our stuff packed up," Mike said. "Link, Zelda, the both of you get a bag packed, right now. No dawdling."

Zelda didn't think she'd ever heard her uncle use the word *dawdle* before. It seemed like such an old man word. He wasn't even in his forties yet.

So, of course, she dawdled. She needed to hear what the plans were as Mike spoke with the officer.

"How long do you think we should be out for?"

The man looked as though he was trying his best to be understanding and accommodating, but that was difficult considering most humans didn't get the nature of pack life.

"Hard to say for sure with these kinds of things. At the very least, make sure you have enough for two days and nights. Toiletries, that kind of thing. When you know where you're going, give my number a call. You'll probably be asked some more questions tonight before you can go to bed. Just keep that in mind."

Mike nodded, took note of how Zelda was still dawdling, and shooed her away. "Hurry up, get your shit packed up."

"I will."

Though Zelda was more interested in what was happening, which led to her walking away as slowly as possible.

What was Mike thinking? Saying they were going to have a place to stay for the night? She doubted it, unless he was planning on getting a hotel room.

Fuck her sideways. He probably was.

Link would demand to help pay for it. If he did that then Zelda would do the same. She wasn't going to let him shoulder that burden on his own.

Mike looked at her, his eyes glaring and wide before he waved her off again. "What are you, a little spy? Get out of here; go get your bag packed up. We have to go."

Zelda clenched her jaw. There was no point in going over this a million other ways. Mike was clearly not going to let her get away with standing around like this.

So she went, quickly. She didn't want to miss anything, any details that might be useful.

Not that she knew what to do with any of them, but all of this was happening because of her. That just seemed unacceptable to her. If there was anything she could do, she needed to do it.

Which meant only one thing, as far as she was concerned.

Zelda didn't expect Victor to follow her. She didn't even notice him until he was in her doorway. He still had some of Steve's blood on his clothes, though he'd been allowed to wash his hands.

Zelda looked at him. She didn't know what to say. What could she say? Everything was so utterly fucked that she didn't think a word existed to describe this.

And Victor looked as though he'd aged ten years in the span of a couple of hours. His cheeks were pale against his dark hair and beard stubble, which seemed more haggard in that moment.

A teensy, tiny part of her brain thought that maybe it would be the best if she gave him some space.

It was the tired expression in his eyes that did her in, the pain and barely-there ability to hang on that pushed her forward.

His hands settled on her hips, keeping her from entirely pressing against him as she kissed him, but he didn't push her away. Victor kissed her back as though he needed all of this and more.

His lips never felt rougher, but it was the fact that he wasn't pushing her away, that he was drinking her in that let Zelda know she was doing the right thing.

"I'm sorry," Zelda gasped, her lips barely parting from his. "I'm so sorry."

Victor shook his head, but he still said nothing. It was all in his eyes.

"I wasn't there."

"Yes, you were."

"No, I wasn't. I wasn't fucking there for him."

"You saved his life. If you want anyone to blame...blame me. I was the one distracting you, remember?"

He looked at her, his tormented gaze suddenly clear. "No." Victor shook his head again. "Don't you fucking think about putting that on you."

"But I—"

"No."

Victor's pained expression turned hard, and she could see he was determined to not let Zelda put this on herself.

Even though she had been the one to distract him from what they were supposed to be doing, which was her self-defense training.

She was the one who'd wanted sex. Hell, he had his phone on him, maybe Steve had been texting him and he hadn't noticed because Zelda was busy grabbing at Victor's hair and begging for more?

She was willing to take the blame, but too much of a coward to ask if he had received prior messages from Steve.

"What will happen?"

Victor sighed. "I'm going to be questioned. They'll want my clothes, which is why I'm keeping my distance."

"What will they want your clothes for? I mean, isn't it all...?"

Victor shook his head. "If any of the blood on here belongs to anyone other than Steve then it might help us figure out what the hell is going on."

"You sure there were four wolves?"

"Positive."

Zelda thought about that. "Is it possible they had nothing to do with...well, me?"

Everything kept coming back around to her. She hated that. There were other people involved as well, other people who were getting hurt. She hated bringing herself up so much.

"Anything is possible. Since they were wolves, detectives are going to go back to the wolf pack and ask more questions. Whether or not anyone will answer them is something else. It could have been just a bunch of punks trying to stir up some shit and things went wrong, or it could have something to do with your ex."

"Who is still in jail, right?"

Victor nodded. He rubbed her arms. "I know it's a stupid thing to say at this point, but try not to worry about it too much. See if you can't get your stuff packed up. If your uncle can't find anywhere for you to stay in the pack then I'll buy a hotel room for the lot of you."

"No." Now it was Zelda's turn to shake her head and lay down the law. "No, that is not your burden to bear."

Victor's hand on her cheeks threw her off. "Yes, it is."

Zelda's stomach tightened. The words she wanted to say were snatched right out of her mouth by the sincerity in his voice.

As though he'd made peace with the fact that this was something he was going to do.

She couldn't let him. Much as the idea of being saved by a tall, dark, and handsome alpha male was a turn-on, she wasn't going to throw away everything he'd tried to teach her.

"You told me that I can't let other people take care of me."

The corner of his mouth quirked. "Pretty sure I didn't say that to you."

"Well, whatever, the point was the same. If we have to get a hotel room, Link and I will help Mike pay for it."

Victor looked at her in a way that seemed shockingly a lot like a glare.

That glare vanished, his eyes popping wide open when she finished her sentence.

"I won't be staying with them."

CHAPTER 20

"You want to say that again?"

Zelda let her hands slide away from Victor's shoulders, which had suddenly become tense beneath her fingers as she let him know her evil scheme.

Zelda was already practically living out of the travel bag she'd come here with, so it was just a matter of grabbing it and putting her makeup and underwear back inside.

Victor's voice was dangerous behind her. He was suddenly up close enough that she felt the warmth of his breath and body against her back.

"What do you mean, Zelda?"

Yeah, he definitely wasn't the sort of guy that liked being ignored.

Because of what he'd just gone through, Zelda had mercy on him.

"When Mike and Link go and get their hotel room, I won't be going with them."

He didn't move from behind her, his voice sounding very much as though he was barely holding back from strangling her. "All right. Want to explain to me exactly *why?*"

Zelda zipped up her bag. "Because I'm not going to let what happened to Steve happen to Mike or Link."

"They're adults. They can be the ones who decide on that risk."

"Well, I'm an adult too." Zelda pulled her bag over her shoulder. She faced her mate. "And I'm deciding they're not going to take that risk."

Even though she had to look up at him and he narrowed his eyes down at her, in that moment, she felt powerful. In control. She preferred that to the feeling of helplessness. Maybe that was why she kept giving the whole confidence thing a try.

Had Victor not had the blood of his friend on him, she might have teased him about the way the little vein at the side of his neck pulsed.

"Am I going to be able to talk you out of this?"

Zelda shook her head. "No."

"If I get your uncle in here, will he be able to talk you out of this?"

"No."

She was determined. Zelda squared her shoulders just to make sure Victor could see how serious she was.

He rolled his eyes, sighing. "I shouldn't have given you that pep talk."

She grinned at him. "Yeah, well, too late for that." Zelda glanced at his clothes again, her heart aching at the sight. "Go and get changed."

Victor lifted a brow. "What? You're not going to fight me if I want to come along?"

"Of course not." She was insulted he would believe such a thing. "You're my mate and my bodyguard. My two for one package deal. I'm not leaving you behind for anything."

Victor grinned at that.

"Plus, you're the one with the car."

He barked a laugh.

As it turned out, Victor didn't have a car. At least, not anymore.

Because it had been his vehicle he'd used to drive Steve back to the pack, back to safety. The police wanted to check out the vehicle.

According to victor, there wasn't a lot of blood in his car, but there was enough that he didn't want her sitting in the passenger seat where there was likely enough blood to stain her clothes.

Shit. There went that plan. It meant that not only did she have to explain to Mike that she wouldn't be sticking around, but she also had to ask him if he could give them a lift to the nearest car rental.

Of course Mike wasn't happy with her decision, and he absolutely refused to take any of her money to help with paying for a hotel room.

She'd never seen anyone's nose wrinkle so much at the sight of cash before. It wasn't even that much, but she might as well have tried to hand over a clump of used kitty litter with the way he looked at it.

Link sure as hell had a lot to say about it, too, but shockingly, it was when he realized Zelda was taking Victor with her that he seemed to calm down.

The two men looked at each other, and maybe it was a guy thing, but something unspoken seemed to pass between them.

They even nodded at each other, as though they were having some sort of telepathic conversation.

Great. Her brother and her mate were communicating with their minds about her.

Which made it all the weirder when Link handed over the keys to his truck.

"It's a piece of shit, so you don't have to worry about keeping it pristine or anything. Just don't drive it into a ditch."

"Are you sure about this?" Victor asked, clearly not understanding Link wasn't being sarcastic with the *ditch* comment.

There was a reason why Link and Mike usually shared a ride to work.

Link's truck was probably illegal when on the road.

She wasn't going to tell him that, however. No damned way. He was a little too Captain America when it came down to certain things, and she didn't want him to not drive it.

"Just drop it off in the parking lot somewhere and text me to let me know where it is. I'll pick it up later."

Mike shook his head, his arms crossed as he growled and paced around the sitting room. He glared at Victor and at Link, as though they were both conspiring to keep Zelda away from him.

Zelda had to give her uncle a hug before she left. She didn't like leaving him like this, but what choice did she have?

"You don't have to do this," he said, holding her tight.

Zelda relished the warmth of his arms, letting herself feel protected in them for just a little while longer. "I'll be fine." She pulled back to look into Mike's pained face. "Victor's with me."

"There's safety in numbers. All of us together would be better."

Since he wouldn't listen if she appealed to his safety, Zelda appealed to Link's while he and Victor got the truck out of the garage.

"If something happens to Link like what happened to Victor's partner, I won't be able to handle it. I have to do this."

It was manipulative and probably a little shitty to say something like that to her uncle. She was basically asking him to choose between her safety and Link's.

And that was a choice he was incapable of making because he really was the best uncle in the world.

His mouth thinned, completely unhappy with what she'd said, of course, so Zelda held him again and went outside to meet with Victor.

She couldn't hop into the truck fast enough, barely stopping to give Link one last hug goodbye.

For the most part, she'd wanted to get out of there before either her uncle or her brother could convince her what a stupid thing it was she was doing, but at the same time, she couldn't just allow herself to stay.

And she needed to go before Victor realized what a shit box they were riding in.

Still, as Victor put the old truck into drive and they slowly made their way out of the pack, Zelda's heart felt suddenly heavy.

Stupid. So stupid. It wasn't as though she was never going to see them again. Of course she was. This thing was going to end at some point, and Victor was here to watch her back. She was only leaving to make sure they wouldn't get hurt because someone wanted to go after her.

"How are you feeling?" Victor asked after two minutes of heavy silence.

Apparently, even he couldn't stand it.

Zelda cleared her throat. "Fine."

Victor didn't press it. Zelda was glad.

He'd had a change of clothes by the time she got out of there, carefully putting his bloody ones into a clean garbage bag and handing it over to the detectives who had come up before they'd gotten into Link's truck, which meant that he didn't smell too much like blood anymore.

The only thing she could make out was the smell of oil from all the work Link had been doing in and on the truck to keep it functional.

Because of the time of night, and the fact that there was only one road leading into the pack, it was easy enough driving by the scene where Steve had been attacked. An officer wearing reflective road gear just had to wave them through.

It wasn't a car wreck, but Zelda still found herself glancing to the side of the road, waiting to see something.

Through the darkness and flashing lights, she thought she could make out a dark splotch on the road.

Zelda pressed her lips together and looked away from it.

She shouldn't have tried to see that.

She made a quick glance in Victor's direction to see if he'd noticed what she'd done.

If he had, he didn't mention it.

Again, letting her off the hook.

A few minutes later, he spoke up. "I think I get now why your brother told me not to drive off the side of the road in this."

Zelda barely bit back a smile. "How are you handling it?"

"Barely," he admitted. "It keeps trying to pull me to the right. We're getting a rental the first chance we get and then we're getting a room somewhere."

Zelda nodded.

"I'll find somewhere close to the hospital. I know it's not ideal, but I want to be close to Steve."

"No, that makes sense."

She just hoped Link and Mike didn't put it together that a hotel room close to the hospital would likely be where they were heading.

There weren't many motels or hotels in Lakeview, so the selection was fairly limited.

Unfortunately, at this time of night, even with how close to the city Lakeview was, there were no car rental services open.

They had to wait until the morning before that would be an option.

The closest hotel to the hospital was a Best Western. It was small enough that there were only two floors. Victor picked them out a room on the second floor. It was a room on the corner of the hotel itself, closest to the fire escape.

He seemed to have a plan for absolutely everything.

The only problem was that, in order to get that corner room that was nicely positioned next to the fire escape, the room had to be with one bed.

Zelda looked at it, her tail swaying as she desperately tried not to let this get to her head as Victor surveyed their room, as though he expected someone to be hiding in their bathroom.

"Yeah, yeah, smirk all you want," Victor said, peeling off his jacket and shirt. He tossed them into the chair in the corner, ignoring the look on her face as he flopped down onto the mattress, face up.

This was certainly new. Zelda went to his side of the bed, standing over him. Her shadow was cast from the lamp behind her, directly over his face. He opened his eyes when he realized she was there, and yet she still couldn't stop smiling.

"I guess this means you're not going to get a cot ordered for in here?"

He somehow managed to look tired, bored, and affronted at the same time. "Knowing you, if I brought the thing in here you'd just burn it, so I didn't think I should bother."

"I won't confirm or deny that would have been a possibility."

He shut his eyes again, breathed deeply through his nose, and then let it out.

His chest rose nicely when he took in a breath like that. The fact that he was lying in bed, shirtless but still wearing a pair of jeans...

He could model for a magazine if he wanted to. He didn't just have the body for it, but he also had the face, and he was by far the most handsome man she'd ever met.

Zelda couldn't believe her luck. From going from a guy like Harry to a natural mate like Victor, who was not only handsome, but healthy, honorable, and brave, made her feel as though she'd won the lottery. It seemed almost ridiculous that she could have that kind of luck.

Zelda climbed into bed. Though she was sorely tempted to straddle Victor's waist, she decided a good spooning was in order instead.

He didn't push her away, though there was something a little colder about him.

"I mean it this time."

Zelda looked up at him.

His eyes were still closed, he still faced the ceiling, but his voice was entirely aware. He wasn't at risk of drifting off to sleep.

"No more sex."

Zelda's heart twisted. "No sex?"

"No sex." Victor nodded. He opened his eyes, turning his gaze down at her.

There was none of that stick up the ass seriousness about him. His words were not cruel and his tone not insensitive. He was simply stating the way things had to be.

"What happened to Steve was my fault. I made a rule, and I kept breaking it."

"We only had sex the once."

"And I'd let myself kiss you multiple times before then, too. I can't do that anymore, and this time I'm serious." He looked back at the ceiling, his brow furrowing as he lifted his hand, dragging his fingers through his hair. "Christ, this isn't to punish you or me. This has nothing to do with Angie, and you are everything I want in a woman, but I can't do this anymore where I pretend everything will be okay if I let my guard down for five minutes. That's not my job. I know better."

Zelda swallowed. "Was Steve trying to contact you before the shots fired?"

Before he'd told her not to worry about that, this time he answered her honestly.

"Yes, but that's still on me, not on you."

"I was the one who took you away from him. I distracted you."

"You're a shifter and your mate is nearby. It's natural for you to need this, to need the intimacy."

"You need it, too."

"I'm not a shifter. I should be able to control myself." He looked at her again, the corner of his mouth pulling in a wry smile. "No matter how beautiful the object of my affections are."

Heat climbed into Zelda's cheeks and stayed there. She pressed herself closer to his body heat. "That's probably the most romantic thing you've ever said to me. It might be the most romantic thing I've ever heard."

Something flashed in Victor's eyes. He brought his hand up, brushing a lock of hair away from Zelda's eyes. "I'm glad I could give you that then, because from now on, there's not much else I can do for you that would be like a proper mate."

"Because no sex?"

He nodded. "Because no sex."

Zelda thought about it, really tried to put herself in the position Victor was in, and the one he wanted her to be in as well.

The no sex thing...she wasn't going to be so selfish that she over-looked the fact that he would be suffering a well. Talk all he wanted about how he wasn't a shifter, subhumans, and even humans, could still feel the effects of being close to a mate. Especially a new mate.

Not that Zelda had much experience with this since she and Harry didn't have a natural mating, no, they'd just gotten married, but she knew the stories.

People who found themselves mated to each other were usually overcome with lust and hormones and desires they had trouble controlling.

Victor had said he didn't want to get too close to her, that he didn't want to distract himself around her, and she believed him. She already had a sense of his work ethic.

So the fact that he'd broken his own rules, allowed himself to kiss her, to touch her, to make love with her, could only mean that the mating had gotten to him.

He might even break that promise again.

Zelda understood now. The way he'd told her he wasn't having sex anymore. It wasn't that he was telling her. He was asking her to work with him on that, to not try so hard to tempt him anymore.

Because that's exactly what she'd been doing.

All those times she'd pressed herself against him, when she'd wanted to take that little pole dancing lesson, and when she'd encouraged him to kiss her in the kitchen and pulled him to her when he was trying to show her techniques that could save her life…

Maybe if she hadn't done that, he could have held himself back.

Not that he was entirely without fault. He was a grown man with his own agency, but this time, if they worked together in this…

Zelda groaned.

This was going to majorly suck.

Victor chuckled. "It won't be so bad. Imagine it like we're gym buddies. We have to encourage each other."

"Right." Zelda wouldn't have used the term gym buddies, but she supposed whatever worked was fine. "What about what we're doing right now?"

She wasn't about to give up her snuggles.

If she couldn't get laid by her own mate, then at the very least she was going to make sure she had a warm body to cuddle with.

Victor inhaled another deep breath. He seemed to think about it.

"I can handle this if you can."

Zelda sighed. "Thank God."

"But I mean it, this is only to ease the ache of the mating. No touching."

Zelda grinned. "We are touching."

Victor squeezed her. "You know what I mean. No tempting me with your foxy feminine wiles."

Zelda snorted. "*What?*"

Victor smiled innocently up at the ceiling, as though he wasn't aware he'd just said something completely ridiculous.

She pinched his ribs, and was massively pleased when he jumped away from her searching fingers.

"Oh my God, are you actually ticklish."

"No, that was a reflex."

The way he was fighting not to smile told her otherwise, and the devious little fox that Victor was so worried about immediately rushed to the surface to get some sweet, sweet revenge.

She attacked.

Victor was a lot more ticklish than she would have thought. He positively thrashed. She couldn't hold him down because of his strength, and because she got to play the girl card, he didn't shove her off of him.

Which meant that if he wanted to get away from her searching fingers, he was forced to squirm his way to the side of the bed, where he fell off and onto the floor.

And it was so unbelievably funny that, despite everything, Zelda burst out laughing.

Victor growled something she didn't hear, and then it was too late for her when he grabbed her by the ankle and yanked her towards him. He straddled her, grabbed her by the arm and yanked it up so he had full access to her armpit.

Zelda shrieked and thrashed beneath him, desperately trying to buck off his weight as he made her laugh out loud.

She was able to put up a fight. He definitely had to struggle to hold her down, but she was still his prisoner as she was tickle tortured.

Victor's hands flew away from her body at the sound of someone banging on the door.

Zelda held still on the bed, her eyes wide as she came out of that haze she'd fallen into really damned fast.

She sat up. Victor went to where he'd left his jacket and holster, pulling his weapon out. He motioned for Zelda to stay where she was, which was a given, considering she was frozen on the bed

Maybe it was someone coming to check on why there was a screaming woman in the room.

The door banged again. Victor toed his way to the door, but he didn't answer as he stood off to the side, as though someone might kick the door in at any moment.

When Victor gestured to her again, Zelda realized he wanted her to get behind the bed.

Where there was some actual cover.

She quickly did as she was told, hiding behind the mattress, watching the door.

They'd just gotten here, so it couldn't be housekeeping, and any employee would identify themselves, right?

Victor quickly checked the peep hole when he was satisfied Zelda was out of the way. The frown on his face was confusing before the person on the other side called out to them.

"Zelda, it's me. I know you're in there. Let me in, please. I'm not going to hurt you."

That was Ben's voice. Ben. One of Harry's best friends, and the man who, if not had something to do with Maxwell's death, had known about it before anyone else.

Victor pressed a finger to his lips, as if he needed to tell Zelda to be quiet. She nodded anyway, ducking down and staying there as Victor opened the door, being careful to stay behind it so Ben would only see an open entryway.

Maybe it was the desperation of the moment, but Ben didn't seem to think twice about who or what had opened the door for him. He just spotted Zelda hiding behind the bed and stepped forward, a heavy puff escaping him.

"God, am I glad to see you."

Victor didn't let Ben get close enough to reach her with a ten foot pole. He stepped out from behind the door, grabbed Ben by the back of the neck, and did some kind of maneuver where he hooked his leg around Ben's feet as he pushed him down.

"Get on the ground. Stay down! Don't move!"

Zelda shivered, watching the show of skill and strength as Victor pressed his knee to the middle of Ben's shoulder blades, yanking his arms back.

Despite being a beta wolf, Ben couldn't seem to move. He couldn't seem to fight off the man on top of him.

"I'm not moving! Okay? I'm not doing anything!"

"Jesus Christ, Ben, what the hell are you doing here?"

"Doesn't matter, call the police," Victor ordered.

Zelda moved for the phone.

"No! No, wait. Come on. I'm here to help you."

Zelda lifted the receiver, but she hesitated at those words. "What are you talking about?"

Victor shook his head. "Whatever you want to explain, you can explain it to the detectives working the case."

"Gerard is still out there!"

It was the slight change in Victor's eyes that had Zelda hesitating.

She and Victor looked at each other before Victor turned his attention back to the beta on the floor.

"Is Gerard the one who's sending people after Zelda?"

Ben nodded, grimacing as Victor pulled ever so slightly more on his arms. "He is. He's pissed. He's trying to blame it all on Harry because he wants to take over the pack."

She didn't understand. "Wait, but it was Harry who poisoned Maxwell."

"And who do you think gave him the idea?"

Ben tried to look back at Victor, but Victor didn't make it easy for him.

"I don't know who you are and I don't care, man. I just want out of this whole thing. I'll do whatever you want me to do to help, but I am not dealing with the humans."

Victor pressed his lips together. He looked at Zelda, as though trying to decide what needed to be done.

"Do you know where Gerard is?"

Ben shook his head. "No, but I wanted to let you know what was happening."

"Why?" Zelda asked.

Ben looked her in the eyes. "Because I don't want you to get hurt."

The sincerity in his voice got her right in the gut. She hadn't expected that out of him, but that didn't mean she should trust him, right?

And because he was her soul mate, Victor seemed to be on the same page.

"We believe you, but you're still going to tell us what you know with the cops around."

Ben shook his head. "That won't help anything. I'm not the one you want."

"Yeah, well, until we find your friend, you'll do well enough. I'm not taking any risks on you."

Zelda's heart warmed.

He really was her soul mate.

Victor was her soul mate and protector, and when this entire thing finished, she could really be with him.

That was worth putting Ben's ass in jail for sure.

The police arrived in record time. Victor really did have some connections. Zelda was impressed. Men and women in blue were in her room and guiding Ben out in handcuffs faster than she expected them to be, she stood in the corner, watching the scene, her brain trying to make sense of everything. Especially as Ben glanced over his shoulder at her on his way out.

It seemed only a minute or two before when Victor had phoned the police.

Victor's warm hand on her shoulder yanked her out of her daze. "You all right?"

The heat of his body, of his hand, surged through her. God, it was only a touch.

"Yeah. I'm fine. I just can't believe he tracked us down."

"Me neither." The growl in Victor's throat sounded positively alpha. Zelda shivered, but it wasn't because she was scared.

Victor didn't seem to realize that as he removed his leather jacket, placing it around her shoulders. "Here. You must be cold."

She hadn't been, but now the smell of him was all around her, and his jacket felt nice, so she kept it.

"Are we going with them?"

"I will be, and I suppose I can't convince you to stay here and wait for me?"

Zelda shook her hear, batting her eyes, trying to make them look as big and innocent as she could muster. "You wouldn't leave me here *alone*, would you? All by myself?"

He shook his head, though there was a quirk in his lips. He totally knew what she was doing.

"I didn't think so." Victor glanced at his watch, sighed, and dropped his hand. "Let's go."

Zelda grinned, following Victor outside.

When the elevator doors opened, Zelda's ears twitched—the sounds of fighting. The sounds of screaming.

"He'll kill me!"

Victor held out his hand, pushing Zelda back into the elevator. "Stay here."

"What?"

Victor ran off. Was he crazy? He wasn't a shifter. He was a subhuman, but not a shifter. What did he think he was going to do?

Zelda reached out, her hand stopping the elevator before it could close on her.

She wasn't going to run into anything. She knew that wouldn't be a smart idea, but she at least had to make sure everything was going to be all right. That Victor was going to be all right.

Zelda ran around the corner, ducking low when she was in sight of the front desk. She walked awkwardly like that until she was safely behind the marble and wood, watching as Ben, in his full blown monster wolf shape, up high on two legs, threw around the police like they were made of packing peanuts.

He'd broken the handcuffs the police had clasped around his wrists. They hadn't put the silver ones on him. They'd used the normal ones.

Fuck.

Alphas, and most betas, had a secondary shape they could shift into. They didn't just become like the animals they were connected to.

It was much deeper than that. Zelda could only shift into a fox, and only if she concentrated hard enough. A beta or alpha, of which there weren't many foxes, could not only change into the animal itself, but they would become something that was both human and animal.

Ben stood on his hind legs, his long, bushy tail swinging around behind him as he slashed his arms out, shoving the officers back.

Victor was right in the thick of it, grabbing one of the men in blue from under his arms and dragging him out of range of those claws.

Ben's face was that of the wolf. Fur covered his body in patches, but it was his face and head that looked mostly like the shape of his inner animal.

His nose scrunched, lips pulled back, revealing his long canines.

His hands were a mix between normal human fingers and wolf paws. His palms were black with the rough padding, but his fingers were still long, his nails jutting out, thicker, more dangerous than human nails. The fur on his back stood on end.

The sight of him was so terrifying that Zelda almost didn't hear the police as they pointed their weapons and yelled at Ben to get down on the ground.

He was going to run. She could see it in his wild eyes.

Zelda hadn't known Ben was capable of shifting into this other shape. He could, she could see it with her own eyes, yet he was that terrified that Gerard would come and do something to him?

Jesus. How powerful was he?

Ben's nostrils flared. He sharply glanced to the side, his gaze locking on her. Zelda's tail stiffened, her ears popping straight up, as though his stare locked her into place. It practically did. She couldn't move. She couldn't think.

Because Ben's eyes were bloodshot red.

Meaning he wasn't thinking clearly either.

Zelda could hear the sound of her own heartbeat in her throat. Something tickled the back of her neck as it warmly slid down her spine.

Ben growled low in his throat.

Victor shouted her name, scrambling.

Ben charged, but in the other direction. He burst through the glass doors of the hotel, shards shattering around him in thousands of tiny pieces, each one glistening like diamonds around him as his enlarged form vanished into the night with a howl.

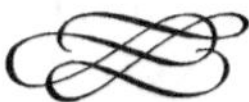

Zelda felt a cold shiver pass through her body as she slumped onto the floor, her back pressed against the front desk of the hotel.

She clutched at her heart. God, she couldn't stop shaking.

Ben had only looked at her, and yet it felt as though she was being stared down by…

"Zelda?"

Warm hands. Zelda blinked. Victor looked down at her. He shook her shoulders a little, desperate to grab her attention.

"I'm fine," she said, not entirely sure if she believed it or not. Not when those deadly red eyes were still burned into her vision. "I'm fine."

Victor deflated with a hard sigh, then his mouth tightened. "I told you to stay back."

Zelda nodded. "Yeah. I'm sorry." She wasn't in the mood to argue with him. What she'd done had been stupid, and she was too spooked by being in the crosshairs of a creature like that to want to defend her actions.

Victor opened his mouth, as though to start yelling at her some more, but he stopped. He looked at her, his dark blue eyes so much more calming and reassuring, even when he was angry.

Except he pulled Zelda to his chest, holding her tight. That wasn't the action of a man who was angry.

Zelda could hardly lift her arms to hug him back.

"Ben is an alpha."

"What?" Victor tensed a little. He pulled away from her, something Zelda hadn't wanted him to do because it meant he was taking his warmth away with him.

He looked at her hard. "What did you say?"

Zelda had to clear her throat. "Ben is an alpha. I…always thought he was a beta." No one had ever told her he was an alpha. He never really acted the part. No one treated him like one.

Most of the time, she could smell the difference. Zelda had never noticed a sharper musk on him whenever he'd been in the house visiting Harry.

Victor's hand was suddenly in her hair. He pulled her close, his mouth coming down onto her lips.

It was one of the few kisses he'd ever given her. It didn't last nearly as long as Zelda wanted it to. He pulled away before she had the chance to really take in the heat of him, or the comfort he was offering.

"Don't ever do that to me again."

The kiss, brief as it was, left her almost as dazed as being given the look of death from an alpha.

Zelda nodded dumbly.

"I have to check on them. Can you please not move from this spot?"

She nodded. She wasn't about to go anywhere.

Victor still hesitated before leaving her side. Zelda figured the only reason she was still somewhat all right with being separated from him was because she could at least see him. He was just a few feet away.

Her brother was right. Zelda didn't know how to take care of herself. She did need someone else to watch over her. It wasn't a good feeling, knowing she could never be as fully independent as she liked.

Watching Victor check on the officers, and then yank off his belt to tie around the leg of another who had been slashed by Ben's claws, made that terrible feeling in her gut go away. If she needed someone, if Zelda was the sort of person who couldn't be on her own, then at least she had Victor now. He wasn't Harry. He was a good man, a skilled man, and he wouldn't take advantage of her shortcomings.

Someone on staff in the hotel came to kneel down next to her, asked if she was all right, then if she was sure.

Zelda quickly pointed anyone who wanted to help her or offer her anything in the direction of the officers who needed it. At the very least, Zelda wouldn't take up time and resources that someone else needed.

An ambulance arrived shortly. Two of the officers were taken away. The one with the injured leg, and apparently another had hit their head pretty bad.

More police arrived. Detectives in plain clothes, people with cameras who took pictures and snagged bits of hair off the shards of glass by the entryway.

There was even a little blood.

Zelda hoped Ben was all right. Even an alpha could bleed out if he was cut too deep.

Somehow, she made her way to one of the small leather waiting chairs instead of the floor. Victor spoke with the detectives first, then they came to her.

Victor didn't sit next to her like she would have wanted, but he did stand next to her, close enough that Zelda was able to feel his body heat, and the protection he offered.

She almost smiled at that.

He was still doing the bodyguard thing, but there was a definite improvement on the way he was acting around her. When he'd first met her, he would have put ten feet between them when she was being spoken to by the police, not ten inches.

She could handle that.

The detective wasn't one of the men she recognized from the station. He was a little younger, probably recently promoted. He handed her his card, introduced himself as Detective Grey, pulled up one of the other chairs to sit across from her, as though getting closer to her level would make everything all right, then started with his questions.

Zelda didn't hear what he'd asked. The first thing out of her mouth was the obvious. "Ben is an alpha."

The detective looked at her, as though waiting for something else.

Zelda repeated herself. "He's an alpha."

"All right, I understand that, did you not know that?"

Zelda shook her head. "I never knew that."

"Did the rest of the wolf pack he was from know it?"

She opened her mouth to deny it, but then stopped. How could she be sure of that one way or the other? Had Harry known? If he had, he'd done a good job of hiding it.

"I don't know."

"Okay, you're going to have to explain to me a little about how the alpha, beta, omega thing works," said the detective. "Give me a refresher so I can make sure all my ducks are in line."

Zelda swallowed. Sometimes she forgot that not everyone knew how all of this worked.

"Most shifters are born omegas. We can change into our animal shapes,"

"You just struggle with it a little more?"

Zelda nodded. "But that's not the only thing, it's in our scent. We can't lead a pack. No one will follow us, and an omega male or female can't turn into a beta the way betas can turn into alphas."

"Why do betas turn into alphas?"

Zelda didn't understand the question. "How should I know?"

The detective gave her a look. Victor cleared his throat. "It's just part of the culture."

Zelda looked at him. He knew it wasn't just a cultural thing. But he softly shook his head at her, as though telling her not to argue the point.

"I see," said the detective, even though he clearly didn't. "So a beta can turn into an alpha, how does that happen?"

Zelda pressed her lips together. She thought of Maxwell, clutching at his throat, choking on his vomit as he struggled to breathe through whatever poison Harry had given him. "You have to defeat the previous alpha of your pack in a fight. Or kill him."

"And this is how your husband was trying to become an alpha?"

Zelda clenched her molars together, responding through her teeth. "Yes, and he's my *ex* husband."

"Right, sorry."

She was getting sick of having to point that out.

"And now you believe this particular shifter was already an alpha?"

Zelda nodded. "I saw it in his eyes. He's definitely an alpha."

"You saw it in his eyes?"

Humans tended to have trouble with this sort of thing about shifters.

If another human was to explain how they knew something deep in their gut, or how they felt something, it wasn't often taken seriously.

When a shifter said those same things, there was more ground to stand on.

"Yes. I could see it in his eyes that he was...*is* an alpha."

"Okay," said Detective Grey in a tone that suggested how little weight he was putting into her words. Still, he wrote them down in his little notepad. She supposed that was something.

Zelda looked up at Victor. "Where is the usual guy?"

The detective answered. "The usual guy?"

"Yeah, the usual guy. What was his name?" She looked up at Victor, but again, Grey answered before Victor could get a word out.

"I can put you in touch with anyone else in the station you like. They might be on their way here. I just happened to be close by when the call came. We're kind of far and out of the way of most things."

Made sense, though she was still irritated with this guy. Hell, he might be putting off his fishing vacation to talk to her.

She didn't care.

"Do you have anywhere to stay?"

"We're in a hotel." Zelda wasn't in the mood to be generous to the guy who had called Harry her *husband*.

Detective Grey at least pretended he hadn't caught the edge in her voice as he smiled and nodded. "Right. Of course. You're staying with her?"

"I am," Victor said, reaching into his pocket. He pulled out a card and gave it to him.

"I see, you're her security?"

"If you can get in touch with the primary detectives on the case, they'll fill you in on what's happening."

Zelda wasn't sure if Victor was speaking that way to the detective because he also wasn't pleased with him, or if he was just being himself in this case.

She suspected it was the latter. Victor was too professional to play games like that, but at the same time, she enjoyed pretending he was being testy with the guy for his screw ups, too.

Victor could be the responsible one and she could be the petty one. That worked out fairly well for her.

Grey nodded curtly. Right. He definitely wasn't happy with this. "I'll make sure they fill me in as soon as possible."

Zelda hoped they didn't fill this guy in on anything. She wanted them to take all the information he had and do what she'd seen countless times on TV. Lock him out of the case and take all the credit when it was nice and solved.

That seemed all right in her books.

Detective Grey closed his little notebook, shoving it in his side pocket before standing. "I'll keep in touch."

"Don't hurt Ben if you find him."

"Zelda," Victor said softy, the look in his eyes suggesting how bad of an idea that was.

"What? He was always...I mean, I don't think he's dangerous."

Victor sighed, as though he was disappointed. In her? Her choice of words? In what?

Detective Grey said nothing else. He nodded to Victor. "I'll keep in touch."

He walked off. Zelda blinked, feeling as though she'd just missed something important.

She looked up at Victor. "What was that?" She wasn't angry, just confused.

Victor sat down in the seat Detective Grey vacated, rubbing his face. "You're sure this guy is an alpha?"

"Yeah, why?"

Victor's hand held onto the back of his neck. "I was getting a similar feel from him."

"You were? I didn't know sub...I mean, I didn't know people like you could..."

"Don't worry about it. I know what you mean. It wasn't a strong feeling, and it's nothing like what you have as a full blown shifter, but it was just a feeling. You confirming it doesn't help much."

"Why not? Ben wasn't the one who killed Maxwell. Harry admitted to it."

"That's just the thing, he's still involved. According to your initial statements, they were in the kitchen together talking about what they did. He might be more innocent than guilty, but he'd still got a nasty part in this."

Zelda's gut clenched. "And now that you know he's an alpha?"

Victor shook his head. "I don't entirely know. It's not good to make assumptions and attribute motives to people. It can lead to all kinds of mistakes."

She waited, knowing it was coming. "But?"

He looked at her. "But, if he's an alpha, it could mean a couple of things. One, that he publicly fought and defeated an alpha, becoming one in the process, and never told anyone in your pack. Or it means he was born an alpha and wanted to help your ex take control of the pack for selfish reasons. He could have wanted Harry to poison Maxwell, getting a powerful alpha out of the way, replacing Harry with himself with a fight that everyone in your pack would have supported."

"Harry wouldn't have allowed that."

"If he'd known."

A major explosion just went off in Zelda's brain. She almost couldn't believe it.

"That's..." She shook her head.

"It's a lot," Victor admitted. "And none of it could be the case, but it's still something to think about. He still attacked the police. We were only going to talk with him. The fact that he ran doesn't look good for him."

"But, he was afraid of Gerard."

"Maybe. Maybe not. There's a whole slew of reasons why people do the things they do. I'm just saying that if Ben gets hurt resisting arrest again, don't be shocked. He's lucky he wasn't killed from that gunshot."

"What gunshot?"

Victor looked at her. "Didn't you see the blood?"

"Wasn't that from the glass?" She wracked her brain, trying to remember the sound of a gun popping off. A lot had been going on and her brain had been kind of scrambled.

"No, baby. Ben was shot on his way out."

CHAPTER 23

Zelda made the decision to not tell her brother and uncle about what happened. If Mike heard that Ben showed up and attacked the police who took him away, then he would have a heart attack. That was the last thing in the world she wanted for him.

If Link heard about what happened, he might just decide to come over and act as her unofficial second bodyguard. Like her, he was an omega. There was no way he would stand any chance against an alpha, so, yeah, more secrets to keep from her family.

Lovely.

The next morning, after Zelda had answered more questions, gave more statements, things looked a little clearer. A little more on the grey and bleak side, but they were clear.

The hotel staff in the morning was entirely different from the graveyard shift, the people who had been there when Ben shifted and attacked.

She imagined they were going to get some paid leave after what happened. The front doors looked...absolutely terrible. Someone actually taped cardboard over the broken doors. The glass was swept away, but now there was a sign there directing guests to use another door in the back, with their sincere apologies.

Victor and Zelda were eating breakfast in the restaurant. There weren't many people there. Fishing season hadn't entirely pulled into swing, but with her long ears, she could hear everyone chatting about what had happened last night. The things they'd seen and what they'd heard.

Of course, a lot of it was gossip that had no basis in anything. One person seemed to think a crazed bear had managed to break into the hotel. Another couple mentioned talk of a shifter, but their take was that it had been a robbery gone wrong.

Zelda had to bite her tongue to keep from correcting each and every one of them. She hated the fact that she had to wear a scarf over her head just to keep her ears pressed down.

News of a shifter attack meant it was probably for the best to not advertise that she was a shifter. Keeping her tail tucked away in the flowing skirt she'd packed was a little easier, but she wanted to wear it to show off her legs, not hide her tail.

Victor smirked a little at her as he forked his hash browns. He knew she didn't like any of this, but Zelda knew how cute he thought she was when she was irritated.

Sometimes Zelda wished he couldn't read her like an open book, though she supposed that, as her mate, this was something she was going to have to get used to.

"Do you really think it's possible that Ben had something to do with Maxwell? More than he already did, I mean."

"Anything's possible," Victor shrugged. "The point is to not rule anything out. The hard part is to not pin down any one single thing either. You end up chasing your tail doing that. Uh, no offense," he said.

Zelda smiled, glad to be the one to see him blush for once at using an offensive saying for shifters.

"None taken." She thought over his main point. "That sounds incredibly hard."

He nodded. "It is."

"But if he's really so scared of Gerard, then that has to mean otherwise, right? Ben is apparently an alpha and he doesn't want to get on Gerard's bad side."

"It could mean that. If Gerard was the one who is the real mastermind behind this whole thing then that could be a problem. Especially since we don't know where he is yet."

Zelda liked his inclusion of the word yet. If he was confident that they were getting somewhere, then she could be confident, too.

They went over a couple more scenarios while their coffee refills came in

Victor's phone buzzed on the table between them. He grabbed it without looking at the screen, putting it to his ear almost as if on autopilot.

"Kincaid."

His demeanor changed considerably. Zelda couldn't *not* notice it.

"Yeah?"

He leaned back in his seat, releasing a long sigh and rubbing his face with his hand. He looked suddenly a lot more somber. More tired.

"When did it happen? Thanks for letting me know. He's sedated? Right. Yes. Understood. Thank you."

When he hung up, Zelda already knew what it was about. She didn't need her sense of hearing for that. "Steve?"

She could still see the blood on her floor, the gashes on Steve's skin after his run-in with the wolves. She hoped none of them had looked like Ben did when he was being attacked.

"Yeah. He's stable now, but he had a change. I guess you already know that."

She shook her head. "No, it was all kind of muffled with this thing on my head." She pointed to the scarf."

He smiled ruefully.

"So, he changed?"

Victor nodded. "He's...a shifter now." Victor seemed to take that in. "Christ."

Zelda swallowed hard, feeling a sense of responsibility coming over her. "He can learn how to control it, how to work his new senses with us. I'm sure the pack will take him in."

"He'll be a wolf, not a fox."

Shit.

"That won't matter. Not too much."

She hoped.

Victor suddenly looked angry. His mouth tightened. His big arms somehow managed to look even bigger as he crossed them over his chest, shaking his head. "It won't matter. If he's going to be a shifter, then he will have all the scents to go with it. He might even be able to identify the fuckers who got him on the road."

Zelda latched onto that good piece of news and held it tightly to her chest. "Right? This will work out, and being a shifter isn't so bad. The best part is he's not a born shifter, so he won't have the goofy ears and tail to bother with. He'll blend in just fine."

Victor didn't take her up on her joke. "He could have died. He could have died on the road or during the change. He's lucky to be alive. When I find those punks who did this to him…" He pressed his lips together, as though he couldn't even speak the words he wanted.

Zelda wasn't going to be able to make him feel better with a joke. She could tell that right now. Too much was happening. Too much was going wrong.

"The point is that he made it. He's still alive."

Victor nodded, though it didn't look as though he'd heard much of what she'd said.

Zelda sighed. "I'll have to put together a gift basket for him now."

Victor blinked, coming out of his angry haze just a little. "A gift basket?"

She shrugged. "Right, for helping to watch over me."

"You're not going to suggest this is somehow your fault?"

"No, not really," though she did feel guilty for it. "I just figured that he should be introduced to his new life as a shifter with a bang. I can, I don't know, get him a subscription to one of those places that deliver all kinds of good steaks every week. I hear those go over well for people."

At least that time she got her laugh out of Victor. He apparently thought it was enough of a good idea that he helped her look up the names of some companies that would do it.

∽

THEY WEREN'T able to visit Steve until the next day. By then, though he was still massively covered in bandages and wasn't allowed to leave his bed, he seemed awake and clear-headed. Almost normal, healthy.

He was definitely happy when Victor walked into his room. Zelda felt good about that, about watching the two men hug each other like brothers. Victor even made a comment on Steve's strength.

Steve's new healing abilities were going to come in major handy for getting him out of here sooner than what would have been possible had he still been human.

"They said I'm going to be a wolf."

Zelda tried not to look too obvious in the room. Guilt still hit her hard for that, even though she knew she shouldn't bear that burden. She wasn't the one who had slashed up Steve's skin.

Of course, he wouldn't be here if it wasn't for her either.

"How you feeling about that?"

Steve shrugged. "Fine, I guess. It's…weird. I'm going to have to get a trainer. Someone to watch over me during my first full moons."

That was right. Zelda didn't even feel the pull of the moon. It was just any other night for her.

Newcomers tended to have two or three where they went…a little wild.

Not always in a bad way, and it was rarely like what the old movies liked to portray it as, but that didn't stop people from putting it into law that anyone new to the life of a shifter needed constant monitoring until they were fit to return to their public lives.

"Well, you know there's not going to be a problem coming back to work, right?"

Steve grinned. "Better damn not be. Someone's got to watch out for your dumbass once in a while."

Zelda snorted a little. She couldn't hold it back.

She'd never heard anyone call Victor a *dumbass* before. Not that she knew him long enough to be that close to him, but it was kind of funny, knowing he and his friends were that close with each other.

Victor gave her a look.

Steve swatted him on the leg. "There, you see? She knows what I'm talking about."

"She doesn't know anything."

Zelda couldn't help but chime in. "I don't know, I'd love to hear all about why your friend would call you a dumbass."

"I've got loads of embarrassing stories for you," Steve promised.

Zelda was only too eager to hear them.

"All right, that's enough of that. I just came here to give you your stupid flowers and make sure you're eating right, not so you could give my client any ideas."

Steve eyed Victor a little funny. "So it's back to client?"

Zelda had never really thought of it before, but now that she did, she figured it only made sense that Steve would know of her and Victor's tentative relationship with each other.

He and Victor weren't just business partners, they were also friends. Very good friends, from the looks of it. He would know Victor had stopped taking payments for watching over her. They would have discussed it, and even if Victor didn't outright tell Steve why, he would have figured it out.

Zelda and Victor looked at each other. She didn't know what he was planning on saying. Zelda didn't know what she should say either. When they'd had sex after her little self-defense class seemed far away, like a one off in the face of everything that was happening right now.

"It's complicated," Victor said.

Which was more than she expected him to say after all that.

It wasn't an *I love you*, but with how seriously he took his position as her protector, and the way she'd been slowly chipping at his defenses, it was pretty close.

He seemed to know it, too. If the little quirk in his lips was any indication.

Despite everything, Zelda couldn't help but feel warmed by the whole thing.

CHAPTER 24

*A*fter that, Zelda felt more confident going to and from the hotel with her ears and tail exposed. Not too many people turned their heads at her, and the ones who did look didn't stare for long.

Many people seemed to be forgetting about the excitement of the shifter who had fought off the police, and she wasn't the only guest with her ears and tail out anymore either.

She kept in touch with Mike and her brother, relieved every time to hear their voices, and everything was almost...normal.

She could almost be having a little staycation with her boyfriend.

Except that Victor didn't touch her in the night. That was the only problem Zelda was forced to deal with.

She went to bed, sometimes wearing only her bra and panties, splaying herself out, making sure all signs pointed to Open, but he never took the hint.

Usually, Zelda fell asleep to the sound of his fingers clacking on the keyboard of his laptop. He was in constant contact with the detectives in charge of her case, always looking over the building plans for the hotel, as though he needed to know where all the exits were blindfolded.

Zelda supposed she wouldn't love and respect him the way she did if he was anything less than diligent. She didn't like the idea that he was staying up until five in the morning going over all the notes and photographs he'd been given access to, but she had to admit, there was something about the way he worked that appealed to her.

She was into hard-working night owls. Basically, the very thing Harry had *not* been.

She dreamed about Harry some nights. She didn't like those dreams, especially on the nights when she couldn't tell she was dreaming.

Sometimes she saw herself back in his house. He was found innocent of Maxwell's murder and she was back to cooking his meals and cleaning up his house, praying he would forget that she was the one who put the attention of the police on him in the first place.

Other nights, she dreamed of the moment she realized Harry had killed Maxwell. She could almost smell the same scents in the house as she snuck closer to the top of the stairs, listening to Harry as he sounded somewhere between panicked and angry.

Ben had been telling him to calm down. Gerard hadn't said anything. His arms had been crossed stoically over his chest. He'd been silent. When Zelda had gotten a look at his face, she could see how tight his neck and jaw were clenched, as though incredibly unhappy with Harry's display.

Not very leader-like, she imagined. He'd probably been thinking about how great it would be when he finally got to knock off Harry as well and take his place as the proper alpha of the pack.

Then Gerard looked up at her.

Zelda froze.

It's just a dream. He can't really see you. He's not really looking at you.

No matter how hard she thought about it, it didn't take away from the terror of having those eyes locked on her while she heard her husband admit to killing Maxwell, to being freaked out by the show he'd made when he'd died, and what the fuck was he going to do with the pack now?

Zelda backed away, into the darkness of the house, heart hammering, waiting for her husband and his friends to come for her, to drag her downstairs and demand to know what she'd heard.

She called the police instead, then hid on the roof of her house until they came.

"Hey."

Zelda snapped her eyes open, her heart still slamming against her ribs, but her relief at the light in the room, at the sight of Victor standing above her, was immense.

Dream was over. She wasn't trapped in the dark, she wasn't waiting on the roof of the house she'd shared with Harry, and she was perfectly safe.

"You all right?"

Victor asked the question as though he would chase away the demons himself if he could.

Zelda rubbed her face, sitting up. "I'm fine."

"You sure?"

His hands were still on her shoulder. She liked that. She liked that he was touching her again, even if it was just like this.

She wanted more than that. She wanted more than just his hands.

"I had a…"

He knew there was only one thing it could have been, but saying it out loud, that she'd been having a bad dream, seemed so childish in the face of everything else.

Of course he knew, and Victor understood. She could see it in his eyes.

"Take your time. You don't have to rush anything for anyone. Don't try proving anything to yourself. It's all right to…feel out of your element in situations like this."

"Would you tell me that even if you weren't my bodyguard?"

His hand cupped the back of her head. "Of course I would."

The way he looked at her, how close he was to her…felt so utterly warm and intimate. Zelda felt an immediate response in her body.

Maybe Victor felt it, too, because right then, his hand fell away from her hair.

Zelda snatched his wrists before he could pull back. "Don't."

He shook his head, his voice heavy. "We really shouldn't."

"It's too late for that."

She knew it. He knew it. She hated having to fight for what she wanted. She hated having to struggle just to feel his mouth on hers, or his hands on her body. He was welcome to her mouth and body whenever he wanted, but he acted as though there was some barrier sitting between them.

Victor looked away from her, his mouth doing that quirking thing it did whenever he was trying to fight off a smile. Of course, he wasn't able to fight it for long. "God, you have no idea what you do to me."

She blinked. "Really?"

Victor looked at her, and in his eyes, she saw something almost animal, that hint of the other side of him that wasn't entirely human. "You know I shouldn't. I know I shouldn't, but every time I do, it chips away at my principles. I don't do this kind of thing with clients."

"Of course not. I'm special." She was happy enough to admit that. "I just wish you wouldn't fight it so much."

"You don't understand. I understand how a mating is supposed to work, but the fact that I can't control this…despite what it could do to you…" He huffed a heavy sigh, shaking his head. "A man can only turn down a beautiful woman so many times, though."

He kissed her. It was sudden, warm, and immediately intoxicating. Zelda's shock melted out of her quickly, replaced with heat and relief as she let her hands slide up his white button-down.

He apparently hadn't gone to bed again last night. Zelda wanted to tell him that if he really wanted to keep her safe, then he should have sex with her and start sleeping instead of avoiding her and staying up all night.

One was definitely healthier than the other.

Victor pushed her back down onto the bed. A soft, hungry growl rippled up his chest and out his throat. The sound excited her. She knew she had him. There was no need to tell him to get his sleep. When she was done with him, he was going to need a few hours as it was.

Victor's hands slid down her body, reaching the end of the T-shirt she'd stolen from him last night in a desperate hope that he would think the sight of her in his clothes was sexy.

When his rough fingers pushed the hem of the T-shirt up her stomach, Zelda became suddenly way more aware of the fact that she hadn't showered yesterday. She definitely needed to shave her legs and armpits, and brushing her teeth seemed like a solid plan.

"Wait,"

"I can't."

She couldn't either. His hands found her nipples, fingers pinching and tweaking them, making her spine arch from the sudden pleasure of it.

Still, she didn't want to go to bed gross.

"Uh, not that I don't like what you're doing, but...God, I think I need to at least brush my teeth."

He froze, yanking his body back, which was a shame because she'd been enjoying what he'd been doing.

"You're worried about that?"

"About morning breath when you're kissing me? Yeah. And my legs are prickly."

He smiled at her, that predatory look back in his eyes as his palm rested on her ankle and slid up her leg.

"No, don't do that."

"Why? It doesn't bother me."

That shocked her. "It always bothered Harry."

Mentioning *his* name when Victor was trying to seduce her was apparently not the best idea in the world.

Zelda grabbed his shoulders before he could pull away from her. "Not that I think you're Harry, or anything like him."

"You're making me hate that guy a lot more than I already do."

Zelda looked at him, searching for any hint of sarcasm, or pandering, or any small signs that he was just saying the things she wanted him to say to spare her feelings.

She wasn't getting any of that from him. It was kind of strange. "It really doesn't bother you that I'm gross right now?"

He looked at her like she was nuts. "You're not gross, Zelda. If you stunk, don't worry, I wouldn't be all over you like this. *This*, on the other hand..." He let his hand slide up and down her leg again. "Is nothing."

"It's pretty bad."

"You're hardly a hairy monkey. It's just the tiniest bit of stubble. I can maybe see it if I squint my eyes." He grabbed her hand, bringing her palm to his face. "Do you like mine?"

Boy, did she ever. Zelda swallowed hard. "It's sexy on a man."

"And I think it's sexy on you. I don't mind a little hair on my women. It's a good reminder that you are a woman."

"Oh?" She lifted a brow, feeling herself relax despite her complaints. "You need reminding of that often?"

"You'd be shocked at how many women insist on having every inch of themselves waxed from the nose down. It's kind of off-putting. I like knowing I'm in bed with a woman."

His hands spread her thighs apart. Zelda thought she should resist, maybe offer to do this with him in the shower so she could clean up and make love to him, but everything he was saying and doing was so perfect. She didn't want to move as he kissed his way down her belly, lifting the T-shirt up her thighs and exposing her to him.

And while she had kept herself decently groomed down there, she did have hair to speak of, and there hadn't been all the time in the world lately to trim the bushes, so to speak.

"I like you just like this."

Victor almost said it as a moan, and when his mouth touched down on her sex, Zelda thought she was going to implode.

Her hands immediately went into his hair, gripping him hard, holding on for dear life, and Victor showed her just how much he liked her as she was.

CHAPTER 25

Victor kissed her with more desire and heat than he had after their brief time after her self-defense lesson. Which was saying something considering he wasn't kissing her mouth.

All thoughts and self-doubts were thrown right out the window as Zelda became lost to her pleasure.

She could hardly think, gasping and panting for air as though there wasn't enough in their hotel room. He pushed his tongue deep; it was so utterly scandalous and shocking that he'd done it with such confidence that Zelda shouted out loud. She clasped her hand over her mouth, staring down at Victor with wide eyes, as though making sure he hadn't noticed the sound.

He kept right on with what he was doing, as though he hadn't heard, but that wasn't possible. He had to have heard it, but he was so focused on his work that he didn't so much as look at up her.

And he was flicking his tongue inside her. Oh God. It was so unfair how confident he was at this, how good.

Zelda wished she could give to him what he was giving to her with the same zest and energy, but she didn't think she would be able to come right out of the gate with that kind of skill.

"G-Gonna practice on you."

Victor apparently heard that. He looked up at her. "What was that?"

Zelda looked down at him, noticed how shiny his mouth looked with *her* fluids, and she thought she was going to die from both the pleasure and embarrassment of it.

"Don't stop!"

It came out sounding more like a whine, but at least Victor got back to work with that wicked grin on his face.

Zelda let her head fall back onto the messy sheets and pillows, running her fingers through Victor's hair, gently scratching at his scalp, then gripping hard whenever he thrust his tongue deep inside her.

He brought her close to orgasm time and again, only to pull back and prolong her torture.

Victor moaned against her sex, sending small vibrations through her that drove her wild again and again. She couldn't take it. She wasn't going to last.

Just when she thought she was done for, her legs and toes clenching in preparation of release, Victor pulled back from her with a sigh, his lips seeming as hot as a small fire as he kissed her thighs.

"It's always been you. God, it's always been you."

What was he talking about? They hadn't known each other for long, though she liked the romantic sentiment that came with words like that.

"Victor."

Victor didn't say anything else. He climbed up her body. Zelda kept her thighs open for him.

Using one hand, he was quickly able to open his belt and drag down the zipper of his jeans, metal teeth grinding open.

Zelda couldn't wait for him. She reached for him, helping to ease his cock out. It was only the second time she'd been able to hold it in her hand, and the fact that she could do so freely came with all kinds of perks.

Like the look on Victor's face when she gently pumped her hand.

"I want to make you feel good, too."

He grinned. "Baby, you make me feel good all the time."

Why? Why was he always able to just spout off easy words like that, as though he'd plucked them mindlessly from the air, and make her face heat up like that? It was beyond not fair. She needed to do something about this. To show that she was at least capable of some control.

Zelda pushed against Victor's chest. With his strength as a subhuman, she doubted she would be able to get him off her if he really didn't want to move, so it was only by his compliance with her wishes that she got him onto his back and straddled him.

He looked up at her with a playful fire in his eyes, his hands casually resting on her hips.

"What do you think you're doing up there?"

Zelda didn't have a mirror handy, but she was pretty sure, she hoped, that the visual she was presenting was a good one.

Her fox ears perked and pointed up at the ceiling, her hair played around her shoulders, and she *knew* he could see her nipples through the T-shirt. She grinned down at him. "You did something nice for me. So I want to do something nice for you."

She could not make that sound sexual to save her life, but she did take note of the slight widening of Victor's eyes, and the flare in his nostrils as she slid down his body until she was in a similar position to the one he'd started off in.

On her knees, between his legs.

Zelda had never much liked doing this to Harry. It had always seemed like a chore, something she didn't get to partake in and enjoy as much as he did.

This time, it seemed like something so much better. It seemed like something she would enjoy as well. She felt an eagerness to do this for him that she had never felt for Harry.

Though she was pleased by it, now she knew better than to bring Harry's name in this space between her and Victor, so she just tested out her theory.

Zelda wet her lips, letting them slide around the enlarged head of his cock. He tasted a little like salt and skin, but not in the unpleasant way she was used to where Harry was concerned. This tasted, not good, but not bad either. Not bitter, not like something she had to get used to. It was just...him.

She liked it. Zelda's confidence was boosted by the sound of his hard and heavy breathing. She glanced up, sliding her mouth down farther and farther around his shaft.

Victor's face was dark with color, as though he was doing everything in his power to hold back, to prevent her from knowing how much she was having an effect on him.

She liked that. It made her want to keep going, to see how much she could make Victor come undone.

Zelda thought of everything she knew about this, about all the things Harry had said he'd liked.

She tried them, slowly, not entirely comfortable with using techniques she'd learned from her murderous ex on her mate, but she didn't have any other teaching to fall back on.

It was as though she was following a map. The best working compass she had was the sound of Victor's breathing, of his moans. He gave her the best guidance simply by those sounds alone, and Zelda did her best to follow along with what he wanted.

He groaned low when she tightened her mouth, dipping down low, until she was able to take almost all of him into her mouth.

She wanted to. God, she so wanted to, but she couldn't quite get there before she had to pull back. Maybe a little more practice was needed before she could quite reach that level of skill.

And Victor was still talking to her, still calling her baby. She liked that, liked his hand in her hair, his encouragement, and the power this gave to her. Because she was doing this. He wasn't the only one who could do this; she could make him come undone, too. She could make him pant and gasp and moan her name.

As she swirled her tongue around the base of his shaft, Zelda felt a tightening, felt his orgasm on the horizon, and she wanted it. She wanted it probably more than he did. She wanted to make him come, wanted to taste him on her tongue.

Except, just as she was starting to find her groove, Victor growled again, sounding more and more like an alpha with every second that ticked by. He grabbed her by her shoulders, pushing her back from his cock until it slipped out of her lips and Victor, with all the strength in his body, was able to easily lift her back up the bed and on top of him.

"Come here."

The sound of his voice, so guttural, so animalistic, brought a shiver from Zelda's body. She curled her arms around his neck, eager as Victor reached between them.

"Lift your hips."

She did, then felt his swollen cock head pressing against her sex.

She gasped, anticipation and excitement making her body tremble.

Zelda sat down onto him, taking all of him inside her before he could tell her to, not giving Victor the chance to prepare her.

Zelda sighed, the sensation of being filled, of having Victor inside her again after the thousand years ago when he'd last been there was exhilarating.

And Victor wasn't just going to lie back and let her do all the work, it seemed. He pushed himself to sit up, looping his arm around her waist, pulling her against his chest.

"You are so fucking sexy." He kissed her on the mouth, his breath warm across her throat as his lips travelled across her skin. "I used to dream of a woman like you."

Zelda didn't understand. "What?"

Victor was silent for a moment, as though regretting saying something like that, but then he continued. "I don't know if it was the mating, but it's always been you. You're exactly my type in every way. I used to dream of someone like you, and I knew she was the one. Everyone else I've ever been with, they've always been you. I was always waiting for you."

Zelda's throat closed. She didn't expect him to say something like that. She didn't expect him to have such an effect on her.

It did. It was better than hearing a love declaration.

"Say something."

She couldn't. Her throat ached too badly.

Zelda grabbed Victor by the back of his head, yanking his mouth forward and crushing their lips together while thrusting her hips forward.

Victor moaned against her mouth. She swallowed the noise,

adjusting her hips until she found a comfortable rhythm, until Victor's hands on her waist gripped her strong enough to bruise.

That was fine. That small pain was nothing compared to the pleasure he gave her as he thrust hard and fast inside her. Victor had to free one hand to steady himself on the bed; their rhythm together was off, but somehow still perfect.

The pleasure was even better than the first time because she was, well, in bed. She was making love with her mate in bed, not outdoors because they were so desperate for each other, unable to control themselves and overcome with such a desperate need that it couldn't be contained any longer.

This almost felt normal. Maybe that was why Zelda liked it so much. The chance to feel normal didn't come to her too often these days.

Zelda couldn't last. Victor was close. She could tell by the groans that left his lips, his perfectly kissable lips.

"Come inside me."

She only had to whisper the words before Victor did as she asked.

Well, she doubted he popped off because she'd commanded it. Even he couldn't have that kind of self-control, but it was a nice thing to think about.

He fucked into her harder, milking his orgasm, and pushing her over the edge as a result.

Zelda cried out, her body clenching tightly around Victor. She couldn't help herself, even as she knew she was gripping him.

He seemed to like it, however, if the way he kissed her after the fact was any indication. Zelda luxuriated in the feeling of his arms wrapped around her, his mouth on hers.

Something had happened here, something other than the obvious sex.

She didn't know how to describe it, but she got the feeling that all of his previous resistance wouldn't be a problem going forward.

It was like he'd said. A man can only resist a beautiful woman for so long.

Zelda had to admit, she felt pretty good after that. Victor growled a little when they were done, and she knew he was disappointed with his inability to control what was a natural function of their mating, but she smoothed away his creased brow with more kisses. She touched his face, his chest, smiled up at him.

Told him she loved him.

That did it. That made the scowl go away.

"When we're outside of our bedroom, it goes back to the way it's supposed to be."

Zelda nodded. "Understood."

"I won't be distracted when I'm supposed to be protecting you, and no more pole dancing classes."

"You are safe from my amazing hips until this is all said and done with."

Victor grinned at that, which was good, because then they made love again, and again.

He really was a subhuman. No normal man could have that kind of stamina. It wasn't normal.

And she wasn't complaining.

When it was over, dawn approached. Zelda couldn't remember the last time she'd ever stayed awake so long, making love and talking all night. She didn't think she'd ever done that with Harry, not even on their wedding night.

And this night was so much more special than her wedding night. She never wanted it to end. "So, what kind of shifter are you supposed to be?"

Zelda lazily played with the dark hairs on Victor's chest. Scratchy soft. She liked them.

"Honestly, a wolf."

Her hand froze, then she settled back into what she was doing. "Really?"

"Are you upset?"

Zelda shook her head. "No. It doesn't matter about Harry or his pack. I actually like wolves." She grinned up at him. "It kind of explains a lot about you."

"Not really. I'll never be able to shift anyway."

"But you've still got all the best qualities."

Like that look of a hunter he got in his eyes whenever he wanted her. Zelda was always going to enjoy that.

Victor grinned down at her. "Well, I think you're the first shifter to come right out and tell me that."

"Really? Why?"

He shrugged, lifting a hand up and settling it behind his head. "Well, most packs, most shifters, look at subhumans like they're just normal humans. It's the full-blooded humans who look at subhumans as though there's anything special about them. Aside from being a little stronger than average and enjoying my steak sandwiches, I feel pretty human."

"Steak sandwiches, I'll remember that."

He nudged her, still grinning.

There were obviously some other aspects to being a subhuman that he wasn't bringing up. Zelda was positive his eyesight went beyond a perfect 20/20. She already knew he had a good sense of smell on top of everything else, and his instincts made him perfect for the career path he'd chosen.

But if he wanted to think of himself as mostly human, she wasn't going to argue with him. It had never occurred to her that subhumans could be treated like that. She'd always assumed they were accepted by all sides. It made more sense, and was a little sad, that he would have trouble finding acceptance by either.

Zelda held him a little tighter. She doubted Victor would want her sympathy. He didn't seem like the type, so she didn't say anything about it, but she would give him all the hugs and snuggles she could muster.

"It was fine. I had a good life. I knew my dad was hoping I would be able to shift, but he was still a good dad."

Zelda hesitated to ask her next question, but so many mysteries about him were being unlocked that she couldn't help herself. "You think part of the reason Angela left was because…"

Victor seemed to think about it. "Maybe. I know it was something she thought of, but I was being honest with you before. We just weren't a good match. Trust me, it didn't feel good to be left at the altar like that, but I got over it." He looked down at her. "And I'm glad she left me. It would be kind of awkward to find your mate when you're already married, wouldn't it?"

Zelda's ears twitched. "I never even thought of that." She looked up into Victor's dark blue eyes. "If Harry didn't turn out to be a complete idiot, I would have still been married to him when we met."

"We wouldn't have met." Victor sighed, looking up at the ceiling. "Christ, now I have something to be grateful to him for."

"That's weird."

He nodded. "Yeah, it is. You and I are going to keep that to ourselves."

Zelda couldn't agree more.

"So, while we're talking…" Victor's fingers slid up and down Zelda's shoulders. She liked the small tickle that left her with. "Zelda and Link?"

Zelda groaned, hiding her face in Victor's chest. She could feel the way his body wracked with laughter.

"I was dreading when you would bring that up."

"I'm guessing your parents liked video games."

"No, they were just…idiot hippies."

"Oh?" Zelda heard the smiled in his voice. "Don't think I ever heard you growl like that."

"They dumped Link and me off on Uncle Mike and took off. Said they were coming back, all that stuff. Poor Mike. He really was too young to get saddled with a couple of kids."

"Your parents are just…gone?"

Zelda heard the serious note in Victor's voice. Oddly, it was enough to calm her down. "Yeah. They wanted to go to some concert or convention. Whatever it was. They didn't come back. To be honest, I don't even know if they're still alive."

Victor rubbed her arm. "I'm sorry, baby."

Now it was Zelda's turn to shrug, as though none of this mattered. "It's okay. I got over that a long time ago."

And she had. For the most part. The dreams she used to have as a little girl of Mommy and Daddy coming back were long gone. Even the tiniest spark of hope that she would hear something from them when she'd married Harry died when there was no word from them.

They'd either abandoned their children or were killed in some terrible event. She didn't know which she hoped for it to be, if she was honest with herself.

Victor was silent in that way that she could tell meant he was thinking.

"Really, I'm okay. Mike was a good second dad. He didn't always know what he was doing, but he was good."

"Well, I'm glad you had him. He does seem like a decent guy."

Zelda wanted off this topic. It was too much talking about her. "What made you want to get into protecting people?"

"Oh, well, that was easy. It was just something I always wanted to be part of. I think part of it was knowing what pack life was like. The sense of community, of looking out for each other. Humans don't always have that. Some people are alone in the world, and if they come to me or Steve, then I want to be able to put their minds at rest."

Warmth filled Zelda's chest. "You're a good person."

She could swear she spotted a dusting of color rising up his neck. "Yeah, well, it's not always romantic or noble. You wouldn't believe how terrible it is when my job is to follow around some woman who may or may not be cheating on her husband so I can snap pictures for the divorce lawyers. Or tail some under aged kids whose parents worry they're doing drugs, or dating the wrong boy."

"Aw, makes you feel a little like a peeping Tom?"

"Try not to sound too amused by that."

Zelda laughed. "Sorry!"

But she couldn't help it, and when Victor spun her around, pinning her down, his merciless hands attacking her ribs in retaliation, she really couldn't help but laugh then.

Victor took her into the shower after that, practically carrying her over his shoulder, caveman style.

Zelda decided she liked caveman style, as well as this new side to Victor. She could really get used to it.

They didn't make love in the water, despite how the only thing between their bodies was the soap suds, but it was still incredibly perfect. Intimate.

This was what it felt like to really be with a mate.

Zelda was getting tired by the end. Even the rush of adrenaline that came with all the sex, and with simply being with her mate, wasn't enough to stop her eyelids from constantly trying to pull shut. Towards the end of her shower, Victor was helping her to rinse her hair. He was shockingly gentle. He knew to cup his hands over her fox ears to keep water and soap from getting in them. He kissed her neck as he washed her back, and she could tell he wanted more. She wanted to give it to him, but she was dead on her feet by the time they were finished.

Zelda had no idea what time it was. She was only able to stay awake because of Victor's constant prodding, and how he toweled her off.

Zelda wobbled to the bed with his help, intent on sleeping well past noon if she could. No sooner did her body become boneless and she flopped onto the sheets did she hear Victor's phone ring.

She groaned. Every time he answered it, it was some bad, weird, or shocking news. She didn't want any of that right now. She wanted her mate to come to bed with her.

"Ignore it," she said as he reached for his phone, still perfectly naked.

He smiled at her. It looked at little forced. "You know I can't."

Zelda grabbed one of the pillows and stuffed her face in it. She hated this. It wasn't going to be some friendly call from Steve who wanted to chat. It was going to be the real world coming in to rain on her parade.

So, of course, she was right about that.

"Kincaid."

Zelda's ears twitched, and she managed to pick up the voice on the other end of the line.

It was the police. One of the detectives on their case.

Gerard had been found. He was dead.

CHAPTER 27

Zelda just wanted to pass out. She wanted to let herself slip into unconsciousness and forget about everything else going on in the world because this was bullshit.

Nothing made sense. The sky was green and the grass was blue and nothing was fitting together.

What in the hell was wrong with the universe?

"I understand. Thank you," Victor said, and he hung up the phone.

Zelda had been too busy groaning and grumbling over this new bit of news that she hadn't caught that last of what was said from the person on the other end of the line. She didn't need to hear it. She knew all she needed to know.

Gerard was dead. Harry was in prison, and Ben was out there somewhere claiming innocence.

The bed dipped beside her. She felt Victor's hand on her back. "I take it you were listening in on that."

Zelda didn't say anything. She wanted to burrito herself in the sheets and not ever come out.

"Until we can find Ben and bring him in, we should probably lay low for a little bit. No going out unless we have to."

Zelda looked at him. "You really think that's necessary?"

Victor pulled his hand away from her. He stood, reached for his pants, and started to get dressed. That was all wrong. He was supposed to stay naked, get in bed, and snuggle with her until they were ready for their next round of lovemaking. Victor looked as though he was getting ready to go to work.

"It's for the best. You told me you were all right with it if we continued on like this."

"Not in private."

He paused in buckling his belt, then continued, looking at her. "I am not holding you hostage in here, but I am saying that we do need to take care. I'm not putting any new rules on you."

Zelda wasn't sure she trusted that. "Are you going to go back to not touching me?"

"When in private? No."

Zelda barely stopped her tail from wagging slightly. She managed to get herself under control quickly, however. "So, you're not going to turn into Mr. Stick-Up-Your-Ass again?"

Victor snorted. "I didn't have a stick up my ass."

Zelda hid her face in her pillow again, but only so he wouldn't see the smile on her face.

He totally had a stick up his ass.

"Anyway, we're going to be cooped up a little, but that's about it. You can still contact your brother and your uncle. Nothing will change. I just want to wait until everything is confirmed."

Zelda pulled her face out of her pillow. "Until what is confirmed?"

Victor was adjusting his shirt around his perfectly narrow waist and muscular chest when she asked.

"You didn't hear?"

"I wasn't spying on *all* of it."

She felt kind of offended that he would think she had been.

Victor shook his head. "So far, the police are thinking it looks like a suicide. With everything that's been going on, it's kind of hard to tell until we have more information."

Zelda sat up. "A suicide? How was he found?"

"In his truck, in one of the small lakes near your pack. Someone noticed the headlights were on in the water and phoned it in, I guess."

Zelda thought about it. "If he did commit suicide, does that mean Ben is telling the truth?"

"Possibly. There are still some other avenues to look at, but it wouldn't be unheard of for someone to take that route out of guilt, but it's not that common either."

Zelda sighed. She rubbed her face. "Why is this so complicated?"

She hated that this wasn't easier to understand, that the answer wasn't right there in front of her.

She didn't take pleasure in hearing that Gerard was dead. It kind of saddened her. It saddened her that Maxwell was dead, that Harry was the one to do it, that he was in jail, Gerard was dead, and Ben was on the run.

She'd known these people, lived with them and laughed with them over barbecues and get-togethers for the year she'd been married to Harry.

Knowing everything was unraveling and shattering into a thousand tiny pieces was getting to her in a way she never thought was possible.

"Do you think he killed himself?" She wanted Victor's opinion.

"To be honest, I was about to ask you the same thing. You knew this man. Spent time with him."

"Not a lot of time."

"Try to think about it anyway."

Zelda did, and she wasn't sure. Gerard always seemed like a happy, confident person. She knew that wasn't always an indication that someone could do something like that, but she also didn't know he, Harry, and Ben were capable of plotting out and executing a murder.

"I don't know. I really don't."

"The police are going to want to hear that."

More interviews then, great.

"We'll know for sure when the coroners get their hands on the body. If there's water in his lungs, it'll point to suicide."

"And if there's not?"

"Then we might have another murder on our hands."

～

THE POLICE DID WANT to speak with Zelda. Victor had tried to get them to come to the hotel for their chase, but it seemed some things were beyond even his control.

She supposed this was one of those things that fell under the category of necessity when it came to leaving the hotel, so they left, and Victor really did turn back into her bodyguard when they were outside.

It was kind of disappointing, seeing that side of him again, the side that was closed off, the side that wouldn't let her near, but at least now she knew this was only until they got back into the private space of their room. She could better handle this when they were out and about.

The police asked her the same question Victor had. Did she think Gerard would be capable of killing himself? She told them the same thing. They also asked a few more questions Victor had prepared her for, namely, if she knew where Ben was, and if she had an idea of whether or not he would try contacting her again.

She was as honest as possible with them, even when it got annoying after they started asking questions she'd already answered time and again.

She knew they were only trying to refresh her memory, to see if there were other details she'd forgotten about the first ten thousand times they'd asked her anything, but still, she hated repeating herself so many times.

"Do you think Ben will try to contact me again?"

That was the main question she wanted to hear from the police.

"It's possible, we're not going to rule anything out."

Why did that make it sound as though they knew for sure Ben was getting ready to contact her? It was as though they didn't want her freaking out over it.

Zelda thought she understood Victor's house arrest rule a little more now. Why wouldn't he tell her about this if he'd worried about it? Did he not want to make her worry, too?

That seemed kind of stupid, and not all that like him.

She wasn't sure how to think about that. She was definitely going to have a little talk with him when she got out of here.

Which was annoying because when she was finished with her interview—a whole two hours long—Victor wasn't waiting for her at the front of the police station. He was apparently having a talk of his own with one of the detectives.

About her, about what his plans were, probably about how he was going to give them every detail of every tiny thing that happened to her or that came out of her mouth when they spoke.

When Victor came out to see her, he took one look at her crossed arms, the way she sat in the waiting area, and his expression changed.

"What's wrong?"

Zelda only then realized she was scowling. She let the expression melt from her face. Why was she angry with him? He hadn't done anything, and if he was making plans with the detectives, it was only because he was trying to help her get back to something close to normal.

Zelda stood, suddenly feeling abashed. "I'm just...in a bad mood. With this whole thing. Sorry. Can we just get out of here?"

Victor did that thing he did where Zelda could tell he was studying her. As though trying to see if she really was all right.

"I'm fine, really." She walked up to him, her arms finding their way around his waist easily. He held her back, which felt great. Even now it felt easy. "I'm sorry I'm in a bad mood."

"You're allowed to be. I get it. Come on, let's head back."

Zelda was only too happy for that. Victor didn't even remind her of their little agreement as she held his hand on the way back to the car.

Zelda couldn't stop her mind from racing on the way back. So many possibilities. There were so many ways this could go.

"The detectives think Ben is going to want to contact me."

Victor nodded, both hands on the wheel, his gaze directly ahead, like a responsible driver. "They do."

"Is that what you think?"

"Yes."

Zelda thought that over a little. "Right, because he already tried to talk to me before."

"And you sympathize with him."

"I do not."

Victor took his eyes from the road for a hair of a second, but it was enough for her to really get a look at the expression on his face, and in his eyes.

"I don't!"

"You kind of do. That's not necessarily a huge problem either. You're a good person. You're sympathetic to other people. That's not always bad."

"Meaning it is bad some of the time?"

"If the wrong person tries to take advantage of that, then yes."

Zelda sighed. She looked out the window, trying to think.

Was she sympathetic to Ben? Maybe a little, but in a sense, she was kind of sympathetic to everyone in this whole mess. Even Harry.

No. Not Harry. She was sympathetic to the person she thought he was. That was the difference.

So maybe it was the same way for Ben.

"Do you think I'm sympathetic to him because I know him?"

"That's usually the reason people are sympathetic to other people," Victor said, though not unkindly. "I imagine you spent some time with these people. You didn't exactly sound happy to hear that Gerard had been found dead."

"No." Zelda shook her head. "Though, to be honest, a real selfish part of me was happy they didn't want me to identify his body."

"They got his mother to do that."

Jesus. That sounded harsh. It made sense, but it couldn't have been a picnic for her to do that.

"What should I do if Ben does try to see me again?"

Victor pressed his lips together. "If he does that, and I, for some reason, am not around, you keep your distance. Don't let him get within ten feet of you. Tell him you understand, you believe him, but that he needs to turn himself into the police for questioning. If he really was afraid of Gerard, then the threat is over with and he can safely talk."

"Right. I can do that." Then something else occurred to her. "What if he goes back to the pack? If Gerard is gone, Harry in jail, and

Maxwell dead, then as an alpha, he'd be able to take control of the pack for himself, right?"

The only reaction she noticed from Victor was the slight twitching in his cheek. Then he pulled to the side of the road, turning his hazard lights on.

Zelda couldn't hide her alarm. "What are you doing?" They weren't exactly on the highway, but it was still a busy road.

Victor pulled out his phone. "Calling the detective on your case. He probably already knows about this and is working on it, but I just want to make sure."

That made sense. Zelda wished she'd thought to ask them if they were going to keep an eye on Maxwell's pack, watching out for that sort of thing, too. They had to be, though, right? After Steve's attack, they were definitely going to keep an eye on what was going on over there. But the scary question was, what if they weren't?

Victor made the call. He didn't have to leave a message. Zelda's ears twitched as she listened to the brief conversation.

She sighed heavily when she realized that, yes, the detectives had thought of that very thing, and they were going to keep an eye on the pack. They weren't going to ignore this. That was good. That was enough to let Zelda sigh and feel easier about everything.

Still, she didn't feel better until Victor started driving again.

With everything going on, all the drama and danger that seemed to be around every corner, she figured the next biggest Fuck My Life event to happen would be if Ben appeared on the road in some dramatic flair to announce that he really was the one who had killed Gerard, it was his idea all along to kill Maxwell, and now he wanted Zelda dead because…

She hadn't figured that part out yet. If this was a movie or a book, that's what she was sure would happen.

But it wasn't a movie. Nothing that happened had to make any sense or happen in any particular order.

Which was hilarious because when Victor pulled into the parking lot of their hotel, he was forced to slam onto the brakes when Ben stepped into the way of the car.

CHAPTER 28

Zelda felt the hairs of her tail stick out on all ends. She smacked the dashboard, an anger building up inside her that she hadn't expected to be there.

"Are you fucking kidding me?"

"Baby, stay in the car," Victor said, as though he was worried she would attempt to jump out and confront Ben.

She wasn't that angry. Or crazy.

She was about to tell him that when Victor suddenly shouted loud enough to nearly pop the vein pulsing at his neck. *"Don't even think about it!"*

Zelda jerked back from him, then realized he was looking behind her.

She turned. Ben had quickly moved to her passenger door. As though he was about to open it. She quickly pressed down on the lock. That wouldn't keep him out if he really wanted to get in. To get at her, but it was something.

"Zelda, come here."

Victor didn't give her the chance to do as he told her before his large hands suddenly grabbed her around the waist. Victor pulled her away from the door quickly, practically in his lap.

He knew perfectly well that if an alpha wolf shifter wanted to get in here, there wouldn't be much stopping him.

Ben put his hands onto the glass, cupping them, as though trying to remove the glare. "I'm not here to hurt anyone."

Victor growled low in his throat. Despite everything, Zelda's heart pounded. "Should we trust him?"

Victor was silent. Thinking again.

"Stay in here, keep the doors locked, and phone the police." He opened the driver's side door.

Zelda grabbed his arm. "Hey, wait! Where do you think you're going?"

"To talk to him. Call the police. I've got this."

She shook her head. She wanted to argue, but Victor pressed a quick kiss to her mouth, and was then out the door. He shut it quickly behind him, gesturing for her to lock it.

She could jump out of the car, to go to him, and demand to confront Ben at his side. Except, she remembered what happened when Ben had been in the hotel lobby. She'd learned her lesson. At least she hoped she had. Zelda scooched into the driver's seat, locked the door, and kept her hands on the wheel before she remembered she was supposed to phone the police.

Her hands scrambled for her purse. She couldn't seem to find her damn phone and looked up at what Victor and Ben were doing. Her fingers trembled as she dug around in there, watching as Victor and Ben both walked around to the front of the car.

Where the fuck was her phone?

"You'd better be here to turn yourself in."

"No. I don't want humans in on this."

"That's not up to you."

Her purse slid to the floor of the car.

Clenching her teeth, Zelda took her eyes off of Victor and Ben, going down for it. She yanked it back up, her phone, thankfully, sliding out and onto the seat. She grabbed it, though Zelda could hardly focus on unlocking it when she was focused on Victor and Ben.

Still, she somehow managed to hit the emergency contact button.

"9-1-1, what's your emergency?"

"Uh, yeah, I've got a problem. Ben, he's a wanted criminal, I guess. The police tried to arrest him because he might be involved in a murder the other day, but he freaked out, shifted, and ran. He's an alpha, by the way. He's here in front of my car."

"All right, sweetie. Are you in a safe place?"

"I think so. My...my boyfriend is outside trying to reason with him. Can you please just send some police, and make sure they have silver handcuffs this time?"

"All right, just give me your current location, honey."

Zelda did. She gave the woman on the other end of the line everything she wanted to hear, which was difficult because her ears were still twitching as she struggled to pay attention to the operator on the other end of the line as well as what Victor and Ben were saying.

Victor was keeping calm, which she supposed made sense. He was a professional. He would know better than to come out of the gate swinging. It almost looked as though he was having a nice conversation with Ben, catching up on old times. Victor's hand rested on the hood of the car casually.

Either he really wasn't all that worried about what was going on, or he was an amazing actor. Maybe a bit of both.

"Sweetheart, can you hear me? Talk to me, honey."

Except she couldn't hear the woman on the other end of the line. Not when Ben suddenly launched his fist into Victor's chest.

Zelda screamed, watching Victor fly backwards and into the nearest parked car.

Ben looked at her, an expression in his eyes and on his face she didn't entirely understand, but she didn't need to as her foot immediately slammed down hard on the gas.

Which did nothing because the car was still in park.

"Fuck!"

Ben moved.

Zelda put the car in drive, never more desperate to run someone over in her entire life.

Too bad Ben wasn't in the way of the car when she floored it.

He ducked out of the way just as she nicked his waist. Ben held tightly to her door, his claws digging into the metal.

Zelda had to slam her brakes to keep from crashing into one of the cars at the end of the lot. That alone was almost enough to get Ben off her, but not quite. It shook him, that was all.

"I just want to talk to you!"

"Fuck you!"

She put the car in reverse. Glass shattered into a thousand tiny, glittering pieces around her face as Ben punched in the window. Zelda cringed, but she didn't stop. She spun on the wheel. The tires screamed and this time the back of the car did slam into one of the other vehicles in the parking lot.

The sudden force of crunching metal hitting each other was shocking enough. The airbag popping in her face was much worse.

It dazed her. Zelda had never been punched in the nose before, but she figured that was what it must feel like, and all the strength in her body to resist, to pull away from the hands reaching in to snatch her out of the car...it was all gone.

"Zelda, Jesus Christ, are you okay?"

That definitely didn't sound like Victor, and for that alone, she was in a bad mood.

Ben's hand touched her throat. Zelda didn't have much strength, but there was enough in her body for her to be able to turn her head to the side and bite down hard on his skin. Ben yelled out loud. When he punched her, Zelda definitely got to experience what the difference was between an airbag and a proper fist.

She didn't remember passing out. Zelda would have thought for sure she would have a memory of that, or that she would at least dream when it happened.

Nope. One second she had the sharp and unexpected pain against her cheek, and then the next, she woke up to the smell of...earth. Earth and pine, and in the distance, water. Birds chirped overhead, and Zelda thought she could see a couple of chipmunks scurrying off.

It was nothing notable, but it wasn't just the smells of Mother Nature that gave her an idea of where she was.

She could also smell people. Exhaust from trucks and cars. The lingering scent of barbecue, and a few other familiar body odors she'd gotten used to while living in Maxwell's pack for a year.

Zelda groaned, rolling onto her stomach. "You've got to be kidding me."

"How do you feel?"

She knew he was there because she could smell him, but Zelda hadn't been aware that Ben had been standing so close.

When he brushed some of her hair out of her eyes, she slapped his hand away. "Don't touch me."

He backed off.

"I really do just want to talk to you."

Zelda pushed herself to her knees. She wasn't bound up in any way. Her clothes were dirty and her face hurt. So did her stomach.

"Did you carry me all the way here?"

She must have been out for a while. Alphas could run fairly quickly, but not as fast as any car.

Ben pressed his lips together. "I just need you to listen to me."

Zelda narrowed her eyes, her anger, her rage, rising to the point where she couldn't control it as images of the way Victor flew backwards assaulted her memories.

"You fucking asshole! Why should I listen to anything you have to say? You might've killed Victor!"

"I just hit his chest. He's fine."

"You're an alpha! You could have broken his ribs!"

What if one of his ribs punctured his lung? An alpha shot right over the heart could kill a man, regardless of whether or not they were human, subhuman, or even shifter.

He could be lying dead in that parking lot right now.

He could be dead.

"Zelda, it's okay, listen to me." Ben got to his knees in front of her. That didn't help. She didn't want him anywhere near her and she sure as hell didn't want him touching her. She slapped his hand away when he tried to grab her shoulder.

"All right, I get it. I understand, you're mad at me. You have every right to be," Ben said. "But I promise he's alive. His heart was beating when I left. I double checked to make sure, okay?"

"You did?" Zelda felt as though she could breathe again. Just barely, but it was something.

Ben nodded. "I promise. He's alive." He paused. "I got your scent on each other. You're together?"

Zelda wasn't sure why she felt compelled to answer. Maybe for the sense of normalcy, but there was also something helpful about this.

Victor had told her how to keep her attackers occupied. Victor had also ended up punched in the chest, so she had to tread carefully here.

"He's my mate."

Ben's eyes flew wide. "He's...what?"

Zelda nodded. "Yeah."

"But...you and Harry—"

"Are not together anymore, and it was an arranged marriage. Not the same thing."

Ben's shoulders sagged a little. "Right, well...that makes sense. I guess."

She wasn't interested in what he did or didn't guess.

"You going to hit me, too?"

She didn't ask it to be confrontational. She tried to keep the sound of that out of her voice. She had to be calm. Like Victor had told her. A few seconds of calm, rational thinking in a tense situation could end up saving her life.

Ben looked horrified when she'd asked the question, as if he hadn't already hit her. "What? No! Of course not!"

She looked at him.

"That was different. You were trying to hit me with your car. You were going crazy."

The tiny muscle beneath her eye twitched. She decided to ignore it. For now.

"Okay, fine. I'm sorry about that, but you did punch my mate in the chest." And he could still be dead. Zelda didn't think she was going to jump straight to believing what Ben had to say about anything just yet.

Please don't let him be dead. Just thinking about it made her heart squeeze and her throat close.

Great. Now she was fighting off a panic attack.

Calm. She needed to breathe. She could do this.

"What do you want?"

Ben pressed his lips together. He briefly looked away from her, then gave her his full attention. "I just need you to help me get back in with the pack."

Zelda's brain didn't pick up on the meaning of what he'd just said. She blinked, feeling stupid. "You...what? Why? Just go back and you'll be fine. They'll hide you."

"They can't do much of anything with the police running around."

"I don't control the police, Ben."

"No, but you can help. I don't want to go to prison for the rest of my life, Zelda. None of this was my idea."

"Okay."

Ben's eyes began turning red. "Harry was the one who wanted Maxwell out of the way. I didn't think he'd actually do it!"

"All right." Zelda reached for him. She grabbed Ben's shoulders, gripping them, hoping he wouldn't punch her or shove her off. She just needed him to focus long enough to get him back to something normal.

To get the wolf hair that was starting to sprout on his face to melt back into his pores.

It did, thankfully.

And Ben looked at her with such a grateful expression that Zelda could almost forget the way he'd made Victor fly across the parking lot.

"I just want your help. I'm not a bad person. I didn't want any of this."

She didn't have to believe what she said next. She just had to say it.

"I believe you. Okay, I'll do whatever I can to make all this goes away."

Not that she knew what she was going to say to make that happen, and maybe Ben figured as much, but he didn't show it. He just looked relieved.

"Thank you. So much," he added.

Zelda sighed. "Okay, so, we can talk on the way back about what I'm going to say, and about your part of the story."

Ben shook his head. "We can't go back. Not yet."

Zelda didn't understand. "I have to go back. Victor might be waiting for me."

Or in pain because he could hardly breathe. She needed to see him again. Zelda needed to put her hands on him and prove to herself that everything was all right. That he was still alive and kicking.

Hopefully. Maybe. Please God, let him be alive.

"He's fine. Just, before we do that, we need to go into the pack."

"Uh, right now? There might be police roaming around. Are you sure it wouldn't be a better idea to just head back to the hotel first?"

Ben glared at her. "I know what you're doing."

Zelda's spine and shoulders tensed. Her tail stiffened and her ears stood on end. "You do?"

"I'm not going back yet. I need to make sure our story is straight. There's no police at the pack yet. They would have told me."

"That's comforting," Zelda squeaked.

Though, not really.

"I just need them to see you."

"The pack hates me."

"Not as much as you might think, and if they can see you, if you can say that you think this whole thing was a misunderstanding, that Harry made a mistake, it'll be easier."

Zelda really didn't think that was the case. Sure, not everyone in the wolf pack despised her guts for leaving Harry. Some would have to understand just from playing a game of numbers alone. But she didn't understand where Ben would get the idea that Zelda's opinion on anything would carry any weight.

"Why go to the pack, Ben?"

He grabbed her wrist. "It doesn't matter right now. Let's just go. We're almost there."

She shouldn't argue, it was dangerous. Ben could attack her at any moment. He could lash out the second she opened her mouth.

Which meant she needed to be careful. Zelda didn't dig her heels into the dirt. She walked with Ben, showing no resistance, submitting to him to calm any raging instincts he might have flaring up within him.

Then she asked her question. "Do they think I'm lying about Harry?"

"No. I mean, some of them do, but pretty much everyone's come to an agreement on this. They know Harry killed Maxwell. They're not happy with him right now."

Okay, so that was out, but Zelda couldn't stop thinking about all the ways this could get even worse for her.

Like if the pack really did blame her and Ben was only bringing her back so she could be judged.

It was very horror movie-esque, but it wormed its way into her brain like a hungry parasite anyway.

She thought of anything else while they walked. They were still a ways from the pack, though the noises in the distance were getting louder. They were almost there. "Did you hear about Gerard?"

Ben grunted something. Then he answered. "Yeah."

Carefully. She had to be really careful here. "It might be a suicide."

Ben said nothing.

"I'm not judging you if you did, but did you have anything to do with it?"

Still no answer.

Zelda's mouth and throat were suddenly dry. "Did you kill him?"

Ben finally stopped. His grip on her wrist tightened.

When he looked back at her, Zelda had her answer. "Holy shit."

CHAPTER 29

"You killed Gerard, didn't you?"

Ben's neck tightened. He wouldn't look at her. They were on pack property now. Zelda could hear the sounds of the people, the children playing and the wolves barking as they chased each other. It was just a matter of time before someone noticed she and Ben were there.

Ben's grip on her wrist was powerful, but Zelda remembered that trick Victor had taught her when he was giving her those self-defense lessons back home.

That time had been so brief, and she didn't get much practice, so she could only hope this worked.

Zelda forcefully angled her wrist so the thinner side of it pointed towards the small gap between his finger and thumb. She yanked hard.

Ben gripped her tighter, not letting her go right away, but Zelda didn't quit.

"Stop that!"

"Let me go!"

She snatched her arm back. Zelda also nearly punched herself in the face doing that, but she was free.

She almost couldn't believe it.

Ben stared at her. He didn't move to grab her again, but his nostrils flared.

"Why did you kill Gerard?"

He rolled his eyes, crossing his arms.

Defensive was not good. That wasn't remotely good.

"Did you have to do it? If you were defending yourself then it's okay. You said you were scared he was going to come after you, right?"

"Right." Ben still didn't look happy. He didn't come near her, and Zelda wasn't going to let him try to, either.

"Is that why you wanted me to go to the pack?" She was still having trouble figuring this out. "I don't think Gerard liked me very much. They won't listen to me."

Ben rubbed his face. "It's not just that. Jesus Christ, Zel, he was the one trying to get you killed."

She blinked. "What?"

Ben turned away from her. His hands settled on his hips. He rubbed at his face as he circled. He didn't seem to know what to do with his hands.

"He was fucking furious when you went to the cops. You don't know the shit he was saying."

Zelda felt relief well up inside her. "So you were defending me."

"I don't want to go to prison, Zelda. It wasn't my idea."

She was starting to feel better and better about Victor, about the idea that Ben was most likely telling the truth about him. The idea that Victor was all right, that he was catching his breath somewhere, that he could be on his way here right now, was the thing to keep her head together.

"Ben, it's okay. If it wasn't your idea to hurt Maxwell, and if you were just defending me, then everything will be okay. We'll explain what happened."

"I'm not dealing with the humans."

"They'll take it easy on you. They'll understand."

"Shifters who go to human prisons are surrounded by silver all the fucking time. We might as well be as good as human. I'm not dealing with that. I can't deal with that shit."

"You're not going to prison. It won't be like that."

Not that she could promise him that, but she was pretty sure that would be the case.

Ben didn't calm himself down. He paced like a caged animal. Zelda had never seen him like this, but she supposed the idea of being targeted in prison would scare the bejeezus out of anyone. Even the calmest of souls didn't take the idea of going to prison with a shrug.

"Ben, honestly, I'll help you. I'll say you did it to protect me, that you were scared and defending yourself. A jury won't just throw you in prison for this."

Ben looked at her. His body simply...stopped. He looked at her as though he was utterly helpless. Only then could Zelda make out the heavy bags beneath his eyes. The bloodshot look to his retinas, and how pale his skin was.

He looked as though he hadn't been sleeping.

"Do you need a doctor? You were shot, weren't you?" Zelda only just now remembered that part. He had a gunshot wound when he'd been carrying her. That couldn't have felt great.

"It's mostly healed over."

"Mostly." She looked him over, trying to see where the shot was. She couldn't see anything on him, so it must have been somewhere beneath his clothes.

"Can I see it?"

Ben tilted his head a little.

Zelda raised her hands. "If you don't want a doctor then at least let me see it. I'll let you take me into the pack and I can look at it."

"There are other people who can look at it. People who are trained."

Zelda pressed her lips together, though she was embarrassed. It was a fair enough thing to point out. She didn't have any medical training, so why would Ben want her hands on him?

"Are you going to come with me or not?"

She wanted to hold back. Zelda still wasn't entirely sure about going with him, but he'd already brought her pretty much the whole way. All she needed was for some kids playing tag to come out here and notice her and Ben standing here, so it wasn't as though she'd be able to get away if she really wanted to.

Might as well go the whole way with this.

"All right."

He held out his hand.

Zelda couldn't help but sneer at it. She walked by him. "I don't need you holding my hand."

He'd already made sure she wasn't going anywhere anyway.

If she was honest, Zelda was hoping she would see the police somewhere around. She gave Ben's name when she was on the phone, so they had to be on their way here, right?

Maybe it was because of her hope of seeing the police that she walked out of the bushes with such confidence, but she hadn't been expecting Ben to grab her arm and yank her back into the shrubs and shadows.

"What are you—"

Ben slapped his hand over her mouth. It really hurt, but he seemed far too interested in looking out among the people who were going about their daily lives.

Guess he knew it was a mistake to just show himself right away, too.

"Right, we're good." Ben released her, then turned away from her suddenly. "Sorry about that."

Zelda rubbed her mouth, glaring at him. "It's fine. Whatever. Let's go."

She had no idea what they were even going to do or who they were going to see. It wasn't as though Maxwell was going to be here to greet them, to hear them out. In fact, Zelda didn't even know who had taken over the pack since Maxwell had been killed and Harry had gone on the run.

Ben walked with purpose, his back straight, fists clenched. Some of the puppies stopped first at the sight of them, shifting into small children with their long ears and tails down as Ben and Zelda walked by.

The females were the second to notice as they made it to the center of the pack.

Many packs, even ones from differing species, were structured similarly. There were trailers, some houses, a few small swing sets purchased from Wal-Mart for the kids, and a well for water, but the alpha's house in this pack, and Zelda's, were placed in the middle of it all.

Zelda walked not too far behind Ben, noting the sound of growling that snapped at her heels. She didn't dare look back.

"Are you sure this is a good idea?"

"Positive."

"Some of the people here tried to hurt the people in my skulk."

"I'm sure they didn't mean anything by it."

Zelda remembered what Steve had looked like in that hospital bed. Even though he'd been awake and seemed to have a lot of energy, that wasn't the point. Someone had put him there and he was going to turn into a wolf during the next full moon because of it.

Zelda was thinking it might have been an incredibly dumb idea to let herself be brought back here, but there was nothing she could do about it. Too many people were looking at her. People she remembered from her time married to Harry.

Most of them gave her a narrow-eyed look. Others seemed genuinely shocked she would show her face here at all.

Of course, someone had to open their big mouth.

"What's *she* doing here?"

"Back off, Linda. Ben asked me to come here."

He'd technically kidnapped her, but she didn't want to share that information with Linda. She'd probably just gloat.

Zelda and Linda never got along. Zelda always suspected it had something to do with Harry, but she'd never had anything to back that up, and Harry had never come home smelling like Linda's perfume, so it was all conjecture.

Linda sneered at Zelda as though she was dog shit beneath her new shoes, then she looked at Ben. "Are you serious? She's the one who started this mess in the first place."

"*What?*"

Linda held up a finger, as though she thought that would silence Zelda.

"Harry was the one who killed Maxwell! You remember Maxwell? Big guy, took care of the pack. Him? He's dead now."

"And we could have handled that without you getting the humans involved, you dumb bitch."

"No, bitches are dogs. That would be you."

There were some things you didn't say to shifters. One of them was calling a she-wolf a bitch. They tended to take that personally.

Linda moved to grab for Zelda's hair. Ben yelled something out, but it was too late.

For Linda.

Zelda went for the woman's throat. She didn't tuck in her thumb, remembering what Victor had told her about breaking it by accident. Zelda didn't even think she got the other woman that hard. It felt like a fairly weak punch. She definitely wouldn't be bragging to Victor about it, but Linda's eyes flew wide. She clutched at her neck and fell back a step, staring up at Zelda as though she'd just performed a move Keanu Reeves, Bruce Lee, and Jackie Chan would have been proud of.

"Whoa, okay, so, try to breathe. You'll be all right, I think."

Zelda tried to touch Linda's shoulder. The other woman swatted her hands away, her claws running down Zelda's arm.

Luckily, the scratches didn't run deep.

"For fuck sakes," Ben growled. "Linda, get the hell out of here and get that seen to. I have better shit to be doing instead of dealing with your jealous bullshit."

Zelda watched Linda walk off, still holding her throat. She felt bad, despite everything. "I didn't mean to hit her that hard."

Ben chuckled. "It was kind of fun to watch."

The door to the alpha's house opened. Zelda snapped her attention to it, forgetting about what happened with Linda and half expecting to see Maxwell walking out, to see him smile at her and welcome her.

Nope. It wasn't Maxwell.

She had no idea who that guy was. In the year she'd spent living here, his face didn't look remotely familiar.

Actually, wait, it did. He looked kind of like…Ben.

Ben seemed to have a bit more spine in his step as he went up the stairs. He and the other man hugged each other, like brothers.

This new face...he was a touch shorter than Ben was. Zelda couldn't tell much beyond that. Was he a shifter? A wolf like Ben? Were they actually brothers or was this just part of her imagination? If they were brothers, why had she never seen this man before?

"Ben, who is that?"

Ben ignored her. He lifted his shirt to the other guy, his teeth clenching in a hiss.

The other man gingerly touched the red lump just beneath his ribs. The bullet wound. It was closed up, but badly swollen, as though something wasn't going all too right inside him.

Ben jerked his head to Zelda, muttered something under his breath, and when the other man nodded, he hobbled his way inside of Maxwell's house.

As though he already had a claim to it.

"Hey! Ben, where are you going?"

She didn't want to be left out here with all these other people. She didn't know what they were going to do to her. Some of the wolves here had already proven they were okay with attacking other people.

The man Ben that hugged came down the deck stairs. His body language didn't give off anything defensive. His expression didn't show any vicious intent.

But that didn't mean it wasn't there.

Zelda adjusted her stance without thinking, half turning so one foot was behind her, just the way Victor showed her.

In case she really did have to run.

"Hi there, you're Harry's wife?"

Zelda shook her head, stunned by the casual note in his voice. "No. I'm his ex wife."

"Right, of course. Sorry about that." He held out his hand. "I'm Bill."

Zelda didn't take it. She looked into Bill's eyes, and was still incredibly aware of all the other eyes around her that stared at her. That probably wanted to hurt her.

Yeah. Really stupid.

"Zelda Wolff."

She shook his offered hand, but only because she didn't want to make a terrible impression.

Zelda didn't think it would be the best idea in the world to piss off someone who might want to hurt her.

"Went back to your old surname? I like it."

She smiled. Tried to smile. "Great. So, how do you and Ben know each other?"

"Right." Bill released her hand and stepped back. "I'm Ben's cousin, actually. I used to live here, but that was a long time before you came. I'm just watching over the place until Ben can take over."

"You're watching the place? Are you another alpha?"

Bill grinned at her, showing off perfectly white teeth, and even a hint of fang.

Too many alphas. That was too many alphas for her liking.

"Oh, okay, great. So, why am I here?"

Bill just smiled at her. Zelda was pretty sure that wasn't going to lead to anything good.

CHAPTER 30

*B*ill brought her inside, which was a double-edged sword for a couple of reasons.

The first being that, all right, it was good she was finally out of glaring sight of those wolves outside, many of whom probably wanted to tear her to pieces for her part in bringing the humans into their lives.

The second was that, well, now she was actually alone in this house. With Ben, an in injured alpha who admitted to killing someone, and his cousin whom she did not know.

Being alone in a room with guys like that didn't seem like the smartest thing in the world.

Bill brought her to the kitchen. Ben was already there. He'd gotten to work quickly. There was blood on the table, a First Aid kit set up, and his eyes were clenched tightly shut as he worked something metal into the swelling beneath his ribs.

Zelda had an immediate freak out at the sight of that.

"What the fuck?" She immediately covered her face with her hands, turning away from it. "What the hell are you doing, Ben? You said you were going to get someone else to do that for you."

Yelling was definitely not a smart move when she wasn't sure what sort of company she was keeping, but she couldn't help it.

"Yeah, I'm supposed to be helping you with that."

Bill walked away from her. Zelda didn't need to look at either of them to know he was helping his cousin. Was Ben trying to take the bullet out? God. She was going to be sick.

This was why she'd never been on top of her first aid lessons. It had always been cooking, crafting, and sewing for her when she'd focused on her education.

The idea of sticking her fingers into someone's bloody wound? No. Just no. She got sick just thinking about it sometimes, and now she was in Maxwell's old kitchen listening as Ben hissed and groaned while he and Bill tried to get the bullet out of his already healing wound.

"Why didn't you do that before?"

"The police were around asking questions. We couldn't risk it." Bill sounded a little too calm while he did his work for Zelda's liking.

She supposed it made sense.

Ben's hissing and groaning turned into a heavy sigh, which was when Zelda figured the bullet had been removed from his body. She still refused to look, not until she heard the clink of metal in the sink and the sound of running water.

When she did take a peek at what was going on, she wasn't all that shocked to see there was still some blood on the table, and even spotted on the floor, obviously, but luckily, now that the sounds of pain and misery were over, her stomach could handle seeing such a thing.

"Zelda, will you help me clean this up?" Bill asked.

Zelda bit down on a groan, but she didn't argue. If she looked as though she was cooperating, then it could put her in a better position.

Also, even though cleaning up potential evidence of…whatever this was, definitely couldn't be good, Zelda had seen enough movies and true crime shows to know that a mop and a little hot water were not going to remove any DNA from anything.

She moved for the wall beside the fridge. The mop hung there. This wasn't her house, but she remembered it from the last couple of times she'd cleaned up after Maxwell. It had been one of her chores. When Maxwell and his mate were out of the house, Zelda came over twice a week to make sure everything was nice and in order. She grabbed it, gently pushing Bill out of the way of the sink to wet it, and then made herself useful.

"So, just so you guys know, the police are probably coming here, too. Very soon," she said. "I called the police just before Ben busted out my car window and grabbed me."

"That's fine. We'll deal with them when they get here."

Bill almost sounded like a total villain when he said that. Not classic cartoon-style villain, but there was an edge to his voice. It was…strange.

"I just need you to stick around for a little while longer, then I can take over," Ben said, clutching at his ribs, the bandage he held over his wound turning a little red around the edges, but that was enough to keep Zelda from staring too long.

"We'll get Zelda to make her statement and that will be the end of it." Bill looked at her. "When the police get here, you can tell them Ben dropped you off with me and he took off. He just wanted someone to talk to and he didn't hurt you."

"Wait, Ben's leaving?" She looked at him, shocked. It had sounded as though he wanted to stay here.

"No, I'll be around, but I can't come out in the open. I'll be arrested."

Zelda clenched her fingers around the mop. She wasn't entirely sure when she'd stopped cleaning, but nothing seemed to matter anymore.

"I won't lie to the police for you, Ben. If you're going to be sticking around then they need to know that."

"It's not a big deal, Zelda."

"You're going to make me an accomplice in…whatever it is you're doing."

Ben's fist moved so quickly Zelda barely saw it fly, but she did jump at the sound of the bang that came when he smashed it hard onto the table.

Zelda also thought she heard a crack.

"Goddamnit, Zelda, I saved your fucking life. You can do this one thing for me."

Except it wasn't just one thing. "Ben, you kidnapped me to bring me here."

"Because I wasn't going to get you to listen with that fucking subhuman running around you!"

Something hot expanded inside her at hearing Victor being called a subhuman. It was what he was, and Zelda had even called him that a couple of times, but not with the same disgusted tone of voice that Ben had used.

"He's my mate, and he didn't want to take a risk with me after everything that happened. That's what a good mate does."

Ben rolled his eyes.

Zelda wanted to claw those eyes right out. "You fucking punched him in the chest and stole me away to come back here where everyone hates me! You're lucky I'm doing anything for you at all!"

Ben's eyes flashed red. He suddenly looked as though his secondary shifter form, that enlarged wolf monster, was closer to the surface than Zelda wanted it to be.

"Okay, okay, that's enough of that." Bill stepped between her and Ben, as though he needed to protect her from something.

Zelda's heart pounded. She wanted to leave. She really wanted to leave, but she didn't know where she stood with these two.

Might as well ask. No point in getting herself worked up if there was nothing to worry about, right?

"You just want me here to tell the pack that you helped me, right?"

Since Ben seemed incapable of answering, Bill did. "It's just a formality. The pack is ready to take Ben as their new alpha. I can't be here forever. I have my own pack to take care of."

"Because you're an alpha?"

"And because he wasn't the one who killed Maxwell. We're wolves, not animals."

Zelda flinched, but it couldn't be entirely ignored that there was some sense of animal instinct that took place here as well. There could be more than one alpha in a pack. Sometimes. Rarely. It didn't always work out because of the clash in personalities, though. Someone always wanted to lead.

Which seemed to be the problem with Harry and Maxwell.

Maxwell had been a good leader. Not everyone liked every single thing he did, but he didn't overcharge the people beneath him for living on his land. He made sure there were always books and toys for the kids, as well as clean drinking water, and transportation to the local schools.

He'd been a good alpha. Zelda hadn't known him long, but he was the reason why living here, away from her skulk, had been bearable.

She could see that now. It wasn't Harry, her own husband, who had made her enjoy her time here. It was Maxwell, and now he was dead because a couple of alphas couldn't stand the idea of not running the pack themselves.

It seemed kind of wrong, that this pack here would be willing to forget Maxwell so soon after his death and take on someone else, but in reality, they had to. They needed someone to follow, to keep their own baser instincts from getting the best of them, to lead them during the hard times when man and wolf fought within their brains.

At least it was Ben. Better for it to be Ben than for it to be Harry. Or Gerard.

But Ben was crazy if he thought he was going to be able to hide out here forever. Even if he managed to avoid being seen or taken in for a year, or two, or ten, something would eventually give, and the longer he stayed away, the worse it would get.

"You have to convince your cousin to talk to the police."

Bill shook his head. "We don't invite humans into our affairs."

"But they already are into our affairs and they think Ben might have had something to do with Maxwell's murder. If we just tell them what happened—"

"The answer is no."

It was the tone of his voice that had Zelda snapping her mouth shut. Complete alpha command. She wasn't a wolf, but that instinct to obey was definitely there.

She pushed passed it. It felt as though she was shoving open a hundred pound door that was trying to slam shut on her. She had to shove against it with everything she had in her small body.

Ben seemed to be aware of this. His eyes widened, and then he smiled. "Are you trying to disobey me?"

She glared at him, mostly because of how difficult she was finding it to push through that barrier. "Maybe."

Bill shook his head, but he didn't stop with that annoying smile. "We're trying to help the pack. They need a leader. I can't be here."

"And they won't get a leader if the humans think Ben is running from them. They're already involved. Ben *does* need to answer for his part in Maxwell's murder, and for bringing me here against my will and attacking my mate!"

That last part came out harder than she intended for it to, but that was all right. She pushed through the barrier. Zelda had her feet planted and she was holding her own. She had no idea how long she would be able to hold her ground like this. It didn't seem like something she would be able to do for long, but she had to try.

And right then, as though the universe was trying to tell her something, her long ears flicked, the sound of sirens coming in the distance.

Bill's ears did the same. He turned towards the front door as though he expected the police to break down the door at any second.

The sirens were still a ways away, but Zelda doubted they had more than two minutes before they arrived.

"They're coming now, and Victor better be with them and not hurt. I won't tell them that Ben isn't here."

Bill narrowed his eyes at her.

Ben came back into the kitchen, his hand still clutching at his side. He'd clearly heard everything she'd just said.

Zelda held her breath, waiting for the other shoe to drop.

Ben's lips thinned. He turned away from her, shaking his head as though he should have seen this coming.

"All right, fine. Whatever. I'll go have a chat with them."

She blinked. "You will."

Ben sneered at her. "Not that you're giving me much of a choice."

She fell back a step at that. "Are you...I thought..."

"What?" Bill asked. "Did you think we were going to hurt you if you didn't do what we asked you to?"

She didn't want to admit that she was kind of thinking that, yeah.

Ben growled low under his throat, his arm hardly pushing hers as he pushed passed her. "Remind me never to do anything for you ever again."

Okay, ouch. That stung, but she couldn't help it.

She was right about this. Wasn't she?

The sirens came closer. They were right outside now. They'd driven right into the middle of pack property and Zelda could make out the sounds of the tires scraping against the earth and gravel.

Victor's voice was a Godsend.

"Zelda!"

Zelda ran out of Maxwell's house. Victor was there, standing beside an unmarked police car, with a couple of cruisers behind him, their lights still flashing. Detective Grey was there, and they seemed to be having an argument about something, which stopped the instant Zelda rushed out.

She and Victor looked at each other. Zelda ran to him. He met her halfway.

Which turned out to be a problem when she jumped into his arms and kissed him.

Victor held her up. He kissed her back, but Zelda heard and felt the groan and cringe he released when she did.

Zelda dropped to her feet immediately. "I'm sorry. Shit. I'm so sorry. Are you okay?"

She wanted to touch his chest, to feel for herself that nothing was wrong and he was perfectly all right, but she kept her hands to herself.

Victor grunted, grabbing her wrist and pulling her away from the house. "Fine. Just knocked the wind out of me."

She doubted that was all that happened, but he wouldn't be standing here, or have taken it so well when she'd jumped into his arms, if he had anything broken, so there was that to be grateful for.

Still, Zelda reminded herself that she needed to take it a little easy on him.

Victor grabbed her arm, his eyes on fire as he stared at the scratches Linda had left behind. "What the hell is this?"

"Oh!" Zelda shook her head. "No, don't worry about this. This was just some idiot with something to prove. Ben didn't do it," she said quickly when Victor glared back at him.

Victor pulled her towards the cruisers. He didn't let go of her hand. She felt the rage and the anger within him and honestly couldn't blame him after what happened, but she was still so utterly happy that he was alive and well, that he was standing there in front of her, that she hardly noticed it.

"Stay here."

She nodded.

"Did they hurt you? Anything else like this?" He tapped her arm, careful not to touch her wounds.

Zelda shook her head, her hands touching Victor's face, the back of his neck and shoulders. As though she needed proof he was actually alive. That he was right here.

Victor barely seemed to notice, not with the way he stared towards the front door.

Zelda could swear she saw a hint of bright red in his eyes, an alpha's anger, but it was gone so quickly she might have just seen the reflection of the red police lights off his blue stare.

Bill and Ben walked out of the house. Bill stayed on the deck. Ben stepped down the stairs.

"Motherfucker." Victor moved forward.

Zelda grabbed him around the shoulders. "No. Don't do that."

"I should fucking kill you!" Victor pointed his finger at Ben as though it was a weapon.

Ben stared back at him as though he was of no consequence. "I barely tapped you and she's not hurt. Don't be like that."

"Idiot! That was kidnapping!"

"She's still technically part of this pack."

Zelda wanted to signal to Ben that he needed to stop talking. Right fucking now. It didn't matter which pack she was a part of when the humans got involved. Their law trumped pack law. Everyone knew that. It didn't matter how much they wanted to fight against it. No matter how much they protested it.

Human law was law. And Zelda had gotten the humans involved.

Some of her former pack mates came out to see what the fuss was about. She doubted many of them had gone back into their homes when Zelda showed up with Ben, but now that there were multiple police cruisers here, lights flashing, men in blue uniform out with their hands on their weapons, they all stared at Zelda with that same angry, glaring expression in their eyes.

And Zelda, for once, didn't feel the need to curl up and hide. Maybe it was a side effect of going against an alpha's orders.

Grey pointed to Ben. "Someone get him into handcuffs."

Ben lifted his hands into the air, waiting for the police to grab him, yanking his arms behind his back. Ben grimaced when the handcuffs clicked into place. They were definitely silver this time if the look on his face was anything to go by.

While Detective Grey read Ben his rights and told him why he was being arrested—kidnapping and assault now added to the resisting arrest he'd done at the hotel, and the suspicion that he was involved in Maxwell's murder.

"Victor, Ben told me that he did kill Gerard."

"What?" Victor looked at her with such a wide expression, then at Ben. That same angry look came over his eyes as before. Zelda thought it was a testament to his self-control that he was able to hold himself back from attacking the other man straight out. The clenched fists and tight shoulders suggested heavily how much he wanted to do just that.

"Grey, can you come over here?" Victor called instead.

Detective Grey looked away from Ben with an unhappy expression on his face. At least he seemed to be done with Ben when he walked over. "What is it?"

"Tell him what you just told me."

Zelda did. "But he said it was because he had to! He said Gerard was the one angry with me about going to the police. He was the one sending people after me. Maybe he was the one who got those other wolves to attack my skulk."

And poor Steve had gotten in the middle of that.

Victor looked at Grey. "What do you think?"

Detective Grey rubbed his narrow jaw. God, he looked so young to be doing this sort of work, but when he turned back to Ben, there was something fierce in his eyes when he went back to him.

Victor walked with him. Zelda held back, but she didn't need to be so close to hear everything as perfectly as though they were speaking to her. "Is that true?"

Ben pressed his lips together, narrowing his eyes at the detective, then he nodded. "Yeah, it's true. I was worried Gerard would want to come after me too. We had a fight. I knocked his ass out."

"Why didn't you leave him like that? You'd already defeated him, hadn't you?"

"An alpha doesn't defeat someone for real unless they kill them or injure them enough to get the message across. That wasn't enough. I didn't want to risk he would go after Zelda again."

Grey looked back at Zelda. Zelda saw how tense Victor's spine was becoming.

Grey shook his head. "That's not self-defense, you just described a murder."

Ben's eyes widened. He looked at Zelda, then back at Bill, as though he expected any of them to do anything. Zelda wanted to do something for him, but she hadn't even stopped to consider the details. If Ben had put Gerard into the truck when he was alive and then push it into the lake, then, yeah, by definition, that was a murder.

Bill, who, as an alpha, would be used to having his own commands obeyed, stepped forward, attempting to be diplomatic. "He was defending the life of one of our own. You there, you're her mate, right? Can you honestly blame him for that?"

Again, Zelda heard that tiny growl rumbling in Victor's throat. "Until I know for sure that story checks out, then I'll treat it for what it is. If he did think he was defending Zelda, then I can still be grateful to him and be comfortable with letting him go his time."

Apparently, Bill's diplomatic attempt was not going to go over well.

Ben dug his heels in a little as the officers tried escorting him to one of their cruisers. "Hey, wait a minute! I tried telling you that at the hotel! You wouldn't listen to me!"

Victor barely looked at him. Zelda didn't understand his cold demeanor until he spoke again. "You told us at the hotel that you were afraid Gerard was going to kill you. I got enough information to know that body was in the water a lot longer than that."

Zelda's eyes flew wide. She looked at Ben, and then, as though someone had flipped a switch, her shock melted away. Of course. Why would she think anyone was telling her the truth at this point? Why would Ben make himself look like anything other than an innocent bystander?

"These are pack matters," Bill said. "I can deal with him."

Did he honestly think the police were just going to let Ben go and hand him over to Bill? They were already starting to put a little more effort into getting him into the car.

One of the nicer officers was trying to tell Ben not to fight him. The fact that he was an alpha was enough to make a few of the other officers stand by a little tense, and Zelda didn't want him to get shot again.

For one thing, the officer shooting might miss and get Victor. That would just be her stupid, idiotic luck with everything that had been going on lately.

Bill stepped forward when he was ignored. Detective Grey stepped into his path. "You're not going to do jack shit. You take one more step and I'll have you in handcuffs with him."

"That's our alpha!" someone shouted.

A woman joined in, thankfully not Linda. "You can't take them. We need them!"

Grey rolled his eyes. "Whatever. Anyone else wants to get in the back of a cruiser, be my guest. I have no problem making a few more arrests today."

Zelda shook her head. The people around him were clearly getting pissy about this whole thing and she didn't want anyone getting hurt.

"Guys, just let them do their job. Everything's going to be all right."

"You shut your damn mouth!"

Zelda looked in the direction of the voice. It was a male, his tail bristled behind him, his ears pointed high, and his face already halfway changed into his more animal shape. "You're the one who invited the police here in the first place."

Victor stepped in front of her before Zelda could say anything back. "You put those claws away before I snap them off your fucking fingers."

The threat wasn't directed towards her, but Zelda's spine stiffened regardless.

Victor was definitely in a bad mood.

Maybe it was the command that did it, Zelda sure as hell felt it, the need to obey. The instinct to give into someone more powerful than she was.

The other shifter clearly didn't want to obey. He wouldn't stop scowling, but he wasn't so eager to challenge Zelda now that Victor stood for her. He couldn't quite make himself hold Victor's stare.

Zelda almost felt sorry for him.

"Victor?"

He didn't look away from the shifter challenging him. "Hm?"

Zelda glanced towards Ben, who was forced into the back of a police cruiser. "Did you mean what you said? Gerard was already dead?"

He briefly glanced back. There was a hesitation there, as though he didn't want her to know, didn't want to tell her something so horrible, but he said it anyway. "Yeah. The full autopsy isn't done yet, but it doesn't take much for the coroner to figure out that much. He was dead before Ben came to pay us a visit."

Zelda looked towards the cruiser. Ben stared at her through the window.

There was regret in his eyes. As well as fear. She couldn't stop looking at him. Victor tried talking to her, but she couldn't quite make out what he was saying.

Victor grabbed her shoulder, finally managing to get her attention. "Zelda, baby, why did he bring you here?"

Zelda could hardly bring herself to look away from Ben. She pitied him, but also feared what he was capable of. "He wanted me to stand beside him and tell the rest of the pack that Gerard…that Gerard was trying to hurt me. He wanted me to say…"

She honestly couldn't get the details right in her head. What specifically had he wanted her to say? He definitely wanted her to help him ease the tensions of the pack. It was strange, since the pack didn't like her, but not so far out of the ballpark that she couldn't fathom it.

But Gerard was already dead? Then…why?

"I don't get it." She shook her head. "It doesn't make any sense. He wanted to bring me here to help him calm the pack, but now…I don't…"

Victor pulled her to his chest. Zelda was worried at first about the idea of hurting him, the injury Ben had given to him, but the way he held her made it almost impossible for her to pull back.

"Try not to think about it, baby."

But she couldn't not think of it. "Do you know why he wanted me here?"

Victor's soft voice became harsh again. "I have a couple of guesses."

And since his guesses usually turned out to be correct, Zelda shivered at the possibilities he was thinking of.

"Come on, let's get out of here."

She nodded, comforted with Victor's arms around her shoulders, but Zelda could still feel the heat of the many glares on the back of her head.

She doubted this was over.

CHAPTER 32

Victor valiantly held back a hiss as Zelda gently touched his chest, trying to rub soothing cream onto the skin without actually doing any rubbing.

The deep purple and blue bruise looked almost like a terrible flower on his chest. Zelda decided not to tell him that as she touched the tender skin. She highly doubted he would appreciate the comparison.

"He got you good, didn't he?"

"Fucker got me worse when I got up and you weren't there."

Zelda stopped tapping cream onto his skin. She looked at him, then set aside the jar. "I promise, he didn't hurt me."

Victor didn't say anything, but his eyes darting down to the bandage wrapped around her arm was answer enough.

"I promise, this was just from some nobody. I told you not many people in that pack liked me."

"No kidding."

They were back in Zelda's bedroom. They didn't go back to the hotel. She'd wanted to come home, to have the scents and smells of family around her, even if Mike and Link didn't know she was here.

Zelda wasn't sure when she would tell them what happened. When

219

she did, she figured it might best to keep some details all to herself. They were going to find out soon enough that Zelda had come home with Victor anyway. It was just a matter of time before someone sent Mike a text, and then he'd call Zelda in return.

"I'm sorry I made you worry."

"It wasn't you that did it."

She smiled. "If it makes you feel any better at all, the person who did this to me," she lifted her arm, "I punched her right in the throat."

Victor didn't laugh out loud like she was hoping he would, but he did smile at her.

"You're really upset, aren't you?"

He nodded. "It shouldn't have come to that in the first place. I should've been able to keep you away from him."

Zelda opened her mouth, then shut it again. She didn't think reminding Victor that he was a subhuman going up against an alpha would do much of anything for his bruised ego.

She lifted his hands, pressing her lips to his knuckles instead. "I'm just glad you came."

Victor's eyes weren't hugely wide, but it was definitely the look within them, the way he inhaled deeply through his nose, that let Zelda know what else was coming.

"Fuck, come here." He grabbed her by the back of her head, yanking her forward, their mouths finding each other in a hard, bruising kiss.

Zelda felt the need of her mate as Victor held her in a bruising grip.

It wasn't just him who needed it. She needed it, too.

Much as Zelda wanted to be careful with Victor's body after what happened to him, she could hardly help it if he decided to grab her and yank her into his lap. She could hardly manage to keep a distance between their chests, and soon, she stopped trying.

The sensation of her fingers threaded through his hair, gripping tight, seemed so much more important.

It was still weird, thinking that this wasn't going to end in a nice, tidy little bow. There were some things Ben hadn't been saying. He'd clamped up when he realized that Zelda's input wasn't going to do much to help him. Victor suspected he had more to do with Maxwell's death than he was letting on, and even if he didn't, murdering Gerard, regardless of why he'd done it, was going to guarantee him some time.

It was over, but there wasn't going to be a whole lot of closure for Zelda. Not for a long time, she suspected.

By why get hung up on that when there was something more important to be handling right now?

With Victor's shirt already off, it gave her the opportunity to touch his chest, to let her fingers slide over the mounds of his perfectly sculpted abdomen, and to gingerly touch and kiss the bruise he'd received because of her.

For her.

"Baby, I need you."

Zelda nodded, warmed by that. "I know."

She pulled back, grabbed at the hem of her shirt, and lifted it over her head. She let it drop. Now she was sitting in his lap with only her bra between her breasts and his hands.

"You should hurry, before Mike and Link come home."

Victor's hand pushed through the hair on the back of her head. He had a look in his eyes that was unlike anything Zelda had ever seen on anyone. No one had ever looked at her quite like that before.

"I don't ever want to hurry with you. Not for the rest of my damned life."

Zelda's breath caught at the meaning behind those words, and she had to kiss him again.

Yeah. For the rest of their lives.

THE END

MANDY ROSKO

CHAPTER 1

*I*f Steve Delany didn't get the hell out of this hospital in the next two minutes, he might have his first crazy wolf-induced casualty on his hands.

Blood. Not the kind that came from a scalpel either.

Well, his claws might be sharp enough that there wasn't much of a difference, but the clean instruments the doctors in this hospital used wouldn't be quite the same as anything that popped out from beneath his fingernails.

And Steve's fingers itched.

He bounced in his hospital bed practically enough that it vibrated around him. "Come on. Come on." He was good to go. He just had to wait for whatever the hell it was that needed to get done. Some official shit that would cost him money, but he had to keep it together.

Being excited to get the hell out of the hospital, a place he definitely didn't want to be, and *needing* to get out because he thought he would lose what little control he had over this new thing that was inside him, were two entirely different things.

His clothes were back on, shoes laced, jacket around his shoulders, wallet and other odds and ends in place.

Now he just had to wait.

Wait.

Steve clenched his hands into fists on his knees and shut his eyes.

He could damn well hear and smell almost *everything.*

Every squeaking footstep from a kid's sneakers along the tiled floor. The sound of a single baby crying somewhere that someone needed to take care of in a hurry, but no one seemed to be getting to. The rattle and hum of the air conditioning drove him insane, and then there was the doctor who had to click his damned pen four times, every time, before he signed anything.

The smells were worse. So much worse. Despite what people claimed, he could make out more than the bleach and cleaner fluid along the walls and in the sheets. The only reason why Steve didn't open his mouth was because he didn't want to *eat* whatever it was that was in the air.

The creature that had taken up residence on the inside of his head whined and circled. It scratched at the underside of his skull, desperate to get out.

No one knew. Not the staff in the hospital. Not even Victor. If they knew he was barely keeping a leash on this thing, they might keep him longer. Worse, put him in a locked room until he had a better handle on it.

He didn't care about the rules. He was getting out of here today. No more waiting.

But, fuck, why was it that in the minutes before he was going to be discharged and finally allowed to get out of here, that the damned animal suddenly developed sharper claws? The headache was starting to kill.

Someone vomited not too long ago in the bathroom. He was pretty sure they had made it to the toilet because Steve also heard the toilet flushing.

Wonderful. The acidic scent clung to the air, blending in with the scent of lavender air freshener, giving him a strange blend of floral smelling puke every time someone opened the door.

He knew where that bathroom was. It was all the way down the hall. Should have been far out of reach of his nose, but apparently it was part and parcel of being a shifter.

Steve didn't much blame the creatures who had done this to him anymore. His attack seemed a little more reasonable now that he knew what it was like to have to live with this kind of suffering.

He *itched*. He couldn't even explain why. It was nothing he could scratch. His wounds were gone. Mostly. All that was left of the slashes left behind by wolf teeth and filthy claws were the faintest of red marks along his arms and legs.

The doctors had said he was lucky. They'd said there was no permanent damage, that not all wolf shifters healed, especially not the new ones.

Steve had only been attacked and shredded five days ago. It was two days ago when he'd felt ready to get the hell out of here. He suspected the staff only kept him for this long because they weren't used to this sort of recovery time and didn't want to risk getting sued if something happened to go wrong.

Of course, Steve wouldn't have minded it if he got to see *her* a couple more times.

Even in scrubs and with those tired eyes, she was the most gorgeous woman he'd ever met.

He imagined he hadn't looked so great the first time she'd seen him. All covered in blood and all, but he was right as rain fairly quickly. Quick enough to notice the slight widening of her eyes when she saw him sitting up in bed on day two of his stay.

Her scent. God, *her scent*. The only good thing he smelled about this place.

She smelled like oranges. Nothing perfume-y either. He was pretty sure that wasn't allowed in a hospital. No, this was natural. Made him think she liked to eat them, maybe kept a basket of them in her kitchen somewhere.

He liked the scent. It worked well with her, and he'd enjoyed watching her cheeks darken as he flirted shamelessly with her.

Then asked for her number.

Then dreamed about her face. What she would look like with her hair down...

The creature inside his head seemed to like that.

Steve just wished he'd gotten her name.

Victor accused the medication of making him overly confident, like an asshole. Uh, no. Steve was just amazing, knew what he wanted, and wasn't afraid to ask for it.

Of course, she hadn't come around since then. It had been a male nurse after that, which made him think he'd either come on too hard when he'd called her gorgeous, or she was strictly a no flirting with patients sort of person.

Fair enough, all the more reason for him to want to get discharged as fast as possible. As soon as he got out of here, he wouldn't be a patient, he wouldn't have to smell that horrible scent that clung to this place. He'd get a new phone since his cracked to shit after the attack, and then he could find the sons of bitches who did this to him.

He had shit to do.

Finally, Steve heard soft footsteps heading his way. His spine instinctively stiffened. The jittering in his legs worsened.

This was it. This had to be it! He wasn't going to walk by again, he wasn't!

He didn't. The male nurse stopped in his doorway, clipboard in hand and professional, tired smile on his face.

"Mr. Delany?"

As if he needed to ask. Steve was already on his feet, trying not to give off the impression that he'd been waiting for this for the last ten thousand years. "That's me. All set. Ready to go."

"Do you need any time to—"

"Nope. Going." He pushed passed the nurse, power walking to get out of here. He'd come back and ask about that nurse when his head wasn't getting ready to explode. When he wasn't sweating over the idea of attacking someone.

He wanted to save that instinct for the shit heads that deserved it.

He headed to the front desk. Steve already knew where it was. He was glad Victor wasn't there to meet him. The man was an awesome friend and he'd offered to pick Steve up, but no. Steve wasn't in the mood for his friend falling all over himself to give Steve the royal treatment after what happened.

Steve was going to make the man repay him in beers, not in guilt favors.

He signed away his life, not looking forward to when his insurance company would call him to reveal they didn't cover werewolf attacks, even though his policy specifically stated that it did.

Fun stuff.

Time to get the hell—

Stop. Oranges. He smelled the oranges again.

She was close. Where was she? Steve turned his head this way and that, searching out the woman he needed most in the entire world, straining his ears for the potential sound of her voice.

"Is everything all right?"

"Yeah, great." Steve waved off the nurse. It wasn't him Steve was interested in, though the guy was nice to look at.

There was one person he was interested, however, and she was…

Finally. She rounded the corner, head down in some papers, pink scrubs on with little bright yellow flowers on it that honestly looked amazing on her.

She walked right up to the front desk, rubbing her forehead, not noticing Steve standing there at all.

"Hey, Denise, those for me?"

Denise. That was her name. He finally had it.

"Yeah," she replied, handing over the papers.

Steve's stupid heart started to pound. He should probably blink. Or look away. Something to show he wasn't a complete creep, but he couldn't.

She noticed. To be fair, how could she not notice when his laser beam was drilling a hole into the middle of her head?

She slowly turned her head, and when her eyes were on him, Steve suddenly moved, turning about face in a nervous rush. Totally not a natural movement, but fuck. He'd just been caught staring at the woman who had been avoiding him, and it was her job to care for the patients here.

He had to go. The thing inside him was whining again, growling, making claws marks on the inside of his cranium as if it had been buried alive and was trying desperately to get the hell out.

He couldn't go yet!

Steve turned again, smiling, ready to say anything.

Except of course she wasn't looking at him anymore. She was speaking with the receptionist.

He turned to go for the door.

Don't leave!

He turned again, then immediately moved to the wall where a painting hung, pretending to be interested in it.

What the fuck was wrong with him? He knew he wasn't a weirdo. He could see someone he wanted standing right there, and so what if she rejected him? Sure, it didn't happen all that often, and it had never devastated him on those few occasions.

Was it because she'd already basically told him to fuck off by ignoring him? By not coming around? All right, fine. That still shouldn't make this so hard.

She looked his way! He could see it in the quick glance to and away from him. As though she didn't want him to be aware she'd snuck a peek.

She could sneak as many peeks at him as she wanted.

"Will you give me one second?" she said. The woman at the front desk nodded, and Steve felt something clench uncomfortably within him when Denise approached.

He hadn't felt this kind of fear since those wolves surrounded him and started turning him into shredded pork with their claws. Now he knew what it was like to be one of those guys who got turned down a lot, and he suddenly sympathized with them a lot more.

Then Denise was standing in front of him, and as she smiled, all that clenching in his gut melted away to nothing. "Hey there."

He smiled back. "Hi."

"Are you waiting for me?"

"Kind of." He scratched at the back of his head, feeling stupid and wishing he'd had the chance to trim his beard. Steve knew he looked all right, but unless Denise was into the scruffy types, now was probably not the greatest time to be trying to catch a date.

"I was just hoping to catch you alone for a bit. I haven't seen you in a couple of days."

"There were other patients."

Words like that were meant to let a man down gently, but it was the way she smiled, and the spark in her dark eyes, that told him, maybe, she liked knowing Steve had been looking forward to seeing her.

"Makes sense. You're a nurse, I bet you're busy. Don't want to get distracted from work."

"Or have patients hitting on me."

Shit.

"No matter how cute they are."

Now they were getting somewhere.

"Great, well, since I'm not a patient anymore, officially released from prison today and everything, I was thinking at some point I could come by and pick you up for dinner? Or just coffee."

He would be totally all right with just a coffee with her.

That smile on her mouth melted a little. "I also don't date werewolves. It's nothing personal."

CHAPTER 2

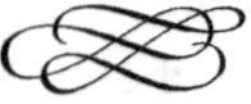

*H*e hid it well. The disappointment. It flickered, clearly there, but then it was gone, as though her words hadn't affected him at all.

"Right, well, I might not be a wolf either. I haven't shifted yet."

She smirked a little. "You had grey fur coming out of your torn up flesh even the day you were brought in. If you're unsure about your shifter status, there's a few numbers I can give you." Denise turned back to the front desk, aware that Steven Delany, the patient, followed the five feet over there.

"Well, to be fair, I could just be a squirrel. Or a rabbit. Recessive shifter genes. That wouldn't be so scary now, would it?"

Denise clamped her lips together. She could hold back a laugh, but not a smile. If there was here was one thing she did enjoy about persistent guys, it was when they turned funny for her attention.

Not that she'd had much of that in recent years.

Of course, the rabbit remark might not be so far off. All guys were horny little rabbits when it came down to it, and this guy definitely wanted her.

And he was cute. And well-built. Denise had seen what he'd looked like, cut up and bloody, as well as on the mend with his shirt open. He could be a model with an abdomen like that. It was the sort of chest she didn't get to appreciate enough of in real life, and he wanted her.

Could there really be much harm in just letting him take what he wanted? She would get what she wanted out of it as well, then she could get her focus back on work.

Ever since she'd seen Steven's chest, only on the second day he was here, mostly healed and so utterly good looking... It was a distraction she didn't need in the work place. That was why she'd asked Greg to take over for her with Delany.

She grabbed the pamphlets. There were a lot of them. They yellowed slightly with age. Despite the shifter population around here, there weren't too many incidents like Delany's, and for those rare occasions, the patients were often too stubborn to take the material, so it didn't need replacing all that often.

Delany, it seemed, was going to be one of those stubborn men. He took the pamphlets, but he didn't look at them. He kept looking at her. Looking into her eyes, as though seeing something within her that made her whole body sound an alarm and put her on high alert. Not the bad kind of high alert either. Not the kind that came with prepping patients for being airlifted out for special care.

This was almost winning the lottery kind of alert.

What was this?

"One dinner date. I'll have you home by ten p.m. and everything."

"You'll be a perfect gentleman, will you?"

Greg called for her from down the hall. "Denise, can I get your help with something?"

She glanced back at him, then at the handsome wolf shifter in front of her who had just enough confidence to be cute about it, and maybe not enough sense.

"Perfect gentleman." He bounced from heel to toe, already aware he was getting what he wanted.

Because of course Denise needed to give it to him. He didn't need to know that she needed something from him, however. She could handle herself now. She wasn't fourteen anymore, and if he did try anything, she would be ready.

Though, from the look in his eyes, Denise was pretty sure he was going to be good on his promise.

Which meant she would have to make him break it when she was ready for it.

"All right. You can pick out the restaurant. I'm good with anything. I'll meet you there tomorrow night."

"I can pick you up."

Denise shook her head. "Not happening. I'll meet you there."

"Denise?"

"Almost done," she called. "I need to get back to work."

"Right. I'll see you tomorrow."

He turned to go so fast with that dumb smile on his face that Denise had to reach out and grab him by the sleeve of his jacket to yank him back.

Mistake. Huge mistake. She meant to grab only at his sleeve, but because the universe hated her, Denise's fingers clamped around his hand instead. The skin to skin contact was heated to the point of discomfort. A bolt of lightning shot through her hand, up her arm, and into Denise's chest. That feeling rushed lower. She yanked her hand away from Steven's before it had the chance to make it to its target.

She stared at him. "What was that?"

He blinked, his hand still stretched out as though she was holding onto it, as though he was waiting for something from her.

"What was...what?"

No way. He felt that, too. He had to have.

Some sort of shifter power? The shifter community, the wolves in particular, were said to be incredibly sexual, their instincts driving them to find their mates, to procreate and have as many children as possible. Hell, it was mostly the wolves that came in and depleted the free condoms that were donated and supplied to the residents of this town.

And yet Steven looked at her as though he didn't entirely understand what had just happened. His cheeks darkened, his long lashes coming to rest at half mast, and his nostrils flared.

Oh yes. He knew what was up.

"Denise!"

Greg was fast losing his patience.

And Denise made up her mind.

"Give me your hand."

He did as she commanded, holding it out for her.

Denise took her spare pen from her pocket and wrote her number onto his palm. That tingling shock of pleasure returned, but at least now that she was prepared for it, she could handle it. "This is my number. You're going to need it if you want to tell me where we're going to dinner."

He nodded. Denise noted the way his Adam's apple worked in a hard swallow.

"Right. Definitely. I guess I need that."

She put away her pen. "Yes, you do." Denise eyed him from top to bottom. How a man like this could still be single, she didn't understand that. All the better for her. At least now she could work at erasing her fear of the wolves. Jumping into bed with one would certainly help with that.

"I guess I won't be ditching you after all."

Steven blinked just as she turned away from him, getting back to work.

"Wait! You were going to ditch me?"

She didn't look back at him. Best if he couldn't see the little smirk on her face.

If she was going to break her no shifter rule for a little sex, then at least she could say the man she was going to do it with was a looker.

THAT THING INSIDE HIS HEAD, which Steve was more that sure was not a squirrel, sighed. It circled, relaxed, and settled.

He could breathe again, but only because he was busy staring at the direction his hot nurse fantasy just walked off in like a hound dog. This was going to be awesome. He had her number on his hand. On his hand. As though they were kids or something. He felt the need to announce to the world that he was never going to wash his hand again, but that was a little too juvenile for his tastes.

Okay, the receptionist and the security guard were giving him funny little smirky looks. He had about another five seconds before those looks became suspicious.

Time to go.

He was glad to not find Victor out in the parking lot. Steve breathed a heavy sigh. At least his friend was able to respect him enough to not want to baby him with a ride—

The black Toyota Avalon his friend drove pulled up to the curb in front of the hospital with the kind of speed that almost made Steve want to jump out of the way before he could get killed.

Because getting killed before his hot date would piss him off.

Victor rolled down the window, revealing his face, because of fucking course it was him. Steve growled, wanting to punch that dumb little smile right off his stupid face. "I told you I didn't want a ride."

Victor put the car in park. "You've got no phone, no ride, and we're not exactly in familiar territory, so shut up."

The word *territory* was enough to make Steve pause. Did Victor mean that because Steve was now a shifter? Or was he just making an honest observation?

Because it was true. Steve would have had to do a lot of walking to the nearest store if Victor didn't come to get him.

"Don't you have a mate to take care of?"

Victor grinned the biggest, stupidest, proudest grin Steve had ever seen on the man. It was unnerving.

"Yeah. She told me she'd kick my ass if I didn't come and get you."

"And since you know she can't, why did you bother?"

Victor shrugged. "It'll make her happy, and honestly, I was feeling kind of guilty about the idea of leaving you to walk."

"I told you—"

"Yeah, yeah, who cares already. Get in the car."

Steve pressed his lips together. Normally, something like this wouldn't have bothered him. He would have maybe punched Victor in the arm or put him in a choke hold at the next possible moment, but there was something about being told what he was and was not going to accept that didn't sit well with him.

The creature inside his head, the one that had settled down to something more peaceful when he'd smelled those oranges inside, heard Denise's name, and got her number, growled a low, warning rumble in his ear.

Worse than that, it was Victor's scent that didn't seem to be helping him with this.

He'd always known Victor was a subhuman. Born to shifters but unable to transform. He was basically a defect, not entirely cast out by the pack, but not respected by them either. It had never bothered Steve before. He hadn't cared. Hadn't noticed.

Now that he could, the idea of being challenged by someone like him seemed so repugnant.

So insulting.

It made him want to fight.

Steve shook his head. "Victor."

Victor sobered, then looked him dead in the eyes. "I am not challenging you. I want to offer you my services and take you wherever you need to go. This is my offer to you."

Steve swallowed hard.

Okay, that helped, a little, but even if Victor didn't entirely mean it, that didn't mean Steve enjoyed making his friend bow and scrape like that.

At least he was able to get into the car.

The engine hummed as Victor drove them out of there.

His car wasn't anything overly impressive. Neither was Steve's, before it got trashed in his attack. With their line of work, it was for the best to keep fairly standard issue vehicles. Made it harder for people to notice when they were being followed.

Though, now that Steve was in the passenger seat, even this wasn't enough, he found. He wanted to be in the driver's seat. He wanted the control. He wanted to be in command of the road. Sitting here like this made him feel like he was a kid again, getting driven home by his old man after a school suspension.

The stupid animal growled again.

"Where would you like me to take you?"

Steve looked the man over. He should tell him there was nowhere he needed to go and nothing he needed. Steve didn't want his help, but fuck, he was going to need that phone if he had any chance of getting anywhere with his sexy nurse.

Denise. He was going to have to look up the meaning of that name. There were always meanings to names.

"I need a phone. Are there any Best Buys in a town like this?"

Lake View was barely a town and more of a stretch of highway between the towns. The only reason there was anything around here at all was the fishing and hiking that occurred in these parts.

"I'm sure I can find you something. I've found a butcher shop that sells deer steaks."

Steve's mouth watered immediately. The last time he'd eaten deer was over four years ago, and he could remember not liking it in the least. Now that it was merely mentioned, he wanted it enough to almost grab the steering wheel, risk the both of them getting into a life-ending accident of the fiery and explosive kind, just to make Victor hurry the hell up and take him to where that delicious meat was waiting for him.

Steve swallowed hard and held back on that impulse instead. "You don't say?"

Victor nodded. "I imagine hospital food hasn't been cutting it for you lately."

"To put it mildly."

Maybe it was because Victor was a subhuman that he understood what Steve needed. Maybe that was why he noticed these changes and went out of his way to not issue any unwanted challenges, and knew to offer some sort of meat product to get Steve turning into putty in his hands.

God, anything to get that food. "I don't even like deer."

"I think he sold moose meat, too."

Even better because, holy shit, Steve loved moose meat.

"Both sound amazing. Christ, is this supposed to be normal?"

He looked at his friend. Victor shrugged, and whatever he was about to say was cut off as Steve suddenly felt a ten ton weight yank against his chest, pulling him forward and into his seatbelt. It still seemed as though his head had come inches from smashing into the glass windshield.

He fell back against his seat, the smell of burning tires assaulting his nose when the car finally screeched to a halt.

And he was pissed.

"Jesus Christ, Vic! What the hell are you—"

He stopped talking. The intensity in Victor's eyes as the man stared ahead was one look Steve knew all too well.

He looked out the windshield, and there, right in the middle of the two-lane highway, were three grey wolves.

CHAPTER 3

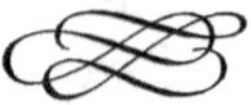

Just as a semi rounded the corner down the road, the three darted off the street and into the trees.

Motherfuckers.

Steve yanked himself out of his seat.

"Steve, wait!"

He couldn't wait. He needed to go after them. He needed to fight them!

Steve practically flew across the road. The horn of the transport truck blared, and he felt the force of it pull against his clothes and body as he just barely managed to stop himself from getting caught into its path or sucked back beneath those massive tires.

Had he been able to give a shit about anything other than catching up to those wolves, he might have had an enormous adrenaline rush from the second near death experience in a day, and the third in less than two weeks.

Didn't matter. Nothing mattered. Find the wolves. Find them and make them submit. Catch them, dominate them, overpower them. That was his only mission.

He could smell them. He could smell them, but he wasn't used to the outside. Steve tried to follow their scents, but he couldn't figure out how. Everything blended in with everything else and he couldn't pick out the scents around him.

Trees. Berries, rodents, snakes, bugs, shit, moss, wood rot, poison ivy. Everything mixed and combined in ways he didn't think was possible. He'd spent a couple of days in the hospital and managed to pick everything out and had learned to figure out where everything was, what they were, and he was pretty sure he would know how to find them if he needed to look.

He was sure he could pick out the scent of oranges in a field of death at this point.

Not so good as he'd thought he was, because fuck, he couldn't find them. He couldn't find them!

Did they split up? Had they done their separate ways to fuck with him?

Steve stopped trying to use his nose to pick out where they had gone. He used his eyes, tried to pick out the sounds of their paws with his ears, but that made it so much worse. The colors began to blend in with each other the same way the smells did. He couldn't see. He could hardly breathe. They were surrounding him. They were coming for him, and he couldn't fucking see where they were!

"Steve!"

Something jumped onto his shoulder. Steve swung.

Victor's face barely got out of the way of the force of Steve's fist.

But it was the way Vic grabbed onto his wrist that made Steve lose his damned mind.

He attacked. He couldn't stop. He barely felt himself doing it, as though he wasn't the one doing it. As though he wasn't in the driver's seat anymore.

Stop. Stop. Stop.

Victor ducked out of the way. He didn't throw any punches back, and the swift way he avoided Steve's rage, oddly enough, made his rage all the worse. He wanted to kill the man. He wanted his best friend to die!

Steve howled. He howled and ran into the nearest birch tree. Purposely. If he couldn't catch his best friend then he would go after one of the closest living things he could that was unable to move out of the way.

Except he didn't attack it. He let himself run into it, smacking his head. White spots exploded across his eyes. Steve fell back, onto his ass, then he got up and did it again.

And again.

Until his head spun so hard that the thing controlling him felt such pain that it was better to retreat than to keep being a prissy little bitch looking for a fight.

Steve panted for breath, his lungs burning more than he thought they were just a minute ago. He held onto that birch tree now just for something to center him. He wasn't interested in smashing his own face in anymore. He just needed to breathe.

His hands. Christ. Steve looked at them, turning his hands from side to side to get a look at the change.

His knuckles were thicker, darker with splotches of fur. What were once his fingernails appeared to be small half-hooks.

They didn't appear to be anything that could do a lot of damage, but he'd been going after his best friend with this shit.

Even as those claws sank back beneath his real fingernails, his hands becoming normal again, he still couldn't stop staring at them.

Victor came to stand next to him, though the man was careful to keep his shadow from falling across Steve's body. He didn't touch Steve either, not that Steve expected him to.

Christ, if Victor tried touching his shoulder then Steve would know he'd really fucked up.

"You good?"

Steve nodded. "Yeah." He looked up at the man, searching for blood with his eyes even though he couldn't smell any. It was a small miracle he hadn't made himself bleed.

"You?"

Victor nodded. "Fine. Did you recognize those wolves? I guess they weren't wild if you went chasing them like that."

Steve shook his head. He pulled himself to his feet. The fact that he couldn't hunt those fucks down hurt more than his head right now.

"They were there. The night I got jumped."

Victor raised a brow at him. "How can you tell?"

"It was obvious."

"Obvious?"

Steve shook his head. "I don't know. I can just tell. I could look at them and see it."

"They all looked the same to me. Every damn shifter I ever lived with or met can tell each other apart like that and I can't figure out how."

That was something Steve never thought of.

Vic was a subhuman, he had some of the instincts, and he was stronger than a normal human male, but it wasn't just the shifting he was stuck without.

Not that Steve had ever been able to fully understand it either, the ability the shifters had to distinguish between each other, but now that Steve apparently had this ability, he couldn't understand how Victor didn't realize who was who.

"Do you know what they look like as humans?"

Steve clenched his jaw. The itch beneath his fingernails returned.

"No. I don't know who any of them are as humans."

And what a bitch that was.

"We should get out of here. I can call up detective Grey, let him know what's happening?"

Steve groaned. "That kid?"

"We need all the help we can get. Come on. You still need a phone and I don't want those mutts coming back our way."

Assuming they weren't watching right now. Steve didn't think they were. He wasn't catching any sounds or scents that would indicate it, but there was so much he had yet to learn about being a shifter and what he could do.

The bastards could be out there watching him right now, hiding their scents from him, as quiet as possible so he wouldn't be aware of them.

He hated that. He hated this entire thing, and what little patience he knew he had seemed to slip through his fingers.

Steve had to take in a deep breath. He closed his eyes, and immediately saw Denise's face.

"I also don't date werewolves. It's nothing personal."

He opened his eyes. Something within him snapped. Or maybe it wasn't a snap so much as it was a light that had switched on.

Christ. If he could barely control himself around his friend, his partner, then how was he supposed to earn her trust?

"What's going on?"

Steve shook his head. "I'll tell you later. Yeah, give that detective a call. Let's get out of here."

They started walking. Steve could tell when Victor was keeping half an ear open, his eyes diligently scanning the woods for signs of attack.

Steve was doing the same thing.

"I know you're thinking about something."

Steve shook his head. "It doesn't have to do with those wolves. I'll tell you when we get to the car."

If the shifters could hear half as well as Steve could, then he didn't want to drop Denise's name and remind his friend of that sexy nurse Steve had been eyeing the last time Vic and Zelda came for a visit.

Victor had parked on the side of the road before chasing after Steve. He unlocked the car and they both entered quickly. Victor started driving again, as though they would be any safer when they made it on the road.

"So, what was the problem?"

Steve rubbed at his mouth. "I was thinking that I'm going to need to learn to control this if I plan on having anything close to a normal life."

Victor's throat went tight; otherwise, there was no reaction out of him at all. "Don't worry about it. I understand."

"It's not you. It's for someone else."

"Well, fuck you too."

"I'm serious. Remember that nurse?"

"The nurse? The one you wouldn't shut up about?"

He hadn't been talking about her that much. "Possibly. I've got her number. I'm going to take her out tomorrow."

Victor raised a brow. "You got yourself a date?"

"I do. Don't sound too shocked by that or anything."

Victor wasn't giving in. "And you don't think you might have some better shit to deal with right now?"

Hearing Victor describe Denise like that, as though she wasn't good enough for Steve to pay much attention to, was enough to make a slight growl work its way up his throat. Even as he knew it was illogical, and that Victor was right. He couldn't help himself.

Victor didn't take his eyes off the road, but Steve knew he'd heard that warning sound.

Being a subhuman in a pack of wolves would also ensure Victor took that warning seriously.

"Is this really important? Can you cancel on her?"

Steve thought on that. The answer was yes. He could cancel on her.

He *should* cancel on her. How fucked up was it that he was still figuring out this thing inside him and he couldn't be bothered to end his date?

It would make him a colossal dickhead if he didn't. He needed to. It was the responsible thing to do.

"So?"

Steve shook his head, hating himself a little. "Don't think so, no."

Victor grunted. "You positive about that? We just got a warning from a couple of the wolves that fucked you up."

Steve clenched his hands to fists. "They won't be a problem. I'm just going to dinner. I can ask her about my new condition," he said when Vic raised a brow at him. He needed some sort of explanation to make this seem a little less selfish.

A little.

And Victor wouldn't stop looking between him and the road and back again.

Steve felt the nonexistent hackles on the back of his neck and spine stand up. "What?"

Victor shook his head. "Nothing. I can hardly judge you after what I got up to with Zelda."

"Zelda is your mate."

"All the same, she was still a client. You seem pretty excited about this woman."

Steve got warm just thinking about Denise's face. "Yeah." He blinked. "Wait, you're not thinking she might be…?" Steve's gut clenched. His heart slammed against his ribs and just behind his ears.

Was that possible? How could it be possible? He didn't know this woman. Well, shifters said all the time about how they could just take one look, get one *smell* out of the man or woman they were meant to be with and *know*. But he didn't know anything. He just really liked this woman. He liked her smell, and she made the thing inside his head calm. It drove the stupid animal damn near crazy when she stopped coming around to check his chart and take his blood pressure.

That didn't necessarily mean anything.

"I don't know what I'm saying. You're new to this. I'll ask Zelda what she knows about how this works. She seemed to know fairly soon what I was to her."

"Okay, and did you know it, too?"

Victor glanced at him. Steve glared back.

This was already fucked up enough. He was talking about how his best friend felt about the woman he'd been in lust with during an ongoing stalking turned murder investigation.

Awkward didn't begin to describe it.

Victor clenched his jaw. "I knew enough to know that, the first time I saw her, nothing was ever going to be the same."

That uncomfortable clenching returned to Steve's stomach. This time it was more of a gut punch.

Because that was the exact thing he'd thought the first time he'd seen Denise, even in a medically induced haze with blood all over him.

Shit.

CHAPTER 4

$\mathcal{D}$enise wished she had the sort of sense that would require her to pick up her phone and text Steven back, telling him she had to bail, something came up.

She was a nurse, and the way he spoke let her know he respected the profession and knew the sort of time that came with the job. Not everyone was aware of the commitment that came with her job, or was patient enough to wait around.

She lifted another outfit, studying herself in the mirror before rolling her eyes and tossing the hangers onto her bed. For some damn reason, everything she owned seemed to hate her today. Denise had a nice collection of good clothes she loved but didn't often get to wear. Now that the chance had arrived, she wanted to scream.

All her shoes were either too loud, too plain, the heels too high or non- existent. Her clothes were either too revealing, too flashy, too conservative, or not conservative enough.

When the hell did she think she was ever going to wear that green dress out in public? Did she think she was going to the Oscars with that thing or what? The cleavage went almost down to her bellybutton.

She should text him. He seemed nice enough. He would understand, and the best part about it was that, if she texted him, she wouldn't have to awkwardly explain using her actual voice why she couldn't make it.

Lying was easier over text.

Denise didn't want to lie. She wanted to go out with a hot guy and, for once, feel like she was...normal?

She touched her chest, rubbed that spot, shook away the dark thoughts that rushed her.

She'd just turned thirty-three, and the last time she'd been on a good date was years ago. She needed to get laid and she wanted to have a good time.

And if she was honest, it was flattering having a gorgeous man stare at her like she was desirable. Very few people did that when she was constantly tired, overworked, and wearing her scrubs that left almost everything to the imagination.

Her phone buzzed. That would be him. Confirming the time and place he'd set up.

Steven had asked if she was sure she didn't want a ride to the restaurant.

No, thank you. She could drive herself.

And if this turned out to be a disaster, he wouldn't know where she lived.

If he couldn't control whatever thing was inside him.

He could control it. It wasn't all shifters. Denise sucked back a breath and rolled her shoulders.

It was a long time ago. Things like that didn't just happen, and Steven had spent days in the hospital with nothing out of the ordinary other than a heavy craving for meat.

Denise pulled another dress to her body, covering the scarring. A simple white piece with what could almost be an animal pattern. She didn't know what it was, but she liked it. The straps weren't too thin, and when she tried it on, Denise remembered why she'd bought it.

She looked good in it. It managed to be tight without being constricting. Stretchy material was amazing.

Denise turned to the side, sliding her hands down the smooth material before she checked out her back.

Her breasts weren't too obvious, and it showed off a nice amount of her shoulder blades without dipping too low, so she wouldn't have to worry about getting cold.

With her hair down, and just a touch of eyeliner and lip gloss...

She could have a good time tonight. Even if it wasn't the dinner part of the date she was looking forward to the most, looking like this was already a confidence boost.

She grinned to herself, changed out of her cotton undies for something much sexier and lacier, then did the same with her bra before adjusting the straps again.

She grabbed for her phone.

If Steven liked looking at her when she was at work, then she couldn't wait to see the look on his face when she showed this off.

Now she just needed a good pair of shoes. That was a little harder.

It was years of working in the hospital that ingrained into Denise the need to be on time.

She drove herself to the restaurant Steven wanted to take her to.

Even with the tourists, hikers, hunters, and fishermen, there wasn't much to choose from in Lakeview. Big enough to be its own space, but small enough to barely justify the things it did have.

There was, however, a Keg restaurant on the water of one of the larger lakes in the area. She didn't often come here. It was a little too expensive for her, but not so far out of left field that she couldn't enjoy a birthday dinner here with her friends or family.

It was a *once in a while* kind of restaurant. The food was good, and she'd been pleased with Steven's choice.

And there was a small hotel a short drive down the lake where she could take him after their meal.

It was roughly a twenty minute drive to the restaurant, but by the time she arrived, it was getting difficult for her to find parking. Until she realized Steven was in the parking lot. She wasn't sure how he knew it was her in this car. Was it because he was trying to get a glimpse of everyone driving by, or was it something to do with being a shifter?

As if he could sense her.

No. Not going to think about that; besides, he was so cute when he smiled and waved her over.

She pulled up, rolling down her window.

"Hey." He leaned down, putting his arms on her door.

Then she got it—that thing Denise had wanted as she frantically picked out her clothes for her date, did her hair and makeup. The sudden bright look in his eyes was exactly what she'd been hoping to see. The exact reaction she'd wanted from him. It was right there. He was impressed.

Steven recovered quickly, though it almost looked as though his face was darkening beneath his beard stubble.

"There's a spot for you over here. Follow me."

Steven darted off before she could get a word out. She followed, driving slowly, desperately trying to pay attention to her speed so she didn't run him over, but...

God, his butt looked good when he ran. Those jeans on him looked good.

Down, girl. She would get what she needed in short order. There was no need to turn into a horn ball over this.

Except he was so cute. Why did he have to be so damned...sexy?

Because that's what he was. Not cute, not handsome. He was sexy.

Well, that was what she'd come here for, after all.

Steven led her to a spot close to the front doors without getting into a handicapped space. What looked to be a waiter, in his black clothes and white apron, stood there. He seemed to recognize Steven as he stepped out of the way.

Steven shook the man's hand in clear thanks, but as Denise pulled up, she could make out perfectly well how something had just exchanged hands. She smirked a little at that. He really wanted to impress her if he wanted to create a reserved parking spot for her.

Did this restaurant even do things like that? She couldn't be sure, but Denise was fairly positive the answer was no.

She stepped out of her car, giving Steven a full view of herself. He gave her that look again, the one that said she'd done a very good thing by wearing this outfit. She tried not to smile, though there was the urge to bask in this glow.

She'd almost forgotten what it was like to feel desirable.

Meanwhile, it wasn't as though she was dressed to the nines. Minimal jewelry, enough makeup to highlight what she had instead of covering her face entirely, just like her mom taught her. Everything else she needed, including a couple of condoms, were in her clutch purse.

"You picked a good restaurant."

She walked up to him. He didn't move. He still looked at her, as though he wanted to take her right then and there, and God, she wanted to let him.

Screw dinner, she wanted to skip straight to dessert.

"You like what you see?"

Steven cleared his throat. "You look beautiful."

Was it just her, or did his throat sound a touch scratchy?

He moved his arm awkwardly, then pulled away from her and walked to the door. She followed, letting him open it for her. Was he trying to give her his arm to hold onto just there?

Did she really have this effect on him?

Oh yes, she was going to enjoy this.

This gorgeous man who oozed sexuality whenever he looked at her, whose eyes whispered into her ear how much he wanted to get her naked, was a bit of a boy scout.

She liked that. It wasn't a mix she would have thought would make sense. An alpha male type who made awkward moves and second-guessed himself before being a gentleman and opening the door for her? Okay, she could work with it.

Denise expected to have to wait ten minutes even with a reservation, but their table was already set for them. The hostess seemed to recognize Steven as he approached, called over another waiter, and then they were being brought to their table.

By the window with a view of the lake, and the sun dipping behind the trees. The colors were beautiful.

Steven pulled out her chair for her. The waiter immediately brought them waters to start, a bread basket, and a bottle of wine.

Denise couldn't believe it. She'd never received service like this when she'd come here.

"Do you come here a lot?"

"No. I just made the reservation."

She lifted a brow, smelling bull. "Did you?"

Steven shrugged, the grin on his face a guilty one. "I might've also given that hostess two hundred dollars."

Denise scoffed at that. "You did not!"

That stupid little smile didn't leave his mouth. Guilty, but not sorry.

"Wow."

"Are you mad? It doesn't mean anything."

"Two hundred dollars always means something."

Her boy scout was trying to get her in bed.

Not that she hadn't seen it coming, but still. "It's a good thing I brought condoms, in that case."

She expected him to snort water through his nose when he took a drink.

He didn't. Steven lowered his glass and looked her in the eyes.

That wanting was there again. Something urgent and heated, and he was directing it right at her. "I brought a couple of things, too."

Denise smiled behind her glass. "Did you? What would you have done if I just wanted a nice dinner and then went home?"

He shrugged. "I would have tossed you over my shoulder and made off with you. I'm pretty sure you kind of want me to do that anyway."

She couldn't tell if he was joking or not. That smile was hard to read at times, but the strange part was...

He was right. She wouldn't mind being carted off caveman-style to be made love to. He wouldn't have to force anything because she wanted it.

Denise leaned forward in her seat. She let her foot slide forward, pleased when his eyes widened ever so slightly as she played with his calf.

Those long lashes, too long and pretty, wasted on a man, slid down to half mast. "And what would you do with me when you got me alone, Steven?"

His grin showed off perfectly white teeth, and a hint of his canines. "Everything you wanted me to do, and everything you don't know you want me to do to you. I can tell you want me to take you right now, but I could hear your stomach rumbling earlier, so I figured I should feed you before fucking you."

Goosebumps flashed across her skin. That sounded good.

"And you can call me Steve."

"Oh? No one calls you Steven?"

"Clients do."

Denise nodded. "Right. You're a detective."

"Private detective. It's a bit different."

"I bet the ladies like it." She sure did.

And it was clear he knew it judging by the smile on his face.

Maybe she'd been wrong. All these years with her no shifter rules, and it turned out that a shifter was the most sensual, sexual man she'd ever sat across from.

It was possible this was because he wasn't a born shifter. He was a changed shifter. A man first and animal second. He might have all the best parts of being that sort of man, with few of the downsides.

Which didn't mean Denise wanted to lose this unnamed game they'd started playing. "Just so you're aware, when you're inside me, I will have protection other than those condoms, so you'd better make good on your promise, otherwise there will be hell to pay."

Something in his eyes changed, those dark browns almost becoming brighter in that moment.

It should have scared her. It didn't.

It excited her all the more.

CHAPTER 5

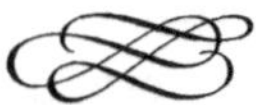

Steve was distracted on about ten thousand different levels, each of which wanted to pull him apart.

It might have been a death by a thousand cuts situation, only worse because, in this case, not only was he trying to pay attention to the vision in front of him, his date, his maybe mate, but he was trying to keep his ears peeled for any suspicious noises. He hoped to catch the scents of anything remotely animal, other than the food, so he could have a warning before an attack came.

And he wanted to drag Denise across the table and crush their mouths together. He couldn't stop looking at her lips.

Every time she spoke, they glistened in the light. She smiled perfectly, and even as she ate…God! He couldn't tell if she was pulling the fork out from between her lips in slow motion or if that was all him.

He was so screwed.

"You seem a little distracted."

"I do?"

She pointed her knife at his plate. "You barely touched your food. Don't you like it?"

He looked down. She was right. The perfectly cooked steak sitting

254

under his nose was going to get cold if he didn't do something about it.

Steve started cutting away at a healthy piece. "I guess I've been craving something other than meat lately."

Only after the words were out of his mouth did he realize how stupid that sounded.

She'd already told him they were going to fuck after this. He didn't need to keep going with the come-ons.

Luckily, Denise grinned, shaking her head. "You're lucky you're cute."

"Yeah," he said, gazing at his date across the table.

He really was lucky.

Something moved into his peripheral vision. A boat on the lake.

Which was what he'd thought until he had a look.

His spine immediately tensed, and the creature inside him growled inside his head at the sight of the wolf sitting on the other side of the glass. It was maybe thirty or forty feet away, but he could make out what it was as it sat in front of the trimmed shrubbery near the water's edge.

Steve would have thought the dark glass reflecting what little light there was left on the water would have made it impossible for the creature to see him.

Apparently not. He seemed to be looking right at him.

Staring directly through him.

Holy shit.

"What?" Denise looked out the window. She didn't seem to see the thing he was looking at; most likely, her gaze was on the water. "What are you looking at?"

"I thought I saw some ducks on the lake." The easy lie didn't sit so well with him, especially when Denise looked at him with a brow raised.

As though she knew he was full of shit.

Her smile faded, and she looked back out the window, searching for the real thing that had his attention.

"Wait."

The wolves were gone. Denise scanned the area, then looked back at him.

Steve could see already that there was no way he was going to make her forget about this and go back to having their nice dinner date.

"What was that?" Her eyes were suspicious, not wide with panic, but searching.

And what was he supposed to do? Tell her the wolves who did this to him were now following him around?"

Vic had been right. This was dumb as fuck.

Steve caught the waiter's eye and signaled him over.

"What are you doing?"

"I think now is a bad time. I'm going to pay for the meal and walk you to your car."

The waiter came. Steve told him to get the bill, had to insist that everything was all right with the meal and that he didn't need a refund on anything, and then the guy was gone.

Denise didn't look pleased. "If you're having an issue with the changes in your body—"

"It's not that."

He was pretty sure it wasn't that.

"It clearly is. Just keep your focus and breathe. If you can feel fur starting to slide through your pores, then focus on holding it back."

She really did think it was his own inner animal that was doing this. Even better, she was trying to help him.

No hint of judgement. Just cool and professional.

If he really was in the middle of having a shifter-style panic attack, then he could see how the sound of her voice, and the words she spoke, might bring him down from the edge.

Since it wasn't him he was worried about, only the wolves outside, he had to get her going.

Steve stood, pulling his phone out of his pocket and sending Victor a text. The man would be waiting for it.

"I promise this doesn't have anything to do with you, and I really am in control, but right now I need to get you home."

He couldn't wait for the bill anymore so he threw down a couple of bills on the table until he was pretty sure that covered it.

Steve stepped up to Denise's chair, held out his hand. "Please."

He couldn't see those wolves anymore, but he could definitely still sense them. He needed to get her out of here. He needed to find those fuckers and figure out what the hell it was they wanted.

Denise surveyed him for no more than a second before she took her clutch purse, and Steve's hand, and stood.

Despite the situation, Steve's chest released a load of tension he hadn't been aware he could carry.

If she hadn't taken his hand, well, that might've signified a fuck up he might not be able to walk back from.

Not that he was going to push his luck and ask for a rain check right now. Much as he wanted to.

Fuck.

He quickly brought Denise outside and to her car.

This was one of the reasons why he wanted a spot for her close to the door. He'd hoped nothing would happen, but if something did, which it apparently was, having her close to the front doors, and not parked all the way in the back where they could get jumped, seemed like the more intelligent option.

The better idea than even that would have been to not go out at all, but Steve's dick had been in charge of tonight's plans.

Which meant he had more reason to get his revenge.

The first being for the attack in the first place, and the second for the way those fuckers were cock-blocking him.

At least he could breathe a little easier when Denise was in her car.

She started the engine and looked up at him, as though waiting for him to say something.

Maybe to apologize, offer an explanation.

He didn't have anything to give to her, so he could only watch as she finally put the car in gear, pulled out of her spot, and slowly left the lot.

Steve didn't take his eyes off her until she turned onto the main road and was driving off.

He sighed.

Then he got mad.

Those *motherfuckers*.

Clenching his fists, Steve made for the spot where he'd seen the wolves.

His phone buzzed in his pocket. Likely a return text from Victor to let Steve know he was on his way.

Steve didn't bother looking at it. He loosened the top buttons on his shirt instead.

He could *smell* them.

Steve tried to hold onto that scent. To catalogue it. People scents were different from *thing* scents. Not as easy to pick out as oranges. So, so easy to keep a memory of.

Especially when they still smelled mostly like wolves.

He could at least follow them when they were this close. Their scents weren't trailing off. They weren't moving in different directions to fuck with his senses.

They were letting him come to them.

Could be a trap.

No. That was dumb.

It was definitely a trap.

Which was what his concealed carry was for.

Much as the animal was still circling, scratching and howling inside his head, Steve trusted the weapon in his hands a thousand times more than he would trust himself in a fight with multiple wolves.

They stayed along the water. It was darker beneath the canopy of trees, the sun was almost behind the mountains in the distance, and yet his vision wasn't being compromised that badly. He could still see as well as though there were headlights above his head.

It was probably a sign that he had to think about that later when he made it to the little clearing that dipped just a touch deeper into the pine trees, and four wolves sat there, as though waiting for him.

Steve paused. The animals didn't move. Their ears pointed straight up, tails curled around their legs. Each of them watched Steve with different levels of interest.

And, fuck, he almost didn't know what to do about this.

It would be nice if Victor was here right now. Steve was starting to remember how these four, and a few others, nearly ripped him to pieces barely two weeks ago.

"What do you want?"

Of course, the wolves said nothing. They didn't even move, showed no signs of shifting into their human shapes. Nothing.

Oddly enough, that was worse than anything they could have done. At least if they'd growled and surrounded him, he would have known where he stood.

"Okay. Why are you following me? If this has to do with your pack, or Ben's arrest, there's nothing I can do to help you with that."

This time, there was a growl. Ah, so he'd been right on target. They were pissed off about the way their pack was falling apart.

Steve swallowed down his annoyance. "Your alpha was killed by a member of your own and Ben was part of it. He was covering his own ass. That's not on me, Victor, or Zelda, so cut it out with this shit. I'm *changing* now because of you."

He didn't want to change. He didn't want to become one of them. He was stuck with this new body and could barely get a date together because of these fuck heads.

Because of that, Steve was kind of glad when they finally decided to move, to surround him.

He reached back for his holster, unclipped his weapon, and pulled it free. He didn't point it at any of the wolves, yet, but he noted the way they paused at the sight of it.

Sometimes, it was enough to show the other man, or wolves in this case, that he was willing to defend himself if it came down to it.

"I don't want to shoot any of you, but I swear to Christ I will if any of you take one more step towards me."

They didn't move, but their heads were bent, ears pulled back. Steve got the impression some of them were debating how quickly they could lunge at him and clamp their teeth around his throat.

The snarling and growling slowly started up again, and once again, he knew what they were trying to say to him without words.

Warning him. They were warning him off.

Uh, what? That couldn't be right. Maybe he didn't know what they meant after all because *they* were the ones who pulled him out here in the first place.

One of the wolves stepped another paw closer.

Steve planted his feet, not willing to give an inch, to show them any weakness.

"I mean it. Stay back."

Another step. Steve pointed his weapon at the wolf's head.

The others released small, warning growls. The sort of noises designed to let him know that if he pulled the trigger, he was dead.

He wasn't so fast that he thought he could shoot them all as they lunged for him. He could get one, maybe two, and considering the fucked up pack these wolves came from, Steve could no longer work under the assumption that they wouldn't be crazy enough to do something.

Fuck. He was screwed.

The wolves closed in. If he moved, he might accidentally touch one of their cold, reaching noses.

Steve didn't move a muscle. He noted the largest of the four, leaning in, close to his hand, those teeth, long and sharp, ready to sink into his flesh.

A bright flash. Steve flinched, and thank God he had his training because he didn't have his hand on the trigger of his weapon, other-wise he might have shot his own foot when the pop sounded, and the flash exploded in front of his eyes.

It burned, like small fireworks happening inches away from his body.

The wolves whined and yelped. Steve could barely keep his eyes open, but what little he did see of them, he noted were running. Awkwardly, as though they also had trouble seeing where they were going, but they were definitely making a break for it.

"Hey! Come back here!"

He raised his arm to his eyes, trying rub away the strange burning sensation.

He didn't want the fuckers attacking him, but he sure as shit didn't want them taking off either!

Something grabbed him. He swung hard.

His fist stopped just before it could touch Denise's perfect nose.

Steve backed off, stumbling a bit before he could right himself. "What the fuck? What are you doing here?"

God, he had to rub at his eyes again, the sting was too much.

"I'm saving your ass."

"I nearly broke your nose!"

Denise grabbed the sleeve of his jacket and started yanking him again. "I'm grateful that you didn't, but we need to get the hell out of here. Right now."

"I can't. Get back to your car. Right now. You'll get hurt."

"You're the one who can barely see." Denise wouldn't stop pulling him, and the burn in his eyes was enough that he didn't want to fight her off anymore.

He wasn't going to track those wolves like this.

"Why did you come back? You could have been hurt." He could at least still be angry about that. She'd put herself in danger and he didn't even know why.

"You were the one who was going to get hurt." She sounded angry. "Running into the woods like that, and you ruined my date for it, too. What did you think they were going to do? Welcome you with open arms? Answer your questions?"

"What are you talking about? What was that thing you threw? Goddamn, it still hurts my eyes."

And it was giving him a headache on top of everything else. He really could have done without that part.

"I told you I had more in my purse than just the condoms."

"*What?*"

He managed to get his eyes open again to see that smile on her face, and only then did he note the sort of smile it was.

The kind that promise to fuck him up sideways if he stepped out of line.

"I know how to take care of werewolves if I have to. That includes you, too."

God, he was so confused right now. And hard. He couldn't ignore that part.

<h1 style="text-align:center">CHAPTER 6</h1>

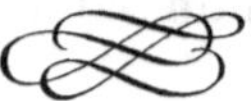

He was clearly confused, but the heat from before, that same heat Denise had basked in at the restaurant, had returned to his eyes.

Steve watched her as though he wanted to pounce on her. Had it not been for the situation, she might have let him.

Down, girl. No time for this. There was really no time. That flash grenade would last only so long, and Steve's eyes weren't looking so cloudy anymore, which meant those wolves might just decide to turn around and come back for them.

She didn't have that much protection in her clutch, so it was better to retreat and live to fight another day in this case.

Luckily, they made it out of the wooded area quickly. Unluckily, there was someone heading in towards them, someone who looked mighty angry.

"Steve? What happened?"

They knew each other. Good. She didn't have to reach for the silver-plated knife in her purse.

Steve rubbed his eyes. "They came back. She chased them off with something that really hurts the eyes. Fuck."

"Sorry about that." Denise couldn't help but feel a touch

guilty now that they were in the clear and it wasn't so dark around her. The parking lot of the restaurant was lit up now with the overhead lamps, it was almost full dark, and she couldn't understand how it was that Steve had been able to see in there.

He was a new shifter. Could he have all the benefits of being a shifter already?

"What was that thing?" Steve asked, reminding her what they were talking about. "Christ, was it silver or something?"

"No. It was just a regular flash bomb with lemon extract. I use silver on my heavier weapons."

"Jesus, you shot a high powered lemon into our eyes?"

"Basically."

The other man, Denise thought she recognized him now, one of Steve's friends who visited him in the hospital, stepped up to his side while Steve continued to rub at his eyes. "You should probably stop doing that. It'll just make it worse."

"You try having lemon juice misted into your eyes en masse. Fuck, Victor, do you have a water bottle?"

"Right this way." Victor started walking, though he glanced back at Denise. "What about you?"

"What about me?"

"She's fine," Steve grumbled. "She was barely there. Got us all by surprise."

"And you're lucky I did. Otherwise, you would have been getting another trip to the hospital."

Victor stepped up to a plain black car parked awkwardly, as though he'd been in a hurry when he arrived. He opened the trunk and pulled out the water bottle.

Damn. Denise must have overdone it with the recipe on that batch of bombs she'd made. Better to go overboard on the citric acid than on the rest of the more explosive components, though.

Steve leaned back, unloading the water bottle right over his face, shaking his hair out when it dripped down his neck, getting some of his clothes. He sprayed Denise a little, but she didn't mind as she watched him, enthralled with the sight of a wet male, red-brown hair dripping. Under the yellow light of the overhead lamps, it looked like bronze. Wet, it shone, too.

She was supposed to be in bed with this man right now. She *would* have been had it not been for those damned wolves, and just like that, she was happy she'd thrown that flash grenade at them.

Had Steve not been there, she would have thrown another just to make their day a little worse.

The pricks.

Steve blinked his eyes wide, face still dripping. Still sexy now that he was soaking wet and looked wide awake.

"You good?"

Steve nodded, handing his friend the bottle. "Yeah, much better. Damn." He looked to Denise. "What would you have something like that in your purse for?"

"I told you that I had protection from shifters."

"You didn't explicitly mention shifters, and I thought you meant pepper spray, not a flash bomb you'd made. Pretty sure that's not legal."

"Pretty sure I don't care."

Steve blinked at her, as if that was the last thing in the world he expected to hear out of her mouth. "Are you serious? You should care. I don't know what the punishment is for making a weapon like that, but if you've got more of them then you need to turn them over to the local police department."

"The local police department knows I have these. Who do you think helped me make them?"

That seemed to confuse even Steve's friend. "What are you saying?"

Denise couldn't believe how she had to spoon feed this to them. "What do you think it means? This isn't the city. There's a shifter population here and anyone human doesn't stand on equal footing with them if something was to go wrong."

"So you're making weapons at home?" Victor stared at her with that same disbelief Steve did.

"It's only for self-defense, and I wasn't about to come on a date with you without something on me to keep myself safe."

Steve raised a brow. "Because I was bitten?"

"Because you might not have control yet."

"Then why bother coming at all?"

She did not want to answer that. "Because I just wanted to."

"You just wanted to be within reaching distance of a guy you were worried might lose control on you? That doesn't make sense."

Victor grabbed Steve's arm. "Steve."

The warning was clear.

"I do *not* owe you an explanation for why I want to do anything." She certainly didn't owe it to him to explain why she wanted to have sex or when she wanted to have it. As sexy as Steve was, she was suddenly regretting ever giving him any kind of chance. It suddenly did feel pretty stupid to want to be anywhere near a brand new shifter with limited control.

Thinking with her libido. She'd almost forgotten the power it had over her, and she didn't like having this pointed out to her. Didn't like being looked at like she was the insane one when he was the one who'd gone off into the woods with just a gun to deal with a couple of werewolves.

"Whatever. You're safe, I'm going home."

"Hey, wait!"

Denise didn't stop. She went to her car, glanced quickly into the backseat to make sure it was still empty, then let herself into the driver's seat.

She closed the door just as Steve made it to her window.

"Come on, don't be like that. I was just worried about you."

His voice, even muffled behind the glass, still sounded sincere, and was enough to make her rethink her position on this.

She started the engine, but Denise left her hands resting on the wheel.

"Please just roll down the window. Don't go like this."

She should just go. She should leave. Right now. She didn't know this man well enough to want to give him any kinds of chances. Coming out with him tonight had been enough of a chance.

But...there was *something* there that made it almost impossible for her to turn away from him.

Denise rolled down the window. Steve's relieved expression was short-lived when she started talking.

"I want to go out with you again, but you need to tell me what's going on with those wolves before I do."

He grinned at her. "You can't just trust that I'm working on it?"

He was clearly trying to play up the fact that he was cute to get her to lay off.

God, if only she could. That smile could melt steel.

It was melting something inside her, that was for damned sure.

"No. If you're in trouble with the local packs, you let me know. Were they the ones who did this to you?"

Steve dropped the cute smile. His jaw hardened. "They are. I don't know what they want."

This complicated a few things.

Denise gripped her steering wheel, staring straight ahead.

Thinking. She was thinking about what she should do. What she should say.

Steve still seemed to be waiting for her to pass judgement, to let the other hammer drop.

He'd just confessed something big to her. Would it be right if she didn't do the same?"

"I know that pack."

She shouldn't say anything.

"You do?"

It was not his business. It really wasn't.

Denise nodded. "Maybe not those exact shifters, but that pack has always been a problem for me."

She couldn't stop talking. Couldn't shut the hell up now that she'd made the decision to let everything out.

"That pack has always had a couple of idiots in it. Stupid people are everywhere, but a stupid werewolf is especially dangerous, and you're mixed up with them."

Steve's eyes darkened, though his voice was oddly soft. Frightening. "What did they do to you?"

Denise looked at him. He wouldn't have seen it right away. She hadn't given him her back, and everywhere else there were any signs of damage was covered.

Denise leaned forward.

Stop, stop, stop. He doesn't need to see.

She pulled the thick strap of her white dress down, freeing her left arm.

She saw it in his eyes the instant he spotted it. The bright, scarred flesh from years passed where teeth and claws had split her skin unevenly.

He wasn't even seeing the whole thing. Just part of one of her bites.

"Jesus Christ, did they do that to you?"

His eyes almost looked red in the lamp light, though she couldn't entirely be sure of that. The only thing she was sure of was that she didn't want pity. "It was a long time ago." She righted her clothes. "Don't know exactly who did it. Maybe it was one of those idiots who murdered their alpha, but I don't care either. Every once in a while, a couple of them come sniffing around my house and I need to chase them off, so you don't get to give me hell for defending myself."

Steve looked as though he was about to fall back a step, but then caught himself. "I wasn't going to do that. That's not...I'm on your side here."

Her heart pitter-pattered. It did a little...

Whatever.

"Just try to stay away from them. Nothing good comes from it, and eventually, they'll leave you alone."

Steve's neck tightened. "Leave me alone? They were the ones who attacked me in the first place."

"And they will stop when you're not in Lakeview anymore."

"You just said they come around to your house sometimes."

Denise clenched her fingers around the steering wheel. She wanted to hit something. "That's different. I've got their smell on me. Some of them are just curious and need to be taught a lesson. You were out there challenging them, and they would have moved in on you if I hadn't stepped in."

"Will they come to you tonight? They must have your scent now, right?"

Most men wouldn't have picked up on that.

Well, he was a private detective.

"If they do then they'll know in a hurry to not stick around. They never do."

That stubborn expression she was getting used to seeing in Steve's eyes came back, only this time, he wasn't playfully asking her out on a date. He looked angry.

Furious, even.

"I won't let them intimidate you."

"It doesn't bother me anymore. This isn't something for you to be worrying about."

"Bullshit it's not! You just said they're going to come to your house."

"And I just told you I have more smoke bombs to take care of them. Your friend is waiting for you. You should go."

"Let me come with you."

Denise footed the break immediately after putting her car into reverse. "Say that again?"

Steve pressed his hands to her door, leaning in, a fight blazing wild in his eyes. "Let me come with you. If they want to prowl around your property then at the very least I should be there."

"No, you'll get into a fight and I'll have to save you again."

"Having me around doesn't hinder you. It would only make you safer. The more people around you, the better your chances are that you won't see anyone at all. There's safety in numbers."

Denise bit the inside of her cheek.

She could handle herself. She'd been doing it for a long time, but he was right. There was safety in numbers.

The wolves already knew where she lived, so what did it matter if one more wolf happened to know on top of that?

He clearly was not a squirrel shifter.

He was something stronger. Powerful. And this chest-pounding, protect my woman bit he was doing was drawing her to him in ways she didn't think were possible.

"If you come to my place then you're going to stay outside."

If she invited him in they were going to have sex, a lot of sex, and doing that the night she knew those wolves were going to show up and start sniffing around her house wouldn't be the best idea.

Steve nodded. "Fine by me. I can do that."

Denise couldn't believe he'd accepted her offer so quickly. "And you don't get to knock on my door asking to use the bathroom or anything."

"I wouldn't do that. Especially not in a professional setting."

Denise waited, still thinking, still trying to see through him.

But the more she looked at him, into those dark eyes, the more she was convinced there was nothing out of the ordinary here.

He was being sincere.

"All right. You can follow me home, I guess. You sure you don't need to go with your friend for anything?"

"I am perfectly fine and ready to go. I'll get my car."

He walked away from her before she could object. Or change her mind.

Victor walked up to her window next, catching her off guard as she thought about her situation.

"You seem like someone who can handle herself, but Steve is a professional. He can be a help to you if you really think you need it."

"He needs it, too. If those wolves are tracking him, then he needs to find out why and stop doing whatever it is he's doing."

"The only thing he did was survive their attack. I've been talking with my mate and giving my old pack a call; this might just be because they see him as part of their own pack now but don't want him. This could go a number of different ways and not all of them have to be violent."

"Your pack?" Denise glanced to the top of his head. She didn't see wolf ears. In fact, his ears were normal, human ears. "You were changed?"

Born shifters had tails and longer ears. Changed shifters, like Steve, didn't.

"No. I'm a subhuman. Don't shift, but I know a little about how this works."

"Oh."

Now she felt kind of bad.

No one exactly knew how to treat the subhumans, so they tended to get hell from their own packs and the human world.

"Don't worry about it." Victor's expression was sincere, his tone calm, professional. "Just make sure you stay safe. I don't want this to go anywhere and I know Steve doesn't want you hurt. We're still not sure how far these wolves are going to be willing to go."

"They're trouble makers for the most part. It's a little hard to believe they were the ones who put Steve in the hospital."

They had yet to break into her home. She was pretty sure the one thing they liked doing the most was pissing around her porch to mark their territory and digging up any flowers she ever tried to plant, but that was enough of a reason to stay on her guard.

She wasn't going to wait for them to try anything before she started taking their presence seriously.

Especially now.

"Just remember that they did put him in the hospital, and since we don't know how much this had to do with the death of their previous alpha, I want to keep all doors open. I don't want you or anyone else getting hurt over something like this."

She nodded. "Fair enough."

Steve was back in his vehicle. He pulled up behind her, gently honked his horn, and then headed to the exit of the parking lot before stopping, waiting for her.

"I need to go."

Victor nodded, stepping back. "I won't be there all the time, but I'll stop by to offer my assistance if you need it. I just need to make sure my mate and her pack are cared for."

"I can't pay you right now."

She didn't know what the services costed for hiring a private detective, in this case, a bodyguard, but Denise was willing to bet it wasn't a cheap fee.

"No charge. Steve wants you kept safe, then I want that too. Besides, I owe him a favor after everything that went down recently."

That was…pretty generous of him. It was one thing for Steve to offer her anything, but something else for this man to do so as well.

Steve might be a shifter, but he apparently associated with some stand up people.

"Thank you."

Steve honked again, reminding her that he was waiting for her to lead the way home.

Other cars were circling the lot, two of them pulled up on either side of her vehicle, and she knew that once she pulled out, there was going to be a bit of a struggle for the spot she held.

She put everyone out of their misery and started driving.

CHAPTER 7

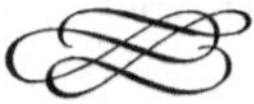

So this was not how Steve expected his date to turn out. Now that he was sitting out in his car in front of Denise's house, doing the usual thing where he watched the property, waited for sudden movements, and logged everything in his notebook for later study, he couldn't lie to himself.

It was the worst fucking date he'd ever been on in his entire life. None of his other dates had ended where he'd had to follow the woman home and, instead of going inside for some fun, was stuck in his car working.

Steve rubbed at his eyes. He could see Denise's shadow from the light coming through her thin curtains as she walked around her home. He turned away from it, forcing his gaze back onto the surrounding property.

Letting himself get distracted would make this whole thing that much more pointless.

At least he knew where her house was. If this whole thing blew over, maybe the next time she would let him pick her up for their date.

Assuming there was a next time. If they really were mated, then

272

would she feel it? Would Denise have any inkling of what was going on between them?

She was neither a shifter, nor a subhuman, so Steve was having trouble figuring that part out.

It could still be in his head, a whole lot of nothing, but it sure as shit hadn't felt like nothing when he'd realized those same wolves who tore him to pieces on the side of the road outside Zelda's skulk were also harassing Denise.

Had put *marks* on her.

He wanted to hurt them for that. Badly.

The problem came when he remembered that his job tended to be boring as hell for the most part.

People sometimes liked to romanticize the private detective profession. There really was just a lot of paperwork, a lot of watching and waiting, and a lot of nothing.

Sometimes something happened, it was rarely exciting, and this was one of those times.

Steve's gaze fell to Denise's windows one more time. Her home modest enough, there was no garden out front, even though the amount of land made it almost the perfect place for flowers.

Denise had seemed like the sort of woman who would like flowers. Steve should have brought them for their date. That might have made the way it ended a little less terrible.

But there was something else about this place that made the hairs on the back of Steve's neck stand up. He almost couldn't place it, not until he briefly cracked his window to let more of the smell in.

Oranges. That was there. He could make it out clearly, but something else, something animal and dominating.

Those wolves had been here before, not in a while. He was pretty sure it hadn't been for a while. The scent seemed…faded. Faded meant it was old.

But they had left something behind that was still sharp in Steve's nose, something that screeched at him again and again to get away. To walk away from here and not come back if he knew what was good for him.

Victor had once described this. The act of marking territory and chasing away other shifters or animals.

Jesus Christ, was that what this smell was? Did Denise *know* about it?

Steve was leaning towards yes, she did know, and that was why she was prepared with all kinds of weapons to keep the buggers away.

He'd confirm it with her when he had the chance, just to make sure, but if Denise knew how to make smoke bombs to scare away the creatures she didn't want around, then it didn't take a genius to realize she'd chased away those wolves a time or two already.

On her own.

Christ, he wished he'd been there to help her through that. Steve's guts twisted with all kinds of anxiety and hatred over the thought of Denise handling those wolves without any help.

Well, she had help now. He was here, and he wasn't going to let those fuckers get away with the shit they'd been pulling.

And wasn't that the fucked up thing? He was *hoping* they would show up just so he could fight them.

Denise's front door opened. Light spilled out of her small home, creating an almost halo effect around Denise's body, preventing him from making out any of her features other than the curve of her hips and upper body as she came down the steps of her small porch.

When she came closer, he realized there was something in her hand.

He rolled down the window.

"Here, I made you a coffee."

Steve took it. She'd put it into a thermos, definitely one that belonged to her if the pink and yellow flowers along the metal base were anything to go by.

"Thanks."

"Don't thank me. I just don't want you out here suffering by yourself." Denise folded her arms. "Are you sure you need to be here?"

She didn't ask it with the same defensive tone she'd taken with him earlier that night when he'd made the decision.

"I won't let them come here and start harassing you." He set the thermos aside. "Are you sure there's nothing the police can do to help you?"

Another shrug. "They tried. I even know some of them. The packs are too tightly knit. No one ever sees anything and no one ever turns anyone in. It's like they've got their own rules against snitching."

Christ, she knew some of the police around here and she still couldn't get results? That bothered Steve on a whole other level.

"Well, either way, you'll learn about how all this stuff works eventually."

"Oh yeah? Why's that?"

"Because you're a shifter now. You'll eventually join a pack and become just like them."

Steve stared up into her eyes. The lights from her house high-lighted all of her best features, her flawless skin, the shape of her throat and jaw.

Even the disappointed glint in her eyes.

"Is that what you're worried about? That I'll be like the people who hurt you?"

Denise shook her head. "Enjoy your coffee, Steve. I'll be inside."

"I'll be out here."

He watched her go. Steve didn't take his eyes off her until the door was shut behind her and she was safely indoors again.

He was no psychologist, but right then, his head spun will all sorts of things that might explain her actions. People did irrational things all the time. Sometimes, they only seemed irrational on the outside; other times, they were still irrational, even with all the explanations out of the way.

Denise didn't seem like an irrational woman. She was an educated nurse, had been taking care of herself for years. That didn't scream irrational to him.

So why bother going out with him if she didn't like shifters?

The mating.

Steve rubbed his eyes.

That was one explanation, he supposed. Shifters spoke all the time about the irrational nature of a mating. Falling desperately in love with someone at first sight, or first sniff, was the most irrational thing in the world.

Steve still wasn't ready to put the mating stamp on whatever it was brewing between him and Denise, but if she'd gone out with him despite her so-called rules, then that could only be another nail in the coffin.

He wouldn't tell her about this. Not yet. There was no point in making her fear him on an even deeper level than she already did.

She didn't want to admit it, but he could tell she did. Knowing she was permanently bound to the type of person, the sort of *creature*, he now was would just freak her out.

Or make her throw another one of those lemon bombs at him. Directly into his eyes this time.

He'd rather avoid that.

Steve took the thermos, unscrewed the lid, and sucked back a heavy gulp of the steaming coffee.

Then spat it back into the thermos, coughing at the strong taste.

"Christ," he choked. He screwed the lid back on and set the thermos aside.

Denise was a beautiful woman and his possible mate, but she didn't know how to make coffee for shit.

He needed his water bottle. God, he had to get that taste out of his mouth.

A flash of light in the distance took his mind off the taste of filth in his mouth.

Steve tensed. He watched the shrubbery and long grass, waited to see that bright flash again.

Denise did have neighbors who lived around here. The houses weren't so close together that anyone would be stepping on each other's toes, but she had said something about the kids who liked to leave their bikes lying around.

Because in the country, apparently no one worried about theft.

Could be the reflection of something from Denise's house.

Or it could be the golden eyes of one of those wolves.

A shadow darted through the long grass, swift and graceful enough that the grass itself barely moved.

That was enough for him. Steve sent a text to Denise with the code word they'd agreed on. She'd keep her door locked and wouldn't step outside.

Steve left the car. He raised his flashlight up high so he could better see what was in front of him.

The strange thing, however, was that when he did that, the bright beam of light contrasted against the darkness made it even harder to see than when he'd been using nothing at all.

Steve squinted. He clicked off the flashlight. Clicked it back on, then turned it off again.

He could see better with the flashlight off.

Steve rolled his shoulders. "All right. Don't think about it."

He kept going. If this was more of his new wolf-ish tendencies rising to the surface, he might as well just go with it.

Steve kept walking. The grass was mowed only to a certain point. He wasn't sure if it was the property line, but when he made it to the tall grass and weeds, he felt farther away from Denise than he had while sitting in his car.

He was going to recommend she get herself a decent fence. This was way too open.

Steve walked forward a little more, listening carefully, searching for any signs of those wolves.

One step forward, then another, and another.

Steve stopped moving. He glanced over his shoulder quickly.

He could still see the light from Denise's windows and the outline of her small house. He thought he could see her in the window through the curtains.

Shit. He should have told her that was a mistake. He didn't think these wolves had brought guns with them, but staying away from the windows would still have been the best idea.

Steve looked back out across the darkness. The wind rustled the leaves in the trees and the top of the grass.

He couldn't see them, and he couldn't hear them, but somehow, *somehow*, he knew they were there.

"I'm not going out any farther, so you might as well cut the bullshit."

He waited. Nothing.

Steve's jaw clenched. "Whatever you want with me, just come right out and tell me, and whatever you're doing coming around this property, it's going to stop. This woman is not part of your pack and has nothing to do with any of you. Understand? And if you think you're going to get me farther away from her so you can run back around to the house, you're out of your damned minds."

The grass rustled again, though, this time, there was no wind.

Steve reached back, his hand fitting around the handle of his weapon.

Three wolves stepped forward, inching from the grass like ghosts, and close. Very close. They could have lunged for his throat and sank their teeth into his flesh before he could touch his gun.

Fuck. That was…impressive and terrifying.

Steve kept his back straight. These creatures respected a man who didn't back down from a fight, right? If that was the point of their whole alpha, beta, and omega system, then he'd give them a fucking alpha.

"Stay off this property. You don't belong here."

The ears of the middle wolf pulled back. It growled low in his throat. That was another thing—Steve could tell they were all male.

And they weren't the same wolves who had nearly killed him and Vic on the road, or ruined his date with Denise.

Steve's brows pulled together. "Who the hell are you?"

The wolf in the middle eased forward. Steve tensed, his arm ready to pull his gun forward.

The wolf froze. Its gaze darted to Steve's arm. It knew.

And yet it inched forward again, just like the wolf from back at the Keg.

Just like back there, Steve was unable to move. Not that he was frozen under some sort of spell, but there was something to this, something natural and easy that let him hold still while the wolf sniffed at his hand, then his leg.

Then his crotch.

"Okay, that's about as much of that as you're going to get."

Right. *Of course* that's what they were doing. Dogs were still dogs, after all.

Not that *he* was ever going to be sniffing at people's asses or their dicks. He didn't care what instinct demanded. That was just a little too gross for his tastes.

The wolf yanked itself back, the ears falling flat again, a low grumble rising from its throat.

"Don't growl at me like that. You're not sniffing at my dick."

All three wolves cocked their heads to the side. The two backing up their leader even looked at each other, as though they didn't entirely understand the problem here.

"What are you doing on this property? What does Denise have to do with you? No more secretive bullshit. One of you change and answer the question so I know what's going on. None of you are leaving until you do."

He didn't have to draw his gun for it to be a credible threat.

The wolf in the middle finally shifted, becoming something that looked much more human.

A naked human. Of course. It was a rare talent for the shifters to be able to keep their clothes on them when they were in their animal forms.

The unfortunate thing was how this guy was taller than Steve by a good two inches.

Fuck.

"Are you threatening to turn your weapon onto myself or my pack mates?"

Booming voice, too. Great.

"I'm saying that if I have to protect my client from intruders on her property, then I will."

"Your client?"

A dark brow lifted on the man. He seemed to be sizing Steve up.

Steve braced himself, his teeth clenching. "Stop that."

The man smirked at him. "You have the smell of one of us on you, but no ears or tail."

He was going to bust one of his molars. "Was it any of you who did this to me?"

"You can smell it on us that it wasn't."

"Prick. I could've been wrong."

The long black wolf ears on top of the man's bald head twitched. "You are not."

"What are you doing here? This isn't your property."

"The woman who lives here is part of no pack and this is our hunting ground."

Steve pressed his lips together. He'd forgotten about this sort of thing when it came down to shifters. "Okay, let me explain it again, this is her property. Her territory. You do not belong here no matter how many trees you might've pissed on."

The two wolves behind the big guy growled. Steve reminded himself that he needed to play this a little smarter than what he was doing now.

They could still rip him up.

"This is our hunting territory, and she also has the mark on her. We are needed here."

Steve didn't get it. "The woman inside is not a shifter."

He'd almost said her name. There was a good chance these wolves already knew Denise's full name, including where she worked and who her family was, but that didn't mean he was going to give anything away.

"The pack that marked her didn't claim her. She has the smell of wolves on her. We come here to make sure there have been no side effects, and that she will not be a danger to others or herself. Her scent draws our kind to her."

"The oranges."

"No, her blood."

"I just told you she's not a shifter. How long have you been coming here?"

"Ever since her mauling."

"Okay, and how long ago was that? Enough time has to have passed that her scent won't bother the shifters around here anymore."

"Sixteen years was when her mark was given and her blood changed. The scent does not leave. It's part of her."

"Sixteen..." Steve glanced back to the house. He could still see the shadow in the window. It looked darker now, as though she was looking out the curtains. Trying to see.

"Does she know any of this?"

The big alpha-looking male shrugged. "It's not our concern."

"Not your…" Now he was mad again. "Motherfucker, *you're* the ones who've been coming around here harassing her. She thinks you're part of the same pack that fucked me up. You can't keep doing this. You're terrorizing her."

"We're *protecting* her."

Steve felt a calm coming over him. "All right. I can work with that. What are you protecting her from?"

"From you."

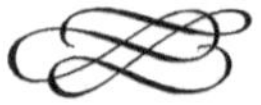

*W*as he in trouble again?

Denise narrowed her eyes, as if that would help her see what was going on out there any better.

Of course, it wasn't helping. She wasn't a shifter.

Not like Steve was.

She really should just leave him out there. It was apparently his job to watch over and protect people. He had a gun, and they had agreed that if anything were to happen, she would need to stay indoors.

"Not because I don't think you can't take care of yourself," he'd said, and Denise had known he was lying to her. "I just don't want to accidentally shoot you in the dark."

Denise still shivered thinking about that.

"I thought you were a professional."

"I am, and as a professional, I want to take the precautions to make sure I don't accidentally kill you because I think you're an intruder."

She couldn't exactly argue with that logic. She didn't want to get shot because she snuck up on the man and his finger was on the trigger.

But if he was in trouble out there and she did nothing either…

No. He was right. She had her little items inside that helped her keep the wolves at bay, but he had a gun. A gun. If she announced herself, she doubted he would shoot her, but that would destroy the point of staying out of sight and out of mind of the wolves he was out there with.

It was killing her not knowing what they were doing.

Not knowing if Steve was in trouble or not.

She texted him. There was the doubt that he would even be able to answer, but she tried it anyway. Just something quick. Asking if he was all right.

She hoped he was all right.

It wasn't as though she wanted him to get hurt.

She didn't want him to get hurt.

Denise dug her nails into the wood of the windowsill. She turned away from the glass and headed back to her room.

Screw it. She'd go out there. She was going to call out to Steve and ask if he was all right. She didn't care if those wolves got a look at her. They already knew she was here.

Denise hurried to her bottom dresser drawer and yanked it open.

If there was one thing she loved, it was keeping her shit organized.

Her smoke bombs were in their own plastic tubs listed from mild, medium, and heavy.

She'd used a medium-level burning bomb at the Keg. She reached for a couple listed as heavy.

She'd made them out of old hair spray cans she'd cut and arranged for the job.

Being into arts and crafts as a kid had really worked in her favor.

She grabbed her silver chains next. They were long, not so heavy that they looked ridiculous or would get in her way if she needed to run, but wearing them would be enough to keep the wolves away from her.

They always seemed to hesitate a little more about getting close to her when she happened to have them on.

The third item was the hunting knife she'd plated with silver. She had two of them. Denise strapped one of the holsters around her ankle, and the other she clipped around her waist and shoulder.

Denise tied her hair back next. Best to not leave it flying around where anyone could grab it, or it could get caught on something.

Her heart slammed as she headed for the back door. It always did before something like this happened. Every close confrontation. She had yet to get used to it.

Suck it in. Hold it back. She didn't get shit done by sticking around on the sidelines.

She opened the back door, making sure she was loud enough that she wouldn't catch her fearless protector off his guard.

"Hey! All of you! It's time to get the hell off my property now. I've already called the police and they'll be here in a few minutes."

She was banking on the fact that they would go just by that threat alone. It was usually the case.

Steve half turned, looking back at her, which confused Denise for a minute because it almost looked as if there was…

Someone else there. Another man, not in his wolf form, and his eyes blazed a bright golden color in the light that Steve's matched.

Her heart stopped.

She was a little girl again. She could see those same eyes staring down at her when they…

It hadn't even hurt the whole time they'd been doing it. The burning in her skin every time their claws and teeth had sliced through her had gone numb at some point, but the sight of her own blood, and simply knowing what they were doing had been enough for her to scream her throat raw.

Denise's knees felt slippery. She managed to hold herself up onto her feet, but barely.

"Denise, you should go back inside."

She blinked. Steve was standing closer to her. Not close, but he was only five feet away this time. That other man and the two wolves a few feet behind him.

She hadn't noticed Steve coming closer. Or those wolves behind him.

Her heart wouldn't stop pounding. She reached into her holster and pulled out her blade. The strong, sturdy grip of the handle in her fingers made her feel better, but not by much.

"Do you know what your eyes look like right now?"

Steve blinked. "What do they look like?"

"They're gold. Like theirs." She briefly pointed the knife to her unwanted guests. "You all need to get the hell out of here. Right now."

The two wolves sat down, as if to make a point that they weren't going anywhere. The naked male crossed his arms. Small, light scars crisscrossed his skin in uneven patterns and places.

They looked like some of the scars she had, only fewer and not so deep.

He'd been on the receiving end of shifters' claws and teeth a few times, too, only he'd clearly been able to fight back.

"Denise, they were speaking to me just now, and if you want them gone, then I'll escort them off the property right now, but you and I need to talk."

"There's nothing to talk about. They were the ones who turned you and now your eyes are gold. The lot of you can get the hell out of here."

It didn't matter how sexy she thought Steve happened to be. No amount of sex appeal was going to make her want to jump into the arms of a man with eyes like that.

He was still making her knees weak, but now it was for an entirely different reason.

Steve blinked, a lot. His brows creased, as though he was actively trying to push back that color in his eyes. He even rubbed at his eyes with his hand.

It wasn't cute. She didn't think it was endearing that he was trying so hard to make it go away just because she didn't like it.

Absolutely, positively not.

"Denise, these aren't the wolves who attacked me. Or you. They've been coming here to look after you."

"Uh huh, and you believe that? Mr. Private Detective?"

He stopped rubbing at his eyes and looked her in the eyes. That gold seemed stronger, more striking when he did that, and Denise's stomach clenched.

"Not necessarily, but I won't rule it out just yet either. They said your scent is attracting other wolves to the area and that's something I need to pay attention to."

"My scent?" Denise glanced back at the man and two wolves behind him. Steve kept his back to them as if he no longer saw them as any sort of threat.

For a man like him to do that, it had to mean something, right?

Didn't mean she was going to let go of her blade. Just in case.

"It's something to do with when you were attacked. It put a scent on you. The wolves around here keep thinking you're one of theirs. Or that you should be theirs."

Denise clenched her hands. "That makes no sense. I don't belong to anyone and this was years ago. Any scent on me should have left. Don't come any closer!"

Steve stopped, his hand on the railing of her deck steps. He didn't look nearly afraid enough considering the knife she held in her hands and was absolutely not going to let go of.

"I won't hurt you."

"Then stop doing that thing with your eyes. I don't like it."

"I'm trying. I can't stop it." Steve glanced back at the two wolves and naked guy still standing stoically behind him. "Could you guys give us some space? It's probably because I can smell you or something."

"No, it's because of her. You want her."

"Okay, that's enough."

"You want to claim her."

"Understood. *Shut up.*"

"It will cement your mating if you do it."

Denise was starting to hear enough of this herself. "What is he talking about? What mating?"

Steve closed his eyes, as though searching for patience.

Denise had no patience to give him. "What is he talking about?"

Steve opened his eyes. That golden color was brighter than ever before, and when he looked at her, Denise could see that same desire that had simmered within him back at the restaurant. The same, but more powerful, and with the hint of his inner wolf within.

Because that's what he was. A wolf. Just like the creatures who'd done this to her.

"I'm thinking, that it's possible, you might be my mate. It could be wrong—"

"It is wrong." Denise backed up a step.

Steve seemed to take that as his permission to get closer. "It doesn't mean I'll attack you, or force you to do anything. I know it could be a mistake. I'm too new at this to know how anything works."

"And you're wrong. I just wanted to go out with you so I could get in bed with you. Not so you could lay some fucked up wolf claim to me! Are you insane?"

Steve took another step forward. "It wasn't like that. I wasn't going to do anything you didn't want me to do."

"She would have wanted you to make the claim when you were in the middle of it."

"God, will you shut the fuck up!" Steve's eyes flashed to bright red when he snapped at the man behind him.

The red was worse than the gold. Denise would almost rather have the gold come back.

Anything but those red eyes.

Steve looked back at her. Denise couldn't see his face. She saw a monster who looked like him.

"You need to go."

"You're still alone here and those other wolves might come looking for you."

"I don't care. I can handle myself!"

"You're trembling right now."

He was right. She was. Denise hadn't noticed, but once she looked down at her hands, she couldn't not see it. Her fingers were cold, numb. She might drop the blade if she wasn't careful.

"I will leave if you want me to. I will get in my car and keep watching out for anyone who tries to come onto your property, but I can't leave you alone."

Denise shook her head. "I don't believe you. No one is that good. No one does something like that for nothing. You want to tie me to you for the rest of my life and I won't let you do it!"

"That's not what I'm doing. I swear."

"Then stop trying to get near me!"

Steve finally stopped. He was on the last step of her deck, looking at her, still taller than her even when he was one step down from her.

And Denise had her back pressed against her door, her free hand scrambling, searching for the door handle. When she did find it, her heart spiked to the realization that the door was locked. She was shut out of her own house, and there were four werewolves in front of her, one of whom wanted to make her into his little baby factory for the rest of her days.

A werewolf wanted to do that to her. Christ, she'd only wanted to have sex with him, not spend the rest of her life with him.

Before she could demand he get the hell off her property again, Steve did something that shocked her.

He sat down.

Denise clenched her teeth. "What are you doing?"

"Trying not to intimidate you. If you're standing over me with the knife, then I'm hoping it will calm you down."

Denise inhaled a long breath, held it, then let it out again.

He was right. What he was doing was helping, a little.

Only a little.

And Steve's eyes went back to their golden color. She wished they would turn dark brown again. She'd liked that color better than the unnatural gold, but she'd take it over the red.

"I am not here to hurt you or to force your hand on anything. Not a single thing. I just wanted to find whoever's harassing you, which were these guys, and keep those other wolves off your back. Then get you in bed, but as beautiful as you are and as much as I want you out of your clothes," —those golden eyes brightened even more— "I have to wait until it's actually safe for you before I can do that."

Denise pressed her lips together. She glanced back at the shifters behind him, the two wolves and the naked man.

"Well, since shifters don't give a shit about walking about in their birthday suits, I'm not all that shocked that you want to get me naked, too."

Steve grinned at her. "Me wanting to get you naked has nothing to do with being a werewolf and everything to do with mutual attraction."

Whatever he was doing to calm her, it was starting to work that much more. The tension in Denise's shoulders melted out of her.

Until that other werewolf behind Steve decided to speak up.

"Others are coming onto the territory. If you want to protect your woman, you should come with us."

"What?"

"What?"

She and Steve had spoken at the same time. They looked at each other, and then back at the other shifters.

Steve got to his feet. "What are you talking about?"

"I can hear them. There are four wolves here. They will be coming for the woman."

Okay, now that panic was coming back again. "I don't have a scent on me."

"It's not something you would be able to smell," said Tall, Dark, and Naked. "You were changed, but you will never be a shifter."

"What do they want me for?"

"The same reason he wants you. To fuck you."

The knife was suddenly feeling a lot better in Denise's hands.

"Christ, you really know how to play it subtle."

Denise wasn't interested in Steve's smart ass remarks. "And you? What do you want?"

"Peace on our territory. If this one claims you then all the better for us. We won't have to keep coming around here to watch over you anymore. You'll have a permanent protector."

"Why would you even bother doing that in the first place? If I'm giving off some freaky smell that pulls shifters towards me, why haven't any of you acted on it?"

She didn't get her answer. The howl in the distance answered for her, and the tall grass beyond the reach of her house lights began to stir as the wolves came closer.

To take what they thought to be theirs.

CHAPTER 9

"You should stay out of the way of this one, little man,"

Steve growled at the barely concealed insult, but there was no time to react to it when he had to react to something else.

Oversized, demonic wolves burst through the edges of the property.

So little time to pull his shit together. Steve sucked it up, noted the two beasts who charged him, and that there were no more behind them.

For now.

Naked man with no social skills stepped forward. Not to be outdone when Denise watched, Steve did the same, fists clenched, his claws punching through his actual fingernails as hair needled through the pores of his skin.

Like back at the hospital, only worse. A thousand times worse.

At least this time he didn't have to hold it back, so why bother trying?

It was a relief when he thought of it that way, and maybe to prove he wasn't so little, Steve rushed at one of those monstrous wolves all on his own.

Because no fucking way was he going to let one of those things anywhere *near* his woman. There was no fucking way he was going to let either of them *touch* her. And there was no fucking way he was going to let either of them *fuck* her.

His body crashed into the thing charging him. It was like throwing his body at a gorilla. Luckily, his head only rattled a little before he remembered he had nearly that same strength.

No. Steve shoved his hands forward and hooked his thumbs against the corners of that huge mouth, back where the teeth couldn't reach. They sure as hell tried. The hot snapping against his face, grazing his cheek, was nearly robotic.

Steve had the teeth contained, barely, but the claws on this thing were like a bear's claws, and they shredded his clothes like butter. The sudden heat nearly made Steve drop his charge. He got angry instead, using all the strength in his upper body, and threw the creature down onto the ground. The earth seemed to bang with the sudden force, as though a huge tree had fallen over.

Of course, the wolf did not stay down. It lunged back to its feet, hackles raised a foot and a half high like some kind of terrifying mohawk. Those thick claws hooked into the earth as though it was getting ready to lunge at him as agilely as it had pushed itself to its feet.

And these things had been stalking Denise and she barely knew it?

A heavy clicking noise sounded behind him. Steve almost paid no attention to it until the bang made him jump and a searing, painful heat caught him on the side of his arm.

The wolf released a terrible cry, curling in on itself as it stumbled, fell, and rolled on the ground before turning and running in the other direction.

The second wolf also made a run for it.

Another gunshot sounded. This time there was no terrible pain, and Steve already knew what he would find when he looked back.

Just because he knew what he would find didn't mean his gut was prepared for the sexual fantasy on two long legs that met his eyes.

Denise, shotgun in her arms, hair around her shoulders and eyes on the prize, stared after the monstrous wolves that ran off her property. Her dark eyes were narrowed. The light from her small home behind her created an almost halo effect.

Like a warrior woman on the battlefield, and it was cheesy as fuck, but Steve wanted to surrender to her as those wolves ran away whining with their tails between their legs.

Denise's chest heaved, as though she'd been holding her breath when firing those shots.

Her gaze flicked to Steve, and the corner of her mouth quirked, highlighting the sexy warrior look she had going on even more.

"You thought you were going to save me, did you?"

Steve thought about it, then shrugged. "Seemed like something I should at least make an attempt at. Chivalry, and all that."

Her grin seemed to brighten, and Steve sank deeper and deeper into the warmth that smile generated.

Until she stopped smiling and he realized he wasn't feeling warm because of her smile.

Steve was bleeding all over himself.

He touched his middle, his hand coming away bright red. Just like when he'd been mauled on the side of the road.

"Oh shit."

He couldn't be sure if it was him who'd said it, or Denise. In that next instant, she was at his side, gun on the ground next to him, pushing him back, her hands tearing open his clothes with ease since they were shredded.

"Goddamn it. Can you not go for a walk around the block without getting your chest ripped open?"

Steve smiled now, even though there was a ringing in his ears and the smell of blood was so thick he could almost taste it on his tongue.

"He is a wolf."

Great. That guy was standing over him now, looking down at him with a massively unimpressed expression on his face.

"You should be healing."

"Uh huh, well maybe it's the sight of your dick right above my head that's causing the problem, so could you do me a favor and take a step back?"

The man grinned, doing as he was asked.

"Oh, look at that, you're actually not a robot."

"Shut up, Steve." Denise's fingers danced lightly over his chest. "You need to focus. I can't see anything."

"What?" He tried to look down.

His chest was covered in hair. Not any natural human chest hair, in fact, but a pelt of fur.

That didn't look right.

"Focus on your healing. I've got some bandages. I'll be back."

"Hey, wait!"

Denise did not wait. She fled his side and ran back into her house, where he could not see her.

Where anything could be waiting for her.

The naked wolf stepped forward again. Steve stopped him with a pointed finger.

"Don't even think about coming to stand over me with your schlong out like that."

Again, another little smirk. "Afraid I will mark you?"

"I just don't like seeing some guy's meatballs and Slim Jim two feet above my head, but that's just me."

"There is nothing *slim* about it."

Steve frowned, but then Denise came back to him, a heavy First Aid kit beneath her arm.

She fell to her knees next to Steve. Her hands did not shake, though there was an undertone of green around the corners of her jaw and neck.

"Are you okay?"

"Don't move."

Steve snapped his mouth shut and did as he was told. How could he not when she commanded him so well?

Above him, that naked guy was smiling, as though he found this whole thing to be amusing or something.

Asshole.

"You have to focus on your healing," Denise said, pressing gauze to his belly and chest before wrapping him up quickly and tightly. "You're bleeding too much."

"I am?"

She looked at him, her eyes suddenly wild and animalistic. "Don't you feel it?"

"Uh..."

"She worries you are dying."

"I am *not* worried, and he isn't dying!"

The guy shrugged and stepped back.

Steve noted his two wolves weren't with him anymore. "Where's your backup?"

"Hunting."

Steve waited. Nothing else came.

"Is that all they're doing? Searching for a snack right now isn't the best of ideas, is it?"

The man sneered. "Who said they were hunting for a snack? They're hunting those wolves."

Steve glared back at him. "I don't need your damned lip when I'm the one cut open like this and your backup is gone."

"Would not have happened if you had not fought so poorly."

"I didn't see either of your wolves offering to help me out. It wasn't three on one like you had it."

"*Enough*, the both of you." Denise grabbed Steve by his jaw, forcing him to look up into her eyes with that painful grip. "You, right now, focus on healing. I don't care if you don't know how to do it, just do it anyway."

She didn't have claws, but she did have fingernails, and they hurt. A lot. So Steve nodded. "All right."

Denise looked at him hard for another two seconds or so. Painful seconds with those powerful fingers digging into his jaw and cheek.

But then she did release him, going back to work over his chest. "I want to get this covered still. We should call an ambulance just in case."

Just the mention of an ambulance was enough to get Steve driving into gear.

"Nope. Don't need one."

"You're bleeding all over the place."

"I'm good. Watch me. I can do the healing thing right now."

And he sure as hell focused to make it happen. He couldn't be entirely sure how good of a job he was doing, or if it was making any sort of difference at all when he was lying on the ground like this, but that wasn't going to stop him from giving it the old college try either.

The naked male shook his head. "Your face is red."

"Right, because I'm focusing."

"You look constipated."

Steve stopped holding his breath and growled at the other man. "You can get fucked, asshole. Maybe it's a good thing if my face turns red because it means I still have blood in me and—"

"Shut up, Steve."

"You're taking his side? Seriously?"

Denise wasn't looking at him. She had her fingers through what little of his furry chest was still exposed. Her gaze was locked onto him, and that panic and desperation he'd seen before was entirely gone.

In its place, was something alight and eager. Something that made Steve take a second look.

Difficult to see through the forest of coarse hair on his chest, but it began to thin and fade, and with it, he noted the way his torn flesh seemed to knit back together beneath Denise's hand.

She continued to run her fingers pleasantly across his skin as it was exposed more and more, as though marveling at the change happening before her eyes.

Relieved, intrigued, and curious.

At least he was the sole focus of her attention now. Steve glanced at the male standing next to them, and he couldn't help but smirk at little.

That was right. Denise was his, and it didn't matter how tall and naked and...*big* he was. She was his and Steve wasn't about to let him get in on this.

The blank expression Steve had returned to him ruined just a little bit of his fun. He wasn't going to lie about that.

"Amazing." Denise shook her head, that same smile on her face as she watched the transformation. "You were in the hospital for two weeks, and that was enough of a miracle, but this is crazy."

Even with his chest completely closed off, her hand continued to slide over his skin, as though marveling at what she felt, and saw.

He sure as hell wasn't going to stop her.

"I guess I'm getting better at healing."

"No shifter can heal that fast naturally."

"Then what is it?" Denise asked, her hand still on Steve's chest.

His mouth thinned, jaw tightening. "I've heard it can be done through the touch of a mate."

Denise's hand yanked off Steve's chest with a speed he didn't think necessary. He wasn't diseased or anything.

Steve sat up. "And you ruined that, so we might as well figure out what to do now that those wolves are gone."

Denise held her hand close to her chest, as though trying to soothe away the same burn that Steve felt. "Right."

"You will both need to come with me."

"Yeah, I got this, pal." Steve came to a stand. He glared at the other man, hating that he was a little taller. Steve puffed out his chest, trying to increase his height, though he stopped when he caught Denise's eye.

"That is not a request. I will have this taken care of today before anything else happens."

Steve blinked. He faced the man head on. "Not a request, is it?"

"No."

A two-by-four smashed into Steve's face before he had the chance to see it coming, or realize it was this man's fist.

For a hair of a second, he thought he was all right, then the dark walls closed in and he went down, Denise screaming his name.

CHAPTER 10

By the time Steve opened his eyes, he was left with the impression that hours had passed, and years of being able to pull himself wide awake on a dime, coupled with the last memory he had, forced him to jump up from where he'd been sleeping, which, from the bang on his skull and bright light exploding behind his eyes, was directly beneath the ceiling.

Children laughed. Steve heard the patter of small feet as he clutched his head and sank back down onto his pillows with a groan.

"The fuck?"

He opened his eyes and squinted through the sudden blur, just in case he was wrong.

Nope. The ceiling wasn't exactly right above his head, but it was close enough that his poor skull took on the full force of it.

Was it *concrete*?

"You're finally awake."

The sound of Denise's voice had him rolling over, which was good because he nearly sat up and smashed his head in again.

He was on a loft of some kind. Denise stood beneath him in a tiny kitchen. She didn't look amused.

"All right, where are we, and who do I have to murder for this?"

"After what Jackson did to you, do you really think you can murder anyone?"

She sounded as though she was trying to be easy-going about this, but the firm set to her mouth said otherwise.

"I can kill that giant son of a bitch any day of the week when the prick isn't sucker punching me."

Steve grabbed the railing next to the futon he was on and pulled himself to where he figured there was a ladder.

There was, but he ignored it and pushed himself to the floor. At least he managed to land on his feet because he was a little sick of not being able to hold his own when Denise happened to be watching him.

As though she was thinking the same thing, Denise asked, "You sure you're all right?"

Steve bit back a low growl. "Just tell me where he is." He glanced around. "Where are we?"

From how much space was between the walls, it appeared he was in a trailer of some kind.

"We're in Jackson's pack." Denise clenched her fists as she said it. "I tried to shoot him when he knocked you out, but he was a little too fast for me to handle."

Steve made a mental note to hate this man. "I'll hold him down so you can shoot him next time. How long was I out for?"

"Long enough for me to get the introductions out of the way, and for Jackson to explain a couple of key details to me."

Again, there was that firm set to her mouth. As though Denise wasn't entirely happy with her current situation, or what had been said to her while Steve had been down for the count.

Fuck.

"Look, about the mating thing, I don't even know if—"

The little door behind him burst open before he could finish. Steve spun around, expecting a threat.

Three barefoot children shrieked, laughed, and ran in the other direction while an adult chased after them with a wooden spoon.

Steve's gut fell out beneath him.

This was not Zelda's fox pack. This wasn't even the wolf pack where she used to live. He'd kind of hoped it would be, even though those fuckers were the reason he was like this.

He had no idea where he was.

Denise's hand gripped his shoulder. Steve looked back at her, and she glanced down meaningfully at his hands.

Where there were claws punching through the spot where his actual fingernails should be.

"Goddamn it." Steve lifted his hands. The claws were ugly, and though those kids hadn't seemed too scared, he could understand why they would run screaming from him.

"You really need to learn how to control that."

"No kidding."

He focused, imagining them sliding back under his fingernails, which had been pushed up as his claws took precedence.

He expected something of a struggle, but that simple focus was all there was to it. He hissed a little as those sharp claws sank back under his skin, as though they had never been there to begin with.

"Does that hurt?"

Steve shook his head, even though it did hurt. "Feels kind of like I'm slowly paper cutting myself."

Denise, naturally, hissed and yanked her hand back. As though she would also feel that terrible sensation if she didn't let him go.

Steve grinned at her and wiggled his fingers. "At least now I know I can bring these suckers out the next time that prick tries to jump me."

He moved for the door, having to duck beneath the loft because he was too tall.

Denise followed him. "I don't think it will come down to that. You shouldn't fight with anyone here."

"Why not?" Steve pushed his way out of the door, grateful when he could stand up straight and didn't feel as though the walls were going to close in around him.

He stopped listening after that. The sight of the area around him… it wasn't the same as Zelda's fox skulk, or the pack of wolves she used to live with. There had been the odd park home in those places, but mostly people lived in cabins and small houses.

Here it was immediately different. Here it looked as though everyone had jumped onto the tiny house craze that had been going around, because every one of the little houses Steve could see were all on wheels, and few of them looked to be over two hundred and fifty square feet each.

Many had little decks attached. There seemed to be a communal garden in what could be called the town center, as well as a couple of swing sets purchased from the local hardware stores for the children to play with.

At the middle of it all, Steve caught the eye of that naked alpha, no longer naked, but wearing regular clothes and a leather jacket, smiling as he approached them.

As if they were friends or something.

"You motherfucker."

Denise took him by his elbow. "Be nice."

"*What?*"

"Your woman is correct, you should be nice."

Steve felt an inhuman growl pushing itself out of his throat, rumbling deep within his chest. "Unless you're going to tell me how to get out of here, then don't talk to me."

"I'm sorry, friend. It was the only way to bring the both of you here. You would not have agreed otherwise."

Steve flexed his fingers. It would feel so sweet to smash this asshole's face in. God, he wanted to do it so badly. He could visualize it perfectly, especially as the asshole continued to smile at him as though everything was all right.

Calm. He was going to be calm and professional.

With that decision made, it became easy to compartmentalize his anger, and focus on what was happening in front of him.

Denise was important. His revenge could come later.

"All right. So why did you bring us here? I could have taken care of her. I have a backup and am trained for situations like this."

"No, you're not, little man."

Keep it compartmentalized. Keep it compartmentalized.

Steve turned to Denise. Had to look away from that other guy before he lost his damned mind.

"You said he explained this all to you?"

Denise did not look remotely happy. She nodded. "Yeah."

His gut sank. "And?"

Denise finally met his eyes. "Is it true? You're smelling mating pheromones on me?"

Steve glanced at Jackson, barely containing his growl. "Yeah."

He would have liked to be the one to explain that to her. To gently ease her into the idea after dinner, sex, a couple of movie dates, more sex.

Instead, he had the option ripped away from him as though all of this was supposed to be for the best.

"She needed to know."

"Yeah, I got that."

"You didn't tell her."

"I didn't get a single date out of her before those wolves came at us, so will you get off my back?"

A few of the adults—Steve figured they were parents by the watchful eye they kept on the kids—turned to look at him sharply at the outburst.

Like he cared. "You succeeded in kidnapping us, so tell us why we're here."

"He brought us here so you can finish the mating."

Steve froze. He looked back at Denise, then shook his head, hardly able to look at the other man when he was so fucking furious with him.

"You motherfucker."

"You were going to do it anyway."

"Yeah, on my Goddamn terms. Not yours."

The whole thing suddenly had a creepy vibe to it. He'd been brought here specifically to fuck Denise? It almost made it out as though neither of them had much of a choice in it. He didn't like that either.

Denise spoke up again. "Not just on your terms, asshole."

Shit.

He turned back to her. Christ, he was really starting to feel as though he was being sandwiched between two hard spots.

"I didn't mean it like that."

The way she looked at him suggested she didn't have much faith in that claim.

Steve turned his body, facing her fully. "Denise, I wasn't thinking of it like that. You saw me when I came into your hospital. You know I just changed. I barely knew you were a mate. I was still debating whether or not it could be true."

Before Jackson opened his stupid mouth.

Denise crossed her arms. She inhaled a breath and seemed to hold it before letting it out. "It's just a lot to take in."

"And I get it. We don't have to do anything you don't want to do."

"Until you make the claim on her, other wolves will be coming for her."

"Will you fuck off with that already?"

Some of the moms got up and went to their children, covering their ears and glaring Steve's way as they carted off the complaining kids from their fun.

Steve didn't give a shit. "If this is affecting her so bad then why aren't any of you jumping all over her?"

Jackson reacted, finally. His face twisted, as though he'd never heard something more vile in his entire life. "Are you asking me why we would not rape her? We are not monsters."

"You said her scent is pulling out a call to other shifters."

"It is."

"And you're not affected? For that matter, why am I not affected? How come I'm not trying to hold her down and have my way with her right now."

"Because I wouldn't let you," Denise muttered.

Steve wanted to believe her, but he had yet to figure out the full extent of her strength, and it still didn't explain why he wasn't under this same spell as the other shifters were.

Jackson took in a breath, doing what Denise had done as he held it a moment before releasing it. As though he was getting rid of all the excess tension in his body.

And Steve hated how much this guy and his mate seemed to have in common.

"What's going on? Those wolves that came at us back at Denise's house weren't from the same pack that did this to me, were they?"

"It's doubtful. Some wolves have been known to travel quite a ways when they get a scent they like."

Steve tensed at that. He looked back at Denise. "How long... No, wait, I think you told me."

She glared at him. "I didn't know it was this bad either. I thought I was just...I knew there were wolves around, and sometimes they would get close, but I thought that was the way of things living around Lakeview. There are all kinds of shifters all over the place around here."

If it hadn't been her saying it, if she'd just been another client he was taking notes off of, he could have handled this better. Steve would have kept his concerns to himself, nodded, and gone right into how she could be protected, and what she could do better from here on out to keep anything else from happening in the future.

This wasn't just someone he'd met for a job. This was...fuck, this was his mate, and she'd been in danger for years of her life and barely been aware of it.

Steve turned back to Jackson, feeling the prickle of coarse fur as it came in through his arms, chest, and around his neck. "You are going to tell me exactly what they want with her and why. Be as specific as possible, because I am done putting up with this shit."

CHAPTER 11

"Your woman is a conduit. She has been tainted with shifter blood, much the same you were, but she will never transform."

Jackson looked Steve in the eye hard. What was he doing? Waiting on dramatic effect?

"So what does that mean?"

Jackson had moved both Steve and Denise to one of the many picnic tables scattered around his territory. The children and parents had come out again, but it seemed as though the parents had done so with some reluctance.

Steve could still feel their irritated eyes on him as Jackson sat them down for their chat.

Denise rubbed her face. She seemed the least pleased by this whole thing, which made sense, all things considered.

"It means I'll make for a good baby making factory." She wouldn't look at either Jackson or Steve. She reached for the canned soda on the table, bringing it to her mouth and drinking while trying not to look at anyone.

The tension in her muscles gave everything away.

Steve's fingernails dug into the wood of the table. "And other wolves want to breed with you now?"

"They always have." Jackson leaned back, his arms crossed over his chest, making him look even bigger than before. "We have been protecting her in secret, and then you came."

Steve gritted his teeth against the unspoken accusation of being unworthy of her.

"So very noble. In my experience, no one does anything for anyone else without wanting something in return."

"Your profession is only helping those for something in return, from my understanding of it."

Steve frowned. He looked sharply at Denise, who still would not look back at him.

"She told you?"

Jackson nodded. "You are a private detective. You help only those who have the money to give you."

His nails dug a little deeper into the wood. "It's not always as simple as that, but fine."

"Regardless, you have proven to be unable to see to her care, and she is clearly too stubborn to accept assistance. It was wise for us to keep our distance, but no more. If you are her mate, then you should make your claim as soon as possible."

Steve was going to puncture holes right through the wooden table. He glanced at Denise quickly, knowing she would not appreciate his next question.

"Would that stop these other wolves from stalking her?"

He felt Denise's eyes on him immediately. He was going to pay for asking that question down the road.

"Possibly?"

"What do you mean, possibly?" Denise finally decided to partake in the conversation. "I thought if my mate made his claim then his scent would be enough to keep the other wolves back."

Jackson shrugged unhelpfully. "There haven't been many like yourself around these parts. I've never seen one, and yet we all knew what you were just from the smell of you. This one is still weak, there's no telling whether he will be enough to keep those other wolves from wanting you."

Steve growled. He didn't recognize the sound of his own voice for a moment. "I'll be more than enough if anyone comes for her."

Denise pushed herself to her feet, taking Steve's attention off Jackson. She dragged her fingers through her hair, shaking her head and keeping her back to the both of them.

Being told she not only had a mate, but that she had to hurry things along in order to keep safe probably wasn't so great. Especially for someone who, until very recently, had a strict no shifter policy.

Steve's cock was going to hate him for this, and he was going to hate himself too, but that was too damned bad.

He stood, though he knew better than to touch her.

No matter how much he wanted to. "Denise, don't even worry about it."

She laughed dryly. "Right, what's not to worry about? Everything's being decided without me. I wanted to have sex with you. I didn't want to feel like we were going to be stuck together for life, or to feel like I *had* to have sex with you."

God, that made his gut twist so hard. He'd already known it, of course, but hearing her plainly say it so loudly that she'd wanted to have sex with him made his groin tighten painfully.

He pulled back that sense of disappointment.

"Who the hell cares what this jackass says? If you don't want me to fuck you, then don't ask me to fuck you. I won't force the issue. Christ, what the hell kind of man do you think I am?"

The idea that she would think he would try holding her down sickened him. Steve tried to push the thought out of his head. Denise was a strong, intelligent, and capable woman. In the short time they'd known each other, she'd already more than proved that to him.

But, right now, she could hardly look at him. "I just need to think about this."

Steve fell back a step.

His first impulse was to get angry, angry at the idea that she apparently thought of him as some kind of monster.

Then, no. No, he knew better than that. This wasn't about him.

She had her reasons for not wanting to be around shifters, but in the end, she'd still decided to go out with him.

She hated that her choices were being taken from her, and he got that.

"I won't do anything you don't want me to do. I swear to God, I won't. I don't give a damn about the mating."

"That's not what he said."

Steve groaned. Didn't take a genius for him to figure out what she meant by that. He glared over his shoulder at Jackson.

"Okay. What the hell did you tell her?"

Jackson, the prick, looked as cool as a cucumber while Steve glared heat rays of death at him.

"The truth. You are a new shifter with the scent of a mate surrounding you. There is the possibility of losing yourself to the instinct to mate."

Steve let that thought sink in. "You're telling me you think I would attack her?"

Not just attack her. Christ, it almost sounded as though he was suggesting—

"There is always the risk with any shifter of losing oneself to the animal. We see this all the time in our young. Why do you think we still have packs?"

Steve shook his head. "I don't care why you still have packs. That's not the kind of person I am, and I would never, *ever* even think about doing that to Denise, or anyone else."

"You can barely contain yourself even now." Jackson gestured to basically all of Steve, and he glanced down.

Fur grew out of the tiny pores of his hands. His fingers turned black, felt rough when he rubbed them together.

Almost as though he was getting ready to grow paws.

"You see? You need control."

Steve flexed his fingers. "I need…I need to find the people who did this to me. They can help me."

"You don't need them. You just need a pack."

Steve looked away from the claws slowly pushing out from beneath his fingernails and back up at Jackson. "What? I thought I needed the people who changed me."

Jackson cocked his head a little. "How many were involved in your transformation?"

Steve growled. "Enough. At least four had their claws in me at some point." He could still feel them at times, but considering the topic, and the hesitant way Denise looked at him, he didn't think it would be the best idea in the world to let out that little detail.

Jackson nodded sagely, those huge arms crossed over his massive chest.

If he didn't look like a living embodiment of *The Rock* then Steve might have attacked him. Unfortunately, Steve knew better than to attack a man who looked like that, much as he wanted to.

"You will become part of my pack. I will take you in and you will learn how to contain yourself."

"Okay, wait, hold on. I'm not going to be part of your pack. I can't be part of anyone's pack right now. I have a life. Responsibilities."

"Your career?"

Steve rolled his eyes. "Yes, that would be a big one."

It wasn't just a career, and despite the man's jab at it, Steve did help people. He put his ass out there to make sure other people stayed safe, and he wasn't about to turn his back on that.

"You will hurt other people, including your woman, if you do not take my offer."

"I would never hurt her. And I've already got some support in place. My friend is a subhuman, and his new mate already has a skulk of foxes."

"That's hardly the same."

"Well, either way, I'm not about to pledge my loyalty to *you*."

Jackson smirked at him, as though Steve had just said something amusing. "You will, eventually."

"Steve, I think you should do it."

Fuck. Steve rubbed his face, looking back at Denise, who still looked hesitant to be standing anywhere near him. "I can handle this. I wasn't lying. You've met my friend. He can help me through this."

She shook her head. "Subhumans are not the same as having an alpha to follow, and I've already seen what you can do. You're sloppy when you lose control, but you're still powerful. Do you really think your new inner animal will be tamed by a group of foxes?"

If he was a wolf, then the answer to that was a big unlikely.

"It's better than nothing."

"You don't have nothing. Jackson is making you an offer right now. If you join his pack, he can help you control this."

"And you would not be a danger to your mate."

"Will you let me talk to her for one minute?" The last thing Steve needed was for the guy making eyes at Denise to throw that in his face right now.

He looked Denise in the eyes. The half grimace on her face suggested all sorts of things. Namely how, mating or no mating, Steve had zero chances with her if he didn't do this.

Because what Jackson told her had been enough to scare the hell out of her, and with what already happened to her, Steve couldn't blame her. The son of a bitch had checkmated him, and he couldn't do anything about it.

"All right, fine." Steve tried not to sound as though he was biting out those words through clenched teeth. "I'll join your pack, but this won't be a permanent thing, and I'm not going to live here or anything either."

"It doesn't have to be a permanent situation for you, but you absolutely will live here until you have a proper sense of control."

Steve growled. That smile never left Jackson's face.

"Your first lesson is now. It's time to see how far that control of yours can stretch in uncertain circumstances."

"What?"

Jackson's fist cracked Steve in the eye before he had the chance to realize it was coming. Which was a terrible reminder of how fast the man was.

Steve didn't pass out like he had the last time, but he couldn't entirely be sure of exactly what happened either when a monstrous roar escaped his throat and he flew at the man.

Everything after that was a haze.

CHAPTER 12

*D*enise screamed without meaning to. The speed at which Steve transformed into a wolf and flew at Jackson was beyond anything she'd known a shifter was capable of.

And she'd thought she'd prepared for something like this. Prepared for when she came face to face with a shifter wanting a piece of her. She had managed to hold her own whenever she caught a wolf, fox, or bear shifter on her property, but this…this was something else.

Jackson actually laughed as the wolf came at him. He managed to lift one of his huge arms, and even when Steve had it in his mouth, teeth clamping down, blood flowing, Jackson hardly seemed to mind it. As though he was excited for the fight. Steve pushed the man back a little. His new body was definitely that of a wolf, but he was bigger than what Denise thought they grew to.

A few of the parents looked up at the fight. Though they quickly moved for their children, gathering them up and moving them out of the way of the scuffle, they didn't appear to have any real panic about them.

The toddlers easily went. The older kids complained how they wanted to watch.

Were fights between the males normal? Or was it an alpha thing? Women could be alphas as far as Denise was aware.

Did that mean Steve was an alpha?

Denise shivered, watching as the massive creature continued biting and clawing at Jackson, who no longer smiled at the display, as though this was going on longer than he'd thought it would.

He pulled his arm free of those massive teeth. Blood spattered everywhere. Jackson grabbed the wolf by the fur of his throat, throwing the creature around, but Steve still managed to stay on his hind legs, front paws still on Jackson's shoulders, claws digging into Jackson's flesh.

Denise couldn't contain herself anymore. "Will you stop him already? Someone's going to get hurt!"

And in that moment, she wasn't too concerned it would be Steve. He seemed as though he could handle himself against Jackson.

Though if he hurt anyone else, one of those excited kids, Denise doubted it would sit well with him after the fact.

Jackson's face changed. Denise could see it in the glow of his eyes first, the way his nostrils darkened and changed, lengthened. His transformation seemed slower at first, but she realized soon that it was much more deliberate. More controlled.

Jackson appeared as though he was shifting into the shape of his wolf, but he stayed upright, kept his opposable thumbs, and held on tightly to Steve's scruff before slamming him down with a roar.

Denise swore she felt the earth beneath her feet rumble with the force of the hit.

Steve didn't go down easy. He snapped his teeth, his hind legs scratching frantically at Jackson's chest and face. Apparently, no one, not even a man as built as Jackson, could hold onto a creature that did something like that.

Denise was so caught up in what she was seeing that she almost didn't notice the two wolves who came to stand on either side of her. She didn't know if they were the same two who had been at her house last night. Didn't care either. "Will you do something? Help him!"

The wolves did nothing. In fact, they sat down. Useless.

Jackson released Steve, who rolled to his feet, hackles raised up high enough that it looked as though a spiked mohawk traveled down his spine as he growled at the other man, head bent, claws digging into the earth as he and Jackson stared each other down.

Denise couldn't breathe. Her heart slammed, though her feet remained locked.

She hadn't felt this since she was a little girl. Since she'd been attacked. She didn't like it, but the fear wasn't entirely for herself this time.

Steve glanced back at her, his pointed ears flicking. Denise's gut twisted.

Steve backed off from Jackson, edging his way towards her, though he kept his eyes mostly on the other man as Jackson slowly followed.

The two wolves next to Denise growled low.

Jackson motioned with his hand, and they stopped, then gave Denise some space.

She tensed. "Hey, what are you doing?"

"Be quiet." Jackson's command was sharp as he refused to take his eyes off the bear-like wolf backing towards her. "Let him come to you."

Denise looked at Steve. No. Not Steve. This was an animal. A wild animal that had a piece of Steve's mind now.

And it was almost on top of her now.

"You've got to be kidding me."

"Let's see what it does."

Denise stared at Jackson, and now she could understand better why Steve clearly didn't like the other man. "You serious?"

The wolf was closing in on her. She could reach out and touch it. It glanced back at her, as though making sure she was still there.

"He wants to protect you."

Denise felt the harsh fur against her hands. She yanked them back, but her feet still refused to move.

The wolf glanced back at her. She could see no sign of intelligence within those eyes. At least not human intelligence, but there was something there. Something that pulled this animal to her.

"Steve?"

The wolf turned his attention back to Jackson, continuing to growl. His tail flicked, whacking Denise in the legs, though she got the feeling the wolf was trying to convey a sense of ownership.

She glared at the back of Steve's head.

He thought he owned her, did he?

Had he not been in his wolf form and she feared he would bite her head off, she might have given him a good smack upside the head for that.

"So what do I do now?"

Jackson had stopped trying to approach her. He stood less than four feet away from where the wolf stood, half curled around Denise's body.

Jackson seemed to be observing the creature.

"I would suggest not moving too much, but speak to him. See what he will do."

"That doesn't sound as though you know what's going on here."

The corner of his mouth quirked, though he did not look at her. He stared intently at the wolf. "Every newborn shifter needs to have their limits tested. This would seem to be the both of yours."

Great.

Denise wet her lips. She looked at the back of the wolf's head, then sighed. "Steve, Steve, if you can hear me, I would really like it if you could shift back into your human shape."

The wolf's black lips didn't pull back so much, though his pointed teeth were still revealed.

"Steve, I know you don't like Jackson, but he's trying to help."

"He does not wish for me to dominate him. Noble enough for a male with a female to take care of."

Denise clenched her jaw. "I don't need taking care of."

"Try telling that to an angry mated wolf."

She was going to tell him in good time. When he wasn't scaring the hell out of her by being in this shape.

"Steve, please, can you change back?" She didn't want to admit to this next part. "It scares me, seeing you like this. Like you're not in control. Please turn back."

She couldn't be sure if he even understood her. That was what made it worse.

But something was getting through. His long ears flicked with every word she spoke. He might not understand. His human mind might be buried a little too deeply in there, but he was *trying* to understand.

"Steve, change back. Turn back, *please.*"

Again, his ears flicked, and this time, the wolf didn't simply glance back at her, but it turned its head away from Jackson, giving Denise its full attention.

Her heart stopped at the sight.

The terror of being so close to something that could rip her to pieces, coupled with her fascination of the powerful creature in front of her, made for an interesting mix within herself, as far as she was concerned.

She wanted to touch the wolf's pelt.

Her hand reached out. Slowly. She barely moved at all. A few seconds ago, she'd yanked her fingers away, but now the compulsion to feel that fur between her fingers was too much for her to ignore.

So close. Those golden eyes watched her, as though waiting for what else she planned on doing.

A low rumble sounded from the throat of the wolf as her fingers made contact. Denise didn't move, but then that soft growl melted away as Denise stroked the coarse fur.

Stroked was being generous. She barely moved her hand, but the thrill of being able to touch a wolf that was nearly the size of a horse… she couldn't believe she'd pulled together the courage to do this.

"Wow." Her heart slammed. It was better than riding a roller coaster. More thrilling than watching a scary movie in the dark while alone, and better than eating ice cream after nine p.m.

The tingle that rose up her fingers made her entire body shudder, and she couldn't pull away from the animal.

An animal that wanted her for himself. A mate.

Maybe this wouldn't be so terrible after all.

Suddenly, the wolf glanced away from her. It growled again, pulling Denise back into the real world as she yanked her fingers back.

But that didn't seem to be the problem. The massive grey and black body of the wolf shuddered, shrank, and then melted down back into Steve.

His clothes were almost entirely torn off around his body as his paws turned into hands and feet. He gasped for breath on the grass and dirt, his eyes wild and face flushed.

His voice was hoarse when he spoke. "What happened?"

Denise blinked when he looked back at her, and the sudden dryness in her mouth left her almost incapable of speaking.

His body… *God*, his body was…

He looked good, she had to give him that. She couldn't spot an inch of fat anywhere on him. Not that she hadn't already seen what he looked like, but that was different. That was back at the hospital. He'd been covered in blood then, or lying in bed recovering. His recovery had been quick, but she was a professional. She didn't moon over patients.

Not too much, anyway.

Steve rubbed his jaw, as though stroking away the aches and pains of his transformation, though his expression became more cautious when Denise didn't answer him right away.

"Denise?"

She shook her head. Someone quickly stepped forward and put a long towel around his shoulders. That helped. "I'm fine. You just…you changed really fast is all."

Now he looked horrified as he tried pushing himself to his feet. "Christ, are you all right? *Guh…*" He groaned and fell back down to one knee. His expression would have been comical had he not just shifted into a wolf.

Denise might not be used to being around creatures like that, but watching Steve sink to one knee brought out the nurse in her. She rushed to him.

"Are you okay?" Had he not already risen to his feet, she would have touched him with more hesitation, though there was still the risk of a neck injury of some kind. "Try not to move too much. Look up at me."

"I'm fine."

She wasn't about to take that risk.

Denise spread Steve's eye wide open, getting a look at the pupil, searching for signs of trauma. She checked his temperature and searched around his throat, then the rest of his body, that she could see, for any hints of a wound.

"I'm okay, Denise. I want to know if you're okay."

She looked him in the eyes, though she couldn't hold the gaze. "I'm all right. I just needed to check you over."

He smiled at that.

"Because I'm a nurse and it's my job," she said, clarifying the mistake she knew he was thinking about.

At the same time, she couldn't deny that he was right. At least a little.

Not that she was going to let him know that.

Though it didn't seem to matter because he was still looking at her like that. Looking at her as though he knew she cared more than she wanted to admit.

"Do you understand the need for a pack now?"

Denise felt the little muscle beneath her eye twitch. Now really wasn't the right time for Jackson to be going on with that. Not as far as she was concerned.

Steve growled, as she expected him to.

"You motherfucker. What did you do to me?"

Jackson narrowed his eyes. "Proving a point. You do not have control. You need control. The fact that you are naked right now is proof of that."

"No, the fact that you did that to me and I could have hurt Denise is on you. You're lucky I don't go over there and—"

Denise slapped her hand over Steve's mouth before he could get out whatever else it was he was going to threaten the man with. "Let me talk it over with him."

Jackson glanced at her, then at Steve. "You have one hour. If he does not step in line willingly, I will make him."

Steve growled, and Denise felt the sudden prickle of fur growing against her hand.

This guy might be in charge around here, but he clearly didn't know how to handle these sorts of things.

"Fine, give me one hour."

Jackson raised his finger to her. "Not one minute more." He turned and walked away, leaving Denise with a very angry shifter to deal with. She'd almost rather call her Nurse Director and ask for more time off. That seemed much easier when compared to this.

She pulled her hand away from Steve's mouth. The way he looked at her was not impressed by any standard of the word.

"You have got to be kidding me. I am not joining his pack! Are you out of your mind?"

"You'll be out of your mind if you think I'm going to have anything to do with a shifter who can't control himself."

That was all it took. One little sentence like that and she saw the light go off in his eyes as he jerked back.

"What?"

Denise looked him right in the eye. "You just had what I'm guessing is your first full blown transformation. You had that in front of me and got into a fight with an alpha before backing up into me as though you thought you owned me. That is not okay."

"All right, you're right—"

"Damn right, I'm right."

Steve leaned closer, his voice urgent. "I cannot join a pack that I know nothing about. These people kidnapped us, and I wasn't kidding. I already have people who can help me with this."

"Jackson said your wolf wouldn't listen to fox shifters, or a subhuman. You didn't see the size you turned into. You might be an alpha."

Steve nodded, as though that information didn't shock him, though it clearly didn't please him either. "Fuck."

Denise wet her lips. "I know you hate this, but it's not forever. You just need their help so you can control yourself." She touched Steve's arm, feeling the sudden change in his body that came with that simple contact. "I know you don't want to hurt anyone. You want to protect me, but this is what you are now, and if you want to protect yourself, and protect me, you need these people to help you."

Steve's jaw tightened. He glanced over his shoulder. Jackson had walked away, but he was still within sight. Denise was pretty sure he could hear every word being spoken with that shifter hearing of his.

"Please, just do this for now. Until you're in control enough to start a pack of your own."

Steve shook his head. "Will it make you feel safer?"

She didn't have to think about it. "Yes."

Steve held her gaze. "Even if I didn't do this, you know you're not stuck with me, right? My decision has no bearing on what happens to you."

Denise felt that fluttering in her heart. The sensation that was becoming a little too common for her lately. "Yeah, it does, actually." Something changed in Steve's eyes. Denise covered his mouth before he could say anything. "Whatever you're going to say, for now, don't. If I really am your mate, then this is something we're going to have to deal with, and I need to have a mate who will take his health and safety, as well as the health and safety of those immediately around him, seriously. Sound good?" She pulled her hand away.

Steve stared at her as though he didn't entirely understand what was going on, but he nodded all the same. "All right."

Denise knew they were far from done with this. If Steve really was an alpha, he would never want to submit to another male, but if it was the only way he was going to gain some control over himself, then it was what she needed him to do.

Steve growled low in his throat, turning his attention back to Jackson. "What does it take to join a pack?"

Jackson didn't smile. Denise thought he would take some pleasure in this.

"Just some of your blood, and an oath."

"Great. You're lucky she's worth this."

Again with that fluttery feeling beneath her ribs. The number of times she could tell herself this was all wrong, that this was a mistake, were dwindling. It was looking more and more as though she had a mate. A mate with a shifter.

Someone somewhere was laughing at her. Denise was positive of at least that much as she helped her new mate to stand, then watched as Jackson snatched out his arm, grabbing both her and Steve by their wrists. He bit Steve's hand first, then, teeth still bloody, sank his long canines into Denise's palm before she could pull away. The heat alone was enough to make her scream before Jackson mashed their hands together.

Steve also screamed, but he sounded more furious than in pain as he snapped at Jackson.

She really hoped the larger man knew what he was doing, because more and more it looked as though he was playing some sort of game with them.

CHAPTER 13

After Jackson bit Steve on the fatty flesh of his palm, in what had to be the most painful thing he'd felt in his entire life, Steve, blinded by the heat and pain, screamed long and loud. The only other sensation he could compare it to was when he'd been torn open by those shifters who Zelda used to live with.

This was...not quite the same.

And he was stupid for not seeing what came next. He should have realized what Jackson planned on doing when he finally pulled his teeth free of Steve's hand.

Steve pounded the man in the head a couple of times when he bit down onto Denise, those big teeth almost looking as though they were going to tear off her slender fingers.

She shrieked and attempted to pull away from him, but it didn't seem to do any good. Jackson was too powerful, and worried Steve would cause the man to accidentally bite off a chunk of her hand, he stopped hitting the other man, waiting until his teeth were free.

Jackson slammed their hands together, holding them in place as though his palms were a metal vice.

The heat subsided, but only a little. Not that Steve cared so much about the pain melting away when Denise sank to her knees.

The terror in her eyes was more than what Steve could handle. He tried pulling them apart, then used his free hand to punch at Jackson's stupid head.

The man either dodged the blows or allowed Steve to hit him.

As though his strength was nothing.

Where was that crazy shifter strength when he needed it? Did it only show up when he was in his wolf shape? Why wouldn't the dumb animal come out now when he needed it to?

"Let this happen."

Jackson's eyes changed to a drastic red color. Steve's knees wobbled at the sight. He nearly fell over, but no. He forced himself to stay on his feet.

This prick was trying to dominate him. He wasn't going to allow for it.

"What the hell do you think you're doing?"

"Stop struggling. You'll open her wound."

Steve froze. He glanced down at Denise. Their hands were still joined, but she remained on her knees, hardly moving, her head bent.

Was she unconscious?

"What are you doing?" Steve snapped through clenched teeth. He wasn't going to let the asshole keep doing this to him, and he was going to get some answers. "If she's hurt, I swear to God—"

"She is not hurt. The heat and the shock must have been too much for her."

Steve was going to explode. "So what is this?"

"A joining. If you will not take your mate through traditional means, then blood will seal the union just as well."

All heat drained from Steve's face at the mention of a union.

He was solidifying the mating.

"I thought that could only be done through sex."

"Blood works just as nicely. Some mates bite each other for that very reason."

Steve was fucking furious. The heat of that anger rose up within him like boiling acid, and he went back to wanting to shred Jackson's face clean off. "She might not have wanted me to mate with her, you dumb motherfucker. That was the whole reason why I was taking my time with this."

Jackson met his stare. God, Steve hated having to look up at the other man. "You do not get that choice and neither does she. A mate will help to keep away the shifters who want her. Your scent is now permanently part of hers."

Jackson released their joined hands. Denise fell over. Steve caught her before she could land on the hard earth. Passed out. Considering how tough she was, he wouldn't have thought that was possible. He swallowed hard. Just because she was his mate didn't mean her fear of shifters would have left her much peace.

Steve growled up at Jackson. "I could have protected her without you needing to do that."

Jackson shrugged. "Perhaps. My pack has done well to keep her would-be rapists at bay, but I suppose if that is a risk *you* are comfortable with taking, then there's nothing I can do to persuade you otherwise."

Everything this man said always made Steve want to tear him to pieces. "I do not want anyone coming after her to rape her! Don't say that shit to me you dumb cocksucker, you have no idea what I would do to protect her."

Jackson sank to his knees, his eyes firm on Steve.

Once again, Steve felt that inkling within him to lower his gaze. To look away. To give this man all power and authority over him.

And, once again, he fought it. He stared back at him hard, refusing to blink until he absolutely had to.

The corner of Jackson's mouth quirked. "You are a fighter. This is good. You will do well for our pack." He pointed at Denise. "She will give you strong alpha children. Your scent on her will make predators think twice about coming for her, but you must still be on your guard."

Steve growled. "Right. Is that why you want me in your pack now? If I'm mated to her and we make babies or something, if puts a couple more alphas under your control?"

"How many times do I have to explain to you that we are not monsters here? Though, to be honest, the urge was always there to make her ours. An intelligent conduit. A nurse at that. Even with fast healing, someone with such talents is always welcome in any pack."

"Right, you just want to help us out of the goodness of your heart."

"I want to help you because you are an idiot who cannot control his powers, and she is helpless without a pack to protect her. If she had ever decided to move away, out of my reach, the next pack she lived closer to might not have had that same control, or mercy, that I did."

Steve clenched his jaw. He said nothing, however. What could he say? Jackson was right. As a medical professional, if Denise ever decided to go work for another hospital, even temporarily, she would have been on her own. From what little he knew of her, that had been the case a time or two in her life, but she'd been lucky.

All it would take would be for one sick freak with thin morals to get a whiff of her scent, get lucky enough to get through her defenses, and then she was done. Forced to mate with someone cruel and disgusting who would use her as a *baby making factory*, as Denise had called it.

Didn't sound too far off the mark as far as he was concerned.

It made him cringe just thinking about it.

No wonder she didn't want to have anything to do with shifters. Hell, Steve had been attacked and changed by them, and he barely wanted anything to do with them.

She'd had to fight them off for most of her life, and she hadn't even been aware of what it was they really wanted. He wouldn't want anything to do with shifters either. She likely wouldn't want anything to do with him when she woke up.

"She will want you. You have nothing to fear in that regard."

Steve tried not to growl at the man. He really did. "It would be amazing if you could not do that around me right now."

Jackson got that look on his face again. The one that suggested he knew something Steve did not. And, after everything, that made him incredibly worried. "What?"

"I've solidified your connection with your mate. I have not yet solidified your connection to this pack yet."

Now he wanted to groan more than growl.

He looked down at Denise, thought of everything Jackson had said. There were people, not just people, but powerful shifters, who wanted to come after her. Wanted to reproduce with her because of some powerful scent she was giving off.

Whether she wanted it or not.

Much as he hated Jackson right now, Steve could not stand by and let something like that happen. No fucking way.

"Right. What do I have to do?"

Jackson brought his hand to his mouth, biting down on it this time. The man barely flinched as he broke the skin and made himself bleed.

Steve barely stopped himself from turning away at the sight. There was always something unnerving about watching someone hurt themselves.

Steve sighed when Jackson finished. "All right." He held out his hand.

Jackson shook his head. "Not with the blood of your mate on there. This will require something different."

Steve frowned, his suspicions rising once again. "Different how?"

Jackson held out his hand. Steve looked at it, then understood. "Goddamn, you don't like making this easy, do you?"

Jackson shrugged softly. "Unless you want my blood intermingling with that of you and your mate?"

"No, no, you're right. This is the best way," Steve said, though he was seriously considering his life choices when he put his mouth onto Jackson's hand and began to drink the blood that pooled onto his palm.

It burned as much going down as his hand had when he'd joined bloody palms with Denise, and almost as much as when he'd changed in the first place.

He was learning how to be a proper shifter. He might as well get used to this sort of thing.

It didn't make him anymore prepared for when three massive wolves charged the property, rushing towards him with their fangs exposed and their hackles raised up high for a fight.

CHAPTER 14

Steve thought he recognized these wolves the moment he caught sight of them. And smell.

The same ones from the road. The same ones who had torn him open, who had left him bleeding to die.

There was only one thing they could be here for, and he sure as hell wasn't about to let them have it.

Steve pulled Denise into his arms. Jackson and two of his other wolves snarled, charging towards the wolves who had suddenly burst onto the scene.

This time, the parents showed a great deal more terror as they screamed and gathered up their children. Steve doubted any of them would be whining or complaining about not getting to see that fight.

He followed the nearest male and female he could spot. They only had one child between them, so at least he wouldn't be putting too many kids at risk here.

"Wait! Please, stop!"

The male didn't slam the door right on Steve's face, but it was close enough that Steve could barely make out any details of the male's face.

"Please, I need to hide her."

The man glanced down at Denise, then back up at Steve. "You've got a place to hide her."

Steve stuck his foot in the door before the man could slam it shut, and that really fucking hurt with bare feet. He snarled through his teeth. "I can't leave her alone."

"We've got a kid in here!"

And this male was clearly no alpha, but two adults watching over her were better than no one at all.

Steve shook his head. "There's a fight going on behind me and I need to help. Please, let me put her inside with you. I'll make it up to you later."

He had no idea how, but that didn't matter. The sounds of the wolves behind him trying to rip each other apart was getting closer and closer as Jackson and his wolves struggled to hold the threat back, and with the taste of blood still in his mouth, Steve wanted to join in on that fight.

The male hesitated for the longest three seconds of Steve's life, and because of that, he could no longer leave the choice up to him.

He pushed his way through the door. The male tried to push back, but the door cracked under the pressure and he was forced to step back or else let it shatter.

"She won't be any trouble," Steve said, moving towards the couch nearest the door to the tiny home.

The female held her child behind her, eyes wide on Steve, as though he was one of the three wolves getting ready to tear shit up around here.

Steve looked away from her, turning his attention to the male, who glared at him.

Steve growled back, letting a little of the wild animal inside him out to play.

And it didn't play as nicely as Steve would have. "I'll come back for her. I find out you threw her outside or something, and I will burn this little hut down around you, understand?"

The man suddenly looked less angry as his eyes popped wide open.

Steve didn't give him the chance to respond as he walked out.

The door slammed shut behind him. Steve noted the sound of

locks sliding into place as he stepped off the tiny porch and went to join the fight.

It seemed fairly even between Jackson and the wolf he dealt with. They appeared to be of a similar size to each other, so Steve didn't get the sense of urgency with that one.

The other two wolves, however, were large enough as to give Jackson's friends some trouble, and more of his wolves had already come in to join the fight. Two of Jackson's wolves against one each of the intruders.

And one of them was getting a little too close to the tiny house where Steve had left Denise.

He needed to let the animal out. He needed to become a wolf again, just like when Jackson had struck him.

He could feel it. Directly beneath his skin, so close to the surface and wanting out. Wanting to fight. Wanting to tear them limb from limb.

But even as he roared and flew at the wolf who overpowered the two working for Jackson, that inner animal still did not come forward. It was just him, but the adrenaline, and the sudden rush of his body caught the wolf off guard as Steve flew at the creature, hooking his arms beneath the neck of the wolf and throwing him backwards.

The wolf swiftly scrambled to its feet, tail flicking, head bent with a growl before its ears flicked, and it looked at Steve suddenly with a touch more recognition. Steve nodded, his fingertips itching. Even naked, he felt as though he could destroy this animal.

"That's right, you remember me? I remember you."

His fingertips weren't just itching. Claws pushed their way out from beneath his human fingernails.

He was shifting, but apparently not as quickly as he would have preferred.

"You try coming near her, and I will rip you apart."

It shocked him when the wolf standing there pushed itself up onto its hind legs, swiftly and easily transforming into a fully clothed male.

A male with soft brown hair, a beard in desperate need of a trim, and a scar down the side of his throat.

Steve drank it all in. He tried to memorize every detail in case the man shifted once more. He would need to describe this guy to Victor, to the local police. He had a description of one of the men now and that would be more than enough to get him off the streets.

Steve almost laughed. "You dumb motherfucker. Did you really think that was going to help you?"

"Thought you would have died by now." The man scrunched his nose. "You smell like something that belongs to me."

His claws became a touch longer. "She doesn't belong to you, dick-face. So you can let your friends know that she's already got an alpha."

"Alpha?" The man sneered at his claws. "You can barely get those little kiddy claws out and ready. Are you serious right now?"

Steve roared. He rushed the other man, swinging for him, but he missed, swiping at only air.

This guy didn't look as though he knew what he was doing, but apparently he did as he ducked low and came back up hard, his fist catching Steve in the gut, knocking the wind clean out of his lungs before he could react.

He went down hard, his arms around his gut. The other man grabbed Steve by his hair, pulling his face up.

He could still hardly breathe. His face burned as the other man forced him to look up at him. His large smile revealed teeth in the stages of yellowing.

"You really think your scent on that bitch will stop me? When I fuck her, I'll be the most powerful wolf in this shithole."

Steve growled. His fist moved almost without his say. Though it wasn't a closed fist. His claws punched out from beneath his finger-nails, painful and bloody before he punched them into the other man's gut.

Air whooshed from the guy's lungs. Every vein in his face seemed to pop as his face turned a comical shade of red as he stared at Steve. As though he honestly hadn't seen that coming.

That strange sense of animal anger, that slipping of control, washed over him so suddenly there was nothing to be done except to go with the flow.

"You touch her and you die. You understand me?" He dug his

fingers deeper into the man's gut. The warmth of blood pooled around his fingers. The scent was heavy in his nostrils. It pulled the animal out of him a little more. His face itched as coarse fur grew in through his extending nose.

The man scrambled to pull himself away from Steve. He began shifting. Steve couldn't allow that. He slammed the wolf down again and again until the animal stopped moving.

Even then, he wanted to kill the other wolf. Kill all the wolves who dared think they could touch Denise. They wanted to touch her with their filthy hands. To hurt her. He'd never let them. Never!

Steve roared. The two remaining wolves, along with Jackson and the wolves who fought with him, came to a sudden halt. They looked at him, as though shocked to hear such a noise.

Not willing to waste the opportunity before he lost his mind to the wolf once more, Steve rushed the lot of them.

CHAPTER 15

*D*enise groaned, opened her eyes, and promptly sat up straight.

A child nearby gasped. "Mommy."

Denise glanced over. She was in one of the tiny trailers. A woman stood by the kitchen counter, a small child next to her, holding her around her waist.

Denise couldn't tell if it was a boy or a girl from the dirt this kid had clearly been playing in, but that didn't matter in that moment as Denise heard what could only be described as a dog fight outside.

A man stood by the door, a rifle in his hands as he stared out the tiny door windows, watching the scene unfold. He looked back at her, his mouth twisting, though he said nothing to her as he went back to guarding his home, and what Denise presumed to be his mate and child.

This was not the trailer she and Steve had been brought to when Jackson kidnapped them. Which meant Steve had dumped her off after their hands had joined and that burning sensation took over.

She pushed herself to her feet, heading for the door. The male didn't move.

She hardly had the patience for this. "Out of my way, please."

He shook his head, not bothering to so much as glance at her as he stared out the window. "Your mate threatened me and my family well enough that I don't think you need to go anywhere."

Steve threatened these people?

Denise glanced back at the clearly terrified female and child. The mother seemed to be trying to get her little one to climb up to the loft to hide, but the kid started to cry.

"What happened?"

The male shrugged. "Three wolves showed up to start some shit. Your mate wanted me to look after you. Don't know who he thinks I am, but I've got a weapon in case they try coming in here." He looked at her briefly. "No offense, but if they come in here, I'm shooting to protect my woman and kid, not you."

Fair enough. "No offense taken." She eyed him. "Can I take a look?"

He looked at her, his lips pressing together as though he didn't entirely trust her. Not that she blamed him for that, but he stepped aside. Which created hardly any room for what she wanted considering how little space there was for her here.

She stepped up to the window to have a look, then gasped at the sight that met her.

It could have been a scene out of a horror movie. She had visions of men standing around caged dogs, pitted together, fighting for prize money for their owners.

Only these weren't dogs. These were people. They just happened to look like wolves in the moment.

One of them was Steve.

She grabbed the door handle. The palm of the male next to her came down hard on the door frame. "No."

Denise gritted her teeth. "I need to get out there."

He shook his head. "No, you don't."

Right. Because Steve had given this guy orders.

Denise nodded. "You're...you're right. I need to stay where it's safe."

He grunted.

"You don't want me in here."

"That's putting it mildly." He stared ahead through the glass, but he might as well have looked back at his mate and child for all the impact those words had.

In that case, she was going to consider what she did next as a favor to him.

Denise's knee came up. It was a move she'd learned through years of self-defense classes that didn't often work on men as much as people seemed to think it did. Men were more guarded of that spot on their bodies than most gave them credit for, and with good reason.

However, this man here didn't seem to think Denise was going to hit him below the belt the way she did. Denise felt badly for him, because he clearly hadn't seen this coming from her if the way he gasped and bent over was anything to go by.

She grabbed his gun.

He let it go easily. Smart move. He didn't want to risk accidentally firing off a shot when in an enclosed space with his wife and child nearby.

If he hadn't let it go almost immediately, Denise would have had to give it over to him instead. It was a risk she wasn't comfortable with taking either.

"Sorry," she muttered, opening the door.

The male flipped her off, his face red with pain as he remained hunched over, his mate coming to check on him quickly before the female glared at Denise and slammed the door behind her, locking it.

Right. No love lost there, but she wasn't here for them. Denise propped the rifle properly against her shoulder, going through the motions of how to hold such a weapon, how to aim it, even as her heart slammed and she told herself, screamed at herself, that she needed to hurry, that she couldn't take her time. She did just that.

Denise remembered her instructor, remembered to breathe, to brace herself, and make sure her fingers were in all the right spots as she fired her weapon.

A warning shot. The spot she'd hit exploded in a rush of dirt, but it was enough to cause the two wolves to yank away from each other.

Steve and whoever else that had been.

That was fine by her. She could see the blood soaking in through the fur. Wolf pelts were designed to be thick, for it to be difficult for claws and teeth to get at all the places no one really wanted them to make it to. They would have had to *really* been going at it for that to be happening.

And she was sick of having to come out from hiding with a gun to get the fighting to stop.

"No one is fighting anymore! And no one is fucking me! Do you understand now?"

The wolf that had been going head to head with Steve bent its head, a terrible snarl curling its lips as it stalked towards her.

Steve moved like he rode the wind, flying around the other creature and putting himself between her and the wolf that felt a little too brave for her liking.

Since Steve made for a bigger wolf than the one in front of him, he looked far more intimidating than his opponent did as he bent his neck and raised his hackles up high.

Denise, not wanting to be outdone, stepped around to his side, refusing to let him shield her like that. She kept her weapon pointed.

"The next shot won't be a warning shot."

Steve growled at her over his shoulder, his tail flicking.

Whatever. He could get over it. She wasn't going to run and hide from these things. Keeping the rifle pointed at the thing in front of her helped to boost her bravery, though, she would give it that.

Jackson and his own wolves seemed to have one pinned down between the lot of them. This other wolf standing in front of Steve honestly looked as though he was going to give it a try.

Either ballsy or incredibly stupid. Possibly both.

Steve growled back, warning it off. The wolf hesitated, but then actually stepped another paw forward.

Until another wolf still jumped on him. At first Denise thought it was one of Jackson's pack, but no. This one seemed to be grabbing his friend's attention rather than trying to start a fight.

The two wolves looked at each other briefly, glanced at their friend, who hardly moved a muscle beneath Jackson's weight, then growled at Steve and Denise one more time before turning tail and running off.

The damned things sure as hell moved fast when they were on a retreat.

Tempted, *so* tempted to fire a shot at them for terrorizing her. For making her constantly fear for her safety and the safety of her patients.

If she'd been holding a shotgun, she might have actually made the shot. From this distance, a few shotgun pellets in their asses wouldn't have killed them. Might make them think twice before trying to turn her into a breeding machine.

Denise waited until they were out of sight before lowering her stolen weapon and taking her finger off the trigger. Finding the safety, she clicked it on.

Jackson transformed, becoming his huge human self once more. He approached her with a smile. Steve growled at the other alpha, but reluctantly allowed him closer to Denise.

Something must have happened for that to be possible.

"You did very well—"

He stopped suddenly as the crack of her hand over his cheek cut off anything he was about to say next.

Jackson briefly turned his head with the force of the strike, but then slowly turned his gaze back to her.

"This…" Denise raised her other hand, the one with the bite mark on it. Still burning, still stinging. "Don't you ever do anything like this to me again."

Did Jackson really have to look at her so patiently? Couldn't he at least look at her as though what she'd done had gotten to him? What did she have to do to get a reaction around here?

"It was the only way."

"*Bullshit!*"

"His scent is on you now. It's almost as good as if he'd actually made a sexual claim."

"Then what the hell is he doing here?" She stabbed her finger in the direction of the wolf Jackson's men kept pinned down. The creature seemed to be unconscious, barely making a noise.

"The scent of your mate will be a deterrent. Others will still make an attempt."

Denise glared at the man.

Again, his stoic expression showed no hint of remorse.

"If you were really unhappy with this arrangement, I might have more pity for you, but I think you enjoy it too much."

"You think I *enjoy* this? Are you crazy?"

He eyed her. "Yes. I do think you enjoy this. You enjoy that you no longer have to make a decision. You want your mate but do not want to admit it. This takes away your culpability."

She was going to hit him again. Denise was on the verge of smacking him and her hand itched to do it when powerful fingers wrapped around her wrist.

"Don't, Denise. It's not worth it."

Even before she heard Steve's voice, his touch alone was enough to bring a shiver out of her. The heat of his hand on her skin, knowing he was naked behind her now that he was in his human form again...

Stupid Jackson. The stupid bastard for knowing what she wanted when she didn't even know what she wanted.

Because he was right. Denise had wanted Steve, *still* wanted him, despite everything that was happening, despite how much she hated shifters...Steve's touch on his wrist, the sound of his voice so close to her ear, and the warmth of his body she could not ignore all came together to make her knees weak.

That trembling feeling in her legs had nothing to do with her firing the rifle and helping to scare off would-be rapists.

She slumped against Steve's chest, feeling the sudden tension in his body.

She must have confused him with that, but she didn't care. Denise needed more of that touch. Even if it was an instinct brought on by horny werewolf mating habits, none of it mattered.

She just wanted to feel all right.

Jackson was right. Now that he'd...done whatever the hell it was he'd done to their hands, she no longer had to hold back. Why bother when the damage was done?

Steve growled. "Jackson, you motherfucker."

Again, Jackson had that look on his face that suggested how little he cared. "You will begin working with me immediately. You will learn to control the animal within you if you want to keep your woman, and yourself, safe from harm. You will not leave this property until you have that control. Neither will she."

That woke up Denise almost immediately. "Wait, what?" Adrenaline rushed through her once more. "I can't just stay here. I have a job. Responsibilities at the hospital."

"Would it be part of your job to put the lives of your patients at risk by allowing yourself access to them when there are those out there who would do you harm?"

Denise clenched her teeth. She had no idea what she was going to say to her boss. "I only asked for three days off. I can't stay here. This is my life. My livelihood."

Jackson raised a brow at her, and she had to admit, she felt foolish for wanting to go back to her work when there were those out there who had shown themselves willing to tear apart the hospital just to get at her.

Someone could get hurt if the wolves came for her when she was on the job in her scrubs.

Someone could die.

"You've protected her for years before I showed up," Steve said. "Why can't you let her go back to work while I learn control?"

Denise thought she loved him in that moment.

"Because I am no longer willing to split the manpower of my betas to watch over one female. I will not risk more of those wolves coming back here when half my men are away. Besides, I made it clear to you that this is a temporary situation, and you made it clear in return you have no intention of permanently staying a part of my pack. We will help you, but she is your responsibility from now on."

Denise had so many things she wanted to say to that.

She forced herself to keep her mouth shut. At least for now.

Denise wasn't anyone's responsibility as far as she was concerned, but this wolf seemed to have other ideas.

And while there were people out there who wanted to force her to carry their babies, and Steve struggling to control the brand new wolf inside him, it might be best to go with the flow on this one.

Maybe Steve understood that she was only going to make it easy on them for now. At least, that was the impression Denise was left with when he hesitated before responding.

"She has three days. Will I be able to control this in three days?"

"I doubt it. Not unless you think you're some kind of rock star."

Denise glanced back at Steve just in time to see the way he smiled. As though accepting a challenge.

"Right. Let's get started then."

"Oh? Going to blow our minds, are you?"

Denise's heart slammed. She couldn't look away from Steve's face. Not when he stared back at Jackson like that.

"We've got a prisoner we can question, I'm high on adrenaline, you'd better damn well believe it."

Though it pained him to have to step away from Denise so soon after everything that happened, if Steve was going to learn how to control this new thing inside him in time for her to get back to a normal life without having to worry about an already stressful job being put on hold, and her career possibly ruined, well, he had to get started right away.

Steve growled at the prisoner he'd left bleeding on the ground, the one that too many of Jackson's men had decided needed to be guarded.

As if there was any hardship or sacrifice that came with guarding an unconscious shifter. Especially when Jackson ordered the chains to come out.

Those brought out a shiver from Steve as he watched the prisoner being shackled.

"Is that necessary?"

"Until we get our answers, yes." Jackson eyed the man. He stayed limp as Jackson's men shackled him.

The way they shook out their fingers after putting the chains on him let Steve know all he needed to about those chains.

"Plated in silver?"

"How else do you expect to contain him?"

Steve pressed his lips together. He was about to ask before Jackson cut him off.

"No. Wearing silver plated chains will not help you."

Of course. Why did he expect to hear anything else? "All right. Why not?"

"The silver is designed to contaminate the animal within. Wearing it short term is one thing. That's why the police use it, but if you were to wear it all the time, it would make you sick."

Shit.

No matter how many ways he thought of getting out of this, it always seemed to come back to the fact that he was going to be Jackson's little pet from now on.

At least until he figured out how to control this new thing inside him.

"Right. So can we get to work now?"

Jackson turned his attention away from his men, who were currently dragging off their new prisoner.

Steve wasn't sure he wanted to know what they were going to do to him. He had to ask if he was going to get anywhere with him.

"You are going to keep that man alive, right?"

"Of course. We're not savages."

Jackson didn't exactly glare at him, but his eyes narrowed slightly, and the heat within them was enough to make Steve embarrassed for asking.

He wasn't about to back down, however. "I need to make sure. He might be one of the shifters who turned me. If he has any control over me—"

"He doesn't. That's a myth."

Steve frowned. "No, it's not. Shifters talk all the time about the power the creatures who changed them have."

"And they are working under incorrect assumptions. They are not following the commands of the shifter who changed them just because it's a shifter making the orders. They are following the commands of the alpha that is showing them the way to commanding and controlling their instincts."

Steve pressed his lips together. "And I guess that will be you, right?"

The other man smiled. "With the way you talk sometimes, I was beginning to doubt I would command any control over you for long. You want to set off on your own so badly, and with your woman. I doubt you will be staying for very long."

"Right, so can we get to it?"

"Right now?"

No, tomorrow. Steve bit back the reply. "Unless you have something better to be doing."

That didn't come out sounding much better, but he wasn't going to take it back either.

Jackson grinned at him, and after everything that happened, Steve knew better than to trust that look. "Very well, your first lesson begins now."

Steve saw the fist coming this time. He ducked cleanly out of the way, though he did feel the whoosh of air above his head.

Jackson barked a laugh. "Good! You learn quickly."

Didn't mean Steve liked how the man had gotten him in the first place.

"I know what you're doing."

"Oh? And what would that be?"

Steve stood straight. "You're trying to make me angry again so I shift and lose control."

Jackson nodded. "Anger can do that, but so can anything that takes you off guard, shocks you too deeply. If you think this will be a mere matter of controlling your temper, then you will be in for a terrible lesson."

"Right. I don't think there's anything you could do to me now that would shock me."

"Even if I told you I wanted to take Denise from you?"

Steve flexed his fingers, then let the rush of anger drain out of him. "Right, you're such a liar. Denise has that scent on her to make you want to mate with her because it will make you stronger and give you powerful babies or whatever. You told me yourself you and your pack aren't a bunch of crazy rapists."

Jackson nodded. "All right. You barely seemed to hold it back that time."

"But I did hold it back, and after you talked about Denise like that. I think that means I'm already on the road to proving you wrong. I might have all the control I need in the world in just two days."

"Two days?"

Steve shrugged. "Or a day and a half. I don't see why this has to be so hard in the first place."

Jackson got that look in his eye again, the one that said he was planning something else.

Steve kept his guard up, his stomach suddenly clenching.

"You think you have every angle planned, do you?"

Steve stared back hard. "It's my job to plan for every outcome and to look at every angle."

"In a human's world. Your narrow world."

"Uh huh. I'm mated to the beautiful nurse who took care of me and a bunch of shifters want to stake their claim on her. What else can you throw at me that would make me lose control?"

Jackson stepped forward, going toe to toe with him. Steve refused to step back, but he did remember in that moment that he was entirely naked still. No one had brought him any clothes to wear and he hadn't wanted to show weakness by asking for them. Not wearing anything at all made him much more vulnerable to attack if Jackson caught him off guard in some way.

"I told you, it wasn't just about anger. It's about shocking you, catching you off your guard in any way."

"Uh huh, and that means what?"

Jackson grabbed Steve by his ears and yanked him forward.

He had to admit, it shocked the hell out of him when another man kissed him. He definitely hadn't seen that angle, and when he shoved Jackson off him, the rush of fur sprouting from the pores of his arms, face, and chest came too quickly to itch, too fast for him to stop, and when he sank down to all fours, before the animal side of him completely took over, he heard Jackson's maniacal laughter.

Steve growled and lunged at him. He wasn't sure what happened after that because the wolf didn't let him see it.

~

DENISE WATCHED Steve stumble into the trailer they had been given later that night. The man flopped onto the tiny couch with a groan, blindly reaching up with his scraped up arm and pulling the knitted throw over his backside and shoulders. He didn't seem to be just hiding his face. He looked exhausted.

Considering the fighting she'd heard all day, and the yelling, followed by a few hours of quiet before more fighting and yelling, she couldn't blame him.

At least this time the dog fights he was getting into were with another wolf who wouldn't be doing his level best to hurt him. Still, she'd watched some of that, and Denise couldn't believe he was putting himself through all of this for her.

That he would put his body through the strain.

She needed to get down there, stop watching him from the loft and wipe down those cuts.

Even a shifter could get infections.

Denise climbed down from the loft.

She stopped next to him, setting her hand onto the part of his shoulder that was still exposed.

He jerked slightly, pulling back and looking at her. His smile was exhausted. "Hey."

"Hey."

She waited. That heat climbing up her hand, through the veins of her forearm, and into her shoulder before settling in her chest was wonderful.

Could he feel it, too?

"I didn't know you were up there."

Denise nodded. "Not much else to do around here, and I didn't think it would be a good idea to go walking around if I really am giving off some strange scent that makes all the males of breeding age think I'm open for business."

Steve snorted, then stopped quickly. He looked back at her, though there was still some mirth in his eyes. "Sorry. I know that's not funny."

Denise pressed her lips together, though, in truth, she was trying to hold back a grin of her own. "I guess I shouldn't have said it like that." She waited a beat. "Are you in pain?"

"Mostly my pride." He looked up at her with more concern. "You, ah, weren't watching anything, were you?"

This time, she couldn't help the full-fledged grin that pulled at her lips. "You mean when Jackson kissed you?"

Steve growled. He grabbed onto one of the little pillows and stuck it over his head, though it was too late to hide his burning cheeks from her.

Denise felt badly for laughing at his misery. She really did.

At the same time...

"You have to admit, he caught you off guard, didn't he?"

Steve muttered something from beneath the pillow that she couldn't make out. She didn't need to. She laughed out loud, stroking his shoulder.

"Poor baby. I'm sorry. I really am. Even if I don't sound it."

Steve had shifted quickly after that, lunging at Jackson, who couldn't seem to stop laughing at him. It had been safe to say Steve really hadn't seen that one coming.

"To be fair, I didn't think he would do that either. But now you know in case he tries it next time, right?"

Steve yanked the pillow off his head. "He won't be getting within reaching distance of me ever again."

She couldn't stop smiling. "What if he does that thing you men do again?"

Steve looked puzzled. "What male thing?"

"What you did before he kissed you. Go toe to toe with someone and refuse to step back. You're playing a game with each other when you do that."

"It's not a game."

"But you refused to back down?"

"He would want me to do that. I wasn't about to give him the satisfaction."

It was the way he growled it that made Denise smile. Some men could be so stubborn, it was ridiculous. If he'd stepped back, Jackson wouldn't have been able to shock Steve the way he had.

But no, Steve had to save face, and now he was lying here, face burning from the humiliation of being caught off guard.

Denise couldn't help but rub it in a little. "I thought it was kind of hot when he kissed you."

Steve groaned again, hiding his head one more time with the pillow.

She laughed. "Oh, come on! You had to think it was a little funny in the end, right?"

This time, she could make out what he muttered beneath his pillow. "Not even close."

She laughed again. "Okay, okay. I'm sorry. I'll take your side the next time he does something like that."

Steve yanked the pillow off his head, a note of panic in his eyes. "You think he would do that again?"

"Well..." Denise thought about it. "It's possible. You mean to tell me you didn't notice the way he was looking at you?"

That panic only increased. "What?"

"Yeah." Denise nodded. "Every time I saw him look at you, he always had this...I don't know. Maybe I noticed it because I'm a woman and you're a man."

"He's a man."

"Yes, and I know it's blowing your mind right now, but two men can be together like that. Didn't you know?" She tousled his hair playfully.

He growled at her, but she wasn't threatened by it. "I know that. I'm just saying...you made it sound as though my being a man meant I wouldn't notice if someone was looking at me like that. I notice things like that."

"Yes, from other women most likely."

"That's not the point."

Denise shrugged. "Either way, I recognized the way he was looking at you. I've seen that look enough to know when a man wants something."

Steve grumbled. "I thought he was looking at you."

"Poor baby." She petted his head again, then stopped, pulling back when she realized what she was doing.

Steve was naked beside her. She kept touching his bare shoulder, patting his head, acting so familiarly to him.

He noted the change. "Are you okay?"

Denise nodded. "Yeah. I'm...I'm fine." She thought quickly. "I probably shouldn't be touching you right now. You could have some cuts or abrasions on your skin where I can't see." She got up quickly, moving for where she knew the first aid kid happened to be beneath the kitchen sink.

Which meant barely walking five feet away from Steve.

When she turned around, he was sitting up, watching her, the knit throw around his waist, though Denise already knew what was beneath it.

She'd seen him naked.

The situation had been different, but now, when things were calmer, when her adrenaline wasn't so high and she wasn't threatening a family man with his own weapon...

Steve cleared his throat. "You know, I'm trained in basic first aid. I can do that if you're not comfortable."

Denise shook her head. "I want to do it. It'll help me keep my mind off everything."

She came back to the couch. Steve moved over, allowing her the room to sit next to him.

"You're shaking."

"No, I'm not."

Steve didn't argue with her, and Denise forced herself to get a grip.

She wasn't going to do this right now. She was going to keep her head. She was trained for this. She had prepared herself for stressful medical situations, and she'd prepared herself for those times when she knew she would have to defend herself.

But this was different. This was so far off the mark of everything she ever thought she would go through.

"Do you want to talk about it?"

Denise looked at him. His eyes were so damned gentle, and he was so handsome and strong. "How are you doing that?"

"Doing what?"

She opened the kit. "It feels like you're reading my mind some-times. Though I suppose that's in part to do with the mating."

"Right. We're going to be in tune with each other. Especially now with our blood merged."

Denise paused. She looked at her palm. She'd bandaged it since coming back to her own trailer, but it didn't hurt. It might be healing quickly now.

As fast as that of her mate.

"Jackson told me why he did it," Steve said softly. "He said it was to…his words were something along the lines of, so I could keep my dick in my pants. You don't have to do anything sexual with me now if you don't want to." He growled suddenly. "As if he thought you had anything to worry about."

"What? You don't want to have sex with me?"

He looked at her, his eyes damn near ready to pop out of his head.

It was cute. She wasn't sure if he knew that he was cute. He had the tall, dark and sexy thing going, but it was the little quirks about him that made Denise melt.

And he was still staring at her. His mouth opened, closed, then opened again.

"What?" She crossed her arms. "Did you forget the reason why I wanted to go out with you in the first place?"

She'd only made it clear to him back at the restaurant.

He cleared his throat. "You know you don't have to do anything you don't want to do."

"Do you like sex?"

"Very much so," he said with a nod.

"Well, for a man who likes sex, you sure do try hard to keep from having it."

Steve stood, letting the knit throw fall from his shoulders.

Denise stood with him. He still had to look down at her, and she recognized what this was.

"You positive about this? I'm a shifter, remember?"

He was trying to scare her off. She wasn't sure whether to appre-ciate the effort or be annoyed by it. "Last time I checked, I'm not some little girl. I can make a decision like this without you getting me to sign a waiver in blood."

She grabbed his wrist, feeling that tingle of pleasure rising up her arm just like it did every time she touched him, but she ignored it. Denise barely took her gaze off his face.

She turned his hand palm side up, the hand that Jackson had bitten. It was already healing. Scabs had formed, and beneath those, his skin was likely turning pink, scars forming.

"I'm already stuck with you for life anyway. I might as well enjoy it."

His eyes flashed. Denise felt that familiar thrill of fear at the sight of something so animal, but it melted into the background quickly.

She didn't fear Steve. How could she when he was everything she could possibly want?

Finally, his lips quirked in a smile. "Yeah, I guess you should enjoy it."

She pointed her finger under his nose. "You better make sure I do."

Denise gasped at the feel of Steve's hands on the curve of her ass. He picked her up so quickly she had almost no chance to prepare.

Her legs curled around his waist easily, instinctively.

"Trust me. I will."

CHAPTER 17

*S*teve walked up those thin steps with Denise to get to the loft, then had to stop suddenly before her head could hit the roof of the tiny house. Denise glanced up, then laughed at how close her face was to the ceiling.

He laughed too. "I wanted to carry you to bed."

She lowered her legs, taking his hand and pulling him towards the futon. "You got me most of the way there. Come on."

She pulled him forward, though she didn't need to. Steve allowed himself to be led, a servant to her wants and whims. She could ask anything of him in that moment and he was more than ready to give it to her.

They had to crouch and crawl onto the bed. Denise sat down, pulling herself back to the middle of the futon, her fingers quickly pulling at her clothes.

Since she was the only one currently dressed and Steve wanted something to do with his hands, he helped her to get out of those clothes. He pulled off her boots, then helped pull her tight jeans down around her waist and thighs.

And that look she gave him as he did that was beyond sexy.

What the hell had he been worried about? This was a woman who clearly knew what she wanted. She didn't need him holding her hand in this regard.

Made him feel kind of stupid for holding back. He'd thought being a shifter would be bad enough. She barely agreed to go out with him, but then Jackson came and took them, and then he shifted without meaning to, then the attack…

Denise looped her arm around Steve's neck, yanking him closer. "Whatever you're thinking about right now, stop it."

She yanked his mouth to hers, and he did stop thinking about it because there was nothing else he needed to focus on other than the sweet taste to her mouth, the softness of her lips.

His whole body buzzed. His cock throbbed and as he settled between her thighs; everything cried out in him that he needed to plunge into her.

Steve gasped, melding his body to Denise's. She moaned and held him close, her body so warm, so perfect.

God, he'd thought he would have so much more control than this. He thought he would be able to hold off if he needed to. Thank God Denise wanted this, was even pushing for it, because now that he was getting it, he wasn't so sure if he would have been able to hold himself back for so long.

Not when her tongue tasted so sweet.

There was something else he wanted to taste, however. Something the wolf demanded and would not be denied.

Steve pulled back from her lips, a small crime in and of itself. He slid down her body, his mouth kissing one of her perfectly budded rosy nipples.

Denise sighed, her fingers combing through his hair, nails gently scraping his scalp in a way he liked.

"God, *Steve*."

He hadn't even reached his final form.

He moved farther down until his feet touched the end of the loft. He almost laughed with the lack of space around here, but then there was nothing to laugh about as he kissed Denise between her legs.

And this was something he took great pleasure in. His skill was the type he liked to hone and perfect, and as Denise arched her back and moaned, he knew he was giving her exactly the sort of pleasure she'd been after.

"Oh God. Steve, *God*." Denise arched her knees, crying out as he plunged his tongue deep inside her, flicking it and playing with her. Every noise she made he used to his advantage, as though following a trail; he quickly learned how to best please her.

It wasn't just that, however. There was something else happening within him as he did this to her.

He didn't just mean the throb of his cock either.

The animal inside him, the wolf that still didn't know when to sit and stay at the best of times...Steve felt the creature rumble with a pleasure all its own. As though it too was enjoying this. As though going down on Denise, tasting her, licking inside her, was somehow making his inner wolf...complacent? Not entirely. But at least in the moment, he felt an ease in the wild animal in his head.

All right then. This was apparently something he could work with. If he ever had a problem with the wolf, he could just go down on his mate and that would be the elixir he needed to solve his problems.

If Denise noticed the way Steve smiled as he flicked his tongue over her clit, she didn't mention it.

That was good. He wasn't sure if he would appreciate his revelation until after he finished with her.

Denise's hands gripped his hair almost painfully tight. She arched her back, her thighs quivering, and he knew she was close.

"S-Steve, oh my God, I'm coming. I'm—"

He felt it. The rush of her orgasm as her entire body tightened. Warmth pooled around his mouth, and he moaned. The taste and scent of her nearly drove him over the edge, and he had yet to touch himself as her sex pulsed around his tongue.

He didn't want to pull away, but he needed to be inside her.

"God, come here." He grabbed her ankles and pulled her legs down, encouraging them to wrap around his waist.

They did. Denise sighed as she settled herself onto his lap, her fingers gripping the sheets as he slid inside her.

"Oh, that's so nice."

He grinned. "Good, that's sort of the point."

She smiled back at him. "Right. Here you are pretending to be bashful. You know what you're doing."

He withdrew and surged forward, unable to hold back even as he shrugged. "Trying to be a gentleman here, that's all." He withdrew and surged forward again, groaning as he picked up his speed. "Except for right now."

Denise shook her head, her fingernails digging into his shoulders this time. "Don't be a gentleman if this is what I get out of it." She closed her eyes and sighed.

Her pleasure began to rise again as Steve moved. He could tell from the look on her face, from the sounds she made, and he didn't want to stop.

He couldn't hold himself back. He felt as though he'd been waiting for decades for this moment, and now that he was here, it was going to end so much sooner than he wanted it to.

His orgasm reached its peak. Steve tried holding back, wanting to extend this for as long as possible.

"Don't come. Not yet. Don't come."

Her words were sweet, but the wolf inside him howled, and Steve could not give his woman what she desperately wanted.

He came with a heavy sigh, his body tensing before he slumped, his hips moving to milk himself of the last of his pleasure through instinct alone.

He practically fell on top of Denise's chest. Her thighs squeezed him tightly, and as she sighed, Steve once again felt that clenching sensation. This time, around his prick.

He smirked, pride and a whole different sort of pleasure rushing through him.

He'd gotten her off again. Not that this was the first time it had happened with a woman, to give her two orgasms so close to each other, but it was still something of a rarity.

And he had to admit, it was extra special this time around.

They lay there quietly, the only noises between them was their thudding hearts and the sounds of their breath as their bodies recovered.

Steve would have thought he would be too heavy for Denise, but she didn't complain about his weight on top of her, and he was too comfortable right where he was to want to move.

"Wow."

Steve chuckled, his cheek pressed to her collarbone. "Feedback has been received."

Denise nodded. There was a brief hesitation before she spoke again. "Matings are usually for life, aren't they?"

Steve swallowed. She was a nurse. She would know the answer to this, but he didn't blame her for wanting it confirmed.

"From my understanding, yeah. It's not the same as a marriage. They're not just broken off so easily."

Easily being the important part of that sentence. Steve didn't know what exactly went into breaking apart a genuine mating, but he'd done enough jobs with the public to know it could be done.

Denise was silent again. That silence was killing him.

"You know I would never keep you tied to me, right?"

"Yeah, I figured that."

He pushed himself up onto his hands, looking down at her. "It's the wolves, isn't it?"

She nodded. "I don't like being told where to go or what to do." Denise shook her head, clenching her jaw. "The fact that Jackson thinks he can bring me here and tell me not to leave until you can control yourself drives me insane."

"So then let's go. Fuck him. You and me, we'll walk out tomorrow."

Denise shook her head.

"It's fine," Steve said. "I know we'll have to fight our way out of here—"

"It's not just that."

Steve stopped, then he understood. "Your job?"

She nodded, that irritation back in her eyes. "Jackson is right. It was one thing when I was working at the hospital and didn't know the shifters were willing to go in there and grab me. I sometimes saw them on the outskirts of our small parking lot, but I always thought the public space kept them away. And that if they ever tried anything, I'd be able to fight them off before they made it into the building." Denise shook her head. "Maybe it's because they smell you around, competition, but I can't go back to work if there's a chance it will put patients in danger. My job is to help people recover, not to put them in any unnecessary danger because I'm giving off some weird signal to the rest of the shifter population."

Steve felt a growl rumbling through his chest. "You're not giving off that strong of a signal. Jackson and his wolves haven't tried touching you. The only wolves you have to worry about are the sons of bitches who have no control. Or don't want to control themselves. I wouldn't have left you alone in one of those trailers with another male if I thought it was that bad."

"Yeah, I guess you did do that, didn't you?" Denise touched his face. Steve felt an immediate cooling sensation, the heat of his anger melting away at her touch. He leaned into it, wanting more, but Denise pulled her hand back, clenching her fingers suddenly.

"I'll get control. I'll be able to control this and you'll be back at work in time to get your life going again. You don't have to worry about that."

"Yes, I do." She looked at him, holding his gaze. It was her eyes that let him know how serious this was going to get. "It doesn't matter if you can learn to control your wolf. While there are people out there who think it's a good idea to use the hospital as a place to fight..." Denise bit down on her bottom lip. "I don't think I should go back to work."

"What?" Steve yanked himself back. He sat up on his knees, hardly able to believe what he'd just heard. "No, come on. You don't have to do that."

"I do if my presence isn't safe for patients."

She talked as though she'd already made up her mind. That was not okay.

"Your presence is safe for your patients, and it has been for as long as you've worked there. Jackson kept those wolves back and you said it yourself that you barely saw any wolves around the hospital. When I get control, I'll make sure anyone who even thinks about getting close to you will realize how bad of an idea that will be."

Denise's eyes shined, her face twisting as she struggled to contain herself. "How selfish would I have to be to do that? To put anyone in danger because I liked my job?"

"Baby." Steve cupped her cheeks. "Your job is helping people. It's not selfish to want to keep doing that. I'm going to control this, and when I do, I'll make sure my scent is all over you so no other shifter gets the wrong idea."

Denise frowned.

Steve realized how that sounded. "Uh, but not like that. I can get my scent on you in other, cleaner ways. Ways that will let you walk into work without getting too sticky."

She laughed out loud. Steve didn't think he'd ever heard her laugh like that.

And he had to admit, it was an infectious sound. He kissed her as she smiled and giggled, pleased when she held him by the back of his head and neck, kissing him back.

He was going to take that as his answer.

He was going to control this. He was going to question that shit head who had been captured, and he was going to make sure Denise didn't suffer anymore because of the shifters in her life.

He swore it.

CHAPTER 18

*D*enise watched the scene with her arms crossed. Her mate, face smashed into the ground, growling, eyes blazing red, and seemingly unable to get a good enough grip on the creature above him, or the ground beneath him, to roll to the side and get back to his feet.

Not for a lack of trying.

Jackson grabbed Steve by the back of the head, smacking his face down, and maybe there was a hard patch of earth beneath him because she heard a crunching noise. Denise bit down on the inside of her cheek. She tried not to wince, but one of the other wolves, one of Jackson's main men, saw her and smirked.

She narrowed her eyes sideways at him but didn't want to give him much more attention than that.

This wasn't just a test for Steve. By the way Jackson kept glancing up at her, and the way his betas pointed her way, they wanted to see if she would flip out and try calling a halt to this.

No. She wouldn't. Steve trusted her enough to be able to make her own decisions under pressure, so it wasn't much of a stretch for her to do the same for him.

Besides, he wasn't in that much trouble.

Maybe it was something to do with the mating, but just by looking at Steve, at the way he put just enough pressure back against Jackson's arms, the way he seemed to be waiting…

She could tell he was up to something. Searching for the right moment before he would get to spring.

She appreciated that.

"You give up yet, new guy?"

If Steve had been concerned Jackson would go easy on him after the other man had surprise kissed him on the mouth, then he was sorely mistaken.

Steve growled. Fur had already sprouted on his face and the backs of his hands and arms. He was managing to keep his inner wolf inside, which Denise supposed was part of the point to this exercise.

But it was just barely. Steve's fangs were starting to get noticeable.

"Should I go bring your girlfriend into the mix? She might like a good fight."

Denise's fingers clenched. She crossed her arms, trying to hide the irritation.

Don't play into it. Don't let him get to you. You're better than that. Come on.

For a brief second, she worried Jackson would get to him. The sudden brightening in Steve's already blood red eyes made her think he was getting ready to turn someone into cat food.

And not the dry kind either.

Steve clenched his eyes shut, dust clouding up around his face and mouth as he exhaled hard. He stayed human.

Mostly human.

Pride swelled within her, but it wasn't over.

Jackson still had Steve's arms yanked tightly behind his back. He'd managed to change positions, holding his knee firmly along the back of Steve's head, keeping his face down. The blood that dribbled from Steve's nose was thick, almost black. She would have to set that when they were done here if it was broken. Jackson better not have broken Steve's nose. It was such a cute nose.

Steve snapped his eyes open again. His gaze landed solely on

Denise. Her spine stiffened, worry that he might lose control just by the fact that she was there returning.

Steve did something she didn't expect it to do. He relaxed.

The tension in his muscles, the sudden way he seemed to deflate, took her completely off guard, and as he relaxed, seemingly submitting to the alpha on top of him, Denise found her muscles cramping with the sudden pressure.

Jackson's grin showed off the white of his corner fang, victory in hand, and Denise couldn't believe it. He wasn't actually—

No. He wasn't. Jackson didn't exactly release Steve, but it was clear he relaxed some of that tight grip, just enough for Steve to yank one arm free, to spin around with a hard roar, and the betas standing around the pair suddenly ignited, flaring to life and cheering as the fight became exciting once more.

Denise's heart pounded. She watched the scene unfold in front of her with barely restrained glee.

She knew it. She fucking knew it, and she watched Jackson scramble to take control of the fight again, his claws coming out, thick, protective fur forming on his chest and across his throat, which he needed as Steve's claws began to move.

He'd used his fists at first, relying on the human way of fighting, but now that more of his instinct was taking over, she could see he was getting used to the idea of biting and clawing and mauling his enemy.

She shivered. Denise didn't like that, the reminder that the wolf was a part of him now, but Steve knew where she stood on that front, and she'd made peace with what he was.

A wolf shifter. Not just a wolf shifter, but her mate, and she was going to have his back.

"Come on, Steve! Kick his ass!"

Denise had been silent for the majority of the fight, not wanting to cause any distraction to her mate, but now that he seemed especially focused, and had the ball in his court, she wanted to get in on the same fun that Jackson's betas seemed to be enjoying around her.

Steve showed no signs of hearing her; maybe the noise of the cheering crowd drowned her out, but that didn't matter. She didn't stop.

"Take him down! You got this!"

She felt as though she was cheering at her old high school football field. There was a sudden energy to this now that the end was within sight and Steve had Jackson up against the ropes.

All the while still holding that human shape. A still furry human shape, but so long as it was in keeping with Jackson's rules, they were good.

Watching Steve go, Denise felt a rush of energy and hope rising within her. He moved fluidly, like a creature of water, naturally in his element as he slashed and struck out at Jackson, pushing him backwards. Damn near out of the circle they'd created for the fight.

Now the betas were losing their damned minds. Crowd going wild and everything. Denise could hardly believe it. Steve almost had him out of the circle. Just one…more…step…

Jackson's face transformed. Fur sprouted out through his pores as though he'd been stabbed with thousands of tiny needles as he suddenly found the strength to push back against Steve, throwing him off his feet.

He tried to jump back down onto him. Steve rolled out of the way.

Several men pushed ahead of Denise, shouting and roaring as the fight heated up, as though they were watching a cage match.

"Hey!" She tried to push through, but they barely noticed her, pushing her back blindly without even glancing at her. They didn't notice her, or they didn't care in favor of the blood sports.

Dammit. An opening. She needed an opening.

The crowd cheered again. Denise was nearly punched in the face when someone shot their fists up.

Assholes. She needed to see!

She found a spot just a few feet away. Small enough that she was stunned the betas hadn't filled it or crowded closer.

Someone pushed through just as she made it there.

Denise saw red. She didn't care if these bastards were wolves or that she didn't have her weapons. Someone was going to get hurt and it wouldn't be her if she didn't get through.

She found a crease in the line up of sweaty bodies and pushed hard. Someone yelled at her. She didn't care. She ignored it, shoving to the front so she could see...

See Jackson getting his arm looped around Steve's throat. His very wolf-like throat. He hadn't been able to hold back the transformation. Jackson bled, his expression no longer amused as he held onto the struggling wolf in his arms.

The way Steve fought and kicked in this form was faster, wilder than anything he'd put up when he'd still had his opposable thumbs. Denise was impressed even an alpha like Jackson could hang onto him

The bloody claw marks down his chest were a good indicator of what would keep happening to him if he didn't hang on.

Denise stepped forward, then pulled back.

No. The point to her being here was to set Steve off, to make him lose control. Or make it easier for him to lose control. If she stepped forward now, he'd just get worse. His animal instincts would fly through the roof, and thinking he was protecting her, Steve might end up doing more damage.

That didn't mean it was fun watching as Jackson choked Steve out, the man's large arms trembling as he fought to keep a proper grip, and Steve's body became more and more slack. His struggles slowing, a small, puppy-like cry escaped his snout with what had to be the last of his breath.

Only when he stopped moving, and when Jackson released the wolf, did Denise rush forward. A few of the other betas had stepped into her way. She shoved them back. They moved easier this time now that the shouts for blood and war cries had died down.

She fell to her knees, pressing her hands to the coarse pelt of her mate.

She knew what to do in the case of a human. If Steve looked more like a man right now, it wouldn't have been a problem for her to check him physically, but for now, she could only open his eyes and confirm there was brain activity before she glared up at Jackson. "You didn't have to do that."

His eyes popped wide open at her, one hand gently touching the long scratches Steve had carved out on his chest. "Are you sure? It looked like I did."

She wasn't impressed by his stupid shocked face, or his excuses. "I didn't have to be here for this. You could have tested him without me ten feet away."

He cocked his head at her, then stood. "I would have expected better of you."

"I'm not trying to impress you."

The sudden steely-eyed look he gave her didn't impress her much either.

"Did you really think I would have approved of this sort of thing to this level?"

"You approved enough to stand by and watch."

Denise bit her tongue. For one, because he had her, sort of. She only had stayed to watch because it was apparently important for Steve to learn how to control his new shifting ability. "Whatever, can you help me get him inside? Does anyone around here have any smelling salts?"

The chances were good that he would wake up soon enough on his own, but she wasn't in the mood to wait.

Jackson bent down, his hands coming under Steve's furry body with much more care than how he'd handled him a minute ago.

Two other betas stepped forward to do the same, putting their hands beneath Steve's body. They didn't need to, Jackson clearly had it, but maybe it was a respect thing. Denise didn't need to help either, but she wasn't about to let them put their hands on Steve without her there to have her hands on him, too.

It didn't have to make sense. Steve had done what he needed to do, and now it was as though keeping her fingers on his fur or skin in some way made up for the lack of support she was able to give to him when he was in the middle of his training with Jackson.

They didn't make it two feet to the little trailer where she and Steve were staying when the sound of a car horn blared, and everyone glanced up.

The dark vehicle came to a strong halt, kicking up dust and rocks less than three feet away from where Denise stood.

A man stepped out. Denise recognized him from before. Victor.

His eyes blazed at the sight of the wolf between Denise, Jackson, and the other shifters holding on. "Get away from him, don't touch him."

The two betas backed away. Jackson didn't, neither did Denise. She knew the command wasn't meant for her anyway, though Victor did growl a little at the alpha.

He would have made a great alpha if he hadn't been born subhuman.

Jackson, of course, didn't so much as give any hint that he was even annoyed by the command. He stared at Victor as though he was one of his own, and Jackson was unimpressed with his tardiness.

As they walked with Steve back to the trailer, even Denise had to admit that Jackson held himself pretty well.

"I came as soon as I got the call, what happened?"

Denise beat Jackson to the punch. "Steve spoke with the shifter they nabbed last night, and Jackson wanted to give him something to work on after the fact."

The three of them carrying Steve managed to get into the tiny trailer. By then, just as Victor and Denise set the large wolf onto the tiny couch, it began to stir. Within seconds, he would be awake. He was already growling and twitching. Denise and victor both stepped back from him.

"I wish you hadn't questioned your…prisoner without me there."

Denise caught that, the way he said the word prisoner. Steve had warned her about this, and had admitted to feeling somewhat the same.

Steve wanted to bring in the law for this. Victor would want the same when he arrived, though he might reluctantly understand.

But now that Steve was down for the count at the worst time, Denise had to make sure Victor would be on her side with this.

"Jackson agreed to bring the police in on this soon enough. Right now, the pack is just covering its bases."

Victor raised a brow at her. "Why would you need to cover your bases?"

Jackson continued to attempt pulling off the aloof thing with Victor, but, like with Steve, it didn't last long.

"We have been having issues with these wolves for years. I would want to be certain they would not accuse me or any of my wolves of being involved with trying to rape a conduit."

Victor looked at her, though Denise only saw this from the corner of her eye since she didn't want to give much attention to that. She was still getting used to the whole idea of being a conduit for the wolves, and being among a pack at the same time.

Victor didn't question the shoddy excuse before he moved on, as though he knew he wouldn't be getting the answer he wanted. "I looked into it, but didn't find much. Explain to me what this is."

Steve replied. "It means she'll produce alphas to whoever impregnates her, guaranteed."

"*Steven!*"

Denise turned. He was back in his human form, hand on the back of his neck, hunched over with a miserable expression on his face. He glared at Jackson. Denise was happy he was awake and all right. She went to him, stopping herself before she could fall into his lap with her arms around his neck.

The way he rubbed at it stopped her.

"Does your neck hurt? Let me see."

"I'm good."

He pulled away from her hands before she could touch him. Denise noted the soft rise in color on his cheeks before he turned away from her and went back to growling at Jackson.

Denise couldn't help herself, she smiled. She tried not to, but it was difficult. Was he angry with himself for losing that fight in front of her?

It was cute. She was…kind of flattered he'd wanted to impress her.

She could have insisted, she kind of wanted to just for his own sake, but for now, Denise decided to give this to him.

He'd fought hard and nearly won against an alpha, a man who had years more experience with his animal side, with control. It was impressive how close Steve had come to besting Jackson. If he didn't want to be treated as though he was breakable now, she'd give him that.

Until they were alone. That would be another story. Then he was all hers.

Victor didn't make any mention of the fight Steve had been in, or the fact that, until a few seconds ago, he'd been unconscious, as though there was some unspoken male rule about not showing an inch of weakness in front of other people.

"You questioned the other wolf?"

Steve rolled his neck and shoulders. "Yeah. The sack of shit and his dumb friends seem to have a few things mixed up as far as Denise is concerned."

Victor glanced at Denise. "How so?"

"They think fu…having sex with her will make them more powerful betas. Or alphas. The entire point is that she's supposed to be able to bear alpha children. Not make whoever's, uh, inside her stronger."

He sounded embarrassed to mention that. Probably thought it was impolite to talk about having sex with her so casually in front of two other men.

He would be right. The more time she spent with Steve, the more she liked him.

"Have you spoken to the wolf yet?"

That darkened Denise's mood considerably. "No. *They* won't let me."

She jerked her head at Steve, but it was clear enough she meant the both of him.

To her extreme anger, Victor nodded. "Right."

She frowned. "What do you mean *right?*"

"You're not in a proper facility to make that meet-up a possibility right now. If anything, the police should have been called hours ago so he could be properly interrogated. If you want to speak with this guy, you should only do it with shatter proof glass between the both of you."

"That's what I said," Steve grumbled.

Denise glared at him. "Don't make me hurt you more than he did."

She wasn't in the mood to be generous to his ego when Victor wasn't on her side either.

Steve's body tensed, his eyes flared at her, but he said nothing.

Denise had assumed Jackson kept her away from the prisoner because of the way her scent worked on him, and he didn't want to risk there would be some sort of effect on him. Maybe that he would develop the strength to escape. For Steve, she'd assumed he hadn't wanted her near a potential rapist because the mating brought out his protective instincts for her.

She didn't know Victor, but he was neither the alpha of this pack, nor her mate, so she'd expected he would take her side and back her up when it came to speaking with one of the wolves who wanted to take her for himself.

Jackson shook his head. "I do not need to be here for this sort of spat. When you have more to say, come and find me outside. Steve, your control needs more work."

"Yeah, I got that."

Jackson left, and the air of annoyance around Steve was thick enough to see. Denise crossed her arms, not speaking up again until the door was shut behind Jackson.

"I want to speak to him."

"No."

She clenched her jaw. "You seriously think you get to tell me what to do just because you've been inside me? Is that a wolf thing or is my being a conduit turning you into a control freak?"

The way Steve's hands clenched into fists did not go unnoticed by her. "You're out of your mind if you think this is about controlling you. Victor, who has no connection to you at all, just mirrored what I said to you before the fight. It's too dangerous, and this isn't a proper facility for that sort of thing."

"Didn't stop you from going to see him."

"Yeah, and the guy is handcuffed to a wooden chair. I don't know his strengths, but even a wolf shifter can escape silver handcuffs if he has the strength to do it. Maybe you really do make wolves stronger just by being around them. I don't know enough about what it is that's making these wolves go crazy, but I've even seen the way Jackson and some of his wolves look at you. I'm not taking the risk that he gets away and slashes your throat when you're less than five feet away from him with nothing between you."

"Well, it's a good thing it's not your risk to take."

"No, it's Jackson's risk, too, and since he's in charge of the pack, it's his call."

Denise glared at him, and in that moment, she was really starting to question this whole mating thing to begin with. "You were so eager to walk out of here when I wanted to last night. Now that you know you can control me, you want to stay. That's typical."

"*Who do you think is trying to control you*? I'm trying to keep people from assaulting you!"

"I can handle myself!"

"It's not worth the risk!"

"Okay, cut it out, the both of you."

Victor stepped between them. Steve hadn't come to a stand, but the presence of another person between her and Steve made her snap out of it, as though there had been the risk of a fight of some kind.

Denise didn't like even thinking that. She crossed her arms, uncomfortable that she had been that close to losing control in the first place. Steve leaned back on the couch, rolling his eyes and cracking his knuckles.

"Christ, aren't you two supposed to be mated?"

"She's the one trying to put herself in front of a would-be rapist."

Denise cringed. "I am not trying to do that. I just want to know why he thinks it would be worth it."

"You want to know the logic a deranged pervert would have for molesting you?"

The way he said it, as though it was one of the stupidest ideas he'd ever heard, was the thing that made her turn around and walk out of there.

"Denise, come on, wait,"

She didn't wait for anything, and as she walked out and away from the trailer, she still made out what Victor said to Steve.

"You really fucked that up."

CHAPTER 20

When Denise left the trailer, needing air to think, and to breathe without a couple of men around her telling her what she did and didn't have to do, she felt an immediate punch of regret.

It had to be the mating itself that did it to her, which was why she shoved that feeling away.

She'd done nothing wrong and there was no reason for her to feel badly about walking away.

Steve was being a possessive asshole. She'd managed to handle herself with a full-time career just fine before he'd shown up, and now he was the one trying to take that control away from her.

Of course, she didn't want to be in front of that shifter by herself. She wasn't crazy. She would have wanted Steve there with her.

Because he was the only other shifter around here she trusted.

Jackson clearly had no interest in her, regardless of what kind of scent she put off, but now that she was outside, walking to nowhere in particular, she could feel eyes on her.

From the males predominantly, and even some of the females.

She ignored it. It could be innocent. Some of them might simply be curious about what she was, and the smell she gave off.

"You looking for the alpha's place?"

"No, I know which house is his."

She was just going for a walk, a walk by the shed where she knew the creep was who came to her house, and who tried attacking Jackson's pack to get a piece of her ass.

She wasn't going to go inside, however. Just stand around, maybe check if the door was unlocked.

Of course there were two betas standing by the door. Probably two more on the inside of the shed as well.

They'd been laughing over something, sitting on a couple of three-legged stools with a small table of cards between them. Denise knew she was good at going unseen, but there was no way two shifters wouldn't notice her walking towards them for long.

They immediately stood, their gazes changing as they clearly recognized her. "You're not supposed to be here."

"I know." She stuck her hands into her pockets, trying to look small and uninteresting. "I just thought I'd check up on how well the prisoner was being kept. He hasn't tried fighting to get out, has he?"

The two betas looked at each other, then back at her. There were no weapons in their hands. They didn't appear to have anything on them that could be used to fight off an intruder, and they were dressed casually in T-shirts and khaki shorts with sneakers and sandals.

Denise took in a breath. She kept expecting to see someone with a pistol, or at least a rifle. Any sort of weapon she could relate to.

She had to keep reminding herself that everyone here was armed. They just had the sort of weapons she couldn't immediately see.

"I don't think that's something you need to be worrying about."

"You probably shouldn't be near us either."

"But why?" Denise asked it as innocently as possible, though she already knew the reason why.

These men were not bad men, but they were shifters, and they were still inhaling her scent now that she was so close. It might have been the thing to tip her off that she was coming.

They would be affected. They would want to breed with her, but unlike the pervert who was trapped inside the shed, they were attempting some self control.

"I'm sure you guys are fine, though. I don't even want to go inside." A complete lie. "I just wanted to make sure everything was all right here, that he wasn't causing any trouble."

Mentioning that she had no intention of going into the shed seemed to relax them. The tension melted from their shoulders, though they didn't give her a path to the door either.

"We are fine here. He's been quiet inside since the alpha visited."

One of the betas kicked the door, as though to show her it was a solid prison. All he managed to show her was how rickety the thing looked.

He seemed to realize it when he did it, and so did his friend, who glared at him.

"He's in silver handcuffs inside anyway. He can't get you with us watching."

"Uh huh." They thought she was worried about that. Or, more worried than she already was. "You wouldn't be able to open the door and let me have a look, would you?"

Neither man said a word, but they shook their heads at her at the same time, as though on point with that much.

"Not even a little? I'll be quick, and you won't have to—"

"Hey."

Denise jumped, the hand on her shoulder gripping hard as she yanked herself away.

"Don't do that!" Steve yanked his hand back, fingers clenching. He was dressed now; someone had given him an extra set of clothes after he'd destroyed his turning into the wolf. He'd clearly known where to find her. "Denise, you don't need to be here."

"I wasn't doing anything."

He stared at her, deadpanned. "You clearly were. I'm not an idiot."

She crossed her arms. "I didn't say you were one."

"And yet you're here."

Patience. She needed to be patient with this because, if she wasn't, there was no way in hell he was going to let her get out of his sight ever again.

"You can't just tell me what to do and expect that will be enough. I need to see him."

"You don't need to see the guy who wants to rape you, and he's not even the only one."

Denise glanced at the two security guards, both of whom looked as though they wished to be anywhere else in the world other than where they were in that moment.

Denise rolled her eyes and started walking. "Whatever."

She was done with this and clearly wasn't about to see one of the men who thought it was a good idea to fuck her without her permission.

The sigh Steve released was an audible one as he followed her.

"You're walking away from the pack."

"So I am." There was a small path between the trees. Animals had probably made it, she had no idea where it led, but she followed it.

"I thought we agreed to stick this out until I learned control."

"You also said we could leave whenever we wanted."

She heard the grumble behind her. "Will you please tell me why you're mad at me? You know I'm not doing this to control you."

That was the worst part. She *did* know it. She didn't know Steve for that long, but what little she did know of him was enough for her to be comfortable with the knowledge that he wouldn't do that to her.

"Hey." Steve grabbed her arm. She stopped for him. His grip was gentle and so was his tone, and Denise wasn't in the mood to fight. "You know it, right?"

"I know. I just…" Denise rubbed her face. "I hate this so much. I hate that you get to look him in the eyes and demand to know why and I don't get to do that."

Steve pressed his lips together; he seemed to be trying to figure out how to answer that. "I know it doesn't make sense—"

"No, it does. I know what you want. You're not the first person to want it either. This has been my whole life, Steve! My whole life. I just want to look at him and ask him why."

"I know, but, baby, he's not the one leading all of this. He's not the one in charge of whether or not it comes to a stop. He's just one of many who've been looking for an opening to get to you. He hasn't even been doing that well. Otherwise, we wouldn't have caught him."

She nodded. That made sense. She just hated how it made sense. "Weird how that puts me down and makes me feel better at the same time. Knowing he's just one of many."

"It pisses me off," Steve growled, and she caught the way his eyes flicked back in the direction of the cabin.

"Me, too. Why, did he say anything to you when you were alone with him?"

"I didn't get to be alone with him, otherwise he'd be crying right now."

Steve would barely look at her. His jaw and neck were still tight. Denise could only imagine what he was thinking.

"What did he say to you?" she asked again.

A tiny muscle beneath his eye twitched. "You're not going to like it."

"It doesn't matter whether or not I like it. I want to hear it. What did he say to you?"

She wasn't going to let this go, and while there were times when she happened to enjoy the whole *woman mine* thing, now was not one of them.

Luckily, Steve seemed to get this. "He growled at me, a lot. I guess he could smell you on me even after the shower."

Denise nodded, and she struggled not to smile about it. "Good."

Steve raised a brow at her. "Good? That guy is deranged. The fact that he thinks he has any claim to you at all was almost enough for me to break his fingers."

"I assume you didn't?"

Steve suddenly looked uncomfortable. "Jackson threatened to kiss me again if I did anything."

Denise snorted.

Steve groaned, crossing his arms. "It's not funny."

"Yes, it is."

Steve inhaled a long breath through his nose, shook his head, but just as Denise thought she saw a hint of a smile on him, his face suddenly blanked.

Claws, fur, and teeth appeared on his hands, face, and mouth. He reached for her. Denise tried to pull back from him, but Steve's strength was too much for her to fight off as he threw her down onto the ground.

Denise readied herself for a fight now that Steve had lost control again, preparing herself for pain, that she would get scratched and bitten, but she would escape this if she worked hard enough and fought long enough. Those teeth and claws didn't come down onto her.

Steve turned away from her, facing another direction as a huge grey wolf leapt onto him, throwing him backwards, and a dog fight broke out between the two as Denise pushed herself back to her feet.

"Steve!"

He was already tearing out of his clothes, but not well enough. The scraps seemed to get caught around his legs and body, making it difficult for him to get at the other wolf. He hadn't yet mastered how to get out of his clothes with the same speed the born shifters seemed to wield so gracefully.

The horrific sight before her nearly caused her to not notice what was behind her. The growls all bled into each other, and when Denise turned her head, slowly, she was disappointed, though not shocked, to see two more wolves behind her.

They were going to come for her or Steve. Even if they decided to pile onto Steve, to kill him before getting to her, there was no way she could run for help and come back before they would overtake him.

Denise pulled off her belt, looped the leather around her fist, and kept the end with the buckle loose.

Her heart pounded.

All she had to do was wait for someone to notice the sounds of fighting and come. She just had to wait this out for that long.

The pain was going to be terrible. She wasn't looking forward to that part.

"All right, come on then."

CHAPTER 21

Steve pulled and struggled against the clothes still around his new wolf body. He was getting better at keeping his mind focused like this, but the damned clothes were almost as infuriating as the grey wolf snapping at his face

The prick had his hackles raised and kept coming forward, snapping and pulling back before Steve could get at him.

He felt the jeans come off his body first, after much wiggling; he didn't think they tore much at all.

It was his button-down the caused the most problems, oddly enough. He would have thought that would be the easiest to break apart, but with his front two legs held back as they were, it made things especially difficult for him to get up and take a proper stance. He felt the buttons pop, the stitching tear, but the damned thing still seemed determined to hold together just enough to make things difficult on him.

He was so determined, despite the clothes that held him back, to keep this wolf away from Denise so she could have her chance to run, that he almost didn't notice she was still behind him until he heard the sound of a wolf yowling its pain.

What?

He glanced back, a mistake because it let the grey wolf lunge forward, biting at his ear

Steve howled, yanking back, feeling something tear, and something warm trickle through his fur.

He put all his enraged focus back onto the grey wolf, but he'd seen Denise behind him, fending off the other two wolves that had come to attack.

He caught sight of her slamming her belt down onto the snout of one of the other wolves hard just before his ear was bitten.

If this prick bit it off, there was going to be hell to pay, and if either of those two wolves hurt her, he was going to lose his damned mind.

Steve stopped. He focused, ignoring the snapping coming too close to his face, the distraction for what it was. He put that behind him, focusing on the things Jackson had told him to.

The shape of his bones, the feel of his skin, and the strength of his claws.

He thought of these things as being interchangeable between his human shape and his new wolf form.

It didn't make his body feel as though it was turning to liquid, the way he'd been promised it would, but he did feel a sense of ease.

He changed his body just enough to get his opposable thumbs back, though they could hardly be called thumbs with the grotesque way they looked, and if he couldn't tear out of the shirt, then he might as well keep wearing it

He stuck his paws back through the arms of the button-down, and though it felt odd, to say the least, it worked, and he could finally stand on all fours. It was the next best thing to being on two feet, but since he couldn't keep that shape long term, or under much control, this would have to do.

As Steve was finally allowed to stand tall, he noted with some satisfaction that he was taller than the wolf that had been snapping at him.

It seemed it wasn't about to give up anyway, which made it very stupid, or it was more talented than it looked.

Steve knew to keep an eye on it, but he wasn't about to let Denise fend off two other wolves on her own either. He backed up towards her, putting himself in line of sight of the others.

"Steve, don't."

He growled at her. She sounded tired, and he could smell a little of her blood now. She was out of her mind if she thought for one second she could keep him away from her when she was outnumbered like that.

He put himself between Denise and the three other wolves.

When it was no longer one-on-one, he knew he was safer to look at what he was dealing with.

The other two wolves Denise had been handling also had their hackles raised, black lips pulled back to reveal long white teeth. One of them had a bloody snout, likely from the belt buckle she'd been swinging around. The other appeared to be blood free, but that didn't mean she hadn't gotten him good once or twice.

"God, Steve, your ear."

He didn't want to think about it. He pressed his body against her legs, shoving her back a little. She fell back a step, but then no more.

"I'm not running."

Fuck.

Now was really not the time when he wanted her to be stubborn about this sort of thing.

He growled back at her a little, wanting her to run, wanting her to get the hint, but she refused to budge.

Shit.

Denise started swinging the business end of her belt.

"We just have to hold out until someone notices they're here. Someone will smell the blood on these suckers soon enough."

She was right about that. As soon as the words were out of her mouth, a long howl drifted up over the trees, reaching Steve's ears.

Well, his ear. It twitched to the sound, and Denise took that as her cue they'd already won.

"There, you see? You idiots aren't on your territory, and you're not getting a piece of my ass today, so you might as well back off."

He couldn't agree more, but even as she said it, Denise's breath came out tired. She was winded from keeping the wolves back, and Steve didn't yet get the chance to figure out where they'd gotten her.

Some of the blood he smelled came from her, and he didn't like that.

For some reason, maybe they were high on their own egos, or they thought simply being near Denise made them stronger, the three wolves glanced at each other, but they didn't turn and flee as expected.

Denise seemed to lose patience with them entirely. "Get out of here! I don't belong to any of you! Go away!"

She swung her belt again, narrowly missing the snout of the grey wolf Steve had been fighting with.

It growled, lowering its head, but the grey wolf didn't attack.

The one with the already bloodied nose did, jumping at Denise, jaws open and claws out, as though forgetting it needed her alive to make itself powerful in the first place.

Steve lunged forward and up, his hind legs working so the other wolf caught the fur along his chest.

It bit down, but Steve barely felt it. Huh, so he did have enough hair there to protect him from the bites. He hadn't fully believed it until now, but here they were.

He fell backward, the other wolf landing on top of him, biting and clawing.

Steve kicked up his hind legs, trying to push the damned thing off him before it could slice open his belly, but he couldn't seem to do it.

Just as he could never seem to get Jackson off him.

Too new. He was too new at this sort of thing and Denise would be the one to suffer if he didn't get his shit together and fight them off!

"Get away from him!"

She was getting close. He could hear her smacking the belt down on the back of the wolf, and even on the back of its head, but the damned creature refused to be moved. Which meant it had lost itself to its wild side, just as Steve had done before.

Which also meant it wasn't thinking.

Steve bared his chest and throat, letting the other wolf bite him there just as it wanted to. He felt the pressure of the bite and some of the teeth, but despite all instincts screaming at him to get the wolf away from that sensitive and dangerous spot, Steve allowed it.

Which meant the wolf on top of him barely notices as Steve raised his back leg, claws ready.

A dirty trick, but he pressed those claws into the softness of the wolf's belly and pulled down hard until he heard its pained cry.

Only then did it fall off him. The wolf staggered back, fur dropping from its body and legs changing shape as a human appeared where there had once been a wolf.

And he clutched at his belly.

Steve pushed himself to his front paws. Denise smacked the head of the grey wolf as it tried to step closer with her belt, a hard downward swing, and it clearly was still thinking because it yelped hard and lunged back.

Even Steve had to have some sympathy pain. He heard the crack as the metal hit the bone of the skull.

The man with his belly slashed moaned, his hand bright red as he tried to contain the blood.

The two other wolves turned tail and made a run for it, leaving their friend behind. He watched them go, eyes wide, as though stunned they could leave him.

Steve wasn't remotely shocked. He tried to push himself back into his human shape as he approached the man, but his body wouldn't cooperate.

Perfect. He could think straight, but now he was stuck. This was harder than he thought it would be.

"St-stay away from me, man."

Luckily, Denise was there to do the talking for him.

"You'd better hold still if you don't want him attacking again. You need medical care. Not even your healing can make that into something you can't worry about."

"Shut up, you bitch!"

Steve lowered his muzzled and growled.

This prick had better not get it into his head that he could call Denise that.

"Okay! Okay! I'm sorry! All right? Fuck, I'm still bleeding!"

Steve didn't give a shit. He was ready to let this little bitch bleed out right here; unfortunately for him, Jackson and his men finally burst through the bushes to see what was going on.

"What the fuck happened?"

They were still in their human shapes? Made sense as to why it took them so damned long to get over here. He was ready to snap his teeth at them for that one.

"What the hell took you guys so long?"

"We didn't know what was going on!"

Denise didn't sound impressed. "You heard fighting and barking, you assholes."

"Christ, you went out here to have a lover's spat! We weren't about to get in the middle of that!"

That caught Steve's attention. Did they really think he was out here having a physical fight with Denise?

"Whatever, can you do something about him before he bleeds to death?"

The two betas stepped around Steve, giving him a wide birth. They glanced back at him. He glared at them in return for thinking he would be getting physical with his mate like that.

The betas reached down for the new prisoner. They handled him gently, which was more than he deserved as far as Steve was concerned.

He backed towards Denise now that he could safely take his eyes off the shithead in question. Her scent surrounded him. He could already feel his blood pressure sliding lower and lower. Steve groaned, leaned against her legs, and allowed her scent to sooth him.

Denise snorted a laugh, her fingers scratching the top of his head.

He would have thought something like that would annoy him, but he found himself leaning into the touch, tilting his head to get the scratch in just the right spot.

"He lost control again?"

Jackson's voice had him yanking away from Denise's hand. He glanced up, spotting the alpha standing next to her. Steve's ears fell back. He growled at the man.

Victor, who had been standing next to Jackson, raised a brow at him. "Maybe you shouldn't pester him when he's like that. Steve? Hey! Can you understand me?"

"He can understand you." Denise barely took her eyes off him. Steve looked to her, and she smiled down at him. She lowered herself to her knees, her hand touching his muzzle and his cheek. He let her pet him, adoring the touch of her hands in his fur. "He knows everything that's going on right now, don't you?"

He looked at her. Damned straight he did.

CHAPTER 22

$\mathcal{D}$enise had to admit, when she walked back to the houses and trailers, she held her head just a touch higher as Steve walked next to her.

Still in his wolf shape, his chest was out and his ears were perked.

Well, his ear. The other was half gone. She *was* going to have a look at that, but she knew better than to get worked up over it when other shifters were around.

His stupid male pride would kick in and he wouldn't let her touch him, but for now, she, even with all her training, her knowledge of some guns and weapons, had never felt more like a badass than she did with Steve walking beside her like this.

She loved it.

More and more she was beginning to understand why so many men and women hoped to find themselves mated to a shifter. Or an alpha, because the way people looked at her as she passed by, the way they looked at *Steve*, it was a powerful sensation.

Meanwhile, the shifter being carried by Jackson's betas was still moaning and yelping, demanding help, to be stitched up until his healing could take effect.

He seemed to be worried his guts would spill out.

Denise had seen the damage. Steve had gotten the man good, and there was that very real possibility, but not with the way he was being carried.

"Put him away," Jackson commanded, waving off the betas.

"I'll go see him later."

Steve growled at that.

Jackson shook his head. "No, you will not."

Denise wasn't taking it this time. She had a built-in excuse, and she wasn't going to let them push her around. "I'm medically qualified to tend to his wounds; you have betas all over the place to watch everything. I doubt he can get it up to do anything to me while his belly is being stitched shut with my needles."

She was going to have to borrow someone else's needles, but that was beyond the point.

"I'll wait until after I've seen to Steve's ear, but unless you want that man dying on your property, then I will see him."

"I won't do anything if she stitches me," called the man.

Denise didn't look at him, and she felt nothing for him but a sense of glee as one of the betas slapped him hard on the face for speaking to her.

Denise sighed. She looked to Victor. "Come on. You know I have to be the one to see him. He could die."

Victor glanced down at Steve. Denise grit her teeth and prepared for the bro code to come between her and one of these men again, but luckily, it didn't happen.

Victor sighed, looking away from Steve as he pressed his mouth together before facing the wolf again. "You can't stop her from doing it. At least this way she'll be safe."

Steve growled again. His ears fell back. His hackles raised. He looked almost as though he wanted to attack his friend.

Which was the only reason why Denise flicked his wounded ear.

He yelped, diving away from her. Denise squashed down her guilt when Steve looked up at her with that crushed expression. He really could make himself look like a kicked puppy if he wanted to.

"Don't look at me like that and stop growling at him. He's your friend, and he's right."

"You're only saying that because I'm agreeing with you," Victor muttered.

She smiled sweetly at him. "I am, and now that you have, you can do whatever you need to do with Jackson while I see to my man." She looked at Jackson, pointing at him. "Keep him alive until I can see him."

Jackson did a half roll of his eyes, as though this entire thing was bothersome to him.

Well, that was too damned bad. Denise was going to get to speak with one of these monsters and she didn't want the opportunity wasted or destroyed before she had her chance.

She grabbed Steve by the scruff, though her grip wasn't so hard. She was sure he didn't feel so much of it. "Come on, you. We've got to see to your ear before it gets infected."

Steve growled again as she led him into the trailer, a sea of eyes from the rest of the pack watching.

Amazed at how she bossed around her mate? Or how Steve put up with it? She couldn't tell, but she slammed the door behind her.

STEVE HAD TO ADMIT, Denise didn't seem interested in showing him mercy while he was in this form.

Not that she handled his wounded ear too harshly, but the sting of the alcohol she put onto his ear was enough to make him whimper.

And he didn't consider himself to be the sort of man who *whimpered* over anything.

Denise dabbed at his ear, a little smile on her face, the sort that a woman only had when she knew she was in command of the situation.

"It's your own fault, you know. Coming along like that to my rescue, looking like a big shot."

Big shot?

"You know, when you threw me down, I honestly thought you were getting ready to attack me. *Don't move!*"

He spun his head back around, staring at the wall, like he was supposed to.

"Stop moving."

He growled, wanting to tell her that he was *trying* not to move, but she was making it very difficult for him.

"Don't growl at me. I'm the one with the needle in my hand. I'm almost done so try to sit still."

He snorted. Sit still while she lectured him, great.

"I know you think I'm nagging you, and I'm telling you, that's not what I'm trying to do. I'm really not."

It was the change in her tone that made Steve settle.

"I get that you want to protect me, and I am grateful for that, but I still need to talk to one of these guys. I know he's not in charge of this whole thing either, and it might not go anywhere. He could tell me to go screw myself when I'm stitching him up, but even if there's a chance…I need to do this, Steve."

She clipped something, he assumed the stitch, then grabbed his face and had him turn to her again.

She shocked him by pressing her nose to his. "I need your support with this. *Please.*"

He still wanted to fight her. It was in him to struggle against it. To not let her anywhere near one of the pigs who wanted to rape her.

But something inside him told him this wasn't just important to her, but to him.

She'd asked for his support. The first time she'd asked for such a thing in the short time they'd known each other. It would set a precedent. If he continued to fight her on this, she would know for the rest of their days what sort of man he was, and it might spoil things for them forever.

He sighed, nodded, and just in case the message wasn't understood, he licked at her face.

Might as well, she'd basically set herself up for the attack by being so close.

"*Gah!* Steve! Stop it! Hey!"

She was laughing, though, which secretly meant she didn't want him to stop, so he climbed onto her, tail wagging, continuing with his attack.

She pushed against his chest, but she was no match for his strength.

"S-Steve! Steve! Stop! Stop it!"

He really didn't want to, but he figured he should give her a chance to breathe if he planned on keeping her around long term.

He pulled back, letting her catch her breath and sit up, though he had to admit, he enjoyed the way her breasts heaved.

"You're crazy." She smiled at him, her hands on the fur of his chest. She gently touched his wounded ear, but with the work she'd just done to it, he didn't feel much pain, if any at all. "I guess this means you're all right with me going to see him?"

He growled a little, because no, he was not all right with it, but if it meant giving her this closure she needed so badly, then he would have to do it.

Luckily, she knew what he meant. Being mated had its advantages, after all.

"Right, I guess it was a stupid question." She continued stroking his chest, her expression sobering. "I need to see him now. He needs treatment. You coming with me?"

He woofed at her in answer, wagging his tail, trying to give off a positive response.

"All right." She stood. "Let's go then."

He hated this so much, but what choice was there?

On the plus side, Denise would be standing around the man with needles.

Steve had learned after a couple of days in the hospital that there was nothing quite like having someone standing over him with his skin torn open, sewing him shut, to force a sense of respect.

Steve didn't have that advantage when he spoke to their first prisoner, and that man had proven himself to be a stubborn son of a bitch.

Maybe Denise would be able to get farther with this new guy.

CHAPTER 23

*V*ictor grumbled and growled as he followed Denise to the trailer where the new prisoner was being kept.

Denise thought it was kind of cute that he was willing to put up with something he clearly hated to give her what she needed, but at the same time, she knew better than to tease him over this. It was hard for him to sit by and let her do this. It was hard for her to do it, too. She didn't want to be in the same room as a man who wanted to hold her down and violate her, but she needed to know.

She'd brought the First Aid kit from her and Steve's trailer to the one where the new guy was being kept. From outside, she could hear his howls of pain and his angry shouts.

Denise stopped briefly, pressed her lips together, then forced herself to keep going before she could give Steve the wrong idea.

The idea that she was scared, that she was about to change her mind.

Like with the shack, there were two betas standing outside the door. Victor stood with them, questioning them, likely trying to make sure things stayed as legal as possible, but Denise didn't know the law, or how it applied and didn't apply to shifters, so she couldn't be sure what he was doing would even help.

The three men stopped what they were doing to look at both her and Steve when they showed up.

Victor had an expression on his face suggesting he'd wished she had changed her mind.

"I take no one's seen him yet?"

"Jackson is inside right now." Victor sighed, then shrugged helplessly. "You can take a guess about what he's doing to the man."

Denise nodded, cringing at the sound of another shriek of pain. "Yeah, well, I gotta admit, part of me wants to let the bastard rot with Jackson, but the nurse in me won't let this stand. You boys going to get in my way?"

They shook their heads, only one of them speaking up. "We were told you would be coming. It's not a good idea, though. If we can smell you, there's no telling what he can smell."

The beta said it as though disgusted. With the shifter inside the trailer? Or himself for having the same sexual urges brought on by her scent?

Steve must have picked up on that same thing, because he growled low in his throat, his ears falling back, even the messed up one.

"You have self-control. That's all I care about."

Another scream of pain.

Denise had enough of this. She pushed forward, shocked when the door opened for her. Only when she stepped inside did she realize it should have been locked. Maybe there was no point with Jackson here.

The man looked up from his work, his shoulders back and chest out, as proud as ever, and hands much bloodier than when Denise had last seen them. He stood in front of a table, the beta from before lying on it. He looked at Denise, too, and color flooded his cheeks at the sight of her, his nostrils flaring.

"Y-you..."

Steve growled low in his throat again, the door shutting behind them.

Jackson reached for a towel, and he began cleaning off his hands. "I thought you would change your mind."

Denise pressed her lips together. She felt as weak-kneed and warm as the first day she'd been in a hospital, still in school, trying to work hands-on with her first patient. Just as she did back then, she buried that sense of unease and put her mind to work.

"Did you put your hands inside him?"

Jackson smiled at her. "Just to see how injured he really is. Wouldn't want to risk that he was faking it."

Denise noted how Steve didn't growl that time. She glanced down at the wolf. It looked like he was smiling.

She rolled her eyes.

"Is he tied down properly?"

"Proper enough that he couldn't get away from me." Jackson let his fingers dance around the open wound, as though getting ready to put his fingers back inside to play around.

The chest of the shifter rose and fell in heavy succession, his eyes wild and terrified.

Denise stepped forward, plopping her First Aid kit onto the counter. She looked at the table, forcing herself to not dart her eyes away too quickly. Everything she did would be judged. Every action she made, every tiny look. By Jackson, by Steve, and by the man on the table. She would not make herself look weak. She was not weak. She was more powerful than anyone in here could possibly know, and she would prove it to them by the end of this session.

So, she stayed as clinical as possible as she opened the kit. "How do you feel?"

The beta laughed, a short, breathy noise. "H-how do you think I feel? This cocksucker has been stretching my belly open from the minute I got in here."

Denise nodded. She looked at the wound, noting it no longer appeared quite like the clean slice from Steve's claw she'd seen before.

"That looks bad. You're conscious, though. That's a good sign."

The man swallowed, eyeing the bottle of alcohol and bandages she pulled from the kit. "Got any pain killers?"

For a wound like his, even with his healing ability, it would be best to give them over, but she wasn't feeling that generous.

"Nothing that would help in the state you're in. Everything in here is for minor aches and pains." She smiled at the man. "You're in good hands, though. I promise." Not entirely a lie, so she felt no guilt in saying the words.

Denise soaked a clean rag in the alcohol. She listened with little to no care as the man hissed while she cleaned his wound. He squirmed and moaned as she squeezed the cloth, letting the burning fluid drain into his wound.

"You're all right."

"The fuck I am. He split my stomach open!"

Denise shook her head. "If he'd touched your stomach, your intestines or your bowels, wolf or no wolf, you'd be dead right now."

The man didn't seem to much care about her excuse. He snorted, but he was taking some care around her. She could tell by the way he eyed her hands.

He didn't once look at Jackson or Steve when she handled him.

As though he was terrified she would reach into his open wound and start grabbing things and yanking them out.

Instead, Denise stayed quiet, her mind focused as she worked on a familiar canvas. She cleaned and prepped the work station, prepared her threads, then began to sew her masterpiece.

There was a certain amount of pride she took in this part. It used to bother her, the look, the very idea of a needle piercing flesh, but she stopped seeing it as bloodied and broken flesh and started seeing it as her current craft.

And in this craft, the needlework had to be neat and precise.

Denise worked every stitch in as she would any other patient. She shocked herself with that. Part of her thought she would have taken some pleasure in making this as uncomfortable as possible for the man who wanted to rape her, but old habits were difficult to part with.

Halfway through with her work, she finally decided to talk.

"What's your name?"

The man looked at her, jumping a little, but not enough to throw off her work. "Dylan."

Denise heard the choked gasp behind her.

"She asks you once and you tell her? Jesus Christ, man. I was playing around with the inside of your belly a few minutes ago."

Dylan growled at Jackson, his teeth forming before he looked fearfully at Denise.

Denise glanced down at Steve, just for his reaction. Her wolfy friend twitched his ears and nose at her.

She smiled back at him.

It wasn't always the case, but there tended to be a respect and fear for those who could handle sewing together torn skin like this with a straight face.

Especially when in the middle of the act.

She wouldn't tell Jackson that. At least not right away.

"You don't have the ears and tail of a born shifter. When were you turned?" She didn't smile at the man, but was careful to keep her tone as unthreatening as possible. Friendly, but not too friendly.

"Few years back."

Denise nodded. "Do you have much control?"

"A little."

She tugged a little harder than necessary on one of her threads, her gaze hardening on Dylan, watching his pupils dilate and the little vein on the side of his head pulse.

"Enough control to stay away from me?"

Dylan's neck tightened. He glanced down at his stomach, at the needle and thread Denise held. The pressure she held away was just enough to pull his skin up into a fleshy spike.

She could really hurt him if she wanted to. He was tied down, surrounded by two powerful shifters, already wounded, and his care was entirely in her hands.

She wanted to. So badly she wanted to make this asshole suffer for thinking he could lay a finger on her.

That was a card she could play only so many times, so she had to be careful.

"I...I could try harder," he said.

Denise snorted. The answer didn't satisfy her the way she wanted it to, so she went back to work on the next couple of stitches.

She was angry now. Steve groaned next to her, his cold nose pushing against her elbow. She pushed her elbow back against him. She couldn't have him doing that when she was working.

"Just so you know, I am stitching you properly."

"I believe you."

"An idiot could do this and make sure you have a very ugly, noticeable scar for the rest of your life." She ran her finger across the line she'd created so far, noting the shiver. "You're lucky I'm not an idiot."

"Yes, ma'am."

She was going to let the *ma'am* bit slide. He was likely too nervous to know or care about much of anything at the moment.

"So, what do I have to do to keep anymore of your friends from coming after me?"

She snipped off the last of the thread, finishing him off. He just needed the few remaining touches and some bandages, and he would be fine if he held still for a day or two.

Dylan blinked at her. "What?"

Denise leaned her arm on the table, her hand, the one still holding the curved needle, hovering over Dylan's skin. He clearly noticed it. "I do not want you or any of your friends to fuck me. So, who do I have to talk to, to make all of you go away?"

"I don't...I don't..." He shook his head, as though unable to get the words out.

Which was not going to fly with Denise. She let the pointed end of the needle trail down the line work of his stitching, her patience running thin.

"You can do it. Come on. Focus here. Tell me who your alpha is so I can go and meet with him. I'll have a nice little chat, and you and your friend can go home."

Jackson scoffed.

Denise shrugged. "Maybe."

"It...it wasn't our alpha; it was just...I mean he knows, but he doesn't care."

She pricked his skin, feeling his small jump.

Men and women could handle many things, but for those who could not handle the pinch of a needle, Denise was their lord and master.

It was good to know the same held true for this shifter here.

"What do you mean he doesn't care?" Jackson asked.

Dylan started talking fast. Really fast, as though he couldn't quite get the words out that he wanted. "He knows about you, and he doesn't want you! He never sent us! But he said he doesn't care if any of us tries. I was just with the others. I can't always control it! You smelled too good and when I smelled you the first time, I could barely keep away."

"Barely?" She dug the needle a little deeper. Denise felt the tension in the man's muscles. The worst thing a patient could do when there was a needle in their skin.

"I tried! Okay? We all smelled a new wolf around, one you were letting near you. It's harder to fight the instinct when there's competition. If he claims you then our chance will have been gone."

That was the reason for the increase in attacks? The fact that another wolf was sniffing around her and she was letting him near was getting these idiots jealous?

"He already claimed me, and for some reason, you're still coming around."

Dylan blinked at her, as though he didn't entirely understand. She didn't expect him to.

"I don't…I don't get it. I thought…I shouldn't be smelling you then. I mean, I smell him on you, but it should be gone, the need to take you. Knowing he's around made it worse."

Denise clenched her teeth, glancing at Jackson. She'd had the same idea thanks to him. "Apparently not."

Jackson didn't look back at her, though he didn't look happy. She imagined he wasn't proven wrong too many times in his life.

She showed a little mercy and pulled the needle back. Dylan sighed his relief, but she wasn't finished with him yet. "Will others be coming?"

"Others?" Dylan seemed to think on that. "I guess so. They're going to want what you're giving to him. I only came because my wolf couldn't stomach another male on you. The others will feel the same."

So, they weren't done with the attacks then. That was fucking perfect.

"You said you can smell Steve on me. Does that make it any better at all? My scent? Or do you only feel that need for possession?"

"I…" Dylan looked at Jackson, then down at Steve, who growled low at him.

"Don't look at them. Look at me. Is it easier for you to control yourself when you smell Steve on me?"

"Kind of, I guess. Yes and no. I can't describe it, okay? It's instinct. I want to stay away from another male, but I don't want him to have you either."

"What if I wanted him? What if I didn't want you?"

Steve nosed her arm. She pushed him back again. She was too focused and couldn't let herself lose that.

"I don't know. I would have treated you right." Dylan shrugged helplessly. "I've got some family who would like you. I wouldn't have hurt you."

He seemed to have a mixed up idea about what hurting her would mean.

"Do you feel the need to claim me now?"

"I'm not feeling anything right now, but I'm also in a lot of pain from that asshole." Dylan glared at Jackson, ignoring the fact that it was Steve who had sliced his belly.

Didn't matter, because as far as she was concerned, Denise had her answer. "You're so full of shit."

He looked at her, eyes wide, as though terrified she would prick him again. "What?"

Steve growled, feeding off her anger.

"You want to give me that shit about how you can't control it? You're controlling it just fine right now. You're only holding yourself back because you have to."

Dylan shook his head. "That's not it! I don't always…I can't always control it!"

She pushed away from the table, standing as she gathered the supplies back into the First Aid kit. "Fuck you."

"Bitch! Are you serious? That wolf there can't control it either! Why would I be lying about this?"

Steve's hackles stood on end. His ears fell back as he showed his teeth.

Denise touched the top of his head, trying to calm him before he could do something they might regret.

Like kill a bound prisoner.

Steve calmed, but that rage Denise felt bubbling up inside her...not so much.

"Steve was changed into a wolf shifter a couple of weeks ago, and this is one of his first transformations. He hasn't raped me, and I sincerely doubt he ever will. You've had years to get your shit together, so don't cry to me about how you're the victim. You're a pig, and I'm going to make sure you go to prison for what you tried to pull."

The man tensed again before he started fighting against his bonds. "I'm telling you, I can't control it! You're the one that smells like that!"

She was leaving. "Jackson, do whatever you want. Tear the stitching apart again, I don't care."

Jackson threaded his fingers together and cracked his knuckles. "With pleasure."

"Hey! No, hey! Wait a minute! I'm telling the truth! Come on! *Please!*"

She glanced back on her way out, then quickly turned away again when it looked as though Jackson was grabbing either side of Dylan's stomach.

As though he was getting ready to rip open a shirt.

The door slammed shut behind her, but it wasn't enough to block out the intensity of Dylan's scream.

CHAPTER 24

*S*teve didn't want to be in this shape anymore. Even with four legs, he could barely keep up with his mate as she marched away from the trailer where Dylan was shrieking once more.

Victor followed, but he didn't seem to have much more success, and he still had use of his vocal chords.

"I take it things didn't go so well?"

Steve growled low in his throat. No, they sure as fuck did not.

"There's no stopping it. Not even with Steve's scent on me. There's no fucking stopping this."

Steve frowned. Dylan hadn't said that. Was that the impression she'd taken from Dylan?

Victor looked at him, but Steve couldn't figure out how to convey his confusion in a growl.

"Are you sure that's what he said?"

"He might as well have."

This was crazy. Steve needed to get back into his human shape and he needed to do it right now. Denise was angry, and he felt it. He'd been in tune with her emotions while in his human shape, but now that he was like this, those feelings washed over him. He felt them as strongly as though they were his own.

And he wanted to ease that burden from her.

Steve suddenly rushed in front of Victor, halting the other man before he could take another step forward.

Victor stopped, lifted a brow at him, then looked to Denise. "Uh, I think Steve might want some alone time with you."

Steve glanced back, just to see Denise had barely looked at him before she folded her arms and kept right on walking.

"Whatever."

His good ear twitched, his bad ear tried, and it just throbbed.

Victor sighed. "Good luck, man. Try to get into your other shape as soon as you can. I think she needs it right now."

No kidding.

Steve whirled around, darting after his mate. She headed for the trailer Jackson had given them, and thankfully, she didn't slam the door on his nose when she stepped through the door. Denise kept it open for him, closing it when his tail was clear of the doorway.

She climbed up to the loft, flopping down onto the bed.

Steve watched her, his paws up on the thin stairway before he followed.

Denise's face in the pillow, her arms clutching the thing, made it clear she didn't wish for company.

Had he been in his more human shape, maybe he would have backed off, left her to get this out of her system, to think and feel these dark things on her own time.

The animal side of his brain refused to allow that. His woman was in need of comfort, so he would provide it.

Wagging his tail softly, Steve approached the futon. He sniffed around Denise's hair, taking in the scent of oranges still lingering on her, the enticing scent of his mate, and yes, even that little something extra that made him think this woman was not only his, but something special.

He almost didn't blame the other shifters for wanting her. She had the whole package.

The ones who tried attacking her for it, he absolutely did blame them.

Denise lifted her face from her pillow, though she hardly looked at him. "If you pee on me, I will murder you."

Steve snorted at that, though there was no mirth on Denise's face. She looked as though she wanted to be anywhere but where she was now.

Steve kept his tail wagging, trying to look both innocent and cute enough that she would allow him closer still.

Denise looked up at him, and while she hadn't been crying, he could see how close she was to her breaking point.

He woofed at her again, pawing at her shoulder.

She shoved his paw away. "What? You think you're an actual dog now?"

He would be a dog, her emotional therapy dog if that was what she needed.

He couldn't tell if that was a product of the mating or his dumb animal brain trying to problem solve, but this seemed like the best way to soothe her angry heart.

So he kept his tail wagging, pressed his nose to her and licked at her throat and face.

"Steve! Cut it out!"

She was angry, her hands pushing him away. She turned over onto her belly, pressing her face back into her pillow, but Steve refused to give up the fight. He went down with her, rolling onto his back next to her, rubbing his scent onto hers before he rolled to his belly and pressed himself close.

He sniffed around her ear, tail still moving as he snuggled next to his woman.

And then, slowly, he noticed the trembling of her shoulders.

Shit. Was she crying? Had he misjudged this?

Denise turned her face out of the pillow, looking at him, and Steve was saddened, but not shocked, to see the tears in her eyes.

What did shock him was seeing how she laughed even as she cried.

Then she reached for him, her arms curling around Steve's neck. She pushed herself closer to his fur, crying against his chest, using him for her comfort.

He let her. A soft whine escaped his throat, a helpless animal sound he could not control.

Because he wanted to do more and couldn't, so he let her cry herself out next to him.

Her body next to his, the way she held him, it did something to him he could hardly explain. Steve felt a relaxation gently sliding through his body, something familiar, and he focused on it, willing his body to change into the human form he knew Denise needed much more than this canine shape.

And it worked. Just like that, no struggle, no heat, his limbs just changed. Lengthening where they needed to, his muscles changing, his bone structure and even his face.

Whatever fur didn't melt back into his pores fell out onto the futon. Denise laughed, brushing some of those coarse hairs off her clothes and away from Steve's skin.

"All it takes for you to get control is to see me crying. That figures."

He ran his fingers through her hair. "I don't think that was it. Not really." He cupped her cheek. "This will get better."

Her eyes shone as she looked at him. The pain made his heart twist. He'd never felt that before.

"How will it get better? There's no bad guy to stop. It's an endless cycle of shifters who want me to have their babies."

Steve shook his head. "It's not endless. I don't care what that asshole said. Jackson has control. His pack has control." Even if they couldn't keep from looking at Denise in ways he didn't like. "I've already got more control now than I did when we came here yesterday. Victor is going to help me through this. Eventually, my scent on you will be strong enough to keep most of them away, and you're badass enough to scare the rest off."

She snorted. "Right, now I know you're trying to get into my pants."

Steve grinned. "That, too, but I mean it."

He slid his hand down the side of her neck, her shoulder, then back up again, loving the feel of her skin against his.

"Do you really not think you're tough?"

"Tough because I have to be isn't tough."

"You're wrong." He shook his head. "That's the best kind of tough."

Denise pressed her lips together, and he had to admit, in that moment, he didn't think he'd ever seen her so vulnerable. It was a strange thing to see, but he was also glad she was willing to show this side of herself to him.

Denise's expression twisted to something painful. She touched the shell of his ear.

Steve flinched a little. Denise yanked her hand back. "I'm sorry."

"Don't be. I forgot about it." He reached up to have a feel for it, worried and fascinated by what he might, or might not, feel. A good chunk of his ear was still there. Made sense, those wolves hadn't taken the entire thing off, but it was strange for him to feel the top half missing. "Shit."

"You're going to have to get that seen to, by someone in a proper facility. Maybe we can do something about it."

"You mean like a transplant?"

"Anything. I don't want those people to scar you for the rest of your life."

His hearing on that side would be a little fucked, but not so much that he wouldn't be able to do his job, or take care of her.

"I'm sure we'll be fine."

"I'm talking about your ear."

"I'm not."

Steve held onto her face before leaning in and kissing her. He felt her sharp intake of breath, felt the way she leaned into him and the way her body warmed for him.

That fear and anger, the ball of emotion that had been swirling around her head when she'd walked away from Dylan, Steve could feel it sifting away. Her body relaxed, just as his did when he'd been next to her. He opened her mouth with his tongue, gently tasting her sweetness inside.

Denise moaned, pressing her body even closer, her small hands sliding around his waist, shocking him when she pressed her nails into his ass, pulling him flush against her.

There was no way she couldn't feel the heat of his cock. That would be a little too difficult to hide from her.

Her lips pulling into a smile against his mouth let him know he was spot on with his guess.

She pulled back, and the look in her eyes was enough to let him know what she wanted even before she shoved him onto his back and straddled him.

"I think I need something else right now other than a good cuddle."

Her hand on his dick was more than enough to make him agree with her. Agree with absolutely everything she could possibly want from him.

Steve's eyes slid to the back of his head. "You can do whatever you want to me if it makes you feel better."

"I will."

Denise pulled herself out of her shirt. She had to get off him so she could get out of her pants, and when she was on her back, frantically working her belt and the button of her jeans, Steve decided to take matters into his own hands.

He spun around, placing himself on top of her, between her legs. Her thighs wrapped nicely around him, fitting so perfectly it should have been illegal.

He kissed her, loving the feeling of her hands in his hair, clutching tightly, her teeth nipping at his lower lip before he pulled away from her again, just to enjoy the rise in color on her cheeks.

Steve wanted to give her anything and everything she could possibly want.

His love, peace of mind against the shifters who were still looking for any reason to use her as their personal incubator.

And a solid orgasm on top of it all.

"Let me help you out of these."

Steve slid down her legs, hands flush against her hips, pulling her jeans down the rest of the way that they needed to go.

He heard the sound of Denise's heart flutter when they bunched up around her knees, and he looked up, briefly stopping what he was doing.

Denise shook her head, breasts heaving as she panted for breath. "Don't stop."

He blinked. Was she not aware of how loud her heart sounded?

One of his ears had been half taken off, and yet he could still make out the sound of that solid thumping.

Denise blinked down at him, coming out of the haze of her lust enough to push herself to her elbows, to look at him. "Steve?"

Her heart began to calm, and only then did Steve think he understood what this meant.

This was that ability shifters spoke of. The heightened senses. Steve had felt it to some degree ever since he had changed. His smell and taste had gone through the roof, and certain instincts had begun bouncing all over the walls like a kid hyped up on sugar, but the hearing thing...he'd felt a change there, but never had he been able to hone it into something specific, like a heartbeat.

"You okay?"

Steve nodded, grinning as he took off Denise's shoe. "Never better." He pulled the leg of her jeans off, leaving the other on, spreading her thighs apart. "I've just been thinking about this for a little too long."

The sound of her heart thudded again, but that was nothing compared to the noise it made when his mouth touched her sex, the heat of her, the beautiful, wet taste that made him moan against her pussy as he licked her deep.

And that thudding sound could have been the banging of a drum against his ears, and yet Steve felt calm and centered. In *control*.

This was going to be good.

CHAPTER 25

*D*enise moaned, her fingers gripping tightly into Steve's hair, her knees rising as he paid worship to her.

Normally, she wouldn't describe the act as romance novel-isa as that, but there was no other way to describe it when he took such care with her, when he gave this sort of expert attention to her sex, when he licked her deep and flicked his tongue in all the right places.

Already she was coming undone. Already she could feel the rush of orgasm about to hit her, and there was nothing she could do to hold it back, not even warn Steve that it was coming so he could stop.

She wanted it to last longer, longer than this, but she was over that edge and he was pushing her faster down to the bottom of that cliff.

When she hit, it was more of a crash, hard and fast. Her orgasm throbbed through her. The pulling rush got her good, and the only thing she could do was gasp for breath.

Then she looked down, watched Steve lift his face up to gaze at her over the mounds of her breasts, and suddenly, she felt shy.

"Oh God."

Denise covered her face with her hands and rolled over.

There was a laugh in Steve's voice as he pulled himself up and climbed over the top of her. "What's wrong?"

He tried to pull her hands away from her face, but she wouldn't allow it.

"That was embarrassing."

"What? Why was that embarrassing?"

Denise shook her head, squeezing her thighs together now against the pulsing of her orgasm. "It just was."

"That's not exactly what I expected you to say about it, but okay, I guess."

Denise laughed, looked at Steve, who was positively pouting at her, and she laughed harder before reaching for him. "Come here."

He did. He was too cute and the grin on his face was something she couldn't resist.

When he kissed her, she didn't even care where his mouth had been, and even though her sex was sensitive after her orgasm, she didn't complain when he parted her thighs, and she kept right on smiling as he pushed his cock inside her.

Denise groaned. "That's what I want."

She curled her arms around the back of his neck, holding him tight as he plunged into her, surging forward before retracting again.

It was slower than the last time. Their first time together had felt more frantic, as though they wouldn't have this chance again, or they were going to be walked in on.

This was different. This felt as though they had all the time in the world.

Denise touched Steve's face, his chest, his nipples. Her hand briefly fluttered around the wound of his ear, her heart hurting for his injury, but then her gaze always came back to his eyes. His eyes that glowed that beautiful golden color as he looked at her.

He didn't just look at her. He kissed her. He kissed her mouth, her throat, then her breasts, lifting her shirt to get at her nipples.

All the while, they kept their pacing. And it was beautiful.

Denise didn't expect for another orgasm to hit her, but then again, this was a werewolf she was dealing with. Basic sex ed told of the ways they could get a partner raring to go in short order. Something to do with the scent of them. She couldn't make it out with her human nose, but he was a powerful shifter, and her mate; she was clearly under his spell when she felt the gentle rising of her pleasure.

And then it started pulsing harder; she reached back to the top of that peak so much faster, and grit her teeth, groaning and wishing she had the strength to hold it back so this would last forever.

"You close again?"

Denise nodded, groaning again. "I hate you so much."

Steve laughed. He pressed his forehead to her collar bone, even as his hips continued pumping inside her.

"Why, because I make this look so easy?" He slammed his hips forward harder, almost slapping his pelvis into hers, and it was that simple act, the vibration of their flesh hitting each other, that was more than enough to make Denise gasp for breath.

Her brain went wild. She could hardly think or breathe anything other than the unimaginable pleasure.

And Steve did know what he was doing.

"Y-You have lots of control." She pressed her head back into the pillows, clenching her eyes shut. "You have all the control you want!"

Steve said nothing, and she knew he was getting closer by the way he growled, by the intense way his hips suddenly picked up speed, and Denise could only gasp for breath as he filled her, as he pushed her towards that edge.

He grabbed her hand, threading their fingers together and clutching her so tightly it hurt.

She didn't care. She was ready to jump off that cliff with him. To forever look into his golden eyes and see that sexy, confident smile.

And she did.

DENISE BASKED under the glow of her second orgasm, enjoying the heat of Steve's body, and the heat of his mouth as he kissed her. She took it all in, enjoying every touch, the intimacy of it, and the heat.

She touched his face, stroking his cheek and feeling the rough stubble there.

"Don't shave."

He tilted his head a little. "Wasn't planning on it until tomorrow, but if you insist."

Denise smiled, shaking her head. "I'm not telling you to grow a beard, but...just don't shave. You rock the stubble look pretty well."

"Do I?" He stroked his chin, pretending to think on that before he grinned at her.

It was the dumbest, and cutest, thing she could have ever seen.

She loved his playful nature. Loved his body and his convictions, the way he worked hard for what he wanted and how he supported her in what she wanted.

"If you keep up the Prince Charming routine, you're going to make a good impression on my father."

A note of panic entered Steve's eyes, and she laughed out loud. "What? Did you think it would never happen?"

"I was hoping you were an orphan."

She laughed again, her legs twisting in the sheets, and she'd never felt more free.

Despite everything, her talk with Dylan, Steve's lack of control, she was alive, and it felt amazing.

Looking into his eyes again, Denise noticed something else.

"The gold in your eyes hasn't gone away yet."

"No?" Steve blinked hard a couple of times. "What about now?"

Denise shook her head. "No, still there. But it looks good."

Steve rubbed his eyes, but the gold lingered. "I wonder what that's about."

"Can you see things differently? Sharper? It might mean your other half is trying to come out and you don't even know it yet."

Steve's grin widened. "Do I see things sharper? I don't know, let's have a look." He tried to pull off the blanket covering to get a peek at her bare breasts again, and even though he'd already seen them, Denise shrieked a laugh as she tried to hold onto her measly coverings. "No, no! You're not doing that! Steve!"

It didn't matter what she said or how she struggled, he was determined to get his fingers on her belly and tickle her to within an inch of her life, and she was completely helpless to it. She shrieked even as the tickling stopped and he was kissing her chest and neck again.

"You've got to be kidding me. Again?"

He grinned up at her, and *yes,* very clearly he wanted to do this again.

Denise rolled her eyes. "Oh my God. I don't know how I'm supposed to survive this. I really don't."

"I think you'll do just fine," Steve said, still smiling at her as he eased her thighs apart.

Denise shook her head. "You are crazy. Were you this horny before being turned into a werewolf?"

Steve paused in the act of kissing her belly. He pulled back, seemed to think on that. "I think I was."

Denise scoffed. "No way."

"Really!"

"You mean to tell me you had that kind of stamina for sex just because?"

"I was born gifted?"

"Hmm," Denise lifted her leg, giving him easier access. "I can't argue with that, but not for the same reasons you're thinking of."

"Careful." Steve ran his hand up her thigh. "It might sound as though you're insulting me."

"I'd never do that to you."

He scoffed. "Sure."

Denise couldn't stop grinning. She'd never had another lover who put her at ease like this before. She'd never felt so calm and satisfied, never felt the need to make jokes and laugh in bed with another man.

This was almost too good to be true.

So, of course, she had to ruin it by thinking of Dylan, which she hated because she absolutely did not want to bring him into bed with her and Steve.

"I'm sorry."

Steve looked at her. "For what?"

Denise wet her lips. "For not believing you when you said it wouldn't do any good."

Steve shook his head, but she cut him off before he could say anything.

"No, I mean it. If I'd just *listened*—"

"*No.*"

It was the tone of his voice that cut her off. Steve shook his head, his jaw clenching before he turned his attention back to her. "It's not about you listening or not listening, or what he would or would not have said. Most people who are victims of something want to confront their abusers, that's normal. You don't have to explain that to me. Most of the time, what happens is the criminal in question has no remorse, or pretends to, or blames everyone else. That guy...I didn't know which route he was going to take, but his thing about not having control...you were exactly right. He's full of shit."

She slid her hands across Steve's cheeks. "Because you have control."

He shook his head. "That's the thing. I don't. I don't even have control and I can still stop myself from becoming a complete monster. These people...even if they're all on their own, even if they're fighting with each other to see who can get to you first, they're going to have any number of people to blame other than themselves. But we'll get through it. I'll chase off every last one of them if I have to."

Denise smiled, not looking forward to the fight ahead, but enjoying the way Steve spoke of it. Of backing her up.

"And I'll shoot anyone in the ass who comes for me."

Steve nodded. "That's my girl."

He kissed her again, long and deep. Sensually. Denise was ready to give him what he wanted. What he needed, but like clockwork, she made out the sounds of shouting, then the growling and barking.

Steve yanked his mouth from hers, turning his good ear towards the sound of the noise, and then he looked at her.

She sighed. "Right. Can't get one minute's peace around here before the dogs come for dinner."

"Don't worry, baby." He pecked her on the lips. "I'll chase those suckers off and have you back in your birthday suit within the hour."

She sighed. "This might be the rest of my life. The ones who won't stay away from you will keep coming because they're jealous of you, and I don't think I'm even doing anything for you."

Steve shook his head. "You have no idea what you do for me. I'm not giving up on this, and when I'm through with them, even the toughest of them will know to keep their fucking distance." He kissed her again before pulling back. "Within the hour!" He promised.

Even though there were shifters outside who were ready to kidnap and violate her, his promise erased all of that and made her warm.

She growled at Steve as he jumped down the loft. He didn't bother grabbing for any clothes as he ran outside, because he wouldn't be needing them.

"Yeah, you've got the Prince Charming thing down all right."

CHAPTER 26

Steve had something closer to a plan now. He could visualize how to make this work and how to keep Denise safe from here on out.

And it would involve kicking ass so hard these animals would know not to mess with him, or his woman, ever again.

There was already a fight by the time he made it outside.

Not just a small handful, like what had happened in the woods earlier that day, but a whole slew of wolves that didn't belong. Dozens.

Holy shit.

Steve shook his head. Whatever. The challenge would get his blood pumping for his next session with his mate, because the more the merrier as far as he was concerned.

The more of them who saw him like this, who were here to witness his beat down of anyone who tried getting near Denise, the more there would be to spread the story about how he and his mate were not to be fucked with under any circumstance.

Victor had his pistol with him, but he seemed to be saving the bullets for when things became more desperate. Now, he had his nightstick out.

Steve went to him first. Victor saw him coming; he was good at not getting the tunnel vision that came with a fight, so there would be less of a chance he would attack a friend, but still, Steve was glad the man saw him running up to get his back.

"A wolf for a couple of days and you're already through with wearing clothes?"

"Shut up."

Steve threw out is fist, catching one of the wolves who had been jumping at him with its mouth wide open right in the nose.

It cried out and fell over, whining and writhing in pain, but more shifters came to take its place.

Victor swung at another wolf, catching it on the skull.

Some of the animals lay down at his feet from the damage he'd already caused, either unconscious, or possibly dead. Despite everything, Steve hoped not dead.

It was too much paper work, and he didn't want that on Victor's conscience.

"If you're going to get into your wolf shape then please do it now. It could really help."

Steve narrowly ducked out of the way of another wolf lunging at him. He noticed more and more of the shifters were coming up to him and Victor. Likely they could pinpoint Steve's scent and were going to want to take him out as competition for Denise.

Victor was right. If Steve planned on surviving this, then he needed to get his protective fur out so he could have something to keep those claws and teeth off him.

He also needed to get his own claws and teeth ready. These things were going to start sniffing out Denise soon.

Steve inhaled a deep breath, trying to focus. He had to learn how to keep the wolf back when he'd fought with Jackson. Now he needed to pull it forward and control it.

Breathe in, breathe out, imagine his body changing—

"*Aaarghhh!*" Steve screamed long and loud beneath the head of the pain that caught him off guard, shooting up from his ankle, up his leg, and into the rest of his body, freezing him and then torturing him with the mind numbing pain of it.

He brought his fists down hard onto the head of the wolf that had bitten him.

The teeth didn't dislodge right away. He hit it again and again. Victor couldn't help him even as the man stood right next to him, fighting off the other wolves that were taking bites out of him. One of them had their teeth on Victor's forearm, and if Steve didn't change right now, they were fucked.

He'd promised Denise. He'd told her he would take care of this within the hour as though this would be a cake walk for him, and he had every intention of keeping to that promise. He wasn't going to let these bastards take her. He wasn't going to let them hurt her. He wasn't going to lose her to them.

Her smile flashed through his brain. He bashed the top of the wolf's head in again.

He saw the look on her face as she held a gun in her hands, pointing it at her enemies.

Steve struck the wolf again, feeling it stagger.

He thought of the way she'd stood over him in the hospital, the care she'd taken with him, how their eyes had met, even back when she'd been scared of the very idea of being with a shifter. She'd agreed to go out with him.

He smashed the wolf's head in again, and this time, its teeth released him. Bright red blood gushed from his ankle, but Steve didn't feel the pain. He didn't feel anything other than his anger and hatred for these things, these monsters who thought Denise belonged to them, that this was a competition for her. That he was standing in their way.

He grabbed the wolf around the neck. It struggled when it realized Steve was on top of it, but it was too late.

He held the snout and brought its head down hard onto the ground, again and again, not stopping even as the wolf struggled and wormed it's body, desperate to escape.

Claws sliced at his legs and arms, the pain hot, but then he didn't feel that either as Steve brought the wolf down again and again. He didn't stop until the wolf did, until it was no longer moving.

He sighed, pulling his hands back from the creature.

He couldn't tell if it was dead. He kind of hoped it was.

The adrenaline pumped through his body, something animal and wild and he wanted to pound his fists onto his chest and roar.

The roar of pain from Victor halted him, and Steve turned his attention to his friend just as Victor was pushed down onto the ground by no less than three wolves.

One biting at his arm, the other the back of Victor's leg, and the third adding his weight to the pile on to take him out.

Steve did roar this time, and he lunged at the wolves, swinging his arms, smacking two of them away in a single blow. They cried out, a pathetic dog-sounding whine stemming from their throats as they flew into the nearest trees.

One of them stopped moving. The other staggered to its feet, shook its head, took one look at Steve before it turned and ran away.

Steve snarled, turning back to the other wolf that had been biting the back of Victor's leg.

It had let go. Its ears were pressed flat against the top of its head as it backed away.

Steve took one step closer, his claws digging into the earth, ready to slice into the flesh and fur of the thing in front of him.

It didn't give Steve the chance as it turned tail and ran for it.

"Jesus, Steve."

Steve looked down at his friend. Victor's clothes were bloody, some of that blood had splattered his face, but he looked at Steve as though he was the real anomaly here.

As though he was something to be feared.

Only because he *was* something to be feared. Steve was an animal, the alpha, and no one was touching his mate.

He raised his snout and howled, hands clenching to fists, claws digging into his own palms, but he was alive, and he was strong.

He would kill all of them if he had to.

Another howl answered him. He looked up, noting the wolf that was not an enemy. Familiar scent and build. Jackson. Some of the wolves behind him howled as well.

There were others that didn't howl. Some were fleeing, others approached Steve in a pack-like form, groups of threes and fours.

Not many. He could handle them. It would hurt, but he could do it.

He looked away from them, to the trailer.

Denise stood there, the door broken open, but she was standing. There was a kitchen knife in her hand, and it had blood on it. She had a little blood on her as well, and the sight of it drove him wild and forced his body into motion.

He plowed through the wolves as they attempted to jump onto him, to take him down, to bite at his face and fingers, legs and arms. He grabbed one by the tail and smacked it hard onto the ground. He spun around to throw the others off his back, and yet they kept coming.

Let them come. He would die like this. He would take them all with him!

~

Denise's arm trembled at the sight of Steve in that...shape.

She'd seen it before. In medical journals, magazines and the Internet. He'd come close to turning into something like that before, earlier that day, even when he'd been mostly in his wolf form and had grabbed Dylan, spinning the wolf around so he could claw at his belly.

This was different. This was something massive, something powerful.

She'd known he was powerful, but she'd always attributed that to his willpower, to his career of helping people, and his need to survive.

Just as he'd done that day he'd come into her hospital.

Steve stood on his two hind legs, his bushy tail swishing around behind him as he grabbed the wolves currently jumping onto him, throwing them off him, and slamming the others down hard.

He was like a fully grown gorilla.

Only much scarier.

Despite his opposable thumbs, and being on two legs, he was not human. He looked something closer to a wolf. His head was all wolf, and there was fur along most of his body.

Did he even know he looked like that?

He was still able to fall onto all fours with the shape of his legs, spinning again to make the last of the wolves fly off him, but they jumped back on as easily as before.

These weren't betas. They weren't like Dylan, or even that first wolf in the shed.

These were alphas. They were here for all or nothing, and these were the ones Steve was going to impress the most as he grabbed another of the wolves by the throat and slammed it down hard again and again, until it stopped moving.

Denise swallowed. She looked down at her hand, realized she was white-knuckling the kitchen knife, and forced herself to stop before she made her fingers cramp up.

This was Steve. She didn't have anything to fear.

But was it fear? She'd already seen his wolf shape, had walked next to it without fear he would attack her and put more scars on her body.

And yet, she couldn't stop her body from trembling.

Denise inhaled a long breath, glancing back at the stupid wolf that had tried breaking in here and was currently making a bloody mess of the trailer floor.

No. This wasn't fear. This was adrenaline. She was *feeding* off him because he was her mate and he was fighting for his life and for her freedom. And because of the raw power that emanated from him.

He hadn't been kidding when he said he would take care of it. Had he known this was hiding beneath the surface? That this was a form he could reach for and touch?

All Denise knew for sure was, after this, any shifter that came for her would do so only because they had a death wish.

And in some primal way, this excited her.

"Come on, baby. You can do it."

She wanted to shout it to him, wanted to pump her fists in the air and cheer him on, let I'm know she was on his side and everything he did he did with her blessing.

Regardless of how bloody it was.

But she didn't. Denise had no idea the level of control he had in that shape, and even if it was perfect control, she didn't dare raise her voice too much to draw attention away from what he did.

The wolves continued coming for him, circling and jumping on him. At first, they did it one at a time before deciding this was a mistake and going all out, two and three at a time, as though this would help them.

It made sense. Why wouldn't it help them, after all?

But they couldn't hold on. They tried biting at his ears again, but Steve moved and spun with the speed of a wild animal, of a creature that knew it was fighting for its life. The wolves were thrown from his body with chunks of hair in their mouths.

They couldn't seem to get a proper grasp of him. Of what they wanted, his flesh and blood. More came for him, and more failed.

Steve grabbed onto the scruff of one that had jumped onto his back and slammed it down hard, his hackles rising as he roared in the face of the wolf, his teeth and eyes terrifying.

To the credit of the shifters, they kept right on trying. They were stubborn bastards, but she expected that from experience.

Steve was just as stubborn, more so, because he refused to give them an inch, and though they had trouble grabbing onto him, when he got them, it was painful for them.

He was going to win. He could do it. As the wolves stopped moving one by one, either unconscious or dead, and one more making a run for it, Denise was filled with a giddy emotion the likes of which she'd never felt before.

The feeling that this could be it. This could finally be the day she was freed.

She was so caught up in watching Steve fight off the remaining two wolves struggle to hold their ground. One had its tail tucked between its legs, and Denise felt it. This was it. It was already over and she wanted to celebrate right now. She'd pop a champagne bottle if she happened to have one in hand.

A sudden movement to her side was the only thing that pulled her away from the vision in front of her.

Her training was likely the only thing that saved her, because one glance to the right was all it took to stop the wolf from taking another step forward.

Her breath hitched. Denise gripped the knife tighter, adjusting her hold on the handle of the blade so the wolf would see she had it.

And that it still had blood on it.

It wasn't so close, about fifteen feet away, but objectively, a good leap and it would be on top of her.

It was a big wolf, bigger than even the other alphas fighting her mate for her.

Smart, too. At the sight of the knife in hand, it straightened, sat, tail curling around its legs, and watched her.

She grit her teeth.

"Don't even think about it." She muttered the words under her breath, and with the noise all around her, she had to wonder if the wolf could hear it.

It didn't move, however. Not towards her. The wolf did look to Steve, ears flicking, nose twitching.

Watching him? What for?

If it was to gauge his strength, then as far as Denise was concerned, he could do it all day long so long as he got the hint Denise belonged to Steve, and not to anyone else.

"You see that?" she asked, needing to make sure the message was delivered as the next wolf ran away with its tail tucked between its legs, leaving only one left to nervously face off with Steve.

The large wolf didn't so much as look at her.

"That's what will happen to you if you come near me. I don't belong to you. You get me?"

Again, no reaction. It was infuriating.

If these things wanted to take her so badly they could at least pretend as though she had some agency here.

The ears and tail on the wolf flicked again, and it stole one more glance at her.

Did it just narrow its eyes at her?

Without her guns, with only a blade in hand, Denise never felt more naked. This was a big wolf. The one she'd left to bleed out in her trailer was no small fry either, but this thing was something else.

If it tried anything, she would have her work cut out for her. She might not be able to fight it off.

The wolf did nothing. It turned tail and bolted away, leaping easily and swiftly across the pack property before vanishing into the bushes.

The branches and leaves hardly stirred, as though the wolf had been a ghost.

Denise blinked.

What the hell was that about?

The pack cheered, pulling her back to the situation at hand. Denise looked up and around, her gaze honing in on Steve just as the wolf-man creature leaned over his most recent kill, pulled his face up to the sky, and howled as though there was a full moon above him.

Denise exhaled. She hadn't been aware of holding her breath, but now that he was done, the attacking wolves either retreating, unconscious, or dead, a heavy weight fell off her chest.

Her blood chilled when Steve's animal eyes turned up, and he looked right at her before coming closer.

CHAPTER 27

*J*ackson tried getting in his way. That turned out to be a mistake even Denise could see coming from a mile away when it came to what not to do with shifters.

Steve's hackles shot up again; he crouched low into a position that suggested he was going to leap at Jackson and tear his head off.

"Steve! Stop!"

He didn't stop.

Jackson jumped at Steve just as Steve jumped at him. They met somewhere in the middle of the air, crashing together hard before coming back down.

Denise dropped her knife, running towards them.

Victor appeared out of nowhere, grabbing her around the shoulders, pulling her back.

"No, no. Stop. Don't get in the middle of that."

Denise wanted to fight him. She wanted to make Steve stop using any method she had at her disposal.

Maybe he sensed that because he shook her a little. "Look around you. None of Jackson's wolves are interfering. You can't go over there."

He was right. The cheering had stopped, the excitement sapped from the crowd, and not because people were recovering from the fight or dealing with the morbid clean up.

They watched their alpha and Steve roll around, biting and kicking at each other as though the sight of it scared even them.

It scared her. Denise's heart thudded against her ribcage as though it was trying to break out.

"We can't let them do this."

"It's all right. Jackson will take care of it. He won't let Steve near you like this."

That thought brought Denise comfort for about three seconds before she realized something was off.

There was something different about this fight compared to the last couple of fights Jackson had with Steve.

For one thing, Jackson, no matter what he did, couldn't seem to get the upper hand. At one point he, too, tried shifting to some point halfway between a man and a wolf. It was a clear act of desperation, and the creature wasn't as smooth and sleek as what Steve had become.

He created hands for himself instead of front paws. Denise knew their purpose. Jackson used his opposable thumbs to try grabbing onto Steve, to catch him around the throat, to push him back and put a stop to this mess, but he couldn't seem to get anywhere. He couldn't put himself on top the way he'd done just earlier that day.

And more than once, Denise noted how Steve seemed to be trying his best to get to her.

"Holy God, Victor, let go of me."

"You can't go to him."

"No, let go of me! He's trying to get to me. He doesn't want another male touching me! You have to stop!"

Victor released her so fast she damn near fell on her ass.

She shook off her shock, noting the way Victor quickly backed away from her, eyes wide, as though only just realizing how very right she was.

Well, it was certainly nice to be listened to. Considering it didn't always happen, and certainly not right away, Denise hoped this would become a habit for the males in her life, but now she had to deal with Jackson.

Except the two wolves still wrestled, spun around and went for each other's throats as though they were in a ball of death.

She didn't want to get in the middle of that any more than Victor wanted her to. Denise liked all her fingers and toes right where they were, thank you very much.

She had to try. Jackson couldn't stop Steve this time, and if Steve hurt him, or worse, he would regret it a lot more than anything he would have felt for the injured and dead wolves littered around the pack.

"Steve? *Steve!*"

If he heard her, he didn't show it. He continued rolling and fighting, biting and snapping at Jackson's face. At one point, he bit the other wolf on the snout.

Denise cried out, flinching as Jackson whined.

He was going to bite right through if he didn't stop. She needed to make him stop!

Denise ran right up behind the two wolves. She balled both of her fists together and, using all the force and weight in her body, brought them down as hard as she could onto Steve's skull.

She was sure it hurt her more than it hurt him, and he definitely felt it by the way he lunged at her, giant maw opening, her entire throat suddenly within those massive jaws.

"*Steve!*"

He stopped. Denise's body felt as though it weighed five hundred pounds. She could hardly move. Her limbs trembled and the only sound she could make out was that of her own breathing.

And his.

His breath, hot, wet, wafted against her skin, her throat. Otherwise, all was quiet.

Denise felt the pricks of his teeth against her skin. They were sharp, anymore pressure and he would puncture her flesh, but he didn't.

She could see right down his throat.

Denise swallowed. Memories of her childhood, of being attacked, of being scarred and hurt as she screamed her pain flitted through her mind.

She was too scared to speak, and even more terrified to stay silent.

"S-Steve?"

Denise tried to work some moisture in her mouth. It was as dry as desert sand in there, but what if the sound of her voice would help him figure out she wasn't the one he needed to worry about?

"Steve, it's me."

She raised her hand. Her fingers wouldn't stop trembling. They were cold, and she pulled back when Steve growled at her.

Denise clenched her hand, her nails biting into her palm, and she touched him anyway. Despite his clear warning for her to not do that exact thing, she did it anyway.

Denise put her cold, numb fingers into his fur. She reached beneath it, finding his skin.

He was warm. There was blood in his fur. She expected that. She hoped not much of it was his own.

"I'm right here."

Jackson's voice called out to her. He must have shifted back into his man shape.

"Denise, don't move."

"No, don't come near us," she called, keeping her voice firm, but otherwise kept her body still. She didn't look away from Steve. He pulled back just enough, so she was no longer staring at his tonsils, but into those golden eyes.

She was a conduit. His conduit. The wolves thought she could bring them strength? Maybe she could.

Denise lifted her other hand, touching his snout, petting him, stroking him, showing him she was here for him.

"You know me. You can smell me. I'm right here. I'm not going anywhere. I promise."

She kept her hands moving, pleased and encouraged at the soft sound of a rumble, what could almost be a purr, rising out of his chest.

Wolves did not make that sound, she knew that much about this, so it meant he was coming forward.

His eyes weren't quite so dilated anymore; she could see more of the man within, trying to come out.

"I'm right here."

Another soft rumbling noise, a low growl, or a whine.

Steve's teeth pulled back from her.

Denise was able to sit up as he stepped off her, shaking his head around, as though coming up from the depths of a dark haze.

"Steve, come here." She reached for him. The wolf creature looked at her, its tail tucked, and it came to her, pressing its nose into her arms.

Denise held him, petting him.

"You did it, baby. They're gone." She sighed, relieved, letting it hit her. "You did it."

Steve's body changed in her arms. She felt the hairs of his fur loosen, some sliding out of his body, many, many more than when he'd been in bed with her. The rest faded into his pores. He shrank down until she was holding a naked man in her arms, her mate.

Only now could she see the scratches and bites across his skin.

He looked like someone had taken a switch to his back, his arms, and the backs of his legs.

She kept stroking his hair, needing to touch him, to pet him, to prove to herself that he was here, he was real, and they were all right.

Steve inhaled a trembling breath. "Did I scare you?"

Denise grinned through the heat in her eyes, holding him tighter.

"You wish."

*D*enise told him about the other wolf, the one that had tried pulling a fast one and slinking towards her when no one had been looking. The description matched one of the wolves he'd seen on the road with Victor, but there was the possibility it was someone else.

There were a limited number of hair colors for wolves, after all, but the scent he got off the area was similar.

He still needed to work on that, his tracking of smells.

The fact that the sight of him fighting with his henchman had been enough to make the fucker back off was a good sign. Steve thought so, at least.

Victor tried to be serious; he stood in Jackson's home with his arms crossed, face as sour as ever, though Steve could still make out the way his mouth quirked in a stupid smile as Jackson spoke.

Victor hadn't even been the one to fight Jackson, but he was as happy and proud as a pig in shit that Steve had finally managed to kick his ass.

Steve was pleased about it as well, but he wanted to be polite to his host, so he was pretending to not remember it.

The wolf had been entirely in control at that point, and the stupid thing had almost ripped out Denise's throat.

Luckily, she had the magic touch, which was why he gripped her hand and refused to let it go.

She didn't make any complaints as she sat on the arm of the couch next to him.

"I would recommend you become part of my pack. Our family would welcome you," Jackson said. "For the most part."

Right. Not everyone would be so eager to have Steve and Denise here when the wolves had attacked twice in one day.

"I gave Zelda a call," Victor said. "She's going to run the idea of having Steve and Denise with her pack. It's a fox pack, but it will still offer some protection for them."

"Will foxes want to breed with me either?"

"They'd better not," Steve growled.

Denise squeezed his hand.

"Hard to say, maybe, but considering Steve's strength and your own capability, I don't think it would be a problem. Foxes tend to not want to bother wolves too much. Even if any of them had that urge, I doubt they'd risk it."

Steve felt the rumble of a growl bubbling in his chest. Again, he relied on Denise squeezing his hand to pull him back into reality.

"I don't like the idea of other people constantly looking at her like that." He glanced to Denise, his mate. "I thought this would go away if I became strong enough?"

"As much as it can," Jackson shrugged. "You certainly sent a message to the wolves who attempted to take her today. They'll remember that."

"Uh huh." Steve was starting to get the impression that Jackson was winging it a lot more than he was letting on.

Steve didn't like that, but there was still that grain of truth to what he said, so it wasn't as though he could make much of an argument.

"We'll take some time to think about it," Denise said before Steve could get too irritated with Jackson. "Your fox pack is close enough that I could keep working at the hospital, right?"

"It is." Victor nodded. "Steve was brought in to your hospital after being changed outside the skulk. It wouldn't be an issue."

Denise nodded, looked to Steve, and he could tell she wanted to get out of here.

He stood. "Right, yeah, we will think about it. Jackson, is there somewhere she and I can talk privately?"

There was a dead wolf being cleaned out of the trailer where he and Denise had been staying. The fact that evidence and bodies were being cleaned away bugged the hell out of Steve on a professional level, but Victor had managed to convince Jackson to have his pack take pictures of everything before they moved the bodies. The live wolves were another problem entirely he didn't want to think about, but considering the workings of this place, and that it would take some convincing before Jackson would involve the human authorities, he was pretty sure he didn't want to set up shop here and call this pack his home with Denise.

Too many things were out of sync.

Jackson stood. "You can talk in here. I will see to the cleanup. I can tell Victor wants a word with me anyway."

Probably about speaking to the police again.

Victor was going to have his hands full with that one.

Still, he nodded. "Thank you."

Jackson waved it off. Victor took one last look at Steve and Denise before the pair of them left.

No sooner had the door shut did Denise speak up.

"We're not staying here."

He looked at her, stunned. "What?"

Denise's neck clenched for a split second before she clarified. "It's not that I'm not grateful for Jackson for everything he's done for me, and for you. He's watched out for me, and he helped you learn some control, but this place is too old school for me. I don't want to live in a pack where intruders can be killed and we don't report it. Jackson can do whatever he wants, it's his property and his pack laws, but just… no. I can't."

Steve sighed. "God, I love you."

The worry in Denise's eyes was telling. "You're not upset?"

"What? No. God no, I'm *glad*. I don't want to stay here for basically that exact same reason. I'm getting itchy with how long it's taking to call the police in the first place."

The only reason he didn't was because he didn't want this entire pack on his ass for the perceived betrayal.

And if they wanted revenge for that, it wouldn't be just him they came after, if they came after him at all.

Denise had enough to deal with. He wouldn't put her through that. Jackson would have to make the call, and with Victor there to persuade him, Steve was confident he would soon make the right one.

"I just want you safe. Zelda's skulk is a nice one, the people there will like you. Especially since you're a nurse. There is a wolf pack nearby, though."

She nodded. "The pack that changed you."

He sighed. "Still not sure who among them did it."

At this point, he was ready to let it go entirely.

He didn't think he would be lucky enough to simply let something like that fade away. Shit always had a nasty habit of rising to the surface, but a skulk of foxes would be the safest bet for someone like Denise.

She would be able to easily show them who was boss when Steve wasn't around to do it for her. Assuming anyone bothered trying anything, which, again, he doubted.

Denise pressed her lips together. She released his hand so she could push her arms around his waist.

"Are we really going to do this? It's moving really fast."

She asked it as though he was the one who might be put off by that, forgetting all about how she'd insisted on distance when they'd first decided to go out.

Steve shook his head. "You could take all the time in the world, or go as fast as you wanted. I can keep up with your pace."

Denise smiled at him, a slow, easy thing that made Steve want to shout to the world how she belonged to him, because he could see it in her eyes that she felt the same.

"Yeah, you're the only one who ever has, now that I think about it."

She said it with such wonder in her voice, it broke his damned heart.

Steve kissed her long and sensually on the mouth, drinking her in before he had to pull back, his ego thrumming as he wanted to make her smile.

"Baby, that's because I'm the perfect man."

She laughed and swatted him, but was no match as he hauled her over his shoulder and went to find a bed.

It really was Jackson's fault for leaving him alone with his mate at such a vulnerable time, after all.

THE END

MANDY ROSKO

CHAPTER 1

*J*onas MacBride walked into the building with a sense of trepidation he wasn't used to. He'd rushed into house fires with more enthusiasm than this. He tried not to show it, but there was something about a woman, this woman, that was wilder, brighter, and deadlier than any fire.

Also, his size seventeen boots didn't feel as though they belonged anywhere near a child's daycare center. He noted the sign on the front door, reading the times for play, snacks, and naps.

And right about now, it was nap time.

He made it to the front desk, where a small sign with the words, "ring for service" sat, but he didn't ring it.

Seriously? Why have that there at all? Someone should be monitoring the front entrance of a place with so many little kids around.

Jonas grit his teeth. He wanted to turn and walk right out of there, maybe come back another time, perhaps when all the little wet and crying bundles were hoisted off onto their parents.

Or somewhere else entirely.

Not that he didn't like kids. He liked them. He liked it when there were school trips to his firehouse and he got to show them all the cool equipment and see something akin to hero worship in their eyes. But even the bored ones were better to deal with than babies.

Jonas didn't know what to do with the particularly small ones.

And Taylor owned this place? He hadn't figured her as one for taking care of other people's kids, but he supposed it was a living.

In a place like Lakeview, there weren't too many options for people looking to drop off their shifter kids for the day. With so many packs and skulks, and even sloths, living around here, this place was probably a good idea. But considering how hard it was for shifters to get daycare for their kids in communities of mostly non-shifters, and the fighting that went on between breeds... it stunned him something like this could function at all.

Jonas checked his watch. About five minutes in. She might have forgotten he was coming. Or maybe she'd hoped he wouldn't come.

He was not touching that damned bell. If he did, and some little kid woke up from the noise, he'd be damned if the crying was blamed on him.

Did Taylor have a boyfriend? His mind wandered back to the thought that drifted into his mind on his way over here... in between the other things he'd been thinking of.

He snapped back to where he was when the door to his left opened wide. Taylor Daniella Norina stepped out, took one look at him, and froze mid-step. Light from the window bathed her hair and made it gleam and shine. Her skin looked smoother than he remembered, and her mouth much pinker.

He could remember the things she'd done with that mouth, and the only reason he didn't play with those thoughts was because of where he stood.

He smiled at her. "I figured you knew it wasn't me."

She blinked, coming out of whatever spell had taken her, checked behind her, and closed the door. Not before Jonas could tilt his head to the side and see for himself all the little bundles sleeping on their mats.

"How many are you handling?"

She shut the door quietly, as though worried she would wake a beast. "Enough." She turned to look at him, crossing her arms. "What are you doing here?"

Jonas blew out a hard breath. "That's cold."

She pressed her lips together, her fingers digging into her arm. "What are you doing here, Jonas?"

It was cold, but there was a hint of something else he couldn't place. Worry? About what?

He smiled. "You think I'm coming to beg for you back?"

She shrugged. "You show up out of the blue, what am I supposed to think?"

"Hardly out of the blue. I wanted to check up on some things. Completely friendly. This isn't to be pathetic and come begging for your attention. You made it clear you didn't want me around." He couldn't keep the edge out of his voice. He knew it was a mistake to remind her of anything regarding their relationship, and how it ended, when he watched her inhale a sharp breath.

"You should go."

"I need to have a word with you."

"I have an appointment right now. When he walks in here, I won't have time for you."

"With Dallas Burns?"

Taylor jerked back, her long, thick lashes fanning as she blinked. "How do you know about that?"

He shrugged, knowing he was about to give her some news she wouldn't like. "He sent me in his place."

"Sent you... you know him?"

"Yeah, he's kind of my boss."

Her shoulders sagged.

He wanted to laugh at her for that. "Don't look too happy for me or anything."

Taylor shook her head. "No, I mean... I'm sorry. That's good. It's what you always wanted. To be a firefighter, right?"

"Yeah. Not doing too badly either."

He was proud to admit it. He'd been in the middle of training when they were dating, but being out here, with not much going on...and debating whether or not he wanted to get married and have kids with the woman he loved...

"So, have you been fighting a lot of fires lately?"

"Eh." He shrugged, making a seesawing motion with his hand. "Not really. My first two times out were to help a woman who called us to tell us her entire house was lit up."

"That's...pretty terrible. Was she all right?"

He snorted a laugh. "Yeah. Her house was fine too. Her dog just got stuck beneath the porch. She wanted our help getting it out." He'd been spitting mad at the time, but looking back, it was kind of funny. "Second time out was a call from an older guy who called us saying he couldn't breathe. Turned out he couldn't breathe through his nose, but air was going through his mouth just fine. When we got there, the only thing we could do was offer to take him to the hospital. He didn't want to go, so we left."

Taylor smiled, and that was good. That was all Jonas wanted at that moment. He didn't even know he wanted it until he saw it, but God, her smile was just as pretty as he remembered.

"Well, at least no one was hurt?"

"Speak for yourself. I caught that cold."

She laughed out loud, quickly stopping herself and looking back at the closed door.

They were both silent for a few seconds, waiting to hear if any of the toddlers inside would wake up. None did from the sounds of it.

They both breathed a relieved sigh.

When Taylor looked back at him, Jonas found himself strangely lost in her eyes. He couldn't help but remember all of the good times. The plans they'd made. How it felt to touch the warmth of her skin.

Even with the way things had ended, it wasn't enough to dampen his memories of her.

And make him yearn for those times to come back.

But they wouldn't. She didn't want a future with a subhuman. She'd made that clear.

He shoved those feelings away, and fast, trying not to look at the cute little rounded ears on either side of her head. The ears that looked like those of a black bear. "So, how have you been?"

Taylor pushed a strand of hair out of her face, one of those ears twitching. He used to play with those ears in bed. They were very ticklish.

"Fine. Everything's been...great."

"Everything?"

She went back to crossing her arms, not a good sign. "Everything with the exception of the fires. I guess that's what you're here for?"

He nodded. "Something like that. My captain will be coming around to ask some questions of the local business owners, too. You might hear from him later."

"But he sent you for this meeting?"

He nodded. "Yeah."

She seemed to think about that. "Is that even allowed?"

"How do you mean?"

"Well, you and I have a history together. Isn't it a conflict of interest or something to have you come and question me about the fires when someone else could do it?"

"Which is why this isn't exactly official." He looked at her, wishing he could make her understand, wishing he knew what was going on inside that head of hers.

"You're not in any trouble, and I'm not a cop. I just wanted to make sure you're all right."

She pressed her lips together. "Does your captain know you know me?"

"He does."

She nodded. "And he still sent you?"

"He hoped that knowing you would allow me to get some honest answers. This is a shifter community, not too many people around here want to speak to anyone human, or subhuman."

She cringed.

Right. She hated that word. Hated the reminder of what he was.

He didn't have the ears and tail. He was born into a shifter community, and yet he couldn't shift. Few shifters wanted something like that for breeding. Not if there was a chance it could taint a bloodline and bring about cubs who couldn't shift either.

Shifters were a little too extreme on making sure their population remained steady, almost to the point of paranoia.

Some called the declining shifter population genocide. But some people also thought the Earth was flat, the sun revolved around the Earth, and lizard people ruled the government. All kinds of nonsense.

He would have never thought Taylor would end up being one of those people.

"We're just trying to make sure no one gets hurt. That's all we're doing. Looking out for you, your alpha, those babies in there." He pointed to the door.

Taylor glanced back at it, as though she could see the little ones inside.

A look came over her face that he couldn't exactly read. He watched her, waiting for her to give her response, hoping desperately that it would be the one he wanted to hear the most.

"Andrew won't like it if I'm talking to you."

So, Andrew was still her alpha. Made sense, the guy was the steady sort — someone with a good head on his shoulders.

The kind of guy Jonas used to look up to.

"Do you have only bears in that room? Or are there some wolves? Foxes? A few coyotes, maybe?"

"I take care of any shifter children who need me to watch them."

He nodded. "Right, so the packs can get along when they need to."

"This isn't about getting along."

"Taylor, someone is setting fires out here. Big ones. We've been lucky so far that the local teams have been able to put them out, but it won't be long before I get called in to help."

Concern seemed to flitter across her eyes. "No, that won't happen. You're in the city."

"You think we won't get called in if another big fire hits? It took three days to put out the last one, and if it hadn't rained, it could have been much worse. That fire was getting a little too close to your terri-tory. We know someone's doing this. If it's a dispute between alphas, please let me know. I don't want you hurt, and I don't want those kids in there hurt. I know you don't either."

Again, she bit her lips together, but this time, Jonas could tell he had her.

"What do you want to know?"

He sighed, relaxing, taking in the small victory. "Do you or your alpha know who's behind this?"

She looked him dead in the eyes. "No, we don't."

His ire rose right up again. He couldn't help it, and Jonas clenched his hands into fists. "You're a terrible liar."

CHAPTER 2

aylor heaved a sigh as she locked the door to her daycare.

It took the McKormicks an hour longer than usual to come and pick up Danny, which meant she was getting out of here at almost six in the afternoon.

She did have an extra fee, charged by the hour whenever someone happened to pull that sort of stunt on her, but at the same time, she knew the situation of the McKormicks, which meant she knew the chances of being paid that extra time were slim.

She might get lucky, however. Sometimes, they paid her. Other times, they seemed to forget they had any outstanding payments due at all, and she didn't want to fight with them over what they did or did not owe to her.

It wasn't worth the extra twenty-five dollars sometimes.

Meg slept nicely against her chest, however. That was a good thing. She'd had a snack with Danny while they waited for his parents, but it wasn't the same things as a proper dinner for a one-and-a-half-year-old.

Thank God Jonas hadn't seen her. If he had...

Taylor shook her head, moving to her car. He wasn't going to know. She worked in a daycare, so of course it wouldn't look odd to him to see Meg.

She was still a baby.

But she looked so much like her father.

Taylor buckled Meg into her car seat in the back of her car. She shut the door, sighing at the rusted flakes that were coming off at the bottom.

Probably not the safest vehicle in the world for her pride and joy, but it got the job done.

She'd tried to open her daycare at home, but coyotes, wolves, foxes, and even other bears weren't willing to step into territory that was not their own, let alone leave their children behind on it.

Neutral territory was the only way to go, it seemed, and even that was something she could barely get away with. Some parents were still not convinced about leaving their young with her, especially with other breeds of shifters around. The ones who did tended to be parents like the McKormicks, people who had little choice if they wanted to work. She kept her prices reasonably low, was able to thanks to the number of children she did have, and the only extra thing she asked was that parents provide their snacks. In return, she would keep a safe environment for their children.

The drive home was uneventful, though Jonas came back to mind when she passed by the result of one of the recent smaller fires. The dead, charcoal remains of the pines looked like skeletal hands. She was used to seeing the trees bare in the winter, but blackened like that, and standing next to half-burned maples and birch trees was... off-putting, to say the least.

When she got home, she didn't park at her trailer. She went straight to Andrew's house, knocking on his door while holding Meg in her arms. She knew he was home. His lights were on, and she could smell him inside.

She banged her fist on the wood again, waiting for him to open up.

Taylor heard a grumbling inside, then a small bang, followed by cursing the likes of which she wasn't sure she wanted her daughter to listen to, even in her sleep.

Finally, the door opened.

Andrew's glare melted away when he realized it was Taylor standing there. "Oh, did you want to come in?"

She smiled at him. "You stub your toe?"

He shook his head, growling as he opened the screen and stepped away from the door. "Eyes going in my old age."

Taylor smiled, stepped inside, but then she couldn't smile anymore. "Jonas came to see me at work today."

"Who?"

It didn't sound like he was pretending, and that annoyed her. "Jonas. You know? Jonas? Meg's father?"

He looked at her suddenly, eyes wide. "No shit?"

She glared at him.

"She's sleeping, give me a break."

"You're lucky you're the man in charge."

He smiled at her. "You're lucky you're a favorite."

She didn't feel like a favorite. She hadn't felt that way in a long time. But she wasn't his daughter, his niece, granddaughter, or related to him by blood in any way, so what right did she have to complain about not being given special treatment?

"Jonas is here, and he wants me to tell him who's starting the fires."

"So? We don't know who's starting them. Well, not for sure anyway."

"I told him that."

He looked at her, a note of panic in his eyes. "You told him?"

She shook her head. "No, not like that. He asked me if I had any ideas, if I knew of any territory disputes or pack fights. I said I didn't know."

Andrew nodded. "Good," He headed for the kitchen. "You want something to drink?"

"Water would be great if you have it."

She felt as rough as though she'd just run a marathon. Thank God tomorrow was Saturday. It meant a little less than half of her usual group. She could take it easy. Sunday was the only day she kept the daycare closed. Some of the parents wanted it open, but not enough to justify the cost of keeping the doors open. Plus, she wanted that time alone with Meg.

But with Jonas around, she felt like hiding away entirely. She didn't want to go in to the daycare tomorrow at all.

Andrew handed her the glass of water just as Taylor sat herself down at his small kitchen table.

"Did Jonas say anything about..." He trailed off, vaguely pointing with one hand to Meg.

Taylor drank her water, shaking her head. "No. I don't think he saw her. If he did, he must have thought she belonged to one of the other parents."

She hadn't let him in to see the kids. He hadn't asked either. Most likely because he wasn't there for that, but she had caught the way he'd tilted his head to the side when she'd shut the door. There was a small chance he'd seen Meg, but again, if he had, there was no way he could know she was hers.

Which brought her to her next problem.

"I need to ask you a favor."

"Shoot."

"I need you, or anyone else who has the time, to watch over Meg tomorrow."

"What? Why?" He looked at Meg, still sleeping against Taylor's chest, as though she was about to grow a second head and attack him.

Taylor glared at him. "I'm pretty sure you can handle anything she throws at you."

"Don't be so sure about that."

"You've got to be kidding me. You're a grizzly bear."

"And you want to put an infant into my claws? Right. Not happening."

"What? Why?"

"I don't mix well with kids, and I've got other priorities to see to. Like meeting up with the other pack leaders. The wolves and foxes and the like. They haven't been happy in a while, and I want to make sure things keep running smoothly."

Because things had been running like shit lately. The foxes and the wolves had been going at it ever since someone outright murdered the pack leader of a wolf pack nearby. There was a conduit around, too, and that threw a wrench into everything for a while.

Taylor had never been around a conduit before. They were supposed to throw off a super potent scent that called for anyone and everyone to mate with them. The children they produced were alphas or something. She couldn't keep all the rumors straight. Especially now, with some idiot starting fires.

Lakeview hadn't precisely been safe as of late. First the murder, then packs fighting over a conduit, and now this?

"Maybe we should let the humans in on this," Taylor thought out loud.

"No."

"They could probably help us put this to bed before anything else happens."

"They'll also splatter this all over their local and national news and peg us for savage monsters. We're dealing with this on our own."

"They already think we're savage monsters. Letting them in to help us might be the best move. Some of the police are shifters anyway. Some of them are subhumans. Like Jonas."

"Subhumans are worse than actual humans." Andrew sat across from her at the table. "They get up their own asses like you wouldn't believe."

She looked at him. "Jonas didn't."

"Oh no? He was the one who didn't want shifter babies."

She cringed, stroking the soft strands of her daughter's hair.

"Thought I wouldn't remember that, did you?"

Taylor grit her teeth. She wouldn't dare glare at her sloth leader, so she glared down at his table, struggling against the burn in her eyes.

"Ah, shit. Look, I'm sorry, but it wasn't me that did this to you."

"I know."

She wanted to be angry with him, but she couldn't be. She tried to tell him that Jonas wasn't that bad. It wasn't his fault, and he wasn't cruel. He hadn't walked out on her for being pregnant. He hadn't known in the first place, and she was too much of a coward to tell him, and couldn't consider terminating the pregnancy, even though she'd been scared of raising Meg on her own.

And thank God she hadn't. Holding her daughter in her arms made everything worth it.

Taylor just never thought she would see Jonas again. When he left, she'd been under the impression he would never come back. The way he spoke to her, even pretending it was all right, that it was for the best that she didn't want to be with him, she could tell he was angry. She knew how much he hated her for breaking his heart.

But it was for the best. Jonas didn't want to be tied down, and didn't want babies, especially if there was the chance they would be shifters.

With Meg's little bear ears and her tiny tail, everyone who saw her would know what she was.

If Jonas saw her now, he'd be pissed.

No, forget that. He'd be outright furious. He'd want to know why she'd kept this from him, and she wouldn't be able to escape the blame for that.

He might even be angry that Meg was a shifter, and Taylor couldn't handle that. The little girl should never feel disdain from her father.

"Maybe you should tell him."

"What?" Taylor's outburst was so strong she jostled Meg, whose face scrunched up. The starting of a cry sounded, and Taylor knew she was in for it now.

"He's the father. He should know."

Taylor wanted to laugh. "You're the one who said I shouldn't tell him."

He nodded. "Right, that was back when you were considering not carrying the child at all. She's here now. You chose to have her, and now her father is running around out there, and he doesn't know."

This time, she did glare at him, and she didn't give a damn that he was in charge of her position on his territory either. "You're supposed to be on my side here."

He nodded again, and she found herself wishing he would stop doing that because she didn't want to deal with him pretending to be so wise right now.

"I'm on your side. I was on your side when you came crying to me because Jonas didn't want a baby. I was here for you when the elders told you to get rid of the child. I was here for you when you decided to keep it, and I was there for you when you wanted to open your daycare."

Taylor winced. "I know. I'm sorry." Without his loan, she wouldn't have been able to afford the lot to open up her daycare. She would have been stuck here, trying to convince people from other packs that it was all right to leave their children with her.

Which they would not have done. She could see that now.

"I can sense a 'but' in there."

She wished he wouldn't sense anything. "I wish you would have been more than a shoulder to cry on when I broke up with Jonas. When I nearly..."

She didn't like talking about it at all, let alone when Meg was in her arms now. She never wanted her daughter to know that doing away with the pregnancy had been something she'd considered.

Andrew's expression was cold. There was little to no sympathy in his eyes for her. She wanted to hide away from that look, but of course, she couldn't. It felt like being stared down at with disappointment by her father.

"I didn't advise you one way or the other because it was your life and you were an adult. You could make your own decisions. If you chose not to have Meg, that was up to you. If you wanted to give her up for adoption because you weren't ready, also up to you. If you wanted to keep her, then that was going to be on no one but you. It was the same with Jonas. That wasn't my decision to make for you. He didn't want babies, you were pregnant, and the elders advised you to get rid of him. If you're regretting that now then that's on no one but you."

"But the elders told me—"

"No." He raised a finger, his tone firm as he stopped her. "No. You don't get to do that. The elders don't tell anyone to do anything. That is not their job. I wasn't there, but I know for a fact that is not what they did. They advised you. If you felt persuaded, then that's on you. You weren't a child. You were old enough to make up your mind. Jonas is back now, so you have to think about the decisions you made."

That was so not fair. She couldn't help it. He was right. She knew that deep down; certainly, no one had forced her to do anything she didn't want to do. But at the same time, it was still lousy advice they'd given her.

There was the chance he wouldn't have walked away from her.

Of course, now that she could see what he'd become, that he'd followed his dream and was now a firefighter...maybe it had been for the best that she didn't tell him.

"Look." Andrew leaned in close. "It's not too late. She's only a year and a half. Still a baby. He didn't miss out on anything."

She had to disagree with him there. Jonas had missed out on a lot. Still, she nodded. "I guess."

"Right. If you want to tell him tomorrow, you can finally know for sure what he thinks. If he's a rat bastard, he'll prove you did the right thing. If he wants to be part of Meg's life, then you still did the right thing. The man's a firefighter now, got a good career. He wouldn't have had that if he'd stayed here."

She frowned at that. "Why do I get the feeling you're trying to make this out to be better than it is?"

Andrew shrugged. "Felt bad for giving you that tough love a minute ago. Either way, nothing too important was lost. And everything aside, having him around might be good for you with everything going on. Even a subhuman can keep other males away."

"Jonas hates being called a subhuman."

Andrew grinned at her, knocking his knuckles on the table. "There, you see? Already you're defending him like you used to."

Taylor looked down at Meg, who more and more appeared as though she was not going to resume her nap, which meant she had to get out of here and fast. "I don't want to spring this on him."

Andrew shrugged, as though to ask *what can I do?*

"You might not have much choice on that one. If he's coming around, he's going to see you with her. He's going to do some quick math in his head and figure things out. If you tell him first, it will be better than if he finds out some other way."

Taylor swallowed just as Meg gave out her first hungry cry. She stood.

"I hate it when you're right."

Andrew stood with her, walking her to the door. "Just make sure to keep him away from our business if you do give him the news. If I can get the other packs and skulks to come together with this, then we might finally get some peace and quiet around here."

Taylor nodded. She didn't like it. She didn't want forgiveness for someone who was out there starting fires in the forest area around Lakeview. Someone like that had to be unhinged. She sure as hell wouldn't want that person as a neighbor.

Which was why she thought it might be for the best if Andrew decided to let Jonas, and his boss, in on what was going on around here.

Taylor went to her trailer, fed Meg before putting her into her playpen, then pulled out the card Jonas had left her with when he left the daycare earlier that morning.

She put the card to her nose, inhaling his scent.

When he'd been in front of her, it had been a struggle not to fall into his arms, to let that intoxicating smell get the better of her. Scent was tied to so many of her memories. She'd heard it was this way even with humans, who did not have such a strong sense of smell.

For Taylor, scent was everything. She'd smelled him the moment she'd opened the door and spotted him, and she'd smelled nothing but him after, even when she'd been trying to work.

The only thing of his she had on her now was his child and this card.

Taylor had always thought Meg smelled a little like him, but now she knew that was nothing in comparison to having Jonas right in front of her.

Taylor pulled the card away from her nose, then smiled at her daughter, who looked at her strangely while chewing on one of her toys.

"Momma's weird, right?"

Meg didn't reply.

Taylor reached for her phone. She played with the idea of a text; she thought of it long and hard, how much easier that would be.

Instead, she dialed his number, her heart hammering, and Meg held her breath until he picked up.

"I was hoping you'd call."

His voice, smooth like butter in her ear, had her ensnared already. "I want to see you."

CHAPTER 3

*J*onas tapped his fingers on the small table of the little cafe. Lakeview managed to pull in a couple of extra small businesses since he'd lived here. It stunned him to see some of these places, but the hiking trails, rivers, and mountain views were bound to pull people in who wanted the outdoor experience without paying higher prices to other nature towns.

The coffee here wasn't as expensive as in the city, and not as expensive as a full-blown tourist town, but it was a higher cost than he remembered it being.

He was on his third cup, and damn near jittering out of his seat when he finally allowed himself to check his phone.

Taylor was fifteen minutes late. But she'd always been late, so he'd expected that. But as each minute ticked by, he was more and more convinced that she wasn't just late, that she wasn't going to show up at all.

She kept her daycare open on Saturdays, and he'd wanted to pick her up after work, but he resisted the urge to offer. He didn't want to come off as being too clingy. Too eager. That could scare off even the strongest of women.

And considering how they'd ended things...

Taylor said she wanted to meet him, that she had something to show him. But for the life of him, he couldn't think of anything other than how much he wanted to taste her mouth again. All sorts of needs and desires he'd thought were long dead were alive and roaring again now that he was back in this place.

The waitress returned to him, asked him if he wanted another refill.

He looked at his phone. Twenty-five minutes late. If she really was late and not just ditching him, then this was pushing it even for her.

"I'll take the check, please."

He'd wait another ten minutes after that, and then it would be time for him to go. He pulled out some cash, enough to cover his four dollar coffee and the tip and placed it on the table before leaning back in his chair, trying not to let the disappointment get the best of him too much.

"Goddamnit."

Jonas was getting ready to leave when he spotted her, her shiny, black head of hair gleaming in the sunlight just through the windows of the cafe as she rushed down the sidewalk and through the glass doors.

Jonas paused. Relief. He shouldn't feel this kind of emotion when it came to her, but he couldn't help himself either.

He was relieved she was here. So much that it stunned him.

Taylor spotted him just as the waitress came to her. Taylor pointed, indicating she was meeting up with him, then made her way to his table, pulling off the summer jacket she wore.

"Sorry I'm late. One of the parents kept telling me another five minutes, and they were going to be here."

He nodded. He didn't point out that she could have texted him that, knowing how she was with answering any of her messages, and he didn't want to start this off on a fight.

"I was starting to worry you weren't just a little late."

She smiled, as though remembering old times. Or was that just what he was thinking?

"Sorry." Taylor still smiled at him, and there was something...almost scared in that. It got his protective instincts up and roaring in an instant.

Later. If this were what he thought it was, he would deal with that later.

"How've you been?"

Taylor cleared her throat. "Good. Yeah, everything's been real good."

He could tell she was lying. Everything wasn't good.

They used to play a game together. Taylor would tell him something blatantly false, and he would determine whether or not she was lying. About ninety percent of the time, he was always on point. There was the odd time when she could get one over him, but it was so rare that he was confident he could read her like a book.

Now was one of those times. Of course, she could just be trying to make friendly conversation. Everyone made nice conversation even when they were having a shit day.

"Are you ready to tell me what's going on with the fires?"

Taylor sucked back a breath, her spine going straight.

He backed off a little. "You don't have to get into specifics, and you don't even have to give me a name if you don't have it, but anything at all; you can be completely anonymous if you're worried about what the pack will think."

"You know it's not as simple as that. Everyone always finds out something about everyone else around here. If I say anything, it will get back to the people responsible."

His captain would love to hear that confirmed. That there actually was someone responsible for this.

"Is it someone, or someones, who are responsible?"

"Jonas, that's not..." She sighed, and he could tell this wasn't something she wanted to get in to.

That was just too damned bad for her. He was going to get it out of her, even if he had to play this long, slow game.

He leaned across the table, which was relatively easy considering how small it was and that his entire upper body took up most of the space.

"I know how things work. I get it, you don't want to rat anyone out, but this is serious—"

"I am being serious." She glanced around, as though making sure no one with prominent ears or tails could hear them.

Jonas had spotted no shifters, but she still acted as though the walls had ears as she leaned in close. "You know how things work around here. It's not a matter of not wanting to tell who's doing what. It's that I can't. You know that."

She tapped her finger hard onto the table, as though to accent her point.

The worst part was that he did know. It was the reason why he'd wanted to leave. Why he'd gotten so sick of the whole shifter community, he'd wanted to go and take Taylor with him.

But she didn't want to go. She wanted to stay, and she didn't want to be with a man who couldn't shift.

Now, he was getting pissed off. He didn't want that. If he didn't pull that shit back, she was going to sense it, and he was going to get nowhere.

Jonas took in a deep breath. "People could get hurt. People's lives could be ruined."

"And my sloth could get hurt. My—" she paused, seemed to collect herself, then continued. "Shifters don't like bringing humans into their business. I tried talking with Andrew, pointing out that you're not entirely..."

He tried not to grit his teeth together too much. "Human?"

Taylor briefly pressed her lips together. "Yeah. It wasn't enough."

He hated that. He fucking hated how it was such a big deal to the shifters when one of their own turned out to be a subhuman. Born to shifters, but couldn't shift. It led to a mother who always looked at him as though he was the reason his father had left and a perfect romance that dissolved when Taylor couldn't see past it either.

He hated shifters sometimes, he really did.

"You work with children. Toddlers and babies. If one of them got hurt, or worse, because of one of these fires, and you didn't tell me anything when you had the chance, would you feel guilty about that? Or would you be all right with yourself?"

Taylor jerked back, wide eyes blinking, as though he'd just physically assaulted her. "What?"

He shrugged, leaning back in his seat. "It's an honest question. I'm trying to find out who is starting these fires. At this point, I don't even care about why. But the sooner you give that information to me, or the police, the better. Don't give me the name if you don't trust me. Make an anonymous call to the police. You're allowed to do that. But if one of those babies is hurt because of this, it will be on you."

Taylor shook her head. "You can't put that on me."

"I can, and I am. It's on everyone here who knows and is too stubborn to let a bunch of filthy humans in on their business."

Taylor narrowed her eyes, getting angry. Good. He wanted her angry. "Jesus, Jonas, I know you left and everything, but you do remember that packs don't take kindly to shifters who bring humans into their affairs, right?"

"So what? I can protect you."

She jerked back again. "What?"

He hadn't meant to say that. Not really, but it was out there now, and he wasn't going to take it back. Jonas leaned forward, his forearms taking up almost all the space on the little round table. "Come with me. I can keep you safe. You don't have to live under people you're afraid of. You don't need a pack."

She stared at him as though he was speaking in tongues. "You're the one who doesn't like shifters."

"I don't like shifters, but I like you."

Always had. In fact, the L word he wanted to use for her was a little stronger than like.

"I am a shifter."

Jonas leaned back in his seat, sighing.

Taylor looked at him, as though waiting for him to say anything else.

When he didn't have anything for her, she shook her head and crossed her arms.

Jonas frowned. "Wait, did you leave me because you thought I wouldn't want you as a shifter?" Taylor said nothing to that. She barely glanced at him, but it was enough for him to get the message straight. "Jesus Christ, are you serious? You broke up with me because you thought I wouldn't want to be with you? Where the hell would you get an idea like that?"

He shouldn't be angry. It was over. It was years ago. Jonas thought he'd buried the need to know, the need for closure. He should be doing so many things other than rehashing an old relationship, but now that it was here within his grasp, he found himself needing to know.

"You were the one who always said you couldn't wait to get out of here."

"Right, because the shifters here kept looking at me like I was dirt. You knew that. I told you literally everything about me." And he did mean everything. She knew what his home life was like. She knew what his mother thought of him.

Hell, the one time he'd brought her over for dinner, he'd heard his mom asking Taylor if she was all right with the idea of dating a subhuman. Someone who might not be able to give her shifter children.

He'd pretended not to hear that shit, but he hadn't brought Taylor over again.

Then, she broke his damn heart.

"You're the one who didn't want to be with a subhuman."

Her eyes popped wide. "I never said that!"

He reached for his nearly empty coffee mug. "Yes, you did."

Taylor shook her head. "I'm telling you, I didn't say that! I wouldn't say that!"

"Why are you arguing with me about this? I know what I heard."

"I wouldn't say that to you!" Taylor snapped her lips shut, once more glancing around the cafe, and this time, there were a couple of patrons who were looking over at them, as though wondering what the matter was.

Taylor lifted her hands, elbows on the table, as though trying to hide her face.

Jonas wasn't ashamed. He didn't care who heard him. He should care, but he didn't.

"I promise, I didn't say that, Jonas. Maybe you thought you heard it because of...how difficult it was."

"Right, it was just in my head that my girlfriend wanted to leave me because I was a subhuman."

She glared back at him. "Uh huh, and was it in my head every time you complained to me about how terrible shifters were? How we were all tribal and ignorant and cruel?"

"I was never talking about you, and you know it." That she could make his pain out to be about her was seriously making him question why he still had a candle lit for her at all. "It wasn't just that, I was...Goddamnit, you have no idea what I was going through, okay?"

She stared at him, and when he noted the misty shine in her eyes, Jonas's gut tightened.

"I didn't just...I loved you, all right? You knew that it was never something fake for me. But you only wanted me around because being with a shifter made you look better to the elders. You can't put all this on me and pretend you weren't using me to up your status because that's exactly what you were doing. I knew it, and I still loved you, you asshole."

She wasn't yelling this time, but Taylor still glanced around to make sure no one was listening to their conversation.

Of course, someone would be. Even humans could pick up on the fact that something was going on.

And Jonas shook his head. "That was never why I was with you."

Taylor looked at him, her eyes doe-like, and she rubbed at them, grabbing her jacket and standing. "Screw you."

"What?"

She marched to the door. Jonas went after her.

No way. No fucking way was he letting her walk out on him again after dropping something like that.

He rushed out onto the sidewalk after her. "Hey, will you stop for two minutes? Where the hell did you get the idea that I was only with you to look good? What about me hating the elders and the shifter hierarchy made you think I only wanted you for...for that?"

He could hardly put it into words. It was so ridiculously stupid he wanted to yank all of his hair out.

"Go away!"

Her car was parked on the side of the road down the street. She pulled out her keys and unlocked her car door before making it to the vehicle. When she did, Jonas had to hurry. He slammed his palm onto the glass, shutting the door when she tried to open it.

Taylor wet her lips, still refusing to look at him, but he could see the tears in her eyes. "Leave me alone, please."

"No way. You seriously think I was using you? What part of I love you, Taylor, made you think that?"

She wiped at her eyes, took in a breath, and he saw something like shame in her expression that made him understand.

"Was it Andrew who told you that? Or your elders?"

"I went to them for advice when you said you wanted to leave. And for...something else."

"Something else? Are you serious right now?"

She glared at him, and he realized he was probably being too rough.

Jonas took his hand off the car door. She didn't open it right away. She just stared at him.

"You didn't like shifters; that's exactly what I was, and you weren't going to stay. It was never about you being a subhuman to me, not ever."

"Well, I never hated you for being a shifter and never used you to look good to any pack."

"So what? We're both wrong?"

He didn't want to be wrong. He wanted to be right. He wanted to be right and make her apologize. But he wasn't going to get that, and part of him knew deep down that, as much as he wanted to be the one who was wholly innocent, he wasn't.

"I think we both misunderstood some things, and I don't think your elders helped anything out by giving bad advice."

Taylor inhaled deeply, letting it out slowly. "I went to see them because I was pregnant, Jonas. And I didn't know what to do."

He blinked. He was waiting for his brain to turn those sounds into something other than what he'd just heard.

Getting kicked in the nuts would have felt better than this.

CHAPTER 4

Taylor didn't like Jonas' reaction. The way he stared at her, as though demanding to know if what she was saying happened to be a nasty joke of some kind...

She wasn't joking, and she could have told him much easier than that.

Now they were standing here between the cafe and the local laundromat, and Taylor started wishing a fire would start up right now so she could have an excuse to be somewhere else.

Of course, she wasn't sure what Jonas' responsibilities would be if a fire occurred in a tiny town where he didn't work or live.

And he was still staring at her.

"You want to say that to me again?"

His voice was low, dangerous. Even a little scared.

"I was pregnant." She opened her mouth to say something else. Anything else, but nothing would come out other than the most useless words there were. "I'm sorry."

Jonas' spine stiffened. He stepped away from her, rubbing his jaw, his other hand on his waist as he paced the alley.

Occasionally, he would look up at her, his expression one she couldn't read. Taylor had never felt more like a jerk in her entire life than she did at that moment.

When Jonas finally spoke up, she was grateful to hear something other than her own terrified inner screams. "You said were. Past tense. Okay, obviously, that was a while ago. Did...did you keep it?"

"I did."

His eyes flared up. "And you never told me about this?"

"It wasn't...it wasn't like that."

"Jesus Christ, Taylor, what was it like? You're telling me I'm a father?" Something seemed to hit him just then. "One of those kids in that room. One of them was mine."

She nodded. "Yeah."

"That's why you started the daycare."

She nodded again. "Yes."

He looked away from her, shaking his head, his mouth and jaw tightening. "You...fucking bitch."

Taylor cringed.

"Why? What did I ever do to you? I wasn't some abusive prick. I wouldn't have pressured you to get rid of it. I wouldn't have walked out on you. You didn't have any reason to hide it from me or send me away."

She didn't have an answer, which meant Jonas came up with his own.

"Right. You didn't want some subhuman raising your kid, is that it?"

"No!"

He didn't believe her. "Then what? Tell me why you did this to me!"

"I didn't do it to you! It wasn't supposed to be like that! I just...I thought you didn't want anything to do with shifters. I thought you wouldn't want to have a baby with me if you knew, and then you wanted to leave, and I didn't..."

He shook his head. "You should have told me. You had no right to keep something like that from me."

"I know. I meant to tell you after I gave birth, but then I was feeding a small baby, recovering. I wanted to tell you when I could walk again, but by then it was months later, and it felt like it was too late."

He frowned. "You couldn't walk after?"

The sudden shift in his tone shocked her, throwing her off.

"It was…it was a birth. I just needed some time."

"Shifters are supposed to heal faster than humans."

"It was a long labor. I'm fine now. I am, so is Meg."

"Meg." He said the word as though it amazed him. "We have a daughter?"

Taylor smiled. "Yeah, we do. She's beautiful. She looks just like you."

"Show me."

Taylor pulled out her phone, scrolled through some photos. She had lots of pictures of her daughter, but at that moment, she wanted to show off only the best ones to Jonas. She wanted to show him exactly how beautiful their daughter was.

She held the phone up. His hand touched hers, steadying the screen, and he groaned.

"She is pretty."

Taylor nodded, her throat closing as Jonas scrolled through the photos. "She is."

He was going through her older catalog now. She could see herself in some of those pictures. She was exhausted, in bed, holding her tiny daughter, breastfeeding hours after Meg finally deemed it right to come into the world.

"How long were you in labor for?"

Taylor didn't want to say, because she knew it would make him mad. "Almost twenty-four hours."

She'd been right. He was mad. She could see it in his eyes.

"I'm fine."

"I'm trained in first aid; I know that's wading into dangerous territory."

"I know, and Andrew promised to bring me to a hospital for a C-section if it lasted any longer."

"You gave birth at home?"

She grit her teeth. "Shifters do it all the time. It's easier for me to smell familiar things. People. No chemicals."

"Taylor, this is why you can't always do what your pack tells you to. You should have been in a hospital. What if you'd died?"

"That wasn't going to happen because Andrew and the elders were there to take care of us. He promised me he would call for an ambulance if it lasted any longer. He said he would drive me to the hospital himself if it looked dangerous."

The problem was how he didn't look as though he believed her.

"I'm telling you the truth!"

"It's not you I don't believe." He shoved her phone back at her. "When can I see her?"

Taylor pressed her lips together. "I brought her to a sitter before coming to see you. You can come with me to pick her up if you like."

"Who's watching her?"

"Andrew is."

Jonas nodded. Taylor expected him to get angry again, to demand to know why she hadn't brought Meg with her, why she'd left their daughter in the care of her alpha, but he didn't say any of those things.

"All right. Let's go."

She blinked. "You want to come?"

He pulled his keys from his jacket pocket. "Of course I do. I want to meet my kid."

Taylor thought he wouldn't want to be anywhere near her sloth, but she supposed she'd underestimated how much this would affect him.

And she felt like a jerk all over again just for that.

"Right, uh, do want to drive with me?"

Jonas shook his head. "No, I've got my own ride. I'll follow you."

The chill in his voice made her shiver.

She'd never heard him speak like this to her before, and it did something to her. Something deep inside.

It made her want to shrivel up and vanish into a dark hole.

Jonas hated her, and she couldn't blame him for it.

"Are we going?"

Taylor nodded, sucking it up.

She had her daughter to think about, and what she was going to do about the other reason why Jonas was here.

"Okay, I'm parked out back, don't drive off without me."

"Do you really think I would?"

He looked at her, but he didn't answer.

She tried not to cringe.

This was going to be tough.

THEY MADE it back to her territory in decent time. Taylor tried not to look at the charred trees on the ride home, and decided not to think of the words Jonas had said to her back at the cafe. She wasn't going to let anything happen to Meg. She could swear on her life to that. Things were going to be all right, and now that she was bringing Jonas to her territory, maybe he could make his case to Andrew.

They parked in front of her trailer. A few of the parents and cubs looked her way when a truck that was newer, nicer, and had no rust on it parked next to her old Nissan. It didn't look as though it fit the scene, but it didn't matter to her right then.

These people might recognize Jonas, or not. It wasn't any of her concern. She was facing a more important event than her neighbors could imagine.

"This is where you live?"

Taylor had to catch herself before she could glare at him. "This is indeed where I live."

Jonas looked it over. She got the feeling he was silently judging her, and she hated that.

This hadn't been his sloth. Jonas had been born to bear shifters, but they weren't part of her territory.

Not officially.

He'd lived nearby, his mother trying to get into the clan, but she had little to offer, no mate, and her son was a subhuman.

At the time, Taylor had wondered why she didn't just take her son to the city to live with the humans, but as she and Jonas became friends, that became more of a fear as she got older. She hadn't wanted her best friend taken to live with the humans. She'd wanted Jonas to live here with her as an official member of their group.

As they got older, and even as they started dating, she'd realized more and more how that was never going to happen. He resented the way others looked at him for not having his ears and tail, for being unable to shift.

Looking at him now, as Jonas glanced around at the other trailers on the territory, at the people and cubs he'd never met before, she wondered if living with the humans had treated him as well as he'd always hoped.

Some humans loved the idea of subhumans. People with higher than average strength, speed, and recovery time. Other humans, from what Taylor read on the Internet, were as nervous around subhumans as they were around the shifters.

It was as though the subhumans couldn't win no matter how hard they tried.

"That house over there, is it new?"

Taylor nodded. "Yeah, construction started shortly after you left. The elders live there."

He smirked. "So, kind of an old age home for the gossip mongers, eh?"

"What?" Taylor had to stuff her hand over her face to cover the snort that threatened to come out. "Don't say that!"

He shrugged, his grin showing off the whites of his teeth. "Why not? Not like it isn't true? Elders are only useful for giving out terrible advice and pretending to be wise and knowledgeable."

"They are. They're older. They have more experience." Even as she said it, Taylor still struggled not to laugh.

And the way Jonas smiled made it so easy for her to relax. He wasn't giving off the angry vibe from earlier. She couldn't feel anger and heat radiating from him anymore, and it felt nice to act like they used to around each other.

"Experience in what, exactly? Nagging at everyone under a hundred they can get their hands on? Honestly, I don't know why packs have them around anymore. If you want family advice, some therapists are specifically trained for that sort of thing. Degrees and everything."

"Someone's going to hear you talking like that, and you're going to get us in trouble."

He shrugged. "Well, you might get in trouble. I won't."

She shoved him on the arm as they headed to Andrew's small house. "You'll still get in trouble."

"If I don't care that I'm in trouble from a bunch of do-gooder elders, and I don't have to live here, does it still count?"

She knocked on Andrew's door. "That sounds like a tree falling in the woods and making a sound type of question."

"It is, but this one has an answer."

She groaned, wishing he didn't look so good with that stupid smile on his face.

Elders weren't as common as they used to be, and if she was honest with herself, Taylor was grateful for that because she didn't much like the elders either.

Still, she wasn't about to openly insult them when anyone could hear. Hell, the elders themselves might have listened to those comments if they only had their windows open to listen.

Her small ears perked as she heard the footsteps inside. Andrew unlocked his door, opened wide, but he didn't smile.

Because he could clearly see Jonas standing next to her.

"So you've made your decision?"

Any mirth she'd felt after Jonas' teasing left her in a mere instant, and just like that, she was back to this dark place again. "Yeah. Was Meg good for you today?"

"Like an angel after I put on some Shimmer and Shine videos. I think I hate that show now."

Taylor smiled. Jonas frowned. "What's Shimmer and Shine?"

Something long, sharp, and merciless pierced her heart at that.

Jonas didn't know the basics of what her little girl liked to watch. He didn't know what these animated characters were, because she'd denied him that.

"I'll show you, come on."

It wasn't lost on her the way Andrew eyeballed Jonas as the other man stepped into his home. She also noticed that Jonas didn't follow her lead and take off his shoes, though she supposed he wasn't in a mood to convey any respect to Andrew as they headed through his house.

Taylor let Jonas take the lead and followed close behind him. She wanted to keep him within her sights. Wanted to see his face when he saw his daughter. She couldn't even explain why that was.

He came to a dead stop in the entryway to the sitting room. Taylor stopped just behind him, and it was easy to see what had caught his attention.

Her throat closed. Meg was in her playpen, sitting up, her favorite teddy bear gripped tightly in her little arms while she looked up at the bright colors playing out on Andrew's forty-inch flat screen.

Taylor heard a soft, choked noise leave Jonas' throat as Meg turned to look at him, and felt everything around her play out in slow motion after that.

CHAPTER 5

His own eyes looked up at him, from the tiny frame of a little girl set up comfortably inside a children's playpen, surrounded by colorful toys. The cogs in his brain struggled to try to process what he was seeing, to make him believe that this tiny person he hadn't known existed a mere hour ago was actually here.

He kept waiting for her to disappear, for him to come to his senses. It couldn't be real. How could it be real when this morning it hadn't been?

He stepped into the sitting room, aware of the light creaking noise coming from the floorboards beneath his weight. As he approached, the little girl did not vanish, as a figment of his imagination would. Instead, she smiled up at him, and his heart did something it had never done before. Something twisty and painful.

Something on the edge of terror and elation.

Because this was his, he'd made this. Helped make it, really. She was a piece of him.

As he got closer, Jonas was able to take in more details. The little yellow dress she wore, the way her dark curls floofed out on top of her head, and the way she still smiled up at him. It all made no sense. She didn't know him. Was it because Taylor was in the room with him? Her mother around would make this stranger in front of her easier to handle, he supposed.

But the girl, Meg, didn't look to Taylor. She kept looking right at him. Chubby fists were squeezing around the leg of her bear. She lifted it again and again, making unintelligible noises.

He reached his hand down into the playpen, and she reached the bear up, seeming to toss it into his hand.

"I think she wants to share it with you."

Jonas blinked and turned his attention to the spot beside him. He'd been so stuck with this tunnel vision of his daughter that he hadn't noticed when Taylor came to stand right beside him.

Taylor smiled at him. She seemed to be suffering from a similar fear of his own, but he realized it wasn't a fear brought on from realizing she was a parent out of the blue. It was a fear of what his reaction would be.

Jonas swallowed, struggling to keep control over the sound of his erratically beating heart. He took the bear, looked at it, then back down at Meg. "Thanks."

She gurgled, then finally seemed to notice her mother before raising her arms.

Taylor complied, reached in, and pulled Meg out, settling the child with an evident familiarity against her chest. As though she'd held her daughter like that a thousand times before.

Right. So dumb. She had held Meg like that a thousand times before. This ease with which she carried her daughter had nothing to do with her experience running a daycare. This was instinct.

"Hello, baby. Were you a good girl today?"

Meg responded in a string of babbles that sounded like "mama," and emphasized her chatter with harmless fists on her mother's chest, as though trying to beat on a drum while grinning up at Taylor.

Jonas couldn't seem to get his breath.

Part of him thought he should have known. He wasn't a shifter, but he was part shifter. His parents were shifters. Subhumans still had some level of strength. Higher than average muscle mass, stronger bone density, and even a slight advantage to healing time when it came to wounds and the common cold.

He should have known. Something instinctual should have alerted him that there was a tiny person out there in the world who had his blood, who looked like him, who had his eyes, who lived and breathed...he should have known.

Part of him wanted to go back to being angry with Taylor. He was still mad at her. He was pissed off beyond all reason, and yet he couldn't bring himself to do that.

The sight in front of him was too...awe inspiring.

Taylor smiled at the little girl in her arms. Did she know she was bouncing on her heels as she held the baby like that? Was that a parent thing? Would he have to carry Meg like that to keep her smiling for him?

He didn't think he would mind it if that's what needed to be done to keep the little girl gurgling and grinning like that.

Then Taylor looked at him, and her smile melted away.

He'd never seen Taylor so vulnerable before. In all the years he'd known her, she'd never looked so stark scared while looking at him.

As though waiting for the axe to come down on her neck.

"Do you want to hold her?"

Jonas tensed. His hands gripped the stuffed bear hard enough to strangle it, had it been real, and he didn't trust himself to put a fragile baby in his arms.

"Uh, maybe later."

Was that disappointment he saw? Was he imagining that, or...

As Taylor's ears twitched, Jonas noticed for the first time that Meg had little bear ears as well, on either side of her head.

She had human ears as well. Many shifters had both. Some did not, but he noted the way her hair was styled to cover her human ears.

Some shifters, the purists, didn't like the human ears. He imagined Taylor didn't want to start any fights with those in her sloth who didn't want to see them on a little shifter girl.

Meg's hair was so curly that he almost hadn't noticed the bear ears anyway.

"She's got the ears. Does she have a tail?"

Taylor smiled, still looking as nervous as could be. "Yeah, she's got a little poof ball." She turned Meg around and revealed the little brown ball of fuzz.

Jonas glanced behind him to Andrew, to make sure he wasn't going insane, and was disappointed to note the alpha was chuckling at him. He responded with a glare.

"Do you want to be in Meg's life?" Taylor's question pulled his attention back to her. The tone of her voice was serious, but the light in her eyes suggested she knew what the answer would be.

"Y-yeah, of course. I want to...if you're serious, and she's mine. Definitely. I want to be in her life."

And he wanted to catch up on every little thing he'd missed.

"Let's start with holding. Do you want to do that?"

He felt himself gripping the bear again.

Taylor had framed that as a question, but he got the feeling there was only one answer she would accept.

He swallowed hard, set the bear aside, and braced himself. "All right. Sure." He held out his arms. Were his fingers shaking? No, that was in his head.

Taylor looked at his hands, then at him. "She's not made of glass, Jonas."

He clenched his jaw. "I know that!"

Taylor shrugged, then handed the child over a little too quickly for his liking.

Then Meg was in his arms. His little girl. A delicate tiny person. Would she be badly hurt if he dropped her? What if he was too rough? She weighed a little more than he thought, but now Jonas was stuck trying not to grip her too tightly, but still keeping a firm enough hold on her that he didn't drop her.

"You can put her against your chest if you want. It's easier than holding her away from your body like that."

Jonas nodded, his arms already trembling a little from the awkward stance he kept. "Right. I knew that." He pulled Meg to his chest, and he had to admit, it was easier on his arms than what he'd been doing before. He felt as though he could relax somewhat while holding her like this.

Meg chewed on her fist. She looked up at Jonas with wide, innocent brown eyes, and that melting feeling came back to him.

He swallowed hard. "How...how old is she?"

Taylor stood close, watching him, but she also seemed to be enjoying the view. Like a prideful mother.

"A year and six months. Almost seven months."

Jonas counted down the months. That meant she would have been born when there was still snow on the ground — made sense, considering the time when he'd left.

It also meant Taylor had been a couple of months into her pregnancy when she'd broken things off with him. How long had she known?

He didn't ask. Not while he held onto his child. He didn't want to spoil the mood. His daughter was a shifter. Would she be able to sense it if he became upset while holding her? Even human babies were strangely capable of detecting the frequency in the air when it came to the moods of their parents.

Parents.

He was going to have to get used to that.

"I think I need to sit."

He went to the nearest love seat, plopping himself down, and only then realized how weak his knees were. It was a small miracle that he hadn't dropped his daughter in that state.

God. Everything is so messed up.

Taylor sat next to him. She pressed her lips together, eyeing both Jonas and her daughter with something akin to shame in her eyes. "I'm sorry I didn't tell you."

Jonas looked at her, then down at his daughter. He didn't answer her. He touched the little bear ears on her head. They were strikingly soft. He'd touched kittens with coarser hair than that.

Taylor took his silence as a negative, pushing forward. "It wasn't that I meant to keep this from you. It was never my...weeks just turned into months, and then the months turned into two years. I started thinking to myself that it was probably for the best that you didn't know, that I didn't tell you. That it was too late, you know?"

Jonas shook his head. "Not really." He glanced at her, noting the flinch.

Maybe Meg really could read the frequency in the air, because immediately after that happened, she reached out to her mother, babbling for "mama," and Jonas had no choice but to hand her over.

Taylor took her daughter, the shamed expression still on her face as she held Meg close, looking very much like a mother bear guarding a treasure.

He needed to extend an olive branch of some kind. "I don't resent you for having her. I'm just pissed off that I didn't know."

Taylor nodded. "Yeah, I know."

Much as he was looking for a fight with her at the cafe earlier, now knew he wasn't going to get anywhere that way. Looking at Taylor holding his child filled him with mixed emotions. The anger at not knowing was there, but also, strangely enough, something not-so-angry too...

Almost protective. That was the word he was looking for.

Which was kind of stupid because it meant he wanted to protect this woman and little girl from, essentially, himself.

Jonas sighed. "You said it was the elders who convinced you to break things off?"

Taylor looked at him, then stroked Meg's hair. "That's not an excuse. I should have known well enough to make up my mind."

"That's not what I asked. You went for their advice, and they told you to ditch me?"

Taylor pressed her lips together. "Not quite like that, but...ugh, it just makes me so mad to think about it! If I hadn't been so stupid about it, Meg would know you. She wouldn't be looking at you right now like you're a stranger!"

He hadn't realized she looked at him like that, but he also had no idea what any baby look might mean.

"I talked with Andrew yesterday, just after you came to visit the daycare," Taylor started. "I wanted to blame the elders, too. They didn't want me to date you. They worried if we...did anything, that any kids we had would be...you know."

"Subhumans?"

She flinched. "I know you don't like that word."

"Still don't, but...there's no point in getting around it. And, ultimately, I know you don't mean it like they do anyway. I know you're not trying to hurt me, so there's no point in getting mad about it."

Taylor still appeared uncomfortable, but she continued. "Well, they worried that Meg wouldn't be able to shift. They advised me to..." She hesitated, then actually pressed her hands over both sets of Meg's ears. With Meg's size, it was doable. "Terminate the pregnancy."

Jonas felt a familiar spark of anger well up within him at the thought that Meg would not exist if the elders had their way...and it would have been for nothing, too. She was clearly a little shifter. She was everything they wanted her to be, but because of what her father was, there was still the stigma.

Jonas never thought he would see shifters stuck with that same stigma as the subhumans. It seemed so utterly unfair. So backward.

"Why didn't you? You got me to leave. One of the three times in our lives together you tricked me into believing something you'd said even though it wasn't true. I would never have known, and no one here would have judged you for it."

Taylor swallowed, inhaling a deep breath through her nose. "I couldn't do it. Every day that went by she became more and more real. I just couldn't go through with it. I thought of calling you, but I worried you wouldn't take my calls, then I was scared you wouldn't want to come anyway. I didn't know whether to hope she would be a human or a shifter. If she were a human, the pack would treat her badly, but if she was a shifter, which she turned out to be..."

"You thought I wouldn't want her?"

Again, he could tell when Taylor bit the inside of her cheek. "Part of me hoped it wouldn't matter, but again, the days just kept going by, and telling you seemed more and more like something that would never happen as each day went by. I'm sorry, I know that doesn't make any sense."

She looked at him, then glanced away again.

That fragile aura around her wasn't right. He couldn't stand that in her. She was so much stronger than that. She deserved so much better. There was no reason for her to be cowed down to him or anyone else.

"I'm still angry, but the more you tell me, the more I'm not angry at you."

"But you're still angry."

"Yeah, at the elders who gave you their horseshi—uh, their garbage advice. At Andrew for not talking you out of it, and everyone else in this sloth for making you think if you had a subhuman baby that you'd both be lesser for it. It's all a bunch of crap. I'm not mad at you. I'm mad at all of them, and the sloth culture that put you in an impossible situation."

He looked at her, right in her eyes, and he felt a little ashamed of himself. "I'm sorry I called you a bitch."

She smiled softly at him. Almost shyly. And she was so damned beautiful he couldn't stand it.

"It's fine. I get it."

"It's not fine."

"Jonas, I promise. I'm fine."

She looked like she meant it, but he didn't want to leave it like this. He didn't want her to think he hated her.

Before he could get another word out, Jonas heard a commotion outside. Nothing sharp or heavy, but he'd worked with the public long enough to recognize the feel in the air when people were gathering around, shouting at each other, with a touch of panic in their tones.

Taylor's ears twitched. Of course, she heard it, too. Her sense of hearing was better than his. "What's going on?"

He shook his head. "Not sure."

Andrew's heavy boots stomped through the house, down the hall, and to the front door. Jonas and Taylor looked at each other before following him.

Jonas rushed a little faster after the alpha. "Andrew, what's going on?"

"Hell if I know," he replied, pushing his way out the door, Jonas on his heels.

The first thing he noted was the way the sloth gathered around. They were in front of Andrew's house, but not facing it. Not facing each other or the ground either, which would have been the case if they were watching a fight.

No. They stared up the mountain, at the forest that covered it, and as his gaze followed their direction, his nose caught the scent in the air of burning.

A heavy rumble in the sky announced a plane flying overhead towards the pillar of smoke snaking towards the sky.

A pillar that wasn't so far away either.

"Oh my God." Jonas glanced to the side at Taylor's whispered fears. She still had Meg in her arms, the little girl completely unaware of what was going on around her.

Yeah. It was way too close.

CHAPTER 6

"Will we have to leave?"

Taylor saw a familiar look in Jonas' eyes when looked at her. Something urgent, even a little dangerous.

He wanted to go up there. He wanted to be with the plane that was currently dropping water and retardant onto the fire below the cloud of smoke. Ever since they were kids, he'd wanted a job where he could protect and care for people. Now that he had it, Taylor found herself fearful.

For him.

"Probably not, but just to be safe, go make sure you have some essentials packed up. It's better to head out and come back in a bit than to try to wait it out and end up trapped."

Taylor nodded. This fire wasn't as close as the last one, but it was still too close for her comfort.

Andrew was trying to get his people moving, to get them to stop watching the fire and go gather their cubs, but it wasn't until Jonas stepped up beside him that Taylor noticed a change. He drew their attention with a clap of his hands and the boom of his voice. "Okay, listen up. My name is Jonas MacBride, some of you may recognize me. I'm a Lieutenant with the Astraea Fire Department just outside of Washington. Andrew called me in to help keep things as calm and collected as possible in the event of a situation such as this. Everyone who has an emergency bag packed with at least three days' worth of food, water, clothes, and other necessities, raise your hand, please."

Taylor had some things packed away in case she needed to make a hasty exit, but it was not three days' worth. It turned out the majority of her sloth was in a similar boat to her because it looked as though less than ten people raised their hands. Even Andrew didn't.

Jonas nodded. "All right. Those of you who do not have these provisions packed away, go to your homes, grab a gym bag, or your backpacks, whatever you have, and get these things together. Anyone who has battery-powered radios, or First Aid kits, add those to your packs as well."

"Are we leaving?" someone asked, echoing the same question Taylor asked a moment before.

Jonas looked back to the plane circling the pillar of smoke before glancing at her. "That is unlikely for now, but Andrew and I want to make sure you are all prepared for the event of an emergency. Keep your radios on; if there is to be an evacuation, they'll broadcast it to us. Go and pack. Listen to your radios. I will come around to make sure each and every one of you has something of use in your bags. If you have any questions, I will answer them."

People started going back to their homes almost immediately after Jonas stopped talking. He only had to reiterate once that he needed them to start moving and to go right away.

He hid it well, but Taylor could see a level of shock on his face. Was he that surprised that the people were listening to him? He hadn't gotten much respect as a subhuman, but he'd stood tall and showed himself to be a man of authority in an emergency. Even shifters would respond to that sort of behavior.

Andrew slapped Jonas on the back, pulling him out of the trance he'd fallen into.

Andrew laughed. "Good work. Didn't expect that out of you."

"Yeah," Jonas said softly.

Had he not expected it either?

Jonas quickly returned to her side. "Do you have anything packed up?"

"I've got a day bag for her and a first aid kit."

She knew that wasn't enough even before he pointed it out.

"All right. We're going to have to work with a little more than that. Come on; I'll help you out." He took her by the arm. His grip was firm but gentle.

She couldn't describe how it felt. He wanted her to move, but she wasn't getting the feeling that he was in a panic. She felt it in his aura. He knew what he was doing. He could help her get what she needed going, and the air about him wasn't spreading any fear. In fact, his touch calmed her. She could see he was very good at his job. The people he helped were better for having him around.

At her house, he opened the door for her, then stepped aside so she could enter with Meg first.

"Where's your First Aid kit?"

"Under the kitchen sink." She pointed to it, though it was readily observable, connected to her living room in the open-concept floorplan.

He moved to the sink, quick, but again, not giving off any vibes that this was a red line kind of emergency.

"Are you sure we won't have to leave?"

He pulled the kit up and onto the counter. It was one of the bigger ones she'd purchased after the last fire made it a little too close to the territory. On sale. She hoped everything inside it would be to Jonas' standards as he opened it and had a look through.

"No way to know for sure, but it's better to be prepared. This is a good one. You got a radio around here?"

She thought about it. "The stereo over there." She pointed to the spot beside her TV. It was an older CD player with a radio attachment. She'd picked it up on sale as well for about twenty dollars. It was not the sort of thing she could take with her. For one thing, it didn't run on batteries, and it needed to be plugged into the wall. Not exactly the sort of thing a person used in an emergency.

Jonas took note of that. "Yeah, you're going to need something a little more portable."

"If we get into a car, would we really need a battery operated radio?" She felt kind of stupid for asking even as she packed extra diapers into Meg's day bag. Meg sat on the floor, a reminder that even though Jonas seemed calm and business-like, there was a real potential danger in the area that could put their lives at stake.

"We won't always be in a vehicle, and when you're on the run, you don't ever want to keep your gas running, or the car battery turned on. You need to save up as much power as possible." He stopped surveying the living room, as though searching for anything else that could be of use to her. "If you don't have one, someone else will, and if your sloth leaves they'll at least travel together. So we won't worry about that one. Is that where you keep all your canned goods?"

She nodded. "I've got another bag in my closet. Can you watch her?"

"Of course."

How was he so calm? She didn't understand it but knew he had to be trained for this sort of situation, and even if there were some part of him that was in the middle of a mild panic attack, he would know how to hide that from her so well that she wouldn't be able to sense it.

Taylor's hands trembled as she yanked out her gym bag from the back of her closet. She turned it upside down, dumping her yoga gear out and going to her dresser. She put spare clothes for herself inside and then filled it with clothes for Meg. Little socks, dresses. She grabbed all the essentials she could get her hands on that were around her dresser. Wipes for Meg, some extra cash she had lying there, that pack of batteries for her flashlight that suddenly seemed much more critical than usual.

She rushed into her bathroom next, grabbing her toothbrush, Meg's baby shampoo. There were so many other things she was pretty sure she was forgetting, and yet she couldn't bring herself to remember everything. She had to remember to keep room for bottled water and soup cans.

"Hey."

Taylor jumped, her heart hurtling into her throat. "Jesus, you scared me."

Jonas stood in the doorway, holding Meg in his arms. He looked so natural like that, even though he'd just found out he was a father.

"You can relax. The radio isn't calling for an evacuation."

She nodded. "I know, you said they said that probably wasn't going to happen, but I just figured...isn't it a bad thing that I wasn't ready anyway? Shouldn't I have been ready?"

He smiled at her, though there was nothing unkind in it. "The vast majority of people are supposed to have emergency supplies put away in their homes and cars, and almost no one has those things prepared. You've got a First Aid kit in your house. That's so much more than what I see so many people doing for their families. Try not to worry about it."

Taylor pressed her lips together. Her eyes stung, and even though he was giving her an out, even though he was being so good about it when he didn't need to be, she felt awful.

She felt like the worst thing in the world she could be — a bad mother.

Jonas stepped into her bathroom. "Hey, you want to tell me what's going on?"

She didn't want to tell him what was going on, because compared to what might be happening outside, the other people who would need him to help with their emergency packs, what she was feeling was nothing.

"Taylor, come on. You can talk to me. Right?"

She inhaled a sharp breath, rubbed at her eyes even though she hadn't spilled any tears.

Yet.

"I just...I hate that this happened. I feel like such a bad mother. I'm not prepared to leave here in a hurry if anything happens. I never told you about Meg, and now these fires are happening, and I'm driving to and from work every day looking at what they did, and I know I should have left. I know all of that, yet I didn't act. Doesn't that make me a bad mother?"

He looked at her, as though searching deep inside her.

"No, it doesn't. You've got your sloth here to worry about. I get it, you've got rules to follow, and you've got your job. You're a working mother, and I don't blame you for any of this."

That was not what she'd expected him to say. "But I thought—"

"No, forget about what you thought, or what I said to you earlier today. I was a prick. Old feelings came up, and instead of facing the hurt I let myself focus on the anger. I didn't mean any of it. I'm not angry anymore; I see that there are so much more important things going on right now than my bruised ego. If you don't want to tell me what you know about the fires, that's fine. I'll figure out something else, but you're stuck with me, at least for now."

She didn't understand. "You're going to stay?"

He shrugged, looking down at Meg who touched his face and seemed to be exploring the stubble on his cheek and jaw. His smile down at their daughter melted Taylor's heart. "I've got a couple of reasons to stick around now, don't I?"

Not one reason. A couple of reasons. Her heart twisted painfully in her chest.

If this meant there was a real chance...that he didn't hate her for what she'd done...

She shouldn't be that lucky. It seemed impossible that she could be so fortunate after everything that happened between them.

Of course, Taylor probably shouldn't get ahead of herself just yet. There was still the issue to deal with of those fire-starting wolves.

CHAPTER 7

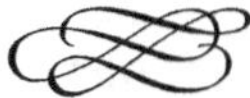

*A*fter Jonas finished with Taylor—and even then, he didn't want to leave her—he had to check on the other bear shifters in the community. He grabbed some emergency checklists from his vehicle and headed to the first house.

He was pleased to find many in the community looking to him for guidance and accepting his help. To be fair, there was a good number of them who didn't know him personally, who hadn't been around when he was shunned for being subhuman. Packs and sloths changed more often than the human population liked to think they did. There was some romantic notion of blood brothers, that those within never left, except for matings or death, but that was not always the case.

Nowadays younger members left the nest, so to speak, all the time. Schooling, dating, and shifters who were choosing to live entirely outside the packs were becoming more common than ever. But there were still those who stayed. Those who wanted the prestige that came with being elders in a pack, who wanted to be like those people who had told Taylor to dump him.

Some of the men and women who Jonas recognized seemed a little put out to ask for his advice, to get him into their homes so he could check their fire alarms and emergency packs. He saw more than one clenched fist and tight jaw when he had to explain what else was needed. One home had way too many electrical hazards for his liking, and it hadn't been fun explaining to a bear shifter that he and his mate were putting their cubs in danger by not taking care of that shit.

He was pretty sure he nearly got punched for that, but even if the advice wasn't the sort anyone wanted to hear, the general population put up with it.

Radios were playing in every home, the local news, so everyone would immediately know if there was a call for an evacuation. Those who had an excess of water bottles shared them with those who did not, and when there weren't enough to go around, he had people cleaning and filling empty soda bottles and filling them with tap water.

Even so, he didn't think the people here would evacuate if there were a call for it on the radio or TV. Even if he recommended it. A few might go, those with young children, but in general, shifters were a stubborn sort. He'd need to get Andrew to listen to him, because then if there was a call to evacuate Andrew could make the others go.

But he had to have Andrew on his side.

If he didn't, Jonas already made the choice that he would do anything and everything in his power to get Taylor and their child to come with him.

He wanted to laugh at that. He'd known he was a father for all of five minutes and already he couldn't stand the thought of leaving Meg here when there were people out there starting these fires.

"You did good, son, really good," Andrew said, clapping him on the back as he was heading back to Taylor's place. It caught Jonas off guard, but he wasn't going to admit to that. He didn't want an alpha knowing he could get the drop on him.

"It might not be enough though. If there's a call to evacuate the area, can I trust that you'll give the order to make them go?"

"What makes you think they wouldn't be going on their own?"

He asked it a little too innocently, and that annoyed Jonas like nothing else.

"Please cut the shit. You and I both know how this works. If there is a call on the radio to evacuate, can I trust that you will command the people here to leave?"

Andrew narrowed his eyes. "I know you like to think we're all a bunch of savage animals, but I can promise you right now, if I think it's too dangerous, I'm sure as hell not going to make anyone stay."

"Uh huh, I'll ask you again because you want to pretend that I'm an idiot and that I'm entirely human." He didn't like that suggestion, and he wanted to make sure Andrew knew it, too. "If there is a call to evacuate, will you give the command for people to leave? I don't care who wants to stay, and I don't care how much you want them to stay; I want to hear you say that you will make them leave."

Andrew looked at him, and something gripped his spine and held on hard. A look like that, from an alpha, it got Jonas somewhere right in his gut. A muffled instinct he suspected had to do with the side of him that belonged to these people. To the shifters in general.

He was being stared at by an alpha. By a male who was stronger than he was and who could snap him in half if he really wanted.

Unlike any other shifters, the beta males and females, or the kids, Jonas was able to fight against the urge to bow his head and submit.

He was only part shifter. Not human enough for the humans to call him a human, and not enough of a shifter to change his form or be taken in by any of the shifters.

It did come with its perks, though, and the ability to resist submitting to the alpha was one of them.

Andrew smirked, crossing his massive arms over his chest, as though trying to remind Jonas of his size. "Sometimes I forget that you were such a stubborn one."

"If you hadn't kicked my mother out of the sloth then it wouldn't have been an issue."

"I never kicked her out. She left after your worthless father did, let's get that straight right now." Andrew's eyes blazed with fire. Jonas nearly fell back a step, and he couldn't believe something so heated, other than an actual fire, was directed at him. "She was ashamed of herself for trusting that no-good loser and didn't want to face anyone in the sloth. Not like she went far anyway; you were always around. You and Taylor got along just fine."

"Until the elders convinced her to dump me when she was pregnant with my kid." He clenched his hands. He wanted to fly at the man, wanted to tear his throat out and demand to know why Andrew had let it all go down like that. As angry as he'd been with Taylor, Jonas could lay a lot of this shit at Andrew's feet, too. "You could have talked her out of it. You could have stopped her, or let me know what was going on."

Andrew sneered at him. "You didn't have a right to know shit. She's the mother. If she didn't want you knowing, you had no business knowing."

"Horseshit."

Andrew shrugged. "Take it up with the courts then. It's not my business anymore anyway." He started to walk off, but Jonas wasn't done. He'd finished checking up on Taylor and Meg and made sure the parents in this damned shithole were packed up if they needed to leave. Now the only task remaining was finding some answers for himself. He saw red and moved in front of Andrew, blocking off the man's path.

He wasn't moving a damned step without them.

"What are you doing?"

"I'm not moving a fucking step until you tell me why you didn't intervene. Jesus Christ, did Taylor tell you what the elders wanted her to do?"

"Yes, she did."

The cold, dead-eyed way Andrew revealed that bit of information had him jerking back. "You...what? You knew?"

"Of course I knew. I'm her alpha. She had her advice, but she wanted a second opinion."

"And she went to you with this?"

"She did."

"And you didn't stop her?"

"It wasn't my decision."

"You're the fucking alpha! Of course it was your decision!"

Sloth members who were outside their house and within earshot stopped what they were doing to look to their alpha, and to the subhuman who was shouting at him. They decided better of it though because they quickly looked away and got right back to packing their items against the checklists Jonas had handed out.

Andrew stared at him with that cold, uncaring look on his face, the one Jonas had gotten used to ever since he was a little kid, sitting on the outskirts of the sloth, wishing he could be within, wondering why his mom wouldn't take him when he was at least half a bear shifter.

He didn't know the rules then. He knew them now, and it pissed him off that those rules had kept him from his child.

Had almost prevented Meg from being here before she was even born.

Andrew took a breath, as though he was the one who was trying to be civil. "It was not my decision what Taylor did with her life or her body. I'm her alpha, not her father or her keeper. If she didn't want to be a mother, if she wanted to get rid of the pregnancy or give Meg up for adoption, I wasn't going to tell her otherwise or judge her for it."

"She was being taken for a ride by the elders. They were giving her shit advice and scaring her into thinking having a subhuman's baby was the worst thing in the world. You could have given her some reassurance."

"I also could have driven her to an abortion clinic and acted as her emotional support there instead of at home. She was an adult and perfectly capable of making her own decisions. I let her do that. I didn't push her one way or the other. I made it clear that this was her life and her decision. That's what an alpha does. I don't control the people here."

Jonas couldn't believe it. "Yes, you do. That's why you didn't ask her to tell me, and that's why you're not going to do shit for these people if there's a call to evacuate."

Andrew chuckled at that, a deceptively friendly noise.

Jonas knew he was trained for heavy lifting, he was fast and stronger than the average human thanks to being a half breed, but even he was shocked by the strength and speed Andrew snapped his hand forward. Just like that, his throat was in a tight iron grip, and Andrew had him yanked forward, their noses practically touching.

"Now you listen to me, and you listen good, you little sack of shit. I did not force her to do anything. Just because I also didn't force her to do what you would have wanted me to do doesn't mean I am in charge of what happened. It's her life. She's in command of it, and you're in command of yours." Andrew shoved Jonas away from him. Jonas stumbled but held his ground. "Maybe if you would have learned not to talk so openly about how terrible all of us are, your girlfriend might not have thought it was a waste to have your kids."

Jonas' throat burned. He clenched his hands, his body tight, ready to go on the attack. Andrew could see it. His smile annoyed Jonas that much more.

"You want to give shifters all kinds of shit for judging you, but you judge us just the same. Do you want to talk about how the elders control the people around here? You want me to control the people here? You just want me to make them do what you want them to do. Where's the difference?"

"You mother—"

"What's going on here?"

Jonas stopped himself before he could say, or do, anything that would have an entire group of bears coming down on him like he owed them money. He turned to see Taylor with Meg in her arms, the baby bag she'd packed over her shoulder.

"Are we leaving?"

Taylor shook her head. "No, not that I'd heard. What were you two doing?" He didn't understand why she would be walking around with the baby bag if she didn't need to have it with her at that moment, but clearly, that wasn't what the issue was here.

"We were just having a friendly chat, nothing to worry about. Right, Jonas?"

Jonas wanted to growl at the man. He still wanted to fight, to get this buildup of rage out of his system, but he didn't. He couldn't. Not with Meg right there.

"Yeah, that's what we were doing." Jonas didn't like Andrew's accusation that Jonas was no better, or that he wanted to control everyone as much as he claimed Andrew already did. Andrew may claim not to control his sloth, but the elders sure as hell had a lot of sway, and he could definitely manipulate the people around him if he wanted to.

Taylor looked at both of them as though she wasn't sure what to believe. Meg's eyes were sliding shut before she forced them back open again and again to stay awake, but it was clear she was going to conk out at any minute.

Jonas looked from them towards the mountain. The smoke was starting to billow a little harder, and more planes were flying in to deal with the fire. If they worked fast enough, had suppressant and a crew already up there to dig a line around the fire, then it could be controlled without spread or other issues.

But it was always better to prepare for the worst. Jonas wanted to be up there with them, and he felt a sense of pride as he watched the hatch of the planes opening up to dump onto the fire. He was hoping the team up there would have their job done quickly, but this wasn't just a campfire put out incorrectly. An accidental fire was one thing, but an intentional one was another. If whoever had done this wanted this to spread...

No. He had to have faith that the team up there would get the job done and stop the fire from heading their way. It was already bad enough that there already was a fire that came a little too close to Lakeview, and this territory in general.

Jonas clenched his teeth. "If either of you has any idea who's causing that," he pointed to the smoke in the distance, "then you both need to tell me what's going on — no more of this bullshit. Taylor, I don't care what Andrew said, what the elders said, or what the people in this sloth want. I care about you, and I care about her." He nodded to Meg. "This could hurt her. This could kill her."

Taylor flinched.

Jonas stepped closer. "The sooner we get a name, the sooner we can put this to bed. My chief is working with the police on this. They can help you even if this is some sort of pack fighting."

"It's not that simple," she said.

"Taylor." There was a warning note in Andrew's voice.

Jonas shook his head, getting in front of Andrew, so Taylor was looking at him instead. "Taylor, if you know anything about what's going on here, and I'm willing to bet you do, then you are actively putting your...our daughter in danger. I know that's not what you want to do here, so please, for the love of God, either tell me or tell the police. If you don't, then I promise that I will do everything in my power to get custody of Meg from you."

Taylor gasped, and the angry, warning growl behind him let Jonas know he'd crossed a line.

Didn't matter. He wasn't going to walk it back. He was serious about this, and he wanted Taylor to know it, too.

"You've got until the end of the day to give me your answer. If you don't give me something to work with, then I'll leave here and get the process started. I can promise you that much."

CHAPTER 8

$\mathcal{J}$onas moved to his truck. He just completely turned his back to her, as if she was ever going to let him get away with that shit.

"You all right?"

Taylor shook her head. "Andrew, hold Meg."

"Come on, now. You don't want to do anything—"

"I said, you need to hold her." She kept her voice calm, didn't raise it, but Meg groaned a little all the same.

It was a good thing she was tired and getting ready for her nap; otherwise, Taylor didn't want to think of how her daughter would react to the vibes Taylor was giving off right now.

She wanted to murder Jonas.

Andrew took Meg and the baby bag. He was the alpha, in command of this sloth of bears and the safety of the people here. She'd never seen that sort of worry in his eyes, even when she'd had her crisis over whether or not to tell Jonas she was pregnant.

She couldn't focus on that train of thought for long. She was already marching after Jonas, catching him just as he got the door to his truck open and reached inside.

Taylor's claws were out as she grabbed him by the back of his neck, yanking him out, slamming him against the side of the truck.

His eyes were wide. She swung at him. He dodged out of the way, which infuriated her all the more.

"You bastard! You fucking bastard!"

She swung again, and again, he ducked out of the way.

It wasn't fair. Andrew had been able to take Jonas by the throat so easily, but he was an alpha, a grizzly bear. She was neither an alpha nor a grizzly. She was a black bear. Even if Jonas was a subhuman, the side of him that was a grizzly gave him enough speed to avoid her punches and her claws.

Which was beyond enraging when she wanted nothing more than to slice his face off.

"You're not taking her from me! She's mine! You understand me?"

She punched again but was clumsier about it this time. And angrier. Taylor threw her back into it, and when Jonas ducked his face out of the way, she punched right through the glass of his back window.

And she yowled with pain.

Blinding. White-hot. She sobbed at the blood even as she pulled her hand back to have a look at the damage.

One of her knuckles looked...a little messed up. Oh God. She'd done that, and every second that went by made it all worse and worse.

"Taylor," Jonas reached for her. She yanked herself back.

She didn't want the sympathy in his eyes or the gentle tone of his voice. Not after he threatened to take Meg from her.

"Don't touch me."

Jonas pulled his hands back. He looked uncomfortable, and it wasn't fair for him to do that. He had no right to look sad or unnerved about anything right now.

"Can we talk inside?"

"No. Go away. Get out of here."

He looked at her pointedly. "You remember what I said I would do if I left here without the answers I wanted, right?"

Taylor clenched her teeth.

She looked back at Andrew. He still held Meg protectively. A few people watched what had taken place with fixed attention, but there were others who were trying not to pay attention. They weren't doing such a great job of minding their own damned business, though. She could tell what they were doing. They were doing such a terrible job of pretending not to watch what was going on that it was insane.

"Taylor, come on. We can talk inside. Please."

She hated him so much right now. "What was all that back at my place? You said you were sorry. You made it out as if you forgave me for..."

Even angry with him, she didn't want to say it, and she flinched at the reminder that she wasn't entirely innocent in this either.

"I do forgive you. I..." He sighed. "Taylor, please, I know you love that little girl. I want to get to know her." He leaned in close, lowering his voice. "If anything happens to her because you didn't let me help, that option won't be on the table anymore. I can protect you. I can protect Meg. I can."

The worst part was she knew he was right. Even if there was a backlash to bringing the humans into this, it didn't change the fact that there was a fire being put out within sight of her home.

She didn't want to worry about Meg's safety. From the wolves, or the fire. The thing was, she could hide from wolves, but even the smallest of children were taught there was no hiding from a fire.

"Andrew?"

"Yeah?"

She looked back at her alpha. He had to know what she was thinking, what she was planning on doing. It had to be written all over her face.

And she'd left her daughter in his arms.

"I'm going to put Meg to bed now."

He looked at her, the wheels turning in his head.

Taylor found herself holding her breath without meaning to.

When he stepped forward, putting Meg into her arms, her little body slumping against her chest in sleep, Taylor felt stupid for thinking the worst of her alpha.

Andrew handed Meg's bag to Jonas. "You do what you've got to do. I'll work something out later."

He meant with the sloth — the people who weren't going to be happy with her decision.

And there would be enough of them to make things difficult for her later on.

Taylor wanted to cry. She really did.

She lowered her head instead, making sure no one could see her eyes. At least not yet.

"Jonas, let's talk inside."

Jonas glanced up towards the fire, the planes still rumbling as they went to and from the fire itself. She didn't see flames, only smoke, and steam. She hoped that meant it was being controlled before it could grow like the last fire.

Still, she wasn't a bad mom. Her little girl against her chest hit it home for her. How much she wanted to give Meg everything. How she couldn't handle the idea of even sort of putting her into harm's way.

That wasn't what she wanted to do, and that wasn't who she was. Not in the least.

She went inside. Jonas followed her, and so did the eyes of everyone in her sloth, all of them knowing she was about to get the humans involved.

~

"You should let me see your hand."

"It's fine."

"You're bleeding." Jonas didn't like that. He didn't have the same heightened senses. Not all of them, anyway, but the blood looked a little redder than he would have liked.

The fact that she got that when her eyes had been that same shade of red, when her face had been sprouting fur and fangs popping out from her teeth, because of him, made it even worse.

"Let me have a look. If it's broken, you don't want it healing wrong."

Taylor dragged a baby play mat over to them and put Meg down onto it. The little girl settled onto her back, eyes closed, completely asleep.

Jonas stepped up beside Taylor and reached for her hand, taking it in his. She pressed her lips together, but she allowed him to touch her anyway.

"This will hurt, but just bear with me."

Her mouth quirked.

He didn't comment on the accidental pun. He focused on prodding her knuckle, making sure it didn't feel out of place.

She hissed; a little blood got on his fingers. "Not broken. Come on; we can wash it in the sink."

"It hurts a lot."

"We'll make sure there's no glass in there. Come on."

She didn't fight him. He was grateful for that.

With her hand beneath the tap, he couldn't help but smile. "I can't believe you smashed my window."

Taylor ducked her head. "I'm sorry about that. I'll pay for it."

He wasn't sure if she would have the money for that, but he didn't mention it.

Luckily, there was no glass. All she needed was a towel over the small wound, and she was good to go.

"I'm sorry for saying I'd take her, but you know I'd only do it to keep her safe, right?"

Taylor nodded.

"And that's not a dig against you as a mother either. If I were doing anything that could hurt that little girl, I'd expect you to do the same with me or anyone else she was in contact with."

"I know."

She just didn't sound happy about it.

He didn't blame her for it.

"I mean it. If the sloth can't take having humans involved, I'll take you with me. We'll leave here together—you, me, and Meg. I've got a nice place. It's comfortable there."

"But it's not territory."

This was one of the few things he never understood about full-blooded shifters. The need some have to be surrounded by their own when others could handle living outside of their packs just fine. What were they doing differently?

"You're right, though." Taylor looked up at Jonas. "I'm…I'm going to get her hurt if I can't separate myself from all of this. She's a baby. She can't protect herself, and the last fire was so close."

"We won't let anything happen to her."

"But what if something happens to the people here because I said something? There are other kids here, Jonas. Other babies. If I get them hurt or killed because I wanted to protect Meg, doesn't that make me a bad mother? Even if they're not my kids?"

"I don't think so. You would be protecting your own. That's a natural thing to do. But you care. You're not heartless. You just have to make a decision. Your child, or someone else's. If the parents here can't be bothered to take their kids away from the dangers coming, that is not on you."

She flinched. Jonas clenched her shoulders, leaning down just enough to look her in the eye, to put them on the same level.

"But I'll do everything I can to make sure that doesn't happen either. We'll do everything possible to keep the people here safe, even if someone tries to retaliate. Okay?"

Taylor exhaled a long breath, relief clouding her eyes.

"There was fighting, between a pack of wolves, not too long ago."

Finally. This was it. This was the information his chief needed, that the police needed.

"Tell me whatever you can. When you're done, we can take Meg and get out of here, just you and me. We'll make sure all of this comes to a stop."

Taylor shook her head, bringing back that sense of unease within him. "It's not that easy. Things have been different since you left."

"I know. I know there was a murder investigation not too long ago."

That would have an impact on the local communities. Even groups of shifters could become victim to the fears that came with hearing their towns and communities weren't so safe anymore.

Taylor nodded. "Did you hear what else happened?"

That didn't sound good. "I heard there were arrests made. And that someone was illegally turned into a shifter." Some states required a license to turn a human into a shifter. Others introduced prison time if it was done against the will of the former human involved. But he didn't get the feeling that was the bit Taylor was worried about.

"Later on, the man who was changed, I guess he found a conduit. Do you know what that is?"

Jonas bit back on a growl. "Yeah, I know what a conduit is."

He'd never seen one in person. He wasn't even sure what the exact rules were when it came to them.

Supposedly, they were in a category similar to subhumans. Only they weren't born conduits. They were humans who had been attacked by a wolf, or bear, or any shifter. But unlike most, who would become shifters after an attack, their transformation didn't take.

Not only that it didn't take, but it changed their scent, making them more desirable to other shifters.

Jonas heard a rumor that anyone who mated with a conduit received a massive boost in strength. Their hearing and sight improved dramatically. Others said the children born from a union were the ones who benefited with power.

The story was rarely straight when it came to them. They weren't exactly as common as subhumans.

"So what happened with the conduit?"

"I guess the wolves that changed the male she was with didn't like that she was with anyone. Look, I don't know the exact details, but a group of wolves came here not so long ago. It was just meant to be a visit with Andrew, to talk about resources, what we could buy and sell. No one had a good feeling about them."

Calm. Jonas felt oddly calm hearing this. Not because it wasn't important, but because he was starting to get to a place where he could do something about it all. There was something about this that made a monster within his chest rumble and gave him a deep, simmering desire to find whoever these bastards were and bring them to justice. Just the idea that these men had been anywhere near Taylor...near his daughter... it was enough to make something dangerous ignite within him.

"Did you see what they looked like?"

"From a distance. I got their scent though."

He cringed. "That's not so much help for me, but maybe we could do something with it. There's always a couple of cops who are shifters." He glanced to Meg, making sure she was still sleeping before giving his full attention back to Taylor. "What did they want? Are you sure they're the ones who started the fire?"

Taylor nodded, pressing her lips together as she glanced down. "Yeah. I didn't know at first, but...Andrew told me. After."

He fucking knew it.

"Don't be mad."

"How can I not be angry?"

The only reason why he wasn't stomping around, cursing up a storm, or grabbing Taylor and kissing her hard on the mouth, was because his child was sleeping mere feet away from him.

"What did they say? Did Andrew tell you what they wanted?"

She nodded. "Yeah. They want our help finding their conduit, and taking over a skulk of foxes. Andrew declined, then the fires started. They're a warning, Jonas. The burned trees on the way up here? Those happened when someone did try to leave. The wolves brought them back, Jonas. We're trapped here, and we can't get the humans involved."

CHAPTER 9

Jonas had a walk around the area where the first fires occurred. He checked the underbrush that remained—dry and singed in some places, dead trees that should have been cut down a long time ago to prevent this sort of thing.

Had it not been for the rain, this could have been much worse.

"What are you looking for?"

Jonas glanced behind him. Taylor stood right there, jeans, a t-shirt, and hiking boots—never looked better. Her hair was tied back, the blue streaks glinting in the sunlight. "What are you doing here? Where's Meg?"

Taylor stepped over some dried roots and branches, her boots crunching on the ones she couldn't avoid. "She's safe. With Andrew. I don't think you're going to find out how the fires started."

"I'm not looking for that. I don't think it matters much right now anyway."

"Really?" Taylor came up to stand beside him. She knelt, surveying the scene with intense eyes. As if she thought there could be some clue hidden within the damage, even though she told him he'd find nothing.

"I'm checking to see how bad it might be if another fire came through here."

"It sounds like they've got the one up the hill mostly contained."

Which was no reason to relax. He wished she would stay with Meg, but Jonas knew better than to tell her that. Taylor had a stubborn streak. She could dig her heels in when she wanted to, and he wasn't about to risk that when the situation was as…delicate as it was.

"So, how bad could another fire get? I mean, it doesn't look like it's going to rain for a little while again, but the local fire department seems to be on it."

Jonas nodded. "Yeah, I might need to make a trip up there later."

From his peripheral vision, Jonas saw the way she jerked back.

"Up there? You mean, up there, up there? For real?"

As she said it, the rumble of a helicopter engine burred overhead, carrying another load of suppressant with it towards the billowing smoke.

Jonas stood, smacking his hands together to dislodge the dirt and soot. "Yeah."

She stood with him. "Wait, are you serious? Isn't that dangerous?"

He headed for his truck. "More fire departments rely on volunteers. If they need the extra manpower around here because of your wolf friends, then I want to know about it."

Taylor chased after him. "My wolf friends? Okay, going to ignore that for now, but I will talk with you about that later."

Fuck. He shouldn't have opened his mouth.

"But aren't you trained to put out house fires? Apartments that catch, car crashes, cats in trees, that sort of thing? Isn't this entirely different?"

"I could still be of use."

He got into the driver's side of his truck, shut the door, started the ignition, and slid the window down. He looked at Taylor. She looked worried. It was in her eyes. In the way her feet seemed to fidget and the way she didn't seem to know what to do with her hands.

"I'm not leaving you, if that's what you're thinking."

"That is absolutely not what I'm thinking."

Was that the truth? He couldn't tell. She'd gotten good at hiding things from him.

"I'm not leaving Meg either, if that's what you're worried about."

She shook her head. "No, I know you wouldn't do that. Now that you know." She smiled at him, a weak, watery smile.

He could barely return it. He didn't want to deal with the heavy load of what it meant that he'd missed out on the first year and a half of his daughter's life any more than Taylor did.

"I'm so sorry about that. I really thought it was for the best at the time and—"

"We're good. Trust me, it's fine."

Taylor snapped her lips shut. She seemed to shrink in a little.

Jonas sighed. "Did you come here in your bear form?"

Taylor nodded. "I heard you'd left. Not that I was trying to catch you or anything. I just wanted to see if you needed anything. Help, I mean, with…" She gestured around her. "Everything that's been going on. You know?"

Jonas nodded, watching her. Had she been worried he wasn't coming back? He didn't want to admit that made him feel pretty good.

"Yeah, I know. You want to come with me?"

Her expression changed. Seemed to get more…open. "Yeah? Really? Wait, won't I get in the way?"

"Not if you're willing to tell the chief of police what you just told me."

She closed up again, backing up a step. "Jonas…I don't think I can do that."

"I've got to tell the people in charge everything you told me. Having your first-hand account will make things easier." He waited a beat. "Taylor, I won't let anything happen to Meg. Not a thing."

He surprised himself with the intensity of how he said it. Jonas had known he was a father for all of five minutes, and yet everything inside of him screamed at him that he needed to protect that little girl from now until the day he died. He wasn't ready yet to examine the strength of his need to protect and care for Taylor too, but it was up there.

And he wasn't about to let some fire-happy wolf shifters playing with lighters hurt his family.

He reached over, pushing open the passenger side door. "Taylor, come on. We have to end this. This can't go on."

Another burr of a helicopter sounded above them. Taylor looked towards it, then him before walking around the front of the truck and climbing into the passenger seat.

"If I'm going to do this, then you should hurry and get me to whoever it is you want me to talk to. Before I think better of it and change my mind."

Jonas grinned and put the truck in gear. "Yes, ma'am."

Jonas' tires got off the gravel and onto the road when Taylor spoke again, her voice much quieter than what he was used to.

"After, if you wanted, I think we should talk a little. About everything that happened."

Jonas clenched his jaw. He couldn't exactly help it. "Yeah. I think you're right."

Taylor sighed, putting her elbow up onto the window of the truck, resting her chin on her fist. "Then, after that, we should find somewhere private to have sex."

He thought about that for about a half second, his pulse immediately picking up as the hairs on his arms and back of his neck stood on end.

"Yeah, I think that sounds like a plan."

CHAPTER 10

aylor stayed quiet in the truck, observing that Jonas seemed to know his way around. Her area of the world was small, and he'd had time to get aquatinted with everything before he'd met up with her at the daycare, so she supposed it made sense.

She couldn't stop her heart from pounding, and Taylor had to repeatedly remind herself that Meg was safe and sound with Andrew. He wouldn't let anything happen to her while she was away. That didn't keep her anxiety at bay though, and a part of her wished she'd taken her daughter with her. Andrew might be strong, but a protective mama bear would stop at nothing to protect their cub.

"Are we going to the police right now?"

"Yes and no. We're heading to your fire station. My chief will be there. I sent him a text saying I was coming. He doesn't know you're with me yet."

She nodded. It made sense. She hadn't seen him pull out his phone since she showed up. "The old fire station was upgraded, you know, it's not where you think it is."

"I know. I had a look around before I came to find you."

Taylor nodded. "Right."

This was a little too awkward. She'd thought she would be light-

497

ening the mood when she told Jonas she wanted to have sex with him, but that lasted for all of two minutes before they went back to this tricky spot they were in now.

"So, how dangerous are these wolves exactly? Do you have names?"

Taylor looked at Jonas, then away as she wet her lips. "I have a few names."

Jonas briefly glanced away from the road, looking right at her before he started paying attention again. "You know I won't let anything happen to Meg, right?"

Taylor nodded. "I know you'll do everything possible to keep something from happening to her, but—"

"But nothing. I won't let anything happen to her."

"You're not in control of everything, Jonas. Things happen that are outside of our limits all the time. This might be one of those times, and I'm just thinking about…the future."

A future where she might have to get her daughter and flee this damned town and everyone in it pronto.

Jonas nodded. "Right. I got it."

"I'm not saying you wouldn't be part of that future if you wanted to be around."

"Okay, since we're on that subject, yes. I do want to be around, and don't want to miss out on any more time with my daughter."

Taylor cringed.

What little they'd already spoken about Meg, and their separation, wouldn't be enough. Taylor knew she had so much more to answer for. She'd been so sure Jonas wouldn't want anything to do with a shifter child that she'd just watched him walk away. So sure he wanted his own life away from her and the sloth. Now she was here, sitting next to the man she'd loved, coming to grips with the fact that she did still love him.

She still wanted him. Raising her daughter and being part of the sloth, working for her living, and then having to deal with the wolves, all of it had given her enough to think about that she managed to pack away her feelings for Jonas. She'd had woken up, cared for her daughter, went to work, then sleep, then started all over again for so many days that she'd managed to convince herself she was satisfied with her life, and over Jonas MacBride.

No. Having him here, and telling him about Meg, and taking in his scent while he sat next to her, brought everything back to the forefront of her mind. She couldn't ignore this.

Which meant making things right, starting with the wolves causing the fires, and then dealing with Jonas.

Though Lakeview was a small town, Taylor almost never stopped by the fire station. She used to drive by the old one when she foolishly hoped that Jonas would turn up working there someday. She'd indulge herself in these moments, thinking about him, and then parking and looking at their old text conversations. She wasn't about to tell him this though; she didn't want to sound weird or anything.

The new fire station was quiet. It made sense, as most, if not all of the people working there would be focused on the fire already burning, or cutting down the underbrush nearby to keep it from spreading.

"Is there anyone even here?" she asked, even though the garage doors were wide open.

"There are some here. My chief would have met up with them to see if there was anything our department could do to help. Come on."

Taylor pressed her lips together and got out of the truck. She scratched at her arm, looking down, and seeing some of her fur poking through her pores. To calm herself and regain control she inhaled a deep breath, exhaled, and then breathed deeply again. This wasn't going to be so bad. It was ultimately for Meg's safety and the safety of the people who lived in and around Lakeview.

She could do this.

She hoped.

Taylor had never seen the inside of this fire station before. It didn't look like anything she'd seen on TV. It was just a long brick building, new, but still with the expected tells of a fire station.

Jonas walked right into the garage, and she followed. The building was new, but the fire truck looked as though it needed replacing. It was probably as old as it was allowed to be before a replacement was mandatory. She could make out many smells from the people who had been here. While some shifters could be overwhelmed by the scents of too many people all at once, Taylor handled it better than others. She'd developed a tolerance for it after working with so many children at her daycare, but this was different.

She had a no-scent policy at the daycare, which not only helped her but also helped the sensitive noses of her little charges. There was no such policy at the police station though. She could smell the pheromones of many men, a few women, shifter and human alike, intermingled with each other as well as with different kinds of aftershave and perfumed deodorants. On top of that, the garage held the strong scent of motor oil, grease, and tire rubber from trucks.

Even so, another scent came at her through the thick soup of smells. Something metallic and familiar.

What is that?

Jonas stopped short right in the doorway leading to another part of the station. "Fuck me."

He bolted forward.

"What? Hey! Jonas where are you—" Taylor stopped short when she came to the doorway.

It looked like the lounge. There was a television going. The fire was on the news with video of the helicopters flying overhead, dumping water and suppressant onto the flames while other men and women dug long ditches around the fire, preventing the spread.

That wasn't what she was paying attention to. On the floor, she realized what the smell was that she'd come across.

Blood. A decent amount of it, too. Jonas flew into action, knowing instantly what he needed to do. Taylor stayed back, knowing better than to contaminate a crime scene.

"Fuck, Dallas? Chief, come on."

Taylor blinked. Somewhere in the distance, Jonas yelled for her, but she couldn't look away. She didn't see the people on the floor anymore. Not as they were. She saw Andrew. She saw the elders of her sloth, her customers, her child. Meg was sitting right there, her little white diaper and chubby legs stained with blood. Her little fist, covered in blood, was to her mouth as she sucked on her hand, all the while looking up at Taylor with those wide, innocent eyes...

Jonas pulled out his phone and dialed while Taylor stood where she was, utterly useless as the sound of everything around her slipped farther and farther away.

"Taylor!"

Taylor snapped out of it, but only when Jonas gripped her by the shoulders and started to push her out of the room.

"You with me?"

She blinked up at him, then shook her head. "Yeah. Yeah, I'm sorry. I…what can I do?"

Jonas glanced back into the room, then at her. "I'd ask you to help me administer first aid, but if you're going to go into shock, it's not going to help anyone. Why don't you step out front and wait out front for an ambulance to get here? You can bring them to me."

She didn't think the paramedics would have trouble finding this place. They weren't out in the woods, so it wouldn't take long, and they would be familiar with the area. He was trying to get rid of her, and after her near panic attack, she couldn't blame him.

"All right." She glanced over his shoulder into the room, tried to, but Jonas took her chin, his grip gentle yet firm as he forced her attention back onto him. "You don't have to look at that."

"Are they dead?"

"I might be able to help some, but the quicker the ambulance gets here, the better. Go on now."

Any other time, Taylor wouldn't have left. She liked to think of herself as being the strong, independent type. She was trained in first aid. She knew how to dislodge food stuck in a toddler's throat, and she had tried herself to be a little obsessive compulsive when it came to keeping anything with peanuts out of her building.

But this was different, and there was nothing that could be solved by sticking around if she was going to freeze up and take Jonas' attention away from the victims. She glanced back towards the lounge. She could hear Jonas inside, speaking to someone. That meant one of them had to be alive. She hoped at least one of them was still alive.

If Taylor couldn't do something for the people in there, then she could do something for them out here. She put her nose to the air and started to get a better whiff, searching through the oil, the chemicals, and the aftershaves.

If this had anything to do with Maxwell's pack, she was going to figure out what it was. She already had a good idea, but if any of the scents here matched the scents she already knew...

"What are you doing?"

Taylor snapped her attention up at the figure entering the garage. A woman with the pointed fox ears and tail, looking right at her.

CHAPTER 11

She was beautiful. Even with the turtleneck on, the tight jeans and hiking boots, it was clear this was a knockout. Taylor wasn't sure why this was the first thing she noticed about the other woman, but it annoyed her, and the fact that this chick was here when there were people hurt in the back...

Wait.

The fox girl took a step forward.

Taylor straightened her back and made sure this chick could see her claws, too.

"Don't take another step."

Fox girl stopped, her eyes flying wide, and then she stepped back. "Okay, uh, I'm not here to start trouble."

Yeah, right.

"What are you doing here? Did you have anything to do with what happened to these men?"

The fox frowned. "Happened to who?" Her eyes flew wide. "Where is Victor?"

Taylor shook her head, not willing to let this woman trick her. "Don't know who that is, but you're not going to take another step until the police get here."

Even now she could hear sirens coming, which eased some of her tension. The fox girl took the slight distraction and marched forward.

Taylor stepped towards her. "You're not going back there."

Jonas was trying to save lives. This bitch might've had something to do with the bloodshed, and she wasn't about to let her get anywhere near her man.

The fox was shorter than Taylor, and the turtleneck didn't give off the impression of bravery, so Taylor was stunned when the woman's eyes started to glow, and her long fox ears twitched. "You're going to want to get the fuck out of my way."

Taylor pressed her lips together. "You're talking to a bear here. You don't want to be throwing your weight around, fox."

There weren't many times when it was better to be a bear, but Taylor loved it right then. Wolves, foxes, and even the cats, always had a sleeker, sexier nature about them. They had ears and tails that were sharper and longer. Taylor always envied the cute fluff to a fox tail over her own little bear ball. But, this time around, the added strength that came with being a bear was something she would embrace to the fullest for the safety of Jonas and the victims he was helping.

The fox girl pressed her lips together, her eyes darting towards the door.

"Don't even think about it."

The fox woman vibrated a rage that Taylor had rarely seen in anyone else. Her hands clenched to fists, her tail whipping around behind her.

"My mate might be back there. I want to make sure he's all right. I can smell blood. Please let me through."

There was never a more unhappy 'please' said in the entire world. That meant something, considering Taylor worked with babies and toddlers who needed to be coaxed to say it on many occasions.

But it was the M word the fox said that made Taylor rethink her position. She could be lying, trying to trick Taylor, but having another woman standing there, asking to be let through because her mate might be in trouble…

If she were in that situation, Taylor would forge her way through anyone who tried to stop her from getting to Jonas.

With a whole lot of blood.

Taylor pressed her lips together. "There are some people back there in pretty bad shape."

Which was the wrong thing to say because the fox girl tried pushing through her. "Then let me see him!"

"Hold on, hold on, your mate might not be back there. He could be fine. I don't know you, and you could mess up the…scene."

That's what the police said about these sorts of things, right? They didn't want someone showing up and stomping all over a crime scene, right?

Shit. The sirens were coming closer. Taylor glanced towards the open garage doors, which was a mistake because the fox girl pushed passed Taylor before she could grab onto her.

"Shit."

"Victor? Victor!"

"Wait!"

The woman ran into the lounge, following her nose. She was way too fast for Taylor to catch up to before she ran into the room.

Taylor stopped in the doorway and saw Jonas sit up to look to the fox woman and then to Taylor. "Where did she come from?"

The fox woman stopped in front of one of the men. He wore a grey suit, he could have been a police officer, but he wasn't dressed the way the other men were. Not in any noticeable uniform.

"Victor? Baby? Shit, come on."

"Don't move him. Don't move him!"

It was too late. The fox woman turned the man over onto his back. A groan came from him, which was lucky; he was all right. Hopefully, nothing else would happen after being moved like that.

Mated pairs tended to feed off of each other. Energies were shared, which allowed humans who mated with shifters to have slightly faster healing times. Still, the fox woman's touch on his cheek shouldn't have been enough to make the injured man open his eyes. But it was.

She smiled down at him, her eyes brimming with tears. The man, Victor, looked back at her as though he was drunk and high at the same time. "What are you doing here?" Victor slurred his words.

The fox woman laughed. "You weren't answering your texts. I was worried."

Taylor and Jonas looked at each other, and Taylor's gut clenched. That was how a mate behaved. That was the worry and love of a mate.

A mate didn't turn her back on the one she loved.

Taylor pushed the thought away. For the moment. She had to. There was too much else to think about, now that she knew this woman was not about to go on a killing spree. There was no time to discuss anything though, because the next thing Taylor knew, there were shouts. She was commanded to put her hands in the air, which she did right away.

The fox girl refused to take her hands away from her mate, and Jonas, his voice as commanding and strong as ever, called out to the men in blue to let them know who he was and what he was doing.

They were all instructed to move away from the victims while paramedics came to tend to the dead and dying. Taylor couldn't help but think it was for the best. These people didn't just have the training, but they also had better equipment on hand. And she was just happy to be taken away from all the blood.

JONAS GRIT his teeth as he was asked for the fifth time his full name, where he lived, and what he did for his living. He knew this tactic had to work from time to time; otherwise, the detectives questioning him wouldn't ever use it. They were only covering their bases and making sure they had all the details.

Still, he couldn't stand this. Being hauled off to the station for questioning was one thing, but being separated from Taylor was even worse. He knew the scene shook her, and he wanted to be able to comfort her and reassure her that everything was going to be okay. Something he couldn't do before, at the scene while there were so many people he needed to try to help.

Detective Grey looked young, almost too young to be a detective, which meant he was either older than he looked or he'd risen through the ranks incredibly fast. Regardless, the man looked at Jonas as if he was the prime suspect in his case now, which Jonas almost couldn't blame him for.

"You're telling me that you're a lieutenant firefighter with the Astraea Fire Department, and your chief asked you to come down here and question your ex-girlfriend about the fires being set in the area?"

"Yes. That's what I'm here for."

Detective Grey raised a brow, and he turned his attention to the other detective in the room as though to ask if Jonas was serious or not.

"I know it's out of the ordinary, but he brought me along because he knew I had connections to the bear clan in the area."

"You don't look like a shifter to me," Grey said, his gaze darting to the top of Jonas' head, noting the lack of ears.

"Subhuman. I don't shift. I used to live around here. I know this sloth."

"Were you one of theirs?"

Jonas shook his head. "Not officially, no. I was allowed to stick around because my mother was a shifter."

"All right, say we believe you. Did you find anything out about the fires?"

Jonas knew this wouldn't make Taylor feel too good, to have everything Jonas had learned about the situation spilled when she wasn't there to confirm or deny it, but she would forgive him for it.

He hoped.

This was for their daughter.

"It's a wolf pack. Something is going on around here, and you can ask Taylor about it if you want more details. I guess a fight broke out with a fox skulk and a wolf pack after an alpha was killed, then there was a fight for a conduit. The wolf pack wanted the bear clan to back them up, and when they refused the started causing trouble. The fires started after some bears tried to leave the area to get away from all of it."

And from the look in Detective Grey's eyes, Jonas knew he'd said something that the man either already knew, or heavily suspected. "Am I right?"

Grey smiled at him, taking a seat across from him. "We'll look into that. Any idea who the fox woman was? Or the man she was with?"

Jonas shook his head. "I barely got a look at her before she ran in. I was too busy trying to make sure my chief was alive." He glared at the other man, "any updates on his status?"

"When I hear anything back, I'll let you know. The fox woman corroborates your story. She said she never met you or the bear shifter before."

Jonas frowned. "Do you know her?"

Ignoring Jonas' question, Grey leaned back, looked to the other detective in the room with them, and when he reached his hand back, an orange envelope was placed in it. He opened the envelope and carefully spilled the contents onto the table, spreading out pictures and papers.

"Tell me what you know about these wolves."

CHAPTER 12

Taylor had never been questioned by the police before. She didn't like it, and she didn't want to make a habit of it in the future either. There was something about not being in control of when she was able to leave this place that didn't sit well with her on so many levels, especially as they asked her questions she wasn't sure she could answer.

Taylor always thought she could handle situations like this with a certain level of grace. All she had to do was tell the truth as she knew it, but sitting at that table with two officers questioning her...it was a lot different compared to what she thought it would be.

Especially since she knew so much.

Taylor ended up telling them everything she knew about the wolves and the skulk of foxes five times. The worst part was all the questions the detectives kept asking, hoping she'd have more information. She had a general idea of what was going on, but her timelines were somewhat off because she wasn't directly involved. At one point, after what seemed like a thousand years had passed, another detective came into the room, and Taylor barely stopped herself from jumping out of her seat.

"It's been hours. Can I go yet?"

"Soon." The detective nodded to the others, and they left the room, leaving her alone with the new one alone.

"I've got a kid at home, and things are crazy right now. Please, I'm trying to tell you everything I know. I just need to get home."

"My name is Detective Grey. I've already contacted your alpha. He knows where you are, and he's taking good care of, Meg, was it?"

Taylor grit her teeth at the mention of her daughter's name. She didn't know how to take something like that. It didn't sound threatening, not really, but this guy knowing Meg's name while she was stuck here didn't jive well with her.

"Yes, that is her name."

Detective Grey smiled at her, but Taylor still wasn't feeling so impressed. "You don't have to be so alarmed. So far, everything you've said checks out with what your friend said."

"Jonas?" Taylor felt a twinge of pain in her stomach. Of course they questioned Jonas, and he would have told them everything he could about what Taylor already knew. He would have had to. He wasn't part of the sloth anymore, and he lived in a completely different world from her. And he'd already said that he was planning on giving as much information to the police as possible. "If Jonas spoke to you then you know it's not exactly safe for me to be without my baby right now. When can I go home?"

"Soon enough. We're just confirming a few things with the vixen shifter who came into the fire station."

"Right, you can ask her. I wasn't there beforehand, and neither was Jonas; we have no idea what happened to all those people." Jonas had seemed especially concerned about one of them. "Are they all right? He was going to meet with one of his friends."

Detective Grey looked her right in the eyes. "Four people were brought into the hospital alive. One died while being airlifted out; one is currently in stable condition, and the other two are still fighting."

Taylor cringed. She thought of Jonas, thought of the name of his boss. What was it again?

"Was there a man named Dallas? Was he all right? Or at least alive?"

The detective's smile was a kind one, and Taylor couldn't figure out if he was trying to be nice but was unable to say one way or the other, or if he didn't want to give her the bad news. Her stomach clenched. "Anyway, I don't want you or Jonas going far. We're going to need to keep in touch. Some of our wolves are sniffing around the station to see if they can come up with anything."

"Wolves? You had wolves sniffing around the station?"

Grey raised a brow at her. "There a problem with that?"

Taylor couldn't believe he didn't see it. "Well, yeah, kind of. You know it was wolves who did this, that a wolf pack is setting these fires."

Detective Grey stared at her as though he couldn't be less impressed. "You know, it is possible for wolf shifters to come from differing packs. I can promise you that the people who work for us are professionals and they will do their jobs efficiently."

Taylor swallowed a little harder than she was used to, embarrassed. "Right. Yeah, sorry." Shifters had enough trouble with humans continually worrying about being attacked, without her adding to it.

"Come on. I'll take you to the front desk."

Taylor said nothing, standing when the detective prompted her to, following him out of that cold, depressing room while she ruminated on her assumptions about the wolves.

She'd given Jonas so much hell for not wanting to be part of a sloth of bears who were constantly pushing him away. She'd allowed herself to be persuaded by the sloth to give him up when he was one of the best things in her life. Then she'd held against him his frustration with how some packs and sloths behaved towards subhumans. Meanwhile, it took her less than a second before she did the same thing to a group of wolf shifters she'd never even met.

Taylor wanted to get out of here. She wanted to go home to her daughter, and she needed to throw her arms around Jonas' neck and kiss him until she purged herself of this terrible guilt.

She let the detective bring her to the front. She signed her name and then waited for Jonas.

When he came out next, she could hardly look at him. He seemed a little too cool, too calm. She knew he was thinking about Dallas.

"You ready to go?"

She jumped a little. Taylor barely noticed when he'd walked up to her, but Jonas always had been good at keeping his footsteps light.

She nodded. "Yeah, I want to go."

When they made it outside, Taylor's eyes scanned the hills in the distance. Smoke still plumed, and the helicopters were still flying to and from the area.

"I think they've got it contained. We should be fine."

She blinked at that, following him to his truck. "How can you tell?"

"A couple of reasons. Because we weren't told to evacuate, the recent rains are probably making it hard for the fire to spread too far even with all the underbrush, and these guys are moving fast. Whoever set the fires put the people around here on edge. They were prepared."

Taylor nodded, moving to the passenger side of his truck, which they'd been allowed to take to the station before their questioning.

"Sorry," she said once she'd buckled her seatbelt.

"For what?" Jonas turned the engine.

Taylor wet her lips, trying and failing to not look at the ink on his fingers. "For everything. I should've…I should've gone to the police sooner. I could've done something."

"You think I blame you for what happened to Dallas?"

"He's your friend, isn't he? I mean, not just your boss? Aren't you angry?"

"I am. I'm fucking pissed, and so will the rest of the guys be when they find out, but I'm mad at the wolves that did this, not at you. You're the one being terrorized; you're the one who fell into this. You didn't do anything wrong."

"Oh." That made her feel a little better, but she still didn't know what to do about…everything else. "Okay then."

Jonas kept right on smiling. "Dallas will be all right. He's a tough old bastard. A subhuman, too, actually. He's not about to let a pack of wolves get the better of him."

Taylor sighed. "That's good."

"The others weren't so lucky."

She cringed. That was right. People had still died, so it wasn't good at all.

"Try not to think about it so much."

"How can I not think about it? This is all my fault."

"How is this even remotely your fault? Let alone all of it?"

Taylor pressed her lips together. "I just...after seeing those people on the floor...don't you at least somewhat blame me? I could have done something so much sooner."

"So could everyone in your sloth. You told me why everyone was keeping quiet about it. I'm telling you, Taylor, I promise you, I don't blame you for this, and you shouldn't blame yourself either. This isn't on you."

Despite his words, she couldn't help but think that it was. At least in some way. It had to be. She'd wanted to protect her home and her daughter, and maybe that would be enough to help her sleep at night, but for now, she wanted to forget.

"Are you going to take me home?"

Jonas nodded. "I think that's the best place for you to be. The police will show up soon after. They might already be there asking questions. I hope you're okay with that."

Taylor nodded. Anyone who had a problem with the humans getting involved at this point could kiss her ass. She'd seen what the wolves were willing to do, to her people as well as the humans, and she wasn't ready to take the risk. Not anymore.

"Do you think Meg and I could stay with you in the city? At least until all of this blows over."

The corner of Jonas' mouth quirked. "Absolutely."

CHAPTER 13

Jonas could tell something was different on the ride back to the sloth. Taylor wasn't usually this withdrawn. She was usually more open. Even her anger would be better than this.

He didn't like to think that the sight of all that blood had traumatized her, or that sitting in a cement room with a two-way mirror for hours on end had finished the job, but there was always that possibility.

He didn't want this for her. He didn't want to come back to upend everything she'd worked for and everything she knew, but even if there were some magical option to turn back time and ease her into this, he wouldn't do it.

He had that little girl to think about.

How strange that he'd only known about Meg for a grand total of fewer than twenty-four hours and he already wanted to protect her with his life. It was as though some powerful instinct had awakened within him, and there was no going back.

That wasn't the only instinct of his that had awakened. Jonas did his damned best to not glance at Taylor as he drove, but it was difficult.

He was a subhuman. He couldn't shift. He didn't have the ears, the tail, or the senses that came with being a shifter, but right at that moment, Jonas was starting to feel more alive than he'd ever felt since leaving this little town.

He shouldn't, but he couldn't help it either. This was a mating pull, and there was no resisting something like that for long.

Not even seeing a good friend struggling for his life.

It stunned him when Taylor was the first to speak up. "You think you could pull over real quick before getting back to the territory?"

Jonas looked at her, gauging the color under her jawline. "You feeling sick?"

Taylor shook her head, her fingernails digging into her thighs. "No, I just want to touch you."

Jonas' heartbeat sped up. By a lot. "You don't have to do anything you don't want to do."

The low growl in Taylor's voice was warning enough. "Please don't patronize me right now. This has nothing to do with what happened back...there. I just don't want to wait anymore. I need to feel you."

They were less than five minutes away. A better man might have resisted a little more, but Jonas never once claimed to be a good man.

He found a path and pulled to the side of the road, turning into the trees and parking. "It won't hide us too well if someone happens to be looking."

Taylor unclipped her seatbelt, her voice throaty. "It's good enough for me." She reached for him, her hands gripping his face as she pulled him to her.

Her lips.

Jonas hadn't tasted them, hadn't felt them, in such a long time. God, he'd forgotten how good she tasted. He'd forgotten how soft her mouth was, and now that he had it, he almost didn't know what to do with himself.

So he held her. As though his body was finally coming alive after almost two years of being frozen stiff, Jonas grabbed Taylor by the waist, his other hand coming to rest on her back right before he pulled her to him.

Taylor's dark hair with those unbelievable blue highlights fell into his face. It wasn't tied back anymore. When did that happen? Didn't matter, because then her arms were looping around his neck and it was so beyond perfect that he didn't know what to do with himself.

The heat and clench of her thighs around his legs, her perfect breasts pressed against his chest, and the way she leaned into his mouth…God, he missed this. He had missed her. So damned much it ached.

And now her tongue was in his mouth.

Taylor had always been a little on the aggressive side—came with being a bear shifter, Jonas had always assumed—but this was more than he anticipated. She kissed him as though she thought he was going to vanish if she stopped. Her nimble fingers worked quickly to undo the buttons of his shirt before she slid her hands against his bare chest, then down to his abdomen.

Jonas groaned, his body pushing up to meet her, his cock jumping to attention but still stuck behind his jeans.

Everywhere she touched him throbbed. Her fingers left behind a trail of fire that made Jonas gasp for breath. Only she could touch him in a way that made him feel as though he'd never been touched. Only she could make his body come alive like this.

How the hell had he gone for so long without her? How did he ever manage to trick himself into thinking he didn't need her anymore? That he was over her? There was no getting over her, and there was no getting over this.

Jonas pulled her waist forward and back, grinding her down onto his erection while giving her a little preview of what was to come. Her small groan of approval was more than he needed to know he was on the right track.

"I forgot."

Jonas blinked his eyes open. "Sorry, what?"

She smiled at him, her full lips darker after being kissed. "I almost forgot what this felt like. I missed you so much."

Her fingers threaded into Jonas' hair, and something in his chest clenched painfully tight. He couldn't take this anymore. He really couldn't. "Come here." He gripped her hair tight enough that it had to hurt, but Taylor gave him no indication she was uncomfortable or in pain as she opened for him, letting his tongue slide forward to lick deep inside, as though their mouths were saying hello to each other after a long time spent apart.

The desperation and need vibrated from both of their bodies. Even with his spacious truck, there was no getting around the fact that dry humping each other on the driver's side made things a little cramped.

Without taking his mouth from Taylor's, Jonas reached his hand down, fumbling for the handle to push the seat back.

His horn blared as Taylor pushed herself up onto her knees to give him space, and then the seat finally pushed back enough to provide them with the room they needed.

And nearly made them head-butt each other.

Taylor laughed. The first real laugh he'd heard out of her since he'd gotten here. She didn't stop touching him. Her eyes danced, and Jonas swore he'd never seen anyone more beautiful in his entire life.

"Taylor—"

She kissed his mouth before he could finish, but it was a quick kiss. She pulled back before he could get a handle on himself. "Don't say anything. Not right now. I don't want to ruin this."

"I won't ruin it."

It could never be ruined so long as she was here with him.

Apparently, Taylor didn't trust him not to ruin the mood with whatever she thought he was about to say because she kissed him again. Her mouth was perfection, so how could he resist her when she was like this?

They didn't remove their clothes so much as they just loosened them, getting to all the good parts that were needed the most to do what they wanted to do to each other.

"I wish I wore a skirt today," Taylor said with that wicked smile on her face, the sort of smile that brought Jonas back to the old days when they were together, and there was almost nothing in the world that could ruin the mood between them. Just the two of them against the world.

Taylor had to lift herself entirely off of Jonas' waist to get her jeans down, and holy hell, this was happening. Jonas quickly rummaged through this glove compartment, searching for just what he needed.

Taylor smiled, taking one of the little packets in her hands and tearing open the plastic, pulling out the latex with a shocking amount of skill.

"Should I be worried that you know how to do that so well?" Jonas could barely take his eyes off her fingers as she held his cock in her skillful hands, rolling the condom down his shaft.

"Should I be worried that you have a box of these in your truck?"

He cleared his throat. "No. I wouldn't think so, no."

She chuckled, that same laugh she used to give him whenever she got the better of him in one way or another. Then she was climbing onto his lap and settling onto his cock.

Jonas hissed low in his throat, gripping her waist and clenching his teeth as the sweet heat of her body, the clench of her sex, engulfed him.

And Taylor was clearly trying to drive him insane by the way she closed her eyes, parted her perfectly puckered lips as she sank inch by sweet inch down onto him. Then she was seated, and Jonas needed a minute to breathe before he could collect himself.

Taylor did, too.

"That feels…" She opened her eyes. "Exactly as I remember it."

Something wild and instinctive rose up and roared inside of Jonas' chest. He knew what she meant because he felt it, too, and even though Jonas was not a shifter, not for the first time, he felt a wild inner side sit up straight. Something animalistic and fierce.

And he wasn't about to hold it back either.

"Let it out," Taylor gasped, already canting her hips back and forth, riding him as though she'd never stopped. "Let me see it."

Jonas growled. "See what?"

She leaned in, her eyes glowing with the eager lust. He could see her inner bear ready to come out. "Let me see it."

Again, he didn't know what she meant, but part of him thought he understood. She was demanding something he didn't have. She wanted to see that wild shifter side to him — a side he didn't have.

But as a subhuman, there was a hint of something, something she could work with. Something she could see, and maybe he felt it, too.

Jonas gripped her hips tightly, encouraging the movement of her body, making her dance for him.

Taylor leaned forward, her face coming close to his chest. He thought she was about to kiss him there. Jonas wasn't entirely sure why, but he was willing to go with it.

Until Taylor pulled the lever that had Jonas falling backward.

No, she just let the seat lean back until it couldn't go any farther, and she laughed again at the look on his face. "You should see yourself right now."

"You should talk, sweetheart."

He didn't want to give Taylor the chance to make fun of him again, so he grabbed her by the back of her head and yanked her mouth down for another beautiful kiss. He bit her lips sweetly, coaxing them open so he could taste her tongue the way he wanted to.

"You look like sex on wheels right now."

Taylor wet her lips. "I better, considering we're having sex right now."

She bit down on her lower lip after that, throwing her head back, and as she moaned, the sound, the vibration of her body, rocked through him. He could understand her need to push the seat back. It gave her all the room she needed to rock his world, and when it came to Taylor, she loved being on top. When she put him into this position, he was more than willing to let her do whatever she wanted.

The only thing he needed to do to keep up the momentum was to thrust his hips up, making her practically bounce on his cock. Jonas had to take some care with this, however. He didn't want Taylor bonking her head while he bonked her.

"I'm close," she rasped, circling her hips in the way she always did when her orgasm was just around the corner.

"Come for me, baby. I want to feel it."

"Are you close?"

Not quite yet, but he was going to get there one way or the other, and Jonas wasn't about to let her worry too much about it.

He reached for her breasts, still behind that sexy, blue lace bra. There was little in the world Jonas loved more than seeing her perfect pair of breasts behind a bra like that. It was almost a shame to undo it, but he needed to get his hands where they had to go.

Her nipples freed, Jonas took one of her perfect breasts in his hand before he leaned in, kissing one of those caramel-colored nubs.

Taylor sighed. "Don't stop doing that."

"Doing this?" He pressed his teeth to her bud, enjoying the shiver that rippled through her body, and the way her sex clenched around his shaft.

"Y-yeah, just like that."

"Then show me." He kissed her other nipple, teasing it while his other hand slid down to her sex. To the curls of hair between her legs that he loved so much.

Too many women waxed absolutely everything off nowadays. He didn't like that. Taylor kept herself groomed, and as he could see, and feel, that hadn't changed. He pressed his fingers to her sex, stroking her, enjoying the feel of scratchy soft hair as Taylor rode him.

"Like this?"

"Yes."

She looped her arm back around his neck, gripping him tight as she rode him, and she was almost there. He could feel it as her pace increased right before Taylor sighed, her body shuddering, and Jonas felt a clenching and unclenching around his cock as she came.

Taylor came, sighing his name. Jonas was going to hold that one over her head for a little while. How could he not as she moved the way she did? As she fucked against him until she had nothing left to give.

"You're not done," Jonas growled, grabbing her by the hair and yanking her head back so he could look into those glowing golden eyes, seeing her wicked smile return after her moment of bliss. He crushed his mouth to hers once more, thrusting up into her, savoring the sounds of her moans as she rode him again. He knew she loved the control that came with the sex they had, especially when he was the one on the cusp of orgasm. She had him right where she wanted him.

Luckily for Jonas, he wasn't too far behind her, so there wasn't much of a chance for Taylor to sex torture him.

Next time. He would lay himself down to whatever tortures she had in mind for him.

"Not yet, don't come yet."

Jonas laughed a low, breathy noise. "D-don't exactly have a say in that right now, sweetheart."

Taylor nodded, her mouth quirking in a sexy, mischievous smile as she focused on the movement of her hips.

"All right. Come on then."

Jonas hissed, his toes curling in his boots as Taylor rode him.

So close. He was damn near there. Just a little bit more and…

Jonas came with a shout, wrapping his arms around Taylor's waist and clutching her tight.

Jonas wished he didn't have the condom on. He wanted to fuck her and claim her the way a real shifter did. Even if he was a subhuman, and even if it didn't necessarily mean the same thing. He wanted it. He wanted her to go back home and for Andrew everyone else who might have told her to turn her back on him to smell his scent all over her.

As he came down off the high of his orgasm, as the crash finished with him, Jonas realized he wanted Taylor for his mate. He wanted her for his wife. This was the mother of his child, and he wanted to spend the rest of his life with her.

He felt her soft stroke on his hair and back, and he pressed his ear to her chest to hear the sound of her beating heart as it calmed. For the first time in years, Jonas felt at peace.

Until he opened his eyes, looked out the front windshield of his truck, and spotted two wolves and a man, staring right at him and Taylor.

CHAPTER 14

Taylor didn't understand why Jonas suddenly stopped moving. When she looked back to see what he had his eyes on, she understood.

She jumped off him and into the passenger seat, pulling on her clothes, trying to keep her eyes on the wolves and the person they were with.

Something flicked. Long ears. She finally noted them, on top of the man's head. A shifter then. Those weren't wolf ears. He scratched at the back of his neck, looking away as color flooded his cheeks.

"Jesus Christ, how much of that were they watching?"

A dangerous growl, a terrible noise that could have belonged to an alpha, rumbled its way out of Jonas' throat. "I'll find out."

"What? Hey, wait!"

Taylor tried to grab for Jonas when she realized what he was doing. Jonas managed to fix his clothes and push his way out of the truck before she could stop him.

He might be subhuman, but he was no match for two wolves, and whatever that guy out there was.

"Stay in the truck! Lock the doors!"

Uh, yeah right. That wasn't about to happen. Much as Taylor occa-

sionally liked letting men pretend at being all protective and possessive, when it came to her and Jonas, she was the one with the claws
around here.

Jonas gave her a hard look when she didn't get back into the truck.
She flipped him off. She had her own bone to pick with people who
watched a woman having sex without her knowing.

"What the hell did you think you were doing?"

"Taylor—"

"What kind of asshole goes around watching someone like that?"

"Sorry, sorry," said the man, raising his hands. He refused to look
at her, as if that was going to help her out now. "I wasn't trying…We
followed your truck after you left the station and found you here. We
weren't watching."

"Bullshit," Jonas growled. "You were standing right there! What the
hell is your problem?"

"Whoa, okay, hold up a minute."

It was interesting how the two wolves did nothing while Jonas
approached the shifter in the middle. They just watched as the guy
stumbled and backed away, as though he feared he was about to get
the crap beaten out of him.

Which looked like it might be the case.

"Steve! Jackson! Will you help me already?"

Jonas snatched the man by the throat, yanking him close enough
that their noses practically touched.

"You're lucky I don't have my ax on me, you little shithead, or I'd
shove it so far up your ass you'd—"

"Jonas!"

They shifted so fast, and Taylor was so distracted by the chest
pounding display that she was late warning him when one of the
wolves transformed. The biggest of the two slammed his hand onto
Jonas' shoulder. "That's enough. Let him go."

"You don't have to hurt him to make your point. He didn't want to
be here in the first place," the second chimed in.

Taylor was so done with this. She let her claws out, a protective
instinct whirling within her as the wolf shifters surrounded her man.
She made sure the bald guy knew she was coming, however. She

didn't want anyone to spin around with their fist ready and catch her off guard. "You'd both better step back right now, or else someone might get hurt. It won't be me, and it won't be him either."

All four men slowly turned to look at her, as though the sound of her threatening voice was somehow a shock to them. Not that she understood what that was about. They didn't have to look at her as if they didn't understand where this was coming from.

Jonas especially, the asshole. She was trying to save him.

The man Jonas held by the throat smiled nervously at her. The other two just stared. Jonas raised his brows, and she could feel the sudden increase of heat in his body.

The bald man turned his attention back to Jonas. "If you would release our friend here, I would like to be able to speak with the both of you before your mate decides to attack us."

"If she did attack, you would all deserve to get ripped apart. I sure as shit wouldn't stop her."

The man Jonas held sputtered. "We just wanted to see you. Th-that was my sister at the fire station. My sister and her mate. We're not here to cause trouble."

"Your sister?" Taylor thought about that, looking at the man's tail. It did look like a fox tail, and so did his ears. It didn't prove they were related, but why would he lie about something like that? The idea that he was worried about his sister did give her pause, and a feeling of sympathy, even though she didn't have siblings of her own.

If Meg ever had siblings, then Taylor would want other people to give her consideration if she ever had to look out for them.

It didn't make any sense, but maybe it didn't need to. Taylor already knew what she wanted.

"Jonas, you think you could let up a little?"

His brows raised high again. "Seriously?"

Taylor let her claws sink back into her fingernails, the itch of fur retracting into her pores tingling across her skin. "I want to hear them out."

Jonas growled, turning that horrible stare back to the man in his hand before he shoved the guy away.

The fox stumbled, caught himself, then rubbed at his throat while glaring at Jonas.

Jonas pointed a thick finger at him. "Don't even think about giving me shit for that. You were the one perving on my mate."

Taylor's heart twisted. She pressed her lips together quickly, trying not to keep her gaze on Jonas for too long.

Was he aware of what he just said?

If that word came to him so quickly, then it meant—

"We just wanted to talk. We want the same thing," said the bald wolf shifter, holding out his hand. "My name is Jackson."

Jonas eyed the hand suspiciously, but then reached out and took it. "You got a last name?"

Jackson grinned. "Dwayne."

"Wait, that's your last name?" said the other shifter, staring at him with amazement.

"There a problem?" Jackson asked, not entirely giving the other man a dirty look, but it wasn't so easygoing either.

"No, I just figured you had something a little different. You know? It doesn't exactly suit you."

Jackson growled, and Taylor was getting sick of this entire thing. "Would you boys just hurry up and tell us why you were watching me and Jonas in the truck? You're giving off serial killer vibes."

Jonas growled at the fox guy again, who took a few more steps backward.

"We're not here to hurt you, and we didn't watch you," said the other wolf. "My name is Steve Delany. I work as a private eye in Astraea. We followed you here and stopped in front of the truck when we wanted to get your attention. We didn't know what you were doing."

Jonas didn't sound too impressed by the explanation, which was good. Taylor wanted to stay angry with these guys, and if she was going to do that, then she wanted Jonas to have her back.

"What we were doing and where we were doing it is not your damned business," Jonas snapped. "What's a private eye doing in Lakeview? The fires here would be outside of your expertise."

"Nothing is outside of my expertise," Steve said, his tone a little too cocky for Taylor.

She cracked her knuckles, reminding the boys she was there and letting her claws return just enough to be noticeable. "So what do you all want?" This had better be good, too. She didn't just have the afterglow of the best sex she'd had in months interrupted because a group of shifters wanted to have a chat. "You said this was about your sister?" She looked to the fox. "You still didn't introduce yourself."

"Right." The guy was still bright red around his neck and cheeks, but Taylor was way too miffed to show him any pity. "My name is Link Wolff, and my sister, Zelda...she used to be married into the pack we think is doing all of this. The paramedics you called saved my brother-in-law's life. We...I owe you for that."

Taylor blinked, such an honest, open answer catching her off guard. "Oh, well...you're welcome."

Link nodded.

Jonas narrowed his eyes. "Your name is Link?"

Link's entire body clenched up, the picture of a male readying himself for a fight. "Yeah?"

"And your sister's name is Zelda?"

For a hair of a second, Taylor didn't get it, but then she did. She didn't even like video games, but the reference wasn't lost on her. And now she was back to staring at the guy, and his two friends, with massive suspicion. "You're telling me that's your name? Your legal name? For you and your sister?"

Link rolled his eyes. "My parents were freaks, all right? Will you just let us talk to you, please?" Even as he said it, Link still seemed to have trouble looking at her.

Whatever.

"What do you think, Jonas?"

Jonas still didn't look happy. He looked like he wanted to throw down and take out all three shifters right here and now, but he sighed and relented. "All right, fine. What do you know about these wolves?"

Steve nodded. "Right, well, for one thing, they are a murderous bunch, and if they're starting fires like this, then they're even dumber than we all thought."

"Arsonists usually are," Jonas agreed. "Tell me something I don't know."

"The conduit is my mate." Jonas and Taylor stared at Steve while he continued to explain that his best friend was Zelda's mate and that his meeting with the conduit had set the war with the wolves in motion and gotten them all involved.

Jackson spoke next, and his words chilled Taylor to the bone. "We think someone in her bear sloth is helping the wolves set the fires."

Taylor caught her breath as her blood ran cold and pieces fell into place in her mind. Without a word, she turned and ran for the truck, which still had the keys in the ignition.

"Taylor, wait!"

She didn't wait. She jumped into the driver's seat and started the ignition. Jonas barely got into the passenger seat before she was on the move.

"Jesus! Taylor! Wait for just a second! We don't even know if what he said is true."

She shook her head. "I don't care. I left my baby back home."

And she wasn't going to stop until she had Meg safely in her arms.

CHAPTER 15

Jonas barely held on for the ride or got his door shut, as Taylor sped down the highway well over the speed limit. She turned onto the road that led to her territory, and Jonas knew he had to think fast.

"Taylor, you need to think rationally about this."

She shook her head, and it was a miracle she was able to drive as well as she did with that wild expression in her eyes.

"If you go storming back home looking like that, and if what those guys said was true, you could give everything away."

"I'm not taking the risk. I want her back. I need her back."

"I do, too, but—"

"You're not acting like it!" Taylor slammed her hand onto the steering wheel, turning that enraged expression onto him before looking back at the road. "We left her there, and she might be in trouble!"

"Of course I do! I would have cared a long time ago if you'd bothered to tell me she existed!" It just came out. He still had anger and hurt about it, but should have kept it inside. The swell of moisture in Taylor's eyes showed that it was too much to think about past mistakes while frantically trying to get to Meg right then.

He focused, bringing calm back into himself. He was no good to anyone, not even Taylor or Meg if he couldn't keep his head. One of them had to. He put his hand onto Taylor's. "Baby, pull over. Please. We've got maybe one chance at this."

Her hand shook. He felt the tickle of hairs under his fingers and palm as she struggled to keep her inner bear in check. She let out a shaky breath before slowing the truck down and guiding it over to the side of the road.

She wouldn't stop trembling. He'd never seen her like this before, and it stunned him. And he wanted to ease her out of that pain. Everything inside him drew him to her. She was a magnet, and he was stuck in her pull. Almost two years away and he'd thought he was over her. He thought there was nothing left between them and now he couldn't yank himself away from her even if he wanted to.

"Baby, nothing is going to happen to Meg."

"Then we need to get home before something does happen."

"I know, and we will, but if what those men said was true and you rush in there looking ready for a fight, it will put them on the defensive and cause them to act. You need to stay calm. All right? If Andrew has anything to do with this—"

"You think he's involved?"

Shit. "No, not necessarily, but maybe he's close to someone who is. The point is that you can't give us away to anyone when we get back. All right? Not yet. Wait until you have Meg safely in your arms and then, when you're out of there, and at a safe distance, the police can get involved and start asking questions."

She looked at him. "Won't you be one of the men asking those questions."

"I've told you, I don't have any actual authority here. I was just here to help, not to carry out any real investigation."

As far as Jonas was concerned, he was done. He'd done his part, Dallas was still alive, and now the police could take over.

"Can we go home now?"

Jonas looked at her. She seemed to be in control again. There was still that edge of panic in her voice, the need to move quickly and get to her destination, but he supposed that was never going to entirely go away when it came to a mother worried about her baby.

"All right, but remember what I said. We have to be careful about this. As controlled as possible, so no one sniffs anything out about us. All right?"

Taylor put the truck back into drive, not looking at him as she nodded.

Jonas was pretty sure he was going to regret this, but he sat back and let her go, not saying another word until they were driving up the road and into the territory, houses and trailers coming into view.

"Remember what I said."

Her jaw tensed. She nodded as she drove right up to Andrew's deck, parking practically right in front of the wooden steps before hopping out of the truck. Jonas clenched his teeth, but he didn't say anything to her while he tried to ignore the sloth members who watched them from their houses. He decided not to look in any particular direction, knowing that any one of them, or even several of them, could be helping to set the fires.

But why? What purpose did the fire serve other than to terrorize a community? Was that the only point? Or was he looking for hidden layers that weren't there? He'd been in houses set aflame by people who loved their lighters a little too much. Sometimes, most of the time actually, there was no point. There was no big revenge plot. There was nothing other than the need to see something burn, to terrorize, and see things made clean by the fire. This could very well be that sort of case, but Jonas wasn't about to lower his guard or stop looking either.

Just in case.

Andrew stepped out of the front door, Meg in his arms, and the hairs on the back of Jonas' neck stood on end. He wanted to rush up there and yank his little girl from Andrew. He didn't trust anyone other than Taylor to hold her after what Steve, Jackson, and Link revealed on the side of the road.

And if this was what he felt, there was no telling how hard it was for Taylor to handle this.

"Made it back alright?"

"Yup." Taylor put on a mask that sure as hell would have had him fooled if he didn't know what was going on. She trotted up the stairs and reached for Meg, smiling as easily as though she was getting off from a day at the daycare and was eager to see her child again.

"Did you miss Mommy?"

"She was very good while you were away." Andrew seemed a little too easygoing as he eased the child into Taylor's arms.

It was sweet the way Meg reached for her mother while sucking on her soother.

Then Andrew looked down at where she'd parked. "Ah, you miss the usual spot?"

"Sorry," Taylor said, smiling as though embarrassed about her parking capabilities. "It's been a long night. I was just a little eager to get home and see her. Right, baby?"

Meg smiled around her soother.

She didn't look like she was suffering from any trauma, but would a one-year-old baby, almost one-and-a-half, be able to pick up on that kind of vibe? Would she know it if she was in any danger?

Jonas couldn't be sure, and it didn't matter. The point was that he had Meg and Taylor here with him now and he was getting them out of here.

"Taylor, come on, we're going to be late."

"Right," she said, smiling at him with that wide-eyed, open expression, as if she knew what they were going to be late for. "You're right. Sorry. I'll just get her bag, and we'll be on our way."

"Where are you both off to?"

He said it so casually. The worst part about the tone of voice was the way Jonas couldn't tell if there was anything sinister about it. If anything was underlying in those words.

"I'm going to stay with Jonas for a bit." Even Jonas knew the best lies were the ones laced with a bit of truth. "He needs to get back to work, and I think it's a good idea to go to the city with him. Give him a chance to get to know Meg a little more."

He looked at that little girl, and he wanted to get to know her. He wanted to watch her grow up and protect her along the way. If Andrew had anything to do with the fires around here, or if he was covering for someone…Jonas wanted his daughter nowhere near him in that case.

Andrew shrugged, not giving any resistance to the plans he and Taylor gave. "All right, but you make sure to come and visit now, understand?"

Taylor blinked, giving the first little slip of her mask. "Really? Just like that?"

"Why not? You're a grown woman. You can do whatever you want."

Jonas didn't want to risk that this was a trap, or that this might not be what he thought, or hoped that it was. "Taylor, come on. Let's go and get Meg's things." He didn't want to take the time to get the damned baby bag. They could easily get more supplies in the city, but it would look suspicious if they rushed out too fast.

Taylor nodded, heading down the stairs, "I'll contact the parents and let them know the daycare will be shuttered for a while."

"Good luck," Andrew called after them.

Jonas settled his arm around Taylor's waist, walking away with her, back to her trailer so he could grab some things.

A few men stepped in his way. Black bears he'd known from his days living just outside the sloth. "Guys, we're in a bit of a hurry."

"Right," said the man in the middle, narrowing his eyes at Jonas. Trevor always was a sack of shit. He was skinnier than Jonas was, and not that tall, but he knew he could outmatch him because of his abilities, which he'd liked throwing around when they were kids.

"Did you guys go to the police?"

"What? No, of course not."

Taylor spoke a little too quickly for Jonas' liking. Even he could hear the lie in her voice, and he was the one who wanted to give her the most leeway right about now.

Trevor didn't look too impressed. He crossed his arms, as if he was trying to make himself look bigger, which was next to impossible considering his size. "You sure about that? Because you were gone a long time."

Jonas clenched his hands behind Taylor's back. "Why? Did you have a visitor?"

Trevor glared at him. Jonas glared right back.

"You remember that I can kick your ass, right?"

Trevor's lackeys had to grab his shoulders and yank him back before he could get anywhere. Jonas knew better than to think age had made these guys mature out of picking any fight they could. No. They stopped because Andrew was still standing on his deck, watching them.

Trevor looked up at Jonas, then shook his head. "You're lucky boss man is watching you right now, or you would be dead in the water."

"Why? Are you hiding something?"

"Jonas, let's just go." Taylor grabbed him by his sleeve, trying to pull him away from the confrontation.

His feet felt as if they were weighed down with irons. He didn't want to move, but ultimately, he did. He had to. This was not the time for a fight even if there was a chance he could win it. Which there wasn't.

He couldn't fight when there was a baby to think about, and he needed to get Taylor out of here before they drew too much of a crowd. As he passed Trevor, he noticed some marks on his arms looked like the tell-tale signs of a run-in with the wolves at one point. Jonas wondered if the wolves could be threatening Trevor if he didn't help them. Even dickheads like Trevor still had family to protect. People to watch out for.

He and Taylor rushed inside her trailer. Jonas locked the door behind him, but he knew that wouldn't stop a shifter who wanted to get in.

"You think they know?" Taylor asked, her voice low, a little scared even.

Jonas put his finger to his mouth. He wasn't about to take the risk that someone was listening in on them.

Taylor nodded and immediately rushed into action, packing clothes, blankets, diapers, packets of baby food, wipes, powders, and an assortment of other things Jonas wasn't sure if they needed at that moment, but what did he know about caring for a baby?

"Are you ready?"

"Almost." Taylor grabbed something else out of the crib—a Piglet doll, and stuffed it into her bag. Jonas took the bag from her and slung it around his shoulder before the three of them were out the door.

Where they were immediately stopped by the number of people standing between them and the truck.

If Taylor had been a cat shifter, she was pretty sure her hackles would have gone up. If her daughter wasn't in her arms, there was no way in hell she would have been able to keep her head about her as Trevor, Andrew, and the entire Council of Elders stood in a circle around her door.

Meg groaned, as though she was picking up on the strange frequency around her and didn't like it.

"It's okay, baby. Momma's here," and she wasn't about to let a damned thing happen to her daughter.

Jonas dropped the bag, taking a step forward. "Hey, guys. What's going on?"

Taylor looked to Andrew. He looked sorry. He pressed his lips together, but he at least had the decency to look her in the eyes while he betrayed her.

"Andrew?"

Andrew shook his head. "I'm sorry, sweetie. I didn't know about this until this morning."

"Horse shit," Jonas snapped, his shoulders bunching. "Are you fucking kidding me? Are there even any wolves involved in those fires at all?"

"There are," Trevor said, nodding. "And they're going to come here and burn everything down if we don't play nice."

"What does play nice mean?" Taylor asked. "Does it mean I can't take my little girl out of here?"

"None of us can take our little girls out of here," Trevor snapped, glaring at her. "You're not special."

Taylor grit her teeth at that.

No, she wasn't special, and logically she knew her daughter wasn't any better than the young kids who lived and played here either, but if given a choice…

She would still want to take Meg and leave here and damn all the consequences.

Apparently, all it took for Taylor to realize she was a terrible, selfish person was to have a kid of her own, and to realize what she was willing to do for her offspring.

"None of you have to stay here and put up with this. None of you have to be terrorized," Jonas said.

"That's simple for you to say," said one of the elders. Taylor noted the way the older man's hand clenched tightly around the cane he held. Thick knuckles white around the wood as he glared at Jonas. "You're not one of us. You don't have any connections to the land or desire to fight for what's yours."

Taylor winced at that, noting the clench in Jonas' jaw.

"You think that, do you?"

He wouldn't fight an old man, would he? An elderly shifter was probably one of the few shifters Jonas had a chance at besting in a fight.

Though that didn't mean he was set to win, much as Taylor hated to admit that.

"Jonas," Taylor put her hand on his arm, stunned when he yanked away from her.

"Many of you have children here. Just go to the damned police! Trevor! Describe the people who did that to you. You can help put these bastards away and get this over with before someone gets hurt."

"Someone was hurt, you prick! Me! And that fire near the entrance of our sloth? That was a warning, so was the fire up there!" Trevor pointed a long finger up the mountain where smoke still blackened the sky.

Jonas didn't seem impressed. "So what do they want from you? For you to help them get the conduit?"

Taylor tried not to look at him when he mentioned the C word. She didn't want anyone around her knowing she'd met with the people the wolves were searching for. That she might know a little more than she was letting on. It would only spell disaster for her, Meg, and Jonas.

"I know you met up with outsiders. Two wolves and a fox? I heard the whole damned thing."

Taylor sucked back a heavy gasp. She backed up a step, though she felt as though she'd been punched.

Trevor was always known for getting around, for being in places he wasn't supposed to be. For being stealthy and sneaky. It was his best-damned trait. She should have known. She should have seen this coming a mile away. Of course, he could overhear something she didn't want him hearing.

Jonas stepped in front of her, blocking off Trevor's view. It didn't help. Taylor still felt cold all over. Her gaze fell to Andrew. This time, Andrew wouldn't look at her.

No. No. This couldn't be happening.

The head elder spoke. "We need to know where the conduit is."

"Ask Trevor," Jonas snapped. "I'm done here."

"You will go nowhere."

All the elders put their hands up, mirroring the actions of the head elder.

That chill deepened in Taylor's gut.

She'd always thought of these people as being helpers for the sloth. They were here to administer advice on marriage and vegetable gardens and help the alpha handle unruly cubs whose parents weren't all that involved.

Seeing them as they were now, as one unit, gave Taylor an idea of how powerful they really were. These weren't the people who convinced her to walk away from Jonas when he wanted to leave for the city. These weren't just well-meaning elderly shifters that the younger generations looked up to because of their age and wisdom. They had real power in the sloth, and Andrew seemed powerless to do or say anything against them.

Or he was unwilling to say anything against them. Taylor couldn't decide which was worse.

"You're going to help hand over an innocent woman to a pack of murderous wolves? To save yourselves?" she asked.

Andrew closed his eyes. "It's not just me, Taylor. Look at everyone else around here. You're not the only one with a baby to think of."

She flinched at that, and was too much of a coward to look around when Andrew gestured to the rest of the sloth.

The elders weren't having it. "Look at us!"

She jumped, then did as she was told almost against her own will.

She looked around at Trevor, the elders, Andrew, and the other bears who had come to stand around and see what the fuss was about. Some looked on as though they were as shocked to learn all of this as Taylor was. Others seemed resigned, but the one thing that stood out was the cubs in attendance. Toddlers, a few of the younger cubs who came to her daycare from time to time. The older kids, and then the teenagers.

Taylor had wanted to think only about Meg, but these sloth cubs were her family too. She couldn't leave it all behind like Jonas could, she owed her sloth and these kids more than that. Having to look at them put her to shame.

Jonas wasn't having it. "That's enough. She gets the point."

"You were going to leave us, too."

Jonas narrowed his eyes at everyone surrounding them. "I was never part of the sloth, remember? There was nothing for me to leave behind."

"Don't be stupid," Trevor snapped, but then followed up with nothing else.

Taylor was too upset with herself, with everything around her, to even look too much into what Jonas had just said. To wonder if he'd feel the same way if she hadn't agreed to leave with him. Were her and Meg something to leave behind? Either way, it wasn't the time for her to get hung up on petty insecurities.

"Andrew," Taylor called out to him. At first, she thought he was going to avoid looking at her, but eventually, he met her gaze. "Andrew, don't do this."

"It's my job to watch out for our people."

"By keeping them from leaving? Keeping them prisoners here?" Jonas asked. "You were the one who got up and told everyone that you cared about their safety."

"I do."

"You said you cared about Taylor and Meg. You supported her choices before, but when she chooses to take her baby and leave with me, that's where you draw your line?"

Taylor couldn't stand the fighting. Everything felt too personal, too close to breaking out into something that could get violent. There was a time when she would have jumped into any fight with the boys, but that was long ago. Holding a baby in her arms, her baby, had changed all that.

Now she looked to the elders, to the people charged with guiding the bears who lived here, and they stared back at her with the same knowing expressions they always did.

As if they knew better and thought it would be just a matter of time before she could see it their way.

Taylor didn't want to see it their way. She wanted to get out of here. To leave this place with her baby and the father of that child.

"Andrew, I never told you this, but you've helped me out so much over the last two and half years. Longer than that. You've been like a father to me at times, and I've always…I loved and respected you like a father, too. Please, please, I want to go with Jonas. I don't want this for Meg. I don't want to risk being here when fires are being set like this. If the other parents feel the same way, let them leave too. If it's not safe, then let us go."

Something changed in Andrew's eyes. His chest puffed out as he inhaled a deep breath through his nose, but then he deflated when he glanced towards the elders. They clearly had their hooks that deeply into him.

Or maybe he'd never had control to begin with. Maybe they'd only let him, and the sloth, think he had.

"Taylor, nothing will happen to you or Meg. I swear. I will personally make sure of that. All right?"

Now she wanted to cry. Her image of her alpha and her sloth was being shattered. The life she'd invested in, to the point of spending years away from Jonas, was crumbling around her.

"All we have to do is mind our own business. Stay here, don't pay attention to any of the wolves or the conduit stuff. They'll leave us alone," Andrew said.

Taylor shook her head. She couldn't look at him anymore. She didn't see her friend. She didn't see the man who let her cry on his shoulder. She saw a stranger, and she couldn't process that.

"And if we don't agree to that?" Jonas asked. "Because you're all out of your damned minds if you think any of you are getting near Taylor."

Her heart did a painful twist. Even after all of this, after staring down an entire sloth full of angry bears, he was still willing to put himself between her and danger.

"We just want you to sit back and relax for a little," Andrew said. "Don't go into anything irrationally. We can work this out."

"How?" Jonas demanded.

Trevor sneered, liking this a little too much. "How about you get the fuck back inside and stop talking? You're not in charge here, asshole."

"Neither are you, shithead," Taylor snapped.

"Shit," Meg said, and any other time, Taylor might have wanted to curl into a ball of humiliation and die for that, but as she was being shoved back inside the door to her home, all she could think about was how she was going to get her little girl out of this.

CHAPTER 17

onas had to remind himself again and again that he was just a subhuman. He was stronger than most humans without any gym time, and he could damn near hold onto the hose by himself without a second man to steady him, but much as Trevor's face was begging to be punched in, Jonas wouldn't last too long against him.

He had to take it easy. He let Trevor search him and take his phone, growling at the man when he went to do the same to Taylor.

Andrew was nothing but apologetic to Taylor, as if that somehow changed anything. She seemed to have enough of this garbage, though.

"Andrew, it smells like burning wood the second you walk outside. You want me to stay here?"

"I don't have a choice, sweetheart."

"Stop calling me that!"

Meg let out an anguished wail. Even if she weren't a little shifter, it would be next to impossible not pick up on her mother's emotions like this. She knew something was wrong, but the poor kid didn't know what, and Jonas' heart ached for her while Taylor yelled at Andrew.

And, pathetic coward that he was, Andrew stood there and took it.

Jonas was half tempted to take Meg from Taylor's arms so she could really unload on Andrew. He got the feeling that if Taylor tried attacking him, then Andrew would do little to defend himself.

That would be amazing to watch.

"Bet you think you're gonna do something right now, don't 'cha?"

Jonas ignored Trevor. The little peckerhead was still trying his damnedest to bring some reaction out of Jonas. A reaction he was not willing to give the other man.

"Come on, you can admit it. You're looking at Andrew like you want to go ape shit on him."

"Nope, not working, Trevor."

"Sure it is." Trevor pointed a dirty finger less than an inch from Jonas' nose. "I can see it all over you. I'm getting under your skin."

"Wasn't talking about that." Jonas couldn't resist. "I was talking about how your daddy still isn't proud of you."

He should have resisted harder, because the fist that caught Jonas in the gut caught him off guard, even when he saw it coming.

The air whooshed out of his lungs. He couldn't even make out the things Trevor was yelling at him because Jonas was too busy trying not to puke all over Taylor's floor as he coughed and sucked back every sip of fresh air he could get.

He could hear Meg crying, and Taylor yelling. Andrew shouted something. Jonas tried to push himself to his feet, if only to stop the bastard from taking his worthless aggression out on her, but then a strong hand pressed down on his shoulder, keeping Jonas on his knees.

He didn't have the strength to get back up, and his vision only just stopped tunneling, so he didn't want to take the risk of anything else happening to Meg if he fought back.

Eventually, Andrew pushed Trevor out the front door. He seemed to be yelling at the other man the entire time, as if he was angry with him. Maybe he was, but Jonas liked it so much more when Taylor slammed the door behind the both of them and locked it when they were out.

Meg was still crying, but she was safe in her mother's arms as Taylor came back to him, kneeling and checking on him while he coughed up the last of his pride.

"Are you all right?"

"Yeah," Jonas said, feeling very much as though he was choking on those words. He was a little, but he was more embarrassed than anything. "Sorry."

"Don't be. Jesus, he could have broken your ribs."

Jonas didn't want to hear about how fragile he was when he tried to protect Taylor and Meg from all of this. He pushed himself to his feet, ignoring the screaming pull in his stomach as he stretched out those muscles.

"Are you all right to stand?"

Jonas cleared his throat, rubbing at his stomach. "I'll be good. He just sucker punched me is all."

Jonas also knew he was going to have a nasty, bear-shaped bruise on his abdomen by tomorrow morning, and he was going to be in a lot more pain then, so he had to hurry up and get through this before everything went to complete shit.

"We have to get you out of here." Much as Jonas hated that his little girl was crying like this, at least her cries gave cover to everything else he was saying. If Trevor or anyone else happened to be listening with their ears to the outside walls, hoping to catch Jonas and Taylor plotting their escape, then a baby crying was a plausible excuse rather than a TV turned up too high.

Taylor rocked her daughter, but it didn't seem to do much to help as Meg wailed.

He touched her back, wishing he could do something, even if the cries were useful.

The cries continued.

"How are we supposed to leave when they took our phones? My laptop?"

"Do you have anything else in the house? A landline they might've forgotten about?"

Taylor shook her head, the helplessness in her eyes, in the air around her as she tried to comfort her daughter, came through hard. Taylor's eyes swam. She rubbed at her forehead and looked around her own home as though she couldn't understand how it came to be this way, how she'd become trapped here.

Jonas pressed his hands to her shoulders. "I'll figure this out."

Taylor yanked herself away from him. "How? How are you going to get Meg and me out of here? We didn't even…I didn't see this coming. How could I not see this coming?"

"It's not your fault."

"It is my fault! You told me so many times that I needed to go to the police. You told me this would…you said…"

"And you did go. You went to the police with me. You gave your statement; that was all I asked you to do."

Taylor didn't seem to be hearing him. He grabbed her shoulders again, holding on tight. He had no intention of ever letting this woman go. This was the mother of his child. His mate. He turned his back on her once, and he was never going to do that again.

"Taylor, look at me. Hey, look at me."

She did. Her eyes glowed a golden brown, showing how close she was to losing all control.

"We're going to get out of this. So is Meg. All three of us. We're fine. You hear me?"

"How are we fine? We're stuck in here, and Andrew went crazy, and he's letting the elders walk all over him like he thinks they're in charge."

Jonas knew what she meant. Elders were supposed to have some weight in a pack or clan, sloth or skulk, but they weren't the ones who ran things. Everyone knew that. Even the humans. Something else was happening here.

"Maybe they made a deal with the wolves behind Andrew's back. Something could be making him do that, but come on, you know Andrew. He wouldn't hurt you, and I doubt he would ever want to hurt Meg."

At this point, Jonas wasn't entirely sure of that, but it was the only thing he had to work with to keep Taylor calm, so he was going to stick with that story.

"We'll figure out what this is, but we have to keep our heads clear and our eyes open. There's going to be a way out of this, and when we find it, we have to take it. Understand?"

Taylor didn't look as though she wanted to wait for anything to happen. She looked as though she wanted to take Meg and start running in a state of panic right now.

So Jonas was pleased when she inhaled a deep breath and reluctantly nodded. "All right."

Just by looking at her, Jonas could tell her heart was still hammering. He could see it in the fluttering pulse at the side of her throat. He could even hear it a little, and his hearing wasn't that good compared to a shifter's.

"I'll get you both through this. All right? I promise. I'll think of something."

Even now his mind raced, but Jonas couldn't think of much of anything that could be done. He knew people were watching Taylor's trailer. They were listening, hoping to hear something. And making sure they didn't go anywhere.

And that was the problem. Jonas wanted to bust his way out of here. He wanted to roar and pull forward all the strength he had to fight off everyone who would dare stop him and Taylor from leaving here when they wanted to. He was going to to take his mate and daughter to safety.

It wasn't much of a comfort that he knew he wouldn't be able to fight his way out of this situation even if he had been born a shifter. There were too many people to fight against.

If there hadn't been, Andrew might not have bothered going along with what the elders wanted.

The little round, black ears on top of Taylor's head twitched, her spine going suddenly going stiff.

"Do you hear that?"

At first, he didn't, but Jonas strained his ears and waited patiently for whatever it was that caught Taylor's attention to hit him.

Then it did.

Trucks. At least a couple of large vehicles. There were a few of them.

"Andrew expecting someone over?" Jonas marched to the window, pulling the curtain to the side just a crack so he could have a glance outside.

Two white trucks pulled up the dirt road leading out of the bears' territory. Jonas tried to get a look at the plates, but he couldn't make out anything from here. He just saw Andrew standing and waiting for them, and when the trucks stopped and parked in front of him, no less than four men got out.

All of them had wolf ears and tails.

"This is bad."

"What? What is it?" Taylor came to stand next to him, glancing out the window just as Andrew shook the hands of each man. What made it worse was when the elders approached to greet the wolves as well.

As if some sort of agreement had been come to.

"Oh my God. Oh my God, oh my God."

"Don't panic. We can still get out of this."

"How?"

Jonas had no idea, but he was going to think of something. "What else did Trevor and the others take before they left?"

"Uh…" Taylor seemed to struggle with that. "I think just the electronics. Why?"

Jonas hadn't seen anyone spend too much time in the kitchen when they were setting up their kidnapping operation. One guy did walk away with Taylor's wooden block of knives, but Jonas hadn't seen anything else get taken.

He hoped it was because this had been overlooked and not because someone had already been in here before he and Taylor had tried to leave.

He yanked open the top drawer to the left of the sink, and then smiled at what he saw inside.

"They didn't take everything." He pulled out a long, mean-looking butcher knife.

Taylor stepped up beside him, keeping her voice a little quieter now that Meg was starting to tire herself out. "What are you going to do with that?"

"Hopefully nothing. Here, you take this one." She had other knives, including one that was hidden beneath the plastic separator for the forks and spoons. The knife he gave to her had a bright yellow handle, but it also had a matching plastic sheath for it.

That was good. If Jonas was going to give Taylor anything sharp while she had a baby in her arms then at least he could handle knowing there was some protection for Meg.

Taylor hesitated, but then took the knife.

"You'll only use it if you have to. I'll try to keep you out of a position where that's necessary."

Her throat worked in a swallow. "Do you think it will be necessary?"

He hoped not, but with everything going on here, he trusted these people about as much as he trusted a hungry dog next to a steak dinner.

Or a pyro-happy wolf next to a lighter.

"I don't want to hurt anyone, Jonas. This is my sloth. My family."

"She is your family," he whispered, pointing to Meg and wishing she would start crying again so he wouldn't have to hide the sound of his own voice. "If anyone tries anything with her, then your job is to protect her above everything and everyone else."

"Even you?"

He looked at her, his chest aching. "You know the answer to that question."

Taylor winced. Jonas hated to say that to her, but it had to be done. No amount of feeling between them was above the need they both had to protect Meg.

Unfortunately, he didn't get the chance to further prepare her for whatever else might be coming for them, because there was a noise at the door.

Someone was trying to open it, and realizing they couldn't.

Jonas always knew having a door lock while living in a pack of anything was a bit on the pointless side, especially when the door burst open and two of the wolf shifters who had stepped out of the truck, along with Trevor, stepped inside.

And Trevor smiled as though he was getting the best-damned present in the whole world.

Jonas stepped in front of Taylor.

Trevor nodded to them. "He's the one right there who got the police involved. Have at him if you want."

CHAPTER 18

eg started to fuss again as the two wolf shifters came into Taylor's home, mucking it up with a stink that was unfamiliar to her.

Taylor quickly unsheathed her blade, but even then she knew she could only use it as a last resort. She could not fight while holding her child in her arms.

But she had to do something. The two shifters spread out, coming to either side of Jonas.

"You guys don't have to do anything. He's not going to go to anyone or say anything."

"He won't anymore," Trevor sang.

She snapped at him. "Will you shut the fuck up, you pathetic little weasel! No one likes you. No one will ever like you. Especially not your dead dad, so stop trying to act tough already!"

Trevor stepped forward. "You want to say shit to me again, you little—"

He stopped real fast when she pointed the knife at him. "You take one more step towards me, and we'll see how brave you feel when I cut your ears off."

Trevor cursed.

"Yeah, you thought you were careful, did you? Stay the fuck away from me."

"Fuck," Meg said.

"That a girl."

Trevor looked to the two wolf shifters in the room with him. "Well? Aren't 'cha going to do something?"

They chuckled amongst themselves. "Deal with your bitch. Not our fault you can't handle her."

Taylor had never in her life seen the hairs on Trevor's ears bristle that hard, or his face turn that particular shade of red.

It was kind of scary, if she was honest.

She didn't even have to do the threatening after that. Jonas did. "Trevor, I know you're a sad sack of shit, but I swear to God, if you take one step towards her, I will do everything in my power to beat the living piss out of you. Do you understand me?"

"Fuck you, subhuman. You couldn't beat the piss out of my kid sister."

Taylor nearly did a double take. "You don't have a kid sister."

Trevor shrugged and looked at her as if she was ruining some great joke. "If I had one! All right? Christ."

Idiot. God, she couldn't believe she'd ever stood up for him.

She looked to the wolves distrustfully, hating them. "So what do you want? There are no conduits around here for you to rape and impregnate, so you can all go away."

The wolves looked amongst each other, then at her.

"You have the smell of the one who took the conduit from us on you. Tell us where they went and we'll let you go."

Taylor opened her mouth to tell them she had no idea where they went, but Jonas beat her to the answer.

"Her mate's name is Steve Delany; he's a private detective who works in Astraea, and he's got the entire police force behind him, along with his pack of wolves who aren't perverts, so you might as well start looking elsewhere for another conduit because you're not getting that one."

The two wolves looked to Trevor. "Is that true?" asked the bigger of the two males.

Trevor winced, as though there was a threat somewhere in the question.

Maybe there was.

"I think so. I couldn't get that close, but that's pretty much what I heard, too. I think."

Trevor glared at her, as though daring her to contradict him.

Taylor blinked at Trevor, wondering why he didn't tell the wolves where the three men had gone. He'd come back home fairly quickly; maybe he couldn't bring himself to follow after the three shifters when he had to rush back here and rat out her and Jonas.

What an asshole.

Then she got an idea. "Look, you guys, I don't want anything bad to happen to my baby. If you want to know anything, ask, and Jonas and I will tell you everything Trevor kept from you."

Trevor damn near jumped three feet in the air. "What?"

The two wolves looked at Trevor, and he backed up a step, his hands up as though getting ready to ward off an attack. "She-she's lying! I didn't keep anything from you! I swear!"

Part of her felt sorry for this, but another part of her felt alive and powerful. She felt like a warrior ready to lay down her life and safety for her little girl, and she was willing to make this gamble.

Jonas watched on. Either because he had no choice, or he was putting his trust in her that she knew what to do as one of the wolves stepped up to her, ignoring the knife in her hand while his larger counterpart continued to get closer and closer to Trevor.

"This had better be good. What did he hide from us?"

Taylor swallowed. "All right, well, Trevor was there when Steve, the man mated to the conduit you wanted, told us his mate is pregnant with their first child."

Which was something she was totally making up at that moment, but it didn't matter so long as it put all the attention on Trevor, and none of it onto her or Jonas.

"That's a lie! I didn't hear that at all!"

"Trevor, I could see you standing right there. You weren't doing that good of a job hiding. There's no way you didn't hear that."

It had to be the worst lie in the history of lies. Maybe that was why the wolves seemed to believe it. It was such a stupid thing for someone to make up, and too dangerous to risk. That was the explanation Taylor was going to go with as the two wolf shifters turned their backs onto Jonas and Taylor as they suddenly started stalking towards Trevor.

The low growls they let out, along with the way every hair on their tails seemed to stand on end, made it the meanest looking sight Taylor had ever seen, and she was a little sorry to have sicced the wolves after Trevor like that.

Whatever. He would live.

Maybe.

Jonas gestured for the door.

Taylor nodded. Even if they'd face more wolves and bears when they left her trailer, at least they'd be closer to freedom and getting Meg to safety. Hell, she was already planning on shoving Meg into Jonas' arms and having him make a run for it so she could shift into her bear form and give him as much time as he needed to get out of there with their daughter.

They bolted for the door, Jonas skidding in behind her before she could go along with her plans of noble sacrifice.

"Run!" The wolves turned their attention back to them as they realized she and Jonas were making a break for it.

Taylor ran. She wanted to stay, even scared as she was; she didn't want to leave him alone to fight, but she had Meg. It always boiled down to protecting her daughter. So she ran.

Her bear ears picked up the sound of a wolf's high-pitched cry behind her. One of them must have run into the knife Jonas still had. She could see members of her sloth around her as she moved with her child. No one interfered. They watched her go, some looking very much as though they wanted to go with her.

Maybe they didn't think she would get away. Maybe that was why they didn't try stopping her.

She took the road, avoiding the woods for now. If she got lucky, someone might come driving up here. Preferably a non-local who was a little lost. It happened sometimes. She could get a ride.

But if the wolves came for her, she would turn to the woods then.

But she didn't hear anyone coming up behind her. Just the sound of her heavy breathing as she kept her pace steady, and Meg's cries in protest of all the jostling. "It's okay. We're all right." Taylor wasn't sure whose benefit she said it for. "We're okay."

She had to keep going. If she strained her ears hard enough, she could make out the sound of the wolves fighting. She didn't want to think about what they were doing to Jonas, or what he was putting himself through to keep them away from her, to give her enough time.

Five more minutes. Maybe ten. She just had to keep running. She was so close to the main road. There would be more lights there and a better chance of getting a truck to stop for her.

Almost there. Almost.

A bear roared in the background. A noise so terrible and ongoing it made Taylor stop and look back.

Was that...no, it couldn't be. He wouldn't...

Taylor kept going, running away from the danger and horror that was taking place in her sloth's territory.

One foot in front of the other. She repeated it again and again, even when she saw headlights coming up behind her.

She ducked into the trees so she could get a look at the vehicle's driver before asking for help. She was at the part of the woods that had already been burned. The smell of soot here was strong, and she wouldn't have much cover against other shifters who already had next to perfect night vision.

"Taylor! Wait!"

Jonas' voice was the only thing that could have stopped her. She nearly tripped over a burned tree root when spinning around. She could see him, getting out of the truck and limply pulling himself around to the front. He wasn't driving. Someone else was.

Andrew.

"Come on! We have to go."

He waved her over. Even with the way he cradled his arm, he still stood strong. Proud.

Alive.

She ran to him, only just then realizing how badly her side hurt as she gasped for breath, crying.

Jonas opened his good arm, wrapping her and Meg up in it. She felt his lips in her hair and the relief in his voice.

"Let's go."

"You smell like blood."

"I'm fine." He pulled her to the passenger side of the truck, and she realized a lot of the blood was coming from his leg. "Come on."

She didn't fight him on it. Taylor went, pulling herself into the passenger side of the truck and holding Meg on her lap. It put her up close and personal with Andrew, who sat immediately next to her in the driver's seat.

"Hey, kiddo."

Taylor said nothing, and then Jonas groaned as he pulled himself next to Taylor, squishing her between both men.

"Let's get out of here," Jonas rasped, letting his head fall back onto the seat as his good hand rested lightly on Meg's arm.

"You got it." Andrew started to drive, and Taylor had to wonder what planet she was on.

CHAPTER 19

"*L*et me see your arm."

Taylor wasn't ready to look at Andrew to ask what the hell he'd been up to, or why he was bothering with helping them.

"It's fine." It wasn't fine. She could see it in the way his jaw clenched.

"Jonas, please let me see."

He looked at her. She stared back at him. Jonas sighed, leaning a little closer.

The blood wasn't gushing, which was a good sign, but there was still a lot of it, and it was still dark and red and...God, she could smell it. Her inner black bear growled, not at all impressed with the way her mate had been attacked.

She tucked Meg safely in Jonas' good arm, and then pulled some of the torn material of Jonas' jacket and shirt out of the way to get a better look at the wound.

It was a bite wound. He would live, but something had gotten him. She was no doctor, and it wasn't exactly well lit in the truck cab, so she couldn't tell what sort of bite it was. Jonas had the smell of wolves and bears on him, so that didn't help.

"Who was it?" Taylor tried to keep the growl out of her voice and decided to keep from looking back at Andrew. She didn't want to admit that she blamed him for this, but it was there.

"A wolf, but I got him back good, don't worry." He smiled through his pain, but it looked to be genuine. Taylor wasn't so sure how much she trusted that smile, but she would roll with it for now. As long as he didn't look to be in any danger, she would be happy with what he presented her with.

"Found out what the wolves want," Andrew growled.

Taylor looked back at him, trying not to glare, and failing because Jonas' blood was on her free hand, and now she was stuck trying not to touch Meg with it.

"We know what they want. They want a conduit."

Andrew shook his head. "Not just a conduit. They wanted to get someone back. Revenge for someone who wronged a family member. Tale as old as time."

"Revenge?" Taylor didn't know if she believed that. Not after everything she already knew. "We didn't hurt anyone, though. Did we?"

Andrew seemed to take offense to the suspicion in her voice. "Of course we didn't!"

"I thought this was about helping them find the conduit they wanted?" Jonas suddenly hissed, and Taylor yanked her hand back from his arm, only then realizing she was clenching it too damned tight. "I'm sorry!"

Meg fussed again. In a minute or two, she would be full blown crying.

"They did come to me for that, but that wasn't the whole goddamned story," Andrew said. He clenched the steering wheel so hard Taylor worried he might bend it out of shape.

"What did they tell you?" Taylor asked. "Tell me the truth; if you lie to me after the danger you put Meg into—"

"Hey! Don't give me that shit. All right? I kept her safe when those wolves came back here to sniff around. I didn't let a damned thing happen to that little girl, and I never would have. You understand me?"

Taylor growled, but what could she say to that? She still wasn't so sure if she trusted Andrew, but right about now, if her mother had still been around, she might not trust her either.

The person who mattered the most right now was squirming in Jonas' arms. Anyone or anything that behaved suspiciously got little to no benefit of the doubt as far as Taylor was concerned.

"Tell us the whole story, Andrew." Jonas sounded just as pissed off as Taylor felt. "Right now. No bullshit. I want to know what the hell is going on with those stupid wolves. Good people are injured, and some of them are dead."

Taylor winced, remembering those injured in the firehouse. One of whom was a good friend and colleague of Jonas'.

"Apparently, the pack that has the conduit caught a wolf sniffing around her, wanting to make a claim."

Taylor didn't understand where this was going. "And?"

"The conduit's mate didn't like this. He and some buddies caught and tortured the kid for getting too close. Damn near killed him before finally letting him go."

"Kid?" Jonas asked, lifting a brow.

"Not an actual kid, some idiot early twenties type." Taylor had never heard the growl that came from Andrew's voice. It was strange. And it was scary.

"I don't doubt for one minute the wolves played up the story, making their little prick of a friend look more innocent than he actually was, but that's not the point. That kid was the younger brother of his pack's alpha. He goes home covered in blood and crying, and then his big brother wants revenge. They want the conduit, and revenge on the wolf pack that tortured one of their own."

"But they needed to secure alliances before the war started," Taylor surmised.

Andrew nodded. "When we refused to help the first time, the fires started. Now they've set up shop on my fucking territory, and I'm stuck dealing with their shit while trying to keep everyone safe." Andrew looked at her, his eyes narrowed. "You're welcome, by the way."

Taylor's spine stiffened. A sudden wave of shame hit her hard. She had to look away from him just because she didn't like that she'd accused him of something so terrible, that she'd believed he...what? That he might have invited the wolves over? That he might have been involved with the fires this entire time?

Light appeared behind them in the distance. It was a strange thing, to look back and to wonder who was there when Taylor never had to worry about such a thing before in her entire life.

Jonas put his good hand on her shoulder and tried to push her down. At least, that's what Taylor thought he was doing. She couldn't be sure because she was so focused on watching the oncoming headlights that she didn't go down. When the vehicle eventually passed them by, and Taylor was able to see for herself that it was a couple of college-aged girls in the front seat, she relaxed, heaving a sigh when she barely realized she was holding her breath.

"I need to get off this road," Andrew growled. His claws were coming out as he gripped the steering wheel so tight he looked like he was going to bend the wheel. "If they're not getting ready to drive up from behind then they might be trying to chase us down."

"Bring us back to the police station," Jonas said. "We can get everything we need dealt with right there."

Andrew growled a little. Taylor expected a fight for involving the humans, but he nodded. "Yeah, got it."

"You mean you'll take us?" Taylor couldn't believe it. She looked down at Meg, who had stopped fussing, likely due to the comforting rumble of the truck engine.

Things were starting to look up.

Before Andrew could answer, glass shattered inward on the driver's side window.

Everything moved in slow motion. Taylor felt the spray of glass and heat against her face. She turned towards Jonas, trying to protect Meg from the flying shards. Jonas wrapped his arm around her shoulders and pulled her to him. But even without looking back, she felt the teeth snapping behind her, and then Jonas' arms almost didn't seem strong enough to hold onto her as Andrew slammed his foot onto the brake.

The truck screeched and fishtailed. She thought she was going to go flying out the windshield. The momentum pushed her against Jonas instead.

He grabbed onto her, holding tight. She wanted to tell him to hold onto Meg, to keep their baby from being thrown from the vehicle and to not bother with her. But just as fast as the truck was attacked and Andrew slammed on the brakes, it all stopped.

Meg cried, long and loud wails from being disturbed and then being squeezed. Taylor didn't care. She pulled her baby into her arms. Jonas gripped her shoulder with his good arm, tight enough that it should have hurt, but she barely felt it. "Are you all right? Look at me! Are you okay?"

Taylor nodded, looking down at Meg, who was wailing miserably, tears streaming down her chubby cheeks and her soft little bear ears. All Taylor could think about was how happy she was, how utterly grateful she felt, to have her daughter still in her arms. She held Meg a little tighter, even knowing her little girl didn't like it. Taylor kissed her face, her cheeks, and her hair.

Taylor's entire body trembled. She'd been so focused on trying to get away that she didn't think about the lack of a car seat, or how she wasn't buckled in.

Neither was Jonas. Taylor only realized that when his trembling hand released the seatbelt. He must have grabbed onto it, then reached for Taylor the instant Andrew slammed his foot onto the brake.

Which meant he'd held her as tightly as he had with his wounded arm.

His body trembled, and there was so little color in his cheeks considering what had just happened, but he didn't look to be in any pain. No. Jonas seemed as alert and ready as though he was planning on rushing to the nearest house fire so he could put it out.

"You sure you're good?"

The ringing in Taylor's ears eventually came to a stop, and before she could answer, it hit her that there was still someone else in the truck.

"Andrew."

She glanced back at her alpha. Jonas said her name, but he

suddenly sounded so very far away as she looked at the bloody mess that was her leader and friend.

Now she knew why she felt teeth behind her.

With all the blood on his face, the entire left side of his body mangled, she didn't think he would be able to tell her how he felt for a long time.

If ever.

She snapped out of it. "Jesus Christ, Andrew!"

"Don't!"

Jonas grabbed her by the arm, yanking her back before she could grab him, shake him, make sure he was alive.

Please, be alive.

She couldn't hear a heartbeat, but there was still a heavy rumbling all around her and the sounds of Meg's crying.

"Taylor, don't touch him, his foot is still on the brake."

"What?"

Jonas pointed down, and that was when she saw it.

Whether Andrew was dead or not, he was still keeping the truck stopped.

Jonas reached forward, put the truck into park, and then turned the engine. "We have to go."

Taylor reached out, pressing her fingers to the side of his neck. She still couldn't hear a heartbeat, but that could be because Meg wanted to get out of there and was making that need known as loud as she possibly could.

Jonas pulled on her arm. "Taylor! We need to go!"

She didn't want to leave Andrew to die here, if he was even still alive.

"Taylor!"

It wasn't just Jonas screaming for her. Meg's shrieks reminded her that they weren't out of danger yet, and there was no time to spare if they wanted to get away.

Not even for a friend. For someone who was basically her family.

Taylor let herself be pulled outside by Jonas, and she didn't look back at the friend she was leaving behind.

CHAPTER 20

*J*onas knew what he was asking, pulling Taylor away from Andrew. He was more than just a friend to her; he was someone who had taken care of her when she had no one else. He hated to leave Andrew behind, but he'd seen the snapping teeth of the wolf who busted his snout in through the driver's side window, and he didn't want teeth like that coming anywhere near Taylor or his little girl.

His arm started to burn and throb again now that the adrenaline rush of the crash was done and over with.

Fuck. He held onto his arm, trying to hold back the building pressure, but it was difficult.

"Can you smell anything around here? Are they still around?" His sense of smell was ineffective because of all the blood. Taylor's full shifter senses would still be sharp though.

She took in several breaths, holding control of herself despite Meg's hollering in her arms. He wanted to take the little girl to give her mother a chance to focus, but he didn't trust that he would be able to hold her properly with only one arm.

Taylor glanced back at the truck, and then down the road. He could see what she looked at, and he was pretty sure he had a good idea of what it was, but he went to take a closer look anyway.

"Don't." Taylor's eyes were wide. She shook her head. "Don't look."

"Is it dead?"

"I think so, but just...stay away from it. Please."

He wanted to stay back, but he couldn't. Something inside of him compelled to go over there and make sure for himself that it wasn't about to chase after them.

As he approached, he saw the wolf was a big one. It seemed lifeless; the chest didn't rise and fall with any breathing. There wasn't even any sign that the damned thing had been running at all. Even the best of shifters panted for breath when they'd been running like that.

And this was one deathly still.

Jonas could see why when he stood right next to it.

Its tail and hind leg were both mangled. When it crashed into the truck and tried to kill them, it must have gotten caught in the back tire and pulled under, crunching its middle.

That was gross.

Jonas sneered down at the body.

Too bad Andrew couldn't have turned this fleabag into roadkill before it slashed his throat open.

"Jonas, we need to go, please. I can hear others coming."

He nodded. The pain in his arm flared up again. This one must have been faster than the rest, but it didn't matter now because he had to get his mate and child out of here. To safety.

He turned and ran back to where Taylor stood. She reached her hand out. He took it, stunned with the strength she gripped his hand with. "Thank you."

"For what?"

Taylor didn't say. When she pulled him into the woods, he let her lead the way. She was the one with a bear shifter's sense of smell. She would know the best direction to go.

God, Jonas wished he had his ax right about now.

"Can we make it into town?"

Taylor didn't say. Meg wouldn't stop wailing. He wanted to quiet her, but he didn't know a thing about how to keep babies silent. He didn't blame the little girl for being upset after all that had happened, but at the same time, silence would give them a better chance of getting away. She was a siren call to anyone and anything that wanted to hunt them down.

"Taylor, can we make it into town?" Her lack of an answer didn't bode well with him.

He intended on getting her to answer him, except she suddenly stopped, thrust Meg into his arms before he could say a word about it, and backed off.

"What are you doing?" He focused on holding the little girl with his good arm, using his bad one to keep her balance. "Taylor, come on, we've got to move."

"You're not going to get away with Meg like this. I'll hold them off."

His gut clenched. When she shifted into her black bear form, he wanted to yell at her for even thinking it would be a good idea to do something like that without his say.

"Taylor! Don't even think about it! Come on! Right now!"

She needed to listen to him. He needed to get her over here. To get her back before she did something they were both going to regret the hell out of.

He couldn't lose her.

"Taylor!"

She didn't listen. The bear regarded him and Meg, snorted, then turned and faced the sounds of the howls floating up in the distance.

The wolves were almost here.

Meg shrieked louder, as though she knew something was amiss. Her chubby arms reached out as the bear began to charge, but Taylor stopped short when a red fox jumped into her path.

Jonas didn't wait for something else to happen. He rushed forward. Meg still screamed in his arms, but he couldn't stop. He had to get to the black bear before she ran off. Jonas put his hand onto her fur when he made it to her, ignoring the heat and throb in his arm.

"Don't leave. Your daughter needs you."

Taylor seemed to be having a staring contest with the fox. He looked at it when Taylor refused to pay him attention. The fox was dark in color. The only bit of orange seemed to be in a puff on its chest.

He narrowed his eyes at those ears. Wasn't that…

The fox shifted, revealing a slender woman, beautiful—although to him she didn't have anything on Taylor—with dark brunette hair and matching dark fox ears on her head, her dark tail waiving around behind her.

How she managed to move around in jeans that tight was beyond him, but he recognized this woman. This was the woman from the station where he'd found the injured and dead men.

Jonas' first instinct was to step in front of Taylor. He had to stop himself when he realized he was still holding onto his screaming daughter. "What do you want?"

"We have to get out of here." She reached into the pocket of her leather jacket, producing a phone. She showed it to him, and to Taylor. "You met up with my brother and a few friends earlier, right?"

She showed off the picture. He saw Link there, and Steve.

"You're Zelda?"

"That's me."

He still wasn't sure this meant he should trust her, and Jonas found himself holding onto Meg a little tighter despite her screaming. "So what do you want?"

"For you to come with me." She pocketed the phone. "You saved my mate's life. Those people are chasing you. I can smell them coming."

Taylor snorted, as though she agreed with the statement.

Another howl, sounding slower than the previous one, confirmed this.

"Tell me that brother and friends of yours are around here?" Jonas wouldn't mind having the backup right about now.

Zelda shook her head. "They don't know I'm here. Link would kill me. My uncle would help him. I came because it was stupid for them to leave you alone. I just wanted to get close and make sure everything was all right. It's not, so come on."

She started to move, running through the woods in a completely different direction from the road and the sounds of the howls. Jonas looked at Taylor. The bear stared back at him as though she didn't want to trust a woman who just appeared out of nowhere.

Jonas got that, but they didn't have time to think this over. "We have to. For Meg." He chased after the fox woman without glancing back, hoping that Taylor would follow. He smiled when he heard the snorting and snuffling of the bear chasing after him; then he spotted it in his peripheral vision.

He didn't look at Taylor. If he smiled at her right now, it might rub her the wrong way that they were changing course. Even though he wished she would get back into her human shape, he was glad for this.

She wanted to fight the wolves and protect her daughter. This mama bear was going to have to cool it on that one because Jonas did not want her doing that. Taylor could stay in her bear shape all she wanted, waiting for something to attack them, but so long as it didn't come down to that, Jonas was all right.

He had to start paying attention to where he was putting his feet. He might be subhuman, but it was getting to the point where it was too dark for even him to see properly.

And Taylor growled at him every time he caught himself tripping. Meg didn't appreciate that either. Still, he managed to keep up. "Where are you taking us?"

"To my car."

Car? There were no roads out here. Unless one had been built when he was away?

Eventually, with the howls behind them getting closer and closer, they made it to what was definitely not a road. It was more of a path. Probably something the odd hiker and animal used. The car sat there, parked, taking up almost all the space there was for it.

It was as though the trees were trying to hug the damned thing. Or swallow it up.

"You've got to be shitting me."

Another howl.

Close. So close he worried one of the bastards would get the jump on him.

Taylor growled, a dangerous noise, as she looked behind her. She might even be able to see their shadows closing in.

Jonas went to the passenger side of the car. It was difficult to open the door without the branches of the trees immediately trying to get in, but he kept his eye on Taylor as Zelda managed to pull herself into the driver's side of the vehicle.

When she started the engine and Taylor still was not inside of the car, Jonas began to to worry.

"Taylor! Come on!"

If this fox girl tried to drive away without her...

Then Jonas would put Meg into the car and let the both of them go because he wasn't about to run away when his mate needed backup.

Zelda didn't seem to enjoy the wait any more than Jonas did. She yelled out of the driver's side window. "Hurry up!"

Taylor glanced back, as though finally realizing that time was of the essence. She shifted so fast that Jonas could have blinked and missed it. Her eyes stayed a bright shade of gold, however. The animal was still very much there, just beneath the surface and ready to fight if need be.

Finally. She pulled open the door to the back passenger seat and got in. Jonas did at the same time. His ass was barely in place when Zelda hit the gas.

Not one second too soon either. He'd just managed to get the door shut and locked, and was looking back at Taylor, debating if he should kiss her or yell at her, when he caught sight of the wolves running onto them.

"Drive faster," he commanded.

Taylor looked back, too. Jonas heard her growling.

Zelda floored it. He felt the tires spin, and the vehicle fishtail a bit while dust and rocks spit up all around them. The dirt road with all of its bumps and dips prevented her from going as fast as Jonas would have liked, but they kept ahead of the wolves. It was only seconds, but it seemed forever, before the pack grew smaller and smaller behind them, until they were out of view and far enough gone that Jonas could breathe again.

Taylor looked at him. The gold was still in her eyes, but there was something more vulnerable there too. She didn't seem ready for a fight anymore. She looked as though she couldn't believe they'd just escaped.

Then she took note of her child.

"Baby, come here."

Taylor held her hands out. Jonas didn't hesitate to help Meg into her arms. The crying quieted slightly. It only made sense that Meg would be more comfortable in the arms of her mother. She still didn't know Jonas.

The ache he would have felt over coming to terms with that wasn't there. Jonas was more concerned with the woman behind the wheel.

"Tell me what your pack or skulk or whatever has to do with those wolves setting these fires. Right now."

Zelda clenched her hands around the wheel. "All right."

CHAPTER 21

The road didn't get any less dark or bumpy as Zelda started talking. Jonas was still acutely aware of everything around him. Every moving shadow, every scratch on the side of the car from the reaching tree branches. If one of those wolves appeared and tried busting through the windows again, he was going to be ready.

"So because your ex-husband killed your alpha you ran away and then found your natural mate, who happens to be a bodyguard. Then your mate's best friend was attacked by shifters, changed into a wolf shifter, and found his mate who turned out to be a conduit being stalked by a whole other pack of wolves who may or may not be connected to your old pack. This guy, Steve, helped torture one of their members for attempting to rape his mate...Jesus Christ, am I getting this right so far?" Jonas looked back at Taylor to make sure he wasn't hearing things, and when she gave him a similar look of disbelief, he almost didn't believe it.

Zelda's neck tightened. She nodded. "That's basically it. Yeah. Yeah..."

She sounded embarrassed. Jonas wasn't sure why she didn't seem worried. She had every reason to be worried right about now, considering the wolf shifters who were out there wanted to tear into him and Taylor.

He didn't even want to think about the fact that he'd left Andrew behind...

Taylor leaned forward.

"I didn't know any of this. I thought those wolves just wanted us to help them get the conduit they wanted. I never heard anything about a little brother being tortured."

Taylor looked at Jonas. "I swear I never knew that."

Jonas nodded. "I believe you."

Taylor had managed to get Meg to quiet down a little. She hiccupped a little, her chubby little face still wet with tears, and she was gripping her mother's tear-stained shirt with tiny, fiercely-clenched hands.

Jonas nearly reached out to touch her, but he doubted the little girl would want anyone other than her mother after what happened.

So he kept his hands to himself.

"I believe you. You and Andrew are close, but I don't think he would have been comfortable with telling you everything that was going on."

Especially as the alpha of the clan. Every alpha kept a few things to himself. That was just the way things worked with them. They wanted what was best for their packs and clans; they made deals, they kept secrets.

This was apparently one of them.

The wolf pack had come asking for help in retrieving a conduit they wanted, but they also wanted revenge on that same conduit and her mate for the torture of the alpha's little brother.

Jonas didn't need to have siblings to know the lengths some siblings would go to, to defend each other. Or get their revenge.

"The fires weren't all about Andrew's refusal to help. They were trying to lure you and your friends out of hiding, weren't they?"

"Something like that," Zelda said. "My skulk isn't far from here either. Neither is Jackson's pack. This was supposed to be a warning to everyone. They'll burn it all down, even their own land to show us how serious they are. They just want us to burn with them at this point."

"Jesus," Taylor breathed.

Jonas hated this more and more. Why couldn't this shit be simple? Why was nothing ever easy?

Bad guys wanted to get their hands on a conduit. Perfect. He could wrap his mind around that one, no problem.

Bad guys wanted to get their hands on a conduit, and get revenge for a tortured relative, sure... but going on to destroy acres of their own land?

"Wait, this means they're nearby. This is a local pack."

Zelda nodded. "Yeah."

"So, where are we going?" Taylor asked.

"Somewhere safe." The conviction in her voice was so firm Jonas almost trusted her. He was still wary, but with the werewolves chasing after him, and Taylor half ready to go charging into action, he wasn't so sure if he had much of a choice.

He wasn't about to let Taylor rush off and get killed, leaving him and Meg behind. Forget that.

Taylor barely seemed capable of holding back her inner bear even now. She pushed Meg back into Jonas' arms, which was something the little girl clearly wanted no part of, if the way she started crying again was any indicator. He felt weird holding her away from her mother, but the black fur starting to come in through Taylor's pores gave him the feeling that she was getting ready for a fast transformation in case it turned out they couldn't trust Zelda after all.

Or she just couldn't hold it back with the stress she was under.

Jonas looked at Zelda. She kept her eyes on the road, but he knew she was aware of the way he looked at her. "If this turns out to be some kind of trap or trick, it won't matter that I'm a subhuman. I will find a way to make you and everyone you love pay for it."

She didn't cower at the threat. He wasn't sure whether or not that was a good sign. Instead, Zelda nodded. "Understood."

They drove into the night, though it wasn't lost on Jonas the way Zelda's fox ears and Taylor's bear ears both twitched when another long, watery howl sounded off behind them.

When Zelda told them she was taking them someplace safe, Taylor didn't think the woman would actually take them to the local motel where Taylor worked before she opened up her daycare.

She came to a stop in front of one of the doors marked one-one-nine.

"You've got to be kidding me."

"Nope." Zelda killed the engine and exited the vehicle, taking the keys with her before anyone could ask more questions.

Jonas looked at her. "You can take Meg, and I'll go check it out."

She bristled at that. "And what do you think you're going to do if a group of shifters are in there waiting for you?"

"I can hold off a few people, give you and Meg the chance to get out of here. Or we can steal the car and get out of here together. I don't mind either way, just so you know."

The selfish part of her wanted to take that offer, but one look into Meg's unhappy face was enough to push her out of the car and towards the motel room, despite Jonas' protests.

She felt him fall into step beside her. "If anyone tries anything,

Jonas, you're the one who's going to take Meg and run for it. Understand me?" She already had her claws ready.

He glared at her but said nothing.

She had no idea how Zelda or her friends had managed to stay here without the wolf shifters knowing about it, but that could mean there wasn't a lot of time to stick around here. If that were the case, Taylor would pry those car keys from Zelda's fingers herself and make sure Jonas had them.

If he could drive, then his chances for escape would be better.

Taylor just wished she could get her hands on a car seat so Meg would have something safer to ride in, but beggars couldn't be choosers.

She pounded on the door.

It opened for her before her fist finished slamming on the wood.

Jackson stood there. He didn't look remotely impressed to see her, but considering what she'd just gone through, the feeling was mutual.

Taylor inflated her courage, ignoring the reminder that she'd met this man only once, and that was on the side of the road after getting caught making love to her mate. She knew nothing about him that made her believe he was an ally. "Hi. I hear it's safer to be here right now." Her nose picked up scents that indicated several people waited inside.

He nodded. "It might be."

Taylor was not about to let her daughter into that room before she had a few things out of the way. "How do we know you're not working with the wolves? That this isn't some trap?"

The man looked at her. The wolf ears on top of his bald head twitching. He raised a brow at her before looking back at Jonas.

"It's a fair question, we don't know you people," Jonas said, sounding irritable. He didn't enter the room, which was good since he was still the one holding onto Meg.

Taylor was so damned happy he had her back on this. She didn't know what she would have done if he didn't.

"We all want the same thing. A stop to the wolves," Jackson said. "By any means necessary."

Taylor blinked at that. "That sounds real safe. Like the motto of a hoard of outlaws." She couldn't hide how much she distrusted this whole thing, so why bother with trying?

"I can assure you; you are safe here," Jackson said. "The wolves want our heads, too."

"Aren't you a wolf?" Taylor looked at his ears.

Jackson grinned at her. "If these wolves were in my pack, they wouldn't even think about doing half the things they were doing now. They would know there would be consequences. Not all packs have that."

She couldn't shake the weird feeling she had about this guy. Taylor didn't want to be anywhere near him. "Right, Jonas, I still say we can steal the car and get out of here without them."

Jonas inhaled a deep breath, closed his eyes, then looked at her. "Might not be the best thing to say in front of them, sweetheart."

He hadn't smiled at her and called her sweetheart like that in a long time. Strange how she was noticing the little things right when this was entirely not the time.

She smiled right back at him. "I don't care what these people think of me, sweetheart," she said back, batting her eyes before looking right at Jackson. "If they fuck around with Meg or me or you, then I'll take everything they've got and leave them for dead."

After what happened to Andrew, she wasn't about to take the risk that anything else would go wrong.

Jackson smiled. "I like your woman."

"Yeah, great, keep your eyes to yourself, pal."

The people inside the room apparently got sick of the exchange, because a male voice called out to them. "Jackson, will you stop that."

"Let them in already," Zelda's voice snapped. "They're leaving their scent all over out there."

Which was true.

Jackson opened the door wider, revealing his friends inside. Zelda was there, along with the two other men Taylor had met before with Jackson; Link and Steve.

They stared at her with a strange hesitation. As though they didn't know what to do with Taylor or Jonas now that they were here.

Taylor hesitated. Jonas seemed to be waiting for her to make the decision. It was Zelda who was able to get her to come in.

"Come on, before your scent gets out too much." She waved them over.

Maybe it was because it was another woman saying it, but Taylor found the power to step over the threshold. Once inside, Jonas followed her with Meg.

When Jackson closed the door, her inner wild animal puffed itself up.

"Just so you all know, if any of you try anything to hurt that little girl, I can turn into a bear, a big one, and it can do a lot of damage before any of you get anywhere near here. Understand?"

Zelda shook her head, her eyes wide, as though she was hurt Taylor would suggest such a thing. "No one here is going to hurt your baby."

"And you wouldn't be able to carry through with the threat even if we were intimidating her," Jackson said.

Taylor decided she didn't like him. She glared at the other man as he stepped into the center of the room. The others in the room looked at him with equal parts shock and disgust.

Steve stepped forward. His trimmed auburn hair and three-day old shave let Taylor know it had been a while since he'd rested. He looked like he might have been in a scuffle or even a full-blown fight. "Please ignore my idiot friend here. He doesn't human too well."

"No kidding, can you at least tell him he can take his attitude and shove it where..." She trailed off, suddenly aware of something that had been unknown to her before.

Steve was a shifter. He didn't have the ears or the tail, but she felt it in the air. It was so evident by smell, now that he stood so close to her in this confined space.

"You're a wolf." She stepped away. Taylor kept looking up at his head, waiting for something to appear to show her what she already knew. "How?" "I was turned. No ears and tail for me." Steve scratched at his hair, smiling bashfully, and she wondered if it were something he wished he could have. "Couldn't you tell the last time we met?"

She ignored the question. "Turned. And you're the one who tortured the wolf's brother?"

The smile immediately slipped from Steve's face.

Taylor looked at Zelda. "You said your mate's friend's name was Steve, right? The guy who was involved in what happened?"

"I said that."

Zelda looked a little unsure about admitting to that now. In fact, she looked as though she didn't want to be here, period.

Taylor looked back at Steve, then backed up towards Jonas. She was finally starting to piece together everything she'd learned from Andrew, and Zelda, and Steve himself. Starting to understand the depth of trouble that these shifters had brought to her sloth. "Forget this. Let's get out of here."

"Baby—"

"No, this is the guy who brought all this down on us. You tortured some kid? Are you serious? Why am I even in the same room as you?"

Steve narrowed his eyes. "What do you mean kid? What did you tell her?" He looked at Zelda, who shrugged her shoulders helplessly.

"She told us everything. That the wolves are here for your mate, and that the two of you tortured some kid who went after her, and now his big brother is punishing my sloth, went after my alpha because you couldn't control your fucking temper!"

Taylor could barely control her temper either. Otherwise, she never would have sworn like that when her daughter was within hearing distance.

"I didn't say he tortured a kid. Just because he was a younger brother to the alpha doesn't mean he had some youth of innocence to hide behind."

"I don't care."

Ever since Taylor had Meg, anyone under the age of twenty had seemed like a kid to her. Which she knew was a strange way to think of it considering her own age.

Jonas stepped next to her. "Taylor, we need these people."

"No, we don't. How do we know where they draw the line if they're willing to torture?" She didn't look at her daughter. Taylor had her sights on the bastard in front of her, and she wasn't about to look away in case any backstabbing occurred.

"Uh, should we maybe rethink having these people around here?" Link asked. He didn't give off an alpha vibe, which was probably why she'd been able to ignore that he was there until now.

"No," Zelda said. "The wolves are after them now, too. Personally. They've got a baby. We can't just throw them out after we got them involved."

"I wish I knew what the hell you were even doing out there," Link said, glaring at Zelda. Taylor could see the similarities in features between the siblings and understood Link's concern for her, but Taylor's only interest was in Meg. Everyone else could rot in hell for all she cared.

"I was helping the people who are in danger through no fault of their own!"

Everyone was talking over each other. Arguing over whether or not to keep Jonas and Taylor here, what they could or couldn't do, and all the voices were starting to irritate the bear inside Taylor's head. She felt its growling, the way it stomped its massive paws inside her skull, wanting out, wanting to fight and defend.

Wanting revenge for Andrew.

She didn't know how much longer she could hold back. She hadn't had trouble holding the animal back like this since the first time she'd turned, and with so many people in the same room, no one trusting each other, she knew she couldn't just let it out.

But the bear wanted out. So badly.

"All right, everyone stop," Jonas snapped.

Taylor's eyes flew open. She hadn't even been aware of closing them. Jonas glared at each and everyone in the room, shocking Taylor with the way he'd managed to get command of the situation.

She was also shocked by the way he looked at her while he held onto their daughter. "Christ, Taylor, I know you want to protect Meg, but we are not going out there without any backup. End of story. I can see all of your ears twitching. I know you can hear the wolves. They're looking for us right now."

Taylor clenched her hands to fists. She looked at Jonas, at her mate. Strangely, with the way he stood and the way he spoke, the animal inside of her brain acted as though he was the alpha in the room.

And it was hot. As hot as it was annoying, given their present situation. "We don't need them. It might be just as dangerous to be here as it is to go it on our own."

"We can't." The dead look in Jonas' eyes was what got her. "We can't do this on our own. Andrew is gone. You can't go back home with Trevor there, or the wolves." He leaned closer, his voice a cool, smooth balm on her wounded pride, and her pained soul. "You have to put aside the nature of the sloth to hate the other packs, and you have to let us all work together now. It's just you, me, and Meg, and I need you with me on this."

Her heart ached to hear that. She'd wanted to hear words like that for the longest time.

She'd just never wanted to hear them under these conditions.

Taylor sucked back a breath. She felt the itch of her fur sliding back under her pores. Her daughter was quiet now. Meg had cried herself to sleep, and now it seemed as though there was no going back.

This was where they were. This was the situation she had to deal with.

Because the wolves were out there, howling at each other and searching for her and her daughter.

A murderous bunch. That was what Steve had called them.

Before he'd decided to be a complete asshole and hide information from her.

She would not let those wolves near her child.

Taylor inhaled a deep breath. "Will you please help me to keep Meg safe? I can't go home with the wolves there."

Or with Trevor fucking everything up for her.

Link and Zelda both smiled, as though they were grateful for the change in attitude.

Steve's smile was much more subdued. He held out his hand to her. "We'll do whatever we can to get you through this."

Taylor looked at it, then at Jackson, whose expression remained neutral and unreadable.

Jonas' face was just as stoic, but she could see it in his eyes that this was what he wanted.

She took Steve's hand, shaking it. "Thank you."

The bang on the front door made her, and everyone else in the room jump.

They all turned to the door. Steve pulled a gun from a holster hidden behind his back. Jackson growled and revealed his teeth.

Another bang against the door made it bend inwards a little, and then the howling started.

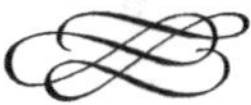

Jonas backed up from the door, his skin crawling when he heard the long scratches down the other side of the door.

The fact that Steve was going to use a gun when he was shifter was comforting.

"I need a weapon," he said, glancing around for anything he could use with one arm holding onto a baby and the other still out of commission.

Meg had woken up at the sound of the banging, but she didn't cry. She rested her head against his chest and whimpered slightly, but seemed to have no strength left to protest.

Holding her, however, was just a reminder of how fragile this little girl was. He didn't want anything coming near her. He wasn't going to let anything go near her.

"Taylor, you need to take Meg. Let us hold them off, and get out of her, find a ride with someone driving by."

Taylor shook her head, the blue in her hair glinting under the lamplight. Fur grew in from the pores on her arms. Her eyes were a bright shade of gold. "No, you hold onto her. I'm going to face this now, not be on the run from them forever."

Even as she said it, Jonas went to the phone and dialed nine-one-

one. He left it off the hook to ring, and took Meg back to the bathroom, the safest distance away from the banging.

Police and other first responders would trace the call and come out if they had the right tracers. He just hoped they heard enough of what was going on to know to send a lot of people.

"They've stopped slamming on the door," Jackson said.

That was what Jonas noticed it, too. There was no more banging, which was strange because one more hard slam and that door would have turned to splinters. It was already cracked open down the center.

Then he could hear the laughing of hyenas. Sounded like it. Maybe they weren't wolves out there after all.

"What's going on?"

Jonas nearly stepped forward to investigate before he remembered there was someone small and fragile in his arms, so he pulled back, letting Jackson do the investigating for him.

"Taylor, seriously, take her."

"No. I can hold them off better than you can."

Jonas couldn't make a decent argument with her in the limited time they had. What was he supposed to say? That he didn't trust himself not to drop his own daughter? That wouldn't go off very well.

Jackson glanced through the cracks of the door, his eyes flying wide before he looked back at Jonas.

No, not Jonas. He looked at Meg.

"We need to get out of here right now."

"What? Why? Can't we fight our way out?" Link asked.

"Not with gasoline."

Jonas got it. Taylor got it when she looked at him. "They can't!"

"They are."

They didn't have time for this. "Taylor, come with me and come with your daughter."

He could already smell the gasoline. The laughter had gotten louder. Someone outside shouted something. Jonas couldn't make it out with all the commotion inside, but he didn't think whatever was being yelled was directed at him.

"Taylor, do not fight me on this. We don't have time for that."

She glared at him. If he hadn't been holding onto their daughter,

Jonas might have had reason to worry that she would get her inner bear out here and go on the attack.

And he wanted her to go on that attack more than she knew.

But not now. Definitely not now.

"We create the distraction. You all run, understand?" Steve asked.

Zelda's dark tail bristled. "Wait, what?"

They didn't give any more time to explain or plan. Link looked terrified to hell, but he still ran behind the other two, roaring with them as they burst through the door.

And then Jonas really could smell the gas. The sudden burst of flames that appeared right after was near blinding.

"Fuck!" Jonas pulled back from the fire.

For the first time in his adult life, since making it his career, fire had him at a disadvantage. Unprepared. Cornered.

He didn't have any of his gear, but he knew he could still manage this. He could do this for his daughter.

"Jackson, give Taylor your gun." Jackson did so. With Taylor armed, she wouldn't need to go into bear form, and he'd hopefully keep her with him. Next, he put Meg down on the floor and ripped the blankets off the bed. "Help me tie this," he told Taylor, as he stripped off his jacket and fashioned the top sheet into a sling for his busted arm. She helped him, and then picked Meg back up and pushed her into his good arm. He pulled his jacket over Meg. He didn't want a lick of flames on her. Or any of the smoke to get into her tiny lungs.

"We have to be fast about this. Got it?" He yelled at Taylor over the sound of the flames.

The fire ate the room around them quickly. It was hungry and alive, reaching for him and his child. But he would protect her.

He held his jacket over Meg's little body, tucking her chubby legs up and beneath it before he rushed towards the sounds of laughing outside, to the heat, to the fire.

CHAPTER 24

Taylor thought her heart damn near stopped for a second as she watched Jonas run towards the fire. It had already started eating its way into the room, crawling along the carpet and walls. The curtains were in flames.

It moved faster than she thought it would, but Jonas was outside of it now, with Meg.

Meg was safe. At least from the flames. Her baby girl was out there, which meant she needed to hurry and follow and face their attackers.

Taylor moved.

It was scary. More so than she would have thought jumping through something that was basically a ring of fire. Hotter, too. She was disoriented when she made it into the air outside that felt oddly cold against the heat of the fire.

The shouting and growling of the wolves around her came second. She spotted Link, doing his best in his fox shape to hold back the attacking. It was a flurry of fur, but none of the wolves paid any attention to her. Now that they had Steve and the others, they were less interested in Taylor and Jonas.

Zelda's car was trashed. Turned onto its side, windows smashed.

She didn't have to use too much brain power to realize how that happened.

If her daughter weren't here, she would have tried to join the fight, to help fight those who'd caused her sloth and family so much trouble. But her daughter was here, and her priority was getting them to safety, as far away from the fire as possible.

Taylor glanced back at the door, to see if Zelda was getting ready to join her. When the fox jumped out, small and graceful, not a single flame marring that perfect fur, the group of fighting shifters was already taking their scuffle into the woods, away from the fire and away from the non-shifters inside.

Taylor turned her back to them and ran in the direction of her mate and child. She would have been able to sniff both of them out even if she were still engulfed in the smoke and flames.

When she found them, Jonas had discarded his jacket and was trying to comfort a crying Meg while trying the handles of the vehicles in the lot. When he spotted her, he smiled. A smile that made her stomach and heart ache. He had soot on his face; his hair was a little singed. She could smell the burn.

But Meg...Meg looked entirely untouched by the fire. Or by anything remotely harmful. Even if she was currently crying her eyes out, pushing against Jonas to try to get away, as though he was the one who had caused her latest upset.

Taylor ran to her daughter. She couldn't stop herself.

Meg reached out for her, and Taylor gave the gun to Jonas before grabbing her little girl out of his arms.

She'd been able to hold herself back before, but now all that bravado was out the window.

"Did you get a car?"

"Not yet." Jonas checked another vehicle. The alarm went off.

Instead of being upset by that, Jonas seemed happy.

"Yes!"

He went to another truck, banging his hands on the hood, and when that did nothing, he rocked a smaller vehicle, which also had an alarm that started to blare.

"What are you doing? You'll call them right to us!"

"That's the point; I need to wake up the people here!" Jonas went to another vehicle, rocking it until the headlights started to flash and the alarm sounded. "They can't be asleep with the fire going, and I can't go back to the building to find an alarm to pull."

Taylor blinked, looking up towards the windows on the first and second floor, which slowly began lighting up one by one. Shouting occurred from the people inside, as they tried to figure out what was going on.

Several loud yells of "Shut the fuck up!" or "Cut that shit out!" sounded from the doors and windows of the various rooms.

"Fire!" Jonas shouted, pointing toward the other side of the building, around the corner where they wouldn't be able to see it. "Evacuate the building right now! Leave everything behind. Do not pack your things and exit the premises!"

He sounded so official when he gave his instructions to the people up there. Taylor pressed her lips together, watching as some of them started gathering up their things, not just their loved ones.

"Hurry up and get out!" She yelled. The few that were already down pulled out their phones. Some ran around to get video footage of the side of the building that was on fire. "You, call nine-one-one!" She'd seen Jonas do it before in the hotel room, but it would help to make sure someone got through to talk to the operator. The woman she'd pointed to did as she was told, stopping filming and pulling up her phone's keypad to dial instead. After what happened with her local fire department, Taylor figured anyone driving in would be whatever volunteers were left over, or maybe even from Astrea.

"People, don't stop here in the parking lot, keep moving. Get across the street. Do not stop." Jonas ushered the people as they ran around from the motel. A couple of small families. A few that looked like day hikers and some random people sprinkled into the mix who were probably just passing through and needed a place to stay for the night in between their travels.

Or to hide their affairs.

Despite Jonas' instructions, many of them had their bags and suitcases with them.

Taylor saw a kid with platinum blond hair, still standing around and filming the fires instead of getting to safety. His pupils were huge, and he smelled like something he was too young to be smoking. He looked too young to be around here, period.

"Give me your phone."

He frowned at her. "Fuck off, no way."

Taylor expected this, which was why she was calm when she let her claws and teeth make an appearance.

"What the fuck!"

The kid tried to step back, but the crowd of people moving through the parking lot was too thick. She was able to grab him by the scruff of his dirty hoodie before he could get far.

She didn't yank him too close. She didn't want him any closer than an arm's length anyway when she had her daughter in her arms. "You will give me your phone right now, or I will cut you." She let her eyes change. That always freaked out the non-shifters. They hated seeing that sort of thing directed at them. "Do you understand me?"

The boy trembled. He didn't piss himself, though, which was at least something. His hand did shake a little as he handed over his phone.

"Thank you."

Between the call from Jonas and the call from the lady she directed, Taylor hoped help was on the way already, but it couldn't hurt to give it one more go.

She dialed, got the operator, and told them exactly where she was and what was happening just in case they needed more information. Taylor didn't bother with staying on the line when the woman on the other end told her to though. She had other matters to attend to.

She called Andrew's home phone number, hoping someone would answer. If he'd managed to survive, he could have made it home by then.

"Come on, come on."

Thankfully, Jonas jogged towards her with a broad smile on his face He'd managed to find a fire extinguisher, and, of all things, an ax.

She supposed that would be his weapon of choice, given the present situation.

He grinned from ear to ear. "I found another gun."

She blinked. "That's great. Uh, was it his?" Behind Jonas, a middle-aged man wearing a black shirt with the motel's logo on it walked, slowly taking in everything around him. He stared up at the growing flames, struck dumb as though he'd never seen anything quite like it.

To be fair, he probably hadn't ever seen his place of employment go up before. If he was the owner, then Taylor hoped he had insurance.

"He came out with some keys too, let's see which car they're for. Don't think he'll notice if we take a company car, do you?" The man was still staring, but had also followed the direction Jonas shoved him in, making his way out the parking lot and across the street with the others. He was the last one of the evacuees that Taylor could see.

She could kiss Jonas right then. She would later. When it was safe to do so. When she wasn't listening to the phone ringing endlessly as she prayed for Andrew to pick up. "Even better."

"I think they're for that truck over there," he pointed towards a truck with a large sticker promoting the hotel's name and number.

As she headed to the truck, someone finally answered on the phone.

It was Trevor, and he sounded uncertain and a little shaky. "Andrew's office."

Taylor knew exploded as Jonas unlocked the passenger side door for her. "Trevor, you massive sack of...you had better have a good reason why you did what you did."

"Taylor?"

"No effing shit, moron!" She could only stop herself from swearing so much, even in front of her child. She was trying, however, which was way more than Trevor deserved.

"You are so lucky I've got my kid in my arms otherwise I'd let you have it. You betrayed us! You disgusting little maggot! I'm going to find you and make you regret this until your last breath, do you understand me?"

Jonas opened the truck door for her, grinning. "Just get in and drive," she muttered. Taylor didn't need to see him smirking at her over her foul mouth right then. She just wanted to cuss Trevor out, guilt-free, and get everything she could off her chest.

She put Meg in first, then climbed in after her. "You seriously think I had much choice?" Trevor's objections were meaningless to her.

"Screw you, weasel shifter, of course, you did. You never liked Jonas, and you were always looking for a reason to prop yourself up."

"I wasn't! All right?"

"Bullshit!"

"Bullshit," Meg repeated, though in a much calmer voice.

Taylor closed her eyes, begged for patience while Jonas still stood outside the truck.

"What are you doing?"

Jonas' gaze was directed back at the burning building. He couldn't seem to take his eyes away from it. "I need to make sure it's empty before we leave."

"What?"

"I'm sorry, I thought I could leave with you two, but you're going to have to hop over there and drive yourself and Meg to safety." He shook his head, and leaned down into the truck, placing his forehead on hers. "I can't leave people in need. But I need you two to get far away from here, from this fire and from the wolves who could decide to come back and finish the job." He reached for her with his good arm and pulled her him, letting their lips speak for everything left unsaid. Then, without another word, he placed the keys in her hand and walked away. He just tucked the ax into the back of his makeshift sling, grabbed the fire extinguisher, and ran back to the motel.

Taylor got out of the truck, pulling Meg along with her. There was no way she was going to drive out of there, past that crowd of people, knowing Jonas could die trying to be a hero. Even with the fire station so close around these parts, some of the volunteers lived far enough away that it would take time to round them up. She hoped they would be there soon to help Jonas, but she'd never be able to live knowing that she just left him.

Now that she was out of the truck, she saw that a few people had made their way back to the parking lot, and they were pointing up at the second floor. The group of teenagers gestured when Jonas went to talk to them.

That was why he'd rushed out of the truck. He'd seen what they were doing. More than just looking up at the growing flames. They'd been screaming out for one of their friends, and he, or she, was not making an appearance.

Taylor watched Jonas nod, and grab a water bottle from one of the teens before he ran for the stairs of the building that was half up in flames. She couldn't take her eyes off of him. She could barely hear Trevor on the other end of the line.

"These guys are crazy. You don't say no to that shit when it comes knocking, Taylor."

"Uh huh, well you can tell that to Andrew when you meet him."

She didn't explain what she meant by that when she hung up the phone.

Taylor was too busy watching Jonas working, fixated on him.

This was his life. This was what he did as a profession.

And goddamn, holding his child in her arms while watching him brave the flames was simultaneously the sexiest and most terrifying thing she had ever seen in her entire life.

"Go get 'em, tiger."

CHAPTER 25

It was differing being among the flames when he didn't have his gear. Not so much as an air tank. Jonas' body was exposed without the added weight, but someone was up here, and he didn't have a choice but to try to help them.

Those kids had been pointing and screaming towards this part of the building. When he'd asked, they said their friend had not met them at the muster point. He gave them instructions to get back over to safety and told them he'd do his best to find their friend.

The fire moved quickly. The heat more intense than he was comfortable with, that was for damned sure.

Jonas kept low. He wasn't in an enclosed space, which meant he had a better chance of avoiding too much smoke inhalation. The path was littered with discarded items, dropped when the occupants had fled for safety. Luckily, he found an abandoned shirt, so he didn't have to use his own. He grabbed the bit of cloth, soaked it with the water bottle contents, and wrapped the material around his face.

He spilled some of the remaining water on his shoulders and chest, and let some more splash down his back. It would make his clothes less flammable.

Using the fire extinguisher, Jonas sprayed the path ahead and below, to the fire licking up through the wooden planks.

He'd done this drill a thousand times before. He didn't have to put it out. He just needed to clear a path for himself and keep it open so he could walk back out again. There was no debris to clear, but the walkway wouldn't hold for much longer. He had to move.

He sprayed around the flooring where he walked. He had no idea how much of the extinguishing agent was inside of the container, so he had to move as quickly as possible. It looked old, so he couldn't rely on it to last long.

Not to mention this was absolutely not what he was supposed to be using for a fire this size.

Thankfully, the wind was with him. For now. It was a simple matter of getting to the room. It was one of the few where the door was still closed, and they'd told him what room number to look for.

The fire licked at the door, but it hadn't caught yet.

Jonas hung the fire extinguisher from the bottom of his sling and pulled the ax out from where he'd tucked it in the material behind him. "If you can hear me, stand back!" He shouted as loud as he could, and waited just a beat before swinging the ax with his good arm, splitting it before he kicked it down.

Smoke billowed out. He ducked down quickly, moving into the dark space.

TAYLOR WATCHED with the same intensity and focus as the people standing around her. She hated them at the moment. The people who pointed, stared with their mouths open, catching flies. Even the ones who were filming it.

She felt a mixture of hatred and sympathy for the people who were worried about their friend. On the one hand, their friend was missing. On the other, if they'd bothered to check on their friend when they were so concerned with packing their bags and getting themselves and their things to safety, then Jonas might not be risking his life right now.

She wanted Jonas to come out of there, get back down here, and be safe.

"He does this for a living. Daddy's going to be fine." Taylor repeated this mantra to Meg but knew she was saying it to try to calm herself more than the toddler. Meg knew that everything was chaos and that they were surrounded by panicked people, but she didn't understand what Jonas was facing.

"He does this for a living. He knows what he's doing." But firefighters also tended to have proper equipment and outerwear before they went into burning buildings.

"Mamama." Meg grabbed a handful of Taylor's hair, sighed, and put her face into her neck.

"He'll be back soon." Where the fuck was he? The seconds ticked by, each lasting a lifetime as she waited to see any movement in the cloud of black smoke.

Taylor nearly jumped out of her skin when a dark figure finally emerged from the smoke. Her heart leaped.

And then it froze in her throat.

Jonas was struggling. The protection she'd watched him put around his face was gone, and his face was black and soot. He moved much too slowly for her taste, and as he made his way through the smoke towards the stairs, she could make out that he had something around his shoulders.

Someone.

With his good arm, he'd managed to get the person over his shoulders. He had that arm wrapped around the person's and then secured across his chest, holding on to the person's arm that was draped over his opposite shoulder. Taylor heard Jonas cough and watched him stumble, but he kept moving forward.

When they disappeared into the stairwell, Taylor snapped out of it. She looked towards the person's friends. "Get over there! As soon as they come away from that building you take your friend so I can take care of mine!" She took off, running back across the street, but not going too close. She'd never forgive herself if she let something happen to him, but she still couldn't put Meg any closer.

The teens came with her, looking ready to run as soon as Jonas and their friend appeared. "Carol! Carol, come on," they cheered, as Taylor held an arm back to stop them from running too close and putting themselves in danger.

She sure as hell would be right there with Jonas if it weren't for Meg.

Jonas' figure emerged from the smoke and fire, moving even slower. "Come on baby, just a few more steps!" Taylor joined in the chanting. When she couldn't wait any longer and got ready to run to him, three men ran past her and the teens. One pulled the girl, Carol, off Jonas' shoulders and put her on his own. The other two helped Jonas, who was almost unable to stand with how hard he was coughing.

Away from the fire and off the parking lot, onto softer dirt and grass across the street, the woman's friends clustered around her like hummingbirds searching for sugar. "Give her a chance to breathe," Jonas said while trying to breath himself.

"What about you?" She was more concerned about her mate than she was this stranger. Taylor didn't care how heartless that made her either.

"I'll be fine. She needs more help." He wasn't coughing anymore, which was good, but his preoccupation with the woman on the ground worried Taylor. She knew she'd have to step up and care for the woman if she wanted Jonas to sit back and let his sub-human strength heal him faster.

"What do we do?" One of Carol's friends cried.

"Is she alive?" The other moaned.

Taylor had taken basic first aid courses but had never had to use any of her skills. After her freeze up at the fire station, she didn't know if she'd ever be able to. Taylor didn't like this feeling. She didn't like that her brain struggled to think of what to do in this situation.

She thought about Andrew, and how she wished she'd had a chance to help him, but she made herself focus. Right now, it was this girl, and no one else was volunteering to help.

"I know first aid." She said, making her way over. "Do either of you?" One of the girls shook her head, the other shrugged — one of the men who'd helped raised his hand.

Taylor looked at Meg in her arms for a moment. She didn't feel safe letting her go, but she couldn't leave her with Jonas, who was too covered in smoke to be healthy for a baby. Finally, she handed Meg over to one of the girls. "I'm going to help your friend, but don't you dare take a step away from me, or momma bear mode is going to come out. It's been a long day, so don't test me." The girl gulped, but nodded and took Meg.

Taylor got down on her hands and knees, by Carol's face. She pointed to the man. "You, do the chest compressions. I'll do the air."

"Check her pupils." Jonas wheezed from a few feet away. "And her airways."

"Right." Taylor did as he instructed, and when she confirmed the airways were clear she nodded to the man, and they began alternating chest compressions and mouth-to-mouth.

When the woman inhaled a sharp breath, a cheer went up. Taylor backed up to give her room to turn on her side and cough. Her friends came closer, the one handing Meg back to Taylor.

Relief washed over Taylor, and she turned back to assess Jonas fully. She went to him, hesitant to touch him. "Are you okay? Do you need a hospital?"

She didn't see any burns on him. Didn't smell any blood, but that didn't mean everything was all right.

"I'm fine."

"Are you sure? Don't give me this tough guy bullshit."

Even now she could see he was taking deep breaths and looking close to the sun to make his eyes water and rinse out the smoke and ash.

"The fire didn't make it into the room. It was just a lot of smoke and heat. Fuck."

Taylor looked at the crowd of people. "Anyone else have another water bottle?"

Preferably sealed.

Luckily, someone had salvaged a cooler full of ice and water from their vehicle. They handed bottles over for Carol and Jonas.

"Tilt your head back."

He did. Taylor couldn't be as careful as she wanted to, so she ended up spilling some of the water down his face and chest, but when he sighed, opening his eyes to the liquid, she knew it didn't matter.

"We still have to get out of here," she said. "The wolves are still in the area."

"Can you still smell them close by?"

That was the problem. She could. "Yeah, but I don't hear the fighting anymore."

Jonas stood up, shaking his hair out and spraying water as if he were a dog.

Some subhumans did keep a few baser animal instincts.

"That's not good."

"Should we stay? Emergency vehicles are almost here."

"Can you hear them?"

Taylor nodded. "Yeah. They're getting close."

She could make out the sounds of sirens in the distance. Realistically, it hadn't been that long since she'd called, but at the moment, with everything going on, it felt like a lifetime.

Jonas glanced around. "Right. We'll stick around, but we need to stay in the crowd."

Taylor nodded. There were people all around them, so there was no need to back off. The truck they had been about to steal wasn't exactly far away, but it was away from the crowd, and around the edge of dim light spilling down from one of the few parking lot lamps.

Not exactly a safe idea to go over there and risk something happening. It would be just asking for someone to grab either of them from the darkness and make their kill.

By the time the firefighters, police, and ambulance arrived, the whole motel burned bright. Maybe half the building could be saved. Maybe. Taylor didn't know much about these things.

When Taylor looked at Jonas, she could see a whole different kind of fire in his eyes. He wanted to join them. He wanted to suit up and handle the hose.

And Taylor was so damned proud of him.

She recognized Detective Grey. His suit looked a touch disheveled as he pulled the jacket back to survey the scene.

"You still have the gun?"

"Yeah, right here."

"Give it to me."

Jonas took it, slipping it into the back waist of his pants with a slight wince. "Don't have a permit, and I don't want to deal with this right now. Let's go and talk to him."

Taylor took Jonas' hand, holding it tightly as they moved.

Jonas still felt a little too warm after being in that building.

They got the detective's attention before the man could move on. He didn't exactly look happy to see either of them.

"What the hell is going on here?"

"The wolves attacked us," Jonas said. "They might have killed her alpha; his truck should be on the side of the main highway leading up to the local bear sloth. A dead wolf should be on the highway. We were brought here, more wolves came, and they lit the place up with gas. This is a revenge thing. The alpha is angry because his brother tried to go after a conduit, and the conduit's mate tortured him for the effort."

Wow. He wasted no time. Taylor nodded. "Yeah, all of that."

Grey looked at her. "You're alpha might be dead?"

It knifed her every time she heard it. "Yeah."

But she hoped he wasn't. God, she was really hoping Andrew was alive.

"All right, give me a second." Grey pulled his radio out. He seemed to be sending instructions out to the other officers around the area. He told them to do a sweep around the motel itself to search for signs of fighting before he turned his attention back to Taylor and Jonas.

"Do you know if anyone is in there?"

"He got everyone out that he could," Taylor said quickly.

"There was a girl passed out on the second floor; I got her out."

"Which is why you look like this? All right, where is she?"

Jonas pointed the way, and Grey made sure the paramedics knew where to go to take care of her before he turned his attention back to Jonas.

"You all right? I know you're subhuman, but say the word, and I'll get someone over here to look you over, all right?"

"I don't need anything other than getting Taylor and my daughter somewhere safe until you can get the cops up to her sloth to take care of the shit that's infested it."

Taylor heard the growl in his voice. Either from being called subhuman, or from the pile-up of everything that had happened, she couldn't be sure, and it didn't matter.

"I can take you to the station. And I'll call someone to get some stuff to help with the little one."

With the sound of all the sirens, Meg had started shrieking a song of painful death in Taylor's ear. Her diaper felt and smelled awful, she hadn't eaten since she'd been with Andrew, and as of right now, her mother was completely done with everything.

Taylor wanted to take care of her daughter, somewhere safe where she could see Jonas and Meg at the same time while knowing something was being done about the wolves.

"Thank you."

"Come on, we can take my car," Grey said.

Before they could get there, a fox landed heavily onto the hood. Screams sounded as a man followed. He jumped up high, landing on the front hood with such force that the front tires burst, and leaving no doubt that the engine was totaled after something like that.

The screaming started. Civilians began to move, the police drew their guns, but it was too late.

CHAPTER 26

*J*onas grabbed Taylor's shoulders, putting his body over top of her and their daughter when the first shots were fired.

Knowing any one of those popping sounds could hit Jonas, could hit their child, made Taylor's heart leap, and her lungs constrict. She couldn't breathe. She couldn't think.

No, she couldn't breathe because Jonas' weight was on top of her. Meg cried and screamed her little lungs out, so she clearly still had room to inhale lots of air.

Taylor swiftly ran her hands over her daughter's body, searching for signs of any wounds, anything that would indicate an injury.

She felt nothing warm and wet, other than her diaper, and she smelled no blood. Meg was fine. The gunfire had stopped.

"Are you all right?"

Taylor nodded, carefully peaking over Jonas' shoulder. "I don't see them."

"They're around."

She knew it, too. She could smell the wolves. They were close.

The chaos would start again soon. Jonas carefully pulled himself off of Taylor's body. He looked around; his eyes were alert while the fire blazed high and bright behind him.

He looked as though he was engulfed in the fire, as though it was already part of him. A man on fire who would protect his daughter, and her. Even though he didn't have the same superhuman strength that they had.

Taylor grabbed him by the back of the neck, ignoring the startled expression on his face as she dragged him down and crushed her mouth to his.

She kissed him. Long and sweet. His mouth softened against hers, eventually, but it didn't last for long before they had to pull back from each other.

"We have to go." Jonas pulled himself up, held out his hand.

Taylor didn't hesitate to take it. "Right."

Jonas yanked her up. He was stronger than she remembered. Taylor couldn't pinpoint exactly what it was. At that moment, he seemed like the most powerful man in the world.

"Grey!"

Jonas started running. Detective Grey had taken cover behind one of the cruisers. He clutched at his side, his face pale. Other officers were down. Three more worked to subdue one of the wolves, striking it again and again with their Tasers when it wouldn't stay down. It looked like they weren't taking any risks with their lives now that some of their friends weren't moving.

Jonas made it to Grey quickly. Taylor knelt with him, but only because she didn't trust herself to remain standing when there were people out there trying to get a look at who to attack next.

"Is it bad?"

"Just a scratch. It better be." Grey clenched his teeth.

Taylor shook her head. "You look like you're in pain. You need a paramedic." She looked up and called out, "Someone help! There's an officer down over here!"

That's what people said when it was a cop who had been injured, right?

"It's fine." Grey grinned, though it looked massively forced under the strain. "It's good to feel pain. If I didn't feel it, I'd be worried. Might think I was dying."

Taylor wasn't sure if that was true or not, and this man was a human. He wouldn't have the healing abilities of a shifter. Or the healing abilities of a mated subhuman.

She glanced at Jonas.

"I don't think they're after you. Not specifically," Grey said through clenched teeth. "They want to get back at Steve and everyone connected to him. There was an attack at the hospital. They tried to get Victor. Didn't work. We were waiting."

"Victor. Zelda's mate." Taylor was still trying to get the names right of all these people. People she didn't know, but whose actions put herself, her sloth, her mate, and her daughter at risk.

Grey nodded. "Yeah. Look, take my car, if it will run." He reached into his pocket with a pained grunt, pulling out his keys. "Get to the station, hide there, wait for everything to blow over and—"

Grey's words were cut short when, not a wolf, but a bear reached around from the top of the car, grabbed him by the top of his head and yanked him clean off the ground.

It threw him away so casually, Grey screamed, but the bear just looked at them.

And Taylor wanted to kill him.

"Trevor! You asshole! What are you doing?"

The bear looked down at her, its eyes popping wide like a puppy kicked for no reason.

He wasn't in a standard bear shape. She hadn't even known he could do this, but she could smell it all over him who this was. It wasn't just in the shape and color of his eyes or the off patches of fur that grew out in shaggy, mismatched directions.

"Do you have any idea what the fuck you're doing? Look at these people!"

She pointed around at the chaos, the people who were down. Several people looked over towards them. The few officers who were still standing brought out their weapons. They had the guns pointed in the right direction, but they seemed unsure, as if all the injured around them were a warning for what would happen to them next.

In his in-between form, Trevor had enough of his original form that he was able to use his voice box, even in this monstrous shape.

"Give them what they want, they go away."

She sneered at him. "They killed Andrew, you know."

Trevor's eyes flew wide. He stared at her, his jaw falling, revealing sharp fangs.

To the officers standing around, he probably looked more menacing than shocked, which was likely why they straightened their backs, shouting out to him.

"You! Get back into your natural shape right now, or we will open fire!"

Trevor stared at her as Taylor continued to back up. Jonas moved with her, though he stayed in front, shielding her and Meg.

"You did this, Trevor. You brought them here, and now everything is going to shit. Give yourself up."

Trevor growled, his snout crinkling as the deep rumble vibrated up through his chest.

The police were losing their patience as well. "This is your last warning! Turn back into your natural form, or we will open fire on you!"

Trevor growled at Jonas. His eyes glowed that of a creature that was angry, that wanted revenge.

Jonas shook his head. "Don't even think about it."

Trevor did think about it. If Taylor didn't have Meg in her arms, she could have done something, something other than let herself be shoved backward by Jonas as Trevor snapped his teeth around Jonas' shoulder and middle.

Jonas screamed from the pain of being bitten. Taylor backed up, part of her screaming that she needed to get into her bear shape and defend him, and the other part of refusing to let her forget she was holding onto something so much more precious in her arms.

"Trevor! Stop!"

"Hold your fire!"

The police opted not to shoot now that the giant bear thing had a victim in its mouth, but Trevor didn't shake Jonas' body around until he stopped moving the way she expected him to.

Trevor turned, leaped neatly off the police cruiser, and darted into the shadows with Jonas, just out of reach of the fire and the motel lights.

No one gave chase because no one here could keep up with a shifter in a form like that.

Taylor could. Maybe those other shifters, Zelda, Steve, Link…

Well, she didn't know if Link was still alive or not, judging by the fact that his fox hadn't moved from where he landed on the car hood, but she had to do something.

"Grey! Detective Grey!"

She hoped he was alive. Prayed for him to be alive. There was no one else she would trust with this sort of task.

"Grey! Detective Grey!"

"Thankfully, he was already groaning and pushing himself onto his side, his face twisting with pain. He clearly wasn't having a good day.

"What the fucking hell—"

"Here. Take her."

"Wait, what? Hey! What the hell do you think you're doing?"

Taylor kissed her child on both of her cheeks, her hands aching to have to let her go, but she needed to move fast. "Keep her safe until I get back, all right?"

"Where the fuck are you going? Do I look like I can look after a little girl right now?"

"The paramedics will help you with that, just watch her! Please."

The detective yelled some more expletives at her, words Meg definitely should not be hearing with her tender, innocent little bear ears, but there was nothing to be done for it. Someone took Taylor's man, and she needed to kick some ass here.

Taylor ran to the edge of the parking lot, where the lights didn't quite reach. She pumped her arms, smelling the wolves all around her as she ran into the trees, flying on the wind.

They were watching her. Maybe deciding when to move in?

Taylor let her claws out. If they tried to come up to her, then she would show them what a mother bear could really do what she was pissed off, and right now, Taylor was angry enough to topple some of the trees around her.

She moved fast, hard, ignoring the sting of branches slapping against her face, arms, and legs. It didn't matter because soon she didn't feel it anyway. She only felt the prickle of her snout changing. Fur sliding in through her pores like thousands of tiny needles.

She no longer had to hold back the bear inside her, and if Trevor hurt Jonas, if he did irreparable damage, or worse…

She'd send Trevor to meet Andrew much sooner than expected, but with a lot more pain.

CHAPTER 27

$\mathcal{J}$onas had no idea where Trevor was taking him for the first minute or so of his kidnapping.

But he figured it out when, twenty seconds after dragging Jonas into the woods, the other man didn't immediately tear him to pieces.

Trevor's bite didn't sink too deep, but deep enough that it fucking hurt, and now it was starting to burn.

Bite chasers would kill to be in Jonas' position right about now, but Jonas wasn't in the mood to risk his life so he could have the chance to turn into a shifter of any kind. He'd already been bitten by a wolf earlier, but it had only been enough to render his arm useless. Now Trevor was working on that same shoulder, and Jonas was losing feeling down that side of his body. The cold sensation that came after wasn't much of a good sign either.

Jonas pounded on Trevor's snout as hard as he could. He reached for his eyes but couldn't get his arm up that high with the awkward angle.

He was going to fuck Trevor up when he got the chance for this. If Trevor of all people was one of the assholes to kill him, then Jonas was going to be massively pissed.

"Trevor! Put me down!"

He'd left Taylor and Meg behind undefended. He needed to get back to them.

Or, no, maybe this was good. Maybe Trevor and the wolves would leave Taylor and Meg and the rest of the humans alone if they had him.

Still, that didn't mean Jonas was going to give up without some fight. Even if Taylor and Meg were safe—well, safer—where there were police, a crowd of people and paramedics, Jonas wasn't going to lie down and die without a proper fight.

He kept smashing his good fist against Trevor's nose.

Even in a bear shifter, that was still a pressure point. Some things were universal. Jonas felt the wince in the shifter every time his fist hit at just the right spot.

"Drop me. Let me go. Put me down. Come on!"

Eventually, Trevor could take no more. His golden eyes had started to water. He spat Jonas out, but Jonas wasn't nearly as fast as a shifter. Trevor grabbed him by his throat with his long, twisted fingers, his claws scraping against the back of his neck, yanking him close.

"Stop that!" Trevor's warm breath blew hot spittle into Jonas' face.

He forced a grin at the man. "You should look into brushing your teeth from time to time. I hear it does wonders for this sort of problem you're having."

Jonas could have sworn he saw blood vessels popping in Trevor's eyes. Enraged, he threw Jonas down onto the ground, his giant foot pressing down on his stomach.

The worst part was that Trevor wasn't even adding a lot of weight, but Jonas grunted under the pressure, holding tightly to his furry ankle, trying his best to keep Trevor's fat ass off him.

"Why did she pick you? Why did you come back?"

Jonas clenched his teeth, hardly able to get the words out. "Are you kidding me? Everything happening and you care about that? Your alpha is dead you sack of shit."

"Because you wouldn't leave well enough alone!" Trevor pointed a clawed finger down at him, and once again, Jonas had to wonder if he was out of his damned mind.

"They came here looking for the conduit. You knew that! You were trying to help them!"

"To get rid of them. They want revenge for their brethren. It's what any good pack would do. You would understand if you weren't a subhuman."

All of Jonas' anger, all of his hatred bubbled up to the surface. He pushed harder against the paw that held him down, sneering up at Trevor as he managed to get the man off him just a little.

Trevor pressed down harder. It hurt. The pain in his side was almost too much, and this couldn't be making it better, but Jonas was determined to keep Trevor's filthy paws off him.

Trevor bared his teeth, barking down at him, but then a very feminine, furious scream broke off whatever he was about to say.

"Let go of me you son of a bitch! I'll kill all of you!"

That wasn't Taylor, thank God, but it sounded like...the fox woman. Zelda.

Jonas took his attention away from Trevor for one second, one second too long, because the deformed bear thing reached down, grabbing Jonas by the throat before lifting him off his feet.

"I'll let them deal with you."

Them?

Trevor took Jonas towards the screaming. It wasn't far. Off the path they'd already been traveling, across a shallow stream, and up a small hill, to a small clearing.

It was dark, the moon shone down on them, but if it weren't for his enhanced eyesight, Jonas doubted he would be able to see much of anything that was going on.

Zelda was there. Her hair was disheveled. Her eyes blazed brightly through the dirt tracks on her face. Blood gleamed on her fingertips as she flew at the men and wolves surrounding her.

They dodged the swipes of her clawed hands with ease, laughing at her, as though it were some game.

Trevor threw Jonas down into the middle of the clearing between them. He grunted, the air shooting out his lungs the moment of impact.

Jonas clutched at his bleeding side, coughing for breath.

And suddenly, all that smoke he'd been fighting not to inhale when he went into that hot motel room seemed to shoot right into his lungs, despite being as far away from the fire as he could get.

Zelda shrieked something next to him, but she didn't sound as though she were in pain, or any real danger, so he ignored her and let her rant while he got control over himself again.

This was such bullshit. If Jonas ever got the chance, he was going to wring Trevor's stupid neck for this.

Jonas rolled to his knees, glancing up, noting how utterly out of control the wolves, and Trevor, seemed to have of Zelda.

She looked more like a wild banshee than a fox as she swung her small, clawed hands out at the wolves around her.

Jonas did a quick count. There were four wolves and Trevor. They seemed to have shifted themselves into the in-between form. They stood on their hind legs, had opposable thumbs, but their bodies looked to be, for the most part, that of wolves. Even their snouts and heads were more wolf-like than human. It was interesting to watch the way they avoided Zelda's claws. Some didn't get out of the way fast enough.

These were the guys who were burning down patches of forest, who burned down homes and business, and yet they avoided a woman much smaller than they were as though their principals refused to allow them to fight back.

They deflected her blows, some laughed over it, but none struck Zelda back.

One of the males eventually grabbed onto her wrists, making a show of how she couldn't get away from him.

It was weird watching a wolf making kissy faces at Zelda while she struggled to get away from him, taunting her as she shrieked at him.

Jonas couldn't take it. He pushed himself to his feet, flying at the wolf, catching the shifter off guard as he put all of his weight and power into the tackle. Shoving his good shoulder into the shifter's middle, he threw it off its feet. Its claws dug into Jonas' chest, trying to free itself.

Jonas had seen shifters fight before, and it was always a gruesome sight to behold. To be in one himself, and to be on top of a shifter while it fought and struggled to get away from him was something else entirely.

The shifter snapped its teeth at him, narrowly missing his face. Jonas managed to pin the arms of the shifter down with his feet. Even with subhuman strength, he only had one working arm, and it took everything he had to hold the beast. It was one hell of a ride as the wolf-man beneath him bucked and tried to roll.

Jonas slammed his fists down again and again on the side of the wolf's head, going for the eyes. He struck the wolf once hard on the nose. That seemed to do it. The wolf whined and turned subdued, looking away with the sudden strike against a pressure point.

Apparently, that was too much for the other wolves standing around, and for Trevor. They must have thought it was funny at first, watching the subhuman going at it with one of their own. But when it got clear their friend wouldn't win, they yanked Jonas away from him.

Jonas roared, pulling against their hands, their claws slicing into him even as he fought them. He cursed them and their mothers. He wanted blood. He couldn't think of anything other than how much he wanted to open their bellies up and let their guts spill out for what they were doing here. For what they'd done to Captain Burns. For what they'd done to Andrew and Grey, and for what they'd tried to do to Taylor and Meg.

Trevor was the guiltiest out of the lot of them. He'd betrayed his sloth, even if he tried to justify it by saying he was trying to get rid of the wolves. Jonas didn't care anymore. He just wanted to crush the man's head in with his bare hands.

"Trevor! You fucking traitor!"

Trevor let out a little whining noise, his bear ears falling on top of his head and holding tightly to his skull, though he didn't say anything.

One of the wolves sucker punched him in the gut, knocking the wind out of him, again, before tossing him onto the ground.

"Stay down," it warned with its growly voice.

Zelda kneeled next to him, worry in her eyes for him before she glared back up at the others.

"If my brother is hurt, I swear I will skin all of you alive and turn you into rugs."

"Your brother..." Jonas thought about that. He'd seen the other fox, but he hadn't looked in a good position.

"Did you see him?"

Jonas thought the fox shifter was alive, but he didn't want to get into too many details with Zelda right now.

No point in worrying her any more.

Zelda sighed, but then she went back to sneering at the men around her, the fur of her tail bristling as she stood up.

"I didn't have anything to do with your stupid brother getting hurt, and I don't know anything about a conduit! You're attacking the wrong people!"

Wait, one of these guys was the brother?

The shifters around him were all around the same size and build, likely all alphas, but there was one that was a touch bigger, a bit wider around the shoulders. He shifted, shrinking down into his human shape.

Even like that, he was still over six feet tall. Maybe even taller than Jonas. That annoyed him.

The man pressed his lips together into a fine line. He put his hands behind his back, the way Jonas had seen cartoon villains do when he was still a kid watching those kinds of shows. He regarded Zelda with cold, unfeeling eyes. Dark eyes. Not the usual sort of dark, but this guy...looked as though a demon possessed him.

"You know the men who hurt my brother. They sent him back to me with strips of his skin missing." He approached slowly, his pace somehow more menacing than if he'd run at her. Zelda backed up. Jonas struggled to his feet, putting himself between the fox shifter and the crazy wolf before he could take another step towards her.

"That's as far as you go, pal."

The man regarded him. "Do you have family?"

He thought of Meg. Of Taylor. "Yeah, I do."

"Good. Then you know what you would do for them if someone were to tie any of them down, were to hurt them. I get the feeling that if I were to seek out that blue-haired bitch you were with and do half of what they did to my brother, you would try to tear me to pieces."

Jonas nodded. "You're right; I would. And you did come after her, so that's one thing. Two is that I doubt my mate and infant daughter would be tearing strips off of anyone in your family, and the third is that female bears aren't called bitches. That's what you would be."

Not the best come back he'd ever thought up. On a scale of one to amazing one-liners, it ranked up there with baby talk, a first timer trying to get a good one in, but it was enough to piss off the wolf in front of him, so when he backhanded Jonas hard enough to throw him into a tree, he had to admit, he didn't really mind it so much.

But only because he didn't feel the strike until well after impact.

By then, the wolf shifter had flown at him, his overly large, clawed hand wrapping around Jonas' throat, holding him up against the birch tree.

That did hurt. This guy wasn't just a normal shifter and had more than just the skill of shifting into an in-between form, something between man and wolf, or man and bear. He had more ability to control his body, his inner wolf, to the point where he could not only bring out his claws and change his eyes, but his entire hand around Jonas' throat felt different, rough and painful. It felt as though the wolf were choking the life out of him when an ordinary-looking, if not larger than average, man stood in front of him.

"This little bitch behind me is the mate of the man who is friends with the man who hurt my brother. You are part of the sloth that refused to help us get justice. You're the one who got the humans involved and a traitor to shifters everywhere."

"Great," Jonas had to choose his words carefully since he could hardly take in a breath to make them. "You gonna go after Zelda's second cousin, too? Maybe my co-worker's grandkids' friends' roommate for not helping you get revenge, too?"

The hand around his throat tightened. Jonas couldn't say a word after that, but as he gagged for breath, he was pretty sure that was something of the point.

"Wait! Wait, stop!" Zelda shouted. She tried to rush to him, but Trevor grabbed her arms. The three other wolves stepped in her way.

As Zelda kicked Trevor in the dick, Jonas was struck with guilt over the way he'd previously thought about her. She was kind of cool, but he still wished her family drama, or whatever this was, hadn't sucked Taylor of Meg into this.

Black started to close in around Jonas' line of vision. He was stunned to realize Trevor wasn't looking at him as though he were glad for this. The man was an asshole. He'd always had eyes for Taylor. The little peckerhead should be loving this.

Whatever. Jonas was dying. His face felt hotter than any fire, and he didn't care anymore.

He slammed his fist into the man's gut.

It didn't have the desired effect. The shifter kept holding onto him and barely grunted. Jonas wasted that precious oxygen trying to get this prick off him.

He slammed another fist into his gut. Then another. The wolf looked at him as though Jonas were punching at the air instead of his ribs. Each strike was weaker than the last.

"Don, I'm sure he understands now."

Was Trevor defending him?

"No, he doesn't understand."

Don? Not exactly the name Jonas expected from a fire-starting villain.

Those eyes glowed bright red, and they were all Jonas could see through the straw hole of his vision.

"Not yet."

Jonas sank into the darkness. He tried grabbing onto Don's arm, to make one last effort to pull the man off, but his fingers touched air as he slumped. It was actually kind of peaceful. He'd just let himself go under before coming back strong.

Yeah, this wasn't over. He was just letting Don think it was done. Jonas just needed to sleep first.

CHAPTER 28

The sinking feeling stayed with Jonas for what felt like hours, until it was no longer a sinking feeling. Now it was just a feeling of dropping.

Down, down, down. Until he slammed hard onto the pavement, through the pavement, bursting through layers of Earth's crust, his body smashing into paste.

Jonas gasped hard, pushing himself up onto his hands and rolling to the side, coughing for breath, the pain in his side almost too much for him to handle as he sucked back precious air.

He wasn't on the road, he hadn't smashed through the pavement, and his body wasn't a pudding of his flesh on impact.

He was still out in the woods. It was still dark except for the moon shining down on him, and he could still hear Zelda going at it with the wolves behind him.

No, not Zelda. Foxes didn't make that sort of deep, skin-tingling roar.

Jonas raised his face, still heated from a lack of blood flow, taking note of the black bear with gleaming blue fur taking swipes at the wolves that surrounded her.

And she was vicious.

Much as it was Jonas' first instinct to be horrified that Taylor was fighting, outnumbered, a group of wolves like this, he couldn't help but admire the way she went at her enemies.

Even outnumbered, she somehow managed to push them back. She kept them on their toes, but they were ruthless. The instant one jumped onto her back and started biting at her neck, Jonas flew into action.

He grabbed the nearest thing he could get his hand on, which was a large, awkward-looking stick.

He would have rather had a rock at that moment, but this did just as well when he came up to the side of his mate's body, jabbing the business end of the stick hard against the side of the wolf's face.

He narrowly missed its eye, but it didn't appear as though that made the strike hurt any less as the wolf cried out and sharply fell off Taylor's back.

The reactions of anyone or anything trying to protect their eyes always tended to border on the extreme.

Another wolf came. Not the biggest one, so it wasn't Don, but Jonas lifted his stick high, wishing he had his ax as he swung it down hard across the side of the wolf's face.

It snapped his stick in half, but at least he now had a much pointier side to work with.

He could use that. He was going to use it.

"Come on! Come and get me!"

Jonas ducked down when he felt something moving behind him, turning just in time to see a dark fox had jumped onto one of the wolves.

Zelda struggled to keep it off her once the tables were turned, kicking her legs up, two sets of teeth snapping at each other.

She didn't stand a chance, but then Jonas barely managed to pull his hand back before it was bitten right off by another snapping wolf.

This one was a big one. Had to be Don.

Jonas lifted his broken stick, holding it as he would a vampire stake. "I will fuck you up if you think about coming near her."

Not that he could do much about it considering two of the other wolves were already giving Taylor trouble. Trevor continued to stand off to the side, being a useless asshole, probably waiting to find out for sure who would win before he jumped in to help.

"I just want the wolf that hurt my brother."

Jones jerked back, stunned the guy could control his shifting ability that well that he could talk while in full wolf form.

Whatever. Jonas didn't have time for this. "She didn't have anything to do with that, neither did Andrew."

"Andrew got in my way. He refused to help. Even a subhuman like you knows shifters watch out for each other. Even a subhuman should know that we take care of our own."

"Yeah, well, the law has something else to say about that."

It was the wrong thing to say. Don flew at him. Jonas barely managed to duck out of the way the first time.

"I'll crush your head between my teeth!"

Jonas nodded. "Yeah, probably, but you're going to have to work for that privilege."

The wolf lunged for him again. Jonas couldn't bring himself to get out of the way fast enough. Don crashed into him.

Jonas brought up his arm, the stake in hand.

The bite on his arm burned. The stake was piercing his own hand as it went through the thick fur around Don's neck.

He knew he'd made it through the protective fur when the wolf screamed out in pain, pulling back.

There was blood at the pointed end of the stake. Jonas looked at it, and the wolf as it staggered back.

But it didn't seem to be enough to take Don down. The wolf stumbled, but it looked at him with bright red eyes.

"You motherfucker," Don growled, his voice sounded as though air bubbles were bursting within it.

Meanwhile, Jonas' arm trembled and felt cold as all hell as he pushed himself back.

He had so many holes in him right now it was a small miracle he was still conscious.

Too bad that miracle wasn't enough to keep Don down. If the damned fleabag hadn't been determined to get him before, then he was right now.

Jonas looked over to Taylor. She was still standing, still holding her own. He hoped it stayed that way and this wouldn't distract her.

He just wished…

Don squared himself, his shoulder bunching as he crouched low before leaping at Jonas one more time.

Those teeth, the warm breath, and spittle that got so close Jonas could see the reflection of his face in it, didn't get the chance to touch him as another bear, a huge brown bear, crashed into Don before he could make his kill.

Jonas blinked. Then he breathed, noting the way the two shifters went at it, and this time it was something else. An actual fight to the death, but one dog happened to be three times the size of the other, and the other was a bear and was already injured.

Andrew.

Jonas sucked back a heavy breath, dragging himself back to the trees, somewhere he could prop himself up. His arm killed, and his side…he didn't even want to think about it, but fuck him sideways. Andrew was alive. He was here.

Which meant Taylor and Zelda had a chance.

He looked back to his mate, and Jonas blinked again, wondering how high he was on adrenaline when he spotted two more wolves helping with the fight.

Steve and Jackson? Had to be. Don's men wouldn't be helping Taylor or Zelda, and the smell was…well, he had trouble smelling anything while caked in his own blood, and his sense of smell was shit compared to an actual shifter, to begin with, but he was getting hints of those other wolves in the air, so he was pretty sure it was them.

Not that it meant he could relax. His body screamed for him to let the others take control now that they were here, but his heart and soul couldn't lie back and do nothing while Taylor continued to fight.

But his body was so damned heavy…

Why were the woods swirling around like that? Jonas blinked a couple of times, trying to keep himself awake, but it wasn't just the need for sleep that was getting to him.

He glanced towards a sound in the trees. He spotted Trevor. Hiding.

A growl worked its way up Jonas' throat. He dug his fingers into the dirt, wanting to go after him, to strangle the bastard for his part in this. Jonas didn't care about his reasoning.

Trevor, even in his bear shape, somehow managed to look a little scared before he turned tail and made a run for it.

Really? That was it? Even when Jonas looked like this, when he felt like this, Trevor ran from him?

Damned pussy.

Jonas searched for something he could use, anything that would help him if someone walked up to him, or tried going for Taylor while her back was turned. He found a rock. It had a slight point. It was dull, but it was good enough.

He kept his eye on the black bear, watching as she roared and slashed out her claws, chasing away. And he was so fucking proud of her.

She was the one. The one he wanted to spend the rest of his life with. If he got a life after this.

He was so fucking stupid to have left her behind. So stupid...

At some point, Taylor noticed him. Maybe it was the way he'd been staring at the back of her head. It was difficult to say, but if a bear could have a terrified look on its face, then Taylor managed to pull it off.

The bear rushed to him, shrinking down, transforming into the sexy bombshell Jonas knew and loved.

Taylor didn't look as happy as Jonas felt when she put her hands onto his cheeks.

She looked as though someone had just run over her dog in front of her. Not that she had a dog, but the idea was the same.

"Oh God, Jonas, baby."

"I'm good."

He touched her wrist. His hand was wet. Was he sitting in a puddle?

"You're not all right! Steve! Jackson!"

What did she think they were going to do?

"Where's Meg?"

Taylor shook her head. "I...I left her with Detective Grey. She's fine. She's safe."

Her eyes were shining. Not just because they were fantastic eyes to look at either. They shone as though she were trying not to cry. Jonas didn't like that. "Did they hurt you? Did Trevor...?"

"No, no, try not to talk so much. You'll be all right." She looked at his arm, then his stomach, her face twisting. "Oh, God..."

That didn't sound so great, and while Jonas knew he should be worried, he felt strangely at peace with this. He was pretty sure Taylor was scared he was going to die, but going out fighting, after doing his job one last time, and helping to take out the wolves that had been starting these fires, protecting his woman and his child, felt pretty good.

It would have been nice to get to know Meg, to watch her grow up, but she would get to grow up, that was better than getting to know her.

Jackson clouded his view by standing over him and Taylor. The man's chest was bare. Slash marks ran down his skin, and his ear looked mangled to all hell, but otherwise, he was stoic as he knelt.

"He needs treatment. He still has a chance, but a human isn't made for this sort of punishment."

"He's not just a human. He's one of us! A subhuman. He can handle it, right, Jonas?"

Only she could make the word subhuman sound like a compliment. Not just a compliment, but a benefit. He loved her so much for that.

She touched his face, Jonas liked that, too, but he didn't like it so much when she gently slapped at his cheeks.

"Don't do that, stay awake."

"Right," he said, forcing his eyes open, and it got a little easier for him to keep them open when he noted the way Steve, now in his human form, marched over to Andrew and Don, who were still in their animal shapes.

"Your piece of shit brother tried to rape my mate. You're fucking right I made him regret it!"

Steve slammed his fist down onto Don's snout, and then he and Andrew worked together to maul the other shifter.

Were they going to kill him? Probably.

Don was right. Jonas was a subhuman, so he did know some of the basic rules. One of them was that you absolutely did not fuck with someone's mate.

Maybe they wouldn't kill him at all. If they wanted to. Don was doing his level best to fuck up their plans if that was the case. He clearly didn't want to be killed, and he fought and struggled with the other wolf shifters to make sure that didn't happen.

Even in the state he was in now, Jonas was angry enough at this entire thing to kind of hope they succeeded.

Then, if Jonas' died, he could find Don on the other side and beat the piss out of him on an equal playing field.

He ignored the fight. There was no point in keeping his eye on it when there was someone much more important to look at right here.

"I'm sorry I couldn't keep you safe."

"Don't talk like that." Taylor faded in and out. She took off the shirt she'd been wearing, pressing it to Jonas' middle, and then he was struggling to stay awake while trying to tell her how much he loved her.

More shouting. He couldn't make out what was going on. Everything burned, and he didn't want to be here anymore. It was an eternity. It hurt so bad he didn't have the words to describe it.

Then, another small eternity later, the shouts and growls seemed to stop, and Steve was there.

"He's bitten pretty bad. In multiple spots," Steve said. The man stood over Jonas, looking down at him as though he were rotting meat that had fallen on his kitchen floor.

Not only did Jonas not like being looked at like that, but he wanted to know what the hell he was doing standing there.

When did he get the time to come over here? Shouldn't he be handing Don his ass to him? Jonas wanted to tell the man to mind his own business and get back to work, but now even his tongue felt heavy.

And Steve looked like absolute shit. So the fact that he could look down at Jonas like that spoke volumes.

"What should we do? Can we move him like this?" Taylor sounded hysterical. He wanted to comfort her, to tell her it was fine. It didn't hurt. The rumors were true. It didn't hurt.

"We have to get him to the hospital. Right now."

"Wait, where's Don?"

"Don't try to talk, baby. Squeeze my hand, instead. Stay with me."

"Where's Don?" He couldn't let it go. They couldn't take him out of here until he knew, but Taylor seemed determined to make Jonas squeeze her hand, as though he would fade away if he didn't.

He tried, he really did, but he couldn't hold his focus for that long, and then Jonas did fade.

Jonas didn't remember anything else after that. He just knew that if Taylor started to cry over him, and Steve didn't kill Don for all those damned fires, then he was going to be pissed.

CHAPTER 29

Everything hurt. Everything throbbed. His body was on fire, and for a while, Jonas just wanted to end it. He swam in a sea of blackness. He couldn't see for miles in one way or another. He went under so many times it was a small miracle he didn't drown.

It felt like drowning, but at least if he were drowning, it would be in the water. This was not the water; this was something else. This didn't cool his heated body; it didn't put out the fire that burned the skin off his hands, legs, and arms.

He could see the bones of his fingers. The tips almost looked like claws.

He was subhuman. He didn't have claws. He didn't shift. He didn't...

Where was he again? Why did this hurt?

Fuck! Taylor! Meg!

He had to get to them. Had to find them. They could be lost in this inky black sea, and he couldn't let them drown, too.

He could hear her. Jonas could hear Taylor's voice. Close at times. So close he could reach out and almost touch her.

Other times, she sounded so far away it was clear he'd gone in the wrong direction to find her.

And the longer he couldn't find her, the more he wanted to roar. The more he wanted to tear himself out of his skin, to become a monster. To rip through anyone or anything that would get in his way.

It was hell. It was limbo, and he wanted to kill anyone who got in his way.

But it was only him. That was the part that was killing him.

When he opened his eyes, it was such a shock that it felt as though he'd been doused in the face with cold water. He didn't know where he was. Who he was. Bright lights and strange smells assaulted every sense he had.

The overwhelming flood of information hurt his eyes, his nose, and his brain. He couldn't stand it. He had to get out!

Wires poked and prodded at him from seemingly all angles. Something was in his nose. He pulled it out and felt the air change, not as crisp or clean, and the smells around him worsened.

Sharp needles were shooting up his nose. That was the only way to describe this.

Jonas rolled out of bed. An alarm sounded somewhere. His eardrums throbbed. Jonas clutched at his ears, but it was barely enough to stop the strange rush of pain that hit him.

People rushed into the room. Don's men. The wolves loyal to him.

They grabbed at Jonas' arms, issued commands, but he ignored them. He pulled at the people who attacked him. He threw them across the room and relished it when their bodies hit the walls.

They smelled strange. He wanted to tear them to pieces.

"Jonas, stop!"

There was only one person in the world that could make his body freeze like that. Jonas didn't move a damned muscle.

Her voice. It was amplified somehow. Taylor's voice always had a specific something to it that could make him stop in his tracks.

He turned towards the sound. The light in the bright room seemed to change when he spotted her. As if all that light was suddenly drawn to her, creating a sort of halo effect.

She looked worried. She looked very much alive. Her clothes were different than what she'd been wearing when they left her sloth.

Clean jeans and a loose white hoodie. Somehow, he could still make out every curve of her shape, from her breasts to her hips, and he wanted her.

So Jonas went to her, but his feet lost strength on the first step. He fumbled to his knees.

That was all right because Taylor was at his side in an instant. Her hands on him were a balm, unlike anything he'd ever felt before in his life.

"Easy, easy. I've got you."

He looked at her, touching her face, marveling at how she could be here.

She smiled back at him. "I missed you, too."

Jonas blinked. "Meg?"

"She's safe, she's fine. Don't you worry about a thing."

That relieved him, but Jonas still wished he could see his little girl. He wanted to confirm with his own eyes that she was all right.

"What happened?"

Taylor's dark eyes shone. "You're not going to believe this, but Andrew is alive. He's alive, Jonas."

Something within him sat up straight and howled. "That's...that's good news. Wow."

He was stunned. He didn't have the words to describe what exactly this meant.

Though he supposed it also made sense on another level.

Of course Andrew would be alive. It took so much more than that to take down a shifter. Especially a bear shifter.

"Wait, did I see him...was he at the..."

Taylor nodded. "I wasn't sure if you would remember that, or how much of it you'd even seen. You were so... Never mind. When his body recovered enough, and he finally woke up and saw we were gone, he came to find us. He helped Steve and Jackson defeat Don."

That didn't sound as though she were saying he was dead.

"Is he alive?"

Her expression changed. Jonas knew the answer at that moment, and he wanted to tear someone's head off for it.

"He's alive." It wasn't a question this time around. It was the truth. "They let him go?"

"No," Taylor shook her head. "It was just too much. He weaseled his way out. They couldn't chase him down. Steve and Jackson didn't want to leave me by myself with you and Zelda, and Andrew was injured. He tried chasing Don down. He was pissed, but he came back only a few minutes later. He knew he couldn't chase after Don on his own."

Jonas looked up and around. The smells were still strong. The general vibe he got calmed to something more acceptable, and when he took note of the nursing staff all around him, some of whom he'd thrown at the wall, he couldn't help but feel ashamed for his actions.

"Come on, let's get you back into bed."

Jonas let Taylor help him to his feet. She eased him back into bed.

"I thought I was somewhere else," he muttered. Jonas couldn't help the rush of embarrassment that hit him now that he realized he'd attacked innocent people.

What the hell had he been thinking?

Taylor rubbed at his arm. That made it easier to let the staff come close and start poking at him again. They put everything back where it was supposed to go. They hooked him in, and then it felt like he was in a hospital again.

"I'm sorry."

Taylor frowned, staring at him. "For what?"

He wet his lips. "I thought I could keep you safe. There are so many times I could have gotten you out of there, but I didn't take any of those times. I just…fucked up at every step of the way."

Taylor was already shaking her head. Jonas didn't understand how she could be so forgiving. "Don't say things like that. You didn't fuck up. You protected me, you kept our little girl safe, and you saved the lives of all those people in the motel. I…" Taylor seemed to think over her next words. "I would have hoped you would want to take care of Meg as much as possible, but the fact that you would still do anything at all for me…after everything that happened."

Jonas grabbed her by her hand, holding onto it tight. He would have pressed his mouth to her knuckles if he didn't feel so out of it.

He held on tight instead. "I'd go to the damned moon and back for you. I love you."

Taylor inhaled a sharp breath. She cleared her throat.

"It's okay if you don't feel the same."

"That's not it," she said, still looking a little too sorry for his liking. "I just thought that, if when your painkillers wore off, when you were a little more focused, and your head wasn't so cloudy..."

"I'm perfectly wide awake right now. I even see the nurses over there as nurses. Not killer clowns with butcher knives."

She smiled at that. That was good. It was always better when he could pull a smile out of her.

Jonas closed his eyes. He could barely keep them open.

"Don't go anywhere. Be here when I wake up."

"Sure. I'll do that."

"You can say you love me back if you want to."

Taylor laughed again. She pulled her hand back long enough to wipe at her eyes. "You know I do."

"Good. Don't ever forget it." He raised a finger. "Or there will be hell to pay."

She laughed again. He felt her lean in, her perfect mouth covering his.

"All right, Prince Charming. You rest now. When you wake up, I will be here. I'll try to make sure Meg is here, too, but that one might get tricky, and when you get out of here, I'll be able to tell you about all the other things that happened. You're going to have to get used to this new shape you've got, and if you want me to, I can help you to control it."

Jonas wasn't sure he caught that last bit, but the only important thing he needed to know was that Taylor said she would be here. His daughter would be here, and they were...all right.

They would still get their chance. This wasn't over.

He could sigh and finally sleep easy knowing that much.

Everything else, as far as he was concerned, was filler.

THE END

ABOUT THE AUTHOR

USA Today Bestselling Author Mandy Rosko is a videogame playing, book loving chick. She loves writing paranormal romances that range from light steamy to erotic, and has some contemporary and historical romances as well. You can find her on all sorts of platforms, including Twitch, Patreon, Wattpad, Radish, and more!

Get all the latest news from Mandy by signing up for her newsletter: http://eepurl.com/bQ8HvT

And get the most up-to date information on releases from Eighth Ripple Press by signing up for our newsletter: http://eepurl.com/gcUObH

facebook.com/MandyRoskoRomance
twitter.com/rizzorosko
instagram.com/mandyroskodraws
bookbub.com/authors/mandy-rosko

Mate of a Dragon Villain

My Angel Lover Have Mercy on Me (M/M)

Bad Boy Billionaire Brothers

Arrangement with a Billionaire

Holiday with a Billionaire

The Billionaire's Fantasy